PUPPETS OF THE TWISTED MIRROR

Karan of Gothryme: To save her people, her land, and her lover, she will have to sacrifice the entire world . . .

Llian of the Zain: Born cursed to serve the Charon, he now must use his knowledge to overcome his very nature . . .

Yalkara of the Charon: The Demon Queen warped the Twisted Mirror to escape Santhenar and the Forbidding, but she may have left her darkest secrets behind . . .

Maigraith: She has the strength to lead armies against inhuman foes, yet she cannot free herself from the one person who would destroy her . . .

Shand: He has spent an eon burying his past but if he does not reveal the truth now, Santhenar may be doomed . . .

Faelamor of the Faellem: The Lady of Illusions plans to lead her people back to their homeworld of Tallallame, even if escape means sacrificing all other worlds to The Void . . .

"A great find! Irvine writes beautifully . . . refreshing, complicated, and compelling."

— ***gon***

Books by Ian Irvine

A Shadow on the Glass
The Tower on the Rift

IAN IRVINE

DARK IS THE MOON

An AOL Time Warner Company

WARNER BOOKS EDITION

Cover illustration by Mark Sofilas

This edition is published by arrangement with Penguin Books Australia, Ltd.

Warner Books, Inc.
1271 Avenue of the Americas
New York, NY 10020

Visit our Web site at www.twbookmark.com.

An AOL Time Warner Company

Printed in the United States of America

First Warner Books Printing: July 2002

10 9 8 7 6 5 4 3 2 1

I would like to thank Simon Irvine for the truly glorious cover concept artwork.

CONTENTS

MAPS

PART ONE

*"You are wrong if you think fortune has changed toward you.
Inconstancy is my very essence."*

BOETHIUS, *THE CONSOLATION OF PHILOSOPHY*

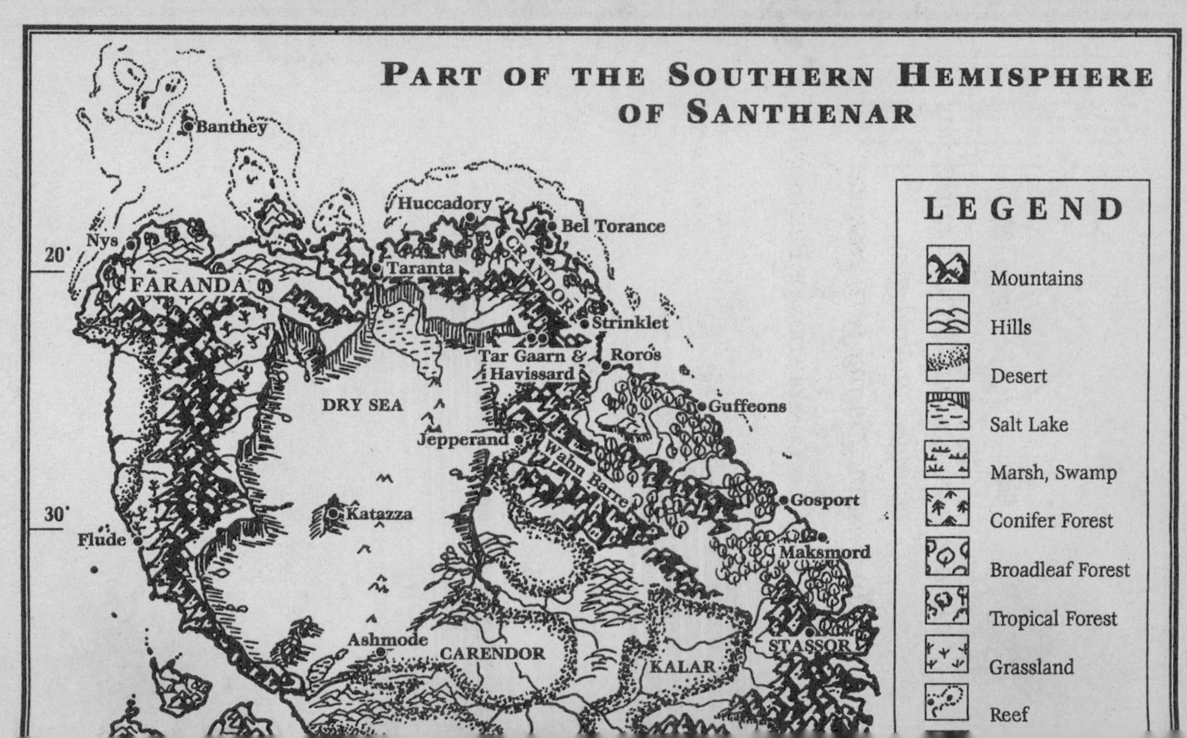
PART OF THE SOUTHERN HEMISPHERE
OF SANTHENAR
LEGEND
Mountains
Hills
Desert
Salt Lake
Marsh, Swamp
Conifer Forest
Broadleaf Forest
Tropical Forest
Grassland
Reef
Banthey
Nys
20˚
FARANDA
Taranta
Huccadory
Bel Torance
CRANDOR
Strinklet
Tar Gaarn &
Havissard
Roros
DRY SEA
Guffeons
Jepperand
Wahn Barre
Gosport
30˚
Katazza
Flude
Maksmord
Ashmode
CARENDOR
KALAR
STASSOR

Maps by the author

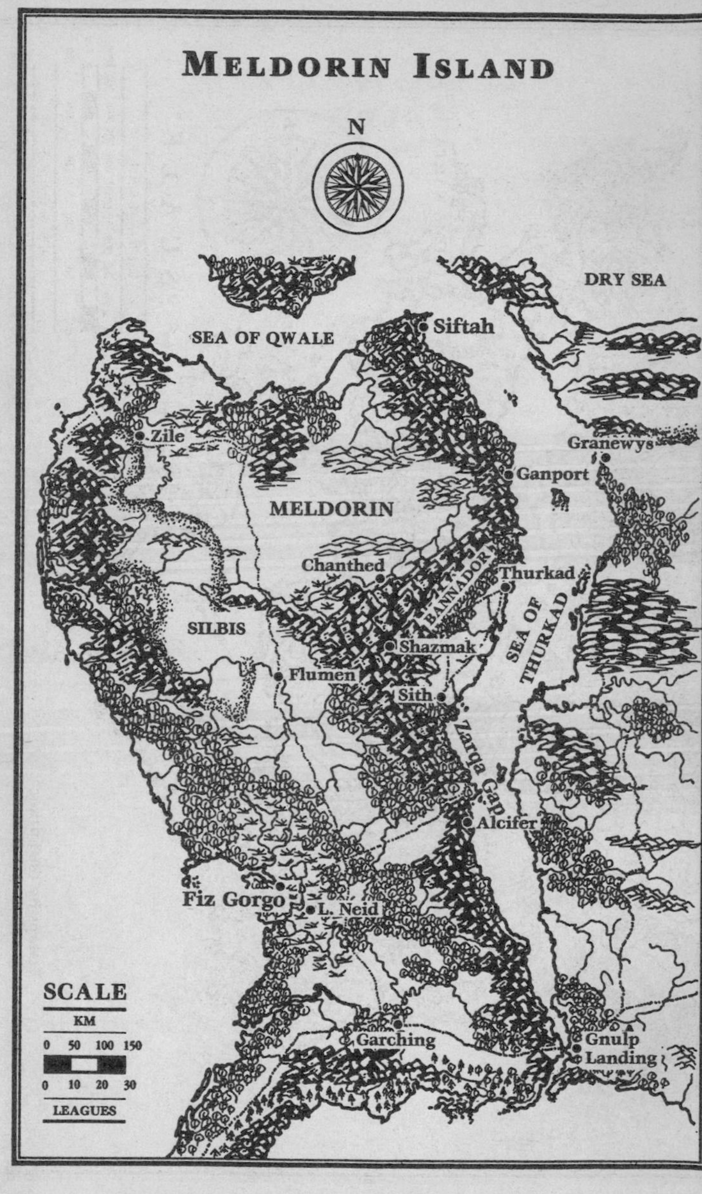
Meldorin Island
N
DRY SEA
SEA OF QWALE
Siftah
Zile
Granewys
Ganport
MELDORIN
Chanthed
BANNADOR
Thurkad
SEA OF THURKAD
SILBIS
Shazmak
Flumen
Sith
Zarqa Gap
Alcifer
Fiz Gorgo
L. Neid
SCALE
KM
0 50 100 150
0 10 20 30
LEAGUES
Garching
Gnulp Landing

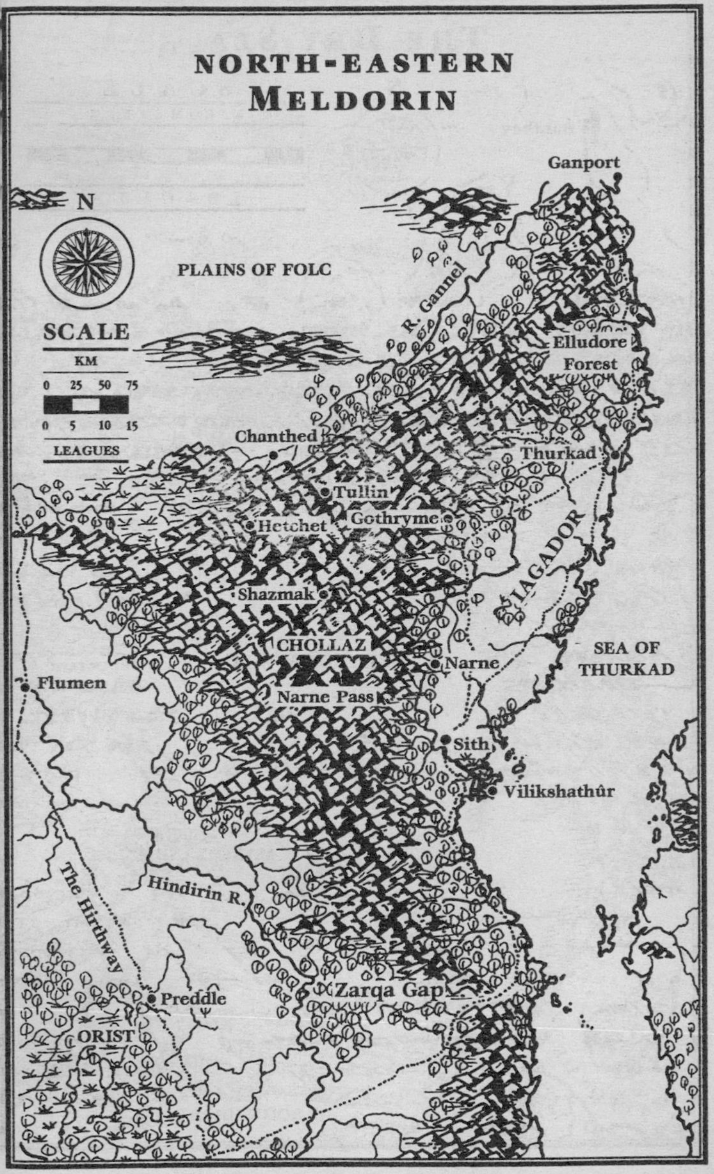

NORTH-EASTERN MELDORIN

N

SCALE

KM

0 25 50 75

0 5 10 15

LEAGUES

PLAINS OF FOLC

Ganport

R. Gannel

Elludore Forest

Chanthed

Thurkad

Tullin

Hetchet

Gothryme

IAGADOR

Shazmak

CHOLLAZ

Narne

SEA OF THURKAD

Flumen

Narne Pass

Sith

Vilikshathûr

Hindirin R.

The Hirthway

Zarqa Gap

Preddle

ORIST

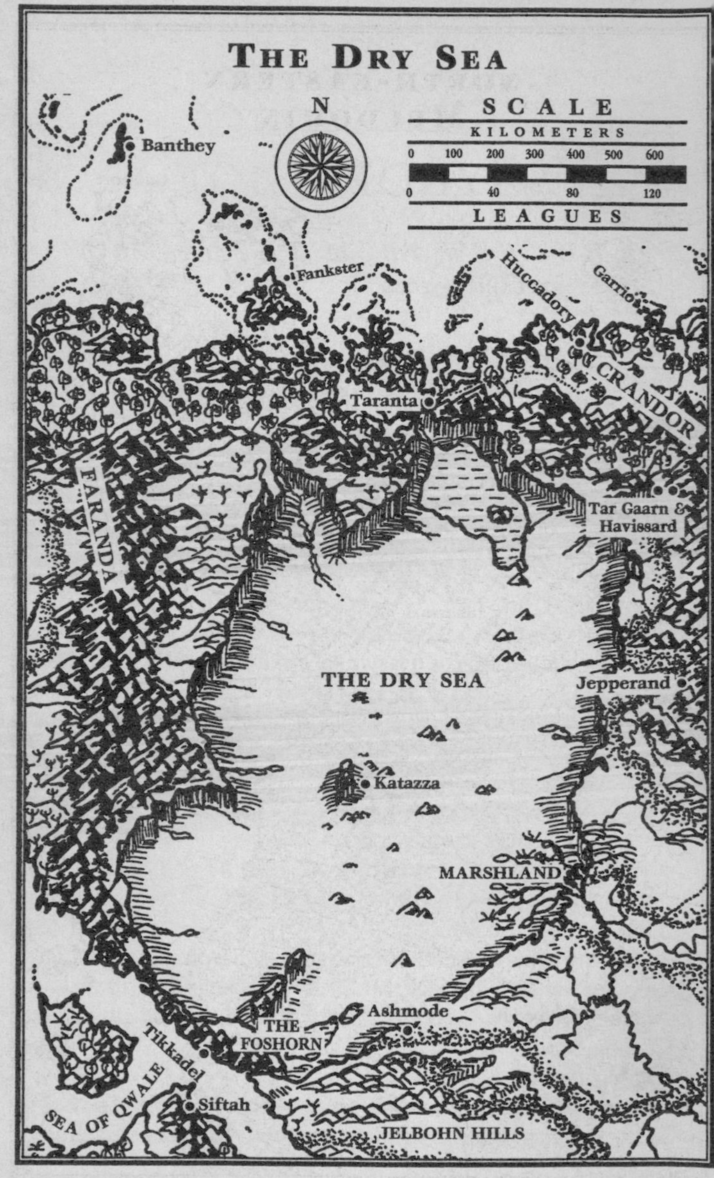
THE DRY SEA
N
SCALE
KILOMETERS
0 100 200 300 400 500 600
0 40 80 120
LEAGUES
Banthey
Fankster
Huccadory
Garrios
CRANDOR
Taranta
FARANDA
Tar Gaarn &
Havissard
Jepperand
THE DRY SEA
Katazza
MARSHLAND
Ashmode
THE
FOSHORN
Tikkadel
Siftah
SEA OF QWALE
JELBOHN HILLS

SYNOPSIS OF

THE VIEW FROM THE MIRROR

The View from the Mirror is a tale of the Three Worlds, *Aachan, Tallallame* and *Santhenar,* and of the four human species that inhabit them: *Aachim, Charon, Faellem* and *old human*. The setting is Santhenar, a world where wizardry—the *Secret Art*—is difficult, and doesn't always work, and every using comes at a price—*aftersickness.*

Long ago a whole race was betrayed and cast into the void between the worlds, a Darwinian place where life is more desperate, more brutal, more fleeting than anywhere. In the void none but the fittest survive, and only by remaking themselves constantly. A million of that race died in the first few weeks.

The terrible centuries ground on. The exiles were transformed into a new human species, but still they could not survive the void. Reduced to a handful, they hung over the abyss of extinction. Then one day a chance came, an opening to another world—Aachan!

Giving themselves a new name, Charon, after a frigid moonlet at the furthest extremity of the void, they took Aachan from the Aachim. The Hundred, as the remaining Charon became known, dared allow nothing to stand before the survival of their species.

But they did not flourish on Aachan, so one of the Hundred, *Rulke*, commissioned the golden flute, an instrument that could open the Way between the Worlds. Before it could be used, *Shuthdar*, the old human who made it, stole the flute and fled with it to Santhenar. Unfortunately for Rulke, Shuthdar blundered. He opened all the paths between the worlds, and the four species scrambled to get the flute for themselves. Rather than be taken Shuthdar destroyed it, bringing down the *Forbidding* that sealed Santhenar off completely. Now the fate of the Three Worlds is bound up with those marooned on Santhenar. They have never ceased to search for a way home, but none has ever been found.

Volume 1
A SHADOW ON THE GLASS

Llian, a brilliant young chronicler at the College of the Histories, presents a new version of an ancient Great Tale, the *Tale of the Forbidding*, at his graduation telling, to unprecedented acclaim. But *Wistan*, the master of the College, realizes that Llian has uncovered a deadly mystery—evidence that a crippled girl was murdered at the time the golden flute was destroyed. The crime must have occurred to conceal a greater one, and even now such knowledge could be deadly, both for him and for the College.

Llian is also *Zain*, an outcast race despised for collaborating with the Charon in olden times. Wistan persecutes Llian to make him retract the tale, but Llian secretly keeps on with his research. He knows that it could be the key to a brilliant story—the first new Great Tale for hundreds of years—and if he were the one to write it, he would stand shoulder to shoulder with the greatest chroniclers of all time.

Karan, a young woman who is a *sensitive*, was at the graduation telling when Llian told his famous tale. She loves the Histories and is captivated by the tale and the teller. Karan returns to Gothryme, her drought-stricken and impoverished home, but soon afterwards *Maigraith* appears. Karan owes an obligation to Maigraith, the powerful but troubled lieutenant of *Faelamor*, and Maigraith insists that she repay it by helping to steal an ancient relic for her liege. Faelamor is the age-old leader of the Faellem, exiled on Santhenar by the Forbidding. Desperate to take her people back to her own world, she believes that the relic may hold the key.

Yggur the sorcerer now holds the relic in Fiz Gorgo. Karan and Maigraith steal into his fortress, but Karan is shocked to learn that the relic is the *Mirror of Aachan*, stolen from the Aachim a thousand years ago. Being part-Aachim herself, she knows that the Aachim have never stopped searching for it. She must betray her father's people or refuse her debt to Maigraith—dishonor either way. And Karan has a dangerous heritage: part Aachim, part old human, she is a *blending*. Blendings, though prone to madness, can have unusual talents, as she has. They are also at risk: sometimes hunted to enslave the talent, as often to destroy it.

Maigraith, captivated by something she sees on the Mirror, is surprised by Yggur. Finally she is overcome but Karan flees with the Mirror into the flooded labyrinth below the fortress, pursued by Yggur's dreadful *Whelm* guards. Karan eventually escapes but is hunted for weeks through swamp and forest and mountains, the Whelm tracking her through her nightmares. In a twist of fate, Karan saves the life of one of them, *Idlis the healer*. She heads toward Chanthed, a place of haunting memories because of Llian's wonderful tale. Pursued by the Whelm and their dogs, she reaches out to him in her dreams.

Mendark, a mancer and Yggur's bitter enemy, hears that the Mirror has been stolen and sends his lieutenants to find it. Learning from *Tallia* that Karan is heading for Chanthed he asks Wistan to find her. Wistan, who would do anything to get rid of Llian, orders him to find Karan and take her to Mendark's city, Thurkad.

At the village of Tullin, Llian dreams that Karan is calling for help and wakes to find two Whelm at his throat, trying to trace her *sending*. He is rescued by *Shand*, an old man who works at the inn but is more than he seems. Llian heads out into the snow to find Karan. Eventually he does, after many perils. Full of mixed feelings about Llian, Karan flees with him into the high mountains. After a number of narrow escapes they lose their pursuers, but Llian gets mountain sickness and Karan has no choice but to head for Shazmak, a secret city of the Aachim, where she grew up.

After they arrive Karan learns that *Tensor* is on his way to Shazmak. She knows she can never keep the Mirror secret from him. Unknown to her, Tensor already knows she has it. Soon Karan is brought to trial, for the Mirror cannot be found. It is impossible to lie to the *Syndics*, but Karan, in a desperate expedient, plants a false dream in Llian's mind, and through a *link* with him, reads it back to the Syndics at her trial. Because Llian believes it to be truth, it is truth, and despite Tensor's protests she is freed. Karan and Llian escape from Shazmak, hotly pursued by the Aachim. Stealing a boat, they flee down a wild river.

In Yggur's stronghold, Maigraith is tormented by the Whelm, who have an instinctive hatred of her. Later, under Yggur's relentless interrogation, she gives away Karan's destination, the city of Sith. Yggur needs the Mirror desperately, for his coming war. However as the weeks pass a bond grows between them, Maigraith finding in the tormented Yggur the complement to her own troubled self.

Faelamor uses her mastery of illusion to snatch Maigraith out of Fiz Gorgo but is furious when she learns that Karan, whom she hates, has escaped with the Mirror. Inwardly Faelamor despairs because the Mirror, which she has sought for so long, has eluded her again. Once before she almost had it, but *Yalkara* the Charon, her greatest enemy, defeated her. Yalkara used the Mirror to find a warp in the Forbidding, the only person ever to escape from Santhenar. Now Faelamor's own world, Tallallame, cries out for aid and she is desperate to return.

Faelamor and Maigraith set off to find Karan. Maigraith falls back under Faelamor's domination. Yggur, finding Maigraith gone, marches to war on the east.

Karan and Llian flee through mountains and caverns, hotly pursued by Tensor and his Aachim. At a forest camp she has a terrible nightmare and wakes to find that the Whelm have tracked her down again. This time she is helpless for they have learned how to control her. Desperate, Karan makes a link to Maigraith, now not far away. Unfortunately the link is captured by a terrifying presence, who uses it to speak directly to the Whelm, reminding them that they are really Ghâshâd, ancient enemies of the Aachim. Llian escapes but Karan is captured.

Not long after, Faelamor is taken by Tensor and sent to Shazmak, where to her horror she learns about Karan's Aachim heritage. Faelamor already suspects that Karan has Faellem ancestry as well. If so, she is *triune*: one with the blood of three worlds. A terrifying prospect—no one can tell what unpredictable talents a triune might have. Faelamor decides that the risk to her plans is too great—Karan must die. Faelamor escapes but the Ghâshâd find a way into Shazmak.

Clumsy Llian somehow rescues Karan, hires a boat and *Pender* takes them down the river to Sith. There they find Yggur's armies just across the river. The city cannot stand against him. Nor is Faelamor there to take the Mirror. Karan collapses, unable to drive herself any further. There is nowhere to go but to Mendark. Karan is afraid of him too.

They reach Thurkad not far ahead of the war to find that Mendark has been overthrown by *Thyllan*. A street urchin, *Lilis*, guides Llian to Mendark's refuge. Mendark and Tallia offer to take Karan in but, angered by Mendark's imperious manner, she refuses him. Shortly, Thyllan captures Karan and the Mirror.

As all the powers gather in Thurkad, Mendark realizes that the only way to recover the Mirror is to call a Great Conclave, which Thyllan must obey. As the Conclave ends, news comes that the army is defeated and Yggur at the gates of the city. Faelamor shatters Tensor by revealing that the Whelm are actually his ancient enemies, Ghâshâd, one-time servants of Rulke, who have taken Shazmak and slaughtered the Aachim there. She lies, blaming Karan for this treachery.

Karan is sentenced to death, while the Mirror is given to Thyllan to use in the defense of Thurkad. Seizing the moment, Faelamor calls forth Maigraith, and Tensor knows by her eyes that she is descended from the hated Charon. He breaks and uses a forbidden *potency*, or mind-blasting spell, that lays the whole Conclave low. Only Llian the Zain is unaffected. Thinking Karan dead, in grief and fury he attacks Tensor but is easily captured. Tensor sees a use for someone who is immune to the potency. He flees with Llian and the Mirror.

Volume 2
THE TOWER ON THE RIFT

Mendark and Tallia wake in the ruins of the Conclave. Tensor and Llian have disappeared, and Karan too. Mendark takes over the hopeless defense of the city but Thurkad soon falls. He flees with his little company: a few guards, Tallia and Lilis, then finds that his boat has been captured. They are forced to take refuge with the *Hlune*, a strange subculture that has made the vast, ancient wharf city of Thurkad their own. Tallia eventually hires Pender's boat and after a series of pursuits, escapes and mishaps they reach Zile, an old, declining city famous for its Great Library. The librarian, *Nadiril*, is a capricious old man who has the knowledge of the world at his fingertips. Nadiril takes Lilis as his apprentice but cannot suggest where Tensor may have taken refuge.

Tensor drags Llian through bloody war to a hideout where a small band of the Aachim wait for him, including *Malien*, his one-time consort. Tensor tells the terrible news about the destruction of Shazmak and the climax of the Conclave, but when he admits that he violated the Conclave with a forbidden potency the Aachim are outraged at his dishonor.

In the uproar Llian tries to get away but is speared in the side. The Aachim flee, taking Llian with them. They are hunted for weeks by Yggur's Whelm. They flee north, escaping many traps, and some among them would kill Llian, the treacherous Zain as they see him, but Tensor has a purpose for him. Llian, grieving for the loss of Karan and plagued by dreams of death and doom, is slow to recover. He often talks to Malien, who is disturbed by his dreams. Finally they are joined by other Aachim, refugees from ruined Shazmak. Their tales drive Tensor into a frenzy of hate and bitterness.

Maigraith and Faelamor are also laid low by Tensor's potency. Maigraith recovers, but Faelamor has lost her powers and sinks into despair. Thurkad is now controlled by Yggur and there is no way of escape. Maigraith has only one recourse—she goes to Yggur. Their meeting is tense, for neither has been able to forget the other and each is afraid of rejection. However, in time they become lovers.

Karan wakes from pain, nightmares and madness to find herself in a dingy room with a stranger. At first she barely knows who she is, and can remember only fragments of the past weeks. The stranger turns out to be Shand, who rescued her from the Conclave. She does not know why.

Karan is devastated to find that Llian has disappeared. As Thurkad capitulates, Shand leaves her in the wharf city, a place that she has a horror of, while he goes to find help. She is put to work at a disgusting and painful job—cleaning jellyfish and packing them in barrels. Finally Shand returns and they go across the sea.

Shand reveals that he knew Karan's father long ago, which is why he rescued her. They travel on, having adventures alternately comical, palpitating and gruesome, and eventually come to a cliff as tall as a mountain, below which is a vast emptiness, the Dry Sea, that was once the magnificent Sea of Perion.

Karan senses that Llian is out there somewhere. Throughout the salt plains there are tall mountains, once islands in the sea, and the largest of them, Katazza, was the seat of the fabulous empire of *Kandor*, one of the three Charon who came to Santhenar for the flute. The empire was destroyed when the sea dried up, but the fortress of Katazza remains.

Karan senses that Llian has been taken there. Shand agrees to accompany her, but it is not a journey to be taken lightly. They set out across the salt, a terrible journey, pursued by bounty hunters and attacked by venomous desert creatures. There is never enough water and at the end, deadly volcanic country to cross before they get to Katazza. There they are stuck, too weak to tackle the great cliffs.

Much earlier, the Aachim also go down onto the Dry Sea. They cross the sea quickly and climb the cliffs and mountains of Katazza to reach Kandor's fortress. Tensor begins his great project, to find within the Mirror the way of making gates from one place to another. He plans to open the *Nightland*, Rulke's prison of a thousand years, and have his revenge.

For a long time Tensor makes no progress, the memories of the Mirror being locked, then one day finds a way in. Only when he begins to make his gate do the Aachim realize what his real plan is. They try to stop him but Tensor seizes Llian, locks the Aachim out of the tower and continues with his work. Soon the gate is ready for its first test.

Back in Zile, Tallia has worked out what Tensor's destination must be. Mendark, his guard *Osseion*, and Tallia set off. After crossing the Dry Sea, to their astonishment they come across recent tracks at the base of Katazza. After a scuffle in the dark they realize that they have found Karan and Shand. Together they climb the cliffs and at the top are met by a deputation of the Aachim.

Mendark agrees to help them against Tensor. Karan is interested in only one thing, that Llian is here, and races off to find him. Unfortunately they can only communicate through a slit in the wall.

Tensor tests his gate but it goes astray, for he has used the Mirror to see the destination. It was often called the Twisted Mirror—a deceitful, treacherous thing. Karan, afraid for Llian, climbs the tower, a terrifying ordeal that she barely survives. Soon after that, Tensor seizes Llian, who is immune to the potency, as a defense against Rulke. Then he opens the gate.

In Thurkad, Faelamor recovers her powers and warns Yggur that Tensor has made a gate, risking their ruin. Yggur manages to draw the gate away from the Nightland to Thurkad, though when it opens he dares not enter. Faelamor curses him for a coward and a fool and leaps into the gate. Later Yggur follows her, leaving Maigraith behind.

In Katazza, Tensor expects Rulke to come through the gate but Faelamor appears instead. She confuses him with illusion, seizes the Mirror and hides. Yggur appears. Shortly after, the gate begins working of its own accord. Tensor seizes Llian, preparing to blast his enemy, Rulke. Karan knows Llian won't survive the confrontation. She hurls a block of rubble in Tensor's face and Llian gets away. Then Rulke leaps out of the gate, terrible in his power and majesty, and the potency fizzles into nothing.

Rulke attacks his enemies one by one. First Yggur, then Tensor, whom he cripples. Faelamor, having found what she wanted in the Mirror, flees back through the gate. The Aachim are broken; Mendark is afraid to act by himself. Finally Rulke turns to Karan and realizes that she is the one whose link he used to wake the Ghâshâd. He needs her for his own project. He advances on Karan. With no other resort, she flings herself through the gate, dragging Llian after her.

Mendark now sees an opportunity, reaches into Yggur's mind and frees him from Rulke's possession of long ago. The tide begins to turn; the allies realize that together they can defeat Rulke, if they have the courage. They attack. Rulke flees to the top of the tower. There they corner him and hurl him out, but he curses them with a foretelling—that when the dark side of the moon is full in *hythe* (mid-winter's day) he will return and Santh will be his.

Shand replies with a riddle, 'Fear the thrice born, but beware the thrice betrayed', then Rulke vanishes. Finally Shand takes the Mirror, 'in memory of the one whose birthright it was', though no one knows what he means.

PART ONE

1

THE STORM

An untuned horn moaned the midnight hour. Maigraith tossed in her steamy bed, her skin on fire with prickly heat. The humid air sweated beads of moisture onto every surface. Two sweltering days had passed, two hot and sticky Thurkad nights since Faelamor had gone through the gate, disguised as Vartila, and one night since Yggur followed her. Neither had returned.

The storm began with a sudden shrieking gust of wind that rattled the windows of Yggur's fortress, an ancient structure whose black stonework brooded over the skyline of the city. The wind withdrew; for a moment there was silence. Without warning a flash of white lightning lit up Maigraith's room as stark and bright as midday. A shattering roar of thunder followed. The calm that sighed into the sound vacuum was eerie.

Leaping out of bed Maigraith ran to a window. A storm was approaching the like of which she had never seen. Bolt after bolt of lightning jagged down, the flashes moving slowly along the hills from the west end to the east. Thunder beat against the great building—measured beats. See what is coming to Thurkad, the pulses said to her. *Fear it!*

No longer could she bear her confining room with its stifling heat and prison-cell windows. The storm called her out. Maigraith flung on a gown, donned glasses that concealed the color of her eyes and ran up the stairs to the tower at the eastern end of the fortress. There, protected by a dome standing on six squat columns of soot-stained stone, she leaned on the marble rail and peered out.

A fitful moon shone through tormented clouds that belched up into towers of black and cream, illuminated from within by lightning that lit up the whole of the city. The billowing stacks were just as quickly rent apart again. Clouds racing nowhere, everywhere! Her scalp began to crawl. The storm was swirling toward one place: the center of Thurkad, Yggur's fortress, the tower in which she stood.

The wind flung itself at the tower from the north, then the east, then the south, one minute dying to a whisper so that the humidity choked her, the next screaming at her from the opposite direction. Maigraith had to twine her fingers in the twisted iron below the rail to avoid being blown out into the night. Roof slates were whirled across the sky like papers before the wind. Chimneys began to topple all around, their long flat bricks streaming onto the close-packed roofs. Now whole roofs were torn up, slates, battens and all, and driven across the city flapping like paper birds. Like paper birds they were crumpled by the gale and tossed into the harbor.

Clouds shut out the moon. It grew calm. An uncanny dark descended, broken every few seconds by a diffuse incandescence, the internal lightning revealing each thunderhead's milky intestines. But the thunder was muffled now, hiding something.

A scrap of paper spiraled up toward the top of the dome, though there was no wind. Maigraith could feel her hair being drawn up too, glowing and crackling.

From the angry clouds above came a pulse of light, so

close that she could feel the heat. Now a double pulse, blinding, blending into a third, the city cast in black and white as if made of lead and plaster. Lightning arched down all around, making an umbrella of light over the tower. The wind shrieked again, wrenching a copper sheet off the dome. Twisted into a knot, it drifted away out of sight. A massive bolt struck the roof, sending sparks and glowing droplets of copper in all directions. The thunder became a cacophony, a roaring, thundering, smashing brutality. Maigraith was lifted and flung onto the floor, wrenching her knee. She lay there for a long moment, afraid to look.

A hot metal stench blew across her face. Opening her eyes, Maigraith saw a river of molten copper running across the floor, dividing into two streams to surround her. As she sprang up her knee collapsed and she had to hop to safety. A fire was burning in fallen timber on the far side of the space. More than half the leaves of the dome were gone, leaving her vantage open to the blistered sky.

At the top of the stair a crowd of people stood. Even before the lightning flashed she knew that they were Whelm. They had not all broken their oath to Yggur; near half had remained behind when the others rebelled and, as Ghâshâd, turned Shazmak into bloody ruin. Why did they stay faithful to a master that they held in contempt? She did not know. Why had Yggur kept them after the rest had turned their coats? She had no idea of that either. Now they went down on their knees and their thin arms reached out and up. But to what?

The first fat drops wobbled down, then the air was thick with rain, teeming down so heavily that within minutes the floor was awash, dammed by rubble and timber in the doorway. As the lightning flashed behind her the air became alive with rainbow colors. Forward her gaze went, to where the remaining leaves of the cupola had been wrenched up to form an arching hood that swayed in the wind. A waterfall cascaded off it.

Lightning struck again with a simultaneous battering of

thunder. She hardly heard it, her ears still ringing from the previous blast. The flash burned her eyes. Maigraith was saturated, the drops flung so hard that they stung her scalp, her arms, her bare feet. She was cold as well, for her only garment was the thinnest of shifts. Every hair on her body stood erect with an icy dread. Shivers began at the top of her head and slowly pulsed their way down her back. She rubbed her eyes; opened them.

Sight slowly returned. Standing massive and terrible before her, beneath that hood so that no rain fell on him, though it smoked about his black-booted, wide-spread legs; dark-bearded; dark mane rippling behind, arms folded across his massive chest, sparks of carmine in his indigo eyes, a look of wild exultation on his face, stood a man that she knew at once—*Rulke!*

Maigraith was paralyzed with terror and longing. He was free! This was the moment that Santhenar had dreaded for a thousand years. Tensor had failed, and Yggur too. Rulke was *here*, proud and terrible. Her fear of him was as black as hatred, for so she had been brought up. Yet she was drawn to him too. Surely *he* was not plagued by the doubts that paralyzed her. What could it mean, his presence here? Had he broken his enemies already? If so, where did her duty lie now? Always a follower, she was not used to such thinking.

From the Whelm came a groan of ecstasy and a young woman leapt forth. Going down on her knees in the water, she threw out her arms toward Rulke. At the same time Maigraith caught sight of a movement on the other side of the space. A lean, hatchet-nosed figure squatted there, watching. It was Vartila, and she had her mouth open, staring at Rulke not in adulation, as the other Whelm did, but in puzzlement. As if she could not understand why he had such a hold over them.

The Whelm gave forth a low, ululating cry. Maigraith knew what was going to happen. They would swear allegiance to Rulke, become his Ghâshâd just as the other Whelm had done last winter.

Rulke turned toward them and spoke in power and majesty. The lightning flashed behind his back, swelling him to the size of his shadow.

"Faithful ones!" his voice boomed above the thunder. "Know that Rulke prizes loyalty above all other virtues. Soon you will have your reward. None has earned it by harder labor, or longer service."

That is a lie, thought Maigraith, shivering. The Great Betrayer, the world calls you. The most treacherous man ever to walk Santhenar. Yet everything about him was magnificent—the powerful body, the intelligent eyes, the sensuous mouth, the confidence that oozed out of him. She could not believe ill of him.

He stretched out his arms like a father to his children, and his voice was nectar. "Come to me, my Ghâshâd. I have been prisoner for a thousand years. There is much I need to know, and so little time. Tell me about my enemies."

They gathered around Rulke like the petals of a flower, speaking around the circle one after another, never interrupting. Maigraith could see their dark eyes shining, the pupils contracted to vertical black slits. After a long time the petals unwound to form a ring around him.

"One more service you must do me," he said, and now his voice was hoarse, the strain telling on him. To Maigraith it was a sign of his humanity.

"Name it, master!" cried an extremely gaunt Whelm with oily-gray, shifting eyes and one shoulder hanging lower than the other. "My name is Japhit. Command me!"

"Go forth, Japhit, make a show of my strength. Show the power of Rulke to all Meldorin. Let none doubt who is master now."

"We will do it!" said Japhit. His voice was a gritty rasp, the sound of a saw grinding against sandstone. "And Thurkad?"

Rulke frowned. "Thurkad?"

"Yggur has disappeared; the people are rebellious."

"Then restore order!" cried Rulke, his voice cracking.

"Bring the Ghâshâd forth from Shazmak. My warrant I give to you, none other. Do not fail me!"

Japhit seemed to glow. "I will not fail, master," he said, his scratchy voice pale beside Rulke's. "You have done me honor."

Rulke began to fade. "Master!" shouted the young woman Maigraith had noticed earlier. She was trembling now with emotion, with yearning for her master. Her black hair was hacked into ragged clumps, yet she was an appealing woman, as Whelm go.

Rulke did not see her. He was barely more than a luminous outline now. "*Master*!" she screamed. Desperate to be noticed, she thrust out her breasts at him. Parting gray lips, she moaned deep in her throat.

As if he would want *you*, Maigraith thought, and knew at once how mean that thought was, and how true.

Rulke reappeared but the exultation was gone; now he was weary and imperious. He stared at the woman. "Why do you call me back? I have many burdens and little time left. Do as you are commanded!"

"Master, my name is Yetchah," she cried, wringing her thin hands. Looking frantically around, her eyes settled on Maigraith. "This one has power, lord. What shall we do with her?"

Rulke peered through the misty dark toward Maigraith's hide. He saw a slender woman with rich brown hair, skin as smooth as honey dripping from a comb, a long beautiful face, though often downcast, and the most remarkable eyes in the world. They could be indigo or carmine, or both, depending on her mood and on the light. But the world feared her eyes, and she had been taught to hide the color with special glasses.

Maigraith crouched down in the rain, water streaming down her face. She did not want him to see her like this. Sodden, downcast, she knew she looked a dispirited lump. And Maigraith, a modest woman, was conscious that her wet shift concealed nothing.

He strode toward her and cold vapor smoked where each boot touched. Examining her from head to toe, he put his hand beneath her chin and drew her to her feet. His hand was hot though the touch was as light as gossamer. He was hardly there, she realized. A breeze glued the shift to her breasts and belly. His scrutiny was unbearable, but she would not be dominated by him; by anyone. She threw back her shoulders, tossed her head and met him eye to eye.

Rulke seemed shocked by her courage. Then a smile broke across his achingly handsome face. "Who *are* you?" he rumbled.

"I am Maigraith," she replied. "I was Faelamor's lieutenant, once."

"You lowered yourself," he said enigmatically. "There is something about you—" He stooped to pluck off her glasses, to look into her eyes. His palms and fingers were cruelly burnt and blistered. She felt his pain. As he touched the glasses his hand shook and he faded to transparency.

"The spell fails already," Rulke said to himself. With an effort he reappeared. He gave a chilly laugh. "No time! Do not harm her," he said to Japhit. "*Hold her until I return. Protect her with your lives.*"

"We will, master!" they cried as one, even a flush-faced Yetchah, though Maigraith did not like the look in her eye.

Rulke raised his arms, gazed back at Maigraith, hesitated, then he was gone in a clap of thunder and the rain teemed down once more.

The Whelm were all staring at her. Maigraith did not move. She was seized by such powerful emotions that momentarily she could not care whether they saw her naked or not. The terror of Rulke, and the longing, was a thousand times greater now.

Japhit stared raptly after Rulke, as if a great truth had been revealed at last. Finally he moved, his jerky gait hardly noticeable.

"The master ordered us to display his strength," he rasped. "Go forth now and do so. Drive Yggur's soldiers from this fortress! Turn his armies on one another. Bring chaos out of order. Take word to our brethren in Shazmak too. Know that we are Whelm no longer. Henceforth we go back to our first name—*Ghâshâd*! And Ghâshâd, know one further thing . . ."

As Maigraith edged past he seized her by the wrist and held up her arm. "Rulke has put his sign on Maigraith. Treat her with courtesy; guard and protect her with your lives. She may do what she wishes, but she may not leave the fortress."

Vartila led Maigraith below to Yggur's apartments. There she lingered by Maigraith's side, picking up things and putting them down again, as if she wanted to speak but could not find the words. Finally the agony burst out.

"*I don't remember him*!"

"I beg your pardon?" said Maigraith with disinterested politeness.

"Did you see how they all cried him master? Was *he* our master once? How majestic he was! My breast aches for him. To serve such a master I would be completed at last."

"Then go and serve him," said Maigraith irritably, desperate to be alone, hating Vartila intruding on this place, her only sanctuary in a pitiless world. Vartila was alien, impossible to understand.

"You don't know what it is like to be Whelm," Vartila replied furiously. She must have been in anguish to display her feelings so—and to an enemy. She had tormented Maigraith in Fiz Gorgo and Maigraith had never forgotten it. "Service is everything to us. Life and death and love, meat and blood. Only one way can I break our vow of service to Yggur—by finding that a previous oath to Rulke still holds." Tears dripped from her sunken eye pouches, but in her anguish even this shame she was oblivious to. "And I know it does. I know in my heart that *he* is the one." Her voice rose until it became a wail. "*But I don't remember him! I am blind to my master*."

"Are you age old?" Maigraith wondered.

"I am thirty-seven, but that is irrelevant. Our oath has the force of a thousand years. My very bones should remember that my forefathers swore it."

What devotion the Whelm must have, thought Maigraith, to have waited for him all these centuries—dying, being born, growing old and dying in their turn, and yet cleaving to their duty to a master that none of this generation, or the past forty generations, had ever seen.

"And the way he looked at you," Vartila continued. "*You of all people*! It burns me. He can never be your master."

"No man can be *my* master," said Maigraith, and all at once she felt weak at the knees and had to sit down. "No woman either, *evermore*."

"Then guard yourself well," said Vartila, "for I remain Whelm and serve Yggur, but most of my fellows are Ghâshâd now. Rulke has put his mark on you; they will never let you go!" She wiped her eyes and stalked out.

Maigraith felt so alone, trapped in the old fortress with her Ghâshâd guard, dreadful enemies of the Aachim. Her enemies too.

Her room felt like a prison cell, but whenever she went out a scowling Yetchah peeled away from the door to follow. Is this what my life is to be like? Maigraith thought. To be shadowed wherever I go, cocooned as a prize for their master? I will not endure that.

She pressed her nose to one of the small windowpanes, gazing at the unchained moon. It was nearly full tonight, and showing only the yellow side. The rugged terrain of the other side was blotched red and black, between which were seas colored a violent purple. The moon's turgid rotation brought the dark side round roughly every two lunar cycles, though thankfully that only occasionally coincided with a full moon. The dark side was an ill-omen, but a dark full moon was a disastrous portent.

Each day and each hour stretched out eternally, and for the few who had remained Whelm too, in their uneasy coexistence with the Ghâshâd. She could see it in their faces. They stalked the corridors of the fortress like hyenas, skittish as if they stood to rise or fall on what was happening far away. They too were come to crisis. And Vartila was more tense than any, going back and forth on her long shanks, her robes rasping together, her sandals slapping on the flags. Her skin seemed grayer than ever, her dog teeth sharper and longer, her face harder than agate.

With the Ghâshâd patrolling outside, Maigraith was reminded of Fiz Gorgo and her previous imprisonment, of Faelamor and her earlier life. Life was a prison: whether of the flesh or the spirit, it hardly mattered. She had not a friend in the world. Karan had offered friendship and Maigraith had rejected her. Maigraith often thought about Karan, about how badly she'd treated her, and what Karan had suffered because of it. Whatever had happened to her? I failed her, not least in Thurkad when she tried to give me the Mirror and I refused it. How arrogantly I forced her to pay back her obligation to me, and yet I ignored my duty to her. I forced her, for a handful of silver.

That thought was followed by a shocking realization—*but Karan was never paid*! Maigraith blushed, breast and throat and face in scarlet mortification. That she had so lectured Karan on duty, honor and obligation, and so failed in her own. I see my failures everywhere. *I must put it right. I will*!

2

A COURSE IN LEADERSHIP

Something crashed against the door. Maigraith jumped, thinking it was the Ghâshâd coming for her. Only days after Rulke's apparition, Thyllan, who had overthrown Mendark and set himself up as Magister before the disaster of the Great Conclave, sailed across the sea with an army, intent on taking the city back. A fortnight had now gone by. Thurkad was besieged and looked set to fall. The Ghâshâd, their subversion done, were hurrying to escape before that happened. If they took her to Shazmak she would never get away.

And the way Rulke had looked at her. *Hold her until I return*, he'd said. *Protect her with your lives*! What did he want of her? The thought of him was frightening, yet exhilarating too. She could not work out why she was drawn to him, for everything she'd ever heard about Rulke had made him a monster—a violent, brutal, treacherous man. Yet that hadn't matched what she'd seen in his eyes.

The noise, when Maigraith went to her peephole, turned out to be someone moving a chest. She paced the room.

Yggur's empire was falling to pieces. How had it happened so quickly?

In two bloody battles outside the city last week, all his generals and half his senior officers had been slain. The armies of Thurkad were now commanded by Vanhe, once the most junior of Yggur's marshals. A stolid, unimaginative man, Vanhe was well out of his depth. He did not know how to deal with the seductions of sinful Thurkad, much less Thyllan's propaganda war or the Ghâshâd subversion.

Maigraith knew what was going to happen—bloody war for the city, street by street. The dead would be piled as high as houses. She remembered last winter's war only too well, huddling in that freezing shed with just a few wormy turnips to eat. That reminded her of the youth who had carried her and Faelamor away from the Conclave, who had been so kind to them, only to immolate himself on the bodies of his slain mother and brothers. The image was wrenching. How many more orphans, as miserable as herself, would this war create?

"I *won't* let it happen again!" she said aloud.

All her life Maigraith had been under the thrall of Faelamor, doing her bidding mechanically, hardly noticing the troubles of the world. She'd always had difficulty making decisions, for she could never believe in herself. But Faelamor had gone through the gate to Katazza, then Yggur. In their absence Maigraith had begun to think for herself.

First she must escape. Being a master of the Secret Art, she had power enough to work the lock, or even break the door if she had to. But the old fortress, once Yggur's headquarters, was now swarming with Ghâshâd. She could not beat all of them.

How would Faelamor get away? Maigraith asked herself. She had often seen her liege use illusion to get herself into, or out of, guarded places. Faelamor had brought them both out of Fiz Gorgo unseen, but she was a master of illusion, possibly the greatest on the Three Worlds. Maigraith, though not unskilful, knew that she could not do the same here.

She'd have to use something much stronger—perhaps a spell of transformation, though that was getting into un charted territory. The spell she knew was only a partial transformation—it would give her a different external form but not actually change her inside. A full transformation, to physically change her into someone else, was the most difficult of all spells. As far as she knew it had never been done successfully, though plenty had died horribly attempting it. And though she knew how to work a partial transformation, she had never done so.

Another problem—who to transform herself into? Here, any stranger would be attacked instantly. She daren't disguise herself as one of the Ghâshâd, for she did not know them well enough. The only person she did know well was Yggur.

Maigraith sat up suddenly, cracking her head on the sloping ceiling. She had been his lover, so it was not improbable that he would come after her. But Yggur was a tall and muscular man, twice her weight. Such physical differences would be a nightmare to overcome.

More yelling along the corridor, and the awkward slap of running Ghâshâd feet. Not much time left. Maigraith began to sketch Yggur in her mind, starting from the inside out. She began with what had attracted her to him in the first place—the cool intellect that weighed every detail before making any decision, and the pain inside him, which found an echo in her own loneliness and emptiness. She recalled to mind his stern but impartial justice, though that had disappeared once the occupation of Thurkad went wrong. Adversity weakened him—he had become mean-spirited, almost brutal to his people.

She tried harder to understand him, as she must if her disguise was to succeed. His anguish at being unable to communicate his feelings had at first drawn him to her, until she realized that he was frozen inside. His terror of being possessed by Rulke again had aroused her sympathies until she saw that he wallowed in his fears rather than trying to overcome them.

After their awkward attempts at coupling, the first in her life, Maigraith had almost thought she'd loved him. Then he shied away from her Charon eyes—lying beside her, Yggur could think of nothing but his enemy. Later, as she grew in her own strength he further diminished, until she began to lose respect for him. Then in a moment of desperate courage or supreme self-sacrifice, he had hurled himself into Tensor's gate and disappeared.

A complex man, Yggur! Hard to come to terms with; impossible to know. Maigraith still cared for him but now knew that she could never love him. More immediately, she felt that she understood him well enough to attempt the spell. It was a dangerous business, normally requiring weeks of preparation. From the sounds outside she would be lucky if she got an hour.

Closing her eyes, Maigraith brought back the memory of his long scarred body lying against hers, the feel of his skin under her hands. His embraces had been as clumsy as her own. Concentrating on her spell of transformation, striving with all her intellect, a likeness began to grow around her. It hurt very much, as if her flesh and bones were being stretched to match his larger dimensions.

When the spell was complete, Maigraith stood up. She promptly fell down again, the top-heavy man's body over balancing her. The feel of those long legs was all wrong. She tried again, more carefully, supporting herself on the bed. A pain ran up her right leg as she moved it. It did not want to support her weight. She'd done her work too well, crippled herself as Yggur was crippled. No time to undo it now.

The body did not suit her at all; she hated it. It was too big, too heavy and clumsy. She wanted her own slim form back, wanted to be rid of the mass of muscle she knew not how to use.

She practiced for hours, limping across the room the way Yggur walked: the halting steps, the rigidity of the right arm, the weak right knee. The imitation was far from perfect—it would take ages to master him.

Someone pounded up the corridor, shouting. Maigraith heard the guttural yelling of the Ghâshâd, then more running feet and crashing sounds. Time had run out. Panicking, she put her hands on the door plate and broke the lock. *Calm down*! She stuck her head around the door. Two people were hurrying along the corridor. They turned the corner. The way was clear.

Tossing an illusory cape over one shoulder, Maigraith strode down the hall as confidently as Yggur at his best. With every movement of her right leg pain jagged up to her hip, as if the nerves were afire. At the corner she collided with a Ghâshâd woman. The impact almost gave her away, for the woman's forehead struck parts of Yggur that were not really there.

"Out of my way!" Maigraith snapped, knowing that she had to keep the initiative, to treat them exactly as Yggur had when they had been his Whelm.

"What are you doing here?" growled Yetchah. She glared at Maigraith, instinctively hostile.

"I've come for my woman," Maigraith said arrogantly, already having trouble with Yggur's deep voice. It was beyond her vocal cords to imitate, and she had to use a form of illusion to disguise it—never very effective with voices. "Where is Maigraith?"

Yetchah let out a cry, half-heard, half-sending, that induced a spiny ball of pain behind Maigraith's temples. The cry was answered and half a dozen more Ghâshâd swarmed around the corner, moving with their awkward ratcheting gait. Several were armed with short spears.

Maigraith's heart turned over. She'd never keep the disguise up before so many. A spasm froze her right leg solid. She tried to speak but the strain paralyzed one side of her face, as if she'd had a stroke. Yggur, my poor man, I begin to understand what life was like for you.

Paradoxically, this seemed to convince them that she *was* Yggur; all but Yetchah, who still stared at her.

"How dare you enter this place!" said a woman she had never seen before. She had a fuller form than the others, and a protruding belly—the only pregnant Ghâshâd Maigraith had ever seen.

"Out!" cried Japhit, running up.

Their voices merged into a muddy clamor. A thicket of spears were aimed at her chest. She froze.

"Move aside, treacherous dogs!" she roared, putting the contempt into her voice that Yggur had always shown for his faithful Whelm servants. It was the first thing that had bothered her about him. "I've come for my own. Not all of you together can stop me!"

"My spear in your heart will stop you," grated Japhit, though she could see the fear in his eyes. "Go back!"

Maigraith dared not turn her back on them. Dared not go forward either, for the spear was at her breast. Worse, she could feel her hold over the transformation slipping. "Where is Maigraith?" she demanded, barely keeping the squeak out of her voice.

"She's gone!" Japhit lied, evidently not wanting to force a confrontation either. "We've sent her to Shazmak."

Maigraith allowed the broad shoulders to slump. "Shazmak!" she said, putting on a dead voice. "I should blast the fortress down."

The Ghâshâd stared at her. Maigraith whirled and stalked away, down the long hall toward the front door.

She did not look back—did not dare, for it would show how afraid she was. She could feel their eyes burning into her all the way, wondering how she had got in undetected, trying to understand what it was about her that was not quite right.

"That's not Yggur!" shouted Yetchah.

A ghastly pain spread out from the marrow of her leg bones, a series of contractions. The spell had failed; she was shrinking back. The floor went out of focus; she felt herself toppling. By an effort of will she recovered, suddenly closer to the ground.

"It's Maigraith!" shrieked Yetchah. "Stop her!"

Maigraith broke into a staggering run, trying to get used to her own body again. Her legs hurt as much as Yggur's had. The best she could manage was a lurching jog.

Ahead was the guard post and the front door. Two Ghâshâd stood there, blocking the way with their spears. Another group came racing up to the right. Even the ones behind were moving faster than she could.

Had she been fit, Maigraith might have used the Secret Art to blast them down, but now she couldn't have blown a gnat out of the air. Then, to her left she saw a series of narrow windows. She clawed her way up onto the sill, kicked out the lead-framed panes and fell through, not knowing whether it was one span to the ground, or ten.

It was far enough to bruise her from hip to shoulder. Japhit appeared at the window, but was too big to get through. Maigraith limped up the street, out of Ghâshâd-controlled territory toward the safety of the military headquarters.

That was only a few blocks, but she was half-dead before she reached it and an angry swarm of Ghâshâd were overhauling her two strides to one.

"Help!" she croaked, still a long dash from the gate.

Neither of the guards at the gate post looked up. "Codgie's offering three-to-one on Squeaker," she heard clearly, "but I think I'll go for Old One-Tooth again." They were discussing the mid-week rat races!

"Help!" Maigraith cried despairingly. They ignored her. Then, like a miracle, in the yard beyond the gate she saw a familiar squat officer addressing a parade. "Vanhe!" she screamed.

Good soldier that he was, Vanhe reacted instantly. He pounded through the gate, the squad just behind him. Vanhe snatched Maigraith out from under the nose of Japhit and threw her over his shoulder like a roll of carpet.

The soldiers formed a phalanx before the gate, others running up to support them. The Ghâshâd froze. Maigraith saw their staring eyes on her. Rulke had ordered them to hold her and they had failed. For a moment it seemed they were going to hurl themselves onto the spears in their desperation to take her back. One man broke free, attempting to do just that, but another tackled him right in front of the soldiers. They faced each other. Maigraith could feel them calling her, their cries tap-tapping at her skull like a chisel-bird after wood grubs.

Yetchah stood at the very front, panting. Hate glittered in her dark eyes. She would have disobeyed Rulke's command right there, had she been able to get to Maigraith.

Reinforcements began to pour through the gate. Japhit took Yetchah's arm. "Come!" he said. "There will be another time!"

The Ghâshâd were shamed and humiliated. Maigraith knew that they would do everything in their power to get her back, to make up for this disgrace.

Her legs hurt for days after, and the narrow escape made Maigraith realize how unfit she was, mentally and physically. Since taking up with Yggur she had been coasting. Having through her life been accustomed to rigid discipline and unending toil both mental and physical, she began an old regimen to get fit again.

This involved grueling exercise interspersed with periods of meditation. At the same time she set herself to solve an abstract problem involving both a chain of logic and leaps of intuition, while improvising a complex chant. In her youth Maigraith had taken refuge in these rituals, exercises and problems, and they helped her now.

About a week after her escape, there came a gentle knock at her door. She knew who it was—a messenger boy, a cheerful little fellow called Bindy, with a round face framed by dark curls. He came every day, always with the same question.

"What is it, Bindy?" she said.

He gave her an angelic smile. "Marshal Vanhe sent me. He wonders if you've heard news of Lord Yggur today?"

Vanhe grew more anxious every day. Maigraith gathered that the war was going badly. "I'm afraid not," she said.

The boy's face fell. "The marshal will be—"

"What's the matter?" She stooped to his level. "Will you be in trouble?"

"Of course not," said Bindy. "But yesterday, when no one was there, he was tearing his hairs out. I'm afraid we're losing the war. My poor mother cries every night. Since father was killed—"

"How did he die?" she asked gently.

"In the first war, last winter. I have three little sisters, and mother can't earn enough to keep us. If it wasn't for the money I earn we'd starve."

"How much does a messenger boy earn?" she asked him, touched.

"Two whole grints a week!" he said proudly. "And my meals and uniform. And when I grow up I'm going to be an officer in the army. I must report to Marshal Vanhe." Swelling his thin chest, he ran off.

Maigraith went back to her exercises, still thinking about the boy. An hour later she was in the final, or *nih* phase, that involved a dance of martial movements, now faster than the eye, now with a dreamlike slowness, almost a parody of a ballet, and her chanting was pulselike, a counterpoint to the dance. Suddenly she felt watched. The solution to the problem that she was working on slipped from her mind. The *nih* ended discordantly.

She opened her eyes, panting, and saw Vanhe there. He was short, only her own height, thick-bodied with a square jaw and a hard skull. Not a kind man, according to rumor, nor a cruel one either. Subverted by the Ghâshâd the other armies were falling apart, but his troops had stayed loyal. Startled, she gestured to a chair and offered tea.

"Thank you," he said, though his look said he would rather get straight to the point. His problems were pressing.

With the war at Thurkad's gates, with no news of Yggur and the violent appearance of a host of Ghâshâd, events were beyond his control. Yggur had been the leader in every respect. Vanhe was adrift and not a little afraid. "Your exercises look . . . challenging," he said.

"They are! When I began this regimen many years ago, I set out to solve the Forty-Nine Chrighms of Calliat. I work at these enigmas and paradoxes while I do my exercises."

Vanhe said nothing for quite a while. When he spoke it was in a rather subdued voice. "And how far have you proceeded? Are there *any* solutions?"

There was no trace of pride or even self-satisfaction in her voice. "Of the Forty-Nine, I have solutions for twenty-seven. Six more are nested—that is to say, they cannot be solved until all the others on which they depend have been solved. The seventh nest rests on the whole—it awaits the resolution of the other forty-eight. Two are improperly formulated, apparently an error of Calliat or her disciples, and must be restated. I have not done that yet. One is a nonsense—I cannot understand it at all. The remainder I have not tried." Her brow wrinkled as if she might even attempt a solution now.

Vanhe's jaw dropped. What she had just said was impossible. Of the Forty-Nine, only one had ever been solved. It had taken a team of scholars a year, and even now their solution was disputed. But he did not doubt her.

Suddenly Vanhe sprang out of his chair, staring at her with the look of a man who had just found the way out of a desperate situation.

"What is it?" she said, rising as well.

"I think I may have the answer to my problem," he said. "Tell me, have you had any news of Yggur?"

"Nothing," she replied, wiping the sheen from her forehead with a silken rag. "What problem are you talking about? The war?"

"Yes! Thyllan outnumbers us greatly—"

Again he inspected her. She felt irritated. What did this

rigid old soldier, with a face as hard and square and red as a brick, want from her?

The brick softened a little. "You were good for Yggur."

Maigraith laughed ironically. "Good in parts, bad in parts, like the famous egg."

"I sometimes wish I'd not given my whole life to the army," Vanhe reflected. "What sadder thing is there than an old soldier? Still, I chose, and I have seen many things. To business!" He gave a sketch of the situation. It was grim. "We're losing the war. Lost it, I should say. Of our five armies, all but my own, the First, have been undermined by the Ghâshâd. I don't have enough troops to defend the city."

"What do you require of me, Marshal Vanhe?"

He swallowed, losing control for a moment. The man was afraid. "Maigraith—"

"Yes?" she snapped. The situation must be disastrous, for him to show it.

Vanhe mastered himself. "You have surprised me." He hesitated.

"What?" she said anxiously. "What do you want?"

"I can't stand up to Thyllan. He knows it, and I know it, and so do my troops. If I try, the army will be annihilated and Thurkad ruined! Will you be our commander until Yggur returns . . . or otherwise?"

Maigraith was completely taken aback. "You jest, sir marshal!"

"Indeed I do not," said Vanhe steadily.

"I know nothing of leadership or armies."

"I'm not talking about war. We need a strong leader to negotiate our surrender."

Surrender! Suddenly Maigraith felt very afraid.

"I cannot do it, nor any of my officers. If Thyllan invades the city it will be bloody! You are clever, you are a thinker. You have power; you are Yggur's . . ."

Don't say woman, or concubine, or any vulgar soldier's term, Maigraith thought, or you will undo your case.

"You are Yggur's partner," said Vanhe. "His equal."

"But I do not know how to command . . . I shrink from dominating."

"I have spies and advisers aplenty. I need someone who looks a leader."

"You want a figurehead," said Maigraith, feeling depressed. The man was as bad as Faelamor. "A puppet!"

"I'm desperate, Maigraith. The city will fall within days."

"What can I do that you can't?"

"Thyllan is a mancer of some skill, and so are you. I'm just a soldier. I can never match him, but you can. Make him think we're still strong, then negotiate favorable terms for our surrender."

"I can't," she said weakly.

"You held Yggur for hours back in Fiz Gorgo. No one else has ever done such a thing." He seized her hand. "I'm begging you. Will you take it on?"

Maigraith took up the teapot, laughing nervously. It was empty. Seizing the excuse, she hurried out to the kitchen for hot water. She had always been tormented by self-doubt, had come to adulthood believing that she was of little worth, that whatever task she undertook would be badly discharged. Faelamor had never been satisfied. This offer was incomprehensible.

On returning, Maigraith realized that the marshal was still waiting, and she had laughed at his offer. Perhaps she had insulted him. She could never understand the protocols, the manners of these people. She squirmed under his gaze.

"I did not mean . . ." she began, but he dismissed her apologies with an inclination of his head. She tried again. "I'm not even master of myself. How can you ask it of me?"

"You do not want power," observed Vanhe. "That is a good start." He repeated his earlier arguments. "We need strength—you are strong! We need wit and guile; you have these things. And to escape a brigade of Ghâshâd the other day . . . My whole army is in awe of you."

Maigraith was afraid. Afraid of daring; afraid of failing. "You need *me*?" she murmured.

"Only *you* can do it," said Vanhe. "If you dare not, Yggur's empire will fail. It does already, for all our efforts. Would you give it away?"

"I don't care for empires," she said quietly.

"Do you care for people? If we fight over Thurkad there will be bloodshed not seen here for a thousand years. Do you want that?"

"I do not," she said, almost inaudibly. "But I am incomplete; insufficient."

"I did not say that you were the best we could hope for," said Vanhe bluntly. "Plainly you are not! But you are the best we have." Then he hit upon a winning formula, the only words that would do. "Do you not see a duty here? Surely, having made this alliance with Yggur, there is a duty that comes with it. Will you not take it up?"

Duty! She hardly heard the rest. How often had that obligation beaten upon her brow. The very word made her withdraw into herself, so that she could not question, once it was put upon her. Why *had* it been her duty to serve Faelamor and obey her will? She scarcely knew. It *was*, and she *did*. Somehow with her alliance with Yggur, duty to Faelamor had failed. Now a new one was forced upon her. All the joy had gone out of the day.

"I will do my duty," she said. "What would you have me do?"

Maigraith sat at the head of the war table, awaiting her first test with an empty feeling in her stomach. Thyllan had come into Thurkad to parley, though not to bargain. His strength was overwhelming.

Vanhe was on her right; the other senior officers on either side. A remnant of the Council and the Assembly were here too, a ragged lot. Time passed. Thyllan was late.

"Bindy," said Vanhe to the messenger boy, "slip outside, run down the street and watch for Thyllan. Keep an eye out for any funny business."

Beaming, Bindy ran out. "The boy loves to feel useful," grunted Vanhe. "He'll make a good soldier one day."

Maigraith's skin prickled. "Now, Maigraith," said Vanhe, "remember what I said earlier. You must look the part. You must steel yourself to power and to command."

"I have never held power. I don't know how."

"Try! You cannot appear to be a puppet."

"But I am a puppet—a mouthpiece for your orders."

He ignored that. "You must learn domination, or appear to have it. No soldier of mine has the discipline or the capability to do what I saw you do yesterday. Just take this as a fiftieth of your puzzles, which you must also solve. But first: Listen! Question! Think! Decide! And when you decide, *know* that you are right. Let the will *burn* within you like a flame. And then *enforce your will*!"

So here she was, maintaining an outward, regal self. In this she was helped by her striking if chill beauty, her stern demeanor and her reputation. Maigraith was little known but the subject of much rumor, from her first appearance at the Conclave to her reappearance as Yggur's consort. Rumor held that she was a woman of terrible power.

Save for Vanhe himself, the officers were sullen, afraid, and in one case openly insubordinate; but they would follow if she could prove her strength. The governing Assembly had always been puppets—they were of no account but to fill up the empty seats. The Council likewise, except for saggy old Hennia, a Zain who had betrayed Mendark's ragtag group at the fall of Thurkad.

"Thyllan is quick-witted, bold, fearless, aggressive," said Vanhe. "A confirmed opportunist. Don't trust him an ell, even though he comes under a flag of truce. If he knew how weak we are he wouldn't be here at all. The best we can hope for is to exact a few concessions in exchange for our surrender."

"I still don't know what you want me to do."

"Look confident, and when it comes to negotiation, consult your advisers and give ground grudgingly. We may yet escape with our lives, and Thurkad intact. Drat that Bindy—why has he been so long?"

At that moment the iron-bound doors were pressed open. A standard-bearer appeared, holding high a blue truce-flag. Marching up the room he slammed the pole into a socket at the head of the table. The flag hung limply, as if ashamed.

"All rise for Lord Thyllan," the standard-bearer thundered.

A tall, red-faced, scarred man stood in the doorway, waiting until every eye was on him. Tossing back his cape, he strode to the empty chair. A smaller man followed, gliding across the floor as on oiled castors. He was beautifully dressed, his black close-cropped hair gleamed with oil and his long mustachioes were waxed and coiled at the ends.

"Berenet!" said Vanhe in her ear. "He was once Mendark's lieutenant, and being groomed to succeed him, but they fell out as Mendark fled Thurkad. Watch him—he's smarter than Thyllan, and almost as cunning."

Berenet sat down at Thyllan's right hand. Thyllan stood, twirling the skirts of the mancer's robes he affected. Further down the table, Hennia kept shifting her dumpy body in her seat, her eyes darting from Maigraith to Thyllan and back again. Maigraith knew her only by reputation—a brilliant woman for all her appearance, but as unsteady as quicksand. Her support could only be relied on when it was not needed.

"Listen to me, all as one!" Thyllan had a booming voice. He played at being an orator, though he lacked the subtlety for it. "I speak as Magister, with the authority of the Council and the Assembly. The old fool Mendark is gone, the upstart usurper fled too, terrified of these Ghâshâd that he liberated but could not control. There is only one authority now—*mine*!"

He strode the length of the table, staring into the eyes of each of them. Maigraith was astounded at his arrogance. His forces had fallen like cornstalks before the march of Yggur. But then, Yggur was not here anymore.

"Your army is a rabble, Vanhe," Thyllan roared in his

face. "Surrender the city and you will be spared! None of us want this war." He thumped away again, thrusting his face at each of them, all the way down.

You're a strutting liar, she thought. This is a charade so you can play the general. "Is he speaking truth?" she said out of the corner of her mouth to Vanhe.

"I doubt it! The only prisoners he takes are those worth ransoming."

The hairs on the back of her neck stirred. If he would not spare a humble foot-soldier, what chance did they have? She felt panicky.

"We are not leaderless, Thyllan," said Vanhe as steadily as he could. "Maigraith was nominated by Yggur before he . . . went away. Our expectation is that he will soon return. Until that time we follow her."

Thyllan was taken aback. His darting gaze weighed her up. Then he laughed, a harsh braying that echoed in the bare room. Maigraith trembled. The explanation was hollow, else she would have taken charge weeks ago, before the war was lost.

"We did not fear Yggur in his strength," he boasted. "Why would we listen to the slut he abandoned when he fled? Let go the strings, Vanhe. Your puppet is a rag woman, and you so gutless that you cower in her knickers."

A different approach might have undone Maigraith but insults never would, for she'd had worse from Faelamor the whole of her life.

"What is your answer?" cried Thyllan. He rasped his sword out of its scabbard. No one spoke. "Would an example help you to make up your minds?"

Vanhe signaled frantically but Maigraith could not think what to do. How could she negotiate with this monster? As she agonized, Bindy slipped through the door. "Marshal!" he cried, sliding between the guards to dart up the room. "Treachery! The enemy—"

He was only half way when Thyllan stepped out in his path.

Maigraith sprang to her feet but she was too far away. "Bindy!" she screamed. "Go back!"

Bindy froze, staring up at the scar-faced man. "The enemy—" he repeated.

"Stay where you are, boy," grated Thyllan.

Bindy trembled as the big man stalked toward him. He wanted to run but was too afraid. Thyllan walked right up close and calmly thrust his sword through the boy.

With a barely audible sigh, Bindy slid to the floor. Thyllan turned to the staring room. "Well?" he roared.

Maigraith ran and took Bindy in her arms. He was in great pain. He did not cry, but his face was wrung with sadness. "My poor mother!" he whispered.

"I will see that she is taken care of," said Maigraith.

Bindy gave her a brave smile, then died.

She laid down the crumpled body. What hopes he'd had. How little it had taken to let the life out of him. Tears grew on her lashes. She did not try to hide them. Inside her a fire had begun to smolder. She fed it into fury.

Treating Thyllan as just another problem to be solved was hard, but she did it. After all, her whole life had been discipline. The man was a butcher. If they surrendered he would slay them all as casually as this poor child. She had no option but to take him, right now. Terror almost overcame her—her life had been submission, too. How could she hope to win?

She took charge of herself and in her expressionless rage she was so beautiful that it was terrifying. "The boy was my friend," Maigraith said quietly. She stood up, a quite slender woman, not tall. "Thyllan, I am arresting you for murder. Yield up your tokens of office. You will be tried fairly."

"Murder?" he said in astonishment. "There is no murder in war!"

"Put down your weapon."

"You refuse my peace offering!" he said with a grim smile. He threw up his arm, holding the stained sword high. "Then I will give you war *until the streets flow with blood.*"

"Making war on children is all you're capable of," she spat.

The room was in uproar. "Maigraith!" hissed Vanhe. "What are you doing?"

"What you put me here for," she said. "The boy is dead. Support me or we will all follow him!"

Thyllan whistled. The double doors were flung open. A band of twenty civilians ran in, but as they came through the door they cast their disguises away, revealing them to be Thyllan's elite troops.

"Treachery!" Vanhe shouted, springing to his feet. It was too late; his guards were already being disarmed. "How dare you violate the blue flag!"

"You see?" said Maigraith sadly. "Bindy was right. Thyllan planned this all along."

Vanhe understood, but he did not imagine she could do anything about it. Hennia the Zain half-rose to her feet, as if trying to make up her mind about whom to support, then sat again. The whole room stared at the soldiers, and down at the messenger boy. Their fate was written in the coils of blood on the floor beside him.

3

BATTLE OF WITS

Rage was burning Maigraith up, fury for little Bindy, dead at her feet, and for all the innocents who would die for Thyllan's ambition. She must bring down this monster even if she died trying. She *would* bring him down! But how? She was unarmed while he had twenty soldiers in the room.

As she hesitated, half a dozen of his most senior officers appeared, come to witness his triumph. Somehow they must be neutralized too.

Thyllan's guards were disarming the people at the table. Suddenly only Vanhe was between him and her. His strategy in ruins, Vanhe snatched out his sword and prepared to die.

Her fingers dug into his shoulder. "Fall back, marshal!" she said, and her voice was one that must be obeyed.

"My duty is to defend my captain," he said. "*I will not* go behind." He moved to one side, but in an instant the soldiers surrounded and disarmed him.

"Take her," roared Thyllan.

Maigraith put on her most arrogant expression. "I challenge you, Thyllan—you against me. Do you dare? Are you the equal of one *frail* woman, or must your dogs do the job for you?"

His face glowed red. He darted a glance at the watching officers. He dared not lose face in front of them.

Without a word he sprang, his sword making a blazing arc in the lamplight. Maigraith put out a slender arm toward him, jerking her outstretched fingers up in the universal gesture of contempt. The action looked incongruous coming from this elegantly attired woman, but it was more than a gesture. Thyllan's legs tangled and he fell on his face, the sword clattering on the floor.

There was a long silence then someone guffawed and most of the room joined in. Thyllan's troops went rigid in outrage, though two of his officers were smiling. They hated him! They followed him only because he was stronger.

Thyllan sprang to his feet, his mouth bloody. Every breath forced scarlet bubbles out of one nostril. Then he hesitated. Maigraith's *confusion* had been so subtle that he could not tell if it had been power or accident. But he could not afford to be shown up. He lunged at her with his sword, at the same time using his Art to weaken her and make her fear him.

There was strength in his sorcery, if little subtlety, and though the strength shook her, fear was the wrong weapon. Her rage for little Bindy burned it to ashes. She'd endured worse from Yggur in Fiz Gorgo: stronger, more cunning, more subtle and for longer. She brushed the attack aside with a casual flick of one wrist, and again Thyllan went flying. Once more he was left wondering what had happened, unsure if she had power at all, let alone what it was.

Berenet shouted advice in a language Maigraith did not understand. Standing well back this time, Thyllan spoke the words of a different spell. It attacked her self-confidence, something she had always been short of.

Maigraith froze, trapped in indecision. Thyllan was a great general, a great mancer too, one who'd overthrown Mendark himself. She was nothing compared to him! There was no possibility of defeating him. The whole room went still. She felt their eyes on her, knowing how insignificant she was. Hope ran out of her, drop by drop.

Thyllan had learned his lesson. He stood with his sword upraised, weighing her up. Blood dripping off the hilt red-handed him. Bindy's blood! Her rage suddenly rekindled; she laughed in his face. He flushed and she knew his weakness. He had a very short fuse; she must drive him beyond the point where he could control himself.

"You're a murderer, a liar and a fraud," Maigraith said. "Your pathetic Art wouldn't have troubled me when I was a child." While speaking, she was using her own talent to reinforce her words. She turned to his officers. "Did you hear how Mendark humiliated Thyllan in the wharf city? How he fled like a cur?"

Suddenly Thyllan snapped. "Die like a cur!" he screamed, and threw himself at her.

Maigraith stood paralyzed for a moment, then she seemed to flicker to one side. As Thyllan went stumbling past, his sword spearing a long strip out of the tabletop, she smacked him contemptuously on the backside. This time all but one of his officers joined the laughter.

Now even Thyllan's uncouth guard began to realize that something was wrong, as Thyllan tried a new attack, a different way. But he had spent the best of his strength; she countered him with only a tightening of the lips. He stood before her, panting, beginning to feel fear.

Forcing a smile, she stepped toward him. For an instant he seemed mesmerized, then he leapt backwards, crying: "Kill her! Kill her with arrows."

One of two archers at the door drew back his short bow. Maigraith turned her gaze on him, her carmine eyes crossed with indigo, and the man let fly his arrow into the ceiling. The other, a short, handsome fellow with curly brown hair, dropped his bow and put his foot on it. The diversion had not achieved the result Thyllan wanted, but it had made time for him. A knife appeared in his other hand. He flung it at her throat.

Maigraith swayed away but not quickly enough. The knife went deep into her shoulder, striking the bone and wedging there, a silver spike rising out of red petals. The pain was intense, piercing. Even her training was not enough to ignore it. She gasped, losing control.

Thyllan sprang at her, trying to spear her in the belly with his long sword. Maigraith threw herself to her left. The blade carved along her side, crimson following its path, then Thyllan slammed into her, knocking her off her feet. She fell flat on her back, sending a spray of bloody droplets across the floor. Grinning in triumph, he raised the sword in both hands to skewer her to the boards.

Maigraith's whole body was shrieking with pain and her left arm was useless. But after all, this was what her regimen had been for, all the years that she had been doing it. She had absolute control over the rest of her body, and her mind too. And she was working on his, whispering into his mind. *Don't strike yet. She's a cunning one. Make sure of her.* She drew her knees up into her belly. Come close, my enemy. Closer!

The sword hesitated for a fraction of a second. Putting on a weak little whimper Maigraith rolled back onto her shoulders, and as Thyllan loomed over her she kicked upwards with both feet. They struck him between his legs so hard that something went crack. Thyllan was jerked off the ground, falling backwards with a shriek that hurt her ears.

Maigraith pushed herself up. Her shoulder felt hideous but her will was stronger. Once more she smiled, showing no pain, and went after him. The fury so concentrated her will that he withered. Now he had no doubt that she had power, and it bettered his.

Thyllan crouched down, clutching his violated organs. "Berenet!" he screeched.

Who was Berenet? The memory was gone. Then, recalling Vanhe's warning, she saw that the dandy with the mustachioes was not in his seat. Where was he?

He came out from under the table behind her, sprang and put his knife to her throat. Maigraith choked. She had failed after all. Thurkad was doomed.

"Shall I do it?" cried Berenet, his perfumed breath all over her.

"Hold her," panted Thyllan from the floor. He glanced at his officers. Some looked openly contemptuous. "I must do the deed with my own knife."

Lurching to his feet, Thyllan took two pained steps toward her, then froze.

Something went *Thunk*! like a butcher's cleaver. The knife flew from Berenet's hand. Blood speckled her throat. Berenet stood up on his toes, staring at his hand. His thumb was missing. A razor-tipped arrow had come out of nowhere, taking the digit clean off. He could not comprehend how the mutilation had come about.

No time to work out why, or who. Maigraith locked Thyllan's eyes with her own. "Take back your knife," she whispered.

Fury almost tied him in a knot, but he was beaten. His hand reached out and with one convulsive jerk he pulled the knife from her shoulder, tearing the flesh open. Blood flooded her cream blouse from shoulder to wrist; another stream ran down her side. The knife hand quivered. Behind her Vanhe gasped, sure that Thyllan would slash her across the throat in his rage. For a moment even Maigraith thought that he might break her hold, but she clenched her will even tighter, his hand fell to his side and the knife cried out against the floor.

Maigraith's face was the color of plaster, but she must complete it. With bloody hand she tore the medals and general's blazon from his breast and ground them underfoot. In his pain and humiliation, his face was almost as white as her own.

"Take up your sword and break it. Submit to me, *on your knees*."

Her voice was harsh with strain. Even now he struggled,

then suddenly Thyllan was done. Stumbling over to the dropped sword, he lifted it high and smashed it sideways against a column. It snapped off cleanly at the hilt. At her gesture he went down on one knee and held up the pieces to her, cringing, holding them up like a shield as if he expected her to strike him down. It was agony for him. She was making a terrible enemy if he ever rose again. She took no pleasure in it, only wanting it to be over.

Maigraith scanned the room. The contempt of Thyllan's officers was evident. "Who among you dares to take his place?"

No one answered. They were mere soldiers, for all their rank, and none had the courage to pit his wits against her.

"Go!" she said softly to Thyllan, still holding the broken sword. "Never return to Thurkad or your life is forfeit."

He hobbled down the room and out the door. The shocked officers and guards turned to follow but she called to them, her voice ringing and echoing off the hard walls.

"Put down your weapons! The war is over. Thyllan is broken; neither Warlord nor Magister ever more. Any who serves him is outlaw. Swear to serve me; or if you still follow him, go weaponless." She looked them in the eye, each one.

Most knelt to give her their oath. Some did so willingly, in awe and respect; others out of fear or opportunism. But one or two put their weapons on the floor and went out quietly, including One-Thumb Berenet. Now it took every measure of her will to stay on her feet, though that no longer mattered. The job was done. Even had she fallen unconscious none would have thought the worse of her.

"Come forward," she said to the curly-haired archer who had saved her. "Who are you, and why did you betray your general?"

"I am Torgsted," he said, giving her a warming smile. "I am on secret duty. I never swore to Thyllan."

"Will you swear to me, Torgsted?" She gasped—the pain! He sprang to support her.

"Would that I could, my lady, but I am Mendark's man."

"Then go and do his work. Though we are at odds, I give you my protection until he returns."

Torgsted bowed and withdrew. She walked slowly back to the head of the table. Vanhe made no effort to aid her. Hennia the Zain, who had been up and down like a jack-in-the-box as the battle swayed first one way and then the other, was slumped in her chair. The whole room was stunned at the unimaginable reversal.

"Your puppet walks by itself," Maigraith said to her marshal.

Vanhe sprang to attention. "Do the officers pledge their loyalty?" he roared. "Does the Council show its support? Does the Assembly subordinate itself to Maigraith?"

They rose as one. "*Maigraith*!" they cried, and the whole room saluted her.

"There will be an election for Magister. I propose that Maigraith be elected. Do any gainsay me?"

Maigraith shook her head. "Nay, do not propose me. The office is not vacant, no matter what claims Thyllan has made. Mendark still holds that honor and can be removed only by death. Does this Council agree? Hennia, what say you? Do you pledge your loyalty, *now that the end is known*?"

Looking sick, Hennia did so. The times had undone her. Pathologically unable to commit to one side, the constant reversals were driving her mad.

The matter was agreed, attested with signatures, and copies distributed.

"Nor propose me for the Assembly neither," said Maigraith. "I hold no office willingly, but Yggur's I will maintain until he returns, or otherwise."

The meeting was closed. The room gave her an ovation, then Vanhe called for an honor guard, who escorted Maigraith back to her chamber. Vanhe himself saw to her wounds, and his attendants to her bathing and dressing. Then she fell into bed, her self-assurance draining away. She should have done better, sooner.

"Poor Bindy," she said. "Why could I not have saved him?"

"He died like a good little soldier," said Vanhe. "That was his fate."

"What kind of times do we live in that children must be soldiers?" she raged uselessly, knowing Vanhe could never understand.

Vanhe was well pleased. The desperate gamble had succeeded beyond any expectation. Even now his people were spreading the tale through the city and couriers galloping to the quarters of the empire.

"You could not have done better save by ridding us of Thyllan. He will always be our enemy, for he has no capacity to serve, only to lead, pathetic failure that he is." He turned to go.

"Vanhe," she cried. "Will you go to Bindy's mother?"

"That is one of my sadder duties," he said.

"And provide her with a pension, or employment."

"Of course. She will be taken care of."

She closed her eyes, feeling aftersickness coming on her strongly. It would be worse than ever this time.

Two days she tossed in her delirium, prey to terrible dreams and bouts of sickness, but on the morning of the third Maigraith woke to find herself better again, though weak and her shoulder very sore. The last time she had slept so long was after Faelamor took her out of Fiz Gorgo.

Vanhe appeared as soon as he heard that she was awake. "You were magnificent!" he said, the smile almost creasing his bullet head in half. "I'm sorry I doubted you. The tale has gone right through the city and won you a million friends, for all that you are a *gangia*, a foreigner. Thyllan has never been liked here save by renegades and opportunists."

Maigraith gave a wan smile. "Then my work is done."

"It's just started! My army is solidly behind you and the Fourth will swear to you tomorrow, if you can walk far enough to review them. Thyllan's forces are already breaking up—we'll have no trouble from them now. But outside Thurkad little has changed and the Ghâshâd may even come down with more fury, to counter you before too many flock to your banner."

"They don't want to counter me," said Maigraith. "They want to take me to Shazmak, to make up for their previous failing."

"They'll have trouble getting through my guard!" said Vanhe. He unrolled a map. "Now we must look to the empire, Maigraith. No matter how miraculous the rumors, to the rest of Iagador you are just a hope that is far away. Bannador suffers cruelly."

"Poor Karan," said Maigraith. "She loved her land dearly. I often wonder what happened to her. Well, you gave me power and I plan to use it. Put it about in Bannador that Karan Fyrn is my particular friend, and if necessary I will lead an army to liberate her country."

He looked startled. "An . . . interesting strategy," Vanhe said. His voice went cold. "Though of course such campaigns require careful thought, not mere whimsy."

He reminds me of my place, Maigraith realized. I am to be a puppet after all. Suddenly feeling too weak to resist, she fell back on the pillows.

"What more do you demand of me?" she whispered.

"For the time: only to rest, gather your strength, learn the art of command and listen to our spies and advisers. We have much work ahead of us: pushing back the Ghâshâd, countering their deceits, rooting out their spies, re-establishing our own. But we are skilled at that. What we don't know is what they will do next. How will they proceed? How can we counter them? These are avenues for you to consider."

"And Thyllan?"

"He's fled with a handful of retainers, One-Thumb among them. Thyllan is sorely humiliated, but a man of much persuasion. A pity you allowed him to live."

Nothing is ever good enough, she thought. Just like Faelamor. "Death is your trade, not mine," she said sharply.

"So it is, and I apply myself to it. Meanwhile there is a great deal for you to do if we are to wage war, in Bannador or anywhere else."

Maigraith said nothing. She would go to war if she had to, though what could be more terrifying than to have command of an army, to know that the lives of hundreds, even of thousands, rested on her whim? Worse still, that any mistake would be measured in lives. She did not have the strength to think about that.

4

The Vast Abyss

It was a glorious spring day in Katazza, the mountainous island that once lorded it over the Sea of Perion, as Kandor had made the sea his backyard and commanded all the lands around in commerce and in might. But the jewel of Perion was no more, dried up and gone long ago, leaving an abyss choked with slabs and bergs of salt, with vicious shards of congealed lava and boiling sulphur springs—the Dry Sea! The surrounding countries were desert. Kandor's empire was gone to dust. His unparalleled fortress city had lain empty for a thousand years, yet its astounding towers, built of plaited cables of stone faced in white and lapis, stood unchanged. The Dry Sea was the most watchful guardian of all.

Orange sunlight streamed in through the open embrasures, catching every mote in the air like a speck of purest gold. A lovely afternoon breeze stirred the motes to a playful dance, a careless rapture. But inside the highest chamber of the Great Tower the company were spent. The conflict with Rulke had hurt them terribly, despite their apparent victory. The burst of elation that came when they all strove together, and seemed to overpower him, was gone. Rulke's foretelling and his arrogant disappearance had put paid to that.

Now aftersickness resulting from their profligacy with the Secret Art was exacting its toll. Only Shand had any life in him, but he felt like plunging out the window. *Rulke was free*! What use anything anymore?

Karan and Llian were gone, lost somewhere in the gate, and the gate was dead as stone. Only Tensor could remake it, but the once-noble Aachim lay a twisted ruin on his stretcher. His face was swollen, his eyes mere slits staring unblinking at the ceiling. Every so often a shudder wracked him from head to foot.

I let you down Karan, Shand thought miserably. Scanning the room, he realized how badly his companions were suffering. There was work to do. Maybe it would help to keep despair at bay.

Yggur was stretched out on the floor, long as a pole. Lank black hair hung over his face like a kitchen rag. His complexion was waxen and covered in droplets of sweat, and he sucked in the air as though he could never get enough.

"Selial needs help more than I do," he panted, as Shand took his hand.

She was crouched on the stairs outside the broken door, heaving, trying to rid herself of a failed life. Her eyes were dead. Shand tried to lift her up but she gave a feeble moan and scrunched herself up into an angle of the wall with her arms over her head. Her nerve had broken—she'd not had the courage to stand up against Tensor and the result was all around her. She would never get over it.

Shand hurried to the next casualty, anxious to complete his work here. A thousand steps below, Malien and Tallia lay abandoned with their injuries. What must they be going through?

Osseion, huge dark warrior that he was, seemed unharmed. Aftersickness had not touched him, but he looked dazed, as if he just wanted to lie down and sleep.

Shand bent over Mendark. The Magister pushed him aside, climbing to his feet unaided. He was suffering as much as any of them, but he hid it so well that Shand could hardly tell. Mendark was not down at all.

"*Selial*!" he roared. "Bring your healers; attend to Tensor; make a stretcher for Malien. The rest of you, get packing! Be ready to leave in the morning. Osseion, make our gear ready." Then he moderated the tone of his voice. "Yggur, get up. We need you!"

Yggur jerked. Failure had sapped him of confidence. He was prey to a vast terror, that Rulke would return more powerful than ever and possess him as he had done before. Yggur would do anything to avoid that. He got up like an old man, yet he obeyed the summons: hesitant; much shaken; much reduced. Part of his memory was gone, from that time before he stepped into the gate at Thurkad to when Mendark reached into his mind and did *something*.

"What happened to me?" Yggur asked, shaking his head in a futile attempt to clear it.

"When Rulke possessed you an age ago, he must have left a hold in your mind that has festered there ever since, weakening you and making you fear him."

"I have had terrible dreams," said Yggur, still shaking.

"They're gone now," Mendark said soothingly. "I broke the hold."

Yggur looked puzzled.

Shand watched this exchange in silence, wondering. The previous roles of Mendark and Yggur had been reversed. Yggur was down but Mendark exultant. The conflict seemed to have burned out of him all self-doubt resulting from the year's failures.

Shand was too exhausted to worry about it. Plagued by his own shortcomings, he threw himself into his work. It did not help—the morbid thoughts about Karan were as strong as before.

"I'm going to see to Malien and Tallia," he muttered.

The rest of the company followed. Several floors below they met Tallia coming up. A broad bandage was bound around her forehead, crimping in her long black hair. Her dark skin looked drained.

"What happened?" she asked.

"When the Aachim blasted their way in you were knocked down by a piece of stone."

"I meant, up there."

Shand explained. "How is Malien?" he asked.

"Sick and sore, but in surprisingly good spirits."

Many stairs later, they entered the ruined chamber that had been Tensor's workroom. It was an odd-shaped space, having the form of a nine-leaved clover, with a carved stone fireplace in each of the bays. The hearth of one of the fireplaces was now a circular hole that led into darkness. Down all the way to the rift, presumably, for the Great Tower had been built over that fuming fissure—one of the most powerful places in all Santhenar to work the Secret Art. Tensor's pavilion, the fateful gate, was a pile of rubble. They set him down beside it.

Shand found Malien on the floor outside, some distance from her blankets. At his footfall her green eyes fluttered open. Her red hair was full of white dust.

"What have you been doing?" Shand asked gruffly, lifting her with an effort. "Crawling about on a broken shoulder. If any of *your* patients did that . . ."

"I had to know what was happening," she said, trying to smile. Pathetic though it was, her courage warmed Shand's heart.

"We didn't win, but we didn't lose either. Rulke has fled, back to the Nightland we suppose. Karan and Llian were forced through the gate before that. We don't know where."

Malien swayed in his arms. "Did no one try to stop them?"

"Who can stop Karan when she decides to do something? We were . . . a little short of courage. It happened too quickly. I tried and I failed. Tensor attacked Rulke. I fear he will never walk again."

"Take me to him!" she cried.

Osseion and Shand carried her in, setting her down beside Tensor. She found the sight of him quite shocking. The withering fury she had previously shown toward him was gone. "Poor, foolish man," she said, laying her hand on his brow. "Just look at you. When first I met you, callow girl as I was, I thought you would be the greatest Aachim of all time. Alas, you have a fatal flaw, Tensor."

Tensor did not acknowledge her. Malien sighed. She pitied him now, and for Tensor that was worst of all. "And Selial, Shand? What of our leader?"

Shand just looked at her.

"She's broken, hasn't she?"

"I'm afraid so."

Malien grimaced as she tried to rise. "Fix me up, Shand. It's up to me to lead the Aachim now, out of the worst peril we have faced since the fall of Tar Gaarn."

"You'll do what you're told!" he said, making a bed for her beside Tensor. "You're not to get up today, or tomorrow." He walked away, shaking his head. "Though how we're going to get you two home I do not know."

With Malien injured, Asper was the only healer among the Aachim. He was a good-natured man with spiky black hair and pupils like black lozenges across his yellow eyes. Asper set to work on Tensor. Shortly Shand added his own hands to the task. They stripped Tensor naked, washed him with wet rags and inspected him all over. The huge frame was powerfully muscled, the chest and thighs those of a wrestler, but one side of his chest was stoved in, his arm dangled uselessly and his whole skeleton seemed to have been pushed out of line.

"This is strange, Asper," said Shand as he worked on the splintered ribs.

"What?" Asper squatted back on muscular haunches,

brushing hair out of his eyes with the side of a bloody hand. He had quite beautiful hands, with the characteristic extremely long fingers of the Aachim, twice the length of his palm.

"The shape and number of his bones don't seem right."

Asper laughed. "We are not made as you are, do you not know? We Aachim have our own . . ." he searched for the right word ". . . race? Tribe? No, that is not right. We are our own species. Close to you, yet different."

"I knew that. I had not realized just how much you differed from us."

The first aid completed, Shand had all the time in the world to worry about Karan and Llian. What had Rulke said? *Did they know where the gate has taken them, they might have been less willing to enter it.*

"Where did they go?" asked Malien. "Has Rulke sent them back to the Nightland?"

"I don't know," said Mendark. "That's not the most important question."

"Then what is?" Shand shouted, so afraid for Karan that he felt like screaming. That would not serve with Mendark. Though not an unkind man, he was a schemer, and it seemed that he had seen an opportunity in this disaster.

"What he wants them for," said Mendark softly. "What are we to do about that? And about him?"

"Let's work out where they've gone," said Tallia, "then we can try to bring them back."

"No!" said Yggur, and though he tried to prevent it, a muscle in his cheek spasmed.

"What's the matter with you?" snapped Mendark. "I've set you free."

"And I intend to stay free," Yggur ground out. "I'm not giving him another chance."

"Had I known that it would turn you into a mouse," sneered Mendark, "I wouldn't have bothered."

"You can never know what it's like," whispered Yggur.

"Bah!" Mendark turned to Shand, putting on a smile that looked genuine. "What say you, Shand, my old sparring partner? What if Karan and Llian are trapped there? Should we even *try* to rescue them, or is the risk too great?"

"Seal the Nightland!" said Yggur in an inexorable voice.

"We'd better make sure he's in it first," said Mendark.

"Of course we must rescue them," said Shand.

"I agree," said Mendark. "Moreover, whatever our feelings toward Karan and Llian—and I care for them too—Rulke is the enemy. If he wants them we must thwart him."

"What if it's a trap?" said Yggur, the nerves twitching in his cheek again. "Maybe they're just bait, to entice us in after him."

"Perhaps," said Mendark. "Or maybe he really does need them. What say you all?" He looked around at the circle of faces. "Do we try to bring Karan and Llian back, or do we run and hide? Better run fast and hide well, if we do."

"We try," said Malien, and one by one the others echoed her.

Mendark raised an eyebrow to his adversary.

"Damn you!" said Yggur. "Of course I'll help—you can't do it without me. But you won't succeed."

"Suppose we do. Or if we fail. What then?" Shand asked.

"Make a gate to carry us back to Thurkad," said Mendark.

"Can we?" asked Malien.

"It's possible! Bury your dead, Malien, then we'll need your artificers to rebuild Tensor's gate and repair the copper mirror. Let's begin!"

The Aachim went about their mournful business. Three of their number had fallen, among them tall Hintis who had so hated Llian. Death had washed away the berserker rage that had characterized his last hours. The woolly hair was powdered with dust, the unlined features at peace, save for a swollen tongue protruding out one corner of his mouth. Hintis looked like an overgrown boy.

His friend Basitor tidied him up, ever so gently brushed

the dust from his hair, then two Aachim rocked the body onto a plank. Lifting him high, and the other bodies, they bore them out of the Great Tower across the western bridge into the fortress.

The Great Tower stood plumb in the middle of a plateau carved from a mountaintop, and was built over a fissure that bisected the plateau. The surrounding area was paved with large flat stones, here and there forced up by the roots of elderly fig trees. Three volcanic peaks stood above the north, east and west sides of the plateau, gently fuming. On all sides the mountain fell steeply, in a series of cliffs and terraces, to the blasted lands below, which were covered in ash and cinder. A road wound its way up to the top. On the shady southern side the terraces were moist and forested, with pavilions, temples and baths peeping out between the trees, offering glimpses of the Dry Sea beyond.

Behind the tower stood Katazza fortress, a large low structure built on a cliffed edge of the plateau overlooking the island and the Dry Sea beyond. Out of the fortress soared other braided towers, miniatures compared to the Great Tower, a thicket of slender minarets and a cluster of mushroom domes. Two stone and metal bridges ran from the fortress to the Great Tower, the only way in or out.

The Aachim were just disappearing into the fortress. Shand followed them across the bridge, musing. The Great Tower was by far the tallest building he had ever seen, and the most astounding. There was no structure like it anywhere in the world. It was built of nine spiraling cables of stone, woven together in a complex braid, the stonework faced with tiles so white that they dazzled the eye. About halfway up, and again just below the embrasures of the top chamber, the braided stone passed beneath collars sheathed in lapis lazuli with a narrow rim of gold at bottom and top. The tower was capped by an onion-skin dome of platinum decorated with crimson.

They carried the bodies into a room that had been cleaned

of every speck of dust and adorned with the beautiful, sensual art that was everywhere in Katazza. All the Aachim went in and shut the door, and apart from an occasional plangent note from inside, Shand never knew what went on in there.

Hours later they came out again. The bodies had been washed and perfumed, the hair brushed into place, each was arrayed in their finest. The Aachim carried the shrouded shapes out of Katazza, four to each one, in stately procession. They stepped carefully down the stone steps, paced across the paving stones, then followed a track that ran off the edge of the plateau. It wound among the boulders and roots of the forest trees, down to the little serpentine pavilion that Malien was so fond of, which looked through the trees over the Dry Sea. Two bore Tensor on his litter, and two more Malien on hers. The last, Tensor's healer Asper, carried the most precious thing that each of the dead had owned.

As the sun set they placed the dead in the ground among the twisting roots of a giant fig tree. Lighting up the tree with lanterns, they kept vigil all night. While their instruments wailed, and the bronze lamplight flickered on their faces, each of the Aachim composed and spoke a threnody for the dead. Far below, the little cones sprinkled around the skirts of the island were erupting, their brilliant lava fountains lighting up the bed of the sea.

At the end of the night the precious things were put beside the bodies, the graves filled and marked each with an obelisk. As the sun flashed its first beam at them from the horizon, a horn called three times three and they turned away.

Selial leaned on Shand's shoulder. "You cannot know what it is like to bury your precious dead on another world," she said in a choked whisper.

"I cannot," he agreed somberly. "But I know what it is like never to know where my dead are buried."

She had no answer to that. In silence they went back to the towers, to begin the perilous attempt on the Nightland.

The Aachim continued their preparations for the journey, in case the work failed and they had to flee in haste. They filled waterbags, packed tents, made sleds to haul gear and water across the salt, checked their water stills, or *trazpars* as they called them, and every other piece of equipment that would be needed. Sufficient food was already packed, for they had prepared it after their earlier rebellion.

Mendark, Tallia and Osseion made their own arrangements just as silently. Tallia collected a number of the glowing globes from the wall brackets, to light the nights of their travel. Only Shand seemed idle, for his preparations took no time at all, and he spent his time with Malien, or by himself at the top of the tower, leaning on the stone embrasure to look out across the Dry Sea, agonizing about the fate of Karan, and Llian too. Despite his well-known prejudice against the Zain race, he liked Llian and wished him no harm.

"Let's begin," said Mendark the following morning.

"How can we?" asked Malien. "We don't know where the gate took them."

"I came through it," said Yggur, supporting himself on Tensor's workbench, for he was still weak. "Had it taken them back to Thurkad I would have known it. They went somewhere else."

"That's my thought too," said Shand. "What say you, Tensor?"

Staring straight ahead, his eyes focused on nothing, Tensor gave no response.

"My guess is the Nightland!" Malien said. "Though I can't think why he wants them."

"Can't you?" said Shand. "I scarcely *dare* think what he might use Karan for."

"Let's get on with it!" Mendark snapped. "If we're hurt,

he is hurt just as badly. If we're weak, so is he! If ever there is a time to carry the attack to him it is now."

"I still think we should seal the Nightland!" said Yggur. "He's had plenty of time to prepare traps, and there's no way to identify them in *that* place."

"You would abandon Karan and Llian to him?" Tallia said coldly.

Yggur bowed his head. "It is harsh, but in war there are casualties, and often the greatest, noblest and cleverest are among them. To go into the Nightland would be to risk everything. That is his world; we know nothing about it. Who knows better than I the consequences of prying into the unknown?"

"Tensor does!" Tallia said.

She sat on a tread halfway up the curve of the stairs watching Mendark. Xarah and her twin Shalah sat together, sharing a joke. The artificers had reconstructed Tensor's pavilion as best they could. The broken columns had been rejoined with metal pins, the dents beaten out of the dome. Finally they lifted it atop the seven columns.

Mendark walked around the stepped pad, inspecting the stonework. There were many cracks and missing fragments. "It looks like a broken pot that's been badly repaired," he said.

"It's a pretty sad attempt," said Thel, the engineer in charge. She was stocky, with a strong jaw that she clenched and unclenched as she worked. "But in the time . . ."

The copper mirror, which Tensor had made to direct the gate after the Mirror of Aachan betrayed him, was equally flawed. A diagonal crease across it had been beaten out, but the mark was still obvious after polishing. Mendark pulled his beard.

"It'll have to do." He took a small stone out of his pocket. "Lift me up!"

Asper made a step for him. Mendark carefully placed the stone on top of the high point of the dome, then scrambled back down. While this was going on, the stair had been blocked with a screen and four Aachim had dragged in a glowing iron furnace surmounted by a contraption of coiled pipes.

"Begin!" said Mendark.

Thel poured some water into a funnel-shaped orifice and immediately steam gushed from the flared ends of seven pipes. Within minutes the air was full of fog.

Mendark held the mirror out in front of him and began to chant. The polished surface shimmered, images fleeted across it, then the pavilion was lit by a crimson flash. With a sharp crack the stone on the dome exploded into pieces, each speck tracing a glowing trail through the fog.

"Fix it, Yggur!" Mendark shouted.

Yggur held up his arms. One hand gripped a glowing red ruby. He grunted. The traces froze in place. There were seven bright ones and an uncounted number of faint trails, some barely visible.

"One, two, close together," said Mendark. "That's you, Yggur, and Faelamor, coming from Thurkad."

Yggur nodded, a dim shape in the mist. "And the third, shorter one, Faelamor departing again. She didn't go back to Thurkad."

"She may have intended to, though," said Malien.

Two more traces began together but halfway across the room spiraled apart, before stopping abruptly. A third, very bright trace followed a similar path, though it faded two-thirds of the way along. "The pair must be Karan and Llian," said Shand, "and the third one, Rulke coming from the Nightland."

"So they *have* gone there!" said Malien.

"Don't jump to conclusions!" Mendark cautioned.

The seventh trace began in a slightly different place, writhed across the room, spikes jagged out of it in all directions, then it too faded. "That's Rulke's departing trace," said Mendark, walking along underneath it. "I don't like the way it ends. Something's not right."

"It's meant to confuse, or entice," said Shand.

"He hasn't gone back to the Nightland," said Tallia.

"That gives me a little comfort," said Yggur.

"It doesn't give me any," growled Mendark. "What's he up to?"

"Can we tell where he's gone?" Tallia wondered.

"No! This only shows paths that begin or end here. Other gates are untraceable."

"Nothing more to learn here," said Malien wearily. "Let's go in, if we must."

"No, I'm worn out," Mendark whispered, sagging down on the step.

"And I," Yggur gasped. He waved a hand and the foggy traces disappeared.

"Shall *I* try to trace the gate into the Nightland?" Tallia asked.

"If you like, but hold back. Don't open it!"

"I won't!"

"How would you begin?" Malien asked.

"Maybe there were two gates," Tallia said. She was on her hands and knees, picking over a pile of rubble beside the pavilion.

"Two?"

"I think the one Rulke came through was separate from Tensor's. I'm trying to find the difference."

"Say it as you think it," said Malien, "and I'll tell you what I think. Perhaps we see the problem from different sides."

Tallia looked up at Malien with sudden friendliness, liking her.

"The gate Yggur came through is dead, but Rulke's may still be capable."

"Why so?" asked Malien.

"The Nightland is still whole, its defenses unbroken. Tensor made use of a flaw that has always been there, though it could only be opened from outside."

"In which case . . ."

"Rulke must hold it open. Let's try to recover the gate. Be careful, he might try to take control of it again."

They set to work. Shand sat on a bench beside the pavilion, watching, but he spoke rarely and only of inconsequential things. Tallia labored for hours, working carefully, cautiously under Malien's direction, trying to conjure up the intangible framework of the gate, that conduit that could tame the very fabric of distance.

Suddenly Tallia flung herself down. "I can't do it!" she said, laying her head on the dusty floor.

"Tell me what you can't do," said Malien, easing her arm in its sling. She climbed off her stool to walk around the pavilion, touching the stone columns with her fingertips.

"It's like trying to catch the end of an oiled thread in a barrel of jelly," said Tallia. "I can't see it or feel it. Even when I do sense it I can't get hold of it."

"And even if you did," said Malien, "there's no way to fix it to anything. But that's what gates are like. You have to sense the unsensable and touch the untouchable. Try to disconnect your rational self."

How? Tallia thought. All my education has been to build that up. Nonetheless, she set to work. An hour later she stopped again.

"I've done everything I can," she exclaimed, "and it hasn't worked." She felt the frustration keenly.

"Just wait!" said Malien.

The sun was setting, flaming through a south-western window, touching the sandblasted glass to little sparks. As the light faded Malien stood back, watching, supported on the other side by Asper.

"I think there's something here," Tallia said shortly.

She was sitting in the shadows with her forehead against the stone of the wall. Her eyes were closed, her palms pressing down on the floor.

"That's funny!" she said, looking puzzled.

Her body began to sway; her head described a circle in the air. Her arms trembled. She arched her back. Her head snapped backwards and she was drawn to her feet as if pulled up by a noose.

"Help!" she cried, vainly trying to beat herself down again with her hands. As she rose in the air a wave appeared to pass slowly through her head, distorting it as if it were being put through a mangle.

Shand ran, stood up on the tips of his toes and caught her by the ankles. "Mendark!" he yelled. Tallia began to choke.

"Gently!" Mendark shouted, running across. "Careful you don't break her neck."

Shand's feet were suddenly jerked from under him. He also began to rise in the air, but upside down. "Yggur! Asper!" he yelped.

"Mendark, *he's here*!" Tallia wailed. "Go back!"

Asper came running. Leaping, he just caught Shand's coattail but was carried up too.

"Help!" he roared.

"Mendark, what's happening?" screamed Malien. Aachim appeared from everywhere but they looked confused, helpless.

"It's a trap!" yelled Yggur. "Close the gate!"

"I don't know how. Mendark, do something!"

Mendark shouted a word. Tallia's legs jerked back and forth as if she'd been hung on a gibbet. The pavilion rocked and one of the columns fell into pieces with a tremendous smash.

On the other side Yggur had his arms out like a sorcerer's apprentice; he seemed to be feeling out unseen shapes in the air. He gave a bloody shriek and shook his hands. Steam rose from his fingertips.

Mendark choked as Tallia's head smacked into the domed roof of the pavilion, lifting it slightly. Her head seemed to pass through the metal, though nothing appeared on the other side. Screaming, "He's taking her!" he rapped out a series of unintelligible words, to no effect.

The dome suddenly became transparent, a ring cutting Tallia off at the waist. Shand and Asper rose into it too.

Yggur ran, leapt in the air and with both hands knocked the dome off the columns. It still hung in the air. He flung down the six remaining columns, one by one, kicking them into pieces on the floor. The dome remained suspended, a gate to nowhere.

Tallia had nearly disappeared now, just her calves sticking through, and Shand and Asper were half-gone too. "Oh, Tallia! I can't do anything," Mendark wept. "Yggur, please help!"

With a grim snort, Yggur brought out his ruby and thrust it high. He shuddered under the strain, went red in the face, then the dome rang like a gong and fell to the floor. He felt around the rim, muttering. With a great heave he lifted the dome and, like a conjurer's trick, the three lay underneath it.

Tallia raised her head then laid it down again. "It feels as if I've been turned inside out," she croaked. "The gate has mutated. I felt a presence, then an instant later it started to pull me in. It was horrible!"

"It's him," said Yggur, quite calmly now. "Rulke's watching us!"

Crawling out, Shand struck his head on one of the fallen columns. He looked more careworn than Tallia had ever seen him. "Oh Karan!" he whispered. "I'm sorry."

"Let's not be hasty," said Mendark. "We'll keep watch."

As night fell they saw a faint glow among the rubble. A luminous gas was seeping out of it, writhing and straining against its imprisonment.

"Oh!" said Malien, very disturbed. "I don't like *that* at all." She rubbed a dusty streak across her brow.

"It's oozed out of the Nightland. The gate is still open."

"And he's on the other side!" Yggur said. "We can't use it!"

"Is there nothing we can do?" Shand pleaded.

"Seal the Nightland!" said Yggur harshly.

"How can we? He's holding it open."

"I hate to say it," said Mendark, "but Yggur is right. The

gate is trapped. We've no option but to seal it." He cast a sympathetic glance at Shand.

Tallia shuddered. She looked around the room as if sizing up her enemy. She bit her lip. "I'd—I've got to try again," she said softly.

"After *that*? You won't!" Mendark snapped.

"How can we leave them there?" she asked. Having abandoned Karan once, she could not think of doing it again. "I'm prepared to risk my life."

"I'm not! It can't be done."

"Mendark—"

Mendark smashed his fist down on the dome. "The whole world is at stake, Tallia!"

"And I can't help thinking that you want it for yourself," she said, suddenly furious.

"I stand on my record, ever since Rulke was first put away."

"And you never stop talking about it," Tallia retorted. "Let posterity be the judge of your worth."

"I will, never doubt it!" he cried.

"I can't sacrifice them," Tallia said stubbornly.

"Pah! Then you will never be Magister after me."

"I don't want it, if it means that I'll end up like *you*!"

"Well, do you oppose me?" He stood up, and Tallia did too, so that he had to look up at her.

"Tallia," said Mendark, "no one cares more for Llian than I do. I . . ." he grimaced, "like Karan, too. But there isn't anything we can do for them. Surely you can see that? Does anyone disagree?"

No one spoke. "Well, Shand," said Mendark. "You've more at stake here than I have."

Shand was quite still. A tear leaked out of one eye and ran down his cheek. "I don't see how we can do anything for them!" He turned away abruptly.

"I suppose you're right," Tallia said sadly. "Do what you must do."

"Well, Yggur," said Mendark. "You have your way after all. How *do* we seal the Nightland?"

"I don't know anymore. I hadn't thought he'd be that strong."

"We don't have power enough to seal it," said Malien. "Unless—" Her eyes slid to the shaft by the fireplace.

"*Yes*!" roared Mendark. "Brilliant, Malien! So far we've failed for want of power. But if we all work together, and tap a greater source of power—"

"I've already tried it!" cried Yggur, his voice cracking.

"We must," said Mendark softly. "We will go down to the seat of Kandor's power. Down to the rift itself."

"No!" Selial screeched, the only word she had spoken in days.

5

THE MAP-MASTER

Tallia sat on the floor with her head hanging. Once again she had failed.

"We hurt Rulke," said Mendark. "And he is unused to the heaviness of our world. Did you see how he labored, climbing the stairs? We've got to act now, before he recovers his strength."

"Ha!" said Tensor in dismal tones. "He has defeated us. Let him have his way."

Malien rose, supporting her injured shoulder with her other hand. "What do you have in mind, Mendark?"

"We three helped to make the Nightland in the first place," he replied. "Me, Tensor and Yggur."

"And when Rulke possessed me you abandoned me!" shouted Yggur. "And Tensor—" His fury overcame him. Yggur stood with head bowed, fists clenched by his sides, his great chest rising and falling. "Tensor betrayed us all! He left a flaw in the Nightland so that he could let Rulke out at a time of his own choosing. Think that I would trust either of you again? Ha!"

Mendark continued calmly. "As I said, we three were there when the Nightland was made. We understand it and we can seal it up again. And when that's done we will tap the power of the rift to make our own gate, and get us straight back to Thurkad."

"The rift failed me two days ago," said Yggur, limping back and forth.

"But you had not the time to study it, to prepare yourself either," Mendark said carefully. "We have that time now."

"It would take years to master," said Yggur.

"Then I'll do it myself," spat Mendark, "with whoever has the *courage* to aid me." He went out.

"The bloody bastard!" said Yggur to Shand.

"I don't like him either," Shand replied, "but he's right." He drew Yggur to one side. "Come and have a cup of chard with me."

They leaned back against the wall with the chard bowls warming their hands. It was cold here, high in the mountains.

"You cannot begin to know what it was like when the Experiments failed," said Yggur. "Rulke clawed his way into my mind. It was like—*I cannot describe it*," he cried, "to have him raging in my head."

Shand met his eyes, silently sipping his chard. Yggur needed to talk. Let him say as much as he wanted to, or as little.

"Ever since I became sane again," said Yggur, "the thought of revenge has sustained me. But now I know I'm not his match. I'm afraid to do anything in case Rulke possesses me again." There were tears of helpless rage in his eyes.

"I know that feeling," said Shand, throwing his arm across Yggur's shoulders. Ahh, Karan, how it hurts.

"Mendark pushes me too far," said Yggur, somewhat petulantly.

"He pushes us all," said Shand, "though no harder than

himself. He's seen an opportunity that will never come again. If he succeeds, we're free!"

"How can he? How can *anyone* beat Rulke?"

"Well, let's at least have a go," said Shand.

Tallia peered over the edge of the circular shaft. The glow from below, that had been so bright when Rulke appeared, had died down to nothing. A massive ladder, crusted in stalactites of yellow and brown sulphur, extended down. It was very dark—she could see only half a dozen rungs.

"What's down there?" she asked. No one answered.

Mendark climbed onto a bench and began unscrewing the polished globes from the wall. "Get yourselves a few of these," he said, putting two in his pocket. "Well, who's coming with me?"

"I will," said Tallia, though she was afraid of the underground.

"And I," Shand said after a long pause. His eyes met Malien's, on her stretcher. You're not ready for it, he seemed to be saying.

"The Aachim must be represented. I will send Asper and Xarah with you." Then Malien paused, staring into nowhere. "No, Selial's failure must be balanced. I must come."

"One more," said Mendark, staring at Yggur, who was fidgeting among a stack of food packages in the corner.

The right side of Yggur's face was quite rigid. "I'll be there," he said in a choked voice, "but let it be known that I opposed this folly."

"As you wish," said Mendark. He slung a bag over his shoulder. "Shall we go?"

Tallia followed him almost as reluctantly. She had never liked confined spaces. Sulphur crusts crunched under foot and hand; she felt her hair drawn up to the rungs as she went down.

The floor below the gate chamber, as they now thought of the place that had been Tensor's workroom, was completely empty, though stains on the floor in one place suggested that experiments had been carried out there. The floor below that, the third floor of the tower, was also vacant. The walls and ceiling were hung with crystals yellow, brown and black.

"It's hot!" Asper said, mopping his brow.

"Not as hot as the Dry Sea will be, if we have to walk it," Mendark said tersely.

A puff of acrid air wafted up, sending them into fits of coughing.

"It burns my throat," choked Xarah, a small woman with yellow hair. She and her inseparable twin, Shalah, were the youngest of all the Aachim.

"This place is perilous," said an unusually quiet Asper, wiping streaming yellow eyes with the back of his hand. "The air burns my lungs."

"Then go back, if your kind do not have the courage!" Mendark snapped. "All our options are perilous."

Asper grimaced, as if his honor had been impugned.

They rested at the ground floor, in a room that reeked of brimstone. It was hotter yet.

Below they passed into a vast space cramped with a myriad of pipes that twisted between the tower's complex foundations. Huge cables like coiled springs swept down in outflaring curves from ceiling to floor, crossing one another before plunging into pocked and scaled sockets. There were nine cables, one running up the middle of each of the spiraling rods of stone from which the tower was made. Smaller cables spun away from each of the main ones, holding them in position.

"Ach!" said Asper, ducking his head to walk underneath. "So that's how it works!"

"What?" asked Shand.

"We could not understand how this tower was held up. Being built over the rift, an earth trembler that moved one side more than the other could bring down the whole structure."

"It's stood for two thousand years," said Mendark, impatient to get on.

Asper wasn't listening. "See how the great cable springs hold the tension, while the foundation blocks can move this way and that. What genius!" Then he said, "Malien, Thel, come quickly!"

"What is it?" Shand asked, weaving though the web of smaller cables toward him.

"This block is at the very limit of its travel," said Asper, pointing.

"What does that mean?" asked Xarah.

"It means," said Thel the engineer, "that the next big trembler could unseat the foundations, in which case the tower will surely fall."

"And it may not take a big one," Shand said. "Look at this!"

They all crowded around, save Mendark, who was disappearing down the shaft. Just above its socket one of the huge spring cables, as large around as Shand's chest, was badly corroded beneath the encrusting sulphur. He picked bits of crust off. "The whole structure is under such tension that if this breaks, the other cables must pull the tower down."

"Maybe, maybe not," said Malien, holding her injured shoulder. She was as pale as paper. The one-handed climb down had hurt her. "Let's hope we don't find out."

"Mendark," Tallia called. "Come back!"

Reappearing, he examined the structure with his lightglass. "Hm!" he said, straightening up. "Up top it looks so solid, and all the time this cancer is eating it away from within. Well, no help for it; let's go down."

"It could fall at any moment," said Tallia, biting her lip. She was strong in the face of a known adversary, but this deadly uncertainty undermined her.

"It could. And Rulke could come back at any moment. Or any one of us could fall down the ladder," Mendark said scornfully. "A hundred chance things could kill us every day."

Tallia had to force herself to follow. They had felt earth tremblers here daily, and every day they were stronger.

Something was going on deep in the rift. The Great Tower now felt to be resting on eggshells, and she was desperately afraid of being entombed beneath it.

They went down a long way, through a well of layered basalt. Finally they reached the bottom, an excavation into solid rock like an upside-down mushroom with the well as its stalk. The vast room was empty but for several crusted benches carved out of the stone of the floor. A closed-up crack bisected the floor directly underneath the shaft. It was clustered with geyser-like mounds stained red, brown and black.

"The rift!" said Tallia.

"Indeed," Mendark replied softly.

She paced around the room and at each quarter-turn felt a breeze on her cheek from a ventilation shaft, though she could not see daylight up any of them.

"How are you going to do it?" Xarah asked.

Mendark frowned at the stone bench. "I'm not sure that I know," he said heavily.

Many hours later, the company had assembled at the bottom of the shaft again, all but Tensor, whom Mendark would not have near. They had collected such objects of power as they could obtain, including a fragment from the gate that Rulke had come through, and the restored metal mirror. Yggur had relinquished his most potent artifact, the grapefruit-sized ruby that he had used previously. The Aachim had worked all night, shaping the ruby into a rod and polishing the ends until they were perfectly parallel. Then they cut down the metal mirror to make a pair of small caps which they fixed over the ends of the ruby with the reflecting side inwards. The whole device was then wrapped around with metal bands, and shaped pieces of stone from Rulke's gate clamped to it.

"What is it?" Tallia asked.

"It doesn't have a name," said Mendark. "I only just thought it up. You could call it an ampliscope, I suppose. Ready, Yggur?"

Yggur trembled. "No!" he choked, standing astride the rift and gripping the device in two hands. Holding it out at arm's length, he nodded, a puppet-like jerk of the head.

Closing his eyes, Mendark held up a carefully chosen lightglass, a polished sphere of green heliotrope the size of an orange. Inside, the stone was spotted with red marks like drops of blood. "Conjure power, Yggur. And aim true, or you'll burn my hand off." He called to the others, "The remaining lights out *now*!"

The Aachim extinguished their lightglasses. The hot room was lit only by the glowing bloodstone, pale green with red flecks. A wisp of vapor drifted up from the rift. The faintest vibration shivered the rock beneath their feet. Tallia's skin crawled. She darted a glance upward but the foundations made no reply.

"Do you recall how the Nightland was made, Yggur?" Mendark asked softly.

"My very cells are imprinted with it," snapped Yggur.

"Good, for we must fit that print to the sphere. I will draw power from this place," Mendark said. "Yggur, you are to focus and amplify it."

A shudder wracked Yggur. His outstretched arms trembled. "Bring it forth!" he whispered. A tiny flare of pink leaked out from between finger and thumb. His whole body began to shake, then with a mighty wrench of will he took control of himself. The end of the ampliscope wavered then steadied, pointing directly at the bloodstone.

Tallia could feel the tension, the strain as if every atom in the room was energized. A tiny hum came from the device. It built to a drone, a whine, a shriek, a blast of sound that hurt their ears. For a fraction of a second a ruby beam of light burst out through the further mirror and struck the bloodstone.

The globe glowed like a cloud of bloody droplets. Mendark grunted, then the radiance spread out to the size of a boulder and hung in the air, frozen light.

"A tiny image of the Nightland, as it was when it was made," said Mendark.

"I did not imagine it would be so easy," said Xarah, holding her sister's hand.

"Ha!" Mendark replied. "This is only the beginning, and a very tentative one at that. Now we must sense out the boundaries of the Nightland, map them to this sphere and drag the map to the correct shape. Only then can we try to close the gate on him."

"Get on with it!" Yggur snarled. "This is like holding a horse over my head. I can't do it all day."

Mendark took a small object from his pocket, a piece of yellow amber in the shape of a comb with three teeth, attached to a band which he put around his head. "I am the only sensitive here, am I not?" He looked to each of them in turn, but no one indicated otherwise. "I will do the sensing while you, Selial, take this comb and map the boundaries of the Nightland onto the sphere." He turned to Malien. "Malien, I would not ask this of you but there is no one else—will you take my place?"

Malien eased her arm in its sling, flinched, then said, "I'll channel the power, as best I can. Begin!"

She gave Mendark her free hand. He closed his eyes; his lips moved. Selial touched the amber comb to the sphere of frozen light and three fine yellow lines appeared there. She scribed the comb smoothly around the circumference of the sphere. The trio of lines followed it, around and under and back, next to the starting point.

"That was hard," said Mendark, dashing sweat off his forehead.

"It's not the hundredth part," said Yggur in a hoarse voice.

"I know!"

They continued. At the beginning of the third circle a tiny wiggle appeared in the scribed lines. Selial steadied herself, but before another quarter-turn her arm began to jerk back and forth, creating a wild series of zig-zag marks. Without warning, she dropped the comb. Her arms fell to her side; her breast heaved; her haggard face crumpled like crepe.

"I can't do it!" she gasped, choking for air. "I can feel him on the other side, watching and waiting. Gloating!"

"Aah!" groaned Yggur, his bad knee buckling. He would have fallen had not Tallia sprung to his side. The sphere of light began to grow dim.

"Hold the sphere!" Mendark roared. "More power, Yggur. Lose it and I may never get it back."

The muscles of Yggur's cheek were working, his eyes darting this way and that. The sphere brightened slightly.

"Are you all right?" Mendark said sharply.

"I . . . I think I can overcome it. You can never know, Mendark, the frightful memories that this brings back."

"I'm supporting you."

"You weren't last time!" Yggur said coldly. "Well, what are we going to do?"

Mendark cast an eye at Selial, a broken wreck on the floor. Her nerve had failed again. He shook his head.

"I'll have a go," said Tallia, "though I've not done this kind of thing before." She bent down to take the amber comb from Selial's limp fingers. Her own shook, more than a little.

"Think of nothing," said Mendark. "Empty your mind completely—just open yourself to my sending."

They started again. Tallia found it incredibly hard work. She began to trace the outline onto the sphere. The trio of yellow lines were all twisted, almost as bad as Selial's last had been.

"No, no!" Mendark yelled. "You're not following me. Concentrate!"

They began again and this time it was a little better, and improved as Tallia learned how to follow Mendark. They had half the sphere done before he suddenly slumped to the floor, breathing hard.

"I've got to rest," he said. "Can you hold it, Yggur?"

"I'll have to, won't I? Be quick!"

"Just a few minutes," Mendark said, hanging his head between his knees.

Tallia was glad of the respite. She felt quite faint, and when she closed her eyes could still see the wavering triplets of lines. As she did so the floor shuddered. Hot gas hissed out of the crack in the floor and caught fire in the air, producing choking white fumes. One whiff and she could feel it searing the inside of her nose, throat and lungs. Her eyes began to sting. She felt suffocated, claustrophobic.

Tallia sprang up, gasping, "Quick! Up the ladder."

The bloody sphere of light, half-woven with lines of yellow, vanished. Pent-up aftersickness exploded in her head. Tallia lifted Malien over her shoulder and ran for the ladder. Each breath was like breathing acid. Most of the Aachim were there already, jostling each other.

"Out of the way!" Asper shouted, trying to carry the helpless Selial through.

"No, you fool!" Malien grabbed at his shoulder. "Let the strong go first, else we will all die here for the weakest."

In an organized panic they clambered up the ladder. Asper was one of the last, panting under his load. Tallia followed, forcing against a sickness that grew steadily worse, and last of all Basitor and tall Blase. The white fumes billowed about them like waves on a stormy sea, one second rippling gently around Tallia's ankles, the next bursting up the shaft in a torrent that had them all hacking and clinging helplessly to the rungs while they tried to heave up their burning lungs like vomit.

"Aaah!" cried Blase.

Tallia looked down to see his fingers slip off the rungs. He fell into the fumes, a dull thud notifying his arrival at the bottom. Basitor started to go after him.

"No!" cried Tallia. "That's certain death!"

He looked up at her with bloody eyes. "Death is certain!" But he did not go down.

They reached the basement where the foundations were. A few white puffs ebbed out of the shaft to dissipate in the open space, and that was the end of it. A few minutes later, looking down with her lightglass, Tallia could see all the way to the body.

"Shall we try again?" asked Malien.

"Have to remake the ampliscope first," said Mendark, taking it apart. One mirror cap was burned through from the intensity of that burst of light. The polished end of the ruby was stuck with drops of condensed metal. "Malien, we'll need as many of these caps as your people can provide."

It took some hours to restore the device to its previous condition—hours when, twice, the living rock trembled all around them with enough force to make the shifting foundations groan. But they did not unseat themselves, the spring cable did not break, the tower did not topple, and eventually the group went down again, knowing that they were past their best.

Blase's body was picked up, honored according to Aachim custom and carried up the ladder. Those Aachim no longer required—half of them—went with it, to prepare for whatever departure they would make. No point risking all their lives in such a hazardous place.

Once more Mendark held up the bloodstone lightglass. Once more Yggur straddled the rift and, as Malien summoned power from it, amplified it within himself and directed it into the ruby rod. Once more that crimson beam blasted through the mirror and pumped up the bloodstone to a sphere of solid light. White-hot sparks blazed curves though the air; molten metal dripped from the end of the ruby.

Mendark swore, a shrill cry of pain. A huge red blister grew on the side of his hand, product of the misdirected ray. He staggered, almost fell, then stood up straight by an effort of will. His hands held the sphere high and did not waver.

"Sorry," said Yggur without sympathy.

"Come on, come on!" Mendark screeched.

Tallia felt sluggish as she moved. She reached out for the three-toothed comb and felt Mendark's sending thump into her mind.

"Now *concentrate*, harder than you ever have before," he shouted.

She began to scribe the yellow lines around the blood-spotted sphere, first tentatively then with a growing confidence, feeling for the first time in her life that she worked with Mendark as one. Finally she drew the last triplet—the sphere was completely encircled. Tallia sighed and made to lower her arm, which was aching almost as badly as her head.

"Not yet!" cried Mendark and Yggur together. "Again, the other way!"

Tallia almost gave up. The work was only half done! The flesh was drooping off Yggur's rigid frame as if pulled down toward the rift. Catching her gaze he drew himself erect.

"I will not give in now," he said limply.

Tallia began again, crossing the previous set of lines at right-angles. By the time she'd finished the sphere positively glowed with bloody droplets, but that was not the end of it either. "My arm!" she gasped.

Asper ran across to massage the cramps away. She had to do it again, obliquely, and once more the other way. When Mendark was finally satisfied she collapsed.

Mendark looked to Yggur, and then to Malien. They were all half-dead with strain. "Still a long way to go," Malien said.

"It's a very poor model of the Nightland, as I sense it now," Mendark replied. "Well, master map-maker, show us how it's done."

Shand came out of the shadows and took up the comb. With the three teeth he caught hold of a yellow thread here and there, or sometimes a whole group of them, slowly teasing them out until the shape was no longer a sphere but more like a knobbly potato, warped, knobbed and pitted all over.

"That's more how I understand it," sighed Yggur.

"And how I sense it," Mendark replied.

"There are more dimensions than these three," said Shand, "but we'd need a better model than this to map them. Still, I think it'll do. Now to find the flaw; the way in."

6

NIGHTLAND

Llian tumbled through empty space. "*Karan*!" he screamed, blinded by the light.

With a smack his nose hit something hard. Snatching at it, he felt smooth warm skin and Llian found that he was holding Karan by the shin. He shifted his grip, looked down and saw her beautiful face upside down near his feet, surrounded by an aurora of white and blue light.

Karan tried to smile, though it was an effort to do so. Holding him was like trying to press two magnets together; an unseen force tried to fling them away from each other.

"What are you doing down there?" she shouted over the roaring of the wind. She held his belt while he twisted around and groped his way up her body. They clung together, lip to lip, breast to chest, thigh to thigh, through a passage that was endless; where time seemed to have no meaning. And in that eternal crossing, even through closed eyes the colors warped all around and in and out.

"Where are we going?" Llian whispered.

"I don't know. I thought the gate would take us back to Thurkad. That's where Yggur and Faelamor came from."

"We should be there by now. When Tensor sent me through his gate I came out the other end straight away."

Karan had a horrible thought. "Maybe this isn't that gate," she said. "What if Rulke came through a different gate?"

Just then something shivered between them. Llian's eyes snapped open in alarm. Karan was staring directly into his eyes and her pupils were so wide that the glorious green disappeared. Her red curls were a riot of waving tangles.

"Something's gone wrong, hasn't it?"

"Yes," she whispered. "Llian, hold me tight. I'm afraid this is the end."

He squeezed her so hard that she could scarcely breathe. "Well, at least we're together," he whispered into her ear.

Even as he spoke, a visible ribbon of the ether insinuated its way between them. It had color and form but was intangible. Then a tiny bubble formed in the middle of it, a hard little bean pressing against Llian's chest. It began to swell rapidly, like a balloon being pumped up, prising them from each other. Llian tried to push it away but his fingers went through it with barely any resistance. Already an arm's length separated them.

"Llian," Karan screamed. "Don't let go!"

She clung to his arms but her hands were slowly forced down his wrists. They gripped hands, straining against the pressure. Their efforts were futile. The balloon burst without a sound and flung them apart.

Llian sought about wildly for Karan but all he could see was her black shadow spinning off, dwindling against the pulsing glare. The madness of thrashing light and sound cut off his senses one by one, and though he cried out to her he had no voice to be heard. Now he lost sight, hearing, touch. He was lost in a dimensionless place for an unknown time, then smashed through a crystalline window and skidded across a floor as cold and slick as ice.

Llian lay there for some time, completely blind and numb.

Pain was the first sensation to return. He woke to feel his body tormented in a dozen places. His tongue, badly bitten from Tensor using him as a shield against Rulke, felt as if he had licked a saw blade. His knee throbbed from some other forgotten accident.

Cold—ice—floor? he thought laboriously. Then either dead or alive, I am no longer in the gate, but somewhere *real*!

He opened his eyes. The madness of his passage had left its after-image there and he could see nothing but colors. Cold crackled against his face.

Fading colors, fading into black. Intense black and an impression of enormous cold space. Definitely not Thurkad! He blinked. The floor was as hard as metal, and might have been. He sat up. The colors appeared again briefly. The air was frigid on his wet face. Wet? Llian put an invisible hand to his cheek, traced the sticky wetness up and flinched—a gash across his temple. Pressing the ridged edges of the wound closed with his fingers, he stood up. There came a spasm in his ankle. Llian kept on going up, his feet lifting off the floor then slowly drifting back down again. He felt only a little pain as he landed, so the ankle must not be broken.

Now the blackness was less than total and he sensed—for he still could not see clearly—that he stood in a vast hall. A black floor stretched out before him. There might have been a black dome above, teasingly beyond his vision. Mist hung near the floor. It had the faintest shimmer but when he moved through it the mist trailed away in slow-moving, coiling banners touched by phosphorescence. Llian had read of the blood-warm seas that glowed when a hand disturbed them, but this was different: a chill, inanimate luminosity that showed every swirl and eddy of the sluggish air.

Where was he? He had never been anywhere like it; had never even read of such a place, though a palace carved out of the mountains of ice at the southern pole might seem like this.

The cold came up through the travel-thin soles of his boots. He had to keep on moving. His ankle was swelling, already pressing against his boot and becoming more painful with every step. Llian's head ached and his stomach roiled; from the gate, he supposed.

"Karan," he said softly, inhibited by the alienness and dimensions of his surroundings. "*Karan!*" more loudly, his breath smoking. There was not even an echo to mock him with temporary hope. He shouted her name but in that vast room his voice sounded lonely and lost, a plaintive bleat—a lost sheep. The image brought the fate of such creatures to mind: prey of wildcats or hunting dogs. What things dwelt in this uncanny place, to gorge upon such pitiful creatures as he?

Where could Karan be? They'd been separated a long time before he landed here. Had she ended up here too? Or was she lost somewhere *between* in a place there was no returning from? Was she dead already? Gates were treacherous devices.

He walked on miserably, with bouncy steps that were the length of running strides. That was strange, but everything was, here. Nothing fitted into the pattern of the world he was used to. And the cold had crystallized in his bones. He could not walk quickly enough to warm himself.

At last Llian could limp no more, not even if he froze. He sat down on the floor and, searching through his pockets, came upon a corner of dark bread, a fragment left over from days before. He chewed the piece slowly, with dry mouth, but it was soon gone and the hunger unabated.

It was too cold to sit. He hobbled on, realizing how much he had come to rely on Karan. He remembered his romantic illusions before he met her, on the road up to Tullin, with disgusted amusement. That foolish youth, his head full of fancy from years of the Histories and nothing else, longing for glory and great deeds. What a callow youth he had been—what a clumsy, vain fool. He was not made to be a hero. He was a chronicler and would never be anything more.

That reminded him of his original quest, forgotten in the turmoil of the past week—what had really happened at the time of the Forbidding, and who had murdered the crippled girl? Llian sensed that he had been near part of the answer; that there was a vital clue he had overlooked, or a vital piece of evidence he had not yet found. Was it here or back in Katazza? Maybe Rulke had the answer. Perhaps he knew where Kandor's records could be found.

He wandered along in these fantasies, oblivious to his vow of only an hour ago. His way in the world was now quite different, and his first purpose to record the *Tale of the Mirror*—now beyond question a Great Tale, and one that must be told whatever the outcome.

Lost in such delightful dreams, Llian had hobbled a considerable distance. Becoming aware of his surroundings again, he found that he was standing in the entrance to another great chamber. Moreover, for it was lighter here, one whose appearance struck a familiar chord. Familiar indeed—the ghostly light showed obsidian pillars as wide as the trunks of forest trees, and beyond, a carven ebony throne . . .

Had he fallen into a nightmare? This was the place he'd seen in his nightmares, and in those he'd shared with Karan long ago. The memories brought back the horror. This must surely be the Nightland, a bubble of nothingness enclosed by an impenetrable cyst—the place made to be Rulke's prison. *The Taking of Rulke* was a Great Tale, one that Llian had studied in all its versions and variants. The Nightland was a dark cold soulless place, a place to sap the will of Rulke, to weaken him.

Well, out of that nothingness Rulke had fashioned an icy palace. Surely within it must be all that he needed to survive. Rulke was flesh and blood too—he must eat, must drink, must sleep. Somewhere sustenance must be found. That set Llian thinking about the Nightland, as he walked along. What was it made from and how had Rulke shaped it since? For the *Tale of the Mirror* he would need to learn all that too. No one had ever written anything about this place. No one had ever been here. If he were the first—but what point to these foolish dreams? If he couldn't find the gate again, here he would remain until he died.

No escape! Llian sank into a bitter despair, a hopelessness blacker than the blackness of the Nightland itself, perhaps the echo of what Rulke himself must have felt at the beginning of his imprisonment. Yet *he* had never given up. All that time he had dreamed and schemed.

If only Karan were here too. But how could Karan find a way out where, for a thousand years, the genius and the strength of Rulke had not been able to?

Already the odor of this place works upon my spirit, he thought, beginning to understand how Rulke's imprisonment must have chafed him. Little wonder he feels such bitterness and malice toward us. And what was Rulke up to now? Maybe he had overcome everyone in Katazza already and prepared to move on the rest of Santhenar.

Llian suddenly felt very small, alone and frightened. Realizing that he was still standing before the vast throne, he hurried away, calling Karan's name in a loud voice. The echoes pursued him across the room.

On the far side he saw the outline of another door. Though closed, when he pushed it moved easily. He entered a smaller room which was faintly lit. There was a large and intricate object in the middle of the room, a machine of some kind, but as the light came from the far side he could see it only in outline. The outline made no sense, even when he walked all around it. In the dim light the complex shapes seemed to shift before his eyes. His skin crawled. Whatever it was he wanted nothing to do with it.

"Karan," he cried in a great voice, making for the door again.

"Karannn . . . araaann," moaned the echoes. There was no reply.

7

The Black Pool

In the gate Llian's arms were torn off Karan and he whirled away, then vanished. Karan, too, went blind and deaf, though she knew exactly where she was going, for like Mendark she was a sensitive, and in her mind's eye she could now see her trajectory as clearly as if it were a paved road extending across the sky. But she had no idea where Llian was. He had simply winked out of existence.

The road dived into a black hole shaped like a corkscrew. She spiraled through until finally it spat her out the other end into an inky pool. Karan bobbed to the surface and tried to swim to the edge. The first stroke lifted her right out of the water, leaving a trail of black drops drifting in the air behind her like soap bubbles. She splashed back down, touched bottom and stood up. Even that pushed her up into the air. The liquid came up to her waist here, and when she stood up it tried to tip her off her feet. She waded out onto the shore, her head beginning to throb, an effect of the gate.

The stuff in the pool was cold but did not wet her; now it

cascaded off her clothes and tumbled slowly down in spheres to form dark shiny pools and little globules on the floor. It was like quicksilver, but light. She shook herself, shivered, emptied fluid out of her pockets and her boots and looked around for something that might be the gate; her way out of here. There was none unless it was beneath the pool, but finding Llian was more urgent than going back in there. Karan wrung black bubbles out of her hair and set off the way she was facing, since every direction looked the same—black ground, black sky. Had Llian also ended up in this place? No way to tell. Better get moving.

Karan walked, or rather bounced, for what seemed like a day and a night, though since the gloom scarcely changed she could only guess the passing of time. She went through rooms numberless, all the kinds that palaces have, but they were empty, silent and cold. None attracted her interest at all; she would much sooner have been home in her cramped and battered manor in Gothryme. Assuming that it still existed after the war. She almost choked on the thought.

She truaged across a throne room and down a grand corridor, looking in each room, calling out for Llian all the while. At the further end she found herself in a bedroom fit for an emperor, though a dismal and depressing one. The floor was red marble, the walls draped in velvet and silk, and the bed a head-high platform raised up on six posts of carven ebony, with a canopy so high that it disappeared in the gloom of the ceiling. Flames roared in a fireplace at the far end but the room was as frigid as everywhere else in this horrible place.

Karan stood by the fire, holding her hands out to the flames, but found they gave off no more heat than a candle. The fire was merely a decoration, a conceit. Maybe Rulke had no need of warmth. Maybe there was not enough substance in the Nightland to make the fire any hotter.

Karan was so cold and tired that even the thought of Rulke had lost its power to frighten her. She pulled a rug over in front of the fire, folded it several times and sat down as close to the flames as she could get. Taking off her boots and socks she put her frozen feet right up on the grate.

There she sat for hours more—a small, forlorn figure, her pale round face resting on her upturned hands. Her curls, red as sunset, were a tangle practically untameable by brush or comb. Once or twice, as she ran her fingers through the mop, a small shiny black globe would be released to drift off like a soap bubble.

Eventually Karan became a little warmer. Suddenly she felt drowsy, as if she had taken a sleeping potion. Even standing up she could barely keep her eyes open. She had not slept for an eternity. Climbing the end of the bed she dragged off her dirty clothes, the same ones that she had climbed the tower in a few days ago, dropped them in an untidy pile at the end of the bed and fell in between chilly silk sheets to sleep, but not to dream. The Nightland *was* a dream, and her sleep was absolute.

"Karannnn!"

The mournful cry jerked her awake, refreshed as if she had slept for many hours. The words had the toneless repetition of one who has long since given up hope of an answer.

"Here!" she shouted.

There was a long silence, then as her eyes cleared she saw, through the end of the bed, Llian's familiar figure at the door. He limped into the room, looking at his wits' end—his long brown hair was like a rat's nest, his cheek and forehead crusted in dried blood, one trouser leg rent and flapping. He scanned the room then turned to trudge out again.

"Llian," she said softly.

He walked around the bed but still did not see her.

"Up here, you nitwit," she cried, leaned out over the end of the bed and shook her lovely breasts at him.

Llian looked up, saw her there with her arms outstretched, and his face showed such a mixture of relief and frustration and lust that she burst out laughing. He took Karan's hand and clambered up into her waiting arms.

"Rulke's own bed!" he said, falling flat on his back. "How bold you are."

"And you are not?" she cried in outrage that was only half-feigned. "What a compliment!"

"I'm too exhausted to care. I just want to sleep."

"Not yet," she said, unfastening his shirt in haste, to stop him from dropping off right away. "I have a bolder plan yet, and I can't do it by myself."

And when Rulke's beard was thoroughly tweaked they collapsed in each other's arms.

"No one has ever done that here," she said, stroking Llian's cheek, "unless *he* conjures phantoms for his pleasure."

Llian did not answer. He was fast asleep. Soon Karan slept too, and dreamed of home.

When Llian woke, Karan was not there. Had it all been a hallucination, a Nightland fancy? After dressing, he automatically reached for the bag that held his journal and the precious notes for the tale. It wasn't there. With a sudden, heart-stopping spasm, Llian realized that he hadn't seen it since Katazza. Had he lost it in the gate?

"Karan," he shouted in a panic, hopping down from the end of the bed and bouncing high again. Pain shot through his ankle. No answer. "Karan!"

"I heard you the first time!" Her soft voice came from the doorway. Running barefoot across the room, she leapt and clasped him around the neck. His ankle gave way and they fell together on the cold floor.

"Aah!" he yelped.

"What's the matter?" She stroked his blood-crusted face. His brown eyes were still bloodshot.

"I twisted my ankle yesterday. Where have you been?"

"I was looking for something to drink; I'm parched." She gave his ankle an experimental poke. His groan was unfeigned.

"Oh, I'm so happy that we are together, even *here*," and she hugged him again and kissed his brow.

The thought of Rulke was a storm cloud blotting out Llian's sun. He lay where he had fallen, holding her hand. "This is the Nightland," he said.

"Where else?"

"What will he do to us when he comes back?"

"I don't know." She felt his ankle all around, more gently this time. "It's not broken. Though sometimes you can walk on a small break. Just twisted, I think. Put the boot back on; that'll support it until the swelling goes down."

"Mm," he said, still distracted by his loss.

"What's the matter with you today?"

"I've lost my bag. The journal, the papers, everything! What am I going to do?"

"It's back in Katazza, silly, hanging on the wall at the top of the tower."

The relief was overwhelming. "I'm really thirsty," he said shortly. "Did you find any water?"

"Not yet. I came back for my boots." She put them on.

"Well," said Llian, "you brought us here. How do we get back?

"I don't know. I thought the gate would take us back to Thurkad, after Faelamor."

"But we don't even know that she went there. Maybe Rulke *sent* us here."

"Did you come through anything that looked like a gate, at this end?"

"I couldn't see anything. I just landed in the middle of a huge room," said Llian.

"I landed in a pool. I don't know whether that was the gate or not. How could it be? How could there be two exits?"

"I don't know. I can't think straight. But you heard what Rulke said. He has need of us. He'll come back."

"If he can," said Karan.

"Then we'd better find the gate first."

"Can you get back to the place where you landed?" She

was not expecting too much. Llian's sense of direction was hopeless at the best of times.

"Probably not."

"Then let's go to mine."

They wandered through the gloom, Llian wondering how Karan could find her way in this place that was so lacking in landmarks. But she did, and a good while later reached the spot she was looking for. Karan waded into the pool, into the shiny liquid that was like black water but did not wet her.

"Can you feel anything?" Llian called, glad that it was her rather than him.

"No," she said, quartering the pool. In the middle it was well over her head. She waded out again, liquid cascading from her in globules that took a long time to fall.

"Then we're trapped. When he returns we must be fearful, and cooperate."

"The first will cause no difficulty," said Karan drily, as they headed back.

"What if he's overcome everyone in Katazza?"

"Let's just keep our wits about us and wait for an opportunity."

"I don't . . ."

"He's unfit, Llian. Didn't you see how hesitant he was against me? How slow his reflexes were?"

Llian had noticed nothing of the sort. Surely she was exaggerating to cheer him, but it only made him feel worse. How dared she pit her wits against Rulke? It bewildered and frightened him.

"He's dull," she went on, "but maybe he hasn't realized it yet. An opportunity must come, and when it does, I'll distract him while you go through the gate. Then I'll follow."

"And he'll follow after. We'll just be back where we came from, or some other worse place, with him on our heels. Ow!" He sat down on the floor, pulling at his boot. The ankle was much more swollen than before.

"It's not far now," said Karan. "Lean on my shoulder."

As they walked along she explained her thinking. "Passing the gate takes a toll—you must have felt it?"

"Yes, my head still aches a bit."

"To actually control the gate must take a far greater toll—you saw how badly Tensor was affected when he used it. After holding it open all this time, surely even Rulke will be sweating. Wrestling with so many powerful enemies must have hurt him, too. *If* he comes, he will be exhausted; why would he follow us if he knows he can come and go as he pleases?"

"Well, if we get the chance, let's get the gate to take us to another place—to Gothryme, even."

"I don't know how to use gates. How can I send it anywhere? Can you?"

"No," said Llian, knowing how foolish his words were. What did he know about gates anyway? It was hard to get them to work at all, and few places were suitable. He knew that from the Histories and from Tensor. A gate could be directed to most other gates, and to a few other special places, though that was much harder and more perilous. Sometimes they failed or went astray, to the death of those using them. But all gates had failed with the Forbidding; Tensor's was the first since that time. Maybe the old rules no longer applied.

"Here we are." Karan pushed open the door of Rulke's bedchamber. "Everything about gates is a risk, particularly going through them. I'm famished. I'm going to look for water and something to eat. Are you coming?"

"My ankle's really sore; I think I'll stay here."

"Good idea." She set off.

After a while Llian felt better, so he limped through the nearby rooms, mentally noting everything for his tale. Going into the next room he stopped abruptly. It was the alarming machine he'd seen before. The light was brighter today; now it was unpleasantly familiar. A complex device: alien curves of dark metal, ominous bulges, curious levers and projections—a *construct*! It was the thing he'd seen in Karan's dream that night long ago, when they had fled from Sith in

Pender's boat. Llian had no idea what it was for, but there was an ugly practicality of shape about it that was menacing.

Llian put out his hand to touch the construct, the hard, blue-black incomprehensible surface of it, but his hand went straight through it. He jerked his hand back out again. *It was not there*! Rulke had made it, complete in his mind, but yet it lacked physical form. Maybe such a thing could not be formed in the Nightland. He walked around the construct, wondering, but it surpassed his understanding.

He touched it again. Again his hand slipped into it without any resistance. Curiosity overcame his fear and he put head and shoulders in. For an instant his senses were disconnected, then the inside of the construct sprang out at him, illuminated by a dark-red light that was unnerving. Everything was fuzzy, slightly out of focus, so that when he moved his head it made him dizzy. He saw two oddly curved seats, a variety of levers, knobs and glassy plates on which colored lines danced—and everywhere, more complex shapes and improbable devices than on the outside.

Something sighed on the other side of the room—he sensed a presence behind him. Karan had been quicker than he'd expected. He said over his shoulder: "Did you ever come across anything like this in Shazmak?" His voice rang with a thousand echoes.

The laughter was rich and deep, so deep that the room seemed to vibrate in sympathy, the construct to waver at the edges. His whole body shivered too, and the hairs on his arms stood up. Llian jerked his head back out, became disoriented, instinctively tried to support himself on the construct and fell straight through it.

8

THE CONSTRUCT

"Master chronicler!" said Rulke in a low, amused voice. "Do you tell me you've not come across a construct before? What did they teach you at your little college?"

"That you're a monster!" squeaked Llian, trying to look like a shadow. Rulke's physical presence was overpowering. As men go, he was the biggest Llian had ever seen; broad-shouldered, wide-chested, long and muscular of limb. But he was more than a man—he was Charon, a different human species, and Llian was so afraid that his mouth had dried up.

Rulke sprang at him. "Maybe I am."

The daydreams vanished in a second. Llian stumbled backwards with his mouth open and his hands in the air. Though he did not realize it, this was the one pose to convince Rulke that he offered no threat. This combination of terror and blank stupidity was a reaction that *he* was most familiar with.

"You wonder about my construct," said Rulke, smiling at him. "It's no longer a secret; I want you to know all about it.

Indeed, who better than a great chronicler to carry the tale of my dread power to Santhenar? I know how you yearn for knowledge—my Ghâshâd have taught me something of you. Anything you want to know, just ask. We can be great partners, you and I."

The sudden appearance of Rulke was shocking enough, even though it had been half-expected, but this . . . Llian was absolutely flabbergasted. Such things do not happen in real life. It is a trick, he told himself. Block your ears, smile and agree to whatever he wants, but know that everything he says is a lie. Rulke the Great Betrayer, the Flatterer, the Seducer.

But I *am* a great chronicler, thought Llian immodestly. At least I was, back when I still worked at my craft. That is no flattery. Maybe he cannot be trusted, but what secrets he must know! To be offered the knowledge of the ancient world, the key to tales that had never been told, was a temptation that he could barely resist.

As they faced each other a shudder passed across the floor. The walls wobbled, the mist forming swelling bubbles of light that slowly dispersed. Only the construct was unchanged.

Rulke cocked his head, watching and listening. His eyes met Llian's and there was a watchful gleam in them. "That's not happened before," he said softly. "I wonder if your friends are probing my defenses. They'll get a nasty surprise if they do." But Llian read unease in Rulke's posture. He could not completely hide it.

Llian examined him with his chronicler's eye, the better to describe him in his Great Tale. He saw that Karan had been right—Rulke's mouth was drawn tight and his jaw knotted, and he moved with an exhaustion that he could not disguise. Perhaps he thought Llian too insignificant to bother.

"Come," said Rulke, "let me show you my construct. It is a machine akin to the golden flute that Shuthdar made for me, before he stole it and brought us all to ruin." Putting out a scabbed and swollen hand he drew the unresisting Llian to him.

Llian trembled. He knew that tale overly well, for his new version, told to such acclaim at the Graduation Telling last summer, had started the whole chain of circumstances that led inexorably to here. It caused his expulsion from the college, leading to his meeting with Karan who had stolen the Mirror of Aachan, the fall of the fabulous Aachim city of Shazmak, Yggur's march to war against Mendark, and outside it all, Faelamor spinning her web to get the Mirror for herself.

And somehow, something about Karan, or something she had done, though Llian did not know what or how, had allowed Rulke to look down from his Nightland prison and use her strange, sensitive talents to wake the Ghâshâd, to prepare the way for his return.

"The patent of the flute was mine," said Rulke, "and the pattern that Shuthdar followed when he made it for me. This is a greater thing by far. What can I *not* do with it?"

Llian said nothing. His veins were boiling; his heart pumped him full of fire but his knees were jelly.

Linking his arm through Llian's as if they were brothers, Rulke led him around the construct, pointing out all its remarkable aspects. Llian gathered that it was a device for making gates from one place to another, and for unstated greater purposes. It was a marvelous machine and a clever one too, but the construct was too complex and the principles that governed its operation too obscure, and Rulke's presence too overpowering for Llian to reach any greater understanding of it.

And all the time Rulke was watching him, saying nothing, measuring Llian with his eyes. He is too strong for me, Llian decided. He knows I am overcome by the dread of him, and tempted by his offer too. And so I am. I should *not* be. Everything I have ever learned, and the whole history of the Zain, cries out—*Beware! Have no part of this! It can only end one way*! But how tempting it is. What if he is genuine? Llian began to fall under Rulke's spell.

* * *

Llian's eye was caught by something in the far corner of the room, a hexagonal pad like a large paving stone. It was glowing faintly, and the luminous mist drifting above it had also begun to shimmer. Could it be the portal through which Rulke had returned? Tensor's gate had been massive, and the air rushed through it all the while that it was open. But this small thing had made scarcely a sound when it opened, just a gentle sigh. Perhaps it was closed to all but Rulke: if so, their rebellion was already lost. Looking within himself, Llian realized that he was just a little bit relieved. He must get away, but not yet. What might he learn in one more hour?

Just then Karan appeared in the doorway, searching for him. She was halfway across the room when Rulke stepped out from behind the construct.

"Welcome to my prison, little one," he said with a thin smile. "I'm glad you came—I have great plans for you." He put out a hand that trembled ever so slightly.

Karan froze, took a single gasping breath, then began to back away. "Llian!" she called.

Suddenly the air above the stone erupted like steam from a boiling kettle. Rulke spun around. "No!" he roared. With a wave of his hand a pane of ice formed between them and him, bisecting the room. It was as clear as glass, but too thick to break, too high to leap, too slippery to climb. He sprinted across to the plate and stood over it with his arms out, chanting words that they could not understand. Shortly the hexagonal gate-stone faded back into the pattern on the floor, the mist resumed its random motions.

He heaved a sigh and trudged back, and with another gesture a porthole appeared in the pane.

"What was that?" Llian asked.

Rulke leaned on the sill of the porthole, his great chest rising and falling. He examined his prisoners. "Your friends are trying to seal me in."

Llian snatched at Karan's hand. "You mean, seal the Nightland back up?" he quavered. "Shut us in with *you*?" Of all conceivable fates, he had not imagined that one. How could they do it to us? he thought numbly.

Rulke bared his teeth. "Careful what you say, Llian. If I truly am the monster your tales make me out to be, I might take offense."

Llian scuttled backwards, trying to drag Karan with him. She resisted. "Did they succeed?" she asked, imagining all her dreams of Gothryme come to nothing.

"*Not this time*! But they could, if they are able to tap the power of the rift. This must put you in rather a dilemma, my friends. Who do you support, them or me?"

Karan squeezed Llian's hand. "We do not wish to die, nor to betray our friends."

"Even though they have abandoned you? You might have quite some time with me, in so far as time can be measured here. It runs strangely in this place—"

In the corner the mist began to stir once more. Rulke reacted instantly. The porthole iced over again as he raced back to the stone with bounds covering five or six spans each.

The mist boiled up all around, much more wildly than before, lit by flashes and streaks of light. All they saw of Rulke was an occasional glimpse through the fog—arms raised, desperately trying to undo whatever was attacking the gate from the other side.

Llian put his arms around Karan. They both stared into the corner. "I hope . . ." Karan whispered.

"What?" Llian said in her ear.

"I feel so guilty, but . . . I hope Rulke wins."

"So do I. I don't want us to spend the rest of our lives here."

After quite some considerable time a bright flash lit up the distant ceiling. A dull boom made the pane oscillate like a wobble board. Rulke shrieked and reeled out of the mist, stumbling blindly toward them until he struck the barrier with his cheek. His staring eyes looked right into Karan's.

He's losing! Karan thought, and he's afraid; terrified that he'll never get out. She could identify with that.

Rulke folded up, his clawed fingernails squealing down the pane. Over in the corner the floor glowed orange and began to dome up like a blob of molten glass on the end of a glassblower's pipe. Orange rays streaked out horizontally. One touched Rulke's cheek, making his beard smoke. Another melted a finger-size hole through the pane. Swearing weakly, he forced himself to his feet and turned back to the stone. The battle went on for a good while, as Karan and Llian watched in terrified fascination. Once, time itself appeared to freeze. Toward the end the ceiling sank visibly lower, the walls thinning until Karan could see through into the next room. Finally the illumination went out once more. This time Rulke could only crawl back to the barrier. He was covered in an icy slush of sweat.

"They're beating me," he said, redissolving the porthole.

"What's the matter?"

Rulke lay his head on his arms, panting. "I'm so thirsty. Do you have any water. No, of course you don't!"

"Tell me where I can find it," said Karan, pitying him despite her fear.

"It's all right. What's the matter, you ask? I've been drawing on the Nightland itself to hold the boundaries together, but whatever power I put there I have to take from somewhere else."

"I don't understand," said Karan.

"The Nightland is not a world, Karan. It is a tiny place: little matter, less energy, and even before this it was running down, leaking its energy into the void. In a while, within your lifetimes, it would have frozen solid, and me with it. My enemies only needed to wait—an irony I'm sure they'll appreciate one day."

"What's happening now?" asked Llian.

"Eventually all this must go." Rulke gestured at the walls around them. "I built this place. If I take back the energy that holds it together, my palace must eventually reduce to the size of a privy. If I can't even hold that together we all die here for lack of air. They're too strong for me here."

"What do you mean, *here*?" asked Llian.

"They have tapped a mighty source of power—the rift itself, I suspect. Though they barely know how to use it, it is more than I can match. The Nightland is a shell, with just enough energy to hold itself together, and me inside."

"That's why it's so cold here," Karan guessed.

"Clever!" said Rulke. "I can make fire here, but it burns cold; there's not enough energy to power it. No, unless I can baffle or trick them somehow, we will soon be dead."

The model was still revolving, very slowly, while Yggur and Mendark went over it with exquisite care, examining every part of it for signs of the flaw in the Nightland. After many hours Yggur shook his head.

"I can't find any evidence of it."

"Maybe the grid isn't fine enough," Mendark said. He looked as if he'd not slept for a week—eyes bleary and sagging, movements sluggish, voice lifeless. "We'll have to do it all over again."

"We've been going more than a day," Yggur said. "Every hour we get weaker, and Rulke becomes stronger. *I can't go on!*"

"We must," said Mendark, though it was evident to Tallia that he was near collapse.

She paced about the light-shape, round and round, while she tried to build a picture of it within her mind. It kept changing—rippling, dimpling, swelling and retreating as, she realized, the Nightland itself must be in constant flux. Then, as her eye rested on a tiny knot of intersecting lines, they shifted, moving apart imperceptibly until there was nothing there.

Tallia rubbed tired eyes, sure that she had imagined it. Where the tangle had been was now a bloody clot that waxed and waned in brightness as the model continued its revolution. Behind her she could hear Mendark and Yggur arguing.

"We've got to give it up," Yggur pleaded. "Before it's too late."

"We've gone too far to give up," said Mendark.

It was hard to concentrate with that going on. Beneath her feet the rock shuddered, more strongly than before.

"Shut up!" she cried, still pacing. "There's something wrong here."

"What?" said Mendark, spinning around.

"There was a little knot of lines just here." She marked it with a fingertip. "But when I noticed them they moved apart. Could Rulke change this model from inside the Nightland?"

"Only by modifying the relevant parts of the Nightland itself. Maybe he has been aware of us all along."

"What did I tell you?" said Yggur, visibly shaken. "He knows everything. He's playing with us!"

"He cannot see *us* from the Nightland," said Malien. "Not at all! But this model is, as it were, a tracing of the shell of that place in smaller dimension, and to the extent that the one corresponds to the other he may be able to detect what we're doing."

"There must be another way to visualize the flaw," said Tallia.

"Do we have anything that Rulke touched after he came through the gate?" asked Mendark. "If we do, one of the principles of the Secret Art—the Principle of Contagion—may show traces of his passage."

"He touched the Mirror of Aachan," said Shand, "though we dare not use *that*."

"What about the emerald?" said Asper. Yggur had empowered it here at the rift, then hurled it at Rulke to destroy him. But Rulke broke the spell and shattered the jewel to emerald sand.

"And he left blood on the floor," said Shand.

"Perfect!" said Mendark.

"Sweep up the emerald sand and scrape up the blood," Malien said to Asper. "Recover every trace of both."

Asper and Xarah hurried up the ladder. The floor trembled again. Tallia looked up at the blank roof, feeling the weight of rock and tower above her, held together so precariously. She found it hard to breathe down here.

The model of the Nightland still revolved in the air, though Yggur was having trouble holding it. It kept fading and flaring. After an interminable wait in the heat the two Aachim reappeared on the ladder. Asper carried the emerald sand in a leather bag while Xarah had a bowl with a scraping of dried blood in the bottom.

"Crush the sand to dust," said Mendark, and that was done—a long process as it was very hard. Finally the glittering dust was ready, the powdered blood mixed though a small amount of it, the light-sphere energized once more with a beam from the ruby rod, then Yggur muttered a command and Xarah blew the mixture though a fine tube aimed at the top of the light-sphere.

The sphere flared bright, then the bloody droplets faded and the green background color too. For an instant the mesh of yellow lines stood out brightly, save in one place at the southern pole where the grid was warped into a funnel with a knot at the bottom, a green cap over the hole—the way in and out of the Nightland. Then, as the dust lost its grip and sifted to the floor, the knot began to fade.

"Fix it!" cried Mendark, and Yggur drew power out of the rift and froze the model of the Nightland in that state.

Everyone breathed a great sigh. "Is it done then?" came Xarah's youthful voice. She was sitting on one of the sulphur-crusted benches on the other side of the room.

"Not near," said Yggur, clutching his jaw. "All we've done is locate the portal."

"The hardest work is yet to come," Mendark said. "And the most dangerous. To seal it up tight."

As he spoke there was a rumble like thunder and the crack in the floor widened perceptibly. Chips of rock fell from the roof, then above them they heard, or felt, the foundations groan as they slid one against the other. They stared at each other. Tallia knew that the terror she saw on Malien's face, and Asper's, was a reflection of her own.

"How can you seal it?" she asked hoarsely.

"The same way we sealed the Nightland in the first place," said Mendark. "But it's a mighty spell. I'm not sure I have the strength for it any longer. My whole body is screaming."

Malien's pale face was spotted with drops of sweat. "And mine," she panted, "far worse than my shoulder does." She rolled over on her good side, retching into the dust of the floor. Tallia helped her back up and wiped her face.

"We can still leave it," Yggur said hoarsely.

"Not like this," said Mendark. "Once started, we've got to go all the way."

Steam began to wisp out from several points along the crack. The floor moved once more. Yggur was partly paralyzed down one side now, terror of his great enemy almost overcoming him.

"Mendark!" Shand shouted urgently. "You're pushing Yggur beyond his limits."

"No more than I push myself," Mendark said contemptuously.

At that, Yggur's head jerked up. "Must—do it!" he forced out, slurring his words, only one side of his mouth moving. His voice droned as if he blew the words down a long pipe. "I'll—prepare."

He wrested control of himself again. "I know the Proscribed Experiments better than any of you. Get the green dust ready. When I say, blow it over the portal and the whole of the model from all sides at once. Mendark—you, Tallia and Malien must keep it there long enough for me to do my work. I will draw power from the rift one last time, energize the ruby rod and fuse the emerald to the model—an impervious coating that will, with luck, seal the Nightland up tight."

"I don't like it," said Malien. "Already—" She was interrupted by a blast of pressurized steam from the crack, then another behind her. "The rift grows unstable. You've taken too much power from it already."

The floor shook underfoot. Steam issued from three or

four places, forming mist in the room. "I think something just shifted below us," whispered Tallia.

"We've no choice," Mendark said. "Just do it!" While they prepared he conferred with Yggur about details of the Nightland and the requirements of the Secret Art.

Tallia squatted down beside Malien. "Better get everyone out who isn't needed," she said, "then if the worst happens, at least some of us will be saved."

"Saved for what?" choked Yggur.

9

SEALING THE GATE

I can feel him sneering at us," Yggur wept, mopping his brow. Though Tallia was just as afraid, she had to resist the urge to smack him in the face.

"Nonsense!" said Mendark. "Get control of yourself."

Yggur straddled the rift, which was now a finger-wide crack running right across the floor, walls and ceiling. A bubbling, hissing sound could be heard in the depths. He strained to lock the dimensions of the Nightland into his mind, and then to summon power from the rift for the last time.

"Ready?" Mendark asked softly.

"Yes!" said Tallia, who held a tube filled with emerald dust to her lips. At the other quarters stood Asper, Xarah and Basitor, each with their own tubes out.

Malien stood by Mendark to aid with the channelling. Shand supported her. The others had already gone up the ladder.

"When I count three," said Mendark, looking over the

barrel of the ampliscope into Yggur's eyes. "And as soon as you are done, get your head down and cover your eyes."

Yggur nodded. His cheek spasmed, then he took control again.

"One!" said Mendark, checking around the circle. Everyone was as ready as they would ever be.

"Two!" He closed his eyes to summon up the image of the Nightland clear and bright in his mind.

The bloodstone sphere glowed in the mist. Tallia felt a cold knot of fear grow in the pit of her stomach.

"He's too strong," Yggur whispered. "He's so strong! I can feel him, holding back our efforts, conserving his own strength until we make a mistake. How can we not? None of us knows what we're doing."

"He's weak!" said Mendark with scorn. "He's bluffing because he has to. Now remember, this is a delicate process. Not too much power. Yggur?"

Sweat was pouring down Yggur's cheeks; his eyes were staring.

"Yggur!" shouted Mendark. "We're hanging over the abyss. Get hold of yourself. Can you do it? If not, then get the hell out of the way so someone else can." He was hard put to keep the contempt out of his voice, and the whole room knew it.

There was a lengthy pause. "I can do it," Yggur said with a shudder. He dashed sweat out of his eyes.

Tallia sighed with relief.

Mendark beat his arm up and down, one, two. "Three!" The word came out like a whipcrack.

As one they blew the dust directly at the model, then dropped flat to the floor with their hands over their eyes. For an instant the dust glittered green all over the sphere, then Yggur erupted defiance, sucked in a mighty breath and a fountain of light roared from the end of the ruby rod.

"Too much!" Tallia heard Mendark scream, then she was blinded by a cataclysmic burst of light from the model. It poured through her hands, her closed eyelids; for an instant it overwhelmed all her senses. Then it was gone into the dark.

It did not begin again for some time. Rulke was quite spent, sitting with his back to the ice pane, dozing but waking every few minutes to check on the gate. Karan fetched a quilt from the bedroom and wrapped herself and Llian in it, watching and waiting. It was a strange feeling to be reliant on their enemy for everything, to identify so closely with his own hopes and fears. Yet at the same time, she knew of his reputation for treachery and trickery, and dared not trust him. Karan was very afraid.

The palace shuddered and the walls thinned further. Karan could see through room after room as if the walls, and the contents of each room, were made of glass. More energy gone, she realized. Only the construct retained its solidity now.

"Ugh!" cried Llian, who had begun to sink into the floor. Even that was failing. She helped him out.

"I'm starving," Llian said hoarsely.

Rulke looked up at him with dull eyes. "In my bedroom, which you have already *used*, you will find a flask and some meal tablets. Bring them here."

Karan ran off, returning with the flask and a handful of little cubes like large dice made of baked dough, which she passed through the porthole. Rulke shared them out equally, washed down with a couple of swallows each from the flask. It did not satisfy but it was better than nothing.

"I've been thinking about what you said earlier," Llian said to Rulke.

"Oh!" said Rulke, uninterested.

"About tricking them. I've been watching the way you fight them. Perhaps I presume too much, to—"

"You do, but get on with it! Damned chroniclers, you never use one word when a hundred will do."

"You go straight at them with all your strength," said Llian. "A poor strategy here, I should think."

"It's served me well enough in the past," Rulke replied listlessly.

"You attack your enemies as though you were stronger than them. Once you were, I know, but not here." Llian paused, searching for the right words.

"Do you have any more advice for me, puny man?"

"I've never been good at physical things," said Llian, "save one."

"Two," Karan murmured, running her hand down the inside of his thigh.

Rulke gave her a disgusted glance. "You're like a pair of rabbits!"

"I was champion arm-wrestler at the college," said Llian. "I often beat men more powerful than me. They think it's a contest of strength, but it's really like staring someone down. It's a battle of wills."

"Go on," said Rulke. "Perhaps you wish to challenge *me* one day." He flexed a bicep the size of Llian's thigh. "What is your tactic?"

"It takes a lot more strength to force than to hold. I—just hold my opponent while he uses up his strength trying to force my arm down. After a few minutes, when our muscles are screaming, I give a little. He forces with all his might, thinking me done, but I hold him again. And again! Finally I put a defeated expression on my face, and the last time he forces, as soon as he stops I slam his arm the other way with all my strength. He is beaten!"

"There's more to you than there appears, chronicler," said Rulke. "Though—"

The ice pane rippled. He lurched back to the plate.

The struggle began again, though before long it was clear that Rulke was losing. The glow of the gate-stone was as bright as the sun at midday, the spears and splinters of bursting light sprayed out in all directions, pocking the pane like a cheese grater. The mist roiled like steam from a volcano.

Gasping, wild-eyed, Rulke fell to his knees, holding out

his clenched fists, his whole body wracked by shudders. The light faded to nothing. He lowered his head to the floor, resting on a tripod of knees and forehead. There was complete silence.

"What's he doing?" Karan whispered.

"I don't know," Llian whispered back. "I can feel pressure building though."

The walls and the pane vibrated, giving out a low gong-sound that made the bones of their skulls quiver. Then the plate exploded with light so bright that they had to shield their eyes. The pane of ice evaporated in an instant. Rulke screamed, a tortured wail that echoed and echoed, ringing like a bell through the spaces of the vast room. He toppled onto his face and lay still.

"That's that then," said Llian in a parched voice.

"Oh, you fool. You bloody, bloody fool!" said Mendark.

Tallia opened her eyes, and at first it seemed that Yggur had succeeded after all. The model hung in the air a moment, lines smeared into a blur of yellow. At one place on the sphere there was a faint tinge of green—the place where the portal had been.

"Yes, you've done it!" she cried.

"No," said Mendark, crushed as if the whole weight of the tower had descended on his shoulders.

There was no green coating on the rest of the sphere. Yggur's blast had boiled the emerald dust to vapor.

Yggur swayed on his feet, eyes staring, mouth open.

As they watched, the light-shape slowly faded, but before it went out a cone-shaped plug of green glass dropped free and cracked in two on the floor. The floor heaved under their feet, steam issuing from a dozen vents.

"You—*cretin*!" Mendark ground out, in a fury so wild that he was practically incoherent. "You used too much power by a hundred times."

"You drove him much too far," said Shand. "I warned you, Mendark."

"I can't see," wept Yggur, watery fluid pouring from his staring eyes. "Can't see anything at all." He still clutched the ampliscope in one hand, though it was useless now, the ruby rod sagging down at the end like rubber. "I am so afraid."

"Is this the end?" Tallia asked. "Can we do no more?"

"We're finished," said Mendark. "No possibility of sealing it now."

"I'm afraid," Yggur repeated in doleful tones.

"You threw away our only chance. I knew you could not be relied upon."

"Then why did you push him?" Tallia snapped.

"Because I had no choice!"

"No point blaming each other," Malien said. "Let's get up the ladder while we still can."

Tallia bent down to pick up the plug of melted emerald. As her fingers closed over the pieces a shockwave passed through the floor and she heard a low, rumbling, grinding sound from underneath. Steam began to belch out all along the vent. Yggur, who still stood straddling the rift, was thrown off his feet.

"Light!" Mendark shouted. Each brought out their lightglasses. One side of the rift had moved up and it now gaped wide enough to put a leg inside. A burning blast of air came up.

"We'll never get out!" cried Xarah, running round in circles through the mist.

Above them the foundations shrieked and groaned. Tallia felt a growing terror—they were going to be entombed here and slowly burned to death.

"Tallia!" Shand shouted. "Help me."

They shepherded the cripples—Yggur and Malien—to the ladder and helped them onto it. The others were already moving up. Tallia was very weak; such aftersickness she had never felt before. The others looked just as bad.

She hung off the bottom of the ladder with Shand,

watching them go. Mendark had already disappeared and Yggur, despite not being able to see, climbed very quickly.

"Go on," said Malien, supporting her shoulder. "I'll be slow. I'll go last."

"No," said Tallia. "You may need my help. You go, Shand."

He folded his arms and smiled. "I've lived more life than I ever wanted, Tallia. After you."

She nodded thanks and turned to the ladder. Malien was climbing slowly, one-handed. Tallia followed close behind, not looking up, for there was a constant rain of dust and pieces of crystalline crust from above. The ladder shook continuously now, once so hard that Malien lost her grip and would have fallen had not Tallia been right against her. Malien gave a grunt of pain, which for her surely indicated that she was in agony. Tallia trapped her between her body and the ladder until she took hold again.

"How is your shoulder, Malien?"

"In the entire span of my life I have never felt worse," Malien replied, sagging against her. "And I think this will be the end of it."

"I think so too."

The earth quaked again. Above them the foundations wailed like tortured demons. Tallia looked down. Shand was just below her feet, climbing steadily. "How are you doing, Shand?"

He did not look up. "All right, though it's getting hot and I can smell the fumes again."

Burning sulphur. Tallia's nose was itching and her eyes watered. "Can you go any faster, Malien?"

Malien accelerated a little, though she could not keep it up. A puff of white fumes rushed past them, sending them all into a fit of coughing, then dispersed in the chamber above. They kept on. The rumbling and groaning grew ever louder.

"How can it survive?" Tallia said to herself.

"The tower? It can't if this keeps up," Shand grunted. "Though it was very well built."

"The foundation chamber is just above," Malien called. "We're halfway. I've got to rest for a minute."

They clambered off the ladder onto solid floor, though that now shifted like waves on the sea. The rest of the group were also resting there, in spite of the danger. Two Aachim were monitoring the shifting foundations, fascinated by the way they were built.

"Why hasn't it fallen?" Basitor panted. "It's already at its limit."

"The rift moved that way," said Asper, pointing. "Should it slide any further in this direction, or move up, over she goes!"

"Look at this cable! The outer spring is broken. The cable must soon snap."

Just then they heard a hollow cry, "Xarah, Xarah!" and her twin hurtled down the ladder, her brown hair flying. Tallia could not help smiling. They were truly inseparable.

"Shalah, I'm here," shouted Xarah. "I'm safe." She ran toward Shalah with her arms out.

As Shalah jumped off the ladder, the rock gave a mighty shudder and one of the subsidiary anchor cables snapped. The free end lashed across the room, just missing Shand's face, to strike Shalah in the chest with the force of a log careering down a mountainside. She was slammed against the wall, slid down it and came to rest on the floor, her head resting against the stone.

"Shalah!" Xarah cried, racing over to her. "Shalah, are you all right?"

Tallia ran too. Shalah's eyes were open. She gave her twin a sad little smile and her eyes glazed over.

"Shalah!" Xarah shrieked. "Speak to me!"

Nudging Tallia out of the way, Asper checked Shalah carefully, though it was clear that she was dead. Her chest was crushed and her neck broken. He arranged her on the floor, closing her eyes with his fingertips. Tallia bowed her head.

"Come on!" Mendark shouted. "That cable is going to go."

They raced for the ladder. Xarah had to be carried, kicking and screaming. She could not abandon her sister, even now. They reached the ground floor and the Aachim rushed around trying to find a way out. There must have been secret doors but, though they hammered everywhere, they could not identify them.

At that moment the earth moved again, a different way, and from below came a shrieking groan that told of the foundation blocks being driven beyond their limits. The whole floor tilted beneath their feet, jerked upwards and jerked again.

"Up, you bloody idiots!" Mendark screamed and they all hurtled back to the ladder.

"Four floors to go," Tallia said. "Then back down two, out of the tower and across the bridge. If we can do that we have a chance."

"Unless the tower falls our way."

A low-pitched zipping sound raced up one side of the tower.

"The cable's gone," said Shand. "That's it!"

"Keep going," Malien gritted.

The tower lurched much more sharply up on one side, tilting the floor and the ladder. Just past the second floor, cracks began to appear in the wall where the cable had run. They widened rapidly, plaster showering down on their heads. As they climbed, stagger-kneed, through the fourth floor, a block of stone slid out of one of the curved bays to crash at their toes. Suddenly with a gush of stone and dust a hole appeared in the wall and they saw the minarets and domes of the fortress beyond.

"This way!" Tallia gasped, pointing to the hole. "Out through the hole."

"No!" cried Shand. "It'll fall that way."

A blast of burning air roared up past them, bringing choking fumes in its wake. Looking down, Tallia saw a red line far below, ebbing out of the rift.

Now they were just below the fifth level, Tensor's gate chamber. "I can't . . . go any further," said Malien.

"It's just a little way," said Tallia, watching the cracks in the wall grow wider.

"Go on! My arm and my legs have cramped. *I can't move!*"

10

The Fall of the Towers

"Is he dead?" Karan whispered when she could see again. They raced across a floor that was soggy in places, an icy slush in others. Blisters were forming on the side of Rulke's face that had been toward the blast.

"No," said Llian, carefully feeling a pulse in Rulke's throat. "But if he dies, we will too. See if you can find some water, *quickly*!"

Karan ran off. Llian squatted down beside the fallen giant—the great enemy who would surely use him if he recovered. But if he did not, they were trapped in the Nightland for the term of their lives.

After a few minutes Rulke groaned and opened his eyes. One eyelid was blistered too, and he seemed to be having trouble focusing. "Is it you, chronicler?" he whispered, putting up a feeble hand. Llian gave the Charon his hand. Rulke hung his head for a minute, panting, then his eyes focused. He flashed a smile that, in spite of their peril, Llian found strangely warming.

"We won," Rulke said. "We beat them! A good strategy, chronicler."

"So they didn't seal the gate?"

"No, it's not even closed."

"Then they could still . . . invade?"

"It's possible. I don't dare close it, chronicler, lest I be unable to open it again."

"Oh!" said Llian, trying to control his reactions. That meant there was still a chance of escape. He stared at the Charon's ravaged face, wondering what would happen to them now. "Are you . . . all right?"

Rulke shoved himself to his feet, but had to clutch at Llian's shoulder for support. "I've not felt this bad in a good age," he said, inspecting his injuries reflected on the construct: the blistered face and bloodshot eyes. His hands and fingers were burned from his encounter with Rulke's emerald rod, not to mention Karan's knife wound through his palm. "Ah, how it wracks me!"

He shook himself, muttering words that seemed to be some kind of cantrip to postpone exhaustion. He flexed his muscles and stood unaided. "But I cannot rest yet. So much to do and to learn. *And you can help me there!*" he said vehemently.

Alarmed, Llian moved back a step. The floor had solidified again. Rulke sprang after him. How could he have recovered so quickly?

"So, will you aid me?" asked Rulke softly. He took Llian by the arm. "I will reward you handsomely if you do. But if you don't . . ."

"Hold on," Tallia said. She climbed around Malien on the ladder, careful of her shoulder, and seized her good arm. "Shand, can you push her up?"

Shand put his head up between Malien's legs, settled her weight on his shoulders, took one, two, three steps up the ladder, then they all tumbled to the floor of the gate chamber.

The walls were beginning to come apart, the nine-leaved

clover shape separating along the seams. The floor tilted even further, part of the ceiling fell, then with a roar one whole bay of the room fell out. Tallia heaved Malien over her shoulder, finding her very heavy for her size, then she and Shand staggered over the rubble, their steps ringing on the crumpled remains of the metal door.

Just outside the door she stumbled over a woman's body. It was the powerfully built engineer, Thel, crushed under a fallen block of stone. The air was so full of dust and smoke that Tallia could not see at all. The stairway was littered with rubble and more coming down all the time. Taking Tallia's hand, Shand led her down, guiding his way by the wall. At the fourth level they could see in one side and out the other. The spiraling cables of stone were unraveling. But even as they watched the tower swayed back, the cracks closing up again.

"Keep going," Shand rasped. "Just a little way now!"

Pieces of rubble were rolling and clattering down the stairs. One bounding fragment the size of a football struck Shand in the backside, knocking him over. To Tallia's relief he got up again, sporting a bloody nose. He grimaced, holding his buttock.

Just ahead was the western bridge that led out of the Great Tower into the fortress. They put on a final, hobbling burst as the tower tilted once again. A gap appeared between the end of the bridge and the landing. Rock was breaking all around them with snaps and roars.

Tallia ran, her knees wobbly. With an effort that she felt was going to burst her heart, she sprang, soaring over the gap with Malien on her shoulders. She landed on the bridge and her knees collapsed, sending them both skidding across the stone.

Malien shrieked in agony. Tallia lurched to her knees, knowing that she could carry her no further. Blood was dripping from her skinned knees. Shand was in a similar state. They began to crawl up the arching bridge, knowing that they were doomed, as the whole world began to shake itself to pieces above them.

A block of stone smashed on the bridge, making it vibrate. Another knocked a piece out of the side. More thudded against the paving stones below. The road cracked under them. Tallia was about to lie down to die when Osseion and a group of Aachim appeared in front of them, the ones who had gone up the previous day. The three were picked up, head and feet, and raced across the bridge as the stonework began to shake free of the metal supporting it.

The whole bridge began to crack apart into plates of stone that slid and shifted, opening crevasses that they had to leap over, then just as suddenly closing up again. The plates slid inward, a chaos that their bearers had to scramble over like goats. Tallia felt the surface drop beneath her, before Osseion flung them both onto the landing. Tallia looked up and saw a sight that would live with her all her life.

The Great Tower leaned a little more. Puffs of dust issued forth from the middle to the top, then the cables separated and the whole tower began to unweave. For a moment it looked as if the nine strands would fall separately, right on top of them; then as the tower leaned further it began to come apart at the top, block by block, and the top half fell in a shattering roar to the right, onto the domes and minarets of Katazza fortress, bringing many of them down as well. Pieces of lapis scattered in all directions, one cutting Shand's cheek. One of the great spring cables went wheeling across the sky, singing, to smash through the largest of the domes.

Last of all the platinum dome fell, soaring through the air to land half on, half off the side of the fortress with an almighty clang. It hung there, suspended, in one buckled piece. The lower parts of the tower began to slide down as well, then boiling dust covered the whole scene.

When all was still and the dust settled, they looked over what remained. Five of the nine stone cables were broken off down to the level of the bridges, while the other four stuck up in a jagged, tilted cluster circled by a ragged annulus of gold and lapis. Spring hawsers dangled out of two of them, still quivering. Behind them and to their left the fortress was undamaged, the towers and domes standing yet, but the other end was a ruin.

"Well," said Mendark, "that's finished us. No chance of making a gate to get us home now. We'll have to walk the Dry Sea in *summer*! That's never been done before. Thank you, Yggur! You've turned what should have been a victory into certain defeat."

"You should not have used the emerald against him," Tensor whispered. "After Rulke had such a victory over Yggur with it, how could you hope to master him?"

"You got us into this, Tensor, and refused to help," Mendark snarled. "Don't bother to advise us now."

Yggur stared with sightless eyes over the ruin that was Katazza. "I was too afraid," he said yet again. "*Too* afraid."

They took stock of themselves. Those who had been down over the rift at the end—Yggur, Shand, Mendark, Asper, Malien, Basitor and Xarah—were burned and blistered about the face and hands from that last explosion of emerald light. Malien's shoulder wound had broken open in the fall on the bridge and urgently needed attention. Tensor was crippled, Yggur blind, and Xarah sat by herself, her eyes turned inward, not even weeping for her lost twin.

"Is there no hope at all of remaking the gate?" asked Tallia. Crossing the Dry Sea in summer was a nightmare that none of them was in any state to face.

As she spoke there was a mighty earth trembler and a fountain of molten rock and ash burst up from the rift on the other side of the fortress, twenty spans in the air.

"That's the fate of Katazza now," Mendark said. "Would you go in there again?"

There was no need to answer.

The Aachim had earlier brought all their packs and stores outside. They checked their gear, heaved packs over their shoulders and with a last look at the wonder and the tragedy that was Katazza they set off for the cliffs that led down to the Dry Sea.

"Shalah!" Xarah wept, her arms and legs thrashing; then they carried her away.

They headed down the winding western road, Shand leading tall Yggur. Then came Mendark and Osseion, the latter's huge frame dwarfed by his pack. Tallia walked by herself, dreading the thought of the Dry Sea, though she was better able to withstand it than most. The sixteen remaining Aachim followed her, nine walking in single file, then two carrying Malien. Two more at the rear bore Tensor on a stretcher, a bier for the living. The Histories had taught Tensor nothing.

What had once been the long island of Katazza was now a mountain chain girt by a series of cliffs and slopes that plunged near two thousand spans to the floor of the Dry Sea. It took five days, with all their cripples and encumbrances, to reach the old shore of the island and climb down the cliffs to the sea bed. The further down they went the hotter, drier and saltier it became.

At the base of the last cliff they climbed out of a shady cleft onto a scree slope crusted with salt. The air was so thick that it clotted in their throats; heavy and desiccating, and when the wind blew, which was most of the time, it carried salt dust that tormented eyes, ears and mouths. The heat was ghastly, like the inside of an oven, the afternoon sun a sledgehammer trying to pound them into scraps of bone and skin.

"This is unendurable," said Shand, holding his cloak over his head as he pushed back into the shade. The others followed. Minutes went by; no one moved, or even spoke. Tallia could see it in their eyes—the Dry Sea had defeated them already.

Some handled the heat better than others. Mendark, huddling at the furthest extremity of the cave, dried out before their eyes. The very skin of his face shrank so that each fiber of his scanty beard stuck out like a hairy goose-pimple.

Yggur was panting like a dog, sweat making rivers across

his brow. He smeared the damp across his face in a futile attempt to cool himself, but the air sucked the moisture off him like a sponge.

"No one has ever walked the Dry Sea in summer," Yggur said. Alone of them all he had not crossed it to get here. "It's madness. I can't do it." He lapsed back into torpor.

"Still seven days till summer," said Shand. "It gets a lot hotter than this."

They sheltered in a cave all day and, come nightfall, had not the strength to begin their trek. The morning after, a debate raged for hours as to whether they could attempt the Dry Sea at all. Even the Aachim were for going back to Katazza until the end of autumn, hopeless and perilous as that seemed. Tallia fanned herself with her hat but did not add to the debate. She knew that they had no option.

Cracks opened in their skin and crusted with bloody salt that the midges sucked at constantly. Shand was so red in the face that he looked ready to explode, while Selial seemed incapable of sweating at all: her pallid skin flaked off her face like dandruff.

"How far was it from here to the lakes?" asked Malien of Osseion.

"Ten nights. But the nights were longer then."

"And cooler," said Tallia, fanning herself languidly. "And we were fit and well. It could take twice as long this time."

Malien eased her arm in its sling. The shoulder, though healing, still gave her a lot of pain. "If we go back we'll die there," she said.

"Or as good as," agreed Mendark. "Give Rulke half a year to prepare and we'll never stop him. I'm for going on, by myself if necessary." There was a trace of the noble sacrifice in his tone.

Osseion laughed disrespectfully. "By yourself, master? You do not command me?"

Mendark flushed. "Just you and me and Tallia!"

"All or none," said Malien.

They trudged through the night, the longest they'd ever suffered. Only one thing raised their spirits the whole time.

"I can see!" Yggur roared at the rising sun. *"I can see!"*

As it turned out he could not see very much; no more than the difference between light and darkness. However, it gave him hope that his sight would return. His bitterness eased somewhat.

In the short nights they walked, as far as the weakest, Yggur and Selial, could go, and that was only for a few hours. But in the broken lava country the passage was unbearably slow, about half the pace of Mendark's leisurely journey out, and even the Aachim found Tensor's litter to be a burden, though not one that they ever remarked upon. All the long days they huddled, packed together, in their tents.

Every day there were windstorms laden with salt dust or crystals, raging across the plains of the Dry Sea at speeds that it was impossible to walk against. Then they must camp in an instant, close all the entrances of their tents, praying that they would not blow away, block nose and mouth and breathe through a pad of cloth. So severely was the water rationed that they were always desperate for it. Their mouths always tasted of salt, and their food, and it got into everything but the waterbags.

On the tenth morning since their departure from Katazza, Shand woke to realize that the air was still, the tent not even flapping. He went outside to enjoy the relative cool of the pre-dawn. Yggur was there too, waiting to see all that he could see—the rising sun. To Shand's surprise he saw a beacon blazing in the blackness.

"That's strange!" he said to Yggur. "There's a light on the mountain."

Yggur allowed Shand to turn him in that direction. He squinted until tears dripped from his eyes. "Rulke!" he said, overcome with helpless terror.

11

CLAUSTROPHOBIA

Karan came hurrying back, carrying a heavy hourglass-shaped bucket with water slopping over the side. She was amazed to see Rulke standing up, looking fully recovered. Karan felt a trickle of fear. A defeated, dying Rulke was one thing; a Rulke miraculously restored to full vigor quite another. She felt an overpowering urge to run away.

But what were they doing? He and Llian stood side-by-side, their backs to her, facing the construct. Llian looked up at Rulke; it seemed a conspiratorial glance. The construct shivered in the air like a mirage. Even from behind she could read Llian's eagerness, his fascination with what Rulke had been telling him. Oh, Llian, she thought, I know you're not Rulke's match, but couldn't you even *try* to resist? Then Llian saw her and his eyes gave her away.

"Karan," said Rulke in a voice like liquid chocolate. "Come, join us."

The word "us" struck her through the heart. Had Llian been swayed in so short a time? She recalled Shand's oft-stated doubts about him. *The Zain can never be trusted. They have proven that over and over. They are fatally curious.*

"Karan!" Llian cried. "We did it. The gate's still open!"

"And if you cooperate too," Rulke said to her, "I may even send *you* back."

Too? What did he mean? Karan felt panicky. There was a pain in her chest. She was panting like a sprinter.

Struggling to control herself, she glanced in the direction of the plate. It was still shimmering, a miracle that she had given up hoping for. She must get Llian to the gate. If only there was a way to link with him without Rulke's knowing. But using her talent here would be doubly dangerous.

"I brought some water," she said in a monotone. Let Rulke think that she was still trying to help. "Would you like me to tend your burns?"

Rulke stared at her, devouring her with his eyes and his smile. His gaze hurt. She looked away, sure that she knew what he was thinking. He was judging her by the tattered clothes and tangled hair, by her smallness, her youth, the lack of guile in her green eyes. Surely he would see her as nothing to be concerned about; her wounding him back in Katazza just a lucky accident.

His words utterly dashed that hope. "I see that I will never sway *you*, my diminutive enemy. I won't underestimate *you* again. Not someone who so resembles my nemesis, Elienor. Not someone who has more courage than all the mighty in Katazza. You are deadly but I will have you anyway. I have need of your other talent; *the one you scarcely know you have.* Indeed, so often have I touched your mind while you slept I know you better than you know yourself."

Smiling a predatory smile, he stepped toward her. Karan felt his presence picking at her mind. It reminded her of the nightmares on the road from Fiz Gorgo. That awful night above Narne, that had been him too. And it had been her link, at least her weakness in using it, that had enabled him to wake the Ghâshâd. Without her, Shazmak would still stand!

Karan recoiled violently and the bucket clattered on the

floor, spreading its contents wide. She bent to pick it up but the water was already glazing the floor with ice. The panic was becoming uncontrollable. If she didn't act now, both she and Llian were finished. She fought it down but it sprang up stronger than ever. Then the glimmering of a plan came to her.

"Touched," she said. "Influenced in some small way perhaps. But use my talent? *Never!*" She spat on his black boot.

Rulke clenched his fist. His arm trembled, and when he stepped toward her one knee wobbled. He could barely stand up now. He shook open his hand, watching her carefully. "I can see into your heart. Give yourself up and I will let Llian go free. Refuse . . ."

"The Great Betrayer!" she said. "Do you take comfort that all hate and despise you?"

"Only because of the lies of the chroniclers." He smiled menacingly.

"That's what I'd expect the Great Betrayer to say," she sneered.

"Don't speak to me about treachery!" Rulke ground out. "I had a partner once. Ask your *friends* Mendark and Yggur and Tensor what they did to her!"

Karan was taken aback. He seemed to be genuinely angry. But then, he was known for his trickery. She kept taunting him, trying to drive him into making a mistake.

"I can read you like a chart on the wall, Rulke. And as for Llian, whom you seek to corrupt with your flattery and your offers, he is nothing but a common harlot—he would sell himself to anyone in exchange for a few scraps of the Histories."

Forgive me, Llian, she thought, seeing the hurt she was doing him. I do not judge you. *I will not!* But if we don't get away he will drive me mad again. I can feel it already. Whatever it takes I will do it, and make it up to you later.

She backed away and Rulke moved slowly after her, just like their dance in Katazza. He put up his hand. "Don't try to anger me. I have borne a thousand insults, a thousand names."

"A thousand years have passed and only one remains," she taunted, trying to draw him away from Llian toward the place where the spilled water had frozen on the floor. "Great Betrayer! Nothing more do people remember of you, treacherous one. There is nothing more."

"Every tale has two sides!" he said furiously. "Maybe I need a teller to tell mine." He gave Llian a significant glance. "Perhaps I already have one."

"Your lies will still be lies even if the greatest teller on Santhenar tells them!" she retorted.

Rulke's face grew dark. His outstretched arm shook. Karan was of no account, her words less than nothing, but he was drained to the dregs and the words stung.

"You anger me, little one," he said hoarsely. He began to exert his mind against her.

The pressure started to build up again, undermining her. Karan began to feel, lurking in the back of her mind, the madness that she had been driven to on the road to Thurkad. It rose up and down like a cork bobbing on waves, still a long way away, but Rulke was a storm that could swamp her effortlessly. She would not go through that again. Blind terror overwhelmed her. Never more!

"Llian," she shouted. How could she tell him to get to the gate without Rulke knowing too? "Remember our plan! Get away from him."

"Think about my offer, Llian," Rulke said, gripping him by the shirt. "There is much profit in it for you. And for you too, Karan. I can give you your heart's desire, and all you need do for me is one little favor."

Karan menaced him with her bucket. Rulke sprang back out of reach, landed off-balance and one foot slipped on the ice. He wavered, flung out his arms for balance, then Karan hurled the heavy container at him. The metal base struck him across nose and eyes, his feet skidded from under him and he hit the floor with a thump that sent luminous shockwaves rolling through the mist.

"Run!" Karan yelled, dashing toward the gate. "Hurry, Llian!"

She had forgotten his sprained ankle and gashed knee. All Llian could manage was a painful hobble, and before he had gone three steps Rulke lurched to his feet. A long gash curved through both eyebrows, weeping blood, and his nose gushed blood onto the ice. Rulke planted his big feet wide, trying to clear his eyes with one hand while the other fist burst brilliant spears of light that carved traces across walls and ceiling. Llian, terrified that Rulke would blast Karan through the wall in his rage, threw himself at the Charon. They crashed onto the ice again.

Karan turned to see where Llian was. He was just a shape in the churning mist, down before Rulke. It looked as if he was swearing allegiance. "What will you not do for your precious Histories?" she screamed, completely losing her presence of mind.

Half-blind, blood pouring into his eyes, Rulke flung his fist out at the plate. The wall beside her dissolved into a ragged hole, then the whole palace thinned to transparency. It was failing!

The pressure of his mind was like a dam bursting above her, making it impossible to think. Madness rolled toward her like a wave driven across the great ocean, swelling until it towered over her, curving over high above, white with foam breaking at the top. Now it thundered down, deluging her, trying to drive her onto reefs of insanity. She tried to fight the panic but it overwhelmed her. As Karan lurched backwards toward the plate, it flared into a corrugated tunnel that shrank away behind her into mist.

The tunnel began to draw her in. Rulke cleared his eyes and knocked Llian out of the way. Only as he went skidding across the floor did Karan understand that Llian had been trying to protect her. In the security of the gate the panic eased and she knew she had made a terrible mistake. Rulke had beaten her—he'd taken her measure very quickly.

"Lliannnnnn!" she screamed, trying to scramble back out. It was too late—the gate was already drawing her away. She leapt up, her arms outstretched like a diver, but it was like trying to jump up an oiled funnel. She was fading, shrinking, being sucked away down the hollow of the gate.

Llian ran toward her, hit a soggy patch of floor and sank into it to the knees. He scratched at the edge. She tried desperately to get back to him but it was too late. Rulke blasted light at the plate again. A line of fire swept through the ceiling, scarred the wall then slashed across the edge of the plate. Air began to hiss out through the roof.

"Back you come!" Rulke roared.

The last thing she saw was Llian scrabbling across the floor on hands and knees. The gate was too far away. Rulke rose over him like a vampire, then the scene was cut off.

Karan was buffeted violently, twisted and hurled about while fireworks flared beneath her eyelids. With a wrench the tunnel began to contract. The air sucked past with a hiss that pulled her hair back toward the Nightland. Karan struggled to remember her destination, Tensor's gate chamber in the Great Tower. Her eyes began to burn; her ears and nose stung; she could taste blood in the back of her mouth.

She was blind, suffocating! Karan opened her mouth to scream and the air boiled out of her lungs. The tunnel shrank around her tight as a stocking: squeezing, choking. Her chest was so compressed that she could scarcely have taken a breath anyway. Karan felt herself falling into unconsciousness. She tried to focus on Katazza with all her talent. *The gate, the gate chamber*, she visualized, using the most vivid and terrifying image that she could think of. *Remember how Tensor held Llian high as he roared defiance at Rulke!*

But the image would not stay in her mind, no matter how she forced. It was as if the gate chamber no longer existed. She riffled through a hundred images of that place but all she could see was Rulke framed by the columns of the pavilion, then its metal dome spinning across the floor. Spinning . . . spinning . . . She was losing it. She was dead.

That image must have been just enough to bring the gate back home, for the tunnel pinched off a bubble of itself, spat her against something hard with a crack that she did not hear, and evaporated.

The impact forced a gasp out of her. Trying to sit up, Karan smacked her head on something hard. She drew in shuddering gasps of air, blinked thick fluid out of her eyes and slowly her sight returned, though it showed nothing recognizable. A trickle of blood came from her nose. Trying to wipe it away, Karan found that she could not move her arm. She brought her other arm up, smearing blood across her face. Turning her head, Karan saw, in dim light, a hard surface curving around her. It was the metal dome of the pavilion—she recognized the shape. The gate had brought her out underneath it.

I wonder how heavy it is. I hope I can lift it off. Feeling around with her free arm, she managed to liberate the other one. She was lying on rubble in a narrow space under about a quarter of the dome. The remainder was squashed flat. Something must have fallen on it since she and Llian had left. She tried to push the dome up but it did not budge. There was no space large enough to crawl through either. She was trapped! She was going to die here. She'd never see Llian again.

Could he have reached the gate after all? Impossible, so quickly had it closed behind her. And that was just as well, for if he had he was surely dead, or abandoned in some place that she could never find. She felt utterly wretched, quite bereft. This was the worst thing she had ever done. A monumental stupidity, an unforgivable betrayal.

To add to her troubles, aftersickness was rising up worse than she'd ever felt it. It pricked her abused body with a thousand spikes of pain, too terrible to fight against. Clearly she was not meant to travel through gates. Her brain throbbed, a migraine sent her blind. Karan curled up on the rubble, surrendered herself to it, and after an eon she slept.

Llian lay frozen, expecting Rulke's terrible rage to strike him dead. One moment it seemed that he would, then as the sound of the air rushing out through the roof rose to a shriek, Rulke reeled away, ripped the door off and began to mold it with his fingers. He soon had a metallic-looking pancake of soft material that was roughly the area of the construct. Awkwardly lifting it above his head, he spun it on his fingertip until it became a disc then sent it flying upwards. The disc slapped against the ceiling, flattened out and the rush of air ceased.

Rulke hung his head, slipped and began to tremble all over, his movements growing more and more exaggerated. He fell to one knee, recovered, the attack came back, then he staggered off, blood pouring down his face. His foray to the reality of Santhenar, and all that had happened since, had sucked him dry. The door banged. Llian's eyes followed Rulke through the transparent walls until he disappeared in the thickening mist. Llian was alone once more.

Alone and terrified. Everything had happened so quickly. Karan was gone before he understood what was happening. Why had she been so angry? He replayed the scene in his mind, trying to see what Karan had seen. He saw her screaming at him in terror, accusing him of collaborating with Rulke. That hurt, for though sorely tempted, he had not. How could she have so mistrusted him? It was so unlike her.

Now that Rulke was gone even the temptation was hard to understand. The Zain had succumbed to Rulke once, and look what it had got them. They had been decimated and decimated again, stripped of every possession, banished from beloved Zile and persecuted for twice a thousand years. And still they were stained by the Curse of Rulke, shameful stigmata that marked them to this day. No one on Santhenar knew it better than Llian. Would he sell himself so easily for such a doubtful reward? Llian told himself that he would not, and hoped that he was never tempted.

What was he to do now? Run and hide? What was the point of that, in Rulke's own realm? He tested the plate but it was as dead as the rest of the floor now; the gate was closed to him. He tried the door, which opened easily. There was no need for locks here. In fact the walls were now so tenuous that he could probably have walked right through them. He tried the nearest, finding it no firmer than a soap bubble. He went back to the construct. Again, when he tried to touch it his fingers disappeared.

Llian walked around the other side, examining the machine tentatively. It was like no device that he had ever seen, and there was no part of it whose function he could recognize. It did not even touch the floor, this sleek, deadly-looking thing. What purpose did it have? Or was it just a whim, a sculpture made to while away the eternal hours? Merely Rulke's empty boast?

The day passed. Llian was so parched that he could hardly think straight. He made a half-hearted journey in search of water—Karan had not been away for very long—but found himself in a part of the Nightland where all the spaces were warped horribly. Even seeing through the walls where he wanted to go he could find no way of getting there. He went back to what was now the relative security of the construct room.

There he stayed for hours more, hours that were damnably hungry and thirsty. He would have eaten the ice on the floor but it was covered in frozen blood. Eventually he found a small clean patch, cracked it with his boot heel and held the shards in his mouth until they melted. The water tasted like metal.

Llian grew drowsy but did not dare to go near Rulke's bedroom. In another room he found a cupboard that was large enough to lie on and less frigid than the floor. There he spent many uncomfortable hours, half-dozing, until finally he realized that fear and hunger had taken away any further chance of sleep. He wandered the halls of the Nightland, looking in every doorway and every cupboard, noting everything down for his tale, but found nothing to eat or to drink.

Eventually Rulke returned, carrying a covered tray. It could not be said that Llian was glad to see him, but at least it gave some certainty to his existence. The Charon had changed into robes of sable silk and looked rested, though the long crescent-shaped gash that passed through both eyebrows was bruised and swollen. He put the tray down on a marble pedestal. Llian's eyes followed it lustfully, almost drooling.

Rulke smiled. "Are you hungry? Well, give me what I want and you shall eat. Ah, but I underestimated your little friend *again*. My time here must have weakened me more than I thought. It is a thousand years since anyone injured me, and no one has *ever* done it twice."

Llian swallowed, tearing his eyes away from the tray.

"In any event, you are no use to me here." Rulke walked off a few paces, musing audibly, presumably meaning Llian to hear his thoughts. "But back there with your friends you might be a great help to me. They trust you."

"What's happened to Karan?" Llian asked.

"That may end up my biggest blunder of all," he said soberly. "I need her, desperately."

"What's the matter?" cried Llian, alarmed by the tone of his voice.

"I don't know where she is. I would have warned her about the gate but she took me by surprise."

"What do you mean, *warned*?" Llian grabbed him by the sleeve. "What's happened to her?"

"The Nightland is failing and it makes the gate somewhat . . . quixotic. And your friends in Katazza haven't helped. Look at it." Rulke waved his hand and projected on the mist Llian saw a field of rubble, above which soared the broken stumps of the Great Tower.

"The gate sent her *there?*" Llian's voice rose to a scream. He groped around blindly. Had Rulke not caught him he would have fallen. He struggled to get away. "I've got to go back."

Rulke held him effortlessly. "She *may* have gone there. You can't always tell with gates."

"Send me back," Llian shouted, whacking at Rulke with his fists.

Rulke caught his hands. "I might, once you give me what I want. Presently I don't have the strength."

"What . . . happened?" Llian asked listlessly, giving up the unequal struggle.

"In Katazza? I'd say your friends took too much power out of the rift and it brought the whole tower down."

"Then they're all dead!"

"I wouldn't be too sure about that, chronicler. My enemies are tough, wily. However, that's all I saw, and without opening the gate and going through it, I can't tell you any more."

He waved his hand again. "This charm requires you to answer me truthfully. Tell me your story, Llian."

Though he wondered if he might not be betraying his friends, Llian could not prevent himself from answering. He told Rulke his whole history, beginning with his childhood in arid Jepperand, where he had been so different from the other children.

"Jepperand!" exclaimed Rulke. "You're Zain!"

"Yes, I am," said Llian, wondering what use Rulke would make of this information.

"Why didn't my Ghâshâd tell me? And no ordinary Zain either. It starts to fall into place. Go on."

Llian spoke of his misery at being sent across half the world to the College of the Histories when he was only twelve, of gradually rising above the ostracism due to a foreigner and a Zain, and suddenly bursting out in that creative explosion that led to his first great telling four years ago, and then to the greater sensation, his triumph at the Graduation Telling last summer when he had told his new version of the *Tale of the Forbidding* and been awarded the honor of master chronicler.

And all the while, Rulke was watching him with those extraordinary eyes, staring as if trying to look into his head. Llian's Zain origins had come as a shock to him.

Llian told the *Tale of the Forbidding* too, and all about the mysterious murder of the crippled girl that had led to his downfall, and the suspicion that had aroused. Someone had crept into Shuthdar's ruined tower unseen and done foul murder. Why, but to cover something up?

"Ah!" said Rulke, his Charon eyes looking through Llian back to that time. "Well told, chronicler! I remember seeing the poor girl's body, though I never knew it was murder. Go on with your own story."

Llian briefly told the events since he'd left the college, including his shameful collaboration with Tensor. How weak I am, he thought. Emmant had a power over me, Tensor a greater power. Now Rulke does just what he wants with me. But at the same time, Llian knew that he wanted to answer Rulke, and to question him. There was so much to learn. "Rulke—" he began.

"Enough!" Rulke said abruptly. "I've got to know what you are."

Taking Llian by the shoulder in one refractory hand, with the other Rulke tipped his chin up. Their eyes came together and locked. Llian's head spun, his mind drifted and he was lost. He felt disembodied, no more than a spirit hovering high up in the mist.

Looking down at his boneless flesh he saw Rulke's hands pass over his face. The thick fingers appeared to press down through his skull just as Llian's own hands had gone through the construct. That was not possible: it must be a hallucination. The fingers roused his brains about, flipping the hemispheres from hand to hand, a sensation that was a cross between a tickle and a sneeze. Rulke's voice spoke to him—commands that might have been in a foreign tongue, for he did not understand a syllable. Finally the fingers withdrew from his head as slowly as they had gone, tugging at the brains as if attached by threads.

The hallucination ended and Llian was back in his body, his brain swarming like an ant city, but ants whose innumerable feet had trod in acid. He saw Rulke stagger back, but after that Llian lost consciousness.

12

UNDER THE RUINS

Karan woke in darkness. She shouted until she was hoarse and after that rapped on the dome for hours, hoping that the company would still be here. Even hoping, bitter irony, that Tensor could reopen the gate for her. But the hours tolled by like funeral bells and, finally, her knuckles bruised and raw, Karan had to stop.

Distantly she heard a roaring sound, then the sound of little stones rattling on the rubble above her. She caught a whiff of pungent gas. It was so hot! Karan realized that she was sweating, her shirt sodden where she pressed against the metal. That was strange, for Katazza was a cool place, high in the mountains. There came another earth trembler and rubble scraped against the dome above her. Something shifted underneath, separating the stones slightly. Suddenly she felt panicky with claustrophobia and began banging her head against the dome, harder and harder, until one blow hurt so much that it brought her to her senses.

A sulphurous stench drifted up through the cracks. Light

began to grow around her—another day. She must have slept again. Karan probed at the rubble under her. Perhaps she could shift some of it.

She picked out the smaller pieces of stone, one by one, stacking them up in the empty part of her prison until it was nearly full. Her excavations exposed a larger piece of stone sitting over a gap between other blocks. If she could lift it there might be a way out. As she slid her fingers down beside the stone the tower shook again and the rubble shifted. Karan snatched her hands out.

The rumbling died away. She tried again. This time the stone moved, though not enough. In the dim light she studied the matrix of rock. If she could get this piece out, the space would be big enough to squeeze head and shoulders in. Did she dare? What if the rubble moved? It would be a miserable way to die, trapped by the head. Well, she was going to die if she stayed here, anyway.

Panic rose up again. She forced her fingers down into the rubble until they bled, gripped the stone and heaved. It moved slightly then stuck. She shook it, feeling her fingernails breaking. The tower trembled again, but this time she used the shuddering of the rubble to ease the stone past the others. With a mighty effort, up it came, revealing a larger space underneath.

Taking a deep breath, Karan looked down. It was light enough to see a network of spaces below, though no way to tell if they went anywhere. Putting her head right in, she rotated her shoulders into the gap and peered round the edge. The earth quivered a long way away. Grit sifted down into her eyes. Karan blinked it out, trying not to panic. The direction she was looking was choked up.

Turning the other way she saw in front of her a space between two flat slabs that extended for a few spans and, beyond it, what looked like the treads of a stair. If she could get that far she might be able to climb out. She withdrew into her cramped space, sucking her bloody fingers, taking deep breaths to overcome the claustrophobia that was building up again. It would be much worse down there. Did she have the courage for it?

The first part almost finished her, for though the space between the slabs was large enough, Karan found that she could not get her body around the corner into it. She almost fitted, but not quite, and her clothes kept snagging on the rough edges. She wanted to scream.

Karan pushed herself back out to lie in the cramped space under the dome. That felt nearly as bad now. It was so hot—she would have killed for a drink. Nothing to do but try again, or die here for want of courage. She was short of courage; there seemed no good reason to keep trying. Then I'd better invent a reason, she thought. She imagined that Llian had come through the gate and was lying helpless not far away, calling out for her with his dying breath. The image was so vivid that she saw him, his face contorted in a scream. It looked as if Rulke had his hands inside Llian's head.

"Llian!" she shouted and the rubble groaned in reply. It was enough. She took off her clothes, knotted her belt around the bundle and went down again, pushing it ahead of her.

The difference was just enough. With much scraping of breasts and shoulders, and not a little skin lost off hips and buttocks, Karan forced herself around the corner into the space between the slabs. There, in spite of the claustrophobia, she had to rest. It was hotter now, her bare skin in contact with the rock. She crawled on, negotiated the space between the slabs which was partly filled with rubble, and shortly found herself in a larger opening on the stair, big enough to stand up in. After her previous prison this was like a palace, though Karan soon realized that there was no way out of it either.

On one side was the curving wall, above were huge blocks of stone precariously perched one against another, and back the other way only the narrow conduit she had just crawled through. Part of the tower had fallen, evidently. There were cracks in the wall too; she could see out over the roofs of the fortress, all battered and broken, though many of the domes and minarets still stood.

The destruction was shocking. Karan wondered what had happened to her friends, but lacked the emotional energy to worry about them. She quickly dressed again then, sitting down to tie up her boots, noticed a hole in the wall near her foot, half-filled with rubble. It did not look quite right.

She levered out several of the larger chunks with a piece of metal lying on the step. There was a hollow space inside—the place where one of the spring cables had run up the inside of the spiral, had she known it, and as the tower collapsed the tension had pulled the broken cable up out the top.

Extracting the rest of the rubble, Karan found a smooth hollow slightly wider than her shoulders. Below was choked, but the way up looked clear for as far as she could see. She began to climb.

It was a hard climb for the inside was smooth, but the coiling passage allowed her, by pressing hard with hands and knees, to get up it. Twice she became stuck and claustrophobia almost made her scream, then finally she saw daylight above. Her head popped out the top. Karan looked over the edge. She was high up: it was a good seventy or eighty spans down to the base of the tower. She was on a cluster of stumps, what remained of the twisted cables of stone, still standing though tilted a long way from the vertical. A long way below, other shards of wall stood up, between which hung an improbably suspended arc of stair. What had been the inside of the Great Tower was a rubble-choked ruin. Beyond, at the western edge of the plateau, a red-hot paste of rock was ebbing out of the rift.

The climb down looked nearly as bad, even for a climber as accomplished as she was, for she had no climbing aids at all. But in the end, not as bad as it appeared, for the destruction had ripped most of the tiles off the outside, leaving a ridged and grooved surface that was quite easy to cling to.

It was nearly dark by the time she reached the bottom,

crept across the rubble-littered paving and into the half-ruined fortress. She made her way through the halls to the part where the Aachim had lived. There she found water and a small stack of food packages where formerly there had been a huge number. Someone must have survived the fall of the tower and set out across the Dry Sea. Let it be Shand and Malien, she thought. She fell on the food like a wolf.

After that Karan inspected herself in a mirror in the bathing room. It revealed a bloody mess covered in dirt which sweat had caked to mud. Her eyes were starred red where their little veins had burst in the gate. Her trousers were worn through at the knee.

What would Llian think if he saw me now? she thought wryly. Then, damn him, he never takes any trouble over his own appearance. The thought of Llian, unkempt but endearing, brought tears to her eyes. The image of Llian on the floor with Rulke looming over him brought the tears down in floods.

Later, to her immense joy, she found her traveling pack where she had left it before she climbed the tower. She took out clean clothes, went to the cisterns, bathed, washed her clothes and her hair, and made herself as presentable as her indifferent facilities allowed. Then she scoured Katazza, even crawling back over the rubble of the tower in case Llian had somehow got through.

Karan did not find him. She did not really expect to. She had abandoned him, her only love, in the Nightland. Fled in mewling terror. And the Nightland was collapsing. He might be dead already.

All the next day she searched; the ruins of the Great Tower again, and the countless rooms of Katazza too. And the rest of the plateau, in case the gate had moved and he had come out nearby, or his body been released into the middle air. Nothing did she find, no trace. Then Karan truly despaired.

He's gone and I must bear the burden of it. I should have protected him better. Either Llian is dead or he remains in the

Nightland where sooner or later Rulke will seduce him to his own purpose. How could Llian possibly resist him? I know I could not.

She had been too afraid for herself, at Rulke taking control of her mind, at being driven mad again. Rulke had woken memories she had tried to forget for half a year; of Emmant; of her madness; of the Conclave.

She had been too eager to believe ill of Llian; had judged him on no evidence at all. How easily Rulke had fooled her. He had done it to drive a wedge between her and Llian. To divide, as he had always divided his foes.

She sat down on the steps outside the broken tower. There was no way of knowing how long ago the company had departed. Perhaps time flowed differently in the Nightland. She judged that she had been there only a few days, yet there were no tracks here, even on soft ground. They might have been gone for weeks. Not months though, for the height of the midday sun was little different from what it had been at the time she'd climbed the tower.

A breeze sprang up, drifting papers across the paving stones. She idly picked one up and recognized the writing—a scroll made by Tensor but overwritten by Llian. Karan ran after the others, knowing how important they were to him. After some searching she tracked the papers back to their source and found his bag, jammed under the edge of the dome by its thongs. She had to cut them off to free it. Inside was his precious journal, in which he had begun to write the first draft of the *Tale of the Mirror.* Flipping through the pages brought back memories of their time together, so strongly that it was unbearable. But the journal might be all that she would ever have of him.

The next day passed as tediously as the first, and the day after. Karan had not felt so lonely in all her adult life. To go or to stay? Either way there were perils. By now the Dry Sea would be a furnace. Even taking the short way of Mendark's, it would be impossible alone. Unless she could catch up to them, she must remain here until the winter. Another two hundred days, and Rulke could come after her at any time.

She must go at once if she was to catch them. But Karan did not want to go. The platinum dome lay half-on, half-off the side of the fortress. She lingered lonely in its shade. Beneath its shelter she and Llian had become lovers, a happening of almost mystical significance for her. The memories made her feel very sad. The night drifted down as softly as her lover's caress. She could not abandon him. Karan wrapped her cloak around her and, holding the journal against her breast, at last she slept.

13

'TIS AN OLD RAT . . .

Rulke recovered before Llian did. He stood staring down at the chronicler, who looked young and defenseless—but then Karan had seemed that way too. Would the *reading* that he had just done actually show true on Llian, a Zain with all their heritage of resistance? Rulke took no chances, going down on one knee and examining Llian more carefully. There was still something that puzzled him about the Zain, something strange and rare.

He wished that he knew more about this one, but information was his weakness now, as before the Nightland it had been his strength. All he'd had was that brief meeting with the Ghâshâd in Thurkad, and at that time Llian had been no more than a name, of the least interest.

Rulke needed spies desperately but those channels were long gone. After he was put in the Nightland only the Ghâshâd remained loyal, but time turned their service into a ritual, all but useless, and in the end even they forgot. He had woken them but they were only a shadow of their former selves. How long would it take to build it all again? Much more time than he had. The world had changed enormously in a thousand years but most of that time was blank to him. His enemies, as they were today, were enigmas.

Llian could help to remedy that. He knew many of them, and as a chronicler he had the right to talk to anyone. Not a perfect spy but a very good one. And he knew the Histories. That was the first thing Rulke wanted from him.

Yet that inexplicable strangeness bothered him. It was just a minor niggle, and there were many other things to think about. Surely Llian posed no risk. No, better be sure! Putting his fingers to Llian's temples, Rulke made the examination once more. Yes! Llian had a rare form of the Gift, the resistance to the spells of the Aachim that Rulke had given the Zain two thousand years ago! Somehow the stigmata did not show in the Nightland. This put a different complexion on things. What could he, Rulke, do with this one? There were still blank parts of Llian, but no one could be known perfectly. He was satisfied that his compulsion would work.

Such an important spy needed what protection he could give him, for the road from Katazza back to Thurkad was perilous. What could he use? The Nightland was made of intangible stuff that would not pass through the gate. Ah! Rulke sensed the imprint of a charm. Llian wore a chain about his neck, from which hung a small jade amulet, a good-luck charm given by his mother when he was sent away to Chanthed. It was the same amulet that Faelamor had enchanted for Emmant so that he could control Karan, though Malien had removed that enchantment long ago.

Unhooking the charm, Rulke tossed it to one side. Then he spat in his hand and out of that stuff fashioned another amulet, identical in all respects. He put it back on the chain, tucking it into Llian's shirt.

"Well, Llian my lad, that's the best I can do. If someone stabs you in the back it won't save you, but it will give you an edge in luck. Though I wouldn't advise you to press it too hard at the gaming tables. Now," he said softly, "when I call, will you come?"

Llian did not move, though his eyes flicked beneath their closed lids. He made a gurgling sound in his throat; foam dribbled out the corner of his mouth and ran down his cheek. He shook his head.

"If you support me I will give you everything you desire," said Rulke, as softly as before. "Wealth undreamed of, the love of beautiful women . . ."

"I care nothing for such things," said Llian thickly, and not entirely truthfully either. His head lolled on his shoulders, but after several spasmic lurches he succeeded in lifting it and stared Rulke full in the face.

A huge smile split Rulke's face. The courage and boldness delighted him; there *was* something to this one, as to the woman. What a pair they made. "Wake, Llian!" and he was himself again. "What then *do* you desire? Tell me and you shall have it."

"I want Karan," said Llian.

"So do I, chronicler!"

Llian felt a stab of impotent jealousy. No one could compete with Rulke. "She's mine!" he said fiercely. "Mine, not yours."

"She's not your property," said Rulke. "She can give herself to whomever she pleases. Besides, she betrayed you; abandoned you."

"It was all a dreadful mistake," said Llian. "The gate pulled her in."

"She accused you of betraying her, Llian. Then she left you behind. Deliberately!"

Llian's faith in Karan was undermined. "Maybe she did. But I still want her safe."

"As do I, chronicler. Believe me, Karan is very important to me. If I was able to get her back I would have done so already."

"Why don't you go after her?"

"In my state, even if I could control the gate, going through it would probably kill me."

"Then send me back," Llian cried, clutching his hands against his breast.

Rulke grinned mirthlessly. "Nice try, chronicler! Do as I want and I might consider it." He glanced up at the ceiling, and Llian did too. Now almost as clear as glass, through it strange constellations could be seen in a blue-black sky. "If you don't you will stay here until you freeze. So you'd better name what I can give you."

Llian felt unbearably tempted. Don't start on that road, he thought. Not a single step.

"You ache to know, don't you?

Llian did, more than anything in the world. Abandoned, betrayed, trapped in the Nightland for eternity, now desire for what Rulke knew burned him. He would do anything for it.

"Just say what you want," Rulke whispered, and even that was a seduction. "Where's the harm in that?"

"I want three things," Llian said, licking his lips. "But I will not bargain with you for them. I am Zain! Warnings about you are burned into every cell and every atom of my being."

"Tell me," Rulke repeated. "I may give them freely."

Llian hesitated. Even to articulate his desires to the great enemy could be a form of treachery. But after all, he had made no promises, nor would he. Something for nothing, if Rulke answered truthfully.

Behind Rulke, one of the walls popped like a bursting bubble. "Better be quick," said Rulke.

"I want the truth about what happened in Huling's Tower after the flute was destroyed," Llian gabbled out. "Who killed the girl there, and why."

"I cannot tell you—I never found out."

"Then I want—" Llian halted, feeling guilty already. "I want to know what Kandor told you. He wrote to you about the matter not long before he died."

"You have indeed been thorough!" said Rulke. "But we

never had that meeting, for he was killed on the way. I suspect that he was murdered to prevent our meeting. His papers must be in Katazza though."

"*Murdered!*" cried Llian. "Who killed him?"

"I was imprisoned here before I could find out. I thought it was Mendark, or Yggur, or one of the Aachim. That is to say, one of *my* enemies, not one of his. But on the other hand, Kandor was paranoid—he even accuses me in some of his writings. And after I took Tar Gaarn, every one of the Aachim had reason to destroy me, had they not reason enough before that. I had papers on that too."

"They will be in Thurkad," said Llian, "in the citadel archives. That's where I first learned about Kandor."

"Well, that puzzle I leave to you. Kandor is long dead and I have my construct, far ahead of the flute and any other device ever made. Who cares what silly secret he discovered? Kandor was always one for trifles. He had no vision, and even if he had uncovered the flute itself, who would be so foolish as to use it after all this time? By now it would be deadly—just like the Mirror that your friends think to be such a treasure. Just how dangerous, they will find out, if they ever try to use it!"

"Where in Katazza?" cried Llian. "I've looked already. It could take a lifetime."

Rulke grinned. "You want it all handed to you, don't you. When I was young I knew that whatever I got, it would be through my own efforts. Still, the murder of any one of us is of surpassing interest to me too; I'm glad you raised it. Now, where did Kandor keep the things he most valued? Here is a clue: *in a place subordinate but fundamental.* I leave it to you to work it out, for I believe that part of Katazza is still standing. What is your next question?"

"The key to unlocking the Mirror of Aachan."

"I don't know what you mean."

"Faelamor said that it was locked by Yalkara, but that she, Faelamor, had a key back in Thurkad."

"I know nothing about that either. I have no idea what Yalkara did with it. Tell me, what has she been up to lately?"

"Lately?" Llian said in amazement. "Yalkara is long gone."

"*Gone!*" Rulke gripped Llian by the shirt. "Gone where?"

Was this betraying his friends? Surely not. Yalkara's departure was common knowledge. "The Histories tell that she used the Mirror to find a flaw in the Forbidding. She made a gate and passed back to Aachan more than three hundred years ago. You did not know this?"

Rulke staggered, then found a seat and sat down on it with a thump, staring through the ceiling at the stars. The luminous mist swirled up around him, blurring the construct into a featureless shadow.

"You're worth more than I thought, chronicler. I have been . . . cut off, here. The greatest event of the past thousand years and I had not an inkling. My need for knowledge is indeed desperate. So, there is a way through the Forbidding. Everything decays over time. That is *very* interesting. Perhaps my compass has been too limited. And your final question? What is it that you want most of all?"

Llian hardly felt guilty at all now. "You already touched on it—the secret script of the Charon. I want the Renderer's Tablet—the stone that contains the key to the script."

Rulke's face darkened. "You ask too much. The Tablet is destroyed. I broke it myself, burned the fragments to lime and scattered the powder across the ocean. That tongue is all that we brought out of the void. None but the Charon may ever know it. You shall not have it." But then he reconsidered. Why not promise him that, he thought. Even if he got it, by then it would not matter.

"Why not?" he said. "When I am finished my work the script will be redundant; only the chroniclers will be interested in it. And why not have the *Tales of the Charon* told by the greatest chronicler of the age?"

He glanced at Llian, to see how he was reacting to the flattery. It was difficult to tell. "Well, master chronicler, I'll think about it. In the meantime, tell me *my* tale. At least, that tiny part where I was betrayed and cast into the Nightland."

Surely telling that tale could harm no one. Rulke sat back with a smile, as with eager anticipation for what he would learn about himself. Llian was amused at the vanity.

"The tale, as we tell it, begins after the fall of Tar Gaarn and the death of Pitlis, designer of that great city as well as your own, glorious Alcifer."

"Ah, Alcifer," sighed Rulke. "How I loved that place."

"Alcifer was magnificent: a city vain and proud; cruel and predatory; majestic; perfect—"

"Cruel and predatory?" scoffed Rulke. "What a lot of adjectives you chroniclers use."

"The very epitome of the Charon, and so Pitlis had designed it. But the city was also a construct, and all its alchemists and engineers, scholars and toilers, and Rulke himself, made a living machine dedicated to a single end, the breaking of the Forbidding!"

"That's not the story the Council puts about," said Rulke.

"I'm telling the Histories," said Llian sharply, "not pandering to any Council or Magister."

"We'll see!"

"Or you either! The tale of Alcifer is a tragic one," said Llian, "for it arose out of one of the most elaborate betrayals of all—the fall of Tar Gaarn. That's how you became known as the Great Betrayer." He glanced at Rulke, whose face was impassive.

"Tell on, chronicler. Thus far you are close enough to the truth, save for the names you persist in giving me. How does your tale begin?"

"Picture a world grown desperate, devastated by the Clysm that lasted centuries and left Santhenar awash with blood. The roads were full of beggars but what was there to beg? The wealth of a world had been dissipated in war. A rich man was one who had food and a table to put it on.

"A terrible plague came. The cities vomited forth their terrified citizens but wherever they went they took it with them. Pestilence came in waves for a hundred years. Then Tar Gaarn fell, the last bastion of the free world, betrayed by Rulke. What remained of the world was squandered on an even greater extravagance, Alcifer.

"Rulke was pre-eminent. Santhenar, desperate. With war, plague and starvation half its people were gone. After the last Death the survivors could barely feed themselves. But much more than this was lost. Of its great libraries only Zile was left. The art and architecture, music and literature, even the Histories of Santhenar were wasted, and those who survived had more urgent tasks than to protect what remained.

"The surviving Council lacked the heart for it. Rulke came to them with an ultimatum.

" 'You will surrender all your devices and tools, your workrooms, archives and other secrets. Do that and you may keep your badges of office, and continue with all the privileges of the Council. Refuse . . .' "

"He did not need to articulate the threat.

"The great Magister Rula was dying, the Council a rabble with a small core of talent: Yggur, Mendark and Tensor—"

"You're right about the rabble," interrupted Rulke, "including those three! Look at them: Mendark—more *cunning* than talent, but always looking over his shoulder. Yggur—brilliant but unstable. He looked down on everyone yet was so easily manipulated. Tensor was the reincarnation of Pitlis—a proud fool addicted to folly, unhinged by hate."

"And so they are still," said Llian, "but they put you here."

"Dishonorably! Go on, chronicler."

"Rula coached Mendark with her last breath—"

"I remember Rula," Rulke broke in. "A great Magister and a worthy opponent. I admired *her*!"

Llian was becoming irritated by the constant interruptions. "Don't you want to hear the story?"

"Your reactions, when I challenge you, tell me just as much!" Rulke said in amusement.

"I'll go on *if you're ready?*"

Rulke sat back, grinning.

" 'You must take over the Council,' said Rula. 'Only you can, Mendark. Alcifer is, in reality, a vast construct designed to give Rulke power over the whole world. We have no defense against it. Just exploring it has destroyed us.'

" 'What can we do?' cried Mendark, on his knees beside her.

" 'Find another way. Find a weakness in Alcifer. There must be one.'

" 'Tensor is already working on that.'

" 'There is one other chance. Exploit the rivalry between Rulke and Kandor. Kandor is on his way to Alcifer now. Use him—' Then Rula died, without further word."

Rulke was no longer smiling. "I cannot believe *Kandor* was involved."

"I don't know anything about that," said Llian. He continued.

" 'I cannot see any choice,' said Mendark. He was in the apathy that follows despair.

"Yggur was silent. 'Shall we submit then?' said Mendark. 'Is the misery of a tyrant's yoke worse than starvation and the utter destruction of Santhenar?'

"Still Yggur did not speak.

" 'For us, perhaps it is,' Mendark answered. 'But for the people of Santh, it might be better . . .'

" 'Shut up, you pompous fool,' Yggur roared. 'There are no simple choices.'

" 'I am sick to my heart of war,' said Mendark. 'I would sue for peace.'

" 'Will you go down in the Histories as the man who sold a world into slavery?'

"The words stung, as Yggur, knowing Mendark's care for his reputation, even then, must have intended them to.

" 'I will try anything—' Mendark said.

"Yggur cut him short. 'Even the Proscribed Experiments? Would you essay even that?'

" 'That is taking recklessness to a folly.'

" 'So you don't have the courage!' Yggur sneered 'You won't give your all for your country and your world.'

" 'I don't know how.'

" 'I do,' Yggur replied.

"At that point Tensor came running in. The only survivor of the previous Council, for months he had been working through Pitlis's plans and notes for Alcifer, searching for any weakness.

" 'There is a flaw in Alcifer!' Tensor cried. 'Pitlis made some tiny changes to Rulke's designs and these were never discovered.'

" 'What will the effect be, when he uses his construct?' asked Yggur.

" 'There's no way of telling,' Tensor replied. 'Probably nothing, unless—'

" 'What?' cried Mendark.

" 'Unless we help it along somehow.' "

Rulke was right up on the edge of his seat now. Llian wondered what he was hoping to learn.

" 'How?' asked Mendark. 'We'd have to be right there, and . . .' He stared at the other two.

" 'Yes,' said Tensor. 'We would have to use the Proscribed Experiments!'

" 'No!' cried Mendark. 'Rula was the greatest Magister of all time, and it killed her. I'm not up to it.'

" 'Nor I,' said Tensor. 'Nor any of our Council, save—'

"They both turned to Yggur.

" 'I might agree,' said Yggur, looking down his long nose at them, 'were things desperate enough. But it would be a terrible risk for me. I would not attempt it without support.'

" 'You'd have it,' said Mendark.

" 'Total support,' said Yggur imperiously, as if he found them inadequate.

"Finally the scheme was ready, the bait prepared, taking advantage of Rulke's only weakness that they could—he was proud as exemplified by magnificent Alcifer. It meant more to him than anything. The Council disguised themselves and rode to Alcifer like a gale. On the way they could feel the fabric of the world distorting as Rulke began to test his city-construct.

"He grasped the levers, compelling the whole of Alcifer and everyone in it, the living construct, to his will. He directed all its force against the shimmering wall of the Forbidding. At once it bulged outward, a great tumor pressing into the void. And if it were not for those tiny changes Pitlis had made long ago he would have broken through. But at the last moment the tumor turned inside out and pinched off a fragment of the void."

The smile had faded from Rulke's face. His eyes burned into Llian. "Go on!" he snapped.

"Yggur began the Proscribed Experiments, the first, less dangerous, summoning part. Rulke took the bait, still suspecting nothing. The pressure was intense, on all of them. He came further. A slight unease prickled him, and he sought the reason for it. The pressure increased. Almost there, and Yggur began the second, very dangerous, capturing part.

"Suddenly one of the Council broke, and another. The carefully built structure began to totter. Yggur felt the horror clawing at the shell of his mind. The Experiments had failed.

" 'Withdraw,' he screamed, panicking under the terror of possession. The Council broke apart and scattered, trying to save themselves.

"Then the scorpion struck—Rulke was inside Yggur's head, clawing and rending. Yggur's mind rebelled against the unspeakable horror of possession. He went into foaming, raging, thrashing insanity.

"Only Mendark did not falter. There was only one way out of the disaster, a terribly risky way, but he took it. He reached into Yggur's mind and trapped Rulke there. For hours they struggled together, but Yggur's madness confused Rulke, and he broke first.

"Mendark had just strength enough, with a last desperate spell, to force him into that tumor, severing his control of

Alcifer. The tumor collapsed to a bubble, the unbreakable prison of the Nightland that touches everything and nothing equally. So Pitlis had his revenge after all.

"And out of that arose Yggur's great hatred of Mendark. But that tale has never been told. Not the full tale, anyway."

Rulke's face was thunderous. "That is a lie," he roared, striking the table so hard with his fist that it tipped over. "A vile deceit."

Llian leapt out of the way. "I didn't make the tale," he squeaked. "I merely tell it the way it has been told for a thousand years."

"A pox on your Histories!" said Rulke, carmine sparks flaming in his eyes. "How can anything you say be trusted when this is such a lie? My name has been stolen from me."

"Where is the lie? Tell me that at least."

"Damned if I will!" roared Rulke. "Only this! I did not fail. I was betrayed and the woman I was to pair with, an innocent, was destroyed. As treacherous an act as has ever been done on this world. Only in her defense was I taken."

Llian was well aware of Rulke's own reputation for deceit and treachery, but he seemed genuine. And if he was, there *was* a great lie in the Histories. Who would have done such a thing?

For a moment they were allies in their outrage. Other aspects of the Histories came to mind, things that had always seemed wrong or inexplicable.

"If it is so, I will make it my life to find out," Llian said softly into the silence. "But not for you, Great Betrayer that I know you are."

"You do me wrong, chronicler," Rulke replied with quiet dignity. "Everything I have done has been to ensure the survival of my species. What nobler aim can anyone have?"

Llian was silent. Rulke's every action since they'd met had been in self-defense. Rulke was noble, he could see that now. He almost believed him. Another question mark over the Histories. "I will find out for myself, and for the beauty of the Histories as I have always known them to be—for pure, unvarnished truth."

"Perhaps there is more to you than I had thought," Rulke said, putting his rage to one side. "Have I found the only honest chronicler in Santhenar?" He regarded Llian thoughtfully. Perhaps he did not need to corrupt him at all. Better yet if Llian would do what Rulke wanted of his own accord. He could answer truthfully when Mendark and Yggur interrogated him. What a wonderful joke!

"I also have papers dealing with this matter," said Rulke, overcome by a fascinating new thought. "I am thinking that I might give them over to you so that you can write the true tale. And if you do that well enough, next I may let you tell the whole history of the Charon since we came out of the void. What do you say to that, chronicler?"

For a moment Llian could hardly breathe. He felt as if he had been snatched from the rack and offered a kingdom. He opened his mouth but could not speak. Remember that he is called Great Betrayer. *Great Betrayer!* I wonder what his price would be?

"I cannot pay your price *here*. That must await my return to Santhenar. But shall I give you an advance?" whispered Rulke. "To show good faith?"

Llian found it impossible to hide his eagerness. He put a hand over his mouth, sure that he was drooling. He gave a jerky nod.

"Here's something that you cannot know," said Rulke, putting his mouth to Llian's ear. He spoke for a minute, and his breath sent shuddering thrills through Llian.

Llian's eyes went wide. Such knowledge he had to offer!

"Just the merest trifle," said Rulke. "So, what do you say?"

The temptation was unbearable. Maybe he could have the reward without paying the price. Karan, the company, his duty to Mendark, all were forgotten in his lust to *know*. "I think . . . we may be able to do business," said Llian. He felt a wild, almost sexual thrill. He'd done it now. No going back!

Rulke smiled. "Good. Remember what you have just learned. Because a thing has been said, or a name given, does not make it true. You must make up your own mind."

"Be sure that I will. The Histories are truth to me."

"That is as well—I have no use for liars! Now you may eat and drink." Pulling the cover off the tray, he passed it to Llian.

The tray contained food totally alien to Llian's experience, for though it looked like shreds of meat or cubes of fish or slivers of fowl, it was light on his fork and fell apart in his mouth as if woven of cobweb. There was other stuff there too, that may have been vegetables, shavings so fine that they were transparent, and the pieces put back together in the shape of different objects: one a fan, another an open book, a third a fluted scallop shell. The flavors were so subtle that he might have been eating perfumed air, after the spicy Aachim food that Llian had grown used to. In between the courses he sipped from a vase of shiny black liquid—it was cold but light and hard to swallow, and its fumes rose straight to his head like spirits of wine.

Finally there were little bite-sized dainties like clusters of crystals growing on black marble: one resembled radiating plates of pink gypsum like desert roses; a second, flat stubby prisms of borax as white as icing sugar. There were feathery balls of hair crystals like fluffy bunnies' tails; fans of green malachite needles intergrown with blue azurite; brown siderite like clusters of maidens' breasts; red corundum; shiny cubes of black galena; and many others that he could propose no names for. Each had a flavor and a bouquet like a flower essence, though he recognized none of them. They were gorgeous, though in spite of their solidity each melted in the mouth like fairy-floss.

"The sole part of our culture that we brought out of the void," said Rulke, watching him eat, "though of course they can never be more than a shadow *here*."

When Llian was finished, Rulke went on. "I am going to put you into a trance. You will stay in this state until you've told me the Histories of the time I've been in the Nightland.

Sort through your mind and tell me everything significant that happened in that time. And your *Tale of the Mirror*, too." He moved his hands in the air.

Llian's eyes went blank. Rulke gave a sigh that carried the weight of a thousand years of imprisonment. "*'Tis an old rat that won't eat cheese!* You will answer my compulsion too, when the time comes. Had you not compromised yourself I could never have done it. But your unconscious mind knows that you are willing."

Llian did as he was bade, speaking until he had run out of things to say, but as soon as he exhausted one topic, Rulke had another question, and another. Every so often the Charon brought more food, or held a mug of the black liquid to Llian's lips, then he continued. At the end of the day he was reduced to a croak. Rulke laid him on a couch, tapped his forehead and Llian fell into sleep. He began to sink into the couch. Rulke pulled him out with a wry curse and solidified the couch at the expense of the adjacent wall, which vanished into fog, while the transparent ceiling above it sagged down like crepe rubber.

Less time than I thought, Rulke said to himself. It'd better be enough!

Only minutes later, it seemed, it was time for Llian to begin again. Several days went by. But there was one last thing Rulke had to do before he brought Llian out of the trance. He bent down to speak in his ear.

"Come to me, when I return to Santhenar, and you will have your reward. My price is a tiny one. One day I will call, and you must come and tell me what you know. If Karan has survived you will bring her too, for I need her more than you. But just in case you don't want to pay your debt, I have put a compulsion on you, chronicler. Should you not come when I call, this is what you will feel. Understand that I take no pleasure from your pain. I do this because I must."

He tapped Llian lightly on the temple and instantly he convulsed, alternately wrapping his arms around his body and flinging them out. His eyes came open, but they were empty. Then Rulke touched him on the forehead again and Llian fell back into his former position.

"So little tolerance for pain," Rulke said to himself. "Truly they are a degenerate and undeserving species." Then aloud:

"Will you come?"

Llian opened his eyes. "I will come," he said, and his voice was startlingly clear. He closed his eyes again.

"Wake now!"

Llian stirred and stood up, looking dazed. "What have you done to me?"

"Nothing you need worry about. I put you into a trance and you told me the Histories—enough to go on. If I need more and cannot find it elsewhere I will come to you again."

"What?" croaked Llian, swaying back and forth.

Rulke steadied him. "Time doesn't mean much here, but in the outside world three or four days have passed since you began. I have no further use for you."

"I can go?" His head throbbing, Llian sensed that a long time had passed, though it did not seem real.

"Yes, tell your friends that you escaped. What ruse you use to explain your escape . . . well, you are a teller. I leave that to you. But be sure that you convince them, or you are no use to me and neither of us will get what we want. No, let me make it easier for you. Little point you being caught out in a lie at once. Sleep for a minute longer."

Llian dropped back into his trance. "Forget what I said," said Rulke softly. "Forget your betrayal too. Go across to the gate. When I wake you again, jump in and believe that you have escaped."

"I'm afraid of the gate," said Llian, his eyes still closed.

"And so you should be. This is the most unstable one I have *ever* encountered. But it's the only way out of here, for you and for me. Imagine if *I* fall victim to the gate when I depart. What a cruel irony that would be. Off you go. I'll send you to a place outside Katazza fortress, for your safety."

Llian got up unsteadily and limped across to the corner of the room. There he stood for a moment, looking puzzled. Rulke followed him, doing something with his hands. Slowly the plate began to glow once more, the luminous air above it to stir, its tendrils rising like steam from a pot. Llian stared at the plate as if he did not understand what he was seeing, or what to do with it.

"Wake!" said Rulke. Llian woke and at the same time Rulke lunged at him.

Llian leapt onto the plate, leaning away from Rulke's hand. The tunnel swelled; Llian fell backwards into it. It slowly closed around him, faded and disappeared.

The Nightland gave an awful screech, the sound of air escaping the mouth of a balloon, then snapped inwards. Staggering across to the construct, Rulke flung himself inside. He was just in time. The Nightland shrank down to the size of the room and kept shrinking, collapsing until it enclosed the construct like a rubber sheath.

Rulke lay inside, gasping. A tremor passed up his arm, the first spasm of the aftersickness that by sheer will he had been holding at bay all this time. What he had done recently would leave him incapacitated for a precious week. Would the Nightland even last that long?

Rulke lay down on the floor. Truly he had a long way to go before he took on the mighty of Santhenar. Fortunate that they did not know that.

14

THE PUZZLE

Not far below the southern rim of the plateau, a little pavilion made of yellow-green serpentine was hidden in one of the pockets of forest that clad the steep slopes. It was a place that Malien had spent much time in. Karan had taken to sitting there too, in her lonely exile, looking out over the sea or down to a series of rockpools and perched bogs among the trees and the shaped stones. It was a place of power, she sensed, but not the same kind of power as the rift offered, not at all. Perhaps that was why Malien had liked it.

Karan hated the fortress—it felt like an alien, broken place, and so she slept in her tent by the pavilion, bathed in one of the pools and dined on figs and other fruit now ripening on the trees.

She had been alone in Katazza for five days. In the afternoon she walked along the edge of the plateau, looking for wild food to supplement her diet. Finding a patch of wild onions, hundreds of tiny bulbs crowded together, she had just bent over to tear up a clump when everything went out of focus, a sensation like being pulled into a gate. A distortion in the air wandered across the open space behind the fortress like a tornado, took a bite out of a moss-covered wall, scattering stone like biscuits, and disappeared over the edge in the direction of the pavilion. A pungent smell drifted on the breeze. There came a liquid, splattering sound, like—she thought in horror—like a body being blown inside out. Trees toppled, creaking and groaning, their impacts shaking the ground.

She sprinted down the path, four steps at a time, scarcely daring to hope. Could it be the gate? She raced through the forest, thorny branches scratching at her. Bounding over lichen-covered outcrops and skidding on wet leaves, Karan hurtled through Malien's pavilion and out the other side.

There she stopped, looking down. Trees had fallen in a tangle of branches across the path. She could not see her bathing pool at all. "Llian?" she called uncertainly.

Karan climbed through the branches. One tree lay right along the path. To get past she had to hop from rock to rock along the sheer edge of the terrace. There was no sign of a gate.

Parting the ferns, she looked down on her pool. It was completely gone, blasted down to half-rotten logs embedded in peat. Black ooze was spattered across the rocks. Decaying strands of vegetation hung from the tree branches, dripping mud.

"Llian!" she shouted. Where once had been tall trees was now a bald patch covered in a mulch of shredded leaves, bark and wood. She trudged through the muddy debris, flinging wood pulp everywhere.

"Llian?" Perhaps a tree had fallen on him. She ran along one side of a fallen trunk, expecting to find him pulverized underneath. Karan clambered through the branches and back along the other side. Nothing! The hope, the thrill of expectation faded. She sat down on the trunk staring into nowhere. He must be somewhere *in between*, lost by the treacherous gate. And her stupidity had caused it.

Behind her Karan heard a faint, squelching plop. She whirled, but there was no one there. "Llian?" she whispered, seeking through the shadowy wreckage.

Something stirred her hackles—a momentary fear of the Whelm who had hunted her so relentlessly. But surely she was safe from them here—they could never have endured the sun of the Dry Sea.

Again she heard that squelching sound. Karan ran back to the empty pond. Nothing to see but stinking black mud and rotten logs. Then a log in the bottom lifted an arm and feebly let it flop again.

"Llian!" she screamed and leapt in, skidding down to him.

He was completely covered in mud, not a vestige of skin or clothing visible. As she reached him he struggled to lift his arm but the pull of the mud was too great. It gurgled around his mouth like a hippo blowing.

She lifted his head. He took a choking breath. "Oh, Llian!" she wept, raking mud out of his mouth. He shuddered a breath then settled down in her arms, too weak to open his eyes. Karan picked muck out of his nostrils with a twig. She scraped his eyelids clean, washed his face with muddy water from a pool that had begun to accumulate in the bottom of the hollow, then just sat there, dazed by the miracle. There was nothing more she could do—he was too heavy to drag up the slippery slope out of the bog.

How had he got free? How could he have escaped from Rulke? Sitting in the cold mud, Karan suddenly began to sweat.

Eventually Llian stirred in her arms. "I was sure you were dead," he whispered hoarsely, his beautiful voice reduced to squeaks and rasps. "I saw Katazza in ruins."

"Llian," she wept, cradling him more tightly. "How did you escape?"

"You were right," he croaked. "He is very tired, very slow."

His eyes touched hers then slid sideways, so that a stabbing pang, a sudden chill went through her. Then his eyelids closed.

"The gate hurts more each time," he mumbled and fell into a dazed sleep.

Suspicion rose again. What had he been doing for the last five days? No. It was my fault. I will be loyal. I will not doubt him.

A few minutes later Llian woke abruptly. "Under the bed!" he shouted.

"What are you talking about?"

His eyes opened. He looked blankly at her. "Karan," he whispered, giving her a wonderful warming smile. Then he looked puzzled. "Did I say that? I don't know." Like a dream, he had lost it again. He tried to get up, his feet went from under him and he slid down into the puddle. "Oh, my head!"

Karan took hold of his arm. They crawled out of the bog to another pool, to wash.

"What happened?" she asked after they were cleaned up. "I thought he was going to kill you."

Llian remembered *that*. "You abandoned me to Rulke," he said furiously. "How could you?"

I didn't, a tiny voice inside her screamed. We had a plan, remember? But you didn't follow and then the gate pulled me in. But Karan knew she had let him down and couldn't bring herself to make excuses. "I should have done better. I'm sorry." She took his hand. "I just . . ."

Llian wrenched her hand out of his. "I thought he was going to kill me. Then he had a kind of a fit and staggered off. I didn't see him again for ages. I could have eaten my arm by that time."

"What did he do to you? Llian, tell me!" She wrung his hand.

He pushed her away again. "He asked a lot of questions. He didn't even know that Yalkara had gone back to Aachan. He put me into a trance. It was like a horrible nightmare, strange but not real. I don't know what he did after that; it could have been anything at all. He said that I told him the Histories of the last thousand years. I could have done, though I remember none of it."

"Well, your voice is quite hoarse."

"My throat hurts. He tried to win me to his side. I was tempted too. Then he woke me and . . ." Llian hesitated, feeling that something was not right about his escape. Before he said a word he knew that it would sound suspicious. But then, she *had* left him behind; what did he have to feel guilty about? He looked her straight in the eye and used his *voice*, that near-magical ability of great tellers to manipulate the feelings of others by the sheer power of their words.

"I escaped the same way you did when you *abandoned me*," he said.

She flushed as red as a rose and he took a tiny pleasure in it, and felt ashamed at the same time. "Whatever he did, it must have hurt him terribly. He looked awful, sick, and somehow I got into the gate. He tried to stop me but it had already carried me away."

Karan was wrestling with her own fears. Llian had not used the *voice* on her since their very first meeting. What was he covering up? So went the winding path of her thoughts, to nowhere.

It took ages to clamber up the littered path to the plateau, for Llian was quite weak. There he stopped, stunned by the extent of the ruin, the broken towers, the shattered fortress. Where the rift ran across the paved area, one side was now upthrust head-high, a wall across their path that steamed and fumed. From the volcanic peak to their north, clouds of ash gushed. The ground shook underfoot, sending up a blast of steam in front of them. The rubble of the Great Tower shifted.

"How did you get out of *that?*" cried Llian, shocked out of his anger.

She told him. "This place doesn't look very safe," Karan continued. "Let's get our packs and get going."

They trudged on. Llian bent to pick up something on the ground—a lozenge-shaped piece of lapis lazuli as long as his hand. "Look," he said. "It's beautiful. I wonder how it got here."

"I broke off a big lump climbing the tower," she said, fingering it. "Bring it, if you like."

"I will." He tucked it into his wallet. "A memento of Katazza."

"Hey!" he cried a little later.

"What?" she asked tiredly.

"I remember now! Rulke set me a puzzle. He said that Kandor would have hidden his most valued papers in a place that was *subordinate but fundamental.* Subordinate, under, and fundamental, *bed.* The answer is, *under the bed.* So obvious I would never have thought of it."

"I've no idea where his bedchamber is," Karan said doubtfully.

"I do. I've been through every room in Katazza."

It required a hazardous scramble over rubble to get to it, for one of the minarets had fallen through the roof of the fortress, partly blocking the hall outside. They found the bedchamber to be even more extravagant than Rulke's. The bedposts were of fragrant cedar wood, gorgeously carven, the head and foot decorated with inlays of a dozen kinds of precious timbers, the edges traced out with silver—decadences showing couples writhing in ecstasies of abandon.

Llian crawled under the bed. Karan stared at the images in open-mouthed astonishment, then snorted and joined Llian underneath.

"I didn't mean to leave you behind," she said. "I'm so ashamed, Llian. Can you ever forgive me?"

"Not now!" he snapped, tapping the floor tiles, feeling the bedposts.

"I've a good idea," she said shortly, rubbing her nose on the back of his neck. He would not be distracted.

"There's nothing here," he said, vexed. "No, it wouldn't be that simple."

"What are you looking for?" Karan asked, intrigued as he prodded and pulled at the underside of the bed.

"A hiding place for secret documents."

"Looks pretty solid to me," she said, feeling up on top of the side frame. "Hullo, what's this?"

As she pushed on a recessed knob, something clicked above her head. She tapped the beam, which now sounded hollow. Karan slid a cover aside, felt up into the hole and pulled out a long metal box. She flipped up the top. It was full of papers, and beneath them was a thin book.

Llian's face lit up. He took the box out into the light. "This is it, Karan!"

There were no other secret compartments in the bed, or in the floor beneath, at least none that they could find. They sat on Kandor's bed eating skagg, a brick-sized cake baked of root flour mixed with dried fruit, nuts and seeds.

Llian sorted through the papers. A tied bundle contained a series of reports of investigations into Shuthdar's death and the destruction of the flute. Most dated from just after the Forbidding. The papers below the bundle were much later, from not long before Kandor's death.

Under the book, on the bottom of the box, lay a very tarnished silver chain made of braided wires.

"It's got a lovely feel," Karan said, stroking the blackened metal against her cheek. "It's all warm and comforting and protecting."

Llian sniffed. "It's just a piece of silverwork."

"You to your talents and me to mine!" she said, irritated. "Anyway, it's beautifully made, and the braid is the same as the Great Tower. I suppose Kandor had it made to remind him of the tower. It feels very old."

He took it out of her hand. "So it is. And since I found it, it's mine."

She looked hurt, but Llian went down on one knee, then slipped it over her head. "Let's start again, shall we?" He kissed her on the tip of the nose.

"Oh Llian," she said, kissing him back.

It took hours for Llian to read everything, but the papers only described dead ends, the results of fruitless investigations. He wearily cast the last to one side.

"It's not here. Kandor must have taken the evidence with him."

There were only two documents remaining, the first a slim book bound in leather as fine and soft as skin, but written in the unreadable Charon script.

He put it aside, perusing the other document. "Hey! It's a letter to Rulke." Then he swore.

"What's the matter?" asked Karan, looking up from the book. "Can't you read it either?"

"I already have. It's a copy of the one I filched from the Magister's archives in Thurkad, that day I tried to rescue you from Thyllan."

He threw it to her, she dropped the book and it fell open at a page toward the back. A folded piece of paper slid out.

"How did I miss that?" cried Llian.

"This has a later date. Months later." He read it aloud.

> My dear Yalkara,
>
> I write to change the date and the place of our meet. I will come to Havissard earlier than I said in my previous letter, and in secret. I am being hunted. It could be the Council but I fear that it is Rulke. He wants my secret for himself. You may be in danger too, since I told him that I had shared my fears with you.
>
> Rulke cares for nothing but his own glory. He's always envied me. I will bring everything I have to you, then go early to Alcifer, to my meet with Rulke.
>
> Salutations,
> Kandor

"Rulke told me that Kandor was murdered!" said Llian. "Probably to conceal the same secret that the crippled girl was killed for, all that time ago. Was Rulke the killer? He said himself that Kandor was paranoid. It just goes round in circles."

"Well, now you've got evidence, and suspects."

"Where was Kandor killed? That's the other thing I have to find out."

Karan shrugged. Then a thought struck her. "Llian! What if it was Mendark or Yggur? Or Faelamor? Go around asking questions and you'll likely suffer the same fate."

"Neither of them was even born when the flute was destroyed."

"Faelamor and Rulke were; and Tensor!" Karan began to feel afraid. "Look, *can't you see!* Whoever did it, if they're still alive, they'll kill anyone else who comes along with awkward questions. That's you. And me too!"

Llian sat down with his head in his hands. "I've got to follow the tale. These letters are crucial."

"I'll carry them secretly," Karan said. "Don't say anything about them, or your speculations, if we ever catch up to the others. You can show the book, since no one can read it. But don't tell anyone that Rulke told you where to find it. Let's get ready. We'll go in the morning.

They ate dinner in an uncomfortable silence. Finally Llian broke it. "Why did you go without me?"

"You were supposed to run for the gate."

"I was trying to *protect* you. I thought Rulke was going to kill you."

"Oh!" she said, staring at him with her hand over her mouth. "I'm so sorry! You were on your knees. I—it looked like you were swearing to Rulke."

"How could you think such a thing?" he cried. Then he went silent, brooding on the events that had led him here. If he had not collaborated with Tensor, would any of this have ever come about?

He, Llian, was as responsible as anyone for this disaster. What an idiot he'd been, meddling in things he knew nothing about, helping Tensor out of desire to see what would happen next, and to further the Great Tale that he planned to make out of it. Well, things would be different now.

He sighed heavily. "I've been stupid, Karan. The temptation to know what would happen next was overpowering."

"But I have no excuse either," said Karan. "Rulke set me against you so easily. I could feel the madness coming back and it was so strong that I panicked—I couldn't stop myself. As soon as I stepped on the plate the gate pulled me in. I've not stopped regretting it since."

She sat up suddenly. "Llian, swear that you . . . haven't sold out to Rulke."

"I was sorely tempted, but I did nothing to be ashamed of." He looked troubled. "Unless I did so when I was in a trance," he said in an undertone that did not escape her.

Llian lay awake for a long time, brooding about his time with Rulke, which had begun to seem hazy, dreamlike. He could not believe his escape either now; it was all too convenient. He had dared to sup with the devil. How long before Rulke presented his bill? Was there anything he could do to get out of it? Well, over their centuries of persecution the Zain had learned how to protect themselves, and as a master chronicler he had his own mind-skills. How could he put them to best use? And what had Rulke done to him in the Nightland? Might he have made a pact with Rulke in his trance, and not even know it?

Afraid that the memories of the Nightland would vanish, he wrote down everything that he remembered in his journal, though nothing incriminating, of course. After that, Llian wandered around Kandor's bedroom, intrigued by the culture of the Charon. The place was full of beautiful, sensual art, things that would be priceless anywhere else, but they remained here because they had not been worth carrying across the Dry Sea. Even the knobs on the bedposts were engraved silver. Conscious that his purse was far from full, Llian climbed up and unscrewed one. It was heavy, many a tar of silver in it. He put it in the bottom of his bag.

That thought led him back to Kandor, and then to Rulke

again. One thing he did remember—Rulke's temptation. The reward that Rulke had offered him, secrets that no chronicler had ever known, kept him on fire for half the night.

The trip down to the Dry Sea took almost as long as it had to come up. Llian was unwontedly silent, and though he had to be watched carefully lest he slip, made scarcely a plaint the whole way. Knowing his fear of heights, Karan found this remarkable, but attributed his silence to anger with her. Or perhaps he had exhausted his capacity to be afraid. As they descended into the thick salty air and the unbearable heat, Karan put her suspicions behind her.

Four long days later they made their camp near the foot of the mountain, just one cliff above the long barren slope that led to the Dry Sea. They ate a scant meal, much less than either wanted. Both were exhausted, so hard and fast had they traveled. Karan picked at the crumbs of skagg in her bowl, dismayed to think of the weeks they must yet travel on their miserable rations. They were perched in a patch of scrub, withered and twisted from the saline westerlies. In the morning their real journey would begin.

"Skagg and onions!" she said. "I'm sick of it already."

He did not reply. It was stinking hot though the heat was moderated by an occasional cooler waft tumbling down the mountainside.

"Tomorrow it begins again," Karan went on. "Water becomes more precious than diamonds." Her pale face was beaded with sweat, her riotous hair now limp, subdued. "I don't think I can bear this, Llian." She wandered off to a trickle, issuing from a cleft, to wash.

He watched her go. He tolerated the heat better than she did. His homeland, Jepperand, which bordered the eastern side of the Dry Sea, was scorching in summer.

Afterwards Karan sat looking west. The sun was setting; the skies so clear that the mountainous peninsula of Faranda could be seen, sixty or seventy leagues away. She was remembering the previous journey with Shand, and dreading the shorter though much hotter one that they were about to make.

She was worried about Shand too. Even in the spring he had found the heat debilitating. How would he be coping now? She imagined the old man getting weaker and slower, until the others had no choice but to leave him behind.

A hand shook her shoulder; she woke from her reverie. It was dark now, cooling down a little. Llian pushed a steaming mug of tea into her hand, which he had made from a bitter herb growing on the cliff top. She took a sip, grimaced, sipped again. "Llian . . ." she began. He was staring out across the sea.

"I saw a light," he said slowly.

Karan stood up on tiptoe, one hand resting on his shoulder, following his gaze. A tiny spark glowed out on the salt.

"*It's them!*" she said, and her face lit up. "They're only a few days ahead. Quickly, let's make a signal fire!"

She began to build a hearth near the edge of the cliff. There was plenty of dry wood about and Llian soon had a pile large enough for a small bonfire. Before they got it going the light disappeared.

"They've gone without us," said Karan.

"They must look back sometime. We'll burn the fire all night."

They did just that, though by the early hours it was a struggle to keep the blaze going, for they had used all the wood that was readily available.

"The sun will be up soon," said Karan, sagging with exhaustion and disappointment. Her eyes were red from the smoke. "We'll never catch them. They'll be too far away by dark."

Just then the light reappeared. It shone steadily for a few minutes then blinked once, twice, three times.

"They're signaling!" said Karan.

"We'd better go carefully, until we're sure," said Llian.

They put on their enveloping desert robes. Karan's pale

skin burned easily, so she was completely swathed in cloth, only her eyes showing through the slits of her eye covers.

Karan was too excited to sleep. She would have kept going all day, in spite of the heat, had Llian not restrained her. They walked fast all night, though Llian was constantly lagging. He was covered in cold sweat.

They began again in the early afternoon. Before dark, Karan, who had climbed a rock pinnacle, cried out, "I can see them!"

She sprang down again and hurried off. Llian followed her gloomily. It was almost dusk. Three shadows appeared on the other side of a broad patch of salt. All Llian could sense was hostility and menace. "Be careful," he shouted. "You don't know who it is!"

Karan kept going. Suddenly she began to sprint. "Malien!" she shrieked, and threw herself at the smallest of the three.

Malien staggered backwards under the impact, wincing.

"I'm sorry," cried Karan, helping her up again. "I forgot."

"It's practically healed." Malien hugged her. "How did you—?"

"Where's Shand?" Karan interrupted. "Is he all right?

"He is," said Malien, and Karan fell down at her feet, crying in relief.

Tallia and Osseion stood quietly by. "You're lucky we came at all," she said. "Some of us thought it was Rulke after us."

They all stood silently as Llian trudged toward them. He knew that they were wondering about the escape. His welcome was just as warm as Karan's was, though. Even Osseion threw his arms around him.

"Well met!" he said. "We'd given up hope long ago."

As they walked along Karan told what had happened in the Nightland, but as soon as she revealed that Llian had escaped separately, days later, Malien stopped dead.

"Llian," she said, giving him the look that he had seen more than once during his dealings with Tensor, "your story had better be true, for you will have to satisfy Mendark and Yggur as well as me."

Karan shivered and held his hand more tightly.

"You might at least hear me first."

"It's going to be a long night after we get there," Malien muttered.

Llian began to wonder if leaving the Nightland had been the right thing to do after all.

15

Crush the Scorpion

Llian hardly said a word during the time that it took to reach the camp. Malien's reaction had frightened him and he knew she liked him. How would his enemies react? What would Basitor do?

The camp was not far away, but it took all night and part of the next day to reach it, for the country was extremely rugged—black lava in flows one atop another, cracked so deep that Llian could have fallen in and never climbed out again, or forming shard-topped spines that were treacherous to clamber over and deadly to fall on, as he remembered from his accident-prone journey to Katazza. Between the flows were pools of hot ash and geysers issuing steam, boiling water or clots of stinking mud. The air had an acrid stench which made his eyes water.

The camp was set on a little field of black ash surrounded by a solid ooze of rock half a dozen spans high. The tents and sleds were hard up against the southern rock wall, clinging to the precious shade. When they arrived a banquet was spread out before them—an extra mouthful of water, an extra slice of skagg.

Fourteen Aachim stood in a ragged semicircle in front of the tents. A few looked pleased to see them—among them Asper, Selial and Xarah, slowly emerging from an abyss of grief at the death of her twin. Most of the others were unreadable—either waiting to judge them or hiding their true feelings. But one—Basitor, who had hated Llian long before the death of his friend Hintis—made no secret of his mistrust. It showed in his eyes, the set of his jaws, the watchful rigidity of his posture.

Tensor was propped up against the rock with his eyes closed. He did not acknowledge their arrival. Mendark looked smaller, dried out and aged, yet more self-assured than the last time Llian saw him. He was smiling. Not a warm smile, but not a bitter one either. Llian knew that Mendark would listen and make up his own mind.

Yggur stood to one side of the group, dark hair shading his cavernous eyes. His very attitude smoldered with suspicion as Karan and Llian appeared.

"What's happened to Yggur?" Karan whispered to Malien.

"Rulke's coming was a terrible blow. Yggur failed in Katazza and it scarred him. We tried to get you back; we nearly lost Shand, Tallia and Asper. There was no choice but to seal the Nightland—" She broke off. "I'm sorry, Karan."

The silence grew uncomfortable. "I dare say you did what you had to," said Karan.

"We tried, down at the rift, but we pushed Yggur beyond his strength, with disastrous consequences. And for him too—he's as good as blind now. Be careful."

Karan, feeling sorry for Yggur, spun around. He started at the sudden movement, stumbled and nearly fell. She sprang forward to steady him. "I'm sorry to hear of your troubles—" she began.

His yellow-filmed eyes shifted, trying to focus but failing. He shoved her away. "I don't need pity," he choked, "especially from *you!* You caused all this in the first place. I'll have the price out of you one day, *my little sensitive!*"

"Karan!" came a familiar shout, and Shand came running from a cleft in the rocks. "I had given you up!"

"I'm as tough as your boots," she said, embracing him.

"That reminds me!" Malien frowned at Karan's feet.

Karan looked ruefully at the boots that she had borrowed from Malien to climb the Great Tower. "Sorry!" she said, squatting down. The boots were extremely battered now.

"I knew this would happen!" said Malien. "You might as well have them." She was smiling though.

"You're a miracle," Shand said, squeezing Karan in his arms. Tears sparkled in his beard. "How did you ever get free?"

"How indeed?" grated Yggur.

Giving him a nervous glance, Llian began his tale.

"Let's eat!" said Mendark.

After their short commons the extra food was a feast, though it was gone long before they had finished their stories. As soon as Llian mentioned Rulke's strange machine, he was interrupted.

"A *construct!*" said Mendark, leaning forward eagerly. "What was it like?"

"It was big. Bigger than the largest wagon, and it looked to be made of metal that was midnight black, shaped into curves and bulges—" Llian struggled to think of words for something so far beyond his experience. He began again.

"It was about four spans long, I suppose," holding his arms outstretched, one span. "Yes, at least eight good paces. And more than two spans wide, and nearly two high. There seemed to be some kind of seat on top, and a number of levers. But the strange thing was, it wasn't supported by anything; it simply hung in the air about knee-high. And inside—"

"You went *inside?*" Yggur demanded, squinting in Llian's direction. People were no more than moving shadows to him.

"My hand went straight through it, so I put my head in as well."

"What did you *see*?" Yggur's voice went hoarse at the end.

Llian described the interior as well as he could recall it—the dark-red illumination, the seats, controls and glowing panels. "I'm sorry," he ended. "It was . . . out of focus. I couldn't see it clearly."

"I don't like it," said Malien, "for all that this construct is not real."

"What do you mean?" asked Tallia.

"I dreamed it long ago," said Karan, shivering in spite of the heat. "And even then it frightened me."

"Nothing real can be made in the Nightland because the very fabric and stuff of the Nightland itself is not real," Mendark explained. "At least, it may seem real there, but outside it can no more *be* real than an image in a mirror is. This construct is just a pattern, perhaps for something that he hopes to make once he returns to Santhenar."

"But the pattern is complete!" said Malien. "All he has to do is bring it with him and put the construct together. How can we stand against such a thing?" She walked out of the light, stabbing the tent pegs back into the crumbly salt.

"What is it for?" Karan whispered.

"Who can tell?" Shand replied. "Though surely it surpasses his previous devices."

"So he wants us to think," said Mendark, "since he took such pains to show it to Llian. But time will tell whether he can make it work. A shape and a pattern in the Nightland, no matter how complete, is an entirely different matter from a device that does what he wants on Santhenar. And just to build it, every material that it is to be made from—metal, glass, ceramic, whatever—must be found, purified and shaped in exactly the right way. Even with Shazmak and the Ghâshâd at his disposal, it will take months. Remember that Shuthdar and a team of Aachim toiled for ages just to make a little flute."

"Just as well!" said Yggur bitterly. "Since we are months away from Thurkad or any place where we can oppose him. Go on with your tale, Llian. Tell us what you learned about Rulke, *and how you got away*."

"Yggur terrifies me," Karan whispered.

Malien put her good arm across Karan's shoulders. They sat together, the two redheads, though the heat soon made the contact unbearable.

"How long do you think it will be?" Karan asked into the silence.

"Until Rulke comes back?" asked Mendark. "Not long!"

Llian went on with his tale. Mendark found Rulke's defense of the gate particularly interesting. "It was so close," he said. "Had Yggur used the right amount of power, had he not panicked, we might well have succeeded."

"Had not this treacherous chronicler given him a strategy to beat us!" Yggur screamed. "The Zain are born traitors, as you found out with Hennia, Mendark."

"Wrist-wrestling!" Mendark laughed outright. "Really, Yggur, I don't think Llian can teach Rulke anything about strategy."

"He's a traitor," Yggur repeated venomously.

"Llian might well say the same of us," said Mendark, "since we did our best to shut him in with Rulke. Though he hasn't. You just can't face up to your failings, Yggur, can you? Go on, Llian."

When Llian told of Karan's escape there was a long silence. The wind wailed outside. More than one eye in the camp looked dubiously at them, doubting the miracle, though they seemed more convinced by Karan's version. Mendark was most interested to hear how the internal structure of the Nightland was failing.

"That's something I had never thought of," he said. "Maybe the Nightland will finish him after all. If only—"

"I wouldn't bank on it," snarled Yggur. "Finish the tale, chronicler."

Llian's tale of his own escape produced an immediate reaction.

"I say that he has sold himself to the enemy!" cried Yggur, leaping to his feet. "Crush the scorpion while it is little, or as sure as I am standing here it will bring the mother down on us!"

Llian jumped. Everyone was shocked; no one spoke. Karan's hand flashed to the knife on her belt but Tallia caught her wrist in an unbreakable grip.

"You are presumptuous, Yggur," she said coldly. "The rule of law applies here just as it does in Mendark's realm. There will be a proper questioning. Then, if we judge that he *has* betrayed us, we will all agree on a penalty. Is that not so, Mendark?"

Whatever his own feelings, Mendark was not going to be dictated to by Yggur. "Indeed! Let him finish his tale first. Llian, be warned that we will weigh your every word."

Llian continued haltingly, knowing he was speaking for his life. The interrogation was worse than any abuse he had suffered from being Zain, but they learned nothing more. Nor did Rulke's compulsion come to light, for that was buried deep and Llian knew nothing about it.

"Tell me again how you escaped," said Yggur, blind eyes glaring through him. He questioned every aspect of Llian's story, over and over. "I'm not satisfied," Yggur said at the end.

"I've already told you a dozen times!" Llian cried.

"Enough, Yggur!" said Mendark. "Karan, Llian, leave us for the moment. Llian, give up your journal and papers."

They read through every word, especially the descriptions of Tensor's gate.

"We need to discuss this further," Mendark said, when they had finished with the documents. "I know that Rulke was exhausted, but even so, how could either of them escape? That both did, separately, beggars credibility. Yet I can find no crack in his story."

"Nor I," said Shand and Malien together. Malien signed for the old man to go first.

"Nor I," Shand repeated. "But the Zain are cunning liars, as we know. How could anyone resist, least of all Llian? He collaborated with Tensor after all."

"Rulke might have *let* them go," said Malien.

"Of course he let them go!" Yggur shouted. "To spy on us! Kill them both, put an end to it."

There was a horrified silence. Mendark sprang to his feet. "They haven't been tried!"

Yggur retreated a step. "Justice is a weakness we cannot afford with Rulke at large."

"Hold on!" replied Mendark. "That's what your war with Thurkad and me was supposed to be all about—justice! I agree with Malien. Even if Llian has sold himself, what can he do but spy? And if so, which I doubt, the spy can tell us as much about his master."

"Just so," said Malien. "We may learn more about Rulke than he does about us."

"You dare, after what Rulke did to me?" said Yggur incredulously. "Be sure, finish him now."

"Then perhaps we'd better be sure with *you* as well," Mendark said coldly. "I believe Llian, and he has many skills that I would put to use. We need his mind and memory at our councils."

They questioned Karan just as carefully, though not as long, and in the end put her under no restraint either. It was as clear as anything could be, where Rulke was concerned, that she had told the truth about her escape.

By the time the investigation was completed it was long past time to set out, so they hurriedly began the night's march. In a few hours dawn came with a brilliant flare in the east, and as soon as the sun rose the heat forced them to set up camp again.

While they were doing that Mendark fell in beside Llian. "There is a matter that I did not raise last night," he said.

"You have an obligation to me for the fifteen years I sponsored you at the college."

"I am aware of it," said Llian. "What do you require of me?"

"Be sure that you do not forget who is your master," Mendark said ominously.

"I'm afraid," Llian said after they had gone to their tent.

Karan lay sweating on a sheet spread out on the crumbly salt. Llian had adapted to the conditions but she could not. "I'm so hot. Fasten the flap, please."

When Llian had done that she took off all her clothes, spread them over the sheet and lay down again, trying to get away from the heat coming up from the ground. Her luminously pale skin was shiny with perspiration.

Llian was peering out through the flap of the tent. "Fan me," she said.

He waved his journal listlessly back and forth. The waft stirred her curls. She sighed. "I don't know how I am going to survive this journey."

"I don't know *if* I am," he replied somberly.

Karan sat up and took his hand, at once contrite. "Llian, I'm sorry! I'm so selfish."

"I'm frightened of Basitor and Yggur."

"Mendark seems to be on your side."

"Only because he wants something from me! I'm afraid of everyone now, except you. And most of all Rulke. Karan, the temptation was unbearable. That time when I . . . when I searched your room for the Mirror, that was nothing to this."

She drew him down. They lay together, saying nothing, but sweating more than the heat required.

Karan had been feeling on edge all the night's march. When they stopped at dawn she ate her skagg silently then went immediately to the tent, which Llian had put up in the shade of a low ridge. She threw off her clothes again and slept, not waking when he came in shortly after.

The day wore on, and it was hot even by the standards of the Dry Sea. The whole camp slept—no need for guards out here.

Karan gave a little sigh and turned over in her sleep. Her eyes began to race under their lids. She began to pant. "Ohh!" she said, making a moaning sound in her throat that could have been pleasure or pain. "Ohh, ohh, ohh!"

Llian woke from his own fractured sleep to see her jerk upright. Her eyes were open, her arms held out like a sleep walker. Rising to her feet, she drew her arms back to her chest, took three deep breaths, standing spread-legged like a weightlifter, then gave a loud, groaning cry and forced her arms straight up as if lifting a weight above her head.

One hand knocked out the ridgepole, collapsing the canvas around her. She struck blindly at the cloth over her face then folded up on the floor, bringing the tent down on them both.

Llian lifted it up again. Karan was awake now, staring at him with a look of hungry despair. "I'm scared, Llian." She took his hand, then the rest of the company were outside the tent, crying out what was the matter.

"Karan had a bad dream," said Llian, putting his head out.

They went away again, though Yggur gave Llian a long smoldering stare as if he could pierce through the veil of blindness and see right into his mind.

"What was your dream?" Llian asked once everyone had gone and the tent was back up.

"I dreamed about Rulke. He was standing on top of his construct like a conquering hero and beams of light were coming out the front of it. The light burned everything it touched. *He's coming*, Llian!"

"Yes!" Llian whispered back. "He's coming!"

She lay down again, staring at the canvas. She could no longer sleep. Karan had left out part of her dream. Llian had been there too, standing at Rulke's right hand like the most faithful of servants.

* * *

The following day Karan and Llian were trudging along at the rear, traversing a landscape of a thousand head-high knobs, pinnacles and winding, maze-like gullies. The others were well ahead. They turned a corner and Yggur stood in the middle of the path, blocking their way. Llian looked over his shoulder to see huge Basitor step out behind them.

Llian froze. "What is it?" said Karan absently, still lost in her own worries.

"Spies!" Basitor spat. "Traitors!"

"Liars!" said Yggur. "Sit down, Karan and Llian. We're going to have a little talk."

No choice but to do so—the rest of the company were out of earshot. They sat on a weathered ledge of salt the color of yellow ocher. Basitor drew a long knife with a chisel point.

"Now, Llian," Yggur said, "you will tell me what happened last night or . . ." He nodded toward Basitor.

The big Aachim squatted down in front of Karan. "Or I gouge out her eyes."

"There's nothing to tell," Karan said calmly. She was terrified but dared not show it. "I dreamed about Rulke. He was standing on his construct and a great light shone out the front of it."

Yggur brought his face right up to hers, staring at her nose to nose. "And that's all?" he asked, his breath sour on her face. His pupils were glazed with a yellow film.

"Yes," she whispered, but her eyes drifted sideways as she spoke. She could not stop them.

"She's lying!" Basitor cried, thrusting out his knife until the point touched her lower eyelid. "Speak true, Karan, or I swear I'll have your eyeballs dangling down your cheeks."

"Karan," Llian yelped, "if there's any more, *tell them*!"

Tears of terror were running down her cheeks. She shook her head.

"Then do *him*!" Yggur grated, jerking his head at Llian.

Llian flung his head to one side, cracking his ear against hard salt. Basitor grabbed him by the jaw, squeezing hard.

His other hand brought the knife up to Llian's eye. Llian went as rigid as an iron gate, staring unblinking at the point.

"Well, Karan?" said Yggur nastily. "What is it to be? Your lover's eyes or . . .?" He slowly brought the knife lower.

"I dreamed that Llian was there too, standing beside Rulke," she said in a rush. "But that's all it was—a dream!"

"That proves his villainy. Is there anything else you want to tell us?" Basitor said, pricking Llian's groin.

"No," she said softly. "There was nothing else." Llian's eyes were watering. She gently wiped the tears from his cheek.

The knife prodded back up. "We haven't finished yet, by a long mark," said Yggur. "Tell us about the Nightland, Llian. Tell us what you really did there *those five days by yourself*."

Llian began to tell the story again, but Yggur interrupted. "We've heard that story. Tell us the *real* story."

Llian shook his head. They would maim him, gouge out his eyes, for he had nothing more to tell. Karan saw their only chance. Yggur was awkward, practically blind. She could get away from him easily. But Basitor was another thing entirely—very fast, very agile. She might escape him but Llian never would.

Karan's hand was on the ground beside her seat. It closed on gritty dust and as Basitor moved the knife between Llian and her, she flung her handful into his eyes.

It blinded him but Basitor kept going, lunging with the knife toward the place he knew Karan to be, throwing his other arm sideways in case she darted that way.

Llian hooked his foot around Basitor's leg, bringing him down. The knife arced toward Karan with all his weight behind it. She jerked frantically to one side, the knife jammed into the salt beside her throat, then Basitor slammed down on top of her, cracking heads.

For an instant he was stunned, just enough time for the normally clumsy Llian to snatch the knife.

"Help!" Llian roared at the top of his voice. "Stay where

you are, Yggur! Help, help!" He twisted his hand in the neck of Basitor's robes and pulled them tight, at the same time pressing the knife hard against the base of the Aachim's skull. "Roll off Karan, very slowly. Any sudden move and I'll drive the knife right through your spine."

Basitor's muscles tensed. Afraid of his enemy, Llian pressed really hard. "*I will*!" he hissed, twisting the cloth until Basitor began to choke. Yggur made a surreptitious move. "Stay where you are," grated Llian, "or I kill your only friend, *blind man*!"

Suddenly the Aachim relaxed and rolled sideways, enough for Karan to crawl out from beneath. There was a huge lump on her forehead and another at the back where it had been driven against the rock salt. She looked dazed.

Llian gave her his hand. "Come on!" he said. "Out of my way, Yggur!" He thrust the knife at his face, making sure that even Yggur could see it.

Yggur pressed back against the canyon wall. "I never forget!" he hissed. "Live in fear for the rest of your life. I swear that I will bring you to ruin, however long it takes."

16

SALTSTORM

Karan sat down on a blocky outcrop of salt, mopping her brow. She reeked, and so did everyone else, for not a drop of water could be spared for washing, and there was no point in changing one set of sweaty, salt-saturated clothes for another just as foul. A desperate, grinding week had passed but their progress had been negligible. Every afternoon there had been a saltstorm that lasted well into the night, precious traveling time lost, and as it was the time of the new moon the nights were very dark. They were still in the lava fields, treacherous country that was dangerous at night, so each day they began as soon as there was light enough to see and walked until the heat became unbearable.

Seven days after Karan and Llian had rejoined the rest of the company, they crossed off the basalt to a place where the salt had been forced up into blocks as tall as towers, or broken into cracks and crevasses, and the upthrust blocks were sculpted by the wind into fantastic shapes.

The path now led along the base of a wind-carved canyon

some eight or ten spans high, with a flat floor of gritty salt that squeaked underfoot. It was hard to walk on but at least there was shade, allowing them a few more hours of travel each day.

Karan and Llian were together at the rear, not the best position because they breathed dust stirred up by those in front. Llian preferred to walk behind because he could see where everyone was. Neither could speak; their mouths were too dry. Anyway, they had exhausted all conversation long ago—everyone was too irritable.

In the mid-afternoon, with flat country ahead of them, they set out again. A murky yellow cloud hung in the hazy distance. They trudged on, wanting to make as much progress as possible before they were forced to camp.

"This looks worse than the others," Osseion muttered. The cloud was much bigger than any other saltstorm they had experienced. It was a monster, the dust towering as tall as thunderheads, an awesome sight on the featureless plains.

"Hoy!" he shouted, cupping his hands around his mouth.

The lead Aachim, far ahead, kept plodding head-down across the salt. Osseion wrenched the hand axe off his pack, banging on the metal base of the water sled to catch their attention.

Clang! Clang! Clang! They woke to the danger and came plodding back. Already the saltstorm covered half the sky.

"Tents won't hold against this," shouted Asper.

"There were caves back there," yelled Karan.

They ran down a split in a buttress of salt. Further along it became a cave blasted out by the storms of ages past.

"No good!" said Shand. "The wind's blowing straight in."

"No time to find a better one," Asper shouted above the noise of the wind. The advance gusts were already stinging their eyes with grit. "If we make a door with our tents and sleds . . ."

"It'll never hold in this wind."

"If it doesn't, we're dead!"

They retreated into the cave, which was twenty or thirty

paces long, winding and multi-branched. The walls and roof were wind-scoured layers of red, brown and yellow-colored salt, the floor salt gravel that crunched underfoot. The Aachim worked furiously, one group unstitching their tents while others took apart the water sleds and reassembled them into a frame the size and shape of the entrance, to which they would fasten the tent canvas to make a door.

"Hurry!" Mendark yelled, but the work could not go any faster.

A dust gale blasted in, whiting out the shelter. Karan scrunched herself up in a corner with her back to the wind. She had her cloak over her face but still the dust got through. Beside her she could hear Llian choking.

Just as the door was being installed the storm struck in fury. The canvas cracked like a whip. Osseion and a group of Aachim, who were holding the frame, were driven hard back against the wall by the wind. Someone yelped, then the door was torn out of their hands and hurled across the cave, right at Llian.

Basitor, who was walking by, threw himself to his right and caught the frame with one hand. It whipped him off his feet, his arms and legs whirled in the air, then the edge of the frame crunched into the wall beside Llian's jaw. Basitor thudded after it.

Llian scrambled up. "You saved my life!" he said incredulously.

Basitor rolled over. Coming to his knees, he spat out blood and a broken tooth. Then he smiled, a warming smile, and Llian realized what a brave friend Basitor could have been, in other circumstances.

Slowly the smile faded. "But what have I saved it for?" said Basitor. He turned away, his arm hanging oddly. "Asper, I think I've dislocated my shoulder."

Asper inspected the injury. "Hold still." With a quick snap that brought tears to Basitor's eyes he popped the shoulder back in its socket.

The canvas was still flapping, the twisted frame trying to

lift itself into the air again. Wind roared in through the door, filling the room with white. Karan sat on it, pulled her hood over her head and waited.

The squall passed. The Aachim stood around the frame, planning how to re-form the twisted metal. After half an hour or so they had the door up again. It flapped, booming like a big drum. Every gust sent puffs of salt squirting in through the gaps. Osseion was covered in layers of white dust, scalloped up his arms like tiny sand dunes. Everyone else was the same.

All that night the wind howled down the canyon, wailing like the wind in Shazmak, though more unnerving; snapping the canvas, putting even the Aachim on edge.

The next day dawned. There were now many more empty waterbags than full ones. The cavern was dimly lit by day with a pale yellow light seeping through crevasses in the salt. Their nights were lit by the globes purloined from Katazza. They went over their situation again and again. Llian's news of the construct had taken away their last hope. Rulke had a potent new weapon, while they were in disarray and faced a journey of months just to return to Thurkad. And what would they find there?

Tensor sat dully, head bowed, taking no account of anything. But occasionally when Llian was talking, or even sitting silently, he would look up to find the Aachim's gaze on him, a stare so impersonal that it stripped away all his petty secrets and self-delusions. Seemingly Tensor's soul was so bare that the secrets of others could not be hidden from him. At such times Llian was reminded of Rulke's offered reward—knowledge that a chronicler could only dream about. Desire for it burned so hot that he was sure it showed on his face. He felt that Tensor was reading him—reading a betrayal that Llian had committed but could not remember. Had he? And if he had, why would Tensor protect his secret?

Llian lay sleeping in an out-of-the-way corner of the cave when he felt a sharp pain in his temple. It was a strange, spiky ache like nothing he had ever felt before. He sat up, gasping, to see the edge of a dark cloak swirl out as its wearer disappeared around the corner. On hands and knees, for the headache was growing steadily worse, he peered after it. No one was visible.

"What's the matter?" Karan asked sleepily.

"A pain in my head. It felt as if someone was trying to prise my skull open."

She ran around the corner but soon reappeared. "I couldn't see anything unusual. It's this place—the heat gives me headaches too. Try to get some sleep."

She dozed then woke again, taking a stroll up to the door. The canvas was still booming in the wind. Someone had plugged most of the gaps around the door frame, though dust still came through.

Osseion was playing a game with Shand, using dice carved out of rock salt. Mendark lay snoring in a corner. Yggur and Basitor had spent most of their time at the rear of the cave, talking together. A group of Aachim sat in an embayment, reciting an epic poem in an eastern dialect that Karan did not know. It went on all day with never a pause. Malien accompanied them on a small instrument with many strings. To one side Asper was manipulating Tensor's back, as he did every day, though so far it had effected little improvement. All was calm, save for the shrieking wind.

Karan ambled down to check on Yggur. At the rear the cave was scalloped into a number of cubicle-sized recesses. Yggur and Basitor were in the furthest. Creeping along the wall she was able to get quite close.

Looking over a knob of rock, Karan saw Basitor with his back to her and Yggur facing him. The fading glow of one of the Katazza lightglasses illuminated the gravelly floor between them. On it sat a curious device, constructed of wire and chips of crystal, in the shape of a round basket. A larger crystal in the center winked ruby-red as she moved. One of the offcuts from the ill-fated ampliscope, she supposed.

Karan felt a pang of alarm, a warning from her talent. As she moved the gravel rolled underfoot. Basitor closed a meaty hand over the light.

"Go away, little snoop!" he said roughly.

Karan turned back to the lighted end of the cave, more worried than ever.

Much later, her sleep was ripped apart by the most horrifying screech that Karan had ever heard. She sprang up, looking around frantically, sure that it had been Llian. The cave was dark, for it was not long till dawn. Her heart was pounding furiously. No one else looked to be awake, or even to have heard what she had.

She fumbled out her own little lightglass, the one Maigraith had given her at Fiz Gorgo. Tallia had carried it all the way from Thurkad. By its light she saw Llian lying asleep. It must have been a dream, she thought, and lay back down.

Shortly she was disturbed again by a whistling hiss like a steaming kettle. She sat up. Llian lay on his side, apparently still asleep, but as rigid as a rod. The sound was air being forced through his clenched teeth. His eyes were staring; his fists knotted.

"Llian, what is it?" she whispered. His fingers clenched round hers so hard that it brought tears to her eyes. Then suddenly she understood.

Karan wrenched her hand out of his. "Malien! Shand!" she shrieked. "Quickly!"

Karan raced toward the back of the cave. Behind her lights appeared as everyone scrambled out of their bedrolls.

She rounded the corner. Basitor loomed in front of her, twice her size. Without thinking she lowered her head and butted him below the ribs. With an explosive gasp he doubled over.

She ran round him to where Yggur squatted, trying to get up. On his head was the basket of wire and crystal, now lit up like a chain of fairy lights. The ruby at its center glowed like the scorpion nebula in the night sky.

Yggur was still mouthing words. Behind her Llian cried out, audibly this time. Snatching Yggur's walking staff, Karan brought it down hard on the basket. It bent slightly then sprang back into shape.

Yggur flung out his fist. Salt exploded off the wall beside her. Master of the Secret Art that he was, Karan knew that he could kill her with a single blast, if he could find her in the dark.

She ducked sideways then drove the end of the staff into his belly. As he doubled over she struck at the basket again, trying to knock it off his head. She gave it two good strokes, but without dislodging it, then she was seized from behind, two long arms went around her chest and began to squeeze.

Karan struggled and kicked, but Basitor was far stronger. The staff fell from her hand. She began to feel an intolerable cracking pressure in her ribs.

Yggur reached out to her, the device on his head glowing brighter than before. Pain erupted behind her eyes. She could feel her ribs about to break. Desperately she tried to take a breath but could draw no air in. She tried to make a sending to block the device Yggur was using, but she could no longer think straight.

Colors appeared behind her eyes. One of her thrashing feet touched the wall. Karan pushed against it with all her failing strength. Basitor lurched backwards, off-balance, and Yggur's blast ripped pieces out of the cave wall. The pressure eased.

"Hold her still!" Yggur grated. He felt around for his staff, found it, and began to raise it above her head.

Karan could feel the strength running out of her. She tried to protect her head with her arm, but was too weak to move.

Basitor went "Ugh!" and crumpled up.

Osseion and Shand stood there. Osseion was rubbing his fist. Shand tore the device off Yggur's head, hurled the staff into the back of the cave, then they all went back to the light.

17

Resolution From Despair

They never did learn what Yggur had been trying to do—force the truth out of Llian, possess his mind, or destroy it. Despite Mendark's threats, Yggur refused to say. He was warned to keep away from Llian, and Malien spoke to Basitor, but that was all they could do.

All Llian knew was a memory of bright pain that had seemed to come from all directions. The attack had so shaken him that he would not even talk to Karan about it. The device—a primitive sensing tool—was destroyed and its components dropped down cracks in the salt.

"If Yggur ever gets control of a sensitive, watch out!" Malien said to Karan.

She knew they would try again—only her vigilance protected Llian now. But the constant attacks on Llian were undermining her faith in him. What *had* he done during those five days with Rulke?

* * *

Another dreary day went by. The storm howled outside, unabated. They were all demoralized, stuck helplessly in the middle of nowhere while their enemy had the world to himself. Both food and water were dwindling rapidly.

"How much left?" Mendark called. Asper was counting the waterbags yet again.

"Eight days, at most."

"And how far to the lakes, Tallia?"

"The same as the last ten times you asked!" she snapped. "Eight or nine days!"

Malien called the company together. "We've still enough water to get there, if we go now."

"We can't go out in a saltstorm," said Shand. "We won't last a day."

"If we stay here any longer we won't make it either," she replied.

No one spoke for a long time.

"If we weren't so encumbered . . ." said Yggur.

"Oh?" said Mendark. "What are you suggesting? That we leave behind Tensor or Selial?"

"Or Llian!" said Yggur. "The weak will probably die anyway. They may as well help the strong to survive."

"I would put blind men in the dispensable category," Mendark said ominously.

"We leave no one behind," said Malien. "Not Tensor, not Selial, not Yggur . . ." Her eyes searched through the faces, settling on one up the back. "Not Llian either."

Llian shivered. Karan did too. "Not while I'm alive!" she whispered.

"We're wasting time," said Mendark. "Since we are stuck here, I propose that we make plans to combat Rulke. We may yet survive, and if we do, we must have a weapon to put up against this construct. Bring out the Mirror, Shand, and let's see what it can tell us."

Shand looked reluctant, but he withdrew the Mirror of Aachan from its case and held it out, a tight coil of black, like a metal scroll. It began to unroll, then stuck and he had to ease it open with its fingers. With an audible snap it formed a hard plane, a sheet of black metal scribed around the edges with silver glyphs. In one corner was a symbol made of three golden balls grown together, set in a circle enclosed by a triplet of crimson crescent moons. Within the written frame was a reflecting surface like stiffened quicksilver. Peering over Mendark's shoulder, Karan saw only the reflection of his face.

Mendark laid the Mirror on the floor of the cave and brought it to life with a touch of his finger. It showed scenes that Karan had seen on it before—gloomy landscapes of the world of Aachan: sooty grass, black hills, endless bogs, mountains like shards of glass, strange towers of fibrous iron leaning over bottomless gulfs. Nothing more. The Aachim gathered round, jostling one another the better to glimpse their home world that few of them had ever known. There were tears in Malien's eyes, and in many others.

"Can anyone here use it?" Mendark asked softly.

"Alas no," said Malien. No one else stirred to take it up.

"Fat lot of use it is!" Karan said acidly. "Or your Secret Art for that matter. Why did you fight over it so long if none of you even know what it's for?"

Giving her a bitter glare, Yggur reached across with an arm as long as an oar and plucked the Mirror off the salt. "I used it to spy on my enemies," he said. Mendark scowled at that. "Though it was not always reliable."

Yggur peered myopically at the Mirror, felt up the edge and touched the symbol. The Mirror went blank, then showed the salty plains and wind-sculpted mesas outside. The view shifted but, though he strained until one side of his face began to freeze, Yggur could extract no scene from it but the Dry Sea.

Mendark called on Tensor to tell them all he knew about the device, but Tensor, still huddled down the back of the cave, did not acknowledge him.

"Here is your chance to redeem yourself, chronicler,"

Mendark said. "What did you learn from Tensor while you were collaborating with him so eagerly?"

Llian shuffled forward. The boyish extrovert had been cowed; he just wanted to hide in the shadows. "I learned that it was made in Aachan in the depths of time, as a seeing device, and Tensor himself smuggled it here to Santhenar at the risk of his life." He paused, seeming, for the first time in his life, self-conscious in front of his audience. "Despite what was always believed, it is not a thing of power—"

"So they would have you believe!" Yggur spat.

"But it contains many, many secrets," Llian went on, "if anyone can unlock it. Most are hidden—even Tensor couldn't find them." He paused, trying to remember something. "Hold on! Faelamor said she had a key to the Mirror in Thurkad!"

"In *Thurkad*?" said Mendark.

"What, an actual key?" Tallia interjected.

"That's all she said."

"What else did you learn?" asked Mendark.

"Well," said Llian, gaining confidence, "we know that Yalkara stole the Mirror from the Aachim at the fall of Tar Gaarn and eventually took it back there when she built Havissard. She added these characters around the border." He touched them with a finger. "Though none of the Aachim knew what they meant. That's right isn't it, Malien?"

"It is so. She must have added this awful moon symbol too." She shuddered.

"Faelamor was sure that Yalkara had done something to it," said Llian. "That it was part of her purpose. I suppose that's why Faelamor wanted it so badly."

"Well, Shand," said Mendark. "You were quick enough to snatch the Mirror up after Rulke was gone, and quick to spout incomprehensible prophecies. What aren't you telling us?"

"I know that I can't use it!" Shand said vehemently. He paced back and forth, the salt gravel crackling underfoot. "The Mirror is like a book of history. It has many tales to tell, and some of them great ones, if you can put them together from the fragments that it allows you to see. But it's a clever, cunning thing, this Mirror of Aachan, and I'm not strong enough to force the truth out of it. None of us are—not even *you*, Mendark."

There was a long silence. The heat grew ever more oppressive. Tensor huddled in a corner, head bowed, eyes closed. No help there, Karan thought, eyeing the ruins of the Aachim with pity tinged with contempt.

Shand limped over to the entrance and eased the curtain ajar. Salt dust blasted in, and air as hot as a furnace.

"Shut the door!" they all cried together.

Shand's thin hair, white with salt, was outlined against the light, then he pushed the canvas back in place.

"So the whole business has been for nothing!" Karan burst out angrily. "All that I went through, and Llian too! The destruction of Shazmak. Yggur's stupid war! All the dead. Poor Rael. How he loved Shazmak . . ." Her voice trailed away.

"Less than nothing," said Tallia, and even her voice was drear.

"Had I left the Mirror in Fiz Gorgo none of this would have happened," Karan said miserably.

"Perhaps," said Mendark. "Or perhaps you just allowed Rulke to advance his plans a little."

"You who have not had Rulke in your mind have never known fear," said Yggur with a shudder.

"I have known fear!" said Karan.

"And will again! I *never* forget an injury, Karan!"

Karan looked up sharply. Yggur was staring blackly at her. "Oh really!" she snapped. "How many people did you kill, trying to get it back? Ten thousand? Twenty? No one could count the people you've injured. If I were to cut your throat right now I'd be doing the world a service." She raised her little fist.

Yggur kept staring right through her. "You won't," he grated. "You're too soft!"

She shivered and turned away to Llian.

"But after all," Yggur said quietly, "your part was only a little part. The criminal folly was Tensor's."

Outside the wind roared. The canvas boomed. Tensor's sagging frame was wracked by a spasm that made him seem boneless. Slowly he raised his noble head to peer at Karan. In this light his huge eyes showed violet, but they were lifeless. Then the shutters came down, to Karan's relief, and he lowered his head again.

Another pause, an even longer one. Karan ended it. "Then what *are* you going to do now, you who have the power to move the world?" There was a fierce icy ring to her voice, and she glared at Mendark, at Yggur, at Tensor, at Malien, even at Shand, though Shand was at the entrance again and had his back to her. None met her gaze. "Do we meekly beg to become his slaves? Or do we creep into some dark hole and wait for him to have his will with our world?"

Shand turned away from the entrance, with the hint of a smile on his blistered lips. "There is one thing you could do, though I cannot imagine it would succeed."

Every eye, save Tensor's, was on him.

"Speak then," said Mendark irritably, when Shand made no move to do so. "It's about time you took some responsibility for this mess."

"The Forbidding came about after Shuthdar destroyed the golden flute. Nothing can move between the Three Worlds any longer."

"Ancient history! Have you anything to tell us that we don't know?"

"Rulke will never stop looking for a way to break the Forbidding," Shand continued equably. "To do so he must remake the flute, or something that can do what *it* did—maybe this construct. How can we stop him? There's only one way—build our own device, banish Rulke back to Aachan and seal Santhenar off from the other worlds forever."

"That is your proposal?" Yggur said incredulously.

"A suggestion humbly put," grinned Shand, "from a village woodchopper to the mighty."

Yggur turned away in disgust. "Stupid old man. If that could be done it would have been done long ago."

His response seemed to sway Mendark the other way. "Really?" he breathed. "That is very interesting, Shand. Go on!"

"The genius of Shuthdar," Shand began, "was not only that he made the golden flute, but that he knew how to use it. For though the making of the flute was a great task, learning how to use it was a far greater one." He turned and began poking the rags back into the cracks around the door frame.

"It seems that a particular talent is required," he went on. "A rare ability. One that is seldom found in the powerful. It is anti-mechanistic, anti-intellectual. A . . ." he sought for the right word ". . . a kind of empathy. The Ways between the Worlds are ethereal, complex, ever-changing, and so the player must seek out and tune himself or herself to the destination, and play a melody that is keyed to the Way that exists at that moment, and no other."

The whole room stared at him. Karan wondered how he came to know such things.

"Rulke designed the flute and helped Shuthdar at the making," Shand concluded. "So it is said in the *Tale of the Flute*. But Rulke never learned how to use it, for when it was completed Shuthdar stole it. Personally, I don't think Rulke would have been *able* to use it, by himself."

"I don't understand," said Karan. "Rulke brought Shuthdar from our world to make the flute in the first place. If he could do that, why did he need to make the flute at all?"

"That was a *summoning*," said Mendark. "The most perilous of all the Secret Arts, for half the time it kills the summoner, or the one who is summoned."

"Or both!" Yggur said gruffly.

"And you can't summon yourself," said Malien. "Rulke wanted to move freely between the worlds; that's why he made the flute. What we don't know is *why*."

"He must have been desperate, to take such a risk," Tallia observed.

"How does it help us?" asked Yggur harshly, wondering if Shand was making a labored joke at his expense. "We don't know how to make such a device."

"Or use it. That knowledge was lost when Shuthdar fell." Shand resumed his seat. "So maybe Rulke hasn't learned how to use his construct either."

"He can't have!" said Mendark. "The Nightland is insubstantial. He can work its fabric into shapes such as his palace and his construct, and into food and drink that will sustain him there, but he cannot make anything real, for there is nothing to make it with. Anything he brings out of the Nightland will revert to the nothingness from which it was made. To make his construct he must come to Santhenar. We've got to know when he does."

"Unless he's here already," Malien muttered. She pulled aside the flap over the entrance. The wind had eased momentarily. "Perhaps he's *out there*, hunting us." She slapped the canvas closed again.

"Gates can only be made to certain places and the Dry Sea is not one of them," said Shand. "Neither can he make his construct without tools and materials, any more than you or I could. He will go to a place where such things can be obtained easily. Right here is the safest place on Santhenar *for us.*"

"Well, Shand," said Mendark, rubbing his beard, "your proposal interests me after all, though I can't help wondering why you made it. What are you up to?"

"I'm not up to anything," Shand said softly. "I just want to go home to Tullin."

"I don't believe you—you've manipulated things too carefully. We'd be happy to have you back, you know, even after all this time. You could still be one of us."

"No thanks," said Shand. "I've retired."

"I thought you'd say that." Mendark did not look upset.

"Getting back to the point, can we find out how to use the flute?"

"I often wondered why Yalkara took the Mirror and kept it for so long," Malien said thoughtfully.

"It was always said that she used it to spy and to twist the perceptions of others, but that never rang true," said Shand. "Had it been said of Rulke or Kandor, or many a human who could have owned it, I would never have queried it. But Yalkara! She was proud, imperious, ruthless . . ." He spoke with admiration. "But she would not spy that way, or sneak, or betray. No! That story grew up after she disappeared and it was meant to hide something."

"Get to the point, pensioner," said Mendark. "You ramble as though there was no tomorrow."

"We have at least fifty tomorrows before we get back to where Pender's boat is, hopefully, waiting for us. I will tell the story in my own way. Long have I studied the Histories of this matter. I've delved into the ancient libraries; scoured the desert caves of Parnggi for their hoards of clay tablets, and crossed the wide lands from *Tar Gaarn* in Crandor to *Kara Agel*, the frozen sea, in the polar south; from the fjords and forests of Gaspé in the east to the bog shores of Larne. And I swear that I've read every inscription on every wall and standing stone in all that way."

How you exaggerate, thought Karan fondly.

"Even then it was quite by accident, and just recently, that I found what I now believe to be the answer. It was seven or eight years ago, if I remember right, and I was at an inn in Chanthed."

Llian sat up suddenly.

"I was at an inn," he repeated, "listening to the young tellers from the college practicing their tales. They were young, mere journeymen and women mostly, but I had been long on the road with only my own thoughts for company and even their clumsy entertainment was welcome. The performances were mostly well worn, and after a time my mind wandered. Then suddenly I was called back by a strange song, a fragment of a tale but chanted in an old mode; one that I, and I fancy my audience, had never heard before. It was bad verse and indifferent music, though told well. It ended with the following curious lines. My translation captures the sense of it, though not the rhyme:

"Twas on a darkling demon's day
That Shuthdar's mournful call,
Shivered time and space in Tara-Laxus.

He vanished through the gateway
Like a hundred times before,
Sneering as he led them to their doom.

But the flute knew what was coming;
It betrayed the master player,
The fabric of the world became unseamed.

Legions fell, but too late, the failing was begun,
And the Twisted Mirror watched it from the wall.

"What doggerel!" Mendark sneered. "The tellers plumb new lows."

"Tara-Laxus?" said Yggur, puzzled.

"The name struck me like a thunderbolt, for Tara-Laxus was the name of an ancient city in Dovadolo, near the Burning Mountain, *Booreah Ngurle*. It was the place that Shuthdar fled from, immediately before he fell."

"The Twisted Mirror?" exclaimed Yggur.

"The *failing* means the Forbidding, does it not?" Llian cried, temporarily perked up by these insights into the Histories.

"I think so. Though it can't mean that the Mirror actually saw the Forbidding, for that did not occur at Tara-Laxus, but days later at Huling's Tower on the Long Lake," said Shand.

"If the Mirror was there when Shuthdar used the flute to

escape," Mendark said excitedly, "perhaps it retains the image of *how* he used it. Tensor!"

Tensor slowly focused on Mendark.

"You can begin to atone for your crimes," said Mendark. "Does the rhyme make any sense to you? How can Shuthdar have had it?"

"Atone," Tensor said in a voice that was the merest husk. "I will atone. My crimes must be scarified from the earth." He turned his piercing eyes on Llian, who retreated again. "*All crimes must be paid for*!"

"Tensor!" Mendark's tone could not be ignored.

"Tara-Laxus? We called it Snizzerlees. I believe that my predecessor, Kwinlis, dwelt there for a while. He had custody of the Mirror then and took it everywhere with him."

"Kwinlis may very well have met with Shuthdar," said Malien.

"Doubtless that's why Yalkara stole the Mirror," Yggur observed. "And why Faelamor fought her for it. And maybe how Yalkara came to find the flaw in the Forbidding."

"When the song was sung I spoke to the singer," Shand continued, "for I was curious to learn where he had found the lines, and if there were any more. But come," he said, gesturing to Llian, who this time had retreated right into the darkness on the far side of the cavern, "you can tell the story yourself."

"Yes, come out," cried Mendark cheerfully. "Earn your keep, chronicler!"

Llian did not move. Karan was surprised at his reluctance, since that was his trade and his livelihood. But the ordeals of the past week had hurt Llian badly; he just wanted to crawl into a dark corner and hide.

"I remember the time," said Llian. "I did not know what the *Twisted Mirror* meant then. Curiously, it is not recorded in the Histories. At least, not in those I had access to in Chanthed. I had forgotten the song, although now that I'm reminded I can, of course, recite the whole of the fragment." He stopped abruptly, moving back in the shadows.

"Anyway," Shand went on, "I'm sure that's why Yalkara wanted the Mirror. Somewhere, buried within its myriad memories, its age-old secrets, there may just be the image of Shuthdar using the flute. Perhaps that's how she found her way through the Forbidding."

"But to make the flute . . ." Tensor rasped from the back, "you must have gold! Only gold from Aachan will suffice."

His head sank down on his chest. Karan noticed Yggur staring at Tensor, his hand trembling. Mendark bore an enigmatic expression. Was he thinking of the ruination of his one-time friend, or of the opportunity that beckoned?

"But there is none to be had," Tensor went on in a subterranean rumble. "That essence which enabled it to be formed into devices like the flute was inimical to the gate. It could not pass between the worlds. Some of us were lost that way, before we realized . . ."

"Do you say, with surety, that there is no Aachan gold to be had?" Mendark demanded.

Tensor had lost interest. Once again his head sagged onto his chest. His eyes closed. They all stared at him.

"You can't just leave it there," said Karan.

His voice came muddy. "I knew only of the flute, and it is destroyed. Perhaps there is more; perhaps someone found a way to bring gold afterwards. In Aachan it was accounted a precious substance, and rare—far rarer than here. I took no interest in gold after the flute. We should never have meddled in the forbidden knowledge. I should have refused. Inquisitiveness was always our downfall." The rambling voice died to a whisper, then swelled into a toneless cold that made them all shiver.

"*That* was what brought the Charon down on us in the first place. Aachan was not enough for us. We thought we were alone in the universe, and we were lonely. We looked beyond Aachan, desperate to find another sentient species, though we were well acquainted with the rules of life on our own world. *Eat or be eaten, only the fittest survive.*

"Xesper—*Curse his name for all eternity*!—found a way

to look into the very spaces between the worlds. But just to look into the void changed it and left a track that led back to Aachan. Our world was hidden no longer. We found that we were not alone at all, *nor fittest*! The Charon came. Would that it were not so."

The silence stretched out to minutes. Llian opened his mouth, then closed it again. Karan knew what he was thinking. No one knew the Charon's origins, before they took Aachan from the Aachim. Tensor had revealed a precious snippet and Llian was desperate to find out the rest of the story.

Karan was not. The void was a nightmare of savagery, as far from her poor but placid life in Gothryme as anything could be. She had nightmares enough already.

"*Nooooo*!" Tensor gave a great bubbling moan that rang out above the wind. "All the troubles of the worlds have come from such meddling, and twice I had a hand in it. You cannot even dream what it will lead to. No more! You hold ruin in each hand."

He lifted his head, straining with his arms, his dark face darkening more with the fury of his exertion. He forced himself to his knees, but will alone could bring him no higher. Two of the Aachim came hurrying but he gestured them away, a savage sweep of the arm that almost had him down again.

"You, girl! We are in this together. Come with me. There is something that I must confess."

Afraid, wondering, Karan took his arm. They went slowly out into the storm.

18

PRECIOUS BANE

Llian rose to follow them, dreading what Tensor might do to Karan in his despair. Shand dropped a hand on his shoulder.

"Stay, Llian! That's not your affair."

"I'm worried," said Llian, staring at the door.

"There is much to be settled between them. Tensor will not harm her. Besides, we need you here."

"Why?"

"To think through this proposition," said Mendark. "Come down the back, Llian."

"You would discuss such things in front of a spy?" said Yggur incredulously. "I don't trust him!"

"And I don't trust *you*," Mendark retorted. "We need what Llian knows."

The five of them—Mendark, Yggur, Tallia, Malien and Llian—went up to the other end of the cave. Selial looked up like a white-haired ghost as they passed, but made no move to join them.

"This plan is senseless!" said Yggur. "We don't have the skill or cunning of Shuthdar. Likely there are secrets of his trade that we can never know. And perhaps the flute simply can't be made here. It was forged on Aachan, remember."

"And once made, we may lack the subtlety to use it," said Tallia perceptively. "As Rulke himself did."

"Such things are often closed to the strong and the wise," said Malien. "Sometimes the operator must be rude and untutored, relying on intuition or a native talent; a sensitivity. But even that needs some training."

"So! The venture may not be possible," said Mendark. "Do we try, and risk wasting all our energies, when they might be better employed with more conventional defenses?"

"I say not," said Yggur. "The flute is the past. It can never be recreated. The wheel has turned too far and not back to its starting point."

"But we must have a weapon to use against Rulke," said Mendark.

"Then let us make a different one!" snapped Yggur. "This flute is a thing of Aachan, not of Santhenar."

"It is a thing of Aachan *and* of Santhenar," replied Mendark, "for Shuthdar made it, and he learned his art here. Shuthdar was human, remember! One of us."

"No—still no!" said Yggur. "It's fighting Rulke with his own weapon."

"What can *you* offer us, Yggur?" Mendark said coldly. "You ever look to the past for security, employing the archaic way rather than exploring the new."

"That was behind our earlier disagreement," said Yggur with a flash of venom. "And one for which I will yet be paid."

"I doubt it!" Mendark's sneer told how little Yggur bothered him anymore. "You can't even master yourself now."

Yggur balled his fists. Llian looked from one to the other. Every day Yggur grew more alienated, more bitter, and Mendark's evident contempt only made it worse. Yggur was terrified of Rulke, and Llian was terrified of Yggur. But Mendark was not finished yet.

"The past has failed us! The Nightland is revealed to have been flawed from the outset; deliberately so. We must look to the future and make a new flute using a new pattern."

The fellowship of the company seemed irreparably broken. Tallia, however, was moved by an urge to conciliate.

"Listen, both of you! It doesn't matter who's right. Surely we must look at all approaches and find the way that best suits our needs and our strengths. If that be the flute, new or old, let us take it and put off the settlement until Santhenar be won—or lost beyond recovery."

Shand nodded.

"Very well, I will put aside my misgivings," said Yggur, though it was clear that he had not. "But where are you going to get the gold?" He gave a sideways flick of his staring eyes that seemed to say, "but this will not end the way you think, just see if it does."

Malien spoke from her crevice. "We Aachim must also take responsibility for our situation. Always we sought to delay the future by taking refuge in the past, just as you have done, Yggur. And too often we abdicated our responsibility, giving in to Tensor when we should have directed him. Our past is gone now; we have no choice but to make a new way in the world. And if we fail . . . Well, what have we to lose? We will aid you, Mendark."

"How can you help us?"

"Small amounts of gold *were* brought to Santhenar. And we know how to work it."

"Really!" said Mendark, with a great gust of a sigh. "How is it that Tensor did not know?"

"Of course he knows!" Her voice dripped scorn. "Pitlis had a circlet of it that he wore about his brow. All the time that he was leader at Tar Gaarn he wore it, and even after the fall, though not into exile."

"What happened to it?"

"Pitlis would have been careful with it. There was another

reason why little gold was brought here—anything taken from one world to another is liable to transmute and become perilous to use. As with the Mirror, so too this gold. But if the circlet passed to another of us it is not recorded. We have ever felt that Rulke took it when he slew Pitlis at the gates of Alcifer."

"Maybe so, but Rulke did not have it with him when he was taken," said Llian, speaking up more boldly than in a long time. "I know those Histories well, and can even recite the inventory of his possessions."

"Doubtless he hid it beforehand," said Mendark. "The gold was one of the precious things we sought, even then. But gold is easily transformed and hidden. Besides, there was not enough to make a flute; not near."

"Though enough for a good start," said Yggur darkly, "and Rulke probably had more, since he knew the value of it better than any. What else do you know, Malien?"

Malien hesitated. "There *was* more—a small golden idol, brought by the second wave of Aachim to come to Santhenar. They came of their own accord, not as Rulke's slaves. The statue is a most ancient and precious thing, the heart of the Aachim of Nastor—a region in the north of Aachan," she explained. "It was kept in the library at Stassor, in the far east. Doubtless it's there still, though it's the grossest blasphemy to even think of using it."

"Was there any more?" asked Mendark.

"Not that we know of."

"Might the Charon have brought some?"

"Rulke and Kandor came with the first wave," said Malien. "They brought nothing."

"Why nothing?" asked Yggur.

"Because nothing could be brought the first time," Llian explained. "Save the flute, of course, but it could be said to have brought itself, since it opened the way. It is recorded several times how they came naked to Santhenar."

"And the second wave?"

"After the Charon had been here for some time—perhaps

fifty years—and realized that the hunt for the flute would be a long one, they sent back to Aachan for aid," replied Malien. "So came the second wave, many of us, and a number of blendings of Aachim and Charon. But as a rule *they* did not share the long life of either Charon or Aachim. Most are dead without issue, for such blendings were generally *sterile—mules*!

"Separately, a host of Aachim came of their own accord. They found a way to bring certain small things that they treasured, ornaments or jewelry or small devices that were useful. That's how Tensor brought the Mirror here, I imagine, for he also came at that time. As did my people, but they certainly brought no gold. That's all I know."

"Not enough," said Yggur. "Why must it be Aachan gold?"

"It has special properties."

"But what use is it if we cannot obtain any?"

Llian's forehead had grown increasingly knotted as he tried to remember something, and now he burst out suddenly:

"Maybe there is more! Yalkara had golden jewelry—a heavy chain, a bracelet and a torc. I've seen a picture of her wearing it. Now where was that?"

Shand gave a sigh, a long outrushing of breath. Llian looked at him curiously, then continued. "But was it Aachan gold? And did she take it with her or leave it behind, as she did the Mirror? The matter is not recorded."

"Why would Yalkara leave it behind if she valued it so greatly?" asked Yggur.

"I don't know," said Llian. "Why did she abandon the Mirror? Perhaps Yalkara lacked the strength to carry it through the gate, for it is said that she was badly hurt in her struggles with Faelamor. Perhaps the Forbidding made it impossible. Perhaps she no longer needed it."

"Those questions cannot be answered," said Malien. "But if you are resolved to attempt the flute, which I caution against, you must go to Havissard, whence she departed. It has never been plundered."

"Then we have two hopes," Mendark mused. "But the first is unlikely. Alcifer was sacked after Rulke was taken and has since lain abandoned. If anything precious remains there it is surpassingly well hidden. Besides, Pitlis's circlet will not be enough. Could it be blended with ordinary gold, I wonder?"

"No," said Malien.

"This is futile," Yggur said irritably. "There's no way to get into Havissard."

"It is *protected*," said Shand. "It cannot be taken by strength save by breaking the foundations, and they are socketed deep into rock. The only hope is from beneath, through the mines."

"The Histories tell that Yalkara reopened the silver mines of Tar Gaarn after that city fell," Llian explained, "and they became the foundation of her wealth, as they had been the basis of the wealth of the Aachim before her."

"But they were abandoned after she departed," said Shand, "and will never be opened again. The pumps failed and no one could repair them. The lower levels are flooded to the depth of a hundred spans."

There was a long silence.

"Do what you want!" said Yggur, now quite agitated. "I'm going back to Thurkad. Unruly people! My empire must be falling to pieces without me, especially with Thyllan lurking just across the sea. I left Maigraith there—abandoned her. How she must be suffering without me. And the Ghâshâd must be curbed—at least, I must make it harder for them to prepare the way for Rulke. Though how that can be done now that they have the resources and defenses of Shazmak . . . From Thurkad I will send people to Alcifer." And even to Stassor, he thought, and seize this precious statue if no other way can be found. The Aachim are failing and eventually even Stassor must fall into ruin. Better that it come into my hands. "But Tar Gaarn and Havissard," he went on aloud, "are beyond me."

"I have long thought that Havissard would be my destination," said Mendark, "and while I was in Zile I searched out the old maps. There's nothing for me in Thurkad now." He directed a ferocious scowl at Yggur, who could not see it. A look that said: *not yet*. "But if the one who knows Tar Gaarn better than any were to come with me . . ."

"Why do you ask, Mendark?" said Shand. "I'm going back to Meldorin with Karan and Llian, and from there, home to Tullin. The gellon will be ripening by the time we get there. You and I have nothing to say to one another. I told you that twelve years ago, if you remember . . ."

Mendark turned away. "I had not thought of you as a coward," he said contemptuously.

Shand shrugged away Mendark's words. "As I was going to say, if you had let me finish: I will make a map for you. No, better still, Yggur and I will make a map together. Yggur!" he gestured, and to everyone's surprise Yggur unfolded his limbs and sat down with Shand. Soon they were chatting as if they had been friends for years. Shand seemed to be able to get on with everyone, save Mendark. He drew on an old scrap of parchment while Yggur corrected him.

Only then did it occur to them to wonder what had happened to Tensor and Karan. Hours had passed since they had gone outside; the brown daylight had long faded from around the edges of the canvas. The wind had died down. All was still. And then a great cry of agony cleaved the silence.

19

CONFESSION

Karan and Tensor found themselves in a hostile, poisonous world. A world of shrieking wind, choking dust and thick air that seared nose, throat and lungs. Tensor stood shakily outside the canvas door while Karan adjusted his face cloth. She gave him her shoulder and they set out, walking ever so slowly along the canyon and up the side of a shallow ridge.

They labored up to a place of fantastically shaped pillars and caverns, buttresses and gullies carved out of the salt. It was layered brown, red and yellow, and the wind had fretted the softer layers away so that a variety of unlikely objects were formed—here a block with the layers resembling the pages of a book; there an outjutting point tapered like the snout of a rodent, even to the trace of whiskers on one cheek.

Karan had time to look closely at these sculptures, so painful was Tensor's progress. Whatever the damage that Rulke's blow had done to him, and none but the Aachim knew how bad that was, it had twisted his back and hip, and the whole of his left side from knee to shoulder; even his left arm hung limp and useless. Only the remnant of that once great will forced him on, blocking out the pain of his twisted frame and torn sinews. But yet he said nothing.

The last part of that climb, into the teeth of the wind, was the worst. Karan's eyes flamed before the end of it. They came stumbling onto the flat top of a peak of salt, the tallest around, and the wind caught her cloak so that it billowed like a sail, lifting her off her feet. Tensor's fingers dug into her shoulder and his weight pressed her back down, and the gust passed.

"Will you sit?" she shouted. Nearby a flange of rock salt stood up to the height of her shoulders, breaking the wind.

His voice came dry and rasping, the sound of one block of salt being rubbed against another. "If I were to sit I might never rise again."

Yellow clouds rushed across the white plains and once more their world was obscured in dust. Karan looked longingly at the shelter, braced her legs against the wind and closed her eyes. Tensor stared unfocused toward the east until his eyes were raw and crusted.

"Endure!" he said. "Endure."

She did not respond, there being nothing to say.

"You are the only hope now," he went on, apparently to himself. "They cannot know where they are led, and will not be told. Only you can see the pattern now. Endure!"

The squall passed; crystals of salt glittered in the air like mica falling through sunlight. Then the sky cleared suddenly and Katazza Mountain stood before them, its pinnacles touched to red by the setting sun, seemingly only a day's march away: mighty; impregnable; fallen. Taking a pebble out of her pocket Karan put it in her mouth, but her mouth was as dry as her hands. Though she sucked at it, no moisture came. Brushing salt dust from her cheeks, she sneezed.

"What did . . . ?" she began.

He turned toward Karan, directing at her that withering stare that she so remembered from her childhood. "I tell you,

Karan, you brought all this on us . . ." He raised his hand as she began to speak. "No, let me have my say! You did us harm, bringing the Mirror to Shazmak, stirring up Emmant, lying to us, stealing it away again. Doubtless they were bitter choices for you, but you made them. You provided a bridge for Rulke to reach out and wake the Ghâshâd. No matter how well-meaning, no matter how ignorant, you were the keystone. Not the shaper, but the vital link. Without you, would the Ghâshâd ever have got into Shazmak? Would Emmant ever have betrayed us? Without you it would not have happened. Because of you it did.

"I do not blame you any longer. Who am I to blame anyone? Your crimes pale to nothing beside my own. Yet you are in it, and you must bear the burden."

Karan was silent. She had not forgotten how bitter her choices had been, nor the consequences of them. You're right, she thought. I cannot ignore my part in this.

Suddenly it flowed out of Tensor like a flood, coming faster and faster, the words tumbling over one another in their haste to escape. "We are responsible both, you and I. As far back as Aachan, eons ago, I chose to help Rulke and Shuthdar forge the flute; I labored with them even knowing that what they did was forbidden. I left the flaw in the Nightland so that I might exploit it later. I chose to take you into Shazmak, to shape you. I set Emmant to spy on you, knowing what a broken instrument he was. I sent Faelamor to Shazmak, ignoring her warnings and her threats. I used power against the hapless Nelissa, violating the Conclave." He gasped a breath, then rushed on. "I used the Twisted Mirror to find the flaw again, even knowing that the Mirror might not show true. And it did not; it betrayed me. I made the gate and failed to protect it, and opened it too soon, ignoring your warnings and pleas, and the warnings of the Syndics. In all the Histories none has been more distinguished, more wholehearted and more consistent in his folly than I. Perhaps the hubris of Pitlis was the greater at the end, but mine has been the creation of a lifetime.

"Were it not . . ." Tensor sagged, the will that held his twisted frame erect failing under the weight of his despair. Karan could not hold him. They fell together onto the salt.

She struggled out from underneath. Tensor had struck the side of his head against a knob of rock salt. A thick strand of blood oozed from his cheek, though it soon stopped in the heat. His dark skin had gone a bilious yellow-green. Breathing shallowly, he looked near death. The wind sang out once more; another squall was on them. There was just time enough to tie the cloth over Tensor's nose and mouth before the blast lifted her off her feet and tried to blow her down into the canyon.

Karan scuttled the few paces to the shelter that she had seen previously. Why had Tensor brought her out here? To drive home her guilt or wallow in his own? She had no illusions about what she had done during that awful time when she carried the Mirror. She had chosen her path, knowing that it must injure the Aachim. She would not wallow in guilt. So many people had used her. Even so, she felt her responsibilities.

The squall eased. Karan ran back to Tensor and shook the dust off his bandage. He opened raw eyes, staring right through her. With a corner of the cloth she picked crusted salt from his eyelashes.

"You said you wanted to confess something to me. Was *that* it? You told me nothing that I did not already know."

Tensor forced until he was sitting upright.

"No," he said, hacking the dust out of his throat. "Not at all. I have done a great wickedness to you." He tried to stand but could get no higher than his knees. Still he could look into her eyes.

"I remember how you came to me in Shazmak," Tensor rasped. "I will always remember how you stood on the doorstep and said, *I have come home.* What an urchin you were; what a tiny bedraggled little thing. And yet, what strength! What dignity! You touched my heart. You were all I would have expected of your father's daughter, rebellious and troublesome as he had been. Even so, I would have sent you away to die."

Karan shivered.

"I would have turned you away, for all that you were a daughter such as I had always dreamed about. You had no right to Shazmak—your father had broken his oath. And broken it again just by telling you of our city. I saw a great danger in you. There is a threat in all blendings, but especially in you. I saw that you would come, but not remain; that you would go back into the world and bring it down upon us. Would that I had turned you away.

"But the Aachim would not permit it. Seldom did they ignore my advice, but this time they were unmoved. From the moment they saw you they were captivated. They thought they knew you. Hah! They knew *nothing*!

"You touched my heart," he rasped, "and I loved you. Not even Rael loved you more. I was afraid of what you would bring—*triune*, a thousand times worse than any blending!"

Karan felt a spear of ice enter her chest. "Triune? What do you mean?"

"*You* are a double blending, Karan, a triune, for you carry the blood of the Three Worlds in you. Three different human species—old human, Aachim, *and* Faellem!"

"Faellem!" said Karan, bemused.

"You did not know that you had a Faellem ancestor? I never told a soul; no one could be trusted with that knowledge. Our Histories speak about the triune, how she would come out of nowhere and move time and space itself. How I wish I had put you out that door." He came to his feet; his big arm went around her slim shoulders. Tensor hugged her to him, very gently.

She looked up at him, unable to take it all in. This changed everything. She wasn't who she thought she was at all.

"But they let you in. All I could do was shape you myself. I took charge of your schooling, trying to prevent the flowering of those talents that I judged to threaten us most. Did I succeed or did I fail? Did I damage you? Certainly you are less than you might have been, and you are now too old, too formed to recover it. Sometimes the *shaping* succeeds, but at other times the force of destiny, the momentum of fate as your mother's people would say, cannot be altered. You did not develop in some ways where you showed great promise. Yet you burst out in other, unexpected ways; talents flowered that may in the end threaten us more. I even tried to suppress all knowledge of the house of Elienor, so that you would never learn of your great heritage. But Malien would not allow that. She undermined me at every step."

Karan was shocked. Shocked to learn of her ancestry. Triune was a curse, a terrible stigma of madness and unpredictability. Shocked at what he had done to her. So that was why she had been pursued for so long. Why everyone wanted something from her, once they recognized something strange and rare in her. How dared he meddle with her so; and without her ever knowing? She could not forgive him for that.

"That is all," said Tensor. "Go back now. Yours is the future, if you can salvage anything from the ruin my folly has wrought."

Karan turned away, hating and despising him. Curse him! Why should he not end it here if he so willed it? Salt sand abraded her cheeks as she went down the path. At the bottom she looked back. Tensor stood tall as a pillar of salt. Snatches of verse came on the wind, a soliloquy of despair and failure. "I am nothing. All I ever stood for is *nothing*!"

A choking cloud of salt struck her. Karan crouched down with her cloak over her face until it had passed. Another squall wailed toward her, and after that another. Hours had gone by since they had come outside. The day was done, a few bright stars out already and the ruddy scorpion nebula brooding above. She peered through the gloom. The pillar was gone; Tensor was not there. Her anger evaporated. Despite his sins Tensor had been as a father to her: she could not let him die alone.

She ran back up, tripping and skidding in the gloom. Tensor lay still, just a rag among the crags. He looked dead, but when she unwrapped the salt-covered cloth and smoothed his cheek his eyes fluttered open. She lifted his head, brushing the salt away.

"Leave me," he begged. "This is a fitting place and a fitting end."

He was giving up, slipping away feeling only self-pity and despair. Something about the gesture pricked at her. It was his pride talking, as it had always done. Karan's compassion disappeared, so diminished was Tensor from what he once had been. How dared he meddle with her so? Let him do something to make up for his follies.

"I have done wrong, I know," she said, "but never did I act for myself. You wronged me and all Santhenar with your vast pride, but what have the Aachim to be proud of save the past? Even there it rests more on glorious failures than on great deeds or lasting works. It is a long time since the Aachim were great in anything but hubris. Now get up! There will come a time when even *your* aid will be needed. *Get up*! Your despair is no more appealing than your pride, and both are rooted in the same source."

"Leave me," he rasped. "I have nothing more to give. It is fitting that I die in this barren and worthless place. So we all pass."

His eyes lost their shine, slowly closing as he let loose the hold of his will on his crippled body.

"Do not dare to die, you *craven*!" she shouted in his face. His eyes flickered open, though so dull that not even the brightest star reflected in them. "It was your wicked folly that brought terror and destruction upon us all. And now that the damage is done you wallow in self-pity, as cursed Pitlis did, then abandon your people without hope. But not this time—I do not allow it."

Tensor's eyes began to glaze over. The coward! In a fury she sprang to her feet and kicked him as hard as she could, right in his injured hip, and was instantly horrified and disgusted with herself.

Tensor convulsed. His eyes flicked open and he let out a

great cry of agony. His arms gripped the abused limb while beads of sweat broke out all over his face, which the starlight touched with points of light. He made no further sound, even though the pain went on and on, ringing back and forth through his body like a bell. He directed her a look of pure rage.

"Why have you called me back, hateful child? My time is finished."

There were tears on her salty cheeks. "As you schooled me, so I school you," she said in an icy voice. "What contempt you must have felt for me, to shape me like an animal, to rob me of my destiny. Well, that is what I feel for you now: *contempt*! You have created nothing. You warped, you twisted, you destroyed, and when all the good you started with lay in ruins you fled because you had not the courage to try and mend what you broke."

Her voice rose above the wind. "It is your pride that tells you to die out here in the desolation. I would have thought more of you if you had gone out alone, rather than bringing me here to lecture me and be a witness to your so-called nobility. This is not nobility; this is not honor, this is *hubris*! Tensor is a craven's name, and yours are a proud, vain coward's deeds, the ruin of all. Get up from your coward's bed, Tensor, or I curse you all the way into the grave, and beyond it. Get up. Get *up*!"

While this was going on the company had come running up. The Aachim looked to go to Tensor's aid but Shand put out his arm and stayed them. They all gathered behind him, watching—impassive, shocked or angry.

Karan saw Llian's hungry eyes on her, but she had no time for him just now. "Get up," said Karan. "Redeem yourself."

Tensor struggled, gave up, looked into Karan's cold eyes, tried again and came to his knees. His skin was an ugly yellow gray, his brow dripping with sweat. "I cannot," he said. "The pain . . ."

"*The pain*?" she shouted in his face. "What is pain beside the pride of the Aachim? What is pain beside honor? To hell with your pain. The Tensor I knew would not have been swayed by it. Stand, if you have the courage."

Tensor squatted with his hands supporting him. He forced, fell back to his knees, forced; fell again. Forced. Fell. Each time he was weaker. Karan could see him failing before her eyes. It was all she could do to stare him down, hating herself. No point, if he could not do it.

"If you have the courage . . ." she whispered, her complexion bleached of all color. The Aachim stirred behind her, but still Shand held them back. Tensor made a supreme effort, pushing himself against the pain and the exhaustion, to the limit of his strength and beyond. He fell again. He looked up at her—old, hopeless, desperate.

"I cannot," he croaked. "Will . . . will you help me?"

It was over. Tears washing gullies down her salt-crusted cheeks, Karan put her arms about his waist and strained to lift him, carefully as ever she could. He staggered to his feet, supporting himself with his hands on her shoulders. Steadying himself, Tensor took a lurching step and would have fallen on his face, but she held him up. They rested for a moment then Karan gave him her shoulder and they made their laborious way past the company, down the hill and into the cavern to the place where Tensor had lain before. The others followed slowly behind, stepping together in pairs like an honor guard at a funeral.

Tensor stood by his litter, leaning on her shoulder, looking down at her. "How would you have me redeem myself?" he asked in a gentle, hoarse voice.

"I've no idea," she replied, "only that a time will come and you will be called."

"I will answer," he said, was lowered to his litter and fell into sleep.

But all that night, and for the rest of their journey across the salt, Karan could not stop thinking about what had been done to her, what she might have been and what she now knew herself to be. A triune—a mad, shameful thing. Suddenly Karan felt dissatisfied with herself, at the part of her that had been lost forever. There was a hollow inside her that she could not fill.

On the other side of the cavern the arguments were still going on when the sun rose. Llian listened, fascinated by the drama and noting everything in his perfect memory for his *Tale of the Mirror.* That cheered him up considerably. It was going to be a Great Tale, the twenty-third, and his name would be on it.

"But how does it help us?" Tallia was speaking now. "We don't know how to make the flute, or how to use it."

"That's a problem for the morrow," said Mendark. "Let's make it first, if we can."

"It is the morrow and we can't keep putting it off."

There was a long silence. The dawn wind flung salt crystals against their door with a gritty hiss.

A croaking, halting voice spoke from the corner.

"I know exactly how the flute was made," said Tensor. "I can tell you, though at the last it will not avail you."

"You!" cried Mendark in astonishment, though whether at Tensor knowing it or at agreeing to help them, it was impossible to say.

"In Aachan," Tensor said wearily, "we became the lesser folk, the toilers, after the Charon took our world. We did the tiresome tasks and the unpleasant. There were many weary tasks in the making of the flute, too many for Shuthdar. He needed an assistant and I was that helper. How could I ever forget such a thing?"

"How is it that you did not make another for yourself, if you knew the way?" Mendark asked suspiciously.

"There was no opportunity in Aachan; and once we came to Santhenar, what need? We were happy here at first. We have never sought power, only freedom. Then, after the Forbidding, what would have been the point? Besides, Aachan gold was needed. Nothing else would suffice." His eyes closed; he slept once more.

They discussed this at length. "Do you think he can be relied upon?" Shand asked. "Better not to even think of using him, if he cannot."

"He has always been honest, after his own fashion," said Mendark. "As honest as any great leader can be. But surely he serves his own purpose. And even if he remembers the making of it perfectly, that is not to say that it can be made anew.

"Four things we will need to find or to learn." Mendark ticked them off on his fingers. "One—enough gold, *the right kind of gold*, for the flute. Two—the way to *make* it. Three—the way to *use* it. Four—the *one* to use it. We have leads on the first and the second. Let's see what we can do with them. If we can find gold and make the flute anew, there will be time to worry about whether we can use it. Perhaps that's one of the secrets of the Mirror."

Perhaps it is, Llian thought, and maybe *I* will be the one to find it. Suddenly all his chronicler's enthusiasm was renewed. What a tale it was going to make, and it was his.

They should have been excited at the prospect that the flute offered, but as Llian looked around the little group he mostly saw dread on their faces. Or despair, that they would put everything into this venture and it would come to nothing. All but Mendark.

"Malien, I must know more about the Mirror. What was written about it?"

"Nothing that I know of, except that it existed, and it was perilous."

He frowned. "Why so?"

"There was no need. Those few who wielded the Mirror knew everything about it. Then it became a quixotic and dangerous thing, and it was put aside and forgotten. After it was stolen, Yalkara wrested it to her own will; changed it. What we knew about it was no longer relevant."

"I can't believe that nothing was written down."

"That was long before my time. You'll have to ask Tensor or Selial. But not even Tensor can tell you what Yalkara did to it."

"Well, I'll start working on the third problem," said Mendark. "The way to use it. I'll take charge of the Mirror now, Shand."

"You won't!" said Shand angrily. "It has come back to my keeping, and the gift of it is mine alone. Listen to what was foretold many years ago: *The Mirror is locked, and cannot be used save by the One who can unlock it. That key lies within the Mirror itself.* Can you resolve that paradox?"

Mendark wrestled with the idea for a considerable time. "No," he said.

"Then *you* will never be able to use it."

Llian was consumed by the paradox but Shand would say no more.

20

Fighting in the Mud

During the day the storm wore itself out. Before dark they gathered their goods together and set off, hauling the sleds with their flabby waterbags along the grit of the canyon floor and onto the crystalline salt beyond, which crunched and crackled under the runners. It was now three weeks since the company had left Katazza, and twelve days since they'd filled their water bottles at the base of the mountain. They had water for another week, but it was eight or nine days to the lakes.

They made better progress in the good conditions, particularly as the latter parts of each night were lit by the new moon rising, though ominously the dark side was now inching toward full.

The days became unbearably hot and tedious—tempers flared for no reason at all. As the moon darkened, seeming to reflect their own troubles, so did the feuding grow worse. Since Karan's attack Yggur's eyesight had deteriorated again, which drove him into a cold, bitter fury with Llian, with Karan and with the whole world.

Karan hardly noticed, so preoccupied was she with Tensor's revelation, and what he had done to her.

One day, Karan noticed that Selial seemed to have aged remarkably. Her silver hair had gone a dingy white and her clothes hung on her.

"What's the matter with Selial?" Karan asked Malien as they trudged across an utterly featureless plain of salt.

"She will die soon. She has given up."

"Is there nothing that can be done for her?"

"Would you make her suffer more than she already does?"

Karan looked back. Selial was stumbling along by herself, head down, arms hanging lifelessly. At that moment she looked up, but did not acknowledge their gaze.

"She was very kind to me in Shazmak."

"Then do her the same kindness. Give her words of comfort and thanks, the best you can make, and leave her be."

That evening, before they set out, Selial summoned the Aachim together. Karan was invited too. They took their places on the ground around her. The moon was three-quarters full, but it gave an eerie light, for it mostly showed the dark side.

"My time has come," Selial said with the dignity that so characterized her. "But my resting place is far from here, so I will keep on. I have chosen to lie beside the Iron Gates of the Hornrace, at the tip of the Foshorn. The Rainbow Bridge was our greatest feat in all Santhenar, and I would share my *forever dreaming* with my great-grandmother who made it. She is buried on the other side. May we meet again when Faranda and Lauralin are linked once more."

"I will come with you and bid you farewell," said Karan with tears in her eyes.

There was little to tell about the journey, save heat, salt dust, thirst and exhaustion. Mirages promised water every day, though they came to nothing but baked salt. One good thing had happened though—since Karan's altercation with Tensor, Basitor had ceased persecuting Llian.

On the seventh evening the water ran out. "How far now?" asked Yggur as they squeezed the last bottles dry.

"At least a day," said Osseion.

They struggled on through the night, and at the end of it were suffering badly from dehydration. "It can't be far," Mendark panted as the first light crept over the eastern horizon. "Surely not much further."

The sun sprang up behind them, revealing flat salt in every direction. "Well," Mendark said, "this is the moment of decision. Stay here and die, or keep on until we die. Either way, it won't take long."

"We can go a little way yet," said Shand, picking dry shreds of skin off his lips.

Karan stopped abruptly, staring about her. The others continued, even Llian, until she was standing all alone.

"What's that?" she said, sniffing the air. Maybe it was her sensitive talent, or perhaps the months on the salt last spring had heightened her ability to smell water.

No one answered; they just kept plodding along. There had been too many false alarms already.

"We're going the wrong way," Karan shouted hoarsely. "I can sense water." She turned around and around. "Yes, it's that way, further south."

No one argued, or even spoke. It was too much effort. But they followed her.

Karan continued for several hours. Every step had become a labor. Her muscles felt as if they had been glued together; her skin itched all over. She recognized the symptoms—advancing dehydration that would lead to her death before the day was over.

As the sun rose higher, mirages shivered on the salt, the most inviting that they had ever seen.

"Which way?" rasped Mendark.

"I—I can't tell," said Karan. Her talent had deserted her again.

"Lift me up, someone," said Llian.

Basitor and Osseion were the biggest. Basitor gave Llian a meaningful stare, but stood patiently beside Osseion while Llian was lifted onto their shoulders. He stood up gingerly and looked in every direction.

"What do you see?" they cried.

"Nothing! I'm not high enough."

Osseion and Basitor each seized an ankle and lifted him above their heads. Basitor's hand was like a manacle.

"I see water," Llian croaked through cracked lips. He pointed further south of their track. "It's the lakes!"

"Another mirage!" gasped Yggur.

"This one has trees," Llian said, and before much longer they could all see them, a little patch of dark-leaved mangroves in the middle of the salt and a long vegetated mud bank running into the distance.

"It is water!" Karan shouted, as if she hadn't quite believed it herself. "Race you to it."

She and Tallia set off toward the lake at a stumbling run. Llian followed slowly; it was too hot for such foolishness. When Karan was almost at the water's edge she sprang off a mound to clear a patch of mud. Landing, her feet went straight through a salt crust and she plunged hip-deep into the salty mud. She burst out laughing. "Whee! It's hot!"

She tried to push herself up but wherever she put her weight on the crust it broke off again.

"Help!" she said, still laughing. Then she slid further down into the mud and suddenly realized that it was serious. "Tallia! It's pulling me down."

Tallia had stopped at her initial cry, but water began to puddle around her feet and without warning the crust under her gave way as well.

"Llian," she shouted. "Run back! Get help!"

Llian kept coming. He was afraid to go for help in case they were sucked right under.

"Go on!" Tallia screeched. "We'll be all right."

"Speak for yourself," said Karan, still floundering in the mud, as Llian ran off. Suddenly she slipped down again until the mud was breast-deep. She panicked and thrashed about wildly.

"Don't move," said Tallia, who had managed to extricate one foot, only to sink so deep on the other that she overbalanced and fell sideways into the mud. She spat out muck and said, "Keep absolutely still. Spread your arms out."

Karan did so and the downward movement stopped momentarily. Llian came staggering back with Shand, Osseion and several of the Aachim, dragging their water sleds.

"Help!" cried Karan. Her shoulders were almost covered now.

Shand burst out laughing. "Keep still! You won't go any deeper."

"It's sucking me under," Karan wept.

"Nonsense! Mud's heavier than water and you can float. How can it suck you under?"

"Get me out!" she screamed. "When I want a school lesson I'll ask for one."

Shand turned one of the sleds over so that its smooth metal surface lay on the crust, then pushed it ahead of him out to Karan's mud hole. Llian followed with the second sled and after much heaving, swearing and disgusting squelching noises they had Karan out again. By this time Tallia had rescued herself, for her long legs had found hard mud underneath the sucking stuff.

Once they were back on solid ground the rest of the company took much amusement from the sight of them. Karan looked like a mud sprite—muck oozing off every surface. And it stank too, with a ripe rotten-egg stench.

"You smell like a hundred-year-old fart," guffawed Llian.

"Don't be disgusting," said Karan, almost in tears.

"Are you thinking what I'm thinking?" Tallia said to her.

"Very probably." Eyeing their tormentors, Karan ran a cupped hand up her thigh, wadded mud into a ball and flung it at the sniggering Llian. It splattered most satisfyingly right in the middle of his chest.

"Hey!" he said and fell over backwards.

At the same instant Tallia's ball smacked Shand right in the ear.

"Right!" he roared. "That's how you show your gratitude, is it?" He scooped mud off the sled and hurled it at Karan.

Then it was on, missiles flying back and forth, everyone laughing and shrieking. Even Basitor joined in, hitting Llian over the head with a mud ball the size of a melon and laughing fit to burst. Llian did too, after he'd got over the shock, and that surprised Basitor almost as much as it did him.

Mendark came running up to see what was the matter and copped one right in the eye, an event that gave Karan a fierce thrill of pleasure, especially as she knew that Tallia had thrown it. Mendark was not amused and the fight petered out soon afterwards. It was too hot for such strenuous activity, and they were too worn out, so they looked for a safe path down to the water to bathe. Karan and Tallia went together, still chuckling.

There were no fish here, for the lake was too shallow and hot, but the salty water was a sovereign feed for the Aachim's sun stills. The first cup of warm, tasteless water was offered to Selial with all the reverence of a noble vintage, and the lifeless Selial perked up and smacked her lips with equal appreciation. Once the trazpars were going they had a party, all the water that they could drink.

At the other end of the lake there were fish in superabundance, so concentrated in the shrinking pools that a single cast of a net would feed them all. They found a vast congregation of birds as well, ducks and divers spiraling in the air then plunging down to gorge themselves before their long pilgrimage north for the winter. Waders stilted across the quickmud that made most of the approaches to the lake treacherous. The place stank of bird manure.

Osseion made a net by unraveling some pieces of cloth

and knotting the threads back together, his thick fingers dancing over the knots.

"I was better at this when I had ten fingers," he said to Llian, rubbing the space where the tenth had been. By the time the sun set he had a coarsely woven net of half a dozen spans length. "Here, hold this end."

"It doesn't look very strong," said Llian, eyeing it doubtfully.

"Well, it doesn't have to be; we'll only use it once or twice."

It was a bright night, a full moon showing just a crescent of yellow. They carried the net down to a place where the crust of salt looked firm enough to walk on, though Llian had no idea where to put his feet and twice Osseion had to haul him out of places that suddenly liquefied under his weight.

"No, put your hands here, and here. Don't you know anything about fishing, Llian?" Osseion rumbled.

Llian smiled. "I've never even wetted a line; nor wanted to before today. But after a month eating skagg I will become the master chronicler of fishing. I have in mind to write a book: *The Compleat Angler*, I will call it."

Osseion roared with laughter, clapping Llian on the shoulder so hard that he fell to his knees and promptly began to sink into the quickmud. "It's been written already, so I've been told," Osseion said, pulling him out again. "But I'm glad to see that you've mastered the first lesson—*never let go of the net.* Now, hold it *down*, otherwise they'll just swim under it."

Llian did as he was told while Osseion waded out into the water until it was up to his waist. His path curved around in a circle, he stamped his feet and turned back to shore. Shortly, after much heaving, they had a catch of half a hundred fat fish, a handful of the crayfish that Karan called clatchers and a red and gold water snake that reared up on top of the pile, its eyes glittering red in the moonlight. Osseion borrowed Mendark's staff to flick it back into the water.

They feasted on the fish, the clatchers and some unfortunate ducks; on lake weed and the pith of reeds that grew along the levee banks high above the salt. Three days they stayed there, drying fish fillets in the sun, then pressed on, much rejuvenated, and in another few days crossed off the salt plain onto the slope leading up to the high plateau. Above the first cliff they found a series of rockpools filled with gorgeously cool fresh water, and in the larger of these they bathed and washed the filthy rags that were their clothes. They stayed two days at that place too, feasting, for fish and fruit were plentiful.

Llian spent most of that time sitting alone in the shade. He was now starting to build the *Tale of the Mirror* in his mind and any kind of company was a distraction. Karan did not worry; she had made a friend in Tallia and they were often to be seen treading water down in the shady end of a pool and talking quietly together—the one tall, black-haired and chocolate-skinned, the other small, flame-haired and pale as milk, with not even a freckle to show for the months of walking under her tent-like robes.

"Come and join us, Shand," Karan called one morning as he went by the pool. He had his head down and did not seem to hear. "Shand!" she yelled.

He looked up vacantly, raised a hand then kept on.

"What's the matter with him?" Karan wondered.

"I don't know," said Tallia. "He's gone all quiet lately. Race you down to the bottom!" She upended, her long legs rising out of the water, then plunged down.

Karan followed more slowly. She knew from experience that no one could match Tallia at diving.

"What will you do after all this?" Karan asked on the last afternoon.

"I don't know," sighed Tallia. "I feel that my life has come to a crossroads."

"You and Mendark are not . . . ?" Karan enquired delicately.

Tallia laughed. "That was brief and ended years ago. I still care for him and for the objectives he strives for. He's done a lot of good for Santhenar, whatever you think of him. But my indenture is over now, and I think I'll go my separate way when this business is finished. What about you?"

"I don't know—I'm all confused. I just want to go home to Gothryme. I can't imagine how I ended up here now. It all seems like a nightmare."

Karan looked up and there was Shand, sitting on top of a lonely rock, staring out over the sea. She followed his gaze. The salt had an eerie beauty from this far away—it looked cool and inviting.

"The Dry Sea is a great tempter," said Tallia.

Next day they went back into the blast of the sun to continue the long climb. They found the high plateau arid, the spring grass long withered, all but the largest rivers broken up into waterholes separated by long expanses of sand and gravel. Yet still there was game in plenty, fruit and nuts ripening on the banks, and they were never more than a day's march from water. Compared to the Dry Sea it was a holiday.

At the first west-flowing river they came to, the Aachim, master boatmakers that they were, stripped huge sheets of bark from trees growing by the water, hardened them over a fire and formed the sheets into bark canoes. After that they padded gently along all day and drifted down with the current for half the night as well. The days were mild and the nights wonderfully cool. Once, as they neared the western side of the plateau, it rained, the first Karan had felt for half a year. It would have been a pleasant journey, save for the ever-present shadow of Yggur at the back of the last canoe.

After another week, more or less, of winding their way down through the eastern mountains, they reached the south road. As soon as they did, Yggur came sidling up to Mendark.

"What do you want?" Mendark asked sourly. He and Yggur had scarcely exchanged a civil word in the past month.

"I'm worried what Rulke is up to," Yggur said.

"Pity you didn't think about that when we had the chance to shut him in!"

"That's done with," said Yggur sharply. "But it's still not too late."

"We must have a weapon first," said Mendark. "The flute, if you remember."

"You can follow *that* path. He is only one man—I have armies back in Thurkad."

"He is Charon! And he has a legion of Ghâshâd."

"I have a hundred thousand troops, blooded in battle. I'll give him plenty to worry about."

"Then you don't need me," Mendark said with a thin smile.

Yggur pursed his lips as though what he was about to ask was repugnant to him. "I . . . I have no money, Mendark. I beg you, lend me gold for my journey back to Thurkad and I will repay it tenfold."

Mendark snorted. "So that you can restore your fortunes and your empire at my expense, and pay me back with my own coin?"

"I cannot deny that I hate you and will do everything in my power to bring you down," Yggur said coldly. "But back in Katazza we declared truce, if you recall, and I hold to that. I know you care, as I do, for the well-being of Santhenar ahead of your own fortunes."

"What is your plan?"

"To get back to Thurkad by the fastest way possible."

"By yourself—a blind man?" Mendark said dismissively.

"I have a little sight. Enough! Will you give me the money?"

Mendark reached inside Osseion's pack, bringing out a small pouch, not much bigger than an egg. "Very well. Take this bag of gold, one hundred tells. See that you repay me a thousand in Thurkad. And after our enemy is defeated, the truce is ended."

Yggur took the gold. "Agreed!" They clasped hands, though only for an instant.

Once on the road it was not long before they reached a sizeable town, where Yggur hired mounts and aides. The half-blind look he gave Llian before he departed was ominous. "Take care of yourself, chronicler," he said. "I won't forget you."

Llian did not answer.

"Send word to me in Thurkad," Yggur shouted, and set off for Flude at a furious pace, there to find a boat to take him home.

They watched his dust spread and fade, then went down to the café tables on the waterfront.

"We'll go to Flude in the morning," said Mendark, "and there, if Pender is true to his word, I will take ship east to Crandor and go overland to Tar Gaarn and Havissard."

"Crandor must be a beautiful country," Karan said, a little wistfully. "I'd love to see it."

"It is beautiful," Tallia agreed, "but then, so is your own land. I came through Bannador on my way back from Tullin last year. I'll visit you in the winter, if I can. You must show me every part of it."

"You will be very welcome, but don't expect too much. It's a poor, droughty place, not like your land, where I hear it rains every month of the year and the soil is ten spans deep and the apples grow as big as pumpkins."

"I think that Crandor has grown rather in the telling," laughed Tallia. "Yes, I'm going home for the first time since I left eleven years ago. I'd love to show you my country too."

"Perhaps you will some day."

"Look, Karan, there's *The Waif*!" Tallia yelled as they hobbled, bow-legged after days of riding, down to the waterfront of Flude.

At last, Karan thought. She was worn out from the months of travel, sick of everybody, even Llian and Tallia, and the knowledge that they were still two hundred leagues from home was unutterably depressing. She just wanted to be alone.

At the end of half a dozen other vessels, as freshly painted and polished as the day they had left it, stood *The Waif*. Only the sails were bleached and tattered to show how far it had been in the past months.

Karan could scarcely credit that the sour and importunate Pender she had first met in Narne could be the master of this lovely vessel. Then a fat, rough-looking sailor appeared on the deck. No one else had quite that shape, or that distinctive waddle.

"Pender!" she cried joyfully, sprinted down to the jetty and sprang right over the gangplank onto the deck.

Pender's grin nearly split his face in half. If anything he was fatter than ever, and more unkempt. Karan's arms did not nearly meet round him.

"Karan!" he yelled, dancing round the deck. "I never expected to find *you* here." They had not seen each other since leaving Thurkad at the end of endre, mid-winter week. It was past mid-summer now. "What have you been up to all this time? And just look at my boat; did you ever imagine such a beautiful creature?"

"Never," she said, sharing in his pleasure, "save that Tallia told me all about her. And, she tells me, she is a part-owner."

"One-fifth," Pender muttered glumly, for though he was fond of Tallia and would sooner have her for a partner than anyone, he would rather not share *The Waif* at all.

Tallia came up and shook hands with Pender. He looked uncomfortable, as if something was preying on his mind. When she stepped back he said abruptly, "I have the books of accounts ready, if you would care to come down and check my reckoning. But I'm afraid that there have been many unexpected expenses . . ."

"We have lost money?" cried Tallia, pretending dismay. "I did not . . ."

Pender was scornful. "Of course not! Rates are as high as the mast, with the war. Do you take me for a fool or a villain, eh? We have a profit, though barely three hundreds of percent. Hardly worth the risk in this business, but I promise the next voyage will be better."

"Hardly worth the risk," Tallia agreed cheerfully. "Well, we want to go to Crandor and come back again, as soon as you can make *The Waif* ready."

"Crandor!" cried Pender, greed wakening in his eyes. "Why, just last week someone asked me the tariff there. He nearly fell off his counting stool when I told him. We will measure our profit by the wheelbarrow load, after such a journey."

"How long to get ready?"

"She is ready now, except for water and fresh food. We could go tomorrow if you wish it. The chandlers serve their customers quickly here in Flude. Unlike some places I could mention," he said with a glint in his eye.

Tallia did not wish to be reminded of their adventures in Ganport last winter. "I don't think Mendark is in quite that much of a hurry," she said, clapping Pender on the shoulder. "Now tell me, have you been keeping an eye out for Lilis's father?"

"Ah, Lilis," sighed Pender, and Karan was surprised to see a tear in his eye. "How I miss her. I keep wondering how she's getting on. The Great Library's no place for a kid, hanging around with books and withered old book grubs."

"But it's just the place for Lilis," said Tallia. "Nadiril is a kind old man. He'll look after her. What about her father?"

Pender sighed. "I've looked at every sailor in every port I've been to, and asked in every inn too, but heard nothing at all. He was taken too long ago. Seven years, eh!" he said, shaking his head. "Pressed sailors don't have a long life. I'm sure he's dead."

21

THE RAINBOW BRIDGE

They stood at the counter of The Typhoon, the best inn in Flude, while Mendark made the financial arrangements.

"I'd like a room to myself," Karan said without thinking. Then she held her breath. Relations between her and Mendark were no more than polite at the best of times, and she expected him to point out that paupers had to take what they were offered. Her debt to others was now so huge that she had ceased to count it, but she felt it on her back every day. She longed to get away from it and from everyone. To have control of her affairs again, at last.

Mendark gave her an enquiring glance, then nodded. Llian looked hurt but she didn't have the energy to explain. Taking the offered key, she ran up the stairs to her room, locked her door and lay on the bed staring up at the ceiling. Peace at last! Blessed solitude! It felt wonderful. The only thing that could improve it would be a hot bath. Her last had been in Katazza months ago. Grabbing soap and a towel, she raced down to the bathroom before anyone else could take it.

After that she locked her door again and went back to the thoughts that had been chasing around her head for most of the journey. What talent did she have that Rulke wanted so badly, and what had Llian and Rulke done together in the Nightland? Maybe the two were related. Did Rulke know that she was triune? What was so special about triunes anyway? She didn't dare ask for fear of arousing suspicion.

After a moment's hurt feelings about the room, Llian had got used to the idea very quickly. Finding that it gave him so much more time, he began to work on his tale every spare moment. That irritated Karan too. He was so adaptable! Annoying man! Much more than she, for in spite of her feelings, she missed him day and night. Night especially.

Mendark seemed in no hurry to head east. They spent several days at The Typhoon, a large, comfortable place built massively in an old style: thick stone walls, slate roof, wide verandas and small windows which left it dark inside. The inn was raised on a little knoll five or six steps above the broad promenade that ran the length of the port. Llian's room had a large bed, a table for working and a balcony veranda outside. The weather was good, and an afternoon sea breeze moderated the summer heat.

Llian found Flude greatly to his liking, and now that Yggur was gone with his accusations and his threats, he felt a great weight lift from him. He rose each day with the dawn, not at all his usual habit, and immersed himself in his papers. From the moment he'd left Chanthed, Llian had begun to make notes of his experiences, and even before they reached Thurkad last winter he had been putting them into a framework for his tale.

He was in his element now, writing furiously all day, surrounded by his notes, enough to make another thick volume. By now every page of his journal, and a collection of scrolls and scraps of parchment, were twice or even thrice overwritten. Here in Flude he bought another journal to write in, a book of many thin pages. The cost was very high, six silver tars, and now Llian began to count with care the dwindling coin in his pouch. Into this book he entered all that had happened since Katazza, and began the first clumsy version, to be rewritten many times, that would become the third book of the *Tale of the Mirror*.

The evenings he spent carousing in the bar or on the terrace, entertaining everyone with his tales, laughing immoderately and drinking even more immoderate quantities of the resin-flavored green wine, or the strong and astringent purple, and staggering up the stairs (sometimes falling down them again) in the middle of the night. Sometimes Mendark joined him in these affairs, and seemed much younger and more carefree, almost as he had been on the road to Zile, years past. They nearly regained the companionship of that journey. Almost, but not quite; Mendark could not quite let go, and his laughter was just a trifle contrived, his gaiety a little forced. Nonetheless, Llian still looked over his shoulder sometimes, imagining Basitor creeping up behind him.

Tallia was better company. She had the knack of being at home with whoever she was with, and making them feel at home as well. Once or twice she joined Llian at the revelry, drank with him bumper for bumper, topping each ribald tale of his with one of her own. She was in the highest of spirits, for she was on her way home. But she had many preparations to make for the journey, and after the second such night, to everyone's regret, she did not come again.

The Aachim, who had gone to a different inn right across town, were morose, indifferent or absent according to their mood, and seldom came to the revels. Their circumstances had cast a pall over all, and when the gaze of the revellers fell upon Tensor sitting silently in a corner, or Selial, white-haired and thin as a bundle of sticks, all the joy fell from them.

Shand joined them on the first night, but like Karan he was withdrawn and became more so with each succeeding day. It was not that he disapproved, rather that the frivolity became less and less relevant as time went by, as he plunged deeper into remembrance of things long gone until he found himself in a place where nothing outside could reach him.

Several days after their arrival, Karan was sitting by herself, brooding, when she noticed someone consulting a calendar on the wall. She idly asked the date.

"It's the seventeenth of Thisto," said the man.

It seemed somehow significant, though Karan puzzled for some time before remembering why. Today was the anniversary of the Graduation Telling. It was a year ago today that she'd first met Llian.

She went back to her chair. Karan often sat there for hours, watching Llian tell his tales, or gazing at the sunset or the moon on the water (for the party was often held out on the veranda overlooking the quay), or the stars, or listening to the waves lapping at the quay. Since that night out on the salt with Tensor she had become more reserved. What she had done to him had shocked her deeply, as her rare fits of violence did. It was as if it had been someone else.

Karan spent her days and nights in introspection, with increasing irritation at Llian's frivolity and his loud enjoyment of life. Haunted by what Tensor had told her about herself, she delved deep into her childhood, trying to find out what her potential might have been. Other curious incidents in her early life came to mind. Her father had been a great shaper, she realized. Even Tensor had not been able to completely undo what Galliad had begun in her. And then the dreams started again.

One night she dreamed of Rulke; the next, about the Ghâshâd, who were leading her across the soaring aerial walkways of Shazmak to their master. Rulke stood spread-legged on his construct, waiting for her. He had always been waiting for her, it seemed. She was the key to his whole purpose.

Did he want her because she was a despised triune? Was that why Tensor had done his best to prevent the flowering of her talents? And had he? Had he broken her or made her? There were no answers.

So the days passed, and then suddenly Mendark was anxious to go. On the fifth morning he appeared on the promenade where Karan and Llian were breakfasting.

"We're off! Don't expect us in Thurkad before the winter to go all that way and return to Thurkad can surely take no less than four months."

"Little need for us to hurry then," said Llian, stretching his legs out luxuriously under the table.

"And remember, keep our adventures secret. Don't go blabbing them in every inn you come to." He fixed Llian with a particularly gimlet-eyed stare. "Especially you, chronicler. I know what you're like. Swear that you will keep silent, or by the powers, when I return I'll make you suffer for it."

"I swear it," Llian whispered.

They waved Mendark, Tallia, Osseion and Pender off at the pier. The Aachim remained, waiting for a boat, for those that had been there on the first night had melted away just when they wanted one.

"Soon a ship will come—tomorrow, or the next day."

So the Harbor Master kept saying. But the days went by and still no vessel had come into port. Karan began to grow impatient. At first she had enjoyed the peace, and being able to have a bath or a swim whenever she felt like it, but once her friends Tallia and Pender went, the delay began to chafe at her. She missed Tallia particularly, missed the long walks they used to take together in the early morning or the cool of night, and the shared confidences about their other worlds. Tallia's life had been so different from hers.

"You're very withdrawn lately," Shand observed the following morning, as they strolled along the beach.

"I've a lot to think about."

"What Tensor told you out on the salt?"

Karan had forgotten how perceptive Shand was. She'd not

told him anything about that night. "That, and other things. Home, mostly."

He did not question her and she volunteered no more.

The pangs of heartache for Gothryme grew ever stronger. A year had passed since she'd set out for Fiz Gorgo with Maigraith. It felt like half her life. When she left Gothryme, her estate had been in trouble after four years of drought. How much worse now, after war as well? How had her people fared in the war? How was poor old Rachis coping? Perhaps he was in his grave and she never knew it. Tears sprang to her eyes and Karan wept bitterly for all that she had left behind. The threat of Rulke meant far less to her than the fate of her own people and her home at Gothryme. Home might not be hers much longer, if she could not pay her debts.

And another need had begun to grow pressing—the little germ of a longing that had sprouted not long after she left Gothryme. The need to provide it with an heir and, just as important, someone to whom she would pass down the family Histories. How was she going to accomplish that amid all these troubles? She wanted to talk to Llian about it but a barrier had grown between them lately and she did not know how to overcome it. She was afraid, without any good reason, that he would laugh at her domestic dreams, or refuse her entirely. So she said nothing, put the dream away and busied herself in another. She must get home.

Several times she went walking with Shand, but they were only short walks now. Shand had come to some personal crisis, but whatever it was he would not talk about it.

"What's the matter with you?" she asked on what was to be the last of their morning strolls. "You seem so sad."

"I—I've a lot of things to think about," he said slowly.

"What things?"

"It's . . . something that happened a long time ago. It was the turning point of my life. I can't get over it."

"Where did it happen?"

"Oh, far from here—near *Booreah Ngurle*, the Burning

Mountain. I sometimes go there on the anniversary. I really don't want to talk about it," he said sharply.

"All right," she said, knowing his moods. The sand squeaked underfoot. "Shand?"

"Yes?" he said absently.

"I'm frightened. I keep having dreams about Rulke. Dreams that I'm helping him."

He answered vacantly, unusual for him. His mind was far away. "Dreams don't mean anything, Karan. They just reflect what you're worried about."

She walked beside him, silenced by his indifference. My dreams have always meant something. *He wants me; I'm triune*! she wanted to say, but Shand had been so remote lately that she could not bring herself to tell him that shameful secret. It was so awful that she had not even told Llian. She hoped that Tensor would take it to the grave.

The next morning she found Shand's note under her door, and all it said was, "Fare well! I will see you in Gothryme in the winter."

Karan felt abandoned. For the first time in ages she ran to Llian, seeking comfort from him. "Llian, Llian, Shand's *gone*!"

That roused even Llian from his stupor of writing and he went with Karan while she questioned the Harbor Master, the fishermen, the ostlers and anyone else who might know where Shand had gone. By the end of the day they learned that he had boarded a fishing boat in the night, but there was no way to find out his destination. Karan was desolate.

"Why did he go alone?" she cried to the empty sea. "We shared so much together. Why would he not share this with me?"

The swell surged and a wave broke over the end of the stone jetty, drenching her with spray. She leapt back; Llian opened his cloak and swept it around them both. He rested his chin on her shoulder and spoke into her ear.

"Shand has a very curious past. Who knows what he's worried about?"

"He did so much for me. Why won't he let me help him?

"He's a strange man," Llian replied. "I keep thinking about what he said to me in Tullin, before I met you. *More than once have I raged against fortune. I raved, I swore, I vowed to stop time itself, even to fling it backwards. It broke me anyway, and took away everything I cared for.*

"Have you seen how angry Mendark gets with him? He asked Shand for help several times in Katazza, but Shand would not. Who *was* he, that even Mendark would look to him for aid? Who *is* he, that he would refuse?"

Karan did not answer, though she had often pondered the same questions. A leaden overcast clogged the pores of the sky. The wind was rising, and the swell; the spray now swept head-high across the end of the jetty, smashing into their faces. She scrunched herself more tightly in Llian's arms, staring out to sea.

"Come inside," he said in her ear, but she made no move, only brushing the wet hair out of her eyes.

They remained there, not speaking, as the wind built up. Darkness came down suddenly, like a bucket of pitch poured over the sea. A lonely lantern illuminated the boards of the jetty. Then distantly, almost as in a dream, Llian heard a cry. He craned his neck, staring toward the horizon.

"Did you hear that?" he shouted over the crashing of the waves.

"It's the landlord calling us in," she said carelessly.

The fellow was running toward them, waving his arms. Llian drew her away from the rapture of the sea, which was becoming dangerous.

"Come on. Wherever Shand is, there's nothing we can do for him."

When they stepped onto the shore the landlord pointed urgently to the north. The clouds were building into a black wall rent by purple lightning. Momentarily the wind died away to just a feathery ripple across the water.

The whole foreshore was deserted now but for people fastening heavy shutters over the windows and doors. "There's a great storm coming, a typhoon," said the landlord, a big, cheerful, freckled man with two fingers missing on his right hand. "Get inside."

"*Typhoon*!" Llian repeated, as if the elements conspired against him.

"I like storms, as a rule," said Karan.

"Well, you'll be a happy woman by breakfast time, if the roof stays on. This is the season of storms."

They hurried up the steps. The door banged behind them and was bolted swiftly: top, middle and bottom. "We had three in a month last year. The third nearly washed us away, though we are constructed so strong and so high."

The storm built up slowly over the evening and the night. They seemed very far from the center of the world and, as waves of wind and driven rain beat at the shutters, very alone. The night grew cool, for all that it was summer. The landlord promised hot soup and spiced ale.

"I do hope Shand is all right," she said as they took a table by the empty fireplace.

"I wouldn't want to be out in any kind of boat in this," said Llian, "much less those cockleshell craft that came in yesterday."

The ale came first, seething from a hot poker, and in Llian's bowl the little muslin bag of spices had burst. He fished it out with a fork. Small pieces of rind and spice husks floated on the surface of the ale. A wave burst over the promenade with a roar that flung spray against the shutters.

Karan skimmed the husks off with her knife. Llian sipped the ale, his eyes meeting hers across the top of the bowl. She saw the old Llian there, her best friend in the world, for the first time in ages.

"Let's go home," she whispered, and suddenly felt terrified that he would reject her.

"Yes, let's," he said. "On the very next boat!"

"I've got to go to the Foshorn on the way, to look at the

Rainbow Bridge that once was, and say farewell to Selial. We'll go home after that. Where do you want to go?"

"Not Thurkad!" Llian said vehemently.

She shuddered. "No, Yggur will be there by now. We are between Shazmak and Thurkad," she said, meaning Gothryme. "Surely that is where it will happen. I must go *home*, to Gothryme. Will you come with me? You once promised that you would." She looked anxious.

"How long ago that seems," said Llian, thinking of that winter night when they'd camped in the hills near Narne, before the world fell to pieces. "I was another person entirely. I told you a tale."

"The tale of Jenulka and Hengist. How I loved that story—and I loved you for the way you told it." She took his strong hand, enclosing it in her fingers. "You were so gentle, so tender. That was the night I first *knew*."

The soup came. It was thin, spicy and liberal with chunks of fish, octopus and mussels, flavored by a pungent yellow herb.

"Of course I'll come to Gothryme," said Llian. "I'm looking forward to it very much."

"It won't be what you expect," she said, suddenly fretting. "It is a poor place and maybe the war has . . . There will be hard work and little else."

"Do you think I'm a rich man?" said Llian, laughing. He tipped the contents of his wallet on the table in between the plates of soup. "This is all I own in the world." He counted the silver coins with his finger. "Twenty-seven tars and a few coppers. Scarcely enough to get us to Gothryme, I'm afraid. How it has gone."

Karan was sobered. "I've nothing; not a grint. What I owe Shand already I can scarcely bear to think about. I will arrive home a bankrupt."

"There are some things I can sell," Llian admitted. "A few bits I picked up in Katazza."

"I wish I'd done the same. The only weight in my pockets is debt."

When the soup was gone they mopped the bowls with yellow bread, lingered over their ale bowls then went upstairs. The wind was still rising and the rain teemed down.

Outside her room she paused, gave him a sudden brief hug, said, "I have to pack," and banged her door in his face.

Llian scratched his head. Karan was moody, doubtless fretting about Shand out in the storm. What was the point in packing until they had a ship? But he was used to her humors by now and went slowly down the hall to his own room. He packed his bag, the work of a minute only, since he simply stuffed in everything lying on the floor, threw off his clothes, blew the lamp out and slipped into bed. The wind was singing in the eaves. The inn was silent save for the wind and the rain.

Used to going to bed after midnight, Llian could not sleep. He lay in the dark, listening to the storm sounds. The roof creaked under the wind. The rain was furious; beyond his experience. It came pouring down the chimney, pooled in the empty fireplace and flooded a filthy slurry of ash and soot out onto the floorboards.

The wind grew to a shattering scream. Something crashed against the shutters outside his window. A louder crash followed it. Llian carried his lantern across. One pane was cracked where something—a wind-hurled branch, he supposed—had broken through the shutter. He went back to bed.

His thoughts kept coming back to Rulke and Karan. Why did Rulke want her? Then he drifted into a kind of waking dream, one where he was back in the Nightland and Rulke was speaking to him, controlling him and he was bowing and smiling and saying, "Yes, perfect master."

This dream—somehow blissful, somehow menacing—was shattered by a violent noise and a thump in the chest. He woke in a daze to find himself lying on the floor in a puddle of water. The wind was louder yet, and his first thought was that the roof had blown off, then the lamp glowed beside the bed and he saw Karan's bare form outlined against the lamp. The lamp flared bright.

"What happened?" he asked with a shaky smile. His head was aching.

"You were dreaming!" she shouted, "and I didn't much like your dream."

He had no idea what she was talking about, even wondered if she had gone mad in the middle of the night. His mind did not seem to be working properly. Why was she staring at him in that way: furiously intense, suspicious, trembling? She had caught the last part of his dream, but Llian had forgotten it already and could not understand the cold horror that she felt. He did not know that his words were the very ones that the Ghâshâd had used after Rulke had wakened them through Karan's link. Was Rulke trying to reach them through Llian? But there was no answer, certainly not in his bewildered eyes.

"Stay here, stay awake," she said abruptly. Throwing a blanket about her shoulders, she ran out. Llian crawled back into bed and pulled the covers up, staring vacantly at the ceiling. It was not cold, but he felt cold and his head throbbed.

Soon Karan came back with her pack over one shoulder and her boots in the other hand. She put them down inside the door, securing it carefully. Llian was now shivering and sweating.

"I need a drink," he said hoarsely. Pouring water into a cracked mug she held it to his lips. He gulped down half the glass and fell back with a groan. Karan dipped the corner of the blanket in the water and wiped his brow.

"That's better," he said, staring at her bare shoulder. It was pale and soft and beautifully rounded. "Thank you for coming," he said softly, reaching up and touching her throat. "Please stay."

His touch sent a delicious shiver down her back. Karan shook the blanket from her other shoulder. "Of course I'll stay," she replied. "I should have known better than to take my eyes off you. Move over."

As she slid between the sheets the whole world went wild. A wind like a solid wall shook the inn to its foundations. The broken pane fell inwards, followed by a pressurized squirt of rain through the shutters.

Karan swore. "I don't like the sound—"

"I thought you liked storms!" he snapped, rolling off the bed and frantically gathering up his soaked papers. Water was dripping off the ceiling. The timbers screamed above their heads. Again water fountained through the window.

"Llian!" she shouted.

He continued his work. Knowing how precious the documents were, she ran to help him. The wailing in the roof grew louder.

"Llian!" she roared in his ear. "I think the roof's going to go. Quick, under the bed."

It was a huge, solid affair, well off the floor. They scrambled underneath. Karan reached back up, dragged the quilt off and wrapped it around them, for neither had anything on. She fastened her pack to the leg of the bed. Llian packed his journal and papers away in his capacious wallet, folded the top over and tied the strings tight, then looped it round his waist.

It was as well that he had, for a wild gust burst the window in, spraying glass and splinters across the room and saturating everything that it did not blow away. A shard of glass stabbed Llian in the foot. The lantern flickered wildly, chasing deformed shadows around the room.

He pulled out the splinter, then took Karan into his arms. They clung to each other as the wind roared higher and louder, then with an ear-piercing shriek part of the roof tore off. The lath and plaster ceiling exploded and disappeared upwards. They both screamed. The bedcovers and mattress were sucked off the bed to disappear through the hole in the ceiling, followed by every other light thing in the room. Llian could feel his hair being drawn up, and the quilt too. Suddenly he and Karan lifted together, cracking their heads on the slats of the bed. The bed moved, then the lamp was blown over, smashed and went out.

They huddled under the bare bed while a deluge poured

down on them, rain such as neither had experienced in their lives. It was miserably uncomfortable sitting in the water, for the rain was coming down faster than it could escape under the door. Every so often a few roof slates would slide in to smash on the bed frame.

Later, when the wind had died down, Llian forced the door open and wedged it, allowing a flood out along the hall and down the staircase. He went back to his perch under the bed, where Karan and he clung to each other for the remainder of the night.

By the morning the worst of the typhoon was over though it was still raining heavily. Llian's clothes had been sucked out of his pack, but Karan's had survived. Her ceiling was intact, though sagging badly.

Wearing a pair of her baggy trousers he went downstairs. The innkeeper was already cleaning up, moving food and furniture into the section of the inn that still had a roof.

"Well, we've survived another one," he said cheerfully, putting down a chair and beginning to crack eggs two at a time with his three-fingered hand. "What can we get you for breakfast?"

Llian was amazed at his good cheer. "The place is in ruins," he said.

"Oh, this happens! Nothing we can do about it. We'll have a new roof on in a week. The stove is going, there's ham and eggs and onions—and plenty of bread left over from yesterday. Sing out your order."

As he ate his breakfast, Llian sweated over the events of the night. Was he being controlled, witting or not, doing Rulke's bidding? Judging by the looks she was giving him from across the table, Karan was worried about the same things.

A few days after the storm a boat limped into port, a tramp that traded up and down the coast of Faranda. Its captain was glad of a hire to the Foshorn and beyond, so much damage had the typhoon done her. By this time Selial was just a collection of bones surmounted by a cadaverous head and white hair like straw, and so frail that she could barely walk.

As soon as the necessary repairs were done they took ship. They had good weather and reached Tikkadel in a few days. There the Aachim bade the captain wait for a week, with half-payment and offers of gold too good to refuse, then headed out into the sandhills not far from the place where they and Llian had crossed on their way to Katazza last winter.

It was a stinking day, hot and humid, and Selial in her litter had to be covered with a wetted canopy, though she was still uncomfortable and the sandflies were a continual torment.

They headed directly around the coast, walking well into the night under a waxing moon, and in a few days more stood before the astonishing chasm of the Hornrace, the black cliffs falling sheer for five hundred spans, surely the greatest gulf in all the worlds. Two stepped black pillars, almost as tall as the Great Tower of Katazza, were all that remained of the Rainbow Bridge that once spanned the strait, linking Faranda with the continent of Lauralin. They stood like sentinels in the mist belching up from the flood. Far below, the waters of two seas raced down this mighty flume, an unimaginable torrent, to cascade over the Trihorn, a waterfall split by three peaks. Down, down and down the deluge poured, cutting through rock like cheese, another thousand spans and more before flooding into the vast salt lake below.

The Trihorn Falls were the greatest on Santhenar, or on the Three Worlds for that matter, but the Dry Sea was master. The lake was a mighty lake, yet just a pond compared to the Dry Sea. Its thirst could never be quenched.

They set Selial's litter down next to the left-hand pillar. She reached up a claw to Malien, who lifted her to unsteady feet. Selial traced the salt-fretted carvings on the stone with her fingertips. Her eyes were closed. She stood in serene attention, as if the pillar sang the *Tale of the Rainbow Bridge* to her. The ranks of the Aachim, and Karan and Llian, waited silently behind her.

Finally her communion was done. "There is another Great Tale for you here, chronicler, if only you could make the stones speak. I promised to tell it to you but I cannot stay to bring it forth. Alas, it will be lost forever."

Selial lurched her way to the very edge of the gulf and swayed there. Malien gripped her elbow tightly.

"Never fear," Selial chuckled, a rusty sound. "I will not jump. This place is sacred to me." Tears ran down her cheeks. "Karan child," she said over her shoulder, "come! You too, chronicler."

They edged up to the brink, hand in hand. "Give me your hands," Selial wheezed. "I will show you a sight as has not been seen for two thousand years."

Karan took one of Selial's hands, Llian the other. "Look out over the chasm," Selial whispered, raising their hands high for a moment.

They looked, and a great whirling cloud of spray burst out of the Hornrace, obscuring everything but the two silent pillars. Then slowly out of the spray grew a glorious arch, a bridge suspended in the air like gossamer. An Aachim structure, magnificently irregular like a cobweb, and beautiful as dew on a cobweb too.

The sun came out and its golden illumination glided along the bridge from one end to the other, touching it with the colors of the rainbow like sun on a cobweb. Then the spray fell back into the chasm, making a rainbow there that arched from one end of the ghost bridge to the other, a symbol of hope out of darkness. It was the most beautiful sight that Llian had ever seen.

"Put that in your tale, chronicler," said Selial. She looked ageless, seer-like, the lines and droop of her face quite erased. "It will never be seen again on Santhenar."

They watched, gripping Selial's hands. The Rainbow Bridge lingered for a few minutes more then slowly began to fade. Suddenly another great burst of spray roared up from the Hornrace, and as it fell back it washed the bridge away like water running down a blackboard. Soon it was all gone, just the black pillars standing up out of the mist.

The hand that he held was cold. Llian looked down at Selial and saw her eyes staring sightlessly into the chasm. She was still standing, but Selial was dead. Llian wiped tears from his eyes.

The Aachim cut out living rock between the two pillars, laid Selial inside and formed the rock back into an arch over her. All night they kept vigil. Then, at the first blush of dawn, each of the Aachim spoke a threnody for her, speeding her off on her long journey into the unknown. Even Tensor, held up on either side, gave her his blessing. Malien spoke last of all. As the sun rose they departed and never came there again.

PART TWO

22

NEMESIS

Weeks went by while Maigraith studied the art of command under the best tutors the empire could provide. It was the hardest work that she had ever done, because it went against all her upbringing and training. Submission to Faelamor's will had been the last lesson every time. But Maigraith was not afraid of hard work; she threw herself into it body and soul. It was good to have a goal even if her progress toward it was imperceptible. And later, when she was forced to command for the first time, she found that, after all, it was a skill that she could learn, if not master. One that might transform her life if she spent long enough at it.

Spring passed into summer. She learned to work with Vanhe, though there was always tension between them. He was afraid that she would become uncontrollable, and she, that he just pulled her strings. But so far neither had challenged the other. The Ghâshâd, mortified by their earlier failure, had made several attempts to abduct her, though each was foiled by Vanhe's ever-watchful guard.

Slowly, after fierce fighting on the perimeters of Thurkad and other places, Vanhe's armies gained the upper hand. The rebellious regiments were overcome; four of the five armies once more did their duty. Maigraith took no part in this, except as a figurehead. It was soldier's work. Yet, strangely, the morale of the troops was as high as it had ever been. Though mostly men, they took to her as they never had to Yggur. They knew she cared.

One day she was studying Yggur's journals, trying to learn something of his strategies and his plans for dealing with the Ghâshâd, when a courier appeared in the doorway. Maigraith looked up. She had come to dread the day's couriers and the night's spies.

One part of the realm was out of control—Bannador! Rather, the Ghâshâd's control had been broken everywhere else, but for some reason they made a stand over this poor and insignificant country. Why was it so important to them? Was it because it was closest to their lair, Shazmak? That question she had not been able to answer. The Ghâshâd were seldom captured, and when they were, nothing useful could be extracted from them. Whatever the reason, Yggur's Second Army in Bannador had been totally subverted. She had to act; better sooner than later.

Maigraith felt more guilty about the suffering of Bannador than about anything she had ever held responsibility for. Of all the countries Yggur had occupied it was the least culpable—it held to its own business and never troubled its neighbors. Its misery came directly from her stealing of the Mirror. And yet if she made war there, thousands would die and the country would be ruined, even if she won. The burden of leadership lay heavily on her.

She beckoned the courier forward. He was a tall, handsome man with yellow hair and a week's growth of yellow stubble, soot-stained like his uniform. A capable young man, she had been told, who knew Bannador well. He had a smiling mouth but he did not smile in her presence. Rumor of her was dour and he wanted only to answer her questions and escape from under her gaze as quickly as possible.

"I am Dilman, lar," he said, using the honorific rather than her name. "I carry dispatches from Captain Trounse in Bannador." Saluting her, he held out the bundle of dispatches.

Maigraith did not open it. "What news from Bannador, Dilman?"

He threw back his shoulders, put on a rigid voice. "It is bad, lar! The Second Army fell on our brigade three days ago. We took heavy casualties. They now hold most of the lowlands of Bannador and threaten us in the east and the south."

"So, it is come to open conflict?"

"Yes! They wage bloody war on us and take no prisoners."

"And what is the condition of Bannador?"

"My country suffers cruelly, lar."

"How so?"

"The lowlands have been razed from Tuldis to Varp." He indicated the area on a map. "Most of the productive land of Bannador has been destroyed. They burned every crop, every home and shed, every haystack and hedge. Every beast was slaughtered or driven off. The country is a wasteland. Fifty thousand people walk the roads; children are starving."

Maigraith was shocked. Having suffered so much when she was young, she could not bear to see children mistreated. "And the highlands?"

"Not so bad—that country is very rugged."

"Why would they do this?"

"I don't know, lar," he added plaintively, for the first time showing the man inside the soldier. "My country does not even have an army."

"Where are they stationed now?"

"Here, at Casyme." He indicated the place on a map.

It was not far from Gothryme. "Why there? Does this place have any strategic importance, Vanhe?"

"None whatsoever! It's not even a particularly good place

to defend. Yet they provoke us constantly. As if they *want* us to attack."

Maigraith felt a prickle of unease, but not being used to following her intuition, she ignored it. "Do you know Karan Fyrn of Gothryme, Dilman?"

"She is mentioned in tales about the Mirror, lar, and I know her to be your friend. I've never been to Gothryme."

"Thank you, Dilman. Take food and rest; I may call on you again."

He saluted and withdrew. Maigraith read the dispatches. "This thorn must be cut out," she said to Vanhe.

"Or starved out! I am minded to blockade them until the spring. A Bannador winter will test their appetite for rebellion."

"And what about the people of Bannador?" Maigraith asked coolly.

"Many would starve," he said, "but that is the cost of war."

"Easy for you to say, since you trade in it. Bannador has done nothing to deserve this war."

Vanhe reacted as if she had blasphemed. "You let personal feelings overcome your judgment. We could lose a whole army there. Our job is to win the war."

"Your job!" she snapped. "To risk an army for so little is folly! The Ghâshâd are not cowed. Our so-called victories have just been strategic retreats by them, but they will be back with a vengeance if we stumble."

"Well, you put me here," said Maigraith coldly. "Do you now withdraw my commission?"

"I appointed you to give us a leader to rally to, not to command my armies."

"I gained a different impression from your earlier arguments," she said in a chilly voice. "Surely my performance has given me legitimacy."

"But not authority! You are no general, Maigraith, to lead an army to war."

"Neither are you, *Marshal* Vanhe." She emphasized his lowly rank.

He flushed. "I did not ask for this command," he said.

"Neither did I, if you recall!"

"Do you challenge me?"

"You forced me to learn the arts of war and command. I saved Thurkad from defeat—saved your life! Your strategy is wrong, therefore I propose my own. Do *you* challenge *me?*"

Maigraith could not read the blank face of the old soldier, but she did not need to. Just the way he stood, the muscles corded in his neck, showed the struggle he was having with himself. He had given her a form of authority and it was scarcely in him to disobey. But on the other hand, marching to war against the Second Army in Bannador was folly. She knew it as well as he did. Good soldier that he was, every one of his troops was important to him.

"You have two choices," she said softly. "Get rid of me and lead yourself, or follow me. I am immoveable."

Now the struggle showed. His square jaw was knotted; she could hear the grinding of his teeth.

She pressed him harder. "Can you lead? Do you *know* where to lead us?

"No and no," said Vanhe with a sigh. "There is . . . some merit in your plan, though it would be a terror to put into action. No, Maigraith, I do not challenge you, for I know I can do no better. If you order it I will lead an onslaught on the very gates of the void. But not without you knowing exactly what the consequences are likely to be."

"Very well," said Maigraith. "I want to be briefed tonight on options for war in Bannador. I want no drawn-out campaign. Give me bold plans; swift strikes; a strategy for quick victory. And all in total secrecy."

"It will be done," said Vanhe, bowing lower than usual.

The following night all roads out of Thurkad were sealed, all bridges guarded and every ford watched, to make sure that the word did not get out. The majority of the First Army moved out before dawn and proceeded, some fourteen thousand troops, by forced marches down the Feddil Road to Bannador, holding all bridges and fords as they went.

Dilman had spoken truly. Bannador was a ruined land. It made Maigraith sick to see it. Why? she kept asking. Why would they do this? What could they hope to gain? On the sixth night Maigraith rode ahead with Vanhe and three of his lieutenants. The following day they were to camp the best part of a league from the Second Army, whose encampment was in a long valley protected by a knife-edged range of slate. Dilman was their guide. He led them up the ridge through a patch of burnt forest to a lookout, where they waited for the dawn.

The sun sprang up, a huge globe, blood-red through the smoke that hung everywhere in the skies of Bannador. It was going to be another scorching day.

"Is this the whole of the Second Army?" asked Maigraith, looking down at the enemy camp, which occupied the lower part of the valley, near the river. Her face was soot-stained. There was ash in her hair.

"No, but it's the best part of it."

"How far are we from Gothryme?"

"Less than a day's march that way." He pointed north, where a rugged arm of the mountains projected east.

So close. Was there a reason for it? "Well, we'll attack at four in the morning, over the ridge."

"No!" cried Vanhe beside her. "Look at their defenses—trenches, palisades, pits and traps. We'll never get through in the dark. And if we do, we'll spend the night killing each other."

"We'd never get through in daylight," said Maigraith. "Word will have reached them by then. Our only chance is to come up over the ridge here, split into two and head down there and there. We'll attack up the road from both sides at once, just before dawn."

"Up the road! They'll cut us down in our ranks."

"I'll make a *deception* to get us to the gates undetected," she said with more confidence than she felt. Such a massive working would have been difficult even if they were not going against the Ghâshâd. "They won't expect that. Look how slack the guards on the gate are." She passed him the field glasses.

"Too slack for guards under the command of the Ghâshâd! Anyway, our troops won't reach camp until this afternoon. You can't do forced marches, push them up over the mountain in the dark and expect them to fight the next day."

"We have the advantage, but it can't last. Surprise is our only chance. *Let it be done!*"

"I will carry out your orders," Vanhe said in a dead voice. "So what *are* you doing about the Ghâshâd? I've heard it said that they can *sense* their enemies."

"I'm working on that too," said Maigraith.

Once they had the layout of the camp fixed in their minds Vanhe and his lieutenants went back to make ready for war. Maigraith, Dilman and her guard remained where they were. Sweat made tracks down her sooty face. One failure and the First Army would be destroyed. And if she succeeded, what would be the fate of the rebels? Why had the Ghâshâd wrought such havoc anyway? What was the point of this rebellion, here of all places? That she could not understand.

But her most crucial problem was how to nullify the Ghâshâd. Some of them were sensitive, together if not separately. If they sensed her the battle plan could not succeed.

She spent all morning staring down at the camp, but whatever the enemy were doing she was blind to it. If only I had a sensitive, she thought unguardedly, but that only reminded her how badly she had treated Karan.

Dilman cleared his throat behind her. "Time to go, lar!"

Yes, time had run out and she knew nothing more than she had the previous day. She went back down to the camp, where her soldiers were already marching in, and the smart salutes of her troops, the whispers behind her back about her strange powers, the boasts of a quick victory tomorrow, were gall in her mouth. She was a facade, an empty shell that the

Ghâshâd would blow apart, and these poor fools would die for it.

Maigraith spent all afternoon and evening trying to design a glamour that would conceal the front ranks of her troops so that they could reach the gates undetected. She had considered every form of the Secret Art that she had any capacity for. Illusion had been her first thought—literally painting pictures in the air to conceal the marching troops. It was probably her best chance, and the darkness would help even though there was a bright moon. But an illusion to conceal an army, from so many of the enemy, would probably be beyond her.

Mesmerism and forms of mass hypnosis she quickly rejected. Such things could not be done from a distance, and in any case Maigraith was not confident that she had the ability. Her lack of empathy with other people was a fatal handicap.

Another option was physical concealment, such as by bringing down fog or mist. But to create mist on a hot summer's night in this drought-stricken land would be difficult. "Where's the nearest water?" she whispered to Dilman after midnight.

"Half a league away, just by their camp."

"Can you take me there?"

"No, lar, I can't. They've got scouts all along the river. Is it important?"

"No," she said, "just one of a few ideas I'm working on." She did not want to alarm him by revealing just how empty her armory was.

"There used to be springs at the bottom of this ridge," he said. "Though they may have dried up in the drought."

"See if you can find one," she whispered.

Time ran out without Dilman returning. She'd have to use illusion after all. Climbing a tree, Maigraith sat in the fork staring down at the road and the enemy camp. Shortly Vanhe appeared, looking up anxiously. "Are you ready?"

"Another few minutes," she said, pretending confidence

that she did not feel. Her preparations had been wasted so far. The best illusion she could do now was also the simplest, just an image of mist on the road. But if the guards wondered at mist on a hot summer's night, if they disbelieved, it would vanish.

"Time to go," said Vanhe, a few minutes later. "Ready?"

She wasn't, but she'd have to be.

It was four in the morning. The night was cloudy, though the moon gave enough light to see the road. The First Army assembled on the brow of the ridge in their two separate wings. Vanhe addressed his lieutenants.

"Go quietly," said the marshal, looking haggard, "until the alarm is raised. Then rush the gates. The quicker you are the easier it will be. Once you're inside I'll send up rockets to light your way."

Maigraith released her illusion. The first ten ranks of soldiers faded to a silvery blur, a file of marching ghosts in the moonlight. A whisper of amazement passed through the army.

"I feel better now," said Vanhe, mopping his brow, surprised though he had known what she was going to attempt. "It's worth half a night's sleep to their morale. Send them out!"

His officers ran to their posts. The two wings began to move.

Let it last, Maigraith prayed. If only it does not break on the Ghâshâd's defenses. But she had a horrible feeling the illusion was not going to last. Something kept interfering, and no matter what she tried she could not overcome it. There seemed to be a shield around the camp. Even this far away it was hurting her. What would it be like at the gates?

Dilman appeared out of darkness. "I found a spring," he whispered. "Not far from here."

"Take me there!" she snapped, feeling the illusion weakening already.

Dilman led her down the hill to a tiny seep coming from

the base of a ledge. A depression in stone held about as much water as a large washbasin. How much fog will that make? she thought, dismayed. Better than none, I suppose! Holding the spell in her mind, she plunged her clenched fists into the basin. A little patch of mist formed in the center. *Hurry. It's nearly too late!*

She concentrated harder, until the mist boiled up around her wrists and spilled over the edge of the depression. Maigraith whipped her arms out. The mist began to pour down the gully.

Climbing onto a pinnacle where she could see the road, she saw her soldiers just coming out of the scrub. To her left the mist shone silver in the moonlight, now splitting to take different paths downslope. Maigraith's head was aching from the strain of nudging her little pools of mist toward the camp. It kept running down the wrong gullies. Weatherworking was a difficult art—no mind could control something so complex.

At last it reached the road near the main gate of the camp, reduced to a few wispy patches drifting with the breeze. Leaving it, she turned her attention back to the two marching columns, which were approaching the road at either end of the camp. Her illusion was fading, the soldiers beginning to appear. She let it go this side of the camp, where her mist was, and put all her effort into holding the other side.

Those soldiers were still some distance from the gates when a roar came from the camp. They had been spotted. Below her the mist was evaporating into the warm air. The moonlit blur on the road suddenly resolved into a column of marching soldiers. They were still fifty paces from the gate. A bell began to clang furiously. Her troops surged forward and were soon involved in bitter fighting.

At the same instant Maigraith was flung backwards off her perch. The illusion had been savagely broken. She lay on the ground in a daze.

"Lar? Lar? Maigraith-lar!" It was Dilman, shaking her. "Lar? Are you all right?" He was practically in tears.

Maigraith groaned. He lifted her to her feet.

"Lar, we need you desperately." His voice positively dripped defeat.

Maigraith realized that she was freezing, shuddering with cold for all that it was a warm night. How long had she lain here? "Don't give up, Dilman," she said with a lying smile. "I haven't begun to fight yet."

They ran for the camp. Dilman had to keep stopping for her, and finally took her on his shoulders for the last dash.

Carnage at the gates, so horrible that she could not bear to look at it. Hundreds lay dead within the sweep of her glance. She had ordered it.

"Come on!" Dilman screeched, dragging her past the hacked corpses.

The Second Army fought as if possessed and, Maigraith realized, probably was. How right Vanhe had been; how quickly her inexperience had been shown up. She had marched as hard as any, and with less rest. By now she was incapable of thinking straight. Her soldiers must be the same.

Flares and rockets went up, lighting their path. One or two fell into the middle of the camp, setting a tent blazing. It was moot whether this advantaged them more than the enemy, though her soldiers did seem to be heartened by the light.

But Maigraith was not. She had blundered and her troops were dying by the score. She had underestimated the Ghâshâd. Their will supported these puppet soldiers and weakened hers. They were the key. If she could not break them the First Army was finished.

She sorted through her recollections of the camp layout, trying to work out where the Ghâshâd would be. It was beginning to get light. She staggered along the rows of tents, through a chaos of running people, burning tents and hand-to-hand fighting. A straggle of her soldiers ran past, weaponless, fleeing back toward the gate. Another band followed, running before the enemy. Maigraith attempted a concealing illusion but it failed utterly.

A tall man with a sword ran straight at her. She gestured in the air, a spell that outside the camp would have had his feet out from under him, but it did not even make him pause. Lurching out of the way of his weapon, she hurried toward the center of the camp. He went after one of her fleeing soldiers, cutting the unfortunate fellow down with one hack.

Maigraith ran around a corner, straight into a battlefield strewn with dead and dying, most of them her own. One of the enemy lay on the bloody grass right in front of her.

Panting, she went to her knees beside him. "Where is the tent of the Ghâshâd?"

The fellow was weeping with pain, mortally wounded. The front of his jerkin was saturated in blood. Putting her hands on his head she lifted the pain from him, a terrible wrench that she would suffer from later.

"Where?" Maigraith screamed in his face.

He raised his hand. "Three rows!" He pointed to the left, "The gray one," and flopped down dead.

Maigraith sprinted down the rows. The wounds Thyllan had given her months ago, shoulder and side, throbbed with each footfall. A great clot of her troops ran the other way. They, too, had abandoned their weapons. The enemy was pushing them back, showing no concern for their own lives. She could feel horror swelling inside her at her folly; she had sent the entire army to their deaths.

There, the gray tent! Shadows moved inside it. No time to think. Maigraith burst in through the flap. Eight Ghâshâd sat on benches in a square, four men and four women, while a fifth woman stood inside the square at a table. They were as alike as clones; she recognized none of them. They were concentrating so hard that she had a few moments before they could react.

A gray board marked with blue and yellow squares covered most of the table. It was scattered with clusters of counters that appeared to represent units of the Second Army, gray, and Maigraith's own, green. As she watched, the woman at the table put out her hand and with evident strain knocked two of the green counters off the board with her gray one. A great roar came from somewhere outside. Maigraith's head exploded.

She moaned involuntarily. All their eyes snapped toward her. She felt so dizzy that she could barely stand up, and fumes of sickness began to cloud her senses. There came a stab in her chest, like a sword thrust—the mortal pain that she had lifted from the man outside. She felt herself slipping into unconsciousness. The battle was lost. All was lost!

23

THE WISE WOMAN

Yggur did not have a good trip back from Faranda. After leaving the company he rode south as fast as his meager sight would let him. He felt overwhelming relief at being rid of Mendark's oppressive presence, and a longing for Maigraith that grew stronger every day. At Flude he hired two attendants and took ship immediately, but the vessel turned out to be a slow, rotten, rat-infested hulk that rolled in the slightest sea. Normally a good sailor, he was seasick for most of the voyage.

Somewhere near Siftah they were chased by pirates, only the weather saving them. Then, as they sailed south down the Sea of Thurkad, dysentery spread through the ship, cramping their bellies and turning their bowels to water. The boat drifted for days, no sailors being well enough to man the masts. The drinking water went a stinking green and one of the casks of salt pork, when they opened it, was a heaving mess of maggots.

The crew knew who to blame for their ill-fortune. The

tall, scowling stranger, the half-crippled blind man they had taken on board at Flude. Rumor said that he was a sorcerer. The luck of this voyage proved it.

One morning Yggur was woken by a disabling blow to the kidneys. It was bad luck to kill a sorcerer, but his hands were bound and he was cast into a dinghy with his hapless attendants. The dinghy, without oars or food, or even water, was pushed off and the boat sailed away.

The attendants untied each other but left him bound. He could not find within him any power to defend himself or even loosen his bonds. They drifted for a day and a night, then next morning Yggur was woken by the sound of breaking waves. They were drifting along a barren, rocky shore. The attendants robbed him of his gold and slipped over the side.

Yggur furiously rubbed his bonds against the thwarts, but the thick rope was still intact an hour later as the dinghy was driven sideways onto the rocks. It overturned. He was flung at the barnacle-covered outcrops, pulled out to sea by the surge then driven back onto the rocks again.

By sheerest luck the succeeding waves were small ones, allowing him to crawl above the breakers. After sawing through his ropes on the broken edge of an oyster shell he staggered across the rocks until he came to a village.

Yggur lurched up to what appeared to be the hut of the village headwoman. She was no more than an outline through his sunburned, salt-crusted eyelids.

"Will you help me?" he gasped. His limbs and body were bloody from a hundred barnacle wounds.

"How may we serve you?" she said in a rather young voice for a wise woman, for such he deduced her to be.

"I need passage to Thurkad," he said.

"You won't find it here."

"Then take me where I can. Please."

"That would cost all of five silver tars," she said, as if she were asking for half the wealth of the world.

He couldn't bear to beg. "I haven't a grint with me, but in Thurkad . . . I am Yggur!" he cried.

After a pause the woman said, "I understand that you are a man of your word. You may send back the coin or . . . there may be other ways to repay me."

Shortly he had been stripped of his tattered clothes, fed a bowl of sea-urchin chowder and his wounds treated with a purple, stinging tincture. He slept in the headwoman's own hut, the greatest honor they could give him, though he lacked the strength to do her the honor she plainly wished for in return. While he slept she had what she wanted from him anyway.

In the morning his garments were returned, repaired and smelling of smoke, for they had been dried over the fire. The wise woman, her prestige now immeasurably enhanced, hand-fed him pickled fish organs. They tasted even worse than they looked. When he was done she bowed, the smiling villagers helped him into a canoe and he was paddled out to sea. A day later he landed at Ganport and immediately boarded a vessel heading for Thurkad. Such kindness, he thought, and they are not even my subjects. They will be well rewarded.

Only when he was landed in Thurkad did Yggur allow himself to think about Maigraith. He'd heard about her humiliation of Thyllan a dozen times already. He would raise Vanhe to general, even commander-in-chief.

On the wharf a ragged street urchin came hobbling up to him, elbowing half a dozen competitors out of the way. His dirty feet were battered, scabbed and covered in running sores. "May I guide you, sir? Please, sir."

"Take me to the military headquarters, boy," he said. "And be quick about it." He was desperate for Maigraith now. He would not shrink from her bed tonight.

As Yggur followed the limping boy, he reminded himself of all the good things about Maigraith—her compassion for his pain; the clumsy way she'd approached him, had drawn him out of himself. It must have been very hard for her.

If only she'd kept her glasses on. If only he'd not looked into her eyes and seen Rulke there. That had undermined him. Mortified, he realized that he'd shrunk from her like a schoolboy from the headmaster's cane. But the barbs Rulke had left in his psyche were gone now and Yggur understood his folly. He had wallowed in terror like a princess bathing in milk; had even taken a kind of masochistic pleasure from it. *No more!* How different things were going to be between them now.

Yggur suddenly felt immensely strong. Back in his own realm with his armies around him, he could no longer imagine why he'd been so afraid of Mendark, or of Rulke. Even his eyesight seemed a little clearer. The first person he met as he limped up the steps of the citadel was the messenger girl, Dolodha, though it wasn't until she spoke that he recognized her.

"Master!" she gasped. Then she shouted out. "The master has come back! Lord Yggur has returned." She fell to her knees before him.

Yggur lifted her to her feet. "Dolodha!" he said. "Faithful servant. I am almost blind. Pay this boy then bring me your indenture. From this moment you are free!"

"Free," she whispered. "But how will I live?"

"You will serve me as adjutant, for one silver tar a week," he said with the utmost good cheer.

"One silver tar!" she exclaimed, as if he had offered a bucket of gold.

"You want more? Then you shall have it. Two silver tars! Now run for your indenture. Scribe," he roared. "Write Dolodha's commission as adjutant. Where's Zareth?"

Zareth the Hlune was found and dispatched back to the village with a bag of silver. Dolodha reappeared. Her indenture was canceled with a row of official stamps and seals, her commission duly drawn up.

"Now, where's Maigraith?" Yggur cried to his adjutant. "Take me to her at once."

Dolodha looked uneasy. "She is in Bannador, master."

"Bannador!"

"She led the First Army to Casyme to fight the Ghâshâd."

"What?" he roared. "When?"

"Five days ago."

As she explained, Yggur felt his heart clutched in a vice, and it squeezed harder every second. To take an army into the wilds of Bannador, against an army just as strong, already dug in, and under the control of the Ghâshâd, was sheer idiocy. Suicide! Maigraith was doomed.

"Who allowed this stupidity?" he raged. "I'll break them. I'll sell them into slavery."

"It was Marshal Vanhe," quavered the adjutant. "Your generals are dead—"

"Vanhe! I'll crucify him! Get my horse ready. We leave for Bannador within the hour."

Such was his fury that the escort was ready to leave before that. They raced south-west down the Feddil Road toward Tuldis.

The army's path was easily followed. At every stop Dolodha leapt off her horse and ran, still in her ill-fitting robes and flapping sandals, to find out how long since the troops had passed that way.

They did not stop day or night, though they changed horses in the afternoon and again in the middle of the night. That was at the city of Muncyte, a steamy, mosquito-ridden place on the floodplain of the Plendur River. All the buildings were up on stilts but still the city flooded every year. On they raced, by gloomy Faidon Forest that ran down to the northern border of Bannador. Reaching dusty Radomin town the following afternoon, they took fresh horses and hurtled on. Yggur's mood became fouler and fouler. He could almost smell the blood.

The sun rose. Dolodha was nearly falling out of the saddle with weariness. She looked like an abandoned waif. He moved his horse closer, holding her upright, surprised that he cared enough to do so. Maigraith had changed him.

The dawn sky was blood-red. There was smoke everywhere, charred ruins and burned animals. The horses were reduced to a plod. "How far to go?" he yelled to the guide as they turned off the main road onto a rutted track that seemed to wind around every hill in Bannador.

"At least eight leagues. Another day, unless we can find fresh horses."

They continued, now in the wilds of Bannador, but found not a single nag all the way. The country had been stripped clean. Yggur was terrified that the army had been destroyed; that Maigraith was already dead.

Maigraith struggled against the dizziness. The fate of the army hung over a precipice and only she could save it. The Ghâshâd did not movc. She sensed that they could not and still maintain *the square*—their control. She stared into the eyes of the woman in the center of the square, pressing with her will, feeling the woman's will and the wills of the other eight opposing her. Maigraith's head was shrieking now.

Don't give up! You can do it. You must! She had overcome them before and surely could again. She allowed the fury to grow in her until it burst out in an explosion of rage that turned the eyes of the woman in the center in on herself. The Ghâshâd gasped, weakened momentarily, then Maigraith leapt in amongst them, kicking out with both feet.

The table toppled, knocking down the two people on the far side. Counters flew everywhere. The woman who had moved them put her hands to her temples and screamed. Another Ghâshâd staggered to his feet, to fall across the overturned table. He tried to claw his way up again but Maigraith knocked him down, seized the board and, swinging it in front of her, cleared the way to the door. Outside she broke the hinges and sent the two halves of the board spinning into an open latrine.

Another roar came from just out of sight. Too late! she thought. The army is beaten; I am too. The Ghâshâd from the tent were just behind her. She could feel the pulse of their will beating against her, sapping her own, now badly weakened by the exploding aftersickness. She tripped over a body and then they were on her, their rubbery fingers sending thrills of disgust up her spine.

"At last!" cried a wrinkled Ghâshâd woman, as if her life's dream had just been fulfilled. Lying with her face pressed into the dust, Maigraith suddenly realized what the summer's campaign had really been about. Her! All this misery and destruction had been to draw her away from her guards, to take her back for Rulke. She had fallen into the trap so easily.

From the corner of her eye she saw someone descending into the latrine. In a few minutes the board would be restored, the square controlling the battle once more. She had created a disaster of her own, far worse than if she had done nothing.

Five Ghâshâd made a wall in front of Maigraith, while two others seized her head and feet and began to carry her away. Maigraith groaned helplessly, too weak to help herself. What a fool she'd been, pretending to go to war in the name of good. She was as culpable as any other warmonger, but more foolish.

They hurried her around a tent, then suddenly dropped her on her back and stood there—frozen-faced. Maigraith turned her head. At least a hundred of her troops surrounded them and more were running up.

"Put down your weapons," shouted one of her officers.

One of the Ghâshâd screamed, a cry of shame and frustration, then threw herself at the soldiers. She fell instantly. Someone wailed. Above Maigraith a knife flashed in the early-morning sun. She watched it helplessly. Another cried "No!" and as the knife stabbed at her breast he flung himself under it. It plunged right through him front to back, pricking into Maigraith's breastbone.

The fellow with the knife rocked back on his heels.

"We swore," said the second to the first, coughed up blood and died.

"I don't understand," said her officer, as the desperate Ghâshâd were led away.

Maigraith rolled over and with an effort climbed to hands and knees. Her clothes were saturated. "They swore to Rulke that they would protect me with their lives," she said, and fell down again.

Her soldiers heaved her up with a triumphant roar. The battle was won; Bannador would soon be liberated, though the cost was too high for Maigraith to take any pleasure from her miraculous achievement.

More soldiers appeared. "Maigraith," gasped an ecstatic Vanhe, holding her hand. "I had not thought it possible. You are a truly great commander! Yggur himself could have done no better today."

Maigraith said nothing. The truth hurt almost as much as the aftersickness. Yggur would never have attempted such a folly, she thought. He would have starved the army and all of Bannador first. Then she fell into the dark.

Vanhe appeared at her tent that afternoon, where Maigraith lay sick and sore in the slanting sun. Her illness was worse, and becoming worse yet.

"I've brought the punishment charter for your approval."

Punishment charter? She could hardly think.

"The Second Army rebelled and warred on their own comrades," he explained. "The guilty must be punished and an example set."

"Read it!" She waved a limp hand.

"The Second Army is to be disbanded and its standard broken; all badges of office and honor stripped and bespoiled; its charter burned."

"Yes," she said. "An example must be set."

"Every officer is to be slain in front of the assembled army, and every eighth soldier too."

"No!" said Maigraith, sitting up despite the pain.

He continued: stolid, inexorable. "All their titles and the goods of their families, up to the second cousin, are forfeit and the families sold into slavery. Every remaining soldier is to be sold into slavery and their families prohibited from title or public office for a generation."

"That's barbaric! I will not sign such a charter." She felt sick at the thought.

"Such is the punishment set out for rebellion," said Vanhe. "The Articles of War are read to the army at all parades; each soldier can recite them by heart. For turning on their own, they are lucky that every one of them is not stoned to death."

"Yggur wrote these Articles?" Maigraith asked, forced to confront unpleasant realities that she had long skirted around.

"He did, and has enforced them more than once. That is the way of war."

"But they were subverted by the Ghâshâd," Maigraith pleaded. "They had no free will."

"My army did not rebel," said Vanhe grimly. "It must be done."

She felt nauseated to think that she had given herself to such a monster as Yggur, a man who cared nothing for the lives of ordinary people. "I can't—" cried Maigraith. Her head felt ready to burst open.

"No matter," said Vanhe. "Sleep on it. I will come back in the morning." He bowed and withdrew.

That was one of her worst nights, and by the time Maigraith finally found sleep she had convinced herself to abandon her army. She would not be responsible for such a crime, far worse than the war. If this was the price of maintaining Yggur's empire it was too high. She would have no part of it, *nor of him either!*

But if she did, what was she to do with herself? If she gave all this away, there would be nothing left of her life.

At midnight the whole world turned upside down again.

Maigraith slept, her long chestnut hair spread across the cream fabric of the pillow. She lay on her good side, for her shoulder had been hurt again in the battle.

Faelamor stepped softly into the tent and stood watching

her. Maigraith stirred, thinking that Vanhe wished to press her further, though it was not his custom to come this late. He was punctilious about the proper courtesies. Her guards would not have let anyone else through, but they could not stop this visitor. Slowly the sleep cleared.

"Faelamor!" The familiar anxiety rose in her. "Where have you been all this time?"

"The gate took me to Katazza, in the middle of the Dry Sea. That is where Tensor went to try his mad tricks."

"How did you get back?"

"Through the gate, though it did not go where I expected. Perhaps that was Rulke's doing."

"Has Yggur come back too?" Maigraith asked apprehensively.

Faelamor mistook her expression for anxiety about him. "When I last saw him he was writhing under Rulke's hand. I imagine he is dead."

"Oh, surely not!" said Maigraith. For all his faults, for all her earlier resolutions, she wished Yggur no harm.

"That fool Tensor broke open the Nightland and let Rulke out. He overcame Yggur in an instant." Faelamor showed no pity, no sympathy, but Maigraith would not have expected that of her.

"Rulke!" Maigraith felt a surge of excitement. "He has been here already. He was terrible in his strength. Poor Yggur; he feared him so."

"Rulke here?" Faelamor was shocked.

"Not *here*—Thurkad. Months ago. Just after Yggur went through the gate."

Yggur dead? It did not occur to her that Faelamor might not know how it had ended, or that she might even lie. If Yggur *was* dead, what was the point of being here at all?

Faelamor gave her a moment to grieve while she thought. She was terrified of Rulke. He'd had so much time to set his plan in motion, yet she had scarcely begun her own. She had to act now. She needed Maigraith more than ever now and this might be her only opportunity. She could afford to be gentle.

"Your lover is surely dead," she said, but kindly this time. "There is nothing more for you here. Why do you cling to these foreigners? Let them fight this war if they must. They love their wars, these old humans, but when it is over nothing will have changed. I am going away now and will never return. Our time is near, the moment that I've worked toward all the long centuries of our exile. There is nothing here for you either." She went to her knees, speaking humbly. "Come with me. I need you, Maigraith."

Maigraith was bemused and off her guard. *She needs me!* Never before had Faelamor said that; it had always been duty. But then, Faelamor's emotions were malleable; always ready to serve her need.

"You say *you* need me, and Vanhe said that *they* needed me. I had to believe that Yggur's work was worthy, else how could I ever have cleaved to him? I should stay here. Here they want me for what I can do for them—I know that! Yet Vanhe has treated me with courtesy. Always you disparaged and humiliated me, made me to be of little worth. What do I care whether the Faellem return to Tallallame or not? They spurned me all my life. I will not go with you!"

"Outside there is talk of death or slavery for the entire Second Army. Did you sign that warrant?"

"No," Maigraith whispered, staring up at her.

"That is all they want you for, now that you have given them back everything they lost. To legitimise revenge and murder a thousand times over. How long will it take to erase that from your conscience? I never treated you *that* cruelly. Once it is done they will be rid of you too."

Faelamor came closer. She looked very controlled, very beautiful. Her eyes were golden in the lamplight. Maigraith had forgotten the compulsion put on her long months ago in the swamps of Orist, and did not think to put up her guard. She leaned away, but there was nowhere to retreat to. All her life and training had been a preparation against this need and nothing would prevent Faelamor from taking her.

The compulsion rewoke with the touch. Maigraith could not dredge up the strengths that had enabled her to defeat Thyllan; that had allowed her to command and to be obeyed. They were lost somewhere deep inside her.

"I beg you, please come," Faelamor said. "Indeed I treated you badly; one of my many crimes. But that is past now and the time you have been trained for is here. Despite everything, I tell no lie when I say that I care for you like a daughter. I have great need of you. Dress yourself. Here is a bag. Gather your clothes and precious things—I will help you."

Maigraith saw a tear in Faelamor's eye. You don't have to go that far, she thought cynically. There was little here that was truly Maigraith's, only her clothes and a gift from Yggur, an ivory bangle, so old that it was quite yellow and the original carving worn away to traces. It appealed to her because of its antiquity and simplicity. She slipped it on her wrist beside the ebony one that her unknown mother had given her at birth. Ebony and ivory—linked symbols of the two phases of her life, in a way.

Dressing took only minutes, for all that she was in a daze: part rebellious, part on-edge, but wholly unable to resist. Soon her bag was full. Faelamor looked around the tent, gathering one or two items of clothing that had been forgotten. Maigraith still stood beside the bed, cradling a journal in her arms, her log of the daily affairs of the army. Tears ran down the cover.

"That is precious? Then bring it, if it comforts you."

"It's over," Maigraith whispered, laying it down again.

Taking one arm, Faelamor drew her outside. Maigraith's troops were everywhere, but the glamour, or other form of illusion that Faelamor used, was so perfect that no one noted their going.

They passed by a tent where soldiers were reeling about, drunk with wine and with their great victory. More than once

Maigraith heard her name mentioned, and always they praised her in voices tinged with awe. Then they went between two hospital tents, and in one a soldier screamed while three people held him down and another sawed off a mangled leg. She peered in through the flap, recognizing the yellow hair. It was Dilman, her faithful guide, his handsome face twisted into a mask of agony. I did that, Maigraith thought. What's going to happen to him? She tried to go to him but the compulsion would not allow her.

"Come on," said Faelamor.

Dawn was breaking by the time they were out of the valley. They slipped into the forest and vanished, heading north.

After riding non-stop for three days, Yggur was slumped in his saddle. Dolodha was tied to her saddle horn, the horse pacing slowly on. Suddenly they rode out of a clot of smoke into a guard post. The sun was rising.

"Name yourselves," shouted the guard, a bandy-legged man with a gray bandage around his head. He wore the uniform of the First Army.

Dolodha roused. "Lord Yggur comes. Who are you?"

"Lord!" cried the guard, saluting. "A great victory."

"Where's Maigraith?" snapped Yggur.

"Resting in the command tent," said the guard, and his face lit up at her name. "That way!"

Turning away from the worship in his eyes, Yggur ran all the way to her tent. He tore open the flap. His eyesight could just make out a lantern flickering in the last of its oil. "Is she here, adjutant?"

He knew the answer, though. The tent was empty. A spasm passed through him. Maigraith was frugal; she would never have left a lantern burning in daylight.

"Where is she?" he roared.

No one had seen her. "Adjutant!"

Dolodha snapped to attention.

"Find her!"

She soon came running back. "She's gone from the camp. We found prints heading south, but no one saw her go."

Yggur went over the tent again. His eyesight told him no more but this time he smelt something familiar, a trace of Faelamor. "Send Private Vanhe to me," he roared.

"You mean Marshal Vanhe?" Dolodha said nervously.

"Adjutant Dolodha, or *slave?*" he said in a deadly voice.

She ran.

Maigraith was gone and no one had the faintest idea where. But Yggur knew, and knew that it was ended too. She had grown beyond him; he would never get her back. The pain was unbearable and there was only one way that he could think of to deal with it. He made himself into a machine, utterly devoid of compassion or human feeling.

He limped out of the tent, grim of face, and his first act was to strip Vanhe of his rank. His second: he signed the death warrants. By sunset the Second Army was no more.

24

A Feast of Bamundi

After laying Selial to rest at the foot of the Rainbow Bridge, Karan and Llian had a rough journey across the sea, beating constantly into westerly winds in their wallowing old tub of a boat. The Aachim were unwontedly reserved, as was Karan. Hardly a word was spoken on the haul back to the boat or the trip across the sea to Meldorin.

Suddenly the long gray shore of Thripsi appeared above the white-feathered waves and Karan woke from her sightless contemplation of the distance to realize that Malien was talking to her.

"What's that?" Karan asked dreamily.

"I said, " 'Where do you want to go now?' " We're sailing west from here, to the Great Library."

"Why there?" Karan had assumed that the Aachim were going back to Thurkad. This raised all sorts of problems, not least how she and Llian were going to get to Gothryme.

"Private business."

"I'm going home," said Karan. "Better land us at the nearest port—Siftah, I think it's called."

"Will you sail to Thurkad?" Malien asked as they went forward to speak to the captain.

"Yggur's there!" Karan exclaimed. "I'm afraid, Malien. Afraid for Llian, and for myself too—Gothryme is the closest place to Shazmak. Rulke might be there already. I don't know what to do."

"Have you had any more dreams?"

"Not lately."

"Well, whatever your troubles, it's better to suffer them under your own roof. But go secretly, by the back roads."

"I will. What are your plans after Zile, Malien?"

"I don't know yet. My heart calls me east, to *my* home, but I daren't go until the business is finished. We've no home in Meldorin any longer."

"Why don't you come to Gothryme? You'll always be welcome in my house, though I don't know how it has survived the war."

"Thank you," said Malien, "perhaps we will, though we've much to do first."

The boat turned onto a new heading that made it wallow uncomfortably, then the two strolled back to where Llian sat in the shade of the sail, hunched over his journal. Their paired shadows fell on him from behind. Llian started up with a muffled cry.

"What's the matter?" said Malien.

"I—thought you were someone else."

We can't be off this boat soon enough, Karan thought. Just me and Llian, and no more troubles.

The following day they approached the fishing town of Siftah, on the north-eastern corner of Meldorin. The hill slopes were clad in herbs, heath and aromatic rosemary, a gray and silver mass that stirred in the breeze. On that hot afternoon they could smell it as soon as they rounded the point.

"I remember this place," said Llian as they sailed up a winding inlet. To left and right rose steep hills of barren conglomerate, brown cobbles sticking out of a yellow matrix like balls of chocolate in a biscuit. "The fisherfolk here are tremendous drinkers."

"I imagine that suited you pretty well," she smiled.

"Not then. I was too worn out. I went to sleep under the table. And a couple of days later the survivors of Shazmak appeared. I lived in fear of my life after that."

Karan looked up to see Basitor staring down at them from beside the wheel-house. Though he had not caused any trouble since the Dry Sea, his presence was a constant reminder of it. She put her arm around Llian, protectively. "It'll soon be over. We're going home."

Siftah was a pretty town, a few hundred whitewashed buildings set on a steep hill that curved around the end of the estuary like an amphitheater, and twenty or thirty fishing boats, most of very rustic design.

Karan and Llian disembarked and said their goodbyes on the wharf. The Aachim waved, all but one, then the boat slipped away. They headed up the street to buy supplies for the long trek south.

"That's that then," Karan said. "We're alone at last."

"At last!" Llian agreed. "I don't have to look over my shoulder anymore."

Karan did just that, then smiled. "Hello," she said, squinting at the fishing vessels anchored on the other side of the harbor. "I know that boat."

"I don't," said Llian, anxious to be going. "Come on!"

"No, it's Tess, I'm sure of it. I'm going back."

Llian sighed and followed after her. The pack was heavy after the days on the boat.

"Tess!" cried Karan, running along the cobbled waterfront, in dire peril of skidding into the harbor.

On one of the boats a big shapeless figure turned from the task she was supervising and her weatherbeaten face broke into a great beaming smile.

"Why, it's little Karan," she said, holding out her arms.

"And you've filled out a bit since I last saw you. Where have you been?"

"Halfway across the Dry Sea and back again," Karan said, embracing her.

"Well!" said Tessariel in amazement. "Your sinews must be made of adamant. When last I saw you, you were just a handful of bones. I wouldn't have thought you could have walked from one side of Ganport to the other. So, did you find what you were looking for? Ah, I can see that you did," she concluded as Llian came straggling up.

"This is my very special friend, Llian of Chanthed," Karan said, dragging him forward. "Llian, meet Tessariel, the owner of this boat. She fishes for bamundi."

Tess inspected Llian minutely, until he grew embarrassed. "The *teller!* You'll do. You were quite famous once, I recall."

"And I will be again, after this is over," Llian muttered.

"What happened to the old man, Karan? Did you leave him out in the middle of the Dry Sea?"

"Shand went his own way from Flude, not long ago," said Karan.

"No matter, all the more for us! Now, come with me." She took Karan's wrist in an iron grip. "You caused me no end of trouble, do you realize?"

Karan looked dismayed, but Tess was smiling. "It's all right, that was half a year ago. Someone in Ganport informed on me—your old friend Gooseface the innkeeper, I suspect. A pox on her inn and her famous bathtub! Llian, did Karan tell you that story, I wonder?"

Karan went red. "I don't believe she did," said Llian with a grin, "but I'll be only too glad to hear your tale."

"Anyway," Tess continued, "when Yggur's captain, Zareth the Hlune—you remember the fellow, I'm sure . . ."

"Well, I never actually saw him," said Karan, "since I was at the bottom of a basket of fish . . ."

"She didn't tell me that story either," said Llian, laughing.

"When he recovered from the octopus venom and found out that I'd helped you get away, he was not pleased. I had to go into hiding. Lucky for you the bamundi season was ending or I'd have had you scrubbing my decks for a thousand weeks to make up the loss." She grinned hugely. Her front teeth, top and bottom, were solid gold.

"Well," said Karan, "when you put us ashore last time I promised to tell you my tale, if ever we met again."

"Why, so you did! And, if I remember correctly, I offered a bamundi dinner in return."

"We will eat bamundi till we are fit to burst," Karan recalled delightedly.

"Indeed, and you are in luck, for the bamundi began to run again only two weeks ago, and I have never tasted better. Will you come to my house tonight?"

"I thought you lived in Ganport!"

"I did, but when I went into hiding I came here, and liked it as much as I hated Ganport, so in Siftah I dwell now and until the end of my days."

It was evident that Tess had done well out of the bamundi trade, for she lived in a magnificent old house nestled into the headland above the town, a villa with sun-drenched verandas and a courtyard inside with a jacaranda tree and a fountain.

The evening was hot so they sat on the veranda while Tess prepared half a basket of bamundi, grilling the vast pink steaks on a hot plate with garlic and rosemary. She served them with a garnish of chopped onion, fresh caper buds and wedges of aromatic limes from a bush growing in the shelter of the courtyard.

A flask of yellow wine was broached, and then another, an intense purple, while Karan told her tale from the day Maigraith had first appeared at Gothryme asking for help. Tess listened without comment, save for expressions of astonishment at each new escapade. Finally, when the stars had curved up across the courtyard and were on their way down again, Karan had finished the story.

"Well," said Tess. "That is the most remarkable tale that I have ever heard. And well worth another bamundi dinner, at least. But," she added, "old miser that I am, I'll save that until our next meeting, so you can tell me how the tale ends. You should have been a teller," she said with a grin and a quick glance at Llian, but he was asleep in his chair. "Hey, wake up boy! There's still half a flask left and you're not pulling your weight."

Llian looked morose and Karan knew why. He had been close-mouthed about their adventures all this time, as Mendark had ordered, and he missed telling terribly.

"So, what are your plans now? I ask because things are not yet settled in Thurkad, you know."

Karan helped herself to another morsel of fish. Even cold it was delicious. "I'm heading to Gothryme, in Bannador, which is my home."

"I have to go to Chanthed first," Llian said abruptly.

"Chanthed!" Karan cried, staring at him. "You are banished, remember! Why do you want to go there?"

"Something Faelamor said in Katazza. I've been thinking about my original quest—who killed the crippled girl?—and I suspect I missed something in the library. I was looking through the sketches from that time just before I left Chanthed but I was . . . er, interrupted." He went silent, reflecting on that night escapade in the library, which had led to his exile from the college. "I've got to go back. Remember that day in Katazza when Faelamor made me tell her about the Forbidding?"

How could she forget it? "Chanthed will add weeks to the trip," Karan said irritably. "Why didn't you tell me before?"

"I'm sorry—I've only just realized what it was. I'm not looking forward to pleading with old Wistan for the privilege of a few hours in his library, but I *have* to go. The Histories are my life."

"They're my life too," Karan snapped. "I still live the ruin my ancestors visited on our family!"

"Anyway, the festival will be on then."

Karan looked ambivalent. Once the Festival of Chanthed had been the height of her ambitions, but home called more urgently now. "Well, we'd better get a move on. I'm not crossing the mountains in winter again."

Tess had withdrawn to the kitchen during the argument. Now she reappeared with steaming mugs of tea. "Perhaps I can help you," she said. "As it happens I'm sailing to Ganport in the morning. Come with me. I'm a little short-handed, so you can work your passage and eat bamundi every evening. That'll save you quite a walk. More?" She held out the platter.

Karan shook her head. "I'll burst."

It took four days to get to Ganport, days of wild weather when they were both seasick and Llian so bad that the whole time he only moved from his hammock to the rail, where he had to be held lest he go overboard at every heave.

They bade farewell to Tess in Ganport and set out upriver following a path that wound beside the Gannel River across the range, then south-west all the way to Chanthed.

The mountain crossing seemed to take ages, though the weather was mild and the track in good condition, relatively easy walking. Llian, utterly sick of travel, just longed for a place of peace and quiet. There was so much to think about, tie together and make sense of, and he could not imagine anything more important than keeping the Histories and writing the *Tale of the Mirror.* Somewhere in the tale there was a great enigma to be puzzled out, one that held the key to the future of Santhenar.

Down on the plains of Folc they came to a town on the Gannel where there were river boats: flat-bottomed, slab-sided vessels that were poled along the meandering channels, or sailed if they were fortunate enough to have a following wind, which they often did. With Llian's dwindling coin they bought passage upriver almost as far as Chanthed. Karan asked after news of Bannador at every stop. She heard plenty about the war, though it was impossible to sort fact from fancy. Nowhere did she learn the news that she longed for so desperately—how Gothryme had fared.

Slowly they sailed on. It was well into autumn now and as

they went south it became cloudier and cooler. Signs of war became more common, though they were still far from the center of things. News of Maigraith's deeds in Bannador were on everyone's lips, and that made Karan wonder even more. She also heard of Yggur's return and the fate of the Second Army. Llian drank all this in, hungry for news, but Karan did not want to know.

The boat ride ended; the Gannel was too shallow at this time of year. They found themselves on the road that led to Chanthed. Karan could not decide what to do with herself; could not find it in herself to make any plans. She must return to Gothryme and take charge of her affairs, but she was deadly afraid of what she would find there.

A week had gone by. "Not long now," Llian said. "Just around the next bend."

Karan trudged at his side, wiping sweat off her forehead. "I know!" She'd been to Chanthed quite a few times, though never from this direction. "Aren't you worried about going back?"

"I've hardly stopped thinking about it since we left Siftah."

They turned the corner. It was late afternoon. The Gannel was on their right hand, low and brown at this time of year. Across the river, fields of wheat were being harvested, the heads butter-yellow in the afternoon light. Karan saw a scatter of villages in the distance, and children diving off the ferry landing into the water.

Chanthed suddenly rose out of the haze in front of them, a tight little cluster of streets on the hillside, surrounded by a plain sandstone wall. It was a town of perhaps five thousand people. The sun slanted down the cobbled streets, warming the old buildings of honey-colored sandstone and green slate. At the very top stood the famous College of the Histories, its ancient buildings a riot of architectural ornamentation. Way beyond, the tips of snowy mountains could be seen.

They labored up the hill to the town gate. Two guards stood there. "We never had guards on the gate in daytime before," said Llian. He looked anxious, shabby and down-at-heel. "What if they won't let me in?"

"I'll do the talking," said Karan. "Stay behind and say as little as possible."

She marched up to the gate. "I am Karan Elienor Fyrn, of Gothryme Manor in Bannador," she said boldly. "And this is my man."

Something flickered in the guard's eyes. It was almost as if he'd heard of her. He looked down at her from his considerable height, then grinned. "You've been long on the road, my lady."

"More than a year! May we pass?"

"Bannador is always welcome here, my lady. And especially Gothryme!" He bowed.

Llian trotted through after her, the guards failing to recognize in this bearded and travel-stained man the acclaimed teller who had been banished a year ago. Just inside, a huge banner stretched from one side of the road to the other, proclaiming the coming Festival of Chanthed, only a few weeks away. The town would treble in size then and a bed could not be had for any kind of money.

"Oh, dear!" said Llian as they passed under the banner.

Not even Chanthed had survived the war unscathed. On their left a whole row of houses had been burnt and were now being pulled down and rebuilt. They saw destruction everywhere. Every coin that the festival brought in would be needed to repair the damage.

"Watch what you're doing!" someone shouted as they went by the last house in the ruined row.

Karan stopped, thinking that the man was yelling at her. Peering over a low wall, she saw two young people, one male and the other female, mixing mortar in a trough. The sloppy mixture was running down the sides. A red-faced overseer was shouting at them from a plank resting on scaffolding halfway up the side wall. Another youth was trying to push a wheelbarrow laden with bricks up a sloping plank. The barrow was too heavy, and kept tilting from side to side, the youth just managing to save it each time.

"Get that mortar up here fast, you clown," the overseer screamed at a girl carrying a hod on her shoulder. "More bloody bricks, you!" He leaned over the scaffolding to roar at the two at the mortar trough. "You've got too much water in it! Bloody students. Why can't I get any decent help? Stay there, I'll do it myself!"

He spun around, straight into the path of the wheelbarrow, which ran over his foot. "Shit!" he cried, dancing on one foot, then took a great swipe at the boy, who let go of the handles in fright. The plank tilted and the wheelbarrow toppled, in a cascade of bricks, into the mortar trough. Gray mortar splattered everywhere. The barrow boy clung to the scaffolding but the overseer followed the load down, landing flat on his back in the trough.

Karan burst out laughing. The overseer slowly sat up, groaning and screaming invective as he tried to clean the stinging mortar out of his eyes. "Bloody useless lot!" he screeched. "Go back to your stupid college."

The girl on the scaffolding calmly tilted the hod and a bucket-sized clot of mortar fell, to splatter on the overseer's head. She laid the hod on the plank, took off her overalls and dropped them into the trough, then sprang over the wall.

The man's eyes lit on Karan, who was still laughing. "Rack off," his mortary finger wavered at her, "or I'll have the dogs on you."

Karan and Llian followed the student up the road, still smiling. They went as far as the college wall. There was plenty of damage here too. The ancient Arch of Knowledge, the gate through which the masters and students passed through into the College of the Histories, had been smashed and defaced. Masons were busy repairing it.

Llian stood looking in through the gate. Karan heard a sniffle. "I thought you hated this place," she said.

"I did, at the end. I couldn't wait to get away. But now that

I'm back . . . Well, it's the greater part of my life. Let's go; there are cheap places just down the road."

"I know," said Karan. "I've stayed at The Orator, and it's the cheapest there is."

"That flea-bitten hole! We're not that poor!"

Karan felt ashamed of her penury. They found a marginally better inn, took a room, and Llian sent a street boy with a message for Wistan. He was still master of the college and the formalities must be observed. They bathed, washed their tattered clothes and went down into the street to a cheap café.

"I used to eat here all the time when I was a student," said Llian.

At that moment someone shrieked "Llian!" A tall, buxom young woman leapt out the door and threw her arms around him.

"Thandiwe," Llian whooped, hugging her and dancing halfway across the road.

Karan examined the competition, scowling. The woman was striking—long in the limb, full in the chest, with sensuous lips and a mischievous sparkle in her eye. Their reunion seemed rather too passionate for Llian to be her long-lost brother.

"I've missed you so much, Llian," said Thandiwe. "What happened to you? Wistan would never say. And have you heard my news? I'm a chronicler now, and I'll be telling at the festival. You must come."

Karan stopped with her hand on the door lever. She felt most uncomfortable. Why were the women that Llian liked all so damnably tall, bosomy and beautiful? And why did she always look as if she'd been dragged through the dirt? She overcame her feelings with an effort.

"Hello," she said, holding out her hand. "I'm Karan."

"Thandiwe Moorn," the other replied, inspecting her minutely. "Are you a chronicler too?" she asked in dubious tones.

Karan felt horribly embarrassed. Her clothes were now

practically falling to bits and she had no profession at all. "No, I'm . . . on the land."

Thandiwe looked amazed, though she hid it quickly enough.

"I'll leave you two to talk," said Karan, desperate to get away. "I'm starving."

She hurried inside, Thandiwe's throaty laughter following her, and the door banged.

Eventually Llian appeared, but to Karan's dismay the woman followed him and sat down at the table. Karan sipped her tea, conscious that the lovely Thandiwe was inspecting her surreptitiously. Eventually she spoke.

"Where are you from, Karan?"

"Gothryme!"

"Where is that, pray?"

"You would not have heard of it. It is in the mountains of Bannador."

Thandiwe stared at her, realization slowly dawning. "Then you are Karan of Bannador—*Karan of the Mirror!*" Her face lit up like a miniature sun.

Karan hated talking about herself to strangers. She always felt so self-conscious. "Yes," she said in an almost invisible voice.

Thandiwe leaned across the table to take her hand. "You are not . . . what I imagined, but what does that matter? You are famous here. I told your tale for my Graduation Telling. But I never expected . . ." She eyed Karan up and down.

Karan felt more embarrassed than ever. "What did you expect—that I would prance about in silks and furs?" she said acidly, withdrawing her hand. She felt an irresistible urge to flee, then Llian took her other hand under the table and gave it a reassuring squeeze. She mastered herself. "How did you hear of it?"

"The tale was all over Meldorin last winter. A scribe fleeing from the war brought it here."

"In Chanthed we have a particular hunger for new tales,"

Llian explained. "Students at the college have been known to fight each other for the privilege of telling a new one."

Thandiwe seemed to feel that her dignity had been impugned. "I did not fight anyone for your tale," she said stiffly. "I had heard parts of it long before it came from Thurkad, and it called to me. I realize why, now," she said, glancing sideways at Llian. "I put my case to Wistan and he agreed that I was the best to make the tale. Perhaps you would like to hear it sometime."

"Perhaps," Karan said very politely, desperate to get away.

"The very idea!" she raged to Llian later that night. "Why, her breasts were practically falling out of her dress. To think that I would want my tale told by *her*."

"You misjudge Thandiwe," Llian said, treading as delicately as he could. "She has the greatest respect for you and tries to show it as best she can. She's just a student, after all—she's done nothing with her life. While you are quite famous in Chanthed. *You are in the Histories!*" He said it with emphasis, as if it was the greatest honor that anyone could wish for. Which it was.

"I don't want to be in the Histories," Karan sniffed. She knew exactly what Thandiwe wanted.

"Then you're the only person on Santhenar who doesn't," Llian retorted. "Better be careful, else the students will think you ill-mannered and proud, and that you regard yourself as being better than them. They are mostly poor, after all, not like you who have a manor and land and forest; no matter how old and shabby that may be," he added to forestall her. "And Thandiwe is one of the poorest. She's worked very hard to stay here."

"Oh!" Karan said, drying a tear. "Was I proud and rude? I would not have her think so. I will try harder next time."

Early the next morning they were summoned to Wistan. Though a year had gone by since Llian's banishment, he was apprehensive about the meeting.

"Karan Fyrn!" exclaimed Wistan, clasping her hands in his gnarled paws. "I have heard your tale more than once, and liked it more each time."

Karan eyed the hideous little gnome uncertainly. Llian's tales had rather colored him in her eyes.

Wistan smiled. "I knew your father. Galliad was a very clever man. He often used the library, though I don't think he found what he was looking for."

Karan was immediately disarmed. "I came here with him many years ago. I sat on the floor while he talked to you—it was over in that corner. And it was you who sent Llian off to find me last autumn, so I owe you more than I can repay."

Wistan glanced at Llian, twisting up his thick lips. "What I did was . . . not from the best of motives. If it turned out well it was not of my doing. Now, to business! We followed your tales eagerly, the fragments that have reached us over the past year. But we're desperate to know what really happened, especially since the Conclave."

The war and the Ghâshâd had shaken the townspeople out of their prosperous complacency. Wistan now understood the value of powerful friends. Despite Mendark's fall last year, it appeared that he was still powerful. No one could afford to be without allies these days, and Llian's name had been mentioned more than once in tales about the war and the Mirror. And Wistan had the chronicler's craving for news. Who better to give it to him?

Llian told him the news, briefly.

"You are much changed," said Wistan at the end of it.

Llian knew that he was. He could scarcely bear to think of the callow youth that he'd been then. He had learned much; suffered much. There was more to the world than himself.

"I am," he said. "I'm sorry for the trouble that I caused you. It was just a game to me then. It's all too real now."

"No matter," said Wistan. "You may do us great service if we survive the coming storm. I am very glad to see you."

"You're different too," Llian observed. Wistan was as withered and ugly as ever, but he seemed less cold now, less manipulating. Perhaps he'd never been as bad as Llian had made him out to be. And the destruction had shocked him, making him realize that he was too old to defend the college any longer. It needed a new master, one who was not only a great chronicler but who had strong allies.

"Tell me," said Llian. "Where's Trusco?" He had not seen the big, cheerful captain anywhere.

"Poor Trusco," said Wistan. "He was killed in the war, defending the college."

"I'm sorry. He was your friend and I liked him."

"I miss him. Enough of that," Wistan said abruptly. "Now, how can I help you? Will you stay for a while? You must tell us the complete tale at the festival."

Llian looked to Karan. "I'd give anything to stay, but I've got to get home," she said.

"I can't; not this year," said Llian. "The business of the Mirror is far from finished, and Mendark does not want it put about. It'll have to be next autumn. I'll come back when it's all over and do my best to make a Great Tale of it."

"That's too far away!" said Wistan. "What if you never return! What if—" The old man stared into the distance. Llian knew that he was thinking about his own death, surely not that far off. Wistan did not want to die without seeing the tale properly set down, to the everlasting glory of the college and, let it be said, himself. "What you have seen already must not be lost."

That was an imperative that Llian could not deny. Wistan called for food and wine, and summoned two scribes. Llian told everything that had happened since he left Chanthed, save for the meeting where it had been decided to attempt to remake the flute. That secret was not his to reveal. The telling took all night and the following day, and two long days after that, and scribes recorded it in a shortened hand, to the extent of twenty-four scrolls each sixty pages in length.

"It is not very satisfactory," Llian frowned after he had checked and amended the scrolls, several more days" work. "Nothing like a tale. But better than nothing."

"It is a wonderful tale," said Wistan, his eyes shining. "A Great Tale in the making, and a great honor for you and the college."

The scrolls were put in a locked cupboard until Llian should return, or to be opened in the event of his death.

After that Llian begged for the privilege of using the library again, and was given a special pass. He could not quite believe that his banishment was lifted, could not put himself in the place of an honored visitor, after so long thinking himself a failure and an outcast. He still felt himself to be the feckless youth who had been thrown out a year ago.

Karan was woken at dawn by a twinge in her wrist, the one she had first broken when she fought Idlis's huge dog last autumn. She felt that she should remember something. Outside they found a dusting of snow in the gutters, months before it was expected here.

While they were eating breakfast at a streetside table she realized what it was. "Llian, it's my birthday!" she sang out. "I'm twenty-five today."

Without a word Llian kissed her hand and ran out to the kitchen.

Karan, briefly alone, reflected on past birthdays. Last year she had woken with Idlis's whelp standing over her. She had only escaped by thrusting her fist down the dog's throat and choking it to death, though she'd been cruelly mauled in the process, and her wrist broken. Later she had shared her chocolate with Idlis in his agony. That was so long ago that it was hard to imagine any longer. A whole year had gone by and she was still buried in the affair of the Mirror, with no expectation of ever getting out of it.

Llian staggered in bearing a great two-handled mug of hot chocolate the size of an urn, covered in whipped cream in a variety of colors, grated nutmeg and shavings of black chocolate. "I know you love chocolate," he said, putting it down in front of her with a bow.

How much was all this? she wondered, licking cream off

a vanilla bean before placing it on the side of her plate. Chocolate cost its weight in silver, she'd learned once when she'd thought to buy some.

The day passed in a whirl as Llian carried her from one of his favorite places to another. It was a wonderful carefree day, one of the best of her life, when all her troubles receded into the background. And as they strolled back down the hill for lunch, Karan carrying a spray of irises, they ran into Thandiwe again. Karan did not feel the least bit jealous now.

"Thandiwe," she said, "I was hoping we'd meet again. What is the news of Bannador? I've been away a long time and I'm worried."

"I haven't heard anything about Gothryme," said Thandiwe. "But I know the lowlands suffered terribly in the war." The tales she told made Karan feel more helpless. She wished she hadn't asked.

"I've got to go to the library," Llian said, clutching his belly after a long luncheon banquet in his honor. "It's why I came to Chanthed. Do you want to come?"

"Not really!" said Karan. "Not if you're going to spend days poring over incomprehensible documents."

"It won't take long," said Llian. "I know what I'm looking for."

Karan raised a sceptical eyebrow. "And that is . . .?"

"It's got to do with the *Tale of the Forbidding*, my original quest. Remember when Faelamor quizzed me about it in Katazza? She wanted to know who was the first to go into the burning tower—she couldn't disguise it. But as soon as I told her, she pretended that she wasn't interested any more."

"So, what *are* you looking for?"

"The drawings made at the time by the war artists. A dozen armies were there and every event was recorded. I'm going to check all the drawings again. Something puzzled me before, but I never got the chance to investigate it properly. Some of the numbers seemed to have been changed."

Down in the archives he checked each of the paintings

and engravings. Several showed Yalkara wearing her gold. So that was where he'd seen it before! He began on the drawings, untying the tapes of one packet. The papers sprang out, all crumpled up where they had been stuffed in carelessly.

Llian was furious. "Who would treat such precious things so badly?"

"Someone in rather a hurry," Karan guessed.

"These are the original sketches made by the artists in the field. All the engravings and paintings were based on them." He went through the sketches one by one, finally stopping at the set that showed people preparing to attempt the ruined tower. "It's never been clear who was the first into the tower after the flute was destroyed. There are so many different versions of the story." He stopped suddenly, frowning at the drawing in his hand. "The numbers don't agree with the catalogue!"

Karan laid the sketches out on the floor, holding each up to the light to check the faded numbers, then putting them in order. Finally she put the pile down carefully, searching the benches and the floor.

"What's the matter?"

"Oh, nothing. There's a couple missing, is all."

"Probably pushed to the back of the shelf," said Llian. "They were all here when I looked last year."

Karan searched everywhere. "No, two sketches are definitely missing."

Llian went through the pile. "That's strange! They're the ones whose numbers seemed to have been changed, last year."

They stared at each other. "Who was here last?" Karan asked.

Putting everything back, they ran out. Llian spoke to the warden of the archives about what they'd found. She consulted the register.

"Only three people have looked at these papers recently," she said. "You did, a year ago, not long before your great telling, and again just after. Wistan did too, when he checked the proofs of your tale."

"I think I can guess the third," said Llian in an aside.

"A visitor with a pass from the library at Tellulior, a university city in the southeast. She was here last summer."

"What name?" Karan and Llian asked together.

The warden squinted at the register, took off her glasses and put them on again.

"Kekkuliel," she said. "A small woman—I recall her now. Golden skin and eyes, and pale hair."

"Faelamor!" said Karan in Llian's ear. "Evil news."

"Thank you," Llian said to the warden. He took Karan's arm. "Let's go somewhere where we can talk."

At the back of the library they sat down in an empty room. "Why did she take those drawings?" Karan asked.

"They told her something—maybe who first went into the tower—and she didn't want anyone else to find out."

Karan shivered, confronted by a mental image: Charon and Aachim, Faellem and old humans, all with their competing devices and their gates, bringing war and bloody ruin upon the whole world.

"What can we do?" asked Llian.

"I don't know. Who can we trust? Maybe we should send to Yggur in Thurkad."

"No!" cried Llian. Yet he knew it was his responsibility to take this news to Thurkad. Mendark must soon return from the east.

They told Wistan what they had learned. "Leave it with me," he said. "Though I can't even send a message at the moment. There's not a skeet left in Chanthed. The war wiped them out."

In the morning Llian and Karan set out for Tullin. Looking over her shoulder as they departed, Karan saw the lovely Thandiwe staring morosely after them.

Just outside the uphill gate they went past a legless beggar sitting in the shade of the wall. His face was covered in sores and flies.

"Alms, lady," he wailed. "Alms, for pity's sake."

Karan felt in Llian's flabby wallet. She came up with a silver tar, a small fortune for any beggar, and even for them, but the poor man looked desperate. She held out the tar, not knowing that it was the last.

The beggar snatched at it, then his pus-filled eyes touched on Llian. With a cry of rage he smacked the coin out of her hand. It rang on the stones at the edge of the road, before it disappeared.

"Curse you, Llian!" he shrieked. "Curse you until the earth bleeds and the black moon rots to pieces."

Llian stared at the beggar open-mouthed. "Turlew!" he cried. "What happened to you?"

Wistan's former seneschal, who had attacked Llian on the road to Tullin last year, spat on his trouser leg. Llian sprang out of range.

"I lost my job because of you. Wistan threw me out of town. Then the war—" He thrashed the stumps of his legs then went on in a gangrenous voice, "I have only one thing to say to you, Llian. Enjoy your success while it lasts, for it won't last much longer. Soon you will not have a friend in the whole of Santhenar. Your very name will be a curse, and before the coming hythe you will wish you were as happy as *Turlew the beggar man!*"

Llian seemed unfazed, but Karan could feel the flesh freezing all the way down her back. "Come on!" she said, dragging him away.

They hurried up the road. After they turned the corner, Turlew dragged his stumps across the gravel. He searched among the stones and thistles until the light faded, but the precious silver coin could not be found.

That night they camped in the hills above Chanthed, among the gellon trees not far from the place where Llian had spent his first night out of the college almost a year ago. Most of the copse bore only shriveled, blighted fruit, but on one single tree the fruits were so ripe that they were bursting, their sweet juice oozing out to form clumps of sugar crystals which attracted bees by the thousand.

Llian seemed to have forgotten the beggar's curse. He had literally been bouncing all day. It made Karan feel grumpy.

"What are you so happy about?" she asked as he ran back and forth, piling up wood for the night's fire. Llian was normally a slacker when it came to camp duties.

"You can't know what it's like to be Zain—an outcast."

"You're right," she said, on hands and knees, gloomily striking flint into tinder. It refused to catch. "I can't!"

"The college was half my life—more—but I never felt accepted there. Not even after the Graduation Telling, when I was made a master." He knelt down beside her and began to fan the smoldering tinder with his journal.

"You'll blow it out," she said irritably. It generally took Llian half an hour to get a fire going.

The fire caught in a blaze that raced up through the kindling. He hurled logs on top.

"Careful!" she said. "You'll put it out again."

In a minute the fire was roaring as high as her shoulders. "But now," said Llian, "to have an honored place at the college—you can't know how much that security means to me. I've not had any since I left home."

Karan knew that she should be feeling glad for him, but her own unease had been growing ever since the discovery in the library. "Then I don't suppose you'll need me anymore," she snapped. "I dare say Gothryme will prove too rustic for you, with all the delights of Chanthed beckoning. Perhaps you want to be the next master of the college."

Llian started. "You're being silly," he said, but just for a minute Karan saw that longing in his eyes.

He'll leave me for Chanthed! He's getting bored with me. Karan kept on. "I saw *her* great cow eyes on you this morning."

"You didn't see mine on her, though!" He changed the subject. "What are your plans now?"

"I have no plans," she said in a faraway voice. She had her

chin cupped in the palms of her hands. It was a clear night and rather cooler than they were used to. Llian edged a little closer to the fire. "No plans. Just dreams and hopes of home. But . . . Bannador was one of the first places to be invaded, and Gothryme lies between Thurkad and Shazmak. Maybe home isn't there any longer. We are an impatient and rebellious people, Llian, and it gets us into trouble. I'm afraid for my country."

"We'll soon be there."

"I can't bear it," Karan said mournfully. "I hope Shand is in Tullin. I miss him."

This was a different Karan again, one who shrank from difficulties. The return to Meldorin had brought back problems over which she had no control; could have no control. And as well, though she said nothing to Llian, last night she had felt again the touch of those dreams that had so troubled her before the death of Selial. What did Rulke want with her now? Yet she was not really surprised. Ever since the Nightland she had been expecting him to appear. A part of her seemed to be looking on, half in awe, half in horror, at what must come. The beggar's curse was just another brick added to the load.

At first it had just been a touch, a fleeting presence, as though Rulke was checking on her. Reminding himself that she existed, and that he had a power over her.

And perhaps that was another reason for her reluctance. With every step of their journey she felt that they were coming closer to him, returning to his domain. And every night after that her dreams were stronger, more immediate, more real.

25

DREAMSCAPES

Four days later they were laboring up the track to Tullin through unseasonably heavy snows. "I wonder what we'll find there," said Llian, warming his hands in his armpits. "How has it survived the war?"

Karan was too immersed in her own worries to reply. They turned around the angle of the ridge and there stood Tullin, embedded in its dimple near the top of the hill, looking exactly as it had done the year before, save that the snow was deeper. The chimneys of the inn were smoking merrily.

"I like Tullin," said Llian. "I've looked forward to coming back for ages. Better pray for good weather though—we can afford one night only."

"I hope Shand is here," said Karan.

They squelched up the path. She thrust open the heavy door of the inn and put her head into the great bar room, where the fire blazed. There were several people at the bar, locals with leathery skin and slow voices. Behind the counter was a shy, black-eyed, rosy-cheeked girl that she recognized as a daughter of the house.

Karan went across to the fire, nodding to the customers. Though she had been here a number of times and knew the innkeeper and his family, recent events had shaken her confidence and she could barely find the strength to talk to people. She stood at the fire for a long minute, warming her fingers at the flames, then took a deep breath and turned around. To her discomfort Llian had not followed her in, but she took her courage in her hands, went up to the bar and said hello.

Llian had gone straight on, through the kitchen and down the stony path to the woodheap. Someone was chopping wood. He half-expected it to be Shand, but coming around the pile he found that it was the innkeeper. Torgen looked up, frowned momentarily then smiled.

"Llian of Chanthed!" he said, rubbing a flattened nose. "Llian the exile! Though perhaps I am presumptuous, since Chanthed is where you've come from. You were here a year ago, before the war. We saw you coming up the road." Putting down the axe, he shook Llian's hand.

Llian was pleased to be remembered, though doubtless he had been spoken about more than once, and it was an innkeeper's duty to remember his customers.

"You went in rather a hurry the last time," Torgen reflected.

"Oh!" said Llian, suddenly worrying about things long forgotten. "I trust the coin I left was enough."

The innkeeper laughed. "Judged to a nicety, if I recall. But I was not alluding to that. I trust your affairs are in better order than they were then?"

Innkeepers also tended to want to know the business of their customers. "They are well enough," Llian said. "I see that the war has passed Tullin by."

Torgen had picked up his axe but now he laid it down again. "Not completely. The fighting didn't get this far, but

Yggur's soldiers did, and your friends the Whelm came back last spring. I gather they have a different name now. The soldiers terrorized us for a day or two. The Whelm found nothing either—what is there to find in Tullin? We've been losing people for years, but since the war we've regained them, and more, fleeing from Bannador and the east. There are more travelers on the roads than I have ever seen. Last summer we even had people sleeping in the stables. A good year for business; though I'd rather we had an ordinary year and no war. Still, that's the way of it in Tullin. People come and people go, but we're always here."

"I'd hoped to find Shand back."

"He went in mid-winter, at the beginning of the war. There was word of him in Thurkad, and he wrote to us from the north; some outlandish place I can't remember. He said he might not be back for a year. But that's Shand. We know him and we don't worry. We miss him though." Heaving a huge log onto his shoulder, Torgen headed up the path.

Llian stood reflecting for a moment, then stacked his arm with as much wood as he could carry and followed slowly. He dumped the wood in the box near the kitchen stove and hurried down for another load, catching the innkeeper just before the woodheap.

"I have more recent news of Shand, if you would like to hear it. He left us in Flude at the end of summer."

"Flude? That must be a foreign place, I dare say."

To the folk of Tullin even Chanthed was a foreign place, so Llian took no account of that.

"Very foreign! Flude is nigh on three hundred leagues away as the wind blows, on the great island of Faranda."

Torgen blanched as if Llian was talking about the dark face of the moon. "Well, you're alive to tell about it, so maybe it isn't quite as deadly as the tales say. Still, you'd know all about that. You can tell your story after dinner. Everyone will want to know what old Shand is up to. And if it's good enough, maybe I won't charge you for your bed. Now, that reminds me of something. Oh yes! The last time you were here you were looking for a woman lost in the snow . . ."

He paused so long that Llian could almost hear the gears creaking in his brain. "I found her," Llian said, "but that tale would take a fortnight. Still, I have plenty of others."

Thus far he had told his tale to no one (excepting at Chanthed, but that was his chronicler's duty), respecting Mendark's demand that the matter be kept secret. But he missed telling very much and was delighted to be asked. There were plenty of stories about Shand that would cause no damage. He would give them the best tale that had ever been heard in Tullin. He needed to, else they would depart penniless.

As they carried their loads, another thought occurred to Llian. "How long has Shand been here?"

"As long as I can remember. He was here when I was a boy, when my grandfather kept the inn. He's always been here."

"But where did he come from before that?"

The innkeeper gave him an enigmatic smile. "Don't know as how Shand would want me to talk about his affairs," he said, and picked up his axe in a dismissing way.

Llian gathered another load of wood and went back inside. Winter was already setting in up here, a month earlier than last year. Even in Chanthed there had been a few flurries of snow, but here it was thick and deep, and the road that wound its way west down the mountain to Hetchet was already closed by deep drifts. No one had come that way for weeks.

"Shand isn't here," he said to Karan, after dumping his load of wood beside the fire.

"I know." She was sitting at a table by herself, staring at the flames. The other customers, after a brief hello, had realized that she was not in the mood for chatter and had gone back to their drinks and their gossip.

"Are you upset?"

"I knew he wouldn't be," she said without expression.

After a stiff silence, Llian took their packs upstairs then wandered over to the counter.

Karan was not thinking about Shand at all, though she had been disappointed to learn that he was not here. Since meeting the beggar she had been feeling jumpy and the further up the mountain they went the more uneasy she had become. The mystery in the library was another part of it. She had many memories tied up in this place, or at least its neighborhood: her first meeting with Llian; but one of her worst nightmares too, the climax of the weeks she had been hunted by the Whelm.

But that was *then*, history. *Now* was different, not only because they were close to Shazmak and the Ghâshâd, but for another reason that she could not articulate, a foreboding that grew ever stronger. The terror she had succumbed to in the Nightland was coming back; a dread that she could not fight against, that induced blind panic in her, that had made her abandon Llian there. Karan was afraid that she would do the same again. She felt as if she was losing control of herself once more.

What had happened to the indomitable will that had driven her halfway across Meldorin? It was not there anymore. Since Chanthed she had come to dread the nights, and Llian was no help at all. After his success at the college he was quite caught up in his Histories again. She had never seen him look so contented.

Karan watched him go, hurt that he had not sensed what she was going through. How could he have escaped from the Nightland unscathed while she was put to such torment? He went up to the group at the counter—a deliciously plump and pretty woman of middle age called Maya (the wife of the innkeeper), her even prettier daughter and two customers with their backs to her.

Soon Llian was the center of attention. He was telling a yarn, smiling and waving his arms in the air. Everyone at the bar burst out laughing. The young woman ladled hot wine into bowls and sprinkled green and yellow herbs on top, as was the custom here in the autumn. Llian carried his bowl in one hand, inclined his head to his companions, took a long and noisy sip and said something that made the others roar with laughter. Maya, who had started to the other end of the counter to serve another customer, looked back then moved away reluctantly. Others drifted across and soon most of the inn surrounded Llian, laughing gaily as if they had known each other for years. The shy daughter was staring at him, but each time he caught her eye she looked away and blushed. The poor girl was smitten.

Karan felt lonely, quite left out, one part of her wanting to join in, the other contemptuous of their levity when the world was in such a state. Drinkers! she thought with disgust, looking down at her own bowl. She loved *proper* wine, the rich purple vintage from the lowlands of Iagador, but this stuff was thin and sour. Moreover the herbs gave it a floral taste which clashed violently with the other flavors.

She took another small sip, gagged, surreptitiously spat it back into the bowl and pushed it to one side. Looking up she saw that Llian's eyes, and the eyes of everyone else at the counter, were on her. One of the men nudged his companions and laughed, and the others echoed him. As Llian turned away she saw that even he was smiling. Karan knew that it might have been anything that amused them, yet she felt her cheeks grow hot, sure that they were laughing at her. Abruptly she got up and, storming upstairs, threw all of Llian's things out into the corridor. Bolting the door she crept into bed, pulled the covers around her neck and lay there, brooding.

So reluctantly had she entered into this relationship with Llian. His every approach she had rebuffed, not because she hadn't cared for him, but rather that she'd cared for him too much, and the wrong way. She had idolized Llian the great teller, but Llian the man, when she finally met him, had been another thing entirely—clumsy, foolish and quite ill-at-ease with life outside his college. She had derided and maligned him at every opportunity, but it had done no good. Even his stupidities in Shazmak, almost a year ago, had not been able to turn her off him. Her reaction then had been all the more violent because of what she felt for him.

She lay staring up at the smoky ceiling boards, smoldering. A long-legged brown spider was repairing a web that ran from the ceiling across to the fireplace. She watched it moodily.

But what did Llian feel for her? He had gone beyond himself for her on that terrible journey to Sith, and in Thurkad too. When first she heard his voice through the wall at Katazza, and touched his hand with her own, she could have died of bliss. But the past few days had renewed the barrier between them that had been built by her failure in the Nightland, and his dealings there, *whatever they were*. She felt miserable, lonely and afraid.

Pinching the lamp out, Karan lay in the darkness watching the firelight flicker on the wall. Occasionally there was a roar from downstairs, doubtless the vulgar guffawing at one of Llian's more uncouth stories. She dozed, woke, put more wood on the fire, dozed again.

Karan was woken suddenly from a restless sleep by the door rattling. It was Llian, heaving at the latch. The fire had burned low again—it must be well after the middle of the night. He didn't seem to understand that he was locked out. Seemed to think that the door was stuck; seemed to find it funny. He gave the door a thump and fell down with another roar of laughter. This would probably go on all night if she didn't do something.

Jumping out of bed, she stormed to the door and pulled it open. Gathering all her misery and frustration, Karan flung it at him.

"Go away, you disgusting drunken pig!" She slammed the door in his face and crept back into bed.

The anger was gone. She felt terribly sad. She should go out straight away and set it right before a little problem turned into a big one. She must, before it was too late. But she could not; did not.

Karan's words had little impact on Llian, but the cold ferocity with which they were offered did. She'd always had an ability to strike him dumb with her anger, and this time she had tried harder than usual. He scrambled to his hands and knees, his good humor evaporating. In truth he was hardly drunk at all, just euphoric with the success of his tale. Gathering his scattered goods he went quietly into the next room, which he found to be empty. It was so cold that he got into bed fully dressed.

He was used to Karan's moods and her need for solitude; more used than she was to his need of people and boisterous company. Even so, she could hurt him. He knew part of the reason for her anger, but he was innocent; they had not been laughing at her at all. Still, her temper was violent but soon over.

There was no fire and no quilt on the bed, just two threadbare blankets. He clutched them about him, lying fully awake in the cold night, suddenly realizing that he was waiting for something to happen. The wind had come up. The shutter near his head rattled once or twice. The wheel turns, he thought, remembering the night in Tullin a year ago when Karan had cried for help in a sending. It could have been this very room. Yes, it was: the fourth on the right, at the top of the stair. The wind had rattled the shutters that night too, though then there had been rain followed by snow. Tonight, just snow.

Llian felt the presentiment strongly now, and an overwhelming sense of déjà vu. Something was building up. Was it Rulke, or just Llian's own pattern-obsessed mind making recurrence out of no more than chance?

The shutters rattled again and for a moment he imagined himself back a year, dozing in his room. He could almost hear the slow crackle of the fire, the rain on the roof, the slow dripping on the hearth. How naive he had been then.

He looked back to that time, that Llian, remaking the night from his perfect memory of it as if rehearsing the events for a telling. Recreating his own frame of mind, that callow young man he had been a year ago, so full of himself and his heroic fancies. Reality was colder, dirtier, more brutal and totally unforgiving. What a crass, vain dreamer he had been. He dozed.

Suddenly the fire was crackling, slowly dying on the hearth. There was a downpour on the roof. It was as real as a year ago; it was! And what was that rhythmical, rising and falling tone in his head? Was Karan trying to send to him, again?

In the next room Karan slept uneasily. She was dreaming, and perhaps something of Llian's year-ago dream passed back to her, touching that link she had made between them long ago in Shazmak. The night's duress had woken it again. She dreamed herself into his mind-meanderings and was shocked to find herself alone on that cold mountainside of a year past, in the wind and the rain.

Her camp was a knife-edged ridge, falling sheer to the right, steeply to the left, and rising up just as steeply before her to the plateau and the ruins she was making for. While the moon was out she'd felt that she hung on a spire that touched the vault of the sky, a dizzying, awesome feeling, but the thick clouds quickly covered it again and she clung to the topmast of a ship in a storm, tossed one way then the other in the darkness.

Now the wind rose, blowing more strongly than she had ever felt before; at any moment she might be blown right off the ridge and flung across the sky like a rag. What if the Whelm came at her here? They were close, but how close?

Karan gripped a vertical blade of slate with her good hand. She could not defend herself here—to stand up was to be blown away. Was that a shadow moving below? The moon was gone again; the wind peppered her with sleet. Her fingers were frozen lumps. Oh, for a fire! No wood; no courage! The moon peeped out once more, and briefly the lower fall of rock swarmed with shadows. Even after it disappeared again they danced in her eyes. She rubbed her gloves across her face, trying to rid herself of the demons. She was so tired that she could have slept standing.

Karan stirred in her sleep, reaching out for the comfort of Llian's solid back, but he was not there. How lonely she was.

He was not there! Had never been there; she had not even met him. Surely she dreamed awake, clinging to her spur of rock, a romantic fancy built on someone she had seen just briefly. A magical tale told at a festival, a teller who had wrung her young heart with his tale. He had looked at her as he told it, and in her mind she'd felt that he spoke just to her, that he reached out to her alone. That was the dream. She could almost feel the warmth of his body, then the shrieking wind tore it away.

No longer could she think that thought, dream that dream. She was too cold and too afraid. She must never allow herself to give up. How could the Whelm be this close? On the snow she would have seen them half a league away. These must be phantoms, delusions drawn out of her tormented mind like waking nightmares.

Then, just as her courage was coming back, the clouds parted above her and the moon shone brightly down on her pale face. Moon? But it was too high in the sky, too large, too red and black. Was the dark face of the moon glaring down at her too? No, more like the giant, carmine-eyed figure of her dreams. More like Rulke watching her!

A moan rose in her throat; she could not keep it down. But she must! Karan knew that if she cried out the terror would feed on itself and she would be lost. She put her finger in her mouth and bit it as hard as she could. Pain cut off the moan and the eye faded, the light dimmed, the moon waned. Then out of the corner of her eye she saw the shadows dancing, and the terror, which had just hidden in the dark spaces of the room, returned more strongly than ever.

Llian's pendulum was swinging from the present to the past as well. He kept dreaming, waking again—one minute in this room *now*, the next in last year's room *then*, and somehow linked to Karan's *now* and her *then* dreams as well. Fleetingly he saw her where she huddled on that ridge, and knew exactly how she felt. He had clung at the same spot a day later, as he followed her to the ruins.

But the eyes, which were a symbol of terror to her, were familiar to him. He suddenly remembered what Rulke had made him forget—their talk in the Nightland, and the outrage they'd both felt that the Histories had been corrupted. And what Rulke had offered, knowledge that no other chronicler had access to. In his half-dreaming state Karan's terror now seemed self-indulgent. Why could she not see? Rulke was their friend. There was no danger from him, only a wonderful opportunity. Rulke could give him everything he had ever dreamed about, and more: things that he had *never* been able to dream about. And for practically nothing in return.

"Aahhhh!" The cry came right through the wall. It was Karan. But when he tried to get up he was punished with pain like a spear through his brain. Everything was too hard. He lay down again. *Karan will be all right*, something sighed in his brain. *I'll take care of her for you.*

Karan sat up abruptly, the blankets sliding off her bare shoulders. Her finger was bitten so badly that it bled, but she knew nothing about it save that she'd had a terrible dream. She was wide awake now, or thought she was. The foreboding grew more terrible and urgent. What was Llian doing? It felt like her trial in Shazmak, when she had read her dream back from him and told it to the Syndics. Only now she was dreaming *his* dream. But Llian was dreaming a lie and dragging them both to damnation.

She tried to get up but could not; awake or asleep she must keep traveling that dream. *How has this come about?* the conscious part of her mind wailed, while the rest of her was on that windswept ridge, watching the flitting shadows and the clouds slowly parting above. The moon—the eye—glared down at her: cold, manipulating, treacherous. Bending her to its will.

No, I will not! But at the same time her other self was raising her hands to keep away the terror, seeking, *crying out for a friend* . . . No, that was yet another time, when the Whelm had come for her near Narne and she had made the fateful link to Maigraith that had betrayed them all. Was Rulke trying to force that link from her again?

Llian's dream of a year ago began to dissolve into two parts. One part was himself in this room in Tullin, dreaming that he was at the festival, telling the greatest of the Great Tales, the *Tale of the Forbidding*. The other part was with Karan on the mountainside, and she was crying out, "Help me! Help me!" He reached out to her slowly, and more slowly, and yet more slowly still, as the telling reached its climactic phase where the mad Shuthdar, surrounded by his enemies, capered on the high tower, cursed them and blew that fateful blast on the flute that sent the whole world spinning into madness.

Karan caught the dreaming and it wrenched her heart, for it was the tale and the teller that she had yearned for ever since the Graduation Telling. He brought it to a triumphant conclusion and her heart went out to him. And the dream went out from the *now*-Karan in Tullin to the *then*-Karan on the ridge, and she cried out in desperation and wonder and hope, "Help me; help me!" and to her joy the answer came back, *"Where, where?"*

The *now*-Karan wept with anguish. This was much more than a dream—look what it had led to before. Her link to Maigraith had been captured by Rulke, used to wake the Whelm to their true identify—Ghâshâd—and set in motion the holocaust. She had opened that box. How much worse would it be now that Rulke was free? In her mind's eye she could see the *now*-Llian sitting up in his bed, reaching up to Rulke, and the other Llian of a year ago looking up in terror, trying to shield himself. And she saw the Karan of a year ago (the images repeating and disappearing and merging into each other as if seen in a pair of mirrors) protecting her face with her hands. This was not at all what she'd imagined when she made that first sending for help, a year ago.

Karan's dream blurred into Llian's. Had he sold himself or was he compelled, overpowered? Whatever it was, she had to break it now. Perhaps if she used the link cunningly enough she could snatch away Rulke's control. Karan tried to sense her way into Llian's dreams but instantly the whole world-view tipped upside down and began to revolve sickeningly. Her head spun, her view of Rulke suddenly changed. He was great and majestic and wise. She should follow him. Why did she struggle?

No! Rulke was trying to *compel* her through Llian, using her own link. Karan tried to snap the link but it was now like a rigid cable joining them together. She could not break it! Rulke was far too strong, much stronger than he had been in the Nightland, for they were close to Shazmak here, where a legion of Ghâshâd waited to do his bidding. Then she realized that even if she did break the link she would be abandoning Llian again. She would have bought her freedom with his soul.

To do anything at all was hard—Rulke's will was utterly dominating now. *Come to me, come to me!* he sighed, his very voice a seduction. *I can give you what you most desire.*

I'm coming, I'm coming! she sang back to him, forcing herself to think of nothing else. Don't dare think or it will give you away. But Karan could scarcely think anyway, for the voice was so overpowering that she must follow wherever it led.

Karan fell out of bed. No time to dress, not even capable of thinking of clothes, she forced herself against air that felt as cold and thick as tar, her only drive to stop this before it went to its inevitable, deadly conclusion.

She stumbled to the door, shaking her head, trying to clear the dream/dreams from it while the honeyed voice sighed across the link. Struggling with the door, her thoughts were so sluggish that it was a minute before she remembered that she had bolted it. She wrenched back the bolt. The dream was quite horrible now. The Llian from last year and the Karan on the ridge, sad phantoms of yesteryear, were fading. In his room Llian stood on unsteady knees, reaching out with both arms like a prodigal son to his father. The great figure rose from the stone chair, broken chains glistening at its feet. The air began to swirl lazily in toward the center of the room, making a whirlpool with Llian at its center.

"No!" she cried softly, running the few steps to Llian's door, praying that he had not locked it when he went to bed. Why would he? Tullin had seemed the safest place in all Meldorin.

You fool! Oh, you stupid, stupid fool; you're doing just what he wants.

The door opened easily and she fell in, tripping over Llian's gear inside the door. She crouched there, looking up. The dream and the reality superimposed, blurred, shifted separately—the one seen from where she stood, the other as from the far side of the room.

An image of Rulke formed slowly in the center of the room. She could tell that it was just an image because there was no rush of air as there always had been through a gate, and the image was translucent, wavery. Llian looked rapt, like an acolyte about to receive the first of the great secrets from the master. How could she stop it? The dreams of *then* were almost gone, merging into the reality of *now,* no longer needed. Whatever Rulke had wanted set in motion was flowing now of its own accord. But what did he want of Llian?

The dreams winked out but the compulsion that flowed from Llian was as strong as ever. She had to break it before Rulke crystallized in the room or he would have them both. How? Under the bed she spied an old chamber pot of thick porcelain, thin gray stripes and a heavy handle. In a single movement she picked it up and hurled it at Llian's head.

He did not even look around. The heavy object struck him on the side of the head, beside the temple. One minute he was reaching up and the next he toppled slowly over and lay still. The pot rolled off the far side of the bed and smashed. Karan felt a brilliant flash of pain in her own head, a moment's empathy for Rulke's own pain as the link was abruptly severed. The empathy bothered her. The apparition vanished at once.

"Liannnnnnn!" she wept, thinking that she'd killed him.

Llian was deathly white save for a dark bruise on the side of his head and a curving gash where the side of the pot had caught him. The gash ebbed a small amount of blood but it soon stopped. Suddenly all the anger, all the bitterness, all the feelings of betrayal were gone. He was as much used and abused as she was. How could he possibly resist Rulke? No one could. She leapt up on the bed and took Llian in her arms, cradling his cold head against her breast. Perhaps it was better that he be dead than what he would have become. Perhaps it was better.

He shuddered. Karan put her hand on his throat and felt a pulse beating. She slid down in the bed, pulling the blankets up around them both, holding him tenderly, trying to warm him, oblivious to the curious faces at the door, the innkeeper and his wife come to see what all the fuss was about. Evidently just a lovers' tiff, and they would pay for the damage in the morning. The two went away again.

The room still had an unpleasant feeling, a presence. Karan did not dare close her eyes for fear of seeing that image again. Surely if she dreamed it, it would let *him* back.

She had to get Llian out. Karan could just lift him, with his feet dragging. She staggered up the hall, rolled him onto her bed and folded him into the covers.

Llian lay still as death all night, and just as cold. The room was dark but she did not dare leave him even to light a lantern. Pulling him onto her, Karan settled his head between her breasts, giving the warmth of her body to him. Absently she caressed him, only moving when she could bear her cramped position no longer. She was too fearful of her dreams to sleep. Rulke was abroad with his construct and Llian was overcome. She was all alone, twenty leagues from anyone who could help her. The company were divided and scattered across the earth; even if they could be trusted.

She had to tell someone, but if she did it would be betraying Llian to almost certain death. There was no solution.

Sometime after dawn, as a dim light began filtering in through the shutters, Llian's unconsciousness passed into a deep, still sleep. His breathing became a little deeper, a little stronger. At last she let go. Karan slept too.

26

TAR GAARN

Tallia!" Mendark called, a few hours after *The Waif* had set out from Flude.

Tallia was standing at the bow, staring into the swell, dreaming of Crandor. Her long black hair streamed out behind her in the wind.

"Tallia!" he shouted.

She turned, wiping spray off her eyelashes and forehead. "Yes?"

"A packet came in last night from Nadiril at the Great Library. Some more information on Havissard. This letter was with it. It's taken quite a while to arrive."

Tallia sat down out of the wind to read. The letter was written in a beautiful hand, though a rather ornate style that had gone out of fashion a century ago.

Guffins 18, 3099

The Library
Zile

My dear Tallia,

If you receive this, please write back with your news. Both Lilis and I are very anxious about you. Now to your quest. I have initiated enquiries, even as far away as Thurkad, using up a good deal of Lilis's ransom money in the process. I am saddened to discover how much it takes to buy a customs officer these days. In my time it could be done for a handful of coppers. What a wicked world!

As you recall, Lilis said that her father was taken by a press-gang seven years ago. It was a fast boat with a red sail and a name like *Cutter* or *Dagger*. Unfortunately those are popular names for boats. I attach a list of a dozen that visited Thurkad at that time, and their home ports as set out in the customs registers.

I suggest you pay particular attention to the last seven, all from Crandor and other eastern lands (see Lilis's letter, and mark how well she's learned her lessons).

And Tallia, beware—pressing sailors is a capital offense in most ports; this boat is doubtless a pirate, or smuggler!

Your friend
Nadiril

Tallia turned the page. Written on the other side, in the same archaic style but a more rounded, childish hand, was a letter from Lilis.

Dearest Tallia,

I can't tell you how happy I am. I have been working very hard on my lessons, and Nadiril is pleased with my reading, though he still thinks my writing is TERRIBLE!

You would not believe what marvels I am learning.

Nadiril is teaching me the catalogue, though to tell you the truth, Tallia (and I hope he does not read this bit over my shoulder), it is in rather a MESS. I am working hard at it but there is so much to do.

I've missed you so very much, Tallia, that sometimes I cry at night for fear that you are lying DEAD in the middle of the Dry Sea. I have read everything about that horrible place. Just the thought of it makes me shiver. But you are so strong and clever and brave, I'm sure you will be all right.

I must finish this, for Nadiril keeps reminding me how expensive paper is. I've remembered something about the day Jevi was kidnapped. The men who took him had dark skins like yours, and spoke the same way that you do, so they must have been from the east.

Please say hello to Pender, and Osseion too, and EVEN Mendark. That says how much I miss you all.

Fare well,
Lilis

I miss you just as much, Tallia thought, consulting the list. The seven vessels from the east were: *Ivory Cutter*, *Cutlass*, *The Silver Sword*, *Stiletto*, *Kris Kris*, *Machete* and *Spear of Midnight*. Unfortunately, the ships' details did not include the color of the sails, and red was a common color, so they were not much better off. Three vessels were from Crandor, but the other four were from ports hundreds of leagues apart up the eastern coast of Lauralin. It would take months just to visit them all. The quest was hopeless.

She took the letter to Mendark. He was in a good mood today.

"Lilis says hello to *me*?" he said with a smile. "She *has* mellowed. Well, we'll stop where we can, but don't take too much time. And don't stir up any trouble."

"Me, trouble?" she said innocently.

The trip north up the long western coast of Faranda was tedious, for the rugged land was desert and practically uninhabited. For the first week they had the benefit of a following wind and northward-setting current, and made excellent progress, sometimes more than forty leagues a day. By the time the winds failed, *The Waif* was rounding the tropical northern bulge of Faranda. From then on they had a slow, dangerous passage between the inner and outer barrier reefs that looped their way for a thousand leagues around the top of Faranda and east down the coast of Crandor.

A fortnight into the voyage they stopped at Nys on the northernmost tip of Faranda. Tallia was glad of the diversion. Their progress up the coast seemed imperceptible. Crandor was a longing that was still a month away, and every other thought was a worry. Time ticked by while they rocked on an empty sea.

Nys was one of the centers of the spice trade, a dirty tropical city surrounded by plantations. However, Tallia's family on her father's side had been in the trade for many generations, and the reek of cloves, cardamom and mace from the warehouses on the waterfront brought tears to her eyes.

They only stayed long enough to obtain water, fresh meat and vegetables, for Mendark was driven by the urgency of his mission. Tallia had no luck with her search, though she did manage to cross one boat off the list. *Kris Kris* had been driven onto the reef in a typhoon three years ago, going down with all hands.

A few days later, well out of sight of land, they were struck by a furious storm, one that drove them far to the north. They almost foundered on the treacherous reefs surrounding the isle of Banthey, coming so close that they could see the wreckers and scavengers cavorting like lunatics on the shore. Once again Pender's miraculous seamanship and Rustible's consummate handling of the sails brought them off the lee shore unscathed.

Rustible was a lugubrious-looking man. With his leathery face and bald brown head, clumps of frizzy yellow hair sticking out at the sides, a bulky round-bottomed body with skinny legs and incredibly long, thin feet, he looked the epitome of a sad clown. He acted one too, always expecting the worst, though he was a wonderful first mate, and faster than anyone up the mast to the lookout.

They spent the next five days beating their way back into the wind, down between the inner and outer reefs surrounding a large mountainous island called Fankster, with Rustible constantly predicting their doom. After that it was plain sailing for the best part of another week until they came at last in sight of Taranta, though not even Pender was confident of navigating their way into port on this rocky and deeply indented coastline. They stopped at a pilot station outside Taranta Bay and hired a pilot to take them in and out again.

"Two silver tars a day!" Pender exclaimed as he dropped back on board. "That's the most expensive pilot I've ever heard of."

The pilot turned out to be a grizzled old woman of about eighty, with milky eyes and only four teeth, which were clamped over the stem of a battered pipe for the whole trip. She nipped nimbly between the sailors, took the wheel and began shouting orders in a cracked accent.

Pender mooched about the deck, looking lost. "Silly old cow, she looks as blind as a cabbage."

"Shush!" said Mendark. "You'll offend her."

"Mmph!" said Pender.

"I'm serious! That's old Hetla, and she is blind."

"What!" cried Pender, running to the rail to peer at the rocks, which were only a span or two away and shaped like chacalot teeth.

"Blind from birth, but she's still the best pilot in Taranta. Rain or storm, she hasn't lost a ship in sixty years."

Pender pounded to the other side, not at all reassured.

"She's a sensitive, you prat!" said Tallia, putting her large feet up on the rail.

They found *Spear of Midnight* laid up in dock in Taranta, but it turned out to be a fat little carrier almost falling to pieces with woodworm, nothing like the sleek, dangerous craft Lilis had described. Tallia wrote to Lilis and Nadiril, a long letter with news of their doings in the past half year and the failure of their search so far.

They continued east to Huccadory, and thence to Gariott, where Pender was to unload his cargo and, with Mendark's grudging approval, load spices and cinnabar for the run back south along the coast of Crandor. Tallia had recognized Gariott at once, for they had come in to shore between a pair of smoking volcanoes. The large one was a famous landmark; the other just a dwarf. Each peak made a roughly circular bulge out from the north-east-curving coast of Crandor, the space between forming a deep bay almost ten leagues across.

"Look!" Tallia cried, leaning out over the rail like an excited child. "There's Bel Torance."

Mendark and Osseion came out to admire the view, and Pender too. Bel Torance was a giant, rearing up in a perfect cone so high that even in these low latitudes it had a dusting of snow on its top. Tallia felt the urge to instruct them about her native land.

"Bel BaalBaan over there used to be Torance's twin but, two hundred years ago, it blew its top right off. A wave as tall as a tower washed the old city into the mud, and ash buried everything that was left. Mud rained from the skies for weeks. The dead would have made a cube fifty bodies high and wide and deep. When it was over Bel BaalBaan was gone, save for a ring of islands. See them there! One of them began to smoke anew, and made what we call Bel SusBaal—daughter of BaalBaan." She pointed to the lopsided double peak that fumed further across the bay. "Ah, Crandor! My country has everything!"

"Including volcanoes, tidal waves, earth tremblers, typhoons, floods and mountain slides," said Mendark sourly. "Not to mention the nastiest insects on Santhenar."

"But it's rich!" said Osseion. "Look at the size of those trees."

Tallia could scarcely believe the emotions that swept over her as they drew up to the familiar shore. Before she set foot on the chocolate soil of Crandor she could have told that she was home, for the breeze carried to her that rich sweet moist odor of the tropics, of forest and people; heat and humidity and things rotting quickly. As they drifted along the shore where the children played naked and the water ran dark and rank in the gutters, and the houses were just shelters on stilts, with slatted floors and open window frames, merely affairs to keep out the hot sun and the warm rain, she breathed a sigh of deep contentment. Home! Back where she belonged. And as deep a sigh that she was not back here for good.

"What now?" she asked as they tied up to a wharf faced with cemented pumice-rock.

"Tar Gaarn," said Mendark, "and then Havissard."

"How far is that?" Pender wondered idly. He wasn't interested in any place that you could not get to by boat.

"Quite a way from here," Tallia replied. "We head south down the coast of Crandor for another hundred leagues or so, to Strinklet. From there we take the Great North Road, south and west, then a western path through the mountains to Tar Gaarn." Thinking about what was to come, a headlong flight across her native land, and then back to Thurkad in an equal rush, Tallia felt quite sad. She knew her duty and would do it, but she could not conceal her misery at the prospect of coming so close and passing all by.

In the morning they set off for Strinklet, arriving without incident in another four days. Mendark knew how Tallia felt. He had spent weeks thinking about Tar Gaarn and Havissard. He sensed very strongly that what was needed to remake the flute would be found there. He would share it with no one, not even Tallia. What she did not know she could not be made to tell. And lately she had been acting a little too independently.

They were to sleep on board *The Waif* that night, for there was a festival in the town and all the inns were full. But they could not bear to be cooped up any longer and, while Pender and the crew organized repairs and had the cargo unloaded, they went into town. Over dinner that night Mendark dropped his bombshell.

"Tomorrow I'm going to Tar Gaarn. Alone! So do what you want in Crandor, then meet me back here in fifty days."

"Alone!" said Tallia and Osseion together. She was shocked. Though Mendark was often close-mouthed, she had expected to accompany him to Tar Gaarn, a place she'd not been to but had often wondered about. What was he up to?

"Completely alone!"

"But who will protect you?" said Osseion. "What will I do?" Having guarded Mendark for so long, he could not imagine him even finding his way around by himself, much less protecting himself in this dangerous and foreign place.

"What do I care? I was looking after myself when you were still on the tit," Mendark said crudely. "Have a holiday."

"I don't want a holiday," Osseion muttered.

A part of Tallia rejoiced at the weeks this would give her in Crandor, yet she knew Mendark was going by himself so that no one would know what he did there, or what he found. Perhaps if he did find what he was looking for, he meant to keep it for himself. Tallia was hurt at the lack of trust.

When they rose with the sun next morning, Mendark was gone.

It was a hundred leagues from Strinklet to the abandoned city of Tar Gaarn, the way the road wound through the mountains. Fifteen days by horse, allowing for rests and unforeseen accidents, bad weather, broken bridges and poor roads.

Mendark hired two horses and, riding one and then the other, reached his destination without incident ahead of time, though the time passed very slowly. What if it's not there? he thought. What if I can't find it? And even if I get it back to Thurkad, how am I going to keep it out of Yggur's hands? His resources were meager now, while Yggur had armies at his disposal and the wealth of an empire.

Still, Yggur is unstable. Adversity weakens him but it strengthens me. He lacks cunning. That reminded him of an enemy who had none of those faults. Rulke! Mendark was terrified of the construct and the potential it represented. It was advanced beyond any device that they could conceive, and Rulke could be building it already!

No question that he, Mendark, was not Rulke's match. But he would never give up. Rulke might fail. His construct might have a flaw. The game's not over till it's done! All the more urgent, his quest.

From the top of the hill he looked down on the magnificent ruins with despair, that something so great, harmonious and subtle had been taken so easily, the very heart of the Aachim cut out. Tar Gaarn—the greatest city that they had ever built, the fount of their culture.

And how changed the land was from what it had once been. When the Aachim first conceived the idea of Tar Gaarn the Sea of Perion was still a jewel. It had scarcely begun its long drying, and all the lands around were populated. Now all was empty desert and Tar Gaarn lay desolate.

Though Rulke had taken the city and broken its defenses, not even he had been able to bring himself to destroy it. In this arid land its towers had been living fountains clad with water. Its crystalline domes and soaring arcs of stone were so attenuated and so delicate that they might have been made of spider thread. As with Katazza, it remained much as when the Aachim had abandoned it, more than a thousand years ago. Its most glorious works of art had been taken, those that could be carried, but the rest remained, statuary, carvings, mosaics. Many of the roofs were still intact.

But the greatest work of all was the city itself, and that would endure while the last brick lay on brick and the last stone on stone. Even under its coating of dust and sand, beneath the litter of stone and tiles and time-mottled glass, the magnificence of Tar Gaarn struck him dumb. It was worth the journey just to see it for the last time. Just to see it once again, he corrected himself, though he knew that this was the last. After this business was over he would travel no more. His body was giving out and he knew he could not *renew* it again. Great mancer as Mendark was, even he had reached his limit.

Mendark headed down the swooping, winding road to Tar Gaarn, where the soil was rich and red as Aachan gold, and the boulders scattered by the side of the road were black. He walked among the stones and broken columns, allowing the city to soak into his bones.

It was built on a radial pattern, curving streets and radiating boulevards arising from the city circle and five satellite centers. The circle was a vast open space roofed with a series of concentric glass shells. Once the glass had been mirrored on the upper side, cooling the space underneath, but the mirror coating had failed long ago and many of the glass tiles lay shattered on the ground. It was sweltering inside.

The building opposite, a tower with aerial walkways spinning out of it in five directions, was a broken ruin.

Mendark heaved a heavy sigh. Scarcely had it been completed, the most beautiful city in all Santhenar, than it was destroyed. Tales of Tar Gaarn, and of the tragic fool Pitlis who had designed it, swam in his mind.

Nine days Mendark spent searching the ruins, but before he had been there an hour he knew that it was a folly. There was nothing to shed light on the Mirror or the quest; no information, no books nor, least of all, any Aachan gold. Searching further was hopeless; what he sought was gone, if it had ever been here at all. But he could not drag himself away. To him Tar Gaarn had been the greatest achievement of humankind on this world. It had just been completed when Mendark first saw it. A thousand years after it was abandoned, it was just as beautiful.

And then again, perhaps the Aachan gold had never been here. Had it gone to Stassor, to the great library there? Then it might as well be destroyed, for he knew that the Aachim, despite his bond with them over the years, would never admit him to the secrets they kept there. Where else could it be, save Shazmak, now occupied by the Ghâshâd? Could the book Llian had seen there, *Tales of the Aachim*, hold the secret?

While thinking thus, Mendark had wandered out of the city along the northern road. Walking helped him to think. Continuing up the hill, he eventually reached the crest of the ridge separating Tar Gaarn from the valleys to the north. The wind was hot from the west, but there was a twist-trunked fig tree near the crest that formed a traveler's rest. Mendark sat down on a boulder in the shade, staring down at Tar Gaarn. But now its beauty was overshadowed; a pall was cast over it, and the shadow grew behind him until he could no longer restrain himself from turning that way. For the past week and more he had been avoiding it, hiding from himself all that he knew about it so as not to spoil Tar Gaarn.

He turned to look the other way. Rising to his feet in spite of himself, Mendark found himself looking higher than he needed to. His eyes were tugged to the triple towers, drawn out to needles of metal in their arrogance, their disdain for all natural forces: their tier upon tier, balcony upon balcony, so delicate that it seemed they might scarcely withstand the wind, making no concessions to the practicalities of defense; shining in the sun as if they were made of glass. Havissard! The citadel of Yalkara. Defenseless! Undefendable! Unbreachable! Unbreached! How long was it since she'd fled? Three hundred years and more. No—Yalkara would never flee! She had done what she came to do, thwarted Faelamor, found a way home to Aachan and took it. Why had she come to Santhenar in the first place? None ever knew.

Yalkara! Yalkara the enigmatic. Mistress of Deceits. The Demon Queen. Why did she come so long after the other Charon? Certainly not to aid *them*; at least, there was never any sign of it. Rather the reverse. To watch over them, spy on them? Perhaps. To be a foil to Faelamor? That hardly seemed needful, yet they were rivals from the first. To carry out some other, long-lasting and secret purpose of the Charon—some purpose which might yet be shaping the course of all their destinies?

She had taken no home, no land, no servant or soldier or guide all the while that the Aachim grew in strength, nor opposed them either. But in the instant of their fall she was there and even before Rulke entered the city in strength she disappeared, and the Mirror too. Then she *was* opposed, and Rulke turned away from the sacking of Tar Gaarn (perhaps that was how it had survived) to pursue her across the length and breadth of Lauralin. That would have been the greatest chase and the greatest tale of all, had it been told.

It seemed that the fugitive drama of Shuthdar was to be played out in another key, then Yalkara vanished and could not be found. Rulke immersed himself in another project, the building of his great city, Alcifer, that the hapless Pitlis had designed for him, though not long after it was complete Rulke himself was cast into the Nightland.

Around that time Yalkara had mastered the Mirror, returned to the very doors of Tar Gaarn and on top of the ancient silver mines of Havissard she constructed her citadel and gave it the same name. Why there? Most people said that she desired wealth beyond all things. And indeed, after reopening the mines and following the lode deep into the hot earth, she did become wealthy beyond any dreams. But Mendark had always thought that she built Havissard there to mock and humiliate the Aachim and to ensure that Tar Gaarn was never rebuilt.

Her citadel was made with vast labor and unparalleled magnificence, sumptuous beyond any description—though, strangely, it was said that her own quarters and workrooms were austere in the extreme. Contradictions abounded at Havissard.

Mendark was drawn to the place too; had always been, and each time he visited Tar Gaarn he had also sat here looking at the enigma of Havissard. He had never been able to get inside—no one could. Havissard was *protected* and resisted all attempts. But this time it would be different.

At the Great Library in Zile, last spring, he had sought out and copied ancient plans of the silver mines. That was what he had been doing all those weeks when Tallia thought he was sunken in despair. The maps were from before Yalkara's time and did not show the newer workings, but they were the best he could find. If Yalkara had made her own maps there was no record of them.

Well, better get on with it. Mendark headed on down the ridge, past Havissard without a backward glance and over another hill to the pockmarked valleys, the mullock heaps and slag piles, the shafts and adits out of which lifeless acid water ran. The streams were so stained with iron that every rock was the color of blood.

The mines of Havissard—as ugly as Tar Gaarn itself was beautiful. He consulted his maps again, identified an adit further up the hill, checked his water bottle and one of the lightglasses purloined from Katazza, and splashed in.

The adit led to a labyrinth, as was the way of old mines. Mendark had to check his way constantly, though he soon found that his maps were inaccurate. Doubtless new drives and shafts had been made after Yalkara reopened the mines, while old ones had collapsed or been filled with waste rock.

He kept going, traveling on a hunch about the direction and the level, knowing that he wanted to end up under Havissard. But how was he to enter? Havissard was protected by a mighty spell, as strong now as it had ever been. Normally such things would fail when the mind that made them died, or in Yalkara's case left the world. But to endure so long, this spell must be powered by something inside Havissard, retaining its strength whilever that object still maintained its power until, like a lightglass kept out of the sun, eventually it was drained dry.

Yet Mendark had a plan, which was why he had come alone. He wanted no one to see what he was doing here, what powers he could draw upon and, most of all, what he hoped to find inside.

Past broken ladders he made his way, beside shafts that offered only shattered bones and a lingering death. Up through wooden water ladders three times his height, among snail screws and rag pumps and other devices that had once been used to drain the mines, some broken and rotting on the floor, others seemingly as good as the day they were built. The mine was a museum of every kind of pump ever devised, but here they lay in rotten futility while the water found its level. Nothing could defeat it.

Finally he found a tunnel that ended in a chamber the size of a ballroom, cut into solid rock. It was high up and dry, but empty. Above he could feel the weight and the ages of Havissard pressing down on him, could sense the protection too. *This was it!* The solid rock above was many spans in thickness, and the protection weakest because it did not need to be strong here. If there was any way in, this was where it would be, up through ten spans of solid rock.

Mendark set his lightglass down on a shelf cut into the stone. From a brass box lined with velvet he took a spheroid the size and shape of a large egg. It was black, but when he held it to the light all the colors of the world and the sky danced there. It was a single piece of black opal, polished to the smoothness of agate. Mendark blew the dust off the rock shelf and set the opal down carefully beside the glass.

Now from a leather pouch he took a series of rings, like a puzzle ring that could only be put together in one way. But these rings, of which there were seven, were the size of bangles, and there were several possible solutions. They were made of silvery platinum.

Mendark put his fingertip to the opal, leaving a glowing red mark there. He exerted all his mind and will on that multi-colored spot, and when his senses were focused to a beam so tiny that it might have cut metal, he sought up through the weight of rock above, for Havissard. He found it at once and traced a path through it, seeking some throbbing subterranean thing that empowered the protection of the fortress. Eventually he identified that as well, though it was high up, too far to reach or visualize clearly, much less to break. He would have to try the more perilous way.

His *all-seeing* had given him an inkling of the nature of the protection, but he would have to know it much better before he could try this other way. So he spied it in and out and all around, and while he did so he was working on a solution to the puzzle ring, one that could be tuned to this protection and it alone. Then, as his seeking roved to and fro inside Havissard, it found something: a prickling aura leaking from what was hidden there. Mendark exulted. It was the Aachan gold, concealed by Yalkara long ago; he knew it instantly! He could not tell its location from here, but it would not be hard to find once he got inside. Tonight he would hold it in his hand. Then let his enemies tremble, Rulke especially.

But first he had to know the shapes and spaces of this protection as well as he knew his own mind. He kept on with his sensing and mapping. To compass this spell about and about, and keep all that he'd learned of it in his mind at once, would be a task worthy of the tellers. His own tale, and after this he would require Llian to tell it, would not just be any Great Tale. It would be the greatest of the Great Tales, and he, Mendark, would be known as the greatest figure in all the Histories of Santhenar. He allowed himself to dream for a moment—it was a longing he felt more and more as he approached the end of his days.

It was hard. Three times he had to break off his working and lie on the floor while the aftersickness burned him up. Three times he was sure that he would never complete it and every nerve shrieked at him to give it away. *Never!* he told himself—this is your last gasp, and if you win it will pay for all. The gold! *The Gold!*

He forced even harder on the fourth try, blacking out momentarily. Coming to, Mendark found himself lying on the dusty floor again, wondering who he was and what he was doing here. Then something in his still-writhing fingers clicked into place and he looked down to see that the puzzle ring was solved, seven melded seamlessly into one in a way that he had never imagined. The first part of his working was done. The day went well. The solution was at hand.

No time to rest. Mendark flipped the completed ring over the opal. It wobbled down to make an annulus about the center. The glowing spot began to move around the surface of the opal and to spread out until the whole stone glowed with color. The same colors sparkled on the walls and floor of the cavern until it was as bright as day.

Mendark spoke a word, spun the opal on its base like a top and the colors whirled and shifted, weaving a cage of light around him. He touched the ring with his fingers. The opal stopped spinning; the cage solidified into a sphere. He spoke another word, holding opal and ring up with out-stretched hands. The sphere of light lifted, revolving slowly like a soap bubble, shimmering like a bubble too, and pulled him up toward the roof.

The top of the sphere passed straight through the rock. Mendark held his breath, knowing that if his working had failed the bubble would squash him to a smear against the roof. But it carried him with it, pulled him right into the rock, into the greatest darkness that could possibly exist. His mind could not encompass what was happening. It resisted all the way, and he could feel the rock dragging all the way through him, filling every atom of him with itself. Then with a thump he came up against something impenetrable that he'd thought he had already overcome—the protection!

Mendark panicked. *It was unbreakable!* Solid rock filled his mouth, his lungs, his eyes and belly and bowels. Claustrophobia overwhelmed him. He was going to die here, forever trapped in this geologic prison.

No! his mind screamed, for his mouth was full and his lips embedded in granite and his lungs were petrified.

The whole of reality shuddered as, it seemed, his powers interacted with someone else's. The living rock rang like a temple bell, its very atoms wobbling through him and back the other way, a jelly the size of a mountain. Mendark could not even twitch his lip, but his mind screamed the most powerful opening word of all.

Suddenly the native rock began to slide past as though it *was* jelly. He spat it out of his mouth, wrestled with his courage. His mind swarmed with visions—two women on a rope platform above a river. Then the platform rocked wildly and they were gone. Suddenly he was through. He was inside at last! The place was thick with strangeness; the reality that he understood seemed to have little meaning here. But he was in, inside the lowest basement of Havissard. He stood up, but only for a moment. Aftersickness had never been this bad. The opal and the ring slipped from his hand to roll across the floor. The lightglass smashed and went out. He fell down and knew no more for a day.

27

HAVISSARD

Mendark woke in darkness. Feeling around, he impaled one finger on a shard of the lightglass. That led him to the rest of it, but it could no longer be coaxed to life. Fortunately he had another in his pack, though it was a long time before he remembered it. His brain did not want to follow the simplest directions. He'd done too much. His much-renewed body was giving out too soon. Mendark knew he'd be lucky to make it back to Thurkad.

The slow seepage of dust had covered everything; there was not even a spider's web or trail of rat to be seen. He worked his way up through the basements and dungeons, searching for that perilous something, surely the Aachan gold, that he had sensed from outside. It promised to be a tedious task, for Havissard was huge. But Mendark was so hyped up, so close to his goal that nothing could quash him. Just a few hours and he would have the gold. No need to fear Yggur any longer, or Rulke, or *anyone*. Being a sensitive, he was sure that he could use the flute if he could only make it.

And Tensor knew how. Tensor had been his friend for a thousand years. Tensor would forge it to atone for his crimes. Then the secret of gates would be his!

Mendark spent the best part of his second day searching before he sensed that the gold was near. Quartering that floor, he saw the most unexpected thing of all: fresh footprints! There were two sets, both coming and going, one smaller than the other. Quite small. A faint haze of dust lay in the air here. Following the prints he came upon a door, half-open, through which light showed. He stepped softly through, staff upraised.

Shelved from floor to ceiling were row upon row of journals, bound and clasped and, it appeared, numbered, though not in any script that he could read. He took one or two of them down: a version of the secret Charon script, he discovered. They showed no sign of the years—no rat holes, worm marks or such, though the earlier ones were worn, the bindings stained and scarred. A stone bench ran the length of the wall on his left, while the room was revealed to be L-shaped, the bench extending beyond the corner.

Mendark put his head round the corner. A woman was seated at the far end. She was bent over a book; a small pack sat on the dusty floor. The woman was small, with stark white skin and incongruously black hair. She wore a loose-fitting blouse and pantaloons, both of fine gray material, and gray boots.

He stood staring at her for almost a minute, wondering who she was and how she came to be here. What could have brought the two of them here, surely the only ones to enter Havissard since Yalkara's departure, at exactly the same time? How had she got in? Was that strange warping sensation that he had felt, *her* working? Was that what had allowed *him* entry too? The woman was familiar in some way that he could not identify, some idiosyncrasy of manner that he knew.

Suddenly she leapt to her feet in alarm. Throwing an arm up, she cried out a word. The air between them shimmered and grew thick. He tried to ward her away but his feet were welded to the floor and his tongue swelled to fill his whole mouth. He could not speak, could not even breathe. She spoke another word and monstrous things appeared, vulgar creatures with spiked clubs. They leapt at him.

Mendark shook his head, but he could not clear the cobwebs that were slowly tangling and filming over all his senses. He knew that the creatures were just illusions that could not harm him. He tried to wave them away but his hands were feeble, uncontrollable appendages. The illusions struck at his head with their maces, then he went blind, choked on his tongue, his legs turned to butter and melted and he fell on his face in the dust.

The woman fled as though pursued by her own phantoms, not noticing that her book had fallen to the floor.

Mendark woke with another frightful headache, once more in total darkness. He couldn't move, at first. His body was failing rapidly now. He groped around for his globe but it was gone, rolled across the floor, and took ages to find. When he did so Mendark found that it was cracked, with a large chip out of one side. He touched it to life but the light was feeble, fluttering, occasionally flaring up to a splintered glare that made his head ache worse than ever, at other times dwindling to a spark in the depths of the crystal. He sat down, suddenly afraid. If it failed he would never find his way out.

He wondered who the woman had been. He had been on his guard, had surprised her, yet she had broken his defenses as if they were not there, overcoming him with illusions so strong that even *he* had not been able to protect himself against them. What had she come for? What if . . .?

He prowled the room. The inscriptions on the back of each journal were in a script that he knew to be Charon. Though unable to read it, he recognized that the journals were numbered in order. He took one down, then another from a different section. They might have been year books, though not a single word could he decipher. He had no reason for taking any of them. His foot touched a small, slim volume lying in the dust, the book she'd dropped as she fled. He put it securely in his own pack.

Following the tracks, which cut straight through a labyrinth of corridors, Mendark soon lost all sense of direction. He was well beyond the area that he had earlier mapped. There was no dust in the air now. She was long gone.

Mendark followed the tracks, sometimes one set, sometimes two, for hours. They disappeared as he entered a section where the dust was scanty. Beyond he suddenly found himself in a bedchamber where the dust was untracked. It contained a low wooden bed, a cupboard on which sat a storm lantern and several books, all covered in dust. A desk on the other side of the room was also piled with books and journals. The bed had a red velvet cover. A scroll lay on it, or rather a piece of thick writing paper rolled up and held with a silver band. Beside it sat a small package wrapped in foil made of beaten silver.

Blowing off the dust, he unwrapped the package. Inside was a broad silver ring, beautifully inlaid with gold and platinum in swirling patterns like writing, though again in a script that he did not know. On the inside it was inscribed, in letters that he could read, *Yalkara—Gyllias*, and a symbol of eternity.

Opening the scroll, Mendark read a short message written in common speech, in silverpoint which had blackened over the centuries.

My dearest Gyllias,

Would that I could tell you face to face, but you are still not back and I can wait no longer. Faelamor attacked me again and this time she was very strong. She dealt me a wound which may well prove mortal. My only chance is to flee back through the gate to Aachan. Beware Faelamor!

Alas, my work is not done! I fear that it will never be

completed now. But I beg you, take the Mirror and guard it well, against the possibility that someone will come to restore the balance that Rulke broke with the flute. I have locked the Mirror. Its secrets are hidden to all save the One who has the key.

Take this ring, which I made with my own hands, of ore that I mined and purified here at Havissard, gold and silver and platinum all. It is the key to Havissard, and a form of protection against my enemy, and a token to give you heart in the darkness, to remind you of my undying love.

It grieves me to go this way, but go I must.

Farewell forever,
Yalkara

Mendark was not easily moved, yet he wiped away a tear. Whoever Gyllias was, it was a gift that had never been received, for Yalkara had passed through the gate and her protection had immediately sealed Havissard off for three hundred years. Well, it was of no importance now, save as a historical sidelight that showed her human side. It would interest Llian. He examined the ring. It was a beautiful thing, but had no power that he could tell. He rolled up the scroll, thrust it through the ring and stowed them both in his pack.

Returning the way he had come, Mendark eventually discovered the tracks again. Hours later, with the globe fading, he found himself outside the library, and later still, back at his starting point. Was this another illusion, designed to trap him in a labyrinth of the woman's own footprints? No, here they were, barely visible. They disappeared then reappeared, leading to another sparsely furnished bedchamber, back and forth in that place while his brain whirled with the effort of unraveling her path.

The tracks doubled back to the library, then one set went a different way, to a room where the plaster had been removed and a stone taken from the wall. He put his hand in the cavity, feeling a tiny prickling that disappeared almost immediately.

Mendark choked on bile. He wanted to break holes in the walls, to topple the towers of Havissard and watch them smash on the ground. The gold had been here, but it was here no longer. The woman had it. If only he had come here first! If only he had not lain helpless in the basement for a day. He could have wept. To have traveled so far and lose it by so little.

The regrets were useless, his great dreams now an embarrassment. No point in him even being here. Devastated, Mendark took out the black opal spheroid and the seven-piece ring, set them up in a suitable place and tried to touch the opal to life. It did not respond; it was utterly dead. He fumbled with the seven parts of the puzzle ring, but it was lifeless metal too. His brain could not imagine how to put it together, much less that there was one unique solution that would open the way out of here. After hours of frustration he realized that it was hopeless. He'd have to find another way out or stay till he starved.

The wall lights did not work here. Sitting down wearily in the dust, Mendark searched in his pack for food, then touched the globe to darkness to preserve what remained of the light. What would he do when it failed? Exhausted, he made a meal of dry bread and cheese so oily that it had begun to drip in the heat, washed it down with stale water, lay on the floor with his head on his pack and slept.

He slept indifferently, troubled by strange dreams, and after only a couple of hours roused himself and continued. The globe ebbed down to a glow so dim that it barely illuminated only the tips of his fingers, and he had to walk crouched down to see where he was going. When even that light failed he tore the sleeve off a dirty shirt, twisted it into the form of a torch, smeared it with the oily cheese and struck sparks into it. After many attempts it began to smolder. He swung the torch around his head until there was a dull red glow, no more than his enfeebled globe had given out, barely enough.

Hours he stumbled on, eking out the light. The shirt and the cheese were consumed and he was halfway though a spare pair of breeches when he discovered that the air was cool on his cheek. Following this path, stopping every so often to reassure himself that he was not mistaken, Mendark eventually entered a scullery. The breeze was coming from a chute that must have been used to dispose of kitchen wastes. A way out, perhaps. Or perhaps a trap that he would never escape from.

He crawled into the mouth of the chute, slipped and began to slide down a steep, greasy tunnel. He pressed the toes of his boots against the sides but it made no difference. He couldn't stop! He shot round a shallow bend toward a ragged light.

Mendark realized that it was the remnant of a wooden hatch that had once covered the outlet of the chute. His arms were trapped by his sides; he couldn't even protect his face. He struck the hatch head first, smashing the wormy wood to fragments. A nail scored his shoulder, he plunged through something that stretched like rubber, opened just enough to let him through and snapped closed again. The ring having opened the way, the protection spat him out. Now he was flying through the air, arms beating like the sails of a windmill. It was a long way down; Mendark had time to imagine his fate—impaled on a tree or smashed against rocks. Then he saw that there were dense bushes below him.

Mendark thumped down into brambles that had not been disturbed for centuries. He slapped his hands over his eyes as the wicked thorns tore his clothes to shreds. The whole center of the thicket sank down like a funnel under his weight, a hundred thorns gouged him, then he stopped, hanging upside down in the middle of the brambles. Dusty leaves rained past his face.

Everywhere he looked there were thorns. Blood ran in

rivers down his arms. He wriggled, sank a little further down then stuck fast. No matter what he did it had no effect.

His brief flight had shown that the brambles extended all the way along the base of the wall and down the slope as far as could be seen. They were old, vastly intergrown, with evil hooked thorns and brittle powdery gray leaves that shook down with every touch. Their dust itched abominably.

By concentrated effort Mendark managed to twist the pack off his back, but when he reached inside, his bread fell out and the water bottle nearly followed it. The vertical sun beat down like the heat of a furnace, but the breeze did not even stir the leaves down here.

Mendark tied the nearly empty bottle to his belt. He felt around carefully for his knife, mindful that if he lost it he would never get out. Still hanging like a bat he hacked hopelessly at the wrist-thick bramble canes that enclosed him on all sides.

A day went by. Mendark lay still. His body had failed him. He could feel it coming apart inside. He longed for death, but not this humiliating failure that would undo his life's reputation. The Histories could not show him like this—*he would not allow it!*

One last cast! he thought. Dare I try to renew myself one final time? Even in the best of circumstances renewal was hazardous. But here, with no food or water, no support, no tools or devices, the consequences could be hideous.

But I must! For myself and for Santhenar. Slowly, painfully, he began the rejuvenation spell for the last time.

28

Official Corruption

Fifty days!" Tallia said. "Well, that gives us time to look for *Stiletto*, and I can visit my family too."

Osseion, Tallia, Rustible and Pender were taking breakfast together in the shade of a sail, for the sun was up before they were and it was already hot. Beautifully hot and sticky, the climate she'd grown up in. Osseion was carving pieces from a whole fish cooked in a fiery red sauce, a splendid specimen that from blue lips to rainbow tail stretched the width of the table.

"Not at the breakfast table," said Pender with a shudder as Osseion reached for the eyeball.

"It's the best bit," said Osseion. He popped it out with his thumb, held it up between thumb and finger then flicked it into his open mouth. He chewed for a while, took the eyeball back out, examining it ostentatiously, licked off a bit of red sauce then rolled it along the back of his hand. Pender gagged on a piece of bread and boiled egg.

"Stop teasing him!" Tallia laughed.

Osseion allowed the eyeball to fall through the gap made by the missing finger, caught it neatly in his other hand and popped it back in his mouth again.

Even Rustible, stolidly packing away the fish as if it was his last meal, gave an amused snort. He was a messy eater, his shirtfront spattered with red sauce and strands of fish intestine.

Pender, who was drenched in sweat, turned his head away. He had not been surprised by Mendark's disappearance. "He's a secretive one, eh!" he said to Tallia, recovering enough to spoon down half a dozen soft-boiled eggs. They had been living on hard tack for weeks but the spicy fare of Crandor did not agree with him. "Well, I've got plenty to do this month if you haven't."

Tallia raised an eyebrow.

"While you were busy in town yesterday I had several approaches," said Pender. "Cargoes down the coast of Crandor as far as I want to go. I also have some private dealings that might make both our fortunes."

"As long as they aren't the kind that could lose our heads!"

Pender rubbed the bristly stump that joined head to body, looking unhappy.

"How far do you want to go?" Osseion interjected, mopping sauce off his plate with a slab of bread as long as Tallia's forearm.

"Roros, Guffeons, Gosport—perhaps even as far as Maksmord if the winds are with us. There's buckets of money to be made here, and a cargo to be found for the journey back home."

"I'll go as far as Roros," said Tallia, "where my mother and father dwell. I wouldn't advise you to go much further, Pender, or you'll never get back in time."

While Pender's crew loaded cargo—spices, coconut, smoked clams and a miscellany of other freight—Tallia went back to the Customs House to enquire about the five remaining boats on her list. After lubricating the tongue of a junior clerk with a few silver coins, she confirmed that three had home ports in Crandor—*Ivory Cutter, Cutlass* and *Stiletto*—though a quick flip through the docking records did not show any of them calling here in the last half year.

"I'd be careful if I were you," said the customs clerk, an earnest, spotty youth.

"Oh!" said Tallia.

"It may not be too healthy to ask too many questions."

"Why is that?" asked Tallia, but then the Customs Master returned from lunch. A great, wallowing woman with sagging dewlaps and tiny eyes, she looked like a born bureaucrat.

"What do you think you're doing?" she bellowed. "Those records are confidential."

Though Tallia knew that was not the case, she did not argue. The woman wanted a bribe, a much larger one than she'd already paid to no avail. Not planning to waste any more money here, Tallia merely bowed and went out. That turned out to be a mistake.

Next morning they continued south down the coast, stopping at several small ports on the way to Roros, capital of the rich southern province of Crandor. Roros was a rich old city, larger even than Thurkad. Draped between two hills across a meandering floodplain, it was a city of canals and a thousand bridges, with a waterfront that stretched for a league. After some trouble, for it was also festival time here and the waterfront was packed, they found a berth. Pender hired a team of divers to scrape down the bottom, which was covered in weed and barnacles. They waited for customs to come aboard, leaning on the rail, watching seagulls feeding on scraps in the water.

"I wish they'd get a move on," said Tallia, impatient to see her family.

The customs inspection was brief and efficient. Immediately afterwards Tallia went down to the Customs House to continue her search. She met with a friendly reception until she mentioned the boats she was looking for.

"We guard our privacy here in Roros," said the officer. "Why do you want to know?"

"I'm looking for a sailor," Tallia replied, "on behalf of his daughter, who is from Thurkad."

"Sailors!" sniffed the woman. "I would advise you to look elsewhere."

"I'm a citizen of Crandor and I know my rights," Tallia persisted. "The docking records are public information."

"Not in Roros!"

Tallia patted her pocket, the first step to offering a bribe, usually the quickest way in her country. "Perhaps we can discuss this privately," she said in a low voice.

To her amazement the officer reacted aggressively. "Are you trying to bribe me?" she said so loudly that all the clerks looked up.

"Of course not," Tallia said hastily. "I just . . . never mind. Thank you."

Back at *The Waif* she told Pender the story. "I don't like it either," he said, munching a sandwich gloomily. "There's something funny going on here."

There was a lot to do, so the crew went on with their work and thought no more about it. Tallia went into the city. At dawn the next morning a long sleek boat with a yellow sail cruised past, its captain scanning their vessel with keen interest. *Poniard* was written in gold letters across the stern.

"He seemed to like what he was looking at," said Osseion.

Pender spat over the side. "Corsair or sea robber, or smuggler," he said. "Don't attract his attention—he's as fast as us; maybe faster. How are your family, Tallia?"

"Well, apparently, though they're all out of town on a family holiday." She sighed heavily.

Half an hour later the same ship came back. This time there was no doubt that the skipper was inspecting them carefully.

"I don't like the look of him," said Rustible.

"Cheeky devil," Pender said. "I'll have to take extra precautions. There goes my profit. No wonder shipping costs are so high here."

"Are we . . . carrying anything special, Pender?" Tallia asked carefully.

"Soon won't be," he muttered.

Just then a customs officer reappeared, checked their papers carefully, cocked an eye along the vessel and said, "Come with me if you please, captain."

Pender waddled off behind him, sweat bursting out of the back of his neck. Before they had finished their breakfast, another customs officer, a woman almost as tall and dark as Tallia, though rather meatier, appeared on the gangplank.

"Tallia bel Soon?"

"I am."

"I would be grateful if you would accompany me to the Customs House. Please bring your papers and seal, if it is convenient."

Despite the politeness, Tallia was alarmed. It was an order and would be enforced ruthlessly if she did not cooperate. But then, this was her country, and she knew the procedures well.

She gathered the required articles and went down to the Customs House. "There is an irregularity?" she asked.

"We take our duties seriously in Roros," said the woman, which might mean anything or nothing.

Pender was sitting across a table from the first official, the ship's papers and cargo manifests spread out all around. Tallia sat down beside him. He was sweating profusely.

"*Black Opal* is on our list," said the man. "She is known to have been a smuggler of illegal substances."

Pender gave Tallia a reproachful glare. She knew exactly what he was thinking. *I told you* Black Opal *was trouble, eh! Told you that we would be harried and hindered and maybe put in gaol just because this boat has a bad name.*

"That was long before our time," said Pender. "We

bought her legally from customs in Ganport. She is *The Waif* now. Look, the papers are signed and stamped. The change of name has been properly registered. Here is the seal of customs, and here, that of the Ganport Harbor Master. Everything is in order."

"We have never heard of Ganport," said the woman. "And papers are easily forged, a matter that we will come back to later." She stared coldly at Tallia. "You admit that this vessel was once the *Black Opal*?"

"Ganport is a fishing port about a hundred leagues north of Thurkad," Pender said, answering the first question.

The woman consulted a huge register of stamps and seals from all over the known world. "I can find nothing for Ganport."

"Surely customs comes under the Registry of Trade, in that country?" said Tallia.

The two officials whispered to one another, consulted various charts and maps of ports and turned more pages while Pender sweated. Eventually they agreed that the stamps were valid. Then another difficulty arose.

"Tallia bel Soon! I recall that name in a dispatch," said the customs man.

More searching through papers. "I knew it!" cried the man, running his finger across the page. "Tallia bel Soon, arrested for forging papers that were used in the purchase of *Black Opal*."

"What alias?" the woman asked.

"Jalis Besune."

She almost had a fit. "Besune is my father's name!"

In a great flurry of excitement, everything was examined again. Tallia thought Pender was going to have a heart attack.

"I admit the forgery," said Tallia calmly. "However, it was done to escape from the war! It is not illegal to use another name in Meldorin, or in Crandor, so long as no crime or fraud is involved. I have a right to use the Magister's seal."

"Easy to say; not so easy to prove. Produce the seal."

Fortunately Tallia had it with her, and a warrant from Mendark which was genuine. Introducing his name into the affair caused more complications, for Mendark was known in Crandor, not entirely favorably. But on the other hand, his was a more powerful name than they cared to deal with on their own authority.

"Mendark must come here in person and explain his business."

Tallia answered that Mendark was not even in Crandor. The officials held another whispered conference. For a while it seemed that they would be kept in custody until he could be brought to account, for Tallia wasn't going to tell where Mendark was or what he was up to. She was already anxious about him, all alone.

"Hold on," said Tallia. "Mendark is not an owner of this boat."

"He was when the papers at issue were signed."

"And we have not even started on the transfer papers from him to you two," said the other.

"Really!" said Tallia icily. "This has gone on too long. I call for an arbitrator, as is my right. I will claim that you exceed your authority, to the hindrance of free trade."

"You have the right," said the woman. "Name your arbitrator."

"Dacia bel Rance," said Tallia, crossing her fingers in case she was no longer alive. It *had* been more than ten years.

The register fell closed with an immense clap. "The Deputy Governor!" The woman stared at Tallia, then at her fellow official.

"My aunt," Tallia said coolly. "And I may claim that you are harassing me to cover up your own corrupt dealings."

"We must consult," said the woman. The two officials disappeared through the door behind the counter.

"Pity you didn't speak up as soon as we got here," said Pender, wiping away the sweat.

"I didn't know Aunt Dacia had risen so high. Besides, using influence in Crandor can be a blade with two edges. It must be done delicately, at just the right moment."

Eventually the officials came back and the matter was settled but they were still not free to go. All the manifests had to be examined in excruciating detail, the duties paid. Finally they returned to a very worried Osseion, and the ship was searched with commendable thoroughness. Nothing illegal was found, but a day had been lost.

A few minutes later the corsair's boat came past for the third time.

"I don't like this at all," said Osseion. He stood up, staring at the sleek ship. "A poniard is a sneak's weapon. What kind of a person would give a boat that name?"

"A dangerous man," said Tallia.

Pender was not a brave man. "No!" he said when Tallia proposed that he make enquiries about *Poniard* and her captain. "I value my skin far too much to draw attention to myself in a strange city. We don't know who to trust."

"I don't trust anyone here," fretted Rustible, coiling yellow hair around a finger.

"I can ask my family," said Tallia, "when they get back."

"I'll go," said Osseion. "There are ways of finding these things out." It did not take him long; the boat was known in every waterfront bar.

"*Poniard* is owned and captained by Arinda bel Gorst. A clever and charming man; also ruthless and violent. The boat has a nasty reputation though no one would say anything specific. He's a smuggler, probably a pirate too, but it seems no one has lived to bring evidence to court."

"Why would he be interested in us?" asked Tallia.

"A fast ship, not from these parts," said Pender. "Perhaps he thinks we're in the same business, or trying to take his. If we disappeared no one would ever miss us. *Black Opal*'s reputation seems to have been everywhere."

"More likely his agent in customs told him about our

cargo," said Tallia. "Just what are you carrying in those locked crates, Pender? Silver bars? I noticed you kept the manifests from me back there."

"Nothing illegal. I've learned that the fewer who know, the better."

"I'm your partner, remember," she said sharply.

Pender looked a little nonplussed. "Much better than silver," he said. "Liquid metal. Twenty flasks of quicksilver, each your weight and worth a fortune here. I've invested all my profit in it."

"Enough to kill us all a hundred times, if a flask tips over in a storm," said Tallia angrily. "You should have told me! Well, get rid of it and get the money into the counting house before our friend bel Gorst comes for it."

"I can't," he said gloomily. "It goes to the Alchemical Academy at Twissel, two days down the coast. Osseion, better go out and hire some guards; and make damned sure that they aren't pirates too."

"I think I'll make a few more enquiries about Poniard while I'm out," said Osseion.

"Better hurry. If he gets the cargo I'm ruined."

"If he gets it," said Rustible somberly, "we're dead!"

It was a hot, still, sticky night. Everyone was hoping for a storm but it hadn't eventuated. They slipped out of Roros port under cover of darkness, making their way up the winding channel among the rocks and reefs.

"Are you sure that this is a good idea?" Tallia asked before they had gone very far. Waves could be seen breaking on reefs in every direction.

"It's a bad idea," Pender replied, "but not as bad as losing ship and cargo, and probably our lives as well, to that pirate, eh! I spoke to the pilot and bought the latest charts. The channel's not my biggest worry."

They were moving slowly forward under a rag of sail, Rustible at the bow with a lead line while Pender paced back and forth, sniffing the breeze.

"The wind?" asked Tallia.

"It's just a land breeze, shifting all the time. It'll die as the night goes on. But if it turns around to the east we won't be able to get out."

"Let's go back. Better not risk it," Tallia advised.

Pender pondered. He stared at the sky, rubbing his bristly jaw. Tallia could hear the rasping sound from the other side of the boat. "I think the land breeze will get us out." He shouted for a bigger sail.

The night passed with agonizing slowness; then, at midnight, the breeze suddenly died away and the sails hung limply from their poles.

Pender cursed, but he said confidently, "It'll come again. It's not far to the sea now."

They sat there for the rest of the night, anchored against the tide, but the breeze did not return. It was not a pleasant night, dwelling on bel Gorst coming after them. Only at dawn did a zephyr inflate the sails, just enough to move them out into the open sea.

"At last," Pender cried. "Let's be on our way before they come looking for us."

"Too late," Osseion intoned from halfway up the mast, where, incongruously, the massive soldier was keeping watch. "Yellow sail coming down the channel."

Pender clambered up. "She's caught the breeze and coming with it," he said. "Moving faster than we are, too."

The crew ran to their posts. The breeze stirred the sails and *The Waif* responded, though not with the same spirit as the other boat.

"It's her," Osseion called, "*Poniard*!"

"Farsh, farsh, farsh!" Pender only swore when he was extremely worried. He ran to the wheel.

"What is it?" Tallia asked, resting a hand on his shoulder.

"She's bigger than us, and faster, at least in these light airs. She's a well-crewed boat. Pity we didn't finish scraping our bottom; we're dragging a bit."

"Is there anything we can do?"

"Not much," he said. "Bel Gorst knows these waters better than I do, and the winds too. Pray for a gale, though even then *Poniard* may be our match."

The blue sky was cloudless—no chance of any strong weather. Out to sea they picked up a nor'easter and tacked into it, for after Roros the coastline turned east. They zigzagged along the coast, the bigger boat steadily gaining, while Pender looked grimmer and grimmer. He seemed to shrink, to get shorter and squatter and more miserable. He had everything to lose—and to lose *The Waif* mattered more to him than his life.

"How far?" asked Osseion half an hour later. He meant to Twissel, where Pender was to unload the priceless alchemical quicksilver.

"Not even halfway," Pender grunted, his shoulders sagging even more.

They were now passing along a cliffed coastline, the dark rock wet, shiny and forbidding, cut by clefts and narrow inlets, and yawning sea caves into which the big swell burst, but none offered any hope of hiding or escaping.

It was a long and tedious chase, for at sea everything happens in slow-motion and there was little difference between the two vessels. *The Waif* picked up a little distance on the port tack then lost it and a bit more on the starboard. With every hour *Poniard* crept closer. She would overhaul them well before dark. Already she was only a couple of bowshots behind. Two archers stood at her bow, preparing to shoot for the sails.

"Osseion," called Tallia, "you draw a mighty bow. Think you can tear their sail from here?"

"Not yet! But soon I'll have a go."

Shortly, through Pender's spyglass, they saw the saturnine bel Gorst standing at the rail.

"Look at him gloating!" cried Pender, almost foaming at the mouth. "Shoot the bugger, Osseion."

Osseion drew back his bow, then loosened it again. "Still too far," he said regretfully.

"He's not gaining any more," said Tallia some time later. "Maybe we have his measure."

"I'm afraid not," Pender replied. "Look, he's changed the trim of his sails to make us think that. He's playing with us, keeping just out of bowshot, biding his time until we're well out of sight of Roros."

"I heard that too," said Osseion. "He loves to torment people."

"Is there any way of getting a bit more speed out of *The Waif*?"

"Only by throwing the cargo overboard," Pender said.

"Better to do that than let him have it," she said.

There was a tear in his eye. "I know, I know."

They raced on, but made up no ground. Finally Pender groaned. "All right, but the quicksilver last of all. Start the water over the side!" he yelled.

Tallia ran to the pump and began to discharge their fresh water, while Osseion climbed down into the hold to heave out as much of their ballast—stones—as they could dump without risk of the boat capsizing. The other crew followed, and when the ballast was gone, they lugged the rest of the cargo up—bags of grain, huge flagons of wine and oil, crates of porcelain and dried coconut. With each splash Pender looked sadder and sadder. After an hour and more, all of the cargo was gone save the quicksilver and enough food and drink to do them for a day or two.

The Waif began to inch ahead of its pursuer. "We've done it!" shouted Rustible, banging one fist in the other hand.

For a while it seemed that they had, then *Poniard* re-trimmed its sails, now, it seemed, sailing as fast as it could, and began to make up the distance. Soon it hung on their windward quarter, no closer than before but no further either. It was still too long till dark.

"Get rid of the anchors," said Pender in a dead voice. "Leave only the smallest."

After much grunting and heaving, the two large anchors crashed into the water, and then a smaller one. The distance between the two racing ships began to widen imperceptibly. Then they saw the pirate's crew hauling up something that had been dragging behind, a weighed-down section of sail. Suddenly, swiftly, the sleek craft began to overhaul them once more.

"The devil taunts us!" cried Pender, tears of rage running down his unshaven cheeks. "He had a sea anchor out all the while. There's no hope now. Throw out the quicksilver!"

Osseion ran down the ladder, to stagger back up with a great iron flask on his shoulder. Wobbling to the side he slid it over the rail into the sea, into which it plunged with a small, high splash. Pender stared at the place for a long time, then abruptly dashed the tears from his cheek and roared, "Send it over, quick!"

Those hands who were strong enough went below to help with the task. They could see bel Gorst's bared teeth—*Poniard* had approached so close—but at the sight of the precious cargo going over the side he roared at his archers and a flight of arrows sang toward them. Pender gave him a two-fingered gesture; the arrows sank into their wake.

"He didn't think we'd dump the quicksilver," said Tallia.

"Neither did I," said Pender miserably.

Osseion snatched up his enormous bow, drew back the string until the muscles corded in his arm, then let it fly. The arrow vanished. Suddenly bel Gorst fell back, jerking at something, then dropped into cover.

"Ha! See how you like that," cried Pender.

"Great shot, Osseion," said Tallia. "Did you get him?"

"Very near," said Pender, peering through the glass. "It went through the sleeve of his coat. He won't be so bold next time."

Tallia ran down the ladder to take her turn. Picking up one of the flasks, she heaved it onto her shoulder, instantly realizing that she wasn't quite strong enough. The curved iron was a crushing weight on her shoulder-blade. Twice she thought the flask was going to get away from her as she hauled herself one-handed up the ladder. The boat heaved, flinging her sideways and cracking her hand between the flask and the hull. She almost dropped the flask. Only the knowledge that Rustible was underneath kept her hanging on.

Somchow Tallia forced herself up the ladder with her precious, deadly cargo. As it plummeted over the side, another flock of arrows soared toward them. One actually struck the stern of the boat, drooping down like the tail feathers of a rooster on the chopping block.

"I'm not strong enough," she apologized as Osseion staggered by.

"If anything can be said to be man's work, this is it," he gasped.

On they went, and as the flasks went into the water, once more *The Waif* began to inch ahead of her pursuer. "Laugh now, you miserable bugger!" Pender whispered. "I'll bet you're sorry you didn't take us when you could."

They were rushing along a shore where some of the sea caves had collapsed to form a series of arches, pinnacles and rocky islands—a treacherous area simply marked "uncharted" on Pender's maps. They were sailing close to shore, but at this point *Poniard* moved further out to sea.

"Is he doing that to cut off a sudden dash for the open sea, or because of the danger of the shoals?" Pender said to himself.

"What are our chances now?" asked Tallia.

"Well, the cargo is gone, and that was more than the value of *The Waif*. But he'll still want the boat if he can get it, and bloody revenge on us for the loss of his profit."

"Yes, the pirates of Crandor don't have a pretty reputation. Then if we must die, let's give him a lesson he'll never forget."

"We're eight," said Osseion. "They must have at least twenty on board."

"I've an idea," said Pender, "if you trust me to attempt it."

"With my life," said Tallia. "What is it?"

"I believe we'd have the edge on him downwind. If we were to turn here, we'd lose way and he'd be onto us in a minute. But up ahead"—looking where he was pointing, she spied a group of islands across their path, and others beyond, all cliffed like the shore—"if we went between them, he'd lose sight of us, maybe for long enough for us to turn back to Roros. Then we'll see who's faster."

"I'm not a sailor, Pender, but won't we lose our wind as we go between the islands?"

"Somewhat," he replied, rubbing his chin bristles. "What I plan to do is tack a bit further out to sea, as though I am going around the islands, then on the last tack, dart through the gap between the two biggest. Because he's further to sea, it'll be difficult for him to do the same—those islands out there will be in his way. After we do that, he'll have to guess whether we've gone on to Twissel or turned back to Roros, eh!"

"What if he guesses right and turns back straight away?"

"Then we're finished! Hey, Rustible, come here."

They went into a huddle, reviewing the state of the tide, the probability of wind and currents being weaker between the islands, or stronger, the draught of *The Waif* compared to *Poniard*, surely less with the cargo and some of the ballast gone, and other technical matters that Tallia had no appreciation of.

They were now beating up into the wind on the last tack. *The Waif* edged a little further ahead, just out of bowshot. *Poniard* turned to cover her, moving further out to sea in the hope of catching a stronger breeze. Just ahead was a cluster of small rocky islands, then to their right two larger ones, cliffed all around and with flat tops covered with scrub. Beyond the right-hand one was a chain of smaller islands.

They passed inside the cluster, then turned smoothly on the port tack, picking up the wind and surging forward. Tallia ran to the rail, watching the other boat. It turned as well, staying seaward of the island cluster.

The tension on Pender's face was mirrored on the rest of

the crew. Everything depended on what bel Gorst did next. Pender had been rather clever, Tallia saw, as they ran toward the gap between the two larger islands. Beyond them, the cliffed coast turned sharply south, a shortcut to Twissel and the wind more to their advantage, if they could get there. Bel Gorst must be worried now, knowing that if they got through first they could turn back or pick up the wind and be well away to their destination, while he either went round the long way or worked his way through the islands.

"What's he going to do?" Pender cried, screwing up his face in his agony. He turned sharply, heading between the two larger islands toward the cliffed coastline beyond. They picked up speed with the wind.

"He's starting to turn," Rustible shouted. Pender swore and Tallia's heart sank. "No, he's going straight on, around the outside."

Pender let out a whoop. They drifted into the lee of the island, eddies flapped the sails, then the wind died completely. Momentum carried them on, drifting dangerously close to the rocks. Osseion and Rustible stood ready to fend them away with oars. With agonizing slowness they drifted between the two islands and out the other side, but still there was no wind, for they were in the lee of the chain of islands beyond.

"I thought we'd catch enough of a current to carry us through," said Pender gloomily. *The Waif* was stationary now, the shrouds sagging from their poles. A tiny current rotated the bow around, then died away.

"There's a bit of a breeze over near the cliff," called Rustible from the mast. "Though it'd be a hell of a pull."

A good few hundred spans away the water was feathered with little ripples where the wind was funneled along the cliff line.

"Quick!" Pender cried. "Get the dinghy over the side, and a stout line onto it. Osseion, into the dinghy. You too, Argis," he shouted to the meatiest of the sailors.

In a minute the dinghy was in the water, the two big men

at the oars. "Pull for all you're worth!" Pender roared, "or we're dead!"

They pulled, and slowly the cable tightened, spraying water out of the braids. *The Waif* began to creep toward the rippled sea. And as it did so *Poniard* appeared at the eastern end of the channel, moving swiftly with the wind.

"Farsh!" Pender swore, then fell silent. The situation was too dire for cursing.

29

BRAGGARD'S ROCK

"I don't suppose you could manage another of your illusions?" Pender said hopefully to Tallia. "Or even better, a breeze?"

"Weatherworking is one of the most difficult of the Secret Arts," she replied. "And the least predictable—like the weather itself. I never had any skill at it. But not even Faelamor could hide *The Waif* on a bright day like today. They can already see us."

Poniard was losing speed rapidly in the lee of the islands, though it looked as if she still had enough wind to catch them. And she would do so before the two in the dinghy, now pulling like galley slaves, towed them to that little breezeway over by the cliffs. They watched the enemy's progress in silence. An hour passed, the slowest that Tallia had ever experienced.

The pirate craft was now so close that they could see the dark visage of bel Gorst, and hear the roars and jeers of the crew.

"I can't bear this," said Pender, punching his fist against the tiller.

"Have you any pitch on board?" Tallia asked casually.

"A barrel or two, unless you threw it over as well, eh?"

"We didn't."

He stared at her, then suddenly grinned. "Rustible, a barrel of pitch up here, on the double."

Shortly Rustible came running up the steps with the barrel on his shoulder, banged it down and expertly knocked the top out.

"Pitch up a couple of arrows for me, would you," Tallia said, concentrating with her eyes closed. "And fetch a bucket of coals from the galley."

Tallia sat, cross-legged, lost in her mind as she constructed the separate parts of her illusion and fitted them together in her head. No one said anything, though Pender gripped the rail as if trying to mold the brass to the shape of his fingers. The crew stared at the approaching boat. It was very close.

Suddenly Tallia's eyes flew open. "The bow!" she snapped. A longbow was put in her hand. She drew the string back once or twice, then nodded. "The arrow!" A pitched arrow was handed to her. She tested its weight and balance, then smeared the pitch down with one finger.

Springing up, she touched the arrowhead to the fire bucket and drew it out flaming. She stepped to the rail, drew back the bowstring until the flaming head almost touched the wood, and let it fly. It arced high, descended toward the other boat and slammed into the sail just above the boom. A little patch of flame grew there. Tallia threw the bow to Rustible, crying "Shoot again!" then she swayed on her feet, chanting.

The tiny flame licked at the sail. Another joined it, higher up, from Rustible's arrow, then with a violent roar flames sprang right to the top of the sail, and leapt to the other sails too. The sailors raced to the sides of the boat. Tallia moved her hands in the air and the flame appeared to jump to the ropes, the wheel-house, even the planks of the deck. Half the sailors promptly leapt over the side, while the others crowded at the bow. Bel Gorst ran back and forth, screaming at them and heaving buckets of water at the fire.

Tallia suddenly fell down on the deck and the illusion vanished. One sail was on fire, and its ropes, but that was all. Pender whooped. Everyone stared at the flames. No one moved.

"Hoy!" boomed Osseion's deep voice from the dinghy. "What are you doing? Let's get going!"

Unnoticed, the rowers had pulled *The Waif* into the patch of light air. The sails rippled and began to bell out. Before Pender could give an order the sailors were at their posts. Osseion and Argis clambered up the side, as drenched with sweat as if they had fallen in the water. The dinghy was hauled over the side.

"I've never worked so hard in all my life," Osseion gasped, slurping down a dipper of water.

On *Poniard* the fire had been put out. A hole was burned in the mainsail, and the ropes and spars were charred, but the other sheets, though scorched, were intact. Most of the conflagration had been illusion.

Bel Gorst was working with a cold fury, recovering the sailors who had leapt overboard, whipping them indiscriminately as they began the task of replacing the ropes and sails. But now *Poniard* was herself becalmed, as tantalizingly close to that cliff-line breeze as *The Waif* had been before her, and he was forced to watch helplessly as she set her sails and began to drift away and, once out of the wind shadow of the islands, to gather speed and head downwind in the direction of Roros.

Only then was there time to pick up Tallia, who still lay in a daze, and carry her to a hammock in the shade. They reached Roros not long before dawn, tied up at a wharf, put out guards and slept the day away. That evening they gathered for dinner and a council of war.

"I'm ruined," Pender said, looking haggard as death. The euphoria of their escape had worn off long ago. "I invested all my profits in the quicksilver venture; every grint!" Slumping down in his seat, he thrust the plate away, too miserable to eat.

"I think there might be one flask left," said Tallia.

"Not enough to replace all the other cargo, much less our supplies and anchors." He wrung his fat hands together.

"Well, let's sell it and take on some new cargoes before your debts fall due."

"No one will give me a cargo now. Bel Gorst has marked me—no one will dare! Ruined, ruined!" He staggered across the gangplank, a fat, sad, down-at-heel barrel of a man.

"Pender, I'm sure we—"

"Don't talk to me—I can't think! Leave me alone!" He wobbled up the street.

Tallia watched him go, then turned back to Osseion and Rustible. "Well, what are we going to do about bel Gorst?"

"Do?" said Rustible, licking his thick lips. "We're not fighters. At least, I'm not. Take it to the constables."

"I'll bet they're already in his pocket!" snapped Tallia. "We humiliated him yesterday and he'll want revenge. As soon as we leave port, he'll be after us."

They talked for half the night but did not come up with any plan, and drifted back to the boat to take their turns at the watch and to sleep. However, when Tallia rose at dawn Pender had still not returned.

"Probably got drunk and spent the night at the inn," said Osseion, rolling out of his hammock.

"Probably! He was well on the way when he left us." Nonetheless, Tallia was worried, and after lunchtime came and went and still no Pender, she went out to look for him.

She discovered what had happened at the first inn she came to. "Your friend was so drunk that he couldn't stand up," said the innkeeper, a bright little gnome of a man. He giggled. "Poor miserable sod, he'd just lost his whole life's hope. Lucky his friends came for him."

"Friends?" said Tallia, fighting to keep the alarm out of her voice. "Who were they?"

"The best friends anyone could have," giggled the gnome. "Powerful friends—led by none other than Arinda bel Gorst himself!"

"And Pender went with them?" she asked more calmly than she felt.

"Last night he would have gone with the devil himself, if he'd offered a shoulder to lean on."

"Where can I find bel Gorst?" Tallia asked.

"You're from out of town, eh?" said the innkeeper with a knowing wink.

"I was born in Roros, but I've not been here for many years."

"I thought so. No one from Roros would need to ask!"

"I'm asking," said Tallia, fighting her irritation.

"He has his own island. Braggard's Rock, it's called, up the harbor across from the slaughterers."

Very appropriate, Tallia thought, turning away.

Pender woke in a cramped cell that had a nauseating dead stench about it. Despite the wine he could remember the night clearly—the flask after flask of cheap wine, the agony of his loss, and at the end of the night the friendly sailors who had helped him outside. He could remember bel Gorst's dark face smiling with menace, though the drunken haze had filtered that out at the time. Now it was all too real.

Bel Gorst had said nothing to him, nor harmed him in any way, in the short march down to the wharves and the brief trip up the harbor. Pender was not fooled. The pirate would appear before too long, to torture and kill him in the most agonizing and drawn-out way possible. For revenge, or maybe for the sheer pleasure of it.

After he had been awake for an hour or so the door bolts scraped and the door was opened a crack. A head peered in, then a slight figure slipped inside. A slave child, by the look of her, a dark-skinned girl clad in ragged shorts and tunic. Her black hair was plaited into a series of handles.

"Garish ha! Ploggit!" she said in a voice not at all cowed by her surroundings, nor by him.

"I don't speak your language," Pender said, sitting up carefully. His head ached abominably.

The girl switched to the common tongue of the west. "Bright morning to you, I said." She held out a wooden bowl, darkly crusted around the rim; within was a gray speckled mess like thrice-cooked gruel. It had the dense, cloying stench of fish preserved by rotting, and it smelled repulsive, even for a man as habitually hungry as Pender was.

"What is it?"

"Boiled slubber, of course!" she replied, amazed at his ignorance.

"You can have it. I'm not hungry."

They regarded each other. "What are you doing here?" Pender wondered. "Are you a slave child?"

The girl scooped slubber out of the bowl with her fingers, eating it with, if not exactly relish, exceedingly good cheer. "Of course not!" she said with scorn. "My father and I are *water carriers*."

She said it with as much pride as if they had been master chroniclers, though it was a low, poorly paid job, in most places little better than slavery.

"Aren't you afraid, living on this island of wicked pirates?"

"There is no one in the whole of Crandor would do harm to a child," she said with utter confidence.

"What about me?" Pender said fiercely. "I am not from Crandor but from evil Thurkad, on the other side of the world." He stood up in a rush and a rattle of chains, trying to ignore the pain in his temples and the nausea in his belly.

She placidly ate her slubber. The stench in the hot little room was overpowering. "I can tell that you are a kind man. Besides, there is a guard outside the door."

Pender slumped back down. "So what are you here for, child? What is your name?"

"My name is Twillim and I am sent here to befriend you

and find out who you are," she said candidly, staring at him with wide brown eyes.

"I make no secret of it," he replied. "My name is Pender. I am a sea captain from Thurkad, trading where I can."

"Why were you asking questions at the Customs House?"

"I am looking for a sailor called Jevander, who was lost from Thurkad about seven years ago."

"Why," she asked, licking smears off her fingers.

"Because his daughter, who would be about your age, Twillim, asked me to find him."

"Oh!" Twillim said, rocking back on her heels. "Well, I don't know anyone with that name."

"It was a long time ago," said Pender. "I promised to ask about him; I didn't mean any harm by it."

"I'm not allowed to answer questions," she said, standing up.

"What's going to happen to me now?" Pender asked, feeling the tables quite turned.

"I'm afraid that you will be tortured when bel Gorst gets back," she replied. "To make sure you are telling the truth. I'm sorry, I like you, Mister Pender."

She went out, taking the bowl with her, and the door was bolted again. Pender spent the next day in a paralysis of terror. He could not tolerate pain; in fact had always known himself to be a coward. He could imagine only too well the kind of tortures that bel Gorst would come up with, for sailing was a hard life and sailors' tales were full of cruelty and torment.

Late in the afternoon of the following day the door opened and Pender's nemesis stood there, bel Gorst himself. Tall, lean, with dark-brown hair hanging in braids to his shoulders, a thin, bladed nose offset by rather full red lips, he had a poniard in one hand.

"Come out, captain," he said, unlocking the chains. "I want you to see the bonfire we're making for you. Then you will join me for dinner—your last, as it happens."

Pender went, pricked every so often by the knife, his fat

face a lather of perspiration. He was going to die a miserable, agonizing, coward's death.

Tallia had a busy afternoon, chasing up old contacts to find out all she could about bel Gorst, and why he seemed able to carry out his piratical endeavors unchecked. It was not until nearly midnight that she returned to *The Waif* to find Osseion and Rustible pacing the deck, anxious but not knowing what to do.

"I was beginning to think that he'd got you too," Osseion said, smiling his relief.

She smiled wearily back. "I've grown wary since the last time," she said, referring to her capture back in Ganport last winter. "I wouldn't mind some coffee if the stove is still burning."

Rustible went down to the tiny galley. Tallia sat in a canvas chair to take off her sandals. It was a drenchingly humid night and thunderheads were building up against the mountains behind the city.

"I spoke to Aunt Dacia—the Deputy Governor," she began. "Family are best where there is corruption involved. And the corruption here goes very high indeed. Perhaps all the way to the Governor." Osseion was pacing up and down, hardly taking in what she was saying. "What's the matter?" she asked.

"When you've finished."

"Bel Gorst is wealthy and powerful, while customs is a sea of corruption and the constables not much better. If there is anything to be done about him, absolute proof will be required. Without it, my aunt cannot act."

"So we must do it ourselves. What have you learned about his island?"

Rustible appeared with a pot of coffee and three mugs. Tallia unrolled a chart of Roros harbor.

"Braggard's Rock? It's surrounded by a wide belt of mangroves riddled with snakes and chacalots. Bel Gorst has a great country house there, as well as barracks, slave quarters, storehouses and a watch-tower."

The moon came out between the thunderheads. A breeze sprang up.

"I've learned something too," said Osseion. "There was a ship called *Stiletto* registered here, but it hasn't been seen for years. My informant thinks it's been sold somewhere down the coast. It had a bad reputation."

Tallia stared at him. "How bad?"

Osseion could not contain himself any longer. "As bad as *Poniard*!" he exclaimed. "It had the same owner!"

"Oh!" cried Tallia. "Then we know who to ask about Lilis's father, though I suspect the news will be bad. Bel Gorst is a monster. Poor Lilis! Enough talking! Let's take a look at Braggard's Rock."

They sailed up the harbor for an hour or two, drifting along the channel markers in the gentle breeze. A cluster of large buildings appeared to their left, lit by bright lanterns. The wind carried the vilest of stenches—decaying blood and offal.

"What's that place?" Rustible asked, covering his nose.

There was a single boom of thunder then rain began to pour down.

"The slaughter works," Tallia replied, "and the boiling-down vats beside it. What's left over, they throw into the harbor, so I suggest that you don't even put a finger into the water."

They sailed around the island, well offshore, though in the dark and the rain there was no chance of their being recognized. *Poniard* was tied up on one side of the island, at the end of a long jetty which ran onto a boardwalk through the mangroves. There was a smaller jetty on the other side, reached the same way.

"There's no other way through the mangroves," said Tallia, "on account of the chacalots."

Out of sight of the island they put down their remaining anchor and tried to work out a plan. "Well," said Tallia, "we either do it with an army, or just one. And since we don't have an army—"

"I don't like it," said Osseion. "If someone has to go, better that I do."

"But this calls for cunning, for sneaking and deception, and perhaps for my Art too, if they're expecting us. You're too big and obvious, Osseion, and you don't have what it takes to be a spy. Here's the plan! Dressed in sailor's blues, I'll land on the small jetty before dawn and climb up into the mangrove trees, from there to spy out the lay of the island."

"Pretty dangerous plan if you ask me," said Rustible.

"I can't think of anything better. Can you?"

They agreed on time, place and signals, then Osseion rowed Tallia to the end of the jetty. It was empty. She waved and disappeared into the fog. Osseion rowed back.

The day passed slowly. The time to pick Tallia up came and went, but she did not appear at the rendezvous.

"Tallia must have been taken," Rustible said that night, when it became clear that she was not coming.

"I'll go looking for her," said Osseion. "But we need some kind of diversion. Pity we couldn't get a few of these chacalots to march up into Gorst's bedroom."

"That'd make him hop," Rustible laughed. "There's a thousand of them across the bay at the slaughter works. Don't need to guard that place."

"Let me think," said Osseion. "Is there any chance of sinking *Poniard* at the wharf?"

Rustible shook his head. "Too well guarded. There's two or three on board all the time, and she's always ready to sail."

"Perhaps we're taking on too much."

"We are," said Rustible mournfully.

"I've got an idea," said Osseion a few minutes later.

"Whatever it is, it won't work," Rustible replied morosely. He leaned on the rail, staring at the dark shape of the island. "There's nothing we can do for them."

"I'd hate to explain that to Mendark," said Osseion. "Stay

here; keep watch. I'm going for a row in the dinghy. Argis, come and give me a hand."

"Where are you going?" asked Rustible.

"I'll tell you if it works!"

They pulled away to the other side of the bay. "Rustible's a worrier all right!" said Osseion.

"Ain't he though," said Argis. A taciturn man, he asked no questions.

They found the slaughter works to be lit up, the gruesome business going night and day because of the festival. Osseion went into a huddle with the night manager and for a handsome bribe rented the offal scow, which was almost full, for the night.

They towed it back to Braggard's Rock with the dinghy, running out a trail of blood, guts and offal all the way across. Unseen creatures thrashed in the wake, tearing at each other in a frenzy and churning the water to foam.

"What time is it?" Argis whispered.

"A couple hours short of dawn."

At the small jetty Osseion crept down the boardwalk to the guard post and struck down the solitary guard. He searched along the edge of the mangroves in the dark, even calling Tallia's name softly, but there was no sign of her. Argis and he shouldered a barrel of offal each and staggered up to the veranda of the big house. The door was open, for it was a hot night. There was no guard here.

Osseion swilled his offal in through the doorway. The stench was overpowering in the humid night. They ran a trail back to the boardwalk, and emptied the second barrel onto the mudflat, completing the trail back to where the water foamed and the reptilian eyes shone in the starlight, where the vast serrated tails thrashed and the huge jaws tore playfully at each other.

One chacalot broke away from the others, swimming swiftly through the shallow water, then moving with a sinuous waddle across the mudflats and mangroves to the shore, following the trail. Within a minute a vast pack of chacalots flowed like a river up the bank, snapping up titbits in the grass as they came. They pushed through the open door, finding just enough offal to fight over and to whet their appetites. The house was full of prey—they could smell it.

Osseion and Argis rowed back to *The Waif*, where Osseion explained what they had done. A scream rent the night, swiftly truncated. Osseion chuckled. "Right," he said, climbing into the dinghy. "I'm going after Tallia."

"Better make it quick," said Rustible, who was at the helm. "That lot'll be right across the island in a few minutes. Wait! How are you going to get back up the jetty?"

There was a long pause. "We'll have to use the other one," Osseion said in a rather subdued voice.

"You'll never get past *Poniard* and those guards," cried Rustible, tearing at his yellow hair. "Why didn't you tell me what you were doing?"

Osseion swore. "This captaining lark is a bit harder than I thought. We'll have to take *Poniard* first."

"We?" said Rustible. "I've never used a weapon in my life.'

30

THE CHACALOT FEAST

Tallia landed on the small jetty and crept down to the boardwalk, sweating as an occasional board creaked under her weight. The intermittent moon revealed chacalots dozing on the mudbanks, each four or five spans long with a mouth that could swallow a child whole. The largest eyed her as she went past, waving an enormous scaly tail.

From the boardwalk Tallia swung up into the branches of an overhanging mangrove tree, the only safe way to get to land, for there was at least one guard at the other end of the boardwalk. She slapped away a swarm of midges, then clambered from branch to branch right up into the canopy, so that she was hidden from below. Beneath her the chacalots were still, but after the sun rose she saw more than one eye on her hiding place. There would be good eating tonight.

When it was light enough to see, Tallia moved closer to shore, to a perch high enough that she could see a good part of the island. It was mostly open land, with storehouses and barracks scattered along one side next to the wall of the mangroves, a gently sloping grassy hill and at its top a vast house set among trees. She sweated and swatted on her branch. The day passed with no indication where Pender could be. Tallia took out her lunch, settled herself on a branch and promptly dropped both bread and cheese into the mud. Before she could scramble down to recover it a dozen crabs had torn the bread apart and were scuttling off in all directions.

Evidently there was little work to do today, for a bunch of sailors could be seen kicking a ball back and forth across an open space. People went by occasionally—sailors, officers, guards—but they all looked comfortable with their place on Braggard's Rock. She was looking for someone who wasn't—a slave or a drudge who might tell her willingly where Pender was.

Later a ragged group of slaves began stacking a bonfire in the middle of the lawn. An overseer roared at them periodically, though with two guards standing by there was no chance for Tallia to speak to them. Other slaves hauled burdens between storehouses, barracks and the house, occasionally going past her hiding place, but each time Tallia thought to accost one of them, a guard appeared.

By late afternoon she was incredibly hungry. She eyed off the mangrove roots, which were covered in fat oysters. No one was looking. Tallia crept down, hacked off several aerial roots and scrambled back into her tree.

The day dragged on. She opened the oysters with her knife and ate them one by one. They were plump and juicy though with an unusual flavor. The humidity was stifling. She felt that she had seen everyone on the island a dozen times. Finally the players disappeared.

At dusk a small man staggered out from a storehouse, bowed under the weight of a sack. He looked worn out and defeated; maybe he would talk. Tallia leaned forward, making the branch shake. A chacalot basking on the mudflat below her waved a serrated tail as long as a dinghy. Its yawning mouth showed a hundred teeth, at which a toothpick bird prised merrily. She climbed down onto the ground well away from the reptile, pulled her cap over her face and headed along the shore.

Tallia fell in beside the man, who was heading toward a cluster of sheds. He looked sideways at her from under his broad-brimmed hat, then away again quickly.

"I need to talk to you," said Tallia.

He walked faster, panting under the strain. "Leave me alone or it will be the worse for both of us. Go back to where you've come from."

"How do you know where I come from?"

"You wear no collar."

His throat was encircled by a wide band of spring steel, with a red garnet set in the front of it. The skin was scarred and inflamed all around the collar.

"It's worth my life for anyone from *outside* to speak to me. And yours too. Spies have fed the chacalots three times already this year."

They reached the shed. The man lifted the sack high above his head, struggling to pitch the weight up onto a pile of other sacks.

"I'm not from customs. I'm looking for a friend."

The man set down the sack. "You have friends *here*? Then go and talk to them and leave me to do my work."

He tried to push past her but Tallia barred his way. "Listen!" she hissed urgently. "My friend was taken by bel Gorst the night before last. A fat man called Pender." She described him. "Is he here?"

"I don't doubt that he is," said the man, "though I haven't seen any strangers, bar you. There's talk of an excruciation tomorrow—I've been stacking bonfires all afternoon."

He tried to force his way past her. Tallia attempted to hold him, but the little fellow turned out to be as strong as wire. He pulled free, dodging past. She tackled him, they crashed to the floor and his hat went flying. In the fading light his long hair was the color of platinum.

A shiver went up her spine. Tallia let go his hand, staring at him. The hair, the long pinched face and pointed chin—

suddenly she knew beyond any doubt. The long search was over.

He got up, staring at her too, then hefted up the sack again.

"I've come all the way from Thurkad looking for you, *Jevi*," she said softly.

He dropped the sack, which burst at one end, shooting dried peas across the dirt floor like bullets.

"Who are you? I don't use that name anymore." He was trembling, barely able to stand up. His voice-box bobbed up and down.

"Lilis told me," said Tallia. "Your daughter."

"Lilis!" cried Jevander. Tears started, then poured down his cheeks like rain down a windowpane. He staggered and clutched at her arm. "Lilis is *alive*?" He shook her violently by the shoulders. "Tell me, quick!"

"Alive and well," said Tallia, overcome by his raw emotion. "And everyone she meets, she asks for news of you. She has never given you up."

Suddenly Jevi flushed and let her go. "I'm sorry, I hope I didn't hurt you." He pulled the door of the shed closed and sat down on the bag. Peas rustled on the floor.

"Lilis!" he said again. "This is a dream, surely. Every day I was not there to take care of her was like a thorn dragged down my back. But I was helpless." He looked up through his fingers at Tallia. "I scoured Thurkad for her, the only time I got the chance, but it was like looking for a shell on the beach. I decided that she was dead, that she died soon after I was pressed. It was the only way I could survive." Then, with sudden hope—"She is here in Roros?"

Tallia was sorry to dash his expectations so cruelly. "Alas, Lilis is as far from Roros as it is possible to get. She is in Zile, in the care of Nadiril the librarian."

"She has mighty friends!" Jevander exclaimed in amazement.

"I took her there last winter," said Tallia. "Before that she lived in the alleys for seven years. She's had a hard life but I don't think she's been harmed by it."

"Lilis was the light of my life, after Grazie died," he said. Tears started in his eyes again. "This is worse than not knowing! If there was ever a way to get free I would have taken it. But bel Gorst is a very devil, and he made sure that there was no way. He is a *spelltwister*."

"Is he now?" breathed Tallia. "That is very interesting. So that's how he keeps you here, is it? Don't give up yet. My boat comes back after dark."

Jevander stroked the iron collar. "We're locked up at night, down in that slab shed beyond the storehouses. Nothing could keep me here now that I know Lilis is alive. Nothing, save this fetter around my neck! Each of us has one and it's set to kill if we try to get away. There's only onc way I'll ever leave this island."

"As it happens I also know a little about spelltwisting, as you call it. Let me see." Drawing Jevander to her, she felt the collar, passing her fingers over the iron and the garnet. It was the cheapest of gems, with a flaw running right through it. Jevander flinched as her fingers touched the inflamed skin. "I won't harm you," she said. "I think I know a bit more about the Secret Art than bel Gorst does, if this is the best he can do."

"I've been too long already," said Jevander, looking hopeless. "Get away while you can." But he lingered, questioning her about Lilis, feeding on her replies like a man who had been starved for seven years. Then, hearing someone shouting not far away, he slipped out the door.

Tallia heaved up the forgotten sack for him and headed back to the mangroves. As soon as it was quite dark, not long in these latitudes, she made her way through the trees toward the boardwalk. There she encountered an insoluble snag. The guard was standing right at the only place where the trees hung over the boardwalk. Another pair of guards stood not far away, chatting. The time came and went for the rendezvous but she could do nothing about it. Any attack on the guards would alert the island. She slid back up into the foliage and waited.

Finally the pair of guards moved off and the single sentry strolled down after them. Tallia swung down onto the boardwalk and headed toward the jetty. It was hours after the rendezvous time, but Osseion might still be waiting. On the way she felt a sharp pang in her belly, though it went away again. A solitary lantern burned on the end of the jetty. She flashed the signal from the other side. There was no answer, and before she could move Tallia heard the footsteps of the guard. She ducked behind the rail, took hold of a post and hung over the side. It might be enough to hide her, in the dark and mist.

The sentry stopped some distance away to lean on the rail in the semi-darkness. He was chewing *gatt*, a potent mixture of tree resin, cloves and ginger. Tallia could smell the spices from where she hung.

The guard did not move. If he strolled over to her side of the jetty the mist would not hide her. Her arms were aching and she was uncomfortably aware of creatures stirring, not far below her feet. Suddenly the stomach ache returned, a fierce pain.

She tried the least whisper of a *suggestion*, to see if she could make the guard move away. It was a chancy method; many people were immune to such things. *Go down the wharf,* she sent.

The guard literally sprang in the air, his head darting from side to side. He must have a latent talent for the Secret Art. She tried again, more subtly, and immediately felt a sharp pain behind her eyes. Strong latent talents—he was defending himself against her suggestion without even realizing it.

Tallia felt a sudden spasm of nausea and her bowels turned liquid. Those damned oysters! Her arms went weak; her sandal scraped on the side of the jetty. The sentry ran three steps down toward the boardwalk. In the gloom she could not see his expression, but she could feel the tension. Bel Gorst was notorious for unannounced inspections.

"Is that you, Klari?" the sentry asked.

Tallia could hardly think straight. She came out from under the rail just as he turned back.

"Hey!" snapped the guard, reaching for his cutlass.

She rushed him. Her foot slipped on a wet board and instead of knocking him down she merely struck him in the chest with her shoulder. The guard caught her by the hair then brought his upraised knee up hard into her belly. Tallia fell flat on her back, winded. The back of her head rang like a bell. The guard, well trained in dirty fighting, slammed his heel down at her throat. She had just strength enough to roll out of the way. She staggered to her feet, knowing that if she didn't finish it straight away he'd kill her.

The guard slashed at her with the cutlass. She ducked, caught his arm and, using his momentum, threw him over her shoulder as hard as she had ever thrown anyone. He crashed into the railing, which broke, and with a cry the man fell into the sea. Looking over, Tallia saw a phosphorescent swirl, a gurgle of bubbles and a brief thrashing that stopped abruptly. That was all.

The illness was horrible and getting worse. She hung over the side, vomiting and diarrhea going at once, then cleaned herself up and lay down on the deck. Precious time was running out. Any minute someone could come to relieve the guard, but she was unable to do anything about it.

Eventually a rain shower roused her. She looked up through a gap in the clouds to see that the scorpion nebula had wheeled round the sky. It was now very late, and she felt almost as bad as she had before. There was too much to do and too little time.

Tallia finally reached the prisoners' barracks. They were locked away for the night but only one guard stood on duty outside. This fellow was careless and, despite her condition, Tallia was an expert. Within a minute she had the door open.

Inside, she held up the guard's lantern. A hundred pressed

sailors and slaves stirred under the light. Night visits from bel Gorst were very unwelcome.

"Jevander," she called softly. He appeared at once, fingering his collar. "We'll see what we can do about that," she said. "Should I offer anyone else their freedom?"

"I dare say," said Jevander. "I don't know them well. I keep to myself."

"I have a boat," Tallia said, loud enough that everyone could hear without it penetrating outside. "Anyone wants to come with me, come now."

Two or three stood up. The rest lay in sullen indifference, or fear. Tallia was not surprised—slavery dulled the spirit very quickly.

"Come down to the jetty; our boat will be here soon." She hoped so.

Outside, Tallia took a small copper spike out of her pocket, moistened it in her mouth and pressed the tip to the garnet set in the iron collar. She strained until she was shaking, reading the spell that controlled it, then with a tiny flash of green fire the mineral shattered and fell out of its setting.

"That hurt," she said, bending over to dry retch. "Is it . . .?"

"I'm free," whispered Jevander, tearing off the collar and hurling it into the mangroves. He hugged her. "*Free!* Tallia, are *you* all right?"

"Not really," said Tallia, squinting. She had begun to see double. "Lucky there's only three of you."

"What's that?" hissed Jevi. From not far away there were cries, thumps, cracks and the sounds of breaking timber.

"I've no idea," she said limply.

By the time Tallia had freed the other two she was as weak as a kitten. It was almost dawn; already the eastern sky was pink. The light revealed a horrible sight—bloody-snouted chacalot everywhere, fighting over scraps of meat and bone. One huge old fellow had a man in his jaws and was swinging him back and forth. The man screamed; then something snapped audibly, he sagged and the reptile dragged him off.

"Did you do this?" Jevi asked, amazed.

"It seems my friends have been a little . . . too efficient," Tallia whispered. "Oh, my head!"

Jevi kept his. "Did you find your man?"

"No!" she groaned. "I don't know where he is."

"I kept my eyes open while you were gone. He's in the cells of the big house, down below. Stay here; I'll find him," he hissed in her ear.

"We'll go together. If Pender's hurt, it'll take both of us to carry him."

Tallia staggered across the lawn, hanging on Jevi's shoulder. One of the magnificent doors had been ripped off its hinges, while the foyer of the house was a bloody ruin—a chaise smashed to wickerwork and splinters, palms and orchids ground into the parquetry, pots smashed. And everywhere, blood and hair and bits of clothing. Literally everywhere—there was blood halfway up the walls, a sock hanging from a chandelier.

"Where?" cried Tallia.

"Down the stairs!"

A red snout appeared out of a room running off to their left. Evidently a library, for a leaf from a book was gummed to the creature's head just behind the eyes.

They ran together. Tallia slipped and sent them both down the steps in a tangle of arms and legs. Jevi threw his arms around Tallia to protect her. They came to rest at the bottom of the steps, with him underneath. Tallia clung to him for a fraction longer than was necessary.

They found the lower levels deserted. The guards had fled. The prisoners clung to their bars, silently staring, and not one of them asked to be let out. The sounds and the rumor from upstairs had carried down all too well.

Pender was in the last cell, a sad, unkempt, red-eyed ruin. Like a punctured bladder his rotund corpulence had turned to limp flab. Tallia had no idea where to find the keys, and no longer had the power to burst the lock, but Jevi soon came running back with a crowbar, with which he levered the bars of Pender's cell apart. They dragged the fat man through.

Pender didn't seem to recognize her. Getting out was no easier than in, for they found two chacalots fighting over a grisly relic in the foyer. Jevi helped Tallia and Pender out a side window and down the wall in a heap on the grass. Pender stared around him as if he had arrived prematurely in the underworld.

"Pender!" Tallia cried, shaking him by the shoulders. "Pender, get up! We can't carry you."

Standing up, he hung against the vine-covered wall, panting like a marathon runner.

"Pender! Look! It's Jevi, Lilis's father."

That shocked him back to his senses. Pender stared at Jevi and then a smile of purest joy broke across his fat face. He held out a sweaty hand. "Lilis is my very dear friend," Pender said. "She saved me from the sea. I've been looking for you for half a year."

Tears welled in Jevi's eyes; he took the fat man in his arms and they wept together. Tallia was moved to tears herself, but she did not allow them time to fall. "We must get going."

The grassy lawn was like a minefield. The shed roofs were covered in refugees, including a dark-skinned girl with hair plaited into handles. Twillim waved at Pender, apparently unfazed, but he did not notice. Tallia wavered down toward the small jetty, then stopped. It was swarming with chacalots, tearing at the remains of the offal and at each other.

"Osseion!" cried Tallia. "You bloody idiot, what have you done?"

"We'll never get down that," said Jevander.

"The main jetty?" said Pender.

"Rustible won't know to look for us there," said Tallia. "Besides, that's where *Poniard* is."

"There's no choice!"

Chacalots were still swarming out of the water. Soon there would be no safety but the roofs. They ran across the lawn, a deadly obstacle course. Tallia was beginning to feel really ill—aftersickness on top of oysters. At the same time a small band of people broke free from the back of the house, racing toward the main jetty where *Poniard* was moored. Most got through, including bel Gorst, not so menacing in a silk nightshirt with skinny legs sticking out the bottom.

Their boots clattered down the boardwalk, but one poor fellow fell through a rotten board and hung there, caught by the chest with his legs dangling down into the mangrove swamp. He screamed to his mates to help him out. They kept running. A chacalot a good five spans long stood up on its tail, snapping its jaws on the man's legs. Though he struggled, it was futile—the reptile pulled him straight through the gap between the boards.

Tallia doubled over, retching on the lawn.

"What are we going to do?" cried Pender.

"Keep going. There's nowhere else to go."

A horde came after them, cutting off any retreat. Twice a chacalot almost had Tallia before she fell onto the boardwalk. The trees had been cut back from this jetty; no chance of climbing up into them. It was foggy. *The Waif* was not in sight. She made a sudden decision.

"Let's try to take *Poniard*!"

They crashed down the jetty but were spotted at once. The pirates must have thought that the slaves were free for they panicked, the sails were sheeted home and a sudden gust filled them. The boat slid away from the wharf, gathering speed in the breeze.

Behind Tallia one of the slaves cried out. The chacalots had followed them. Tallia tried to work a desperate illusion to stop *Poniard* from getting away. Too weak!

A shadowy vessel appeared though the mist, dead ahead. Reacting instinctively, *Poniard*'s helmsman spun the wheel, snapped orders, the sailors hauled the lines.

"It's an illusion, you fool," cried bel Gorst, lashing the helmsman with his whip. His dark face was a caricature of terror—eyes like black pits, mouth as round as the hole of a privy. His efforts were too late; the boat curved around and ran back full tilt.

Tallia watched *Poniard* plunge toward them; she was

powerless to move. It ran straight into the jetty, shearing a section of the decking right off and hurling all but Pender, who was well behind, into the water. Tallia landed flat on her back in the shallow water on the other side. A dozen chacalots slid off the mudbank. *Poniard*, sadly crushed about the bows, was pushed off and limped out into the bay. The phantom boat was gone—Tallia wasn't sure whether it had been her illusion or not.

Tallia thrashed through sticky mud toward the fallen deck. One end was embedded in the mire while the other stuck up in the air, resting precariously against one of the jetty piles. The chacalot swerved toward her. A pathetic cry signaled the end of one of the slaves. Tallia was braver than most, but seeing such a death staring her in the face she was hard pressed not to scream. Pender hung above her, caught by the back of his jacket. Plump arms and legs thrashed uselessly.

"Keep still!" she screeched, momentarily diverted from her own troubles, "unless you want to end up down here."

"Tallia, here!" It was Jevander, clinging one-handed to one of the piles. "Onto the deck."

Her eyes followed his pointing arm and she realized that the fallen deck made a ramp that extended under the water. She flailed toward it, feeling like a turtle pursued by a leopard. Something caught at her boot. She gasped, but it was just a twisted mangrove root.

Jevander sprang down the ramp, stretching out his arm, but she could not quite reach it. Over her shoulder Tallia saw the leading chacalot, a big one. She was not going to make it! The beast lunged.

Her boots struck something solid—the deck! She clawed herself up it, gasping, slipping, skidding. The chacalot was close enough to have her, and Jevander too. Its jaws snapped on her boot. The reptile tossed its head, tearing boot and sock right off. Tallia felt a terrible pain in her ankle. She tried to clamber up the boards but her ankle would not support her. The chacalot lunged again.

Jevander wrenched off a loose plank, slipped on the

greasy boards then fell toward the beast. Tallia screamed, but he found his balance and rammed the board into the creature's maw, trying to force it down the throat. The chacalot bellowed, snapped its jaws and sheared the plank in two.

Tallia's outstretched hand touched Jevander's callused hand. They clasped and, showing astonishing strength for a small man, he jerked her up out of the water so hard that it almost dislocated her shoulder. The chacalot's jaws slammed shut just where she had been, tearing a chunk out of a pile and breaking teeth on the iron reinforcing bands. It rolled back into the water, then prepared to lunge again. Tallia thumped into Jevander, almost knocking him down to where grinning jaws waited on the other side.

"Up!" he shouted, springing onto the undamaged part of the jetty and hauling a shocked Tallia up after him, one bare foot bloody and dangling.

"Where the hell's Osseion?" she gasped as a brace of chacalot advanced down the jetty toward them. They were defenseless; her illusions would not work on these creatures. Pender was precariously suspended from the pile, only the collar of his coat holding him up. The chacalot clustered underneath, waiting.

Jevi lifted Tallia onto the top of a pile and climbed up after. She leaned on his shoulder, almost fainting from the pain in her ankle. He put his arms around her again. It felt wonderful. All around them the creatures snapped. The remaining slave squatted on the top of his pile like a gargoyle. The fog thickened.

"Hoy! Hoy!" someone shouted from the water, a hollow cry twisted by the fog.

"It's bel Gorst!" cried Jevi, shaking with emotion. "I'll not be taken by him again. I'll go down among the chacalot first."

Tallia took his hand. "Don't do anything rash. Think of Lilis."

Timbers creaked in the fog. "It's *The Waif*!" Pender yelled. "I know it. Hoy, Osseion, over here. Hoy! Hoy!"

"Hoy!" came the cry again, from the fog. The chacalots snapped their jaws, in time.

"Over here!"

A few seconds later, the most glorious sight of their lives, *The Waif* drifted up to the wharf, handled by Rustible as lightly as thistledown on the breeze. A rather shame-faced Osseion plucked Tallia to safety over the rail. The slave sprang off his post onto the deck. Jevander leapt in. They cut Pender down and headed back to the wharves of Roros.

"Damn fine plan that was, Osseion!" she said, shaking. "You might have given me some warning! I was that close to being in the belly of a chacalot." She measured a tiny space between finger and thumb.

"It was worth it though," said Pender. "Look who we've found."

Osseion stared at the small man; then, overcome with emotion, he embraced him. Jevander sat down, shaking his head, tears running down his face.

"Pity about *Poniard* getting away," Tallia said through clenched teeth.

Rustible pointed through the fog. "The villain didn't get far. I thought we had him the first time."

"So that *was* you?" said Tallia. "I didn't *think* my illusion had worked."

"We ran him aground, though it was a dicey business for a while. I thought he was going to have our bottom out on a reef." The fog parted enough for them to see the beautiful boat stuck fast on a mudbank, surrounded by dozens of chacalots. "There he'll stay, for he has no dinghy. Osseion cut it loose in the fog. About the only smart thing he's done all day." Osseion smiled sheepishly. "The tide is running out and won't be this high again for a fortnight."

"A good morning's work," said Tallia. "Let's get to customs and swear our complaint."

"He has their protection," grunted Pender.

"My aunt is the Deputy Governor, remember. He won't buy his way out of this. Ah, my ankle!"

Osseion took her foot in his hand. "You won't be walking on this for a while," he said. "It's broken."

Tallia spent a fortnight with her family, but by the end she was becoming increasingly worried about Mendark. He had asked them to be ready in fifty days, but forced into inaction by her ankle she could no longer restrain her curiosity at his secrecy.

"I have to find Mendark," she said.

There had been a reward from the merchants of Roros for ridding them of bel Gorst. Though not enough to make up for the lost cargo, it at least rescued Pender from immediate ruin. He was very quiet, not even mentioning the profits that would be lost, so a day later they headed north to Strinklet again, on the great estuary of the Wu Karu. Despite the fact that her ankle was still in plaster and abominably uncomfortable in the heat, Tallia hired horses and set out for Tar Gaarn with Osseion and Jevander.

31

Faelamor's Gate

Faelamor led Maigraith north-east out of Bannador. They trekked through Faidon Forest, where loggers were stripping out the last of the great ironwoods to build the wharf city of Thurkad ever higher above the mud. Fording the Saboth River at Gance, they found its vast gravel banks exposed because of the drought, while a solitary prospector panned the riffles for platinum. Continuing north, Faelamor then turned west toward Dunnet, buried in the heart of the great forest of Elludore. Dunnet was an isolated land hemmed in by mountains on its western side, the rugged lands of Bannador to the south and a chain of barren hills to the north. The journey took about a fortnight, and though they passed through war, blockade and devastation, they were not hindered.

Several times on their wandering journey they heard tales of Yggur's return and the fate of the Second Army. "Just as I told you," said Faelamor. "What do you think of this lover of yours now?"

Maigraith felt the last bond to Yggur fall away. The man was a monster; he meant nothing to her anymore. But with that decision made, what choice did she have now but to serve Faelamor again, the woman who had dominated her for the whole of her life, the one to whom she owed a burden of duty that could never be repaid?

"I am over him," Maigraith said tersely.

From that point on, with every step Maigraith's newfound assuredness was stripped from her, and the misery, despair and nothingness of her previous existence were renewed. All of her confidence and self-worth faded into a memory of another life, and each step woke the nightmare of that life. By the time they reached the refuge that Faelamor sought, deep in the forest-clad lower slopes of Dunnet, the new self that Maigraith had constructed so painfully was gone. Faelamor had taken back her life, commanded everything she did, and though her orders were now clothed in a veneer of courtesy, the bones underneath were as obdurate as ever.

"Here we are at last," said Faelamor, sinking down on a mosscovered stone with a sigh that had the weight of centuries of frustration behind it. "Of all places in Santhenar, this could almost be Tallallame. I can do it, here."

Her refuge was a deep valley whose upper end ran right up against the mountains, terminating in a precipice that reared very high and inhospitable. The ridges on either side were sheer and sharp, hazardous for climbing, a defensive wall. The entrance to the valley was a slot cut by the river through limestone, once a cave whose roof had fallen, and the river rushed deep and fast and cold where the cave had been. The way in was a narrow ledge beside the river. Not impregnable, but difficult of approach and easy to defend. Upstream of the slot the valley belled out, dark beneath giant trees, moist and misty at the upper end where stairstep waterfalls tinkled down a cliff three hundred spans in height. Vines trailed from the trees; ferns carpeted the ground. It was a place much to the liking of the Faellem, a shadow of their own world. Faelamor had discovered it many years ago and remembered it, thinking of such a need as this.

"It is very beautiful," said Maigraith, gazing around her.

Faelamor sprang up again. "Not just beautiful, but *right*! Whatever I do will work better here because of it, and we have much to do. How I need my people now."

"They are still in Mirrilladell, are they not?"

"Most are, three hundred leagues away." Mirrilladell was a land of lakes, swamps and vast cold forests on the southern side of the Great Mountains. "But however far, I must bring them here. This will be the first of your great tasks."

Maigraith held her breath. This was what she had been waiting for all her life. Prepared for, at least. She wasn't sure she wanted it.

"First I will try to link to the Faellem. You will support me! Sit here."

"You can *link*?" cried Maigraith, astonished. "I thought . . ."

"That talent *comes* from the Faellem, though even among us it is rare. I did not teach you that?"

"Then why didn't *you* go with me to Fiz Gorgo, to steal the Mirror?"

"I wish I had," Faelamor said grimly.

The initial link was made, a smooth, sensuous coupling of their minds, as voluptuous as custard. Maigraith liked it no more than Karan had when they had first linked outside Fiz Gorgo last autumn. It was an invasion of her most personal spaces, the only parts kept completely to herself in all the years that she had endured Faelamor's domination. Her mind rebelled and flung off the link; she hurled herself backwards across the grass.

"Keep your distance!" Maigraith choked. "You link with me on my terms, or not at all. Keep out of my mind."

Faelamor rose slowly to her feet, flexing her fingers. Maigraith tensed, wanting to run. Then, whatever Faelamor had been about to do, she thought better of it and sat down again. "As you wish. Only the link matters now. We'll try again, if you are ready."

Maigraith was amazed. Perhaps she had some power over Faelamor after all.

After several more tries Faelamor managed to forge a link that was bearable to Maigraith, one that kept well away from any conscious part of her mind.

Ellami, Ellami, Faelamor called.

The world silence, vast and empty, saturated Maigraith's mind.

"So far away," said Faelamor. "So hard." *Ellami*; *Hallal*; *Gethren.*

"They do not reply," Faelamor said somewhat later.

She called and called and called again. Still there was no answer! Faelamor looked haggard. "Why do they not respond?" she gasped, gripping the log with both hands to save herself from toppling off. "I feel very weak. Give me a little of your strength."

Maigraith felt a sensation as if her lifeblood was pumping out her throat across the link to Faelamor. Suddenly dizzy, she had to prop herself up with her arms. The flow increased to a flood. Beads of cold sweat broke out on her forehead.

Faelamor kept on until tears squeezed out of her eyes. Maigraith felt as flabby as a week-old balloon. She almost fainted and had to lie down on the grass.

At last an answer came, though it was very faint.

Who calls? came a wispy little straw voice. *Is that you, Faelamor?*

It is I, she replied. *It is time. Come to me in Elludore, northwest of the ancient city of Thurkad, on the island of Meldorin. I have made a refuge in the lower mountains, a land called Dunnet.* She did not need to say forest—where else would the Faellem hide if they had the choice?

Maigraith could sense anger, resistance to Faelamor's call.

Why did you not call us before? Where have you been all this time?

No time! Faelamor gasped. *Come! Come! Come quickly and secretly.*

There was no response. *Are you coming?* cried Faelamor. The link began to thin. *Are you coming?* Again no answer. Faelamor was frantic. *Please, Ellami! I'm begging you! You must come.*

Faelamor sank to the ground and buried her face in the grass. *Call me! Call me tomorrow!*

The link faded like the sky after sunset. "They're coming!" Faelamor sighed, sinking to the ground in exhaustion. "They will come. They must!"

Maigraith said nothing. Why must they come? They had exiled Faelamor when Maigraith was but a child. She did not know why, but the mystery of her life and her parents' deaths was at the heart of it.

Faelamor woke next morning in a state of high anxiety.

"What's the matter?" asked Maigraith, watching her pace back and forth.

"The Faellem should have called." Faelamor turned away abruptly.

By the end of the day she was practically beside herself. Normally so controlled, she had even resorted to biting her nails. The call never came.

"Why don't you call them again?" Maigraith said as she prepared dinner.

"I can't!" Faelamor screeched. "To link over such distances can't be done again so soon."

"I thought . . ." began Maigraith.

"To send a link one league is hard. Two leagues, four times as hard. Three leagues, nine times. But to link to someone 300 leagues away—work it out for yourself!" Faelamor was not good at mental arithmetic.

"Ninety thousand times as hard," Maigraith murmured.

"Just so! It has probably never been done in the history of the Three Worlds. I might try a dozen times without succeeding, so weak is the signal. But there are hundreds, thousands of Faellem. If they all link together they can overcome the tyranny of distance."

"If they choose to," murmured Maigraith, to bait her.

A few days later they made a second attempt, but though they forced till Faelamor could not hold her head up, they heard nothing.

"Perhaps they're hiding from you," said Maigraith, half-expecting Faelamor to lash out at her.

Scrunching up her eyes to prevent the tears from welling out, Faelamor whispered, "They are; they've put up a barrier against me! Me, who led them here to Santhenar, and ever after. They leave me no choice but to do what is forbidden."

She did not rise from her couch of boughs and ferns for days. Whenever Maigraith went to check on her, she snapped, "Go away! I'm thinking!" Then one evening, after they had been there for more than a week, Faelamor broke her selfinduced silence.

"I was right," she said soberly.

Maigraith prodded the fire, which she kept alight because it helped to keep the mosquitoes off. She did not feel any curiosity, but Faelamor needed to talk and therefore Maigraith must listen.

"*I was* right, when I embarked upon this great gamble three centuries ago. All that time I have been plagued by self-doubt, by the thought that I had cast aside my honor for a shadow. That I had done this great evil for something that could never be."

Maigraith sat up. What was she talking about? She felt a sudden chill, an urgent need for warmth. She held out her hands to the fire. The air sighed in the treetops. The faintest chuckle came from the river, thirty paces away. It seemed amused by their petty dealings.

Faelamor stared at the coals, speaking in a monotone. "Even before my enemy Yalkara found a flaw in the Forbidding and fled, I suspected that there might be a way. I fought her for it and I was defeated. She had learned too many secrets with the cursed Glass." There was nothing in Faelamor's voice. She might have been describing preparations for their dinner.

"But before Gethren dragged me to safety I had a glimpse in that Glass and I saw a possibility! I collapsed and knew nothing for weeks. But later, as I lay brooding, full of hate and self-loathing, I learned that Yalkara's success was not as great as I'd thought. Her injuries were so grave that she had to flee unready. I learned that she had left something behind to finish her job. Then, as I lay in my bed of pain and misery, bitterness and despair, I conceived a plan. I saw how, by corrupting that gift, I might make of it a tool that I could twist to my own purpose, *and smash the Forbidding*!"

Maigraith was so shocked that she almost leapt up and ran. There had been talk of breaking the Forbidding at the Conclave, but it had never been more than talk. Since then she had sometimes thought about that, and what the consequences might be.

"I was never sure though," Faelamor went on. "It was not until I used the Mirror in Katazza that I knew I was right." Something old and frightening showed in her eyes, then she looked away as though uncomfortable with what she had revealed, or whom she had revealed it to.

So Faelamor *did* plan to break the Forbidding. What would that do to Santhenar? Was it right to help her? The brief taste of power had opened Maigraith's eyes to the world and her place in it. There had to be a role for someone like her, who wanted neither power nor wealth, but only what was right.

Once she had even spoken to Yggur about the Forbidding, for she knew that he had come closer than any to fathoming its essence.

"I don't know what would happen," he had said, "nor, I suspect, does anyone else. No one understands the Forbidding. Why did it come about? We don't know. Did Shuthdar make it deliberately, a last corruption of that most beautiful thing, the golden flute? A last malicious act before he destroyed it and himself? Or did the Forbidding just happen, the balance trying to reassert itself after so long a distortion, and so violent? Or was there another power there at the ending? Rulke was there, Yalkara and Kandor; most of the great of that era. Such an assemblage of strength as has never been seen since. Was the Forbidding a plan, or the failure of one? Did it form at once or slowly crystallize over the following weeks? We do not know, only that when the Faellem and the Charon made to go back to their own worlds, the Way between the Worlds was closed."

"Did Yalkara have anything to do with it?" Maigraith had asked. "She knew enough to find the flaw in the Forbidding when the time came."

"I believe that the Forbidding protects us," said Yggur, "whether it was made for that purpose or not. I do not believe that breaking it will restore the balance that existed before the flute. I think that it will break open *all* the paths between the worlds. Santhenar will lie naked to the void.

"Our world would be like the village below the dam. When the dam bursts, the village is swept away. If the Forbidding is broken Santhenar will be torn apart, for we have no defense against what is in the void. Perhaps there is no defense. Faelamor trifles with what she does not understand."

"Smash the Forbidding!" said Maigraith aloud, and the Yggur in her head was gone. "But what of Santhenar? Would you condemn the world that sheltered you so long?"

The firelight turned Faelamor's cheek to rose, to scarlet. She turned her head to Maigraith, and though her eyes were in shadow, golden specks swam in them, in eyes that were old and deeper than the bottomless sea. Her voice was pitiless.

"When one breaks out of a prison, one does not take care that the gaolers are safe. Santhenar can look to itself. I looked in the Mirror in Katazza and saw what I wanted to see. There is a way. I *can* break the Forbidding. I *will* take the Faellem home, even if all else falls into ruin around me. That I have sworn to do. My duty is clear."

"How will you do that?"

"I dare not tell you, or anyone. Suffice it to say that there are many steps, and much preparation. The first step is done; the instrument is prepared. It is flawed but it will serve. The second—to see the way. That too I have done. In the Mirror I saw Yalkara's path. But there are many things I must have, and many things I must learn, and so little time. It is a race against Rulke, now that he has shown his hand, for whichever of us is ready first will spoil the plan of the other. And perhaps against Mendark too, if he survived Katazza. On my way back from there I discovered a great danger, something that cannot fall into the hands of the Council, or Rulke either. Perhaps an opportunity. No, I will not even think of that.

"Let's get to work. The Faellem have let me down. I prayed that I would not have to take this path, but now I must. We must go to far-off places, but there isn't time. I must make a gate, like to the gate that Tensor made in Katazza. That secret I also had from the Mirror."

"Make a gate!" exclaimed Maigraith. "Aren't you Faellem forbidden to use such things?"

"Indeed. Any gate violates the prohibition against devices that we swore to uphold eons ago. To make one is a sin of mortal dimensions, and in using it I will suffer cruelly. But I need one now and will again at the end, wherever the end will be."

Maigraith knew of the prohibition against the Faellem using *devices*, but not the moral imperative behind it, or the inevitable punishment. It was not relevant to her, though, since she was not Faellem.

Faelamor returned to her couch, more irritable than ever. Maigraith spent the next few days by herself, exploring the forest until she knew every part of the valley. She loved forests, for that was the world she had grown up in, but this one was dark and damp, always shaded by the high ridges, encouraging her morbid thoughts.

Death was everywhere this year, and never far from Maigraith's thoughts either. It had been a scarce commodity in Mirrilladell in the long years that she'd lived with the Faellem. They scarcely aged, and only a handful died or were born in the time she was there. They died by accident or injury, or because they had lost the will to keep on, exiled here on Santhenar.

But since Maigraith had come to Meldorin there had been little else but death, and she had played her own stupid part in it. The Aachim were slaughtered within Shazmak and without, and Iagador burned from south to north; from Sith to Thurkad. Countless people were dead and Yggur had caused most of it. Her war-making in Bannador, supposedly for a noble cause, had slain many more.

How many children starved tonight because their fathers had not come back from the war? How many wives wept for their lost menfolk; how many mothers and brothers and fathers wailed for loved ones they would never see again? How many bold young soldiers had come back crippled and embittered to a brief life of pain and poverty? These were questions that Maigraith had never before had to contemplate, but now they wracked her.

Not even in twenty years would the damage be repaired. And what had they fought for? Because one tyrant or another commanded it. Faelamor was the worst of them all.

Someone has to do what is right for the world, Maigraith thought, and if I don't no one will. I begin to see where my duty lies, and this is one that I owe only to myself: finding fulfilment in what has always been my greatest burden. Well, my training with Faelamor, with Yggur and with Vanhe has given me as many skills as anyone can have for the job. The rest is up to me. When the chance comes I must be ready.

Thereafter Maigraith worked all her waking hours. She wove mats and screens from rushes, sewed them together and braced them with poles until she had a house of sorts, a light but secure shelter, and a hammock to sleep in above the damp. All right for Faelamor to curl up in the fork of a tree but she needed more.

Then she sorted through the round stones in the river bed and occupied herself by making lightglasses. That was a skill that she had learned long ago but not used of late. Each one was different: sometimes she made them of stone, when she could find stone that felt right in her fingers, but more often from mineral. Quartz was easily found but she did not like the brilliant splintery quality it gave to the light. She sometimes used calcite too—it gave out a soft milky light, but did not last long. Topaz was good, though she worked only with crystals she could find herself, and it was rare. Once she had even made a globe from granite—more as a test of her skill than for any need to use it—but the ominous light, welling up out of hundreds of little crystals, clear, pink, milky or black, reminded her of the dark face of the moon. She only used that globe the once.

After a while making globes became too easy, so she amused herself by selecting the least suitable pebbles that she could find, ironstone or basalt, and coaxing them, or on one famous occasion, *forcing* them to light. She hung up her globes in little woven baskets, so that all the trees around the camp glowed with colored light in the evening, and slowly faded as the night wore on.

But these activities were too routine. She needed work that was so hard that it hurt. Maigraith went back to her regimen, becoming more and more involved in it until it took up most of her free hours. But it was as if she practiced in a void. Though she went through the motions like a machine, body and soul, and even solved another of the Forty-Nine, one of the nested Chrighms, she took no satisfaction from it. She was empty inside. The spark had been lit in her but it just smoldered away, lacking the fuel to burst into fire. Where could she find the strength for that, to free herself from Faelamor's domination and strike out on her own?

* * *

Some weeks after their arrival, Faelamor suddenly rose from her bower.

"Tomorrow we make the gate!"

All that night she sat beside the fire, thinking, occasionally scratching marks in the earth with a stick. Several times Maigraith woke and saw her sitting erect, wide awake but unmoving. Then suddenly it was morning, mist rising all along the river, and Faelamor had gone upstream.

Maigraith followed her to a place where the river narrowed between two hillocks. It was only ten or twelve paces wide here, but deep and very fast. The forest was dense; ancient trees framed the river on either side. Over that narrow place they built a hanging platform from vines hung between two trees, a structure based on three large hammocks slung across each other. This they stabilized with vine ropes tied around the trunks and woven together. Above they made another platform in the same way, fixed the two together with slender upright poles and wove a canopy of reeds over the top. All was tied together, guyed and re-guyed, then the stays loosened to allow for the motion of the trunks in the wind.

Faelamor climbed down, frowning at the structure, a basketwork pavilion suspended above the water.

"It will do," she said finally, "though it is too like the thing that Tensor made for my liking. Yet on the other hand, like calls to like. It will be the easier to open the gate for all that. Had there been more time I might have given it beauty and a better shape but, after all, we are not trying to break into the Nightland. We're taking a little journey to save time. And because there is no other way in."

Maigraith remained where she was. "I didn't realize I had to go too," she said haltingly.

"What's the matter? Are you afraid?"

"Of course I'm afraid," snapped Maigraith. "You taught me that such devices were forbidden."

"Only to Faellem."

"I'm still frightened. I saw how tortured Yggur was when he went through one."

"Bah! You're far greater than he is. Get up here!"

They took their places on the platform and Faelamor brought forth from her pouch a piece of pale stone. One side had been shaped and polished smooth, while the other had a curved, glassy fracture.

"I brought it from Katazza," she said. "It was part of Tensor's gate, broken off when Yggur appeared unexpectedly—or was it Rulke? I can't remember."

"Rulke!" said Maigraith, her stomach churning.

Faelamor mistook her. "It doesn't matter who—all that matters is that it was part of a gate. Like calls to like—I hope it will be enough."

She moistened the fragment with her tongue and put it down carefully on the platform, resting her bare foot on it. Sending forth her strength, she drew a link between her and Maigraith.

"First we have to see where we're going."

"Where are we going?" asked Maigraith, dreading the gate.

Faelamor did not answer. She gestured and the world faded. Fog swirled all around them, then Maigraith saw a stronghold on a barren ridge, just a glimpse through clouds, and a ruined city in the valley below.

"Tar Gaarn!" said Faelamor. The city faded, the fog too, and they were looking into a dark chamber. There were soft lights on brackets on the wall, but it was as if they peered through fog—the mists of time, perhaps. The lights had haloes around them, and rainbow colors. The floor was stone with a silk carpet, and at the further end of the room was a table with a small mirror on it.

The Mirror! Maigraith thought with a shivery thrill. She could never forget how it had felt when first she'd held it in her hands in Fiz Gorgo. How it had seemed to call to her. She ached to hold the Mirror again, to look into it.

"Havissard, in the time of Yalkara!" said Faelamor with an involuntary shudder. "We're looking into Yalkara's salon. At least, that's how I remember it. Hope and pray that my memory of three hundred years ago is enough to find it now, for this is a perilous way to direct a gate."

Her voice broke. She staggered, snatching at Maigraith's hand to steady herself. "Help me, Maigraith! We Faellem *can* use simple devices, though it costs us dear. Hold the image while I seek out for the way. Take it across the link and keep it firmly in your mind. Observe carefully. You may have to do it on the return."

Maigraith held the image of Yalkara's salon true while Faelamor did something that her mind could not encompass. Faelamor grunted, apparently satisfied, and did another thing equally incomprehensible. Suddenly a portal blasted open between them. The mist about the platform was buffeted by outrushing air that had a stale, dry smell.

"Keep it true!" Faelamor whispered. "Keep it anchored, else we will never get back. Oh, this is hurting!" She would have fallen had not Maigraith held her up.

Suddenly Maigraith felt dizzy and weak. Faelamor was taking her strength across the link, but it might have been flowing straight down a sink for all the good it did her.

"Stop!" cried Maigraith, clinging to one of the guy ropes. "You'll kill us both."

The draining sensation ceased. Faelamor hauled herself upright. Her shirt was dripping with sweat and her face was ghastly. "We'll have to try another way." She examined Maigraith. "You've changed. You are not what you were before." She looked uneasy, perhaps realizing that her control was slipping away.

Maigraith laughed. A tiny fire had begun to flicker inside her; she was burning up with joy. "In Thurkad I was forced to become a leader—to command and see people obey instantly. It broke the mold that you made me in. That experience has changed me forever. Remember that, the next time you try to control me. Your time is ending but mine has barely begun."

"You haven't seen a fraction of my weapons!" Faelamor

snapped, then decided not to press it. "Let's get on. Here, put your foot on the stone."

Maigraith slid her foot underneath Faelamor's smaller one, feeling the smooth fracture against the ball of her foot. Faelamor's foot was trembling. Maigraith had not seen her under such strain since they had recovered from the Conclave.

"Are you all right?"

"Forbidden deed!" Faelamor whispered. "I will pay for this." She made a working with her hands. "I'll have to practice a few times, to get used to the gate and sense the place out."

"Sense what?"

"The defenses of Havissard. We're going to the place where Yalkara defeated me, and where she fled from."

She tried again and again, but it didn't seem to be working. "I can see where I want to be but I can't get to it. Space is all warped there. I'm too weak."

As she tried again, her knees buckled and Maigraith barely stopped her from tumbling into the river.

"No good," Faelamor gasped, clinging to Maigraith as the platform rocked. "Another attempt and I won't have the strength left to use the gate. I'll have to risk it with the image I have."

"Give it to me," said Maigraith, afraid for them both. "Show me how you control the gate."

"You're not ready for it!"

"You're right! I'm not. But I'm more ready than you are, and I don't want to die because you can't do it." Maigraith had recovered quickly, and the more Faelamor struggled, the better she felt. "Show me how you seek the destination out, and exactly where you are trying to get to."

Realizing that there was no option, Faelamor did so. The images pulsed across the link. Maigraith sought out the destination and there it was, Havissard, as steady as the earth. But it was enclosed in a great transparent cyst.

"It's *protected*!" said Maigraith, puzzled. "But . . . I think I can see a way in."

Faelamor shivered at Maigraith's confidence. She would have to be taken down later. But all that mattered now was to get there.

"Ready?"

Though Maigraith still did not want to go through the gate, she reveled in the expectation of Havissard. Her biggest worry was Faelamor's state of mind.

She opened the gate. "Shall I go through?"

"No!" cried Faelamor in alarm. It was almost as if she cared. "*I* must go first to fix the other end. This is the most dangerous time, particularly for me."

She stepped into the gate and vanished. The platform lurched wildly. Maigraith fell to one knee, almost losing contact with the stone. She could feel that it was a hazardous crossing, and briefly contemplated breaking the anchor while Faelamor was in transit. That would resolve all her troubles. No, that was a coward's way. Then Faelamor was across. Maigraith held the path focused, restrained the wavering and the pinching out, then at last it firmed from the other end and Faelamor's voice, distorted to a whispery croak by the link, called her through.

Maigraith resisted the call for a long moment. After what had happened to Yggur she was afraid of the gate. But Havissard was insistent. She stepped into the portal, hesitated, half-in and half-out, feeling pulled in two different directions. One pull became stronger than the other—it dragged her in. Her entrails twisted themselves in knots, then she emerged head first in a black room, banging her head.

She lay there, her head throbbing. There was dust in her mouth; she could smell it in every breath. A globe glimmered, the swirling motes slowly settled and she saw that they were in the room that Faelamor had visualized. It looked exactly the same, save for the dust, but there was no Mirror of Aachan on the table.

"Havissard!" said Faelamor again, this time in a gasping

breath. All the rose had gone out of her face. She looked old and pallid. "That was harder than I thought. The gate came up against Yalkara's defenses; I almost lost it. Almost lost us both." Her eyes showed dismay at the danger unrecognized. "No one has been here since the time of Yalkara. Her defenses have never faltered, though what they defend is beyond guessing." She sat down on the floor and sank her head on her knees.

I thought it was me, Maigraith thought, reminded of her impulse to break the anchor while Faelamor was in transit.

For a long time after their arrival, reality shivered like ripples on a pond. Faelamor was as blanched as the white of an egg, here in the stronghold of her ancient enemy, but Maigraith was exhilarated.

"Havissard must have been locked on Yalkara's departure," said Faelamor. "Even as the Mirror was, protected against all. Maybe the protection has decayed enough to let the gate open here."

Another burst of unreality shook the walls—for a moment they were in no-time, no-place. There was no Havissard at all, or else they were in a time where it had long fallen into ruin. Waves of transparency passed through the structure, showing them other ages of Havissard: a time when the workers swarmed out of the silver mines; a time when Tar Gaarn was being built. Once, eons ago, when there was nothing here but hillsides clothed in forest, and rock faces over which waterfalls roared, and panthers stalking goats across the slopes of the mountain. Then all around broke a wild, uncontrolled reality that frightened them both, shook them in their ordered, orderly minds. Time and space quivered, they saw what mad ones saw, it quivered again and Havissard was restored.

The place was old, dusty, plain: stone floors, black or steel-blue; bare save for small carpets. Stone walls, gray or the blue of ice. Here an exquisite small tapestry, there an engraving on the stone. Lower, an artwork done in metal threads, a galloping horse, just gray and blue and white.

Maigraith reached up to a lightstrip on the wall. To her surprise it lit up all the way along the corridor. Down this corridor they went, then descended a long flight of stairs. Neither spoke. Maigraith felt disoriented, as if the gate had twisted her brain around in its case. The long bones of her legs and arms ached.

Halfway down, reality shivered again, but this time differently. An urgent, alarming wrench passed through the four dimensions. Maigraith felt violated. She lost her balance and fell the last three steps onto the floor, holding her middle. All the lights went out. Faelamor abruptly sat down on the step to avoid falling. She lifted the globe high and stared at Maigraith. The golden motes swam in her eyes.

"What was *that*?" she whispered, wide-eyed.

Back in Elludore, the platform was flung upwards and sideways by the violence and imbalance of Maigraith's departure, warped by her straining to maintain the gate against the strangeness of Havissard. Then it settled back into its former place, but the piece of stone that Faelamor had carried all the way from Katazza, the anchor for the gate, was gone, falling slowly through the humid air into the current.

32

AEOLIOR

"It felt like someone trying to get in," Maigraith said. She did not know how she knew that, or why she said it, but she did.

Faelamor reached up to the lightstrip again but it was dead. She shivered.

Maigraith knew what was the matter. Here in the citadel of her enemy, Faelamor was afraid. Though Yalkara was hundreds of years gone, Faelamor still feared her! Maigraith took a secret pleasure from that. She was not afraid, not in the least. She had no idea why, but she felt very comfortable with this place.

"I'm worn out," said Faelamor. "The passage has drained me dry." The gate had wracked her, forbidden device that it was.

They could not get the lights to work again. Maigraith brought out another of her lightglasses, one made of marble which emitted a pale green light. It suited her complexion, but Faelamor looked ghastly. They ate fruit and bread from Maigraith's pack.

"I can't suffer this now," Faelamor said. Gritting her teeth, she struck herself with one clenched fist. Her eyes rolled sideways in her head. A thread of saliva dribbled out her open mouth, down her chin.

She spent a minute in that state, while Maigraith stared in consternation, then Faelamor's eyes rolled back and she gasped a breath. She wiped her chin, looking better.

"You have overcome aftersickness?" Maigraith wondered, intrigued.

"I forced it back down like vomit. But like vomit, when it comes up again it will be twice as bad. Come on. We have to find something hidden here. I don't know where. We'll start with her workrooms, her library and her . . ." she struggled to think of the word ". . . personal chamber."

"You mean her bedroom?"

"Accursed tongue—yes, her *bedroom*," she said furiously.

Maigraith decided to pressure Faelamor a little more. "How did it go, your last battle with Yalkara?"

"I have no wish to relive it," said Faelamor in a sulky voice, though she had thought about little else since they arrived. She meant that she could not bear to have her failure so exposed. Especially not here. But after a long pause she spoke.

"I don't know how it began, only that it was a long time ago, not long after Yalkara came to Santhenar. So long!" She rubbed a dusty hand across her brow. "As soon as we met, it was as if we each saw in the other a lifelong enemy. I was afraid, something I never felt from the other Charon, not even Rulke. They were but opportunistic enemies, opposing me as I opposed their ends. But Yalkara had come here with a purpose, and a great part of that purpose was me. She came to oppose me; to hinder and delay me; to frustrate my ambitions and hopes. Why? Why was she appointed my nemesis?" Faelamor shuddered and broke off abruptly. "Let's get on!"

They continued down the passage, Maigraith leading, walking wherever her intuition led her, enjoying the reversal of roles for as long as it would last. For the moment Faelamor was content to follow, although occasionally she suggested another way.

"What have we come for?" Maigraith wondered that afternoon, beginning to understand how Karan must have felt when they broke into Fiz Gorgo last autumn, after being kept in the dark for so long.

"I learned something in my travels, a dangerous secret. My guess it that it is hidden here somewhere."

"Learned what?"

Faelamor's green eyes flashed red in the light. "*I don't know what!* I just know that Yalkara hid something here—a precious, deadly thing. She must have left it for some future need, otherwise why would the place require such strong protections? I hope that I'll recognize it when I find it."

So be it, Maigraith thought. I'll play your game. The longer we spend here the happier I'll be. She wandered off by herself, curious to see what Yalkara's domain had been like, fascinated by everything she saw.

"And that bears on another matter," Faelamor said when they were together again. "This is a lesson for you, and a test; perhaps your greatest before the final one. The one that will free you."

She said this with no particular emphasis, only a fleeting glance at Maigraith, but Maigraith felt a sudden chill, a clawing of pain and terror, a feeling that she stood alone at the entrance of a funnel-shaped well of light, guarding it against a horde that flooded up, snapping and slashing at her. She was very alone and there was no hope. But that feeling passed as quickly as it came, then Faelamor led the way down another corridor.

It was the following morning before they found the first of the places Faelamor was looking for. This was a broad, high room with simple ornamentation on frieze and cornice and architrave, once Yalkara's bedchamber. There was a bed of black steel and brass, very broad and long, with a high head and foot. On either side of the bedhead stood an ebony cupboard; small silken tapestries decorated the mostly bare walls, alien worldscapes in muted colors. A dusty carpet covered the central part of the floor. A door at one end led to a dressing room, and beyond was a bathing room with a square tub as big as the bed. Everything was beautifully made but austere.

Havissard must have been sealed at the moment of Yalkara's departure, for precious things sat everywhere, untouched. And abandoned without haste, for all was orderly, left in readiness for the next owner.

Faelamor's face was forbidding. She gave the room one hostile glance and went into the dressing room. What personal things would the great Yalkara have kept beside her? Maigraith wondered. She opened the door of the cupboard on the righthand side of the bed. There was a drawer below, compartments of varying sizes above, but all were empty. The other cupboard was the same. She found a writing tablet in the drawer, a stylus lying neatly on top and a loosely rolled scroll.

She took out the scroll. It was a small one, and on it were several columns of writing in indigo ink, but she knew neither the language nor the script. She put it back. The tablet was thick paper, the kind for drawing on, and neither brittle nor yellowed, even after all these years. The stylus was made of ebony with gold bands. It had a silver tip, soft silver that was sometimes used for writing in ancient times. At the back of the drawer she found all that remained of a piece of fruit—a scatter of small round seeds, withered like peppercorns, a woody piece of stalk, scraps of desiccated rind.

The stylus was a simple, beautiful thing. She weighed it in her hand. It was very heavy. If Yalkara wrote with it, Maigraith reasoned, she would have had to press hard, to mark the paper with silver metal. What was the last thing she wrote? Something of importance, or utterly trivial? It seemed important that she know something about Yalkara, most enigmatic of all the Charon. Maigraith held the tablet at a shallow angle to the light and saw slight depressions there. Faelamor was still out of sight.

Sprinkling dust over the page, she tapped the excess away. Falling dust twinkled in the light. Dust on the paper revealed what seemed to be a single word. What was it? Something *lior*. Aeolior! Just the word, written near the top of the tablet, as if it had been on Yalkara's mind. Perhaps written absently, for it was surrounded with patterns. As though she had sat for a moment, dreaming.

Aeolior! The very sound of it set up a reverberation in Maigraith's mind. But the name—it was a name, surely—meant nothing. A place or a person? *Aeolior*. It cried out to her. And it was something that Faelamor did not know about. Maigraith did not want her to find out.

A footfall sounded in the bathing room. Maigraith tore the sheet from the tablet, folded it below the name and put it carefully in her pack.

"Here is something," she said, going over to the door to meet Faelamor, showing her the scroll and the tablet.

Faelamor glanced at them absently, unrolled the scroll, frowning, somewhere else, then handed them back.

"There's nothing here," she said, and led the way out and down.

They found the library soon after, a large room that was L-shaped and shelved with books from floor to ceiling. "It's not here either!" said Faelamor from the door. Frustration and fear made her more irritable than usual.

On impulse Maigraith went inside, and Faelamor did not restrain her. Most of the books looked the same, large journals all of a size and bound alike. The symbols on the spines might have been numerals, but Maigraith did not recognize them. The books appeared to be in a sequence, as year journals might have been, and the ones furthest to the right and highest were worn and battered.

"Of course Yalkara would have kept the Histories," said Faelamor, following her in. She took a volume down at random from a middle shelf and opened it at the front, turning the pages idly. "The Charon script, as you would expect. No one can read it." She walked along the rows. All the others were the same, except for the very last and, presumably, latest volume. It was smaller, not half the size of the others, and slimmer too. She opened it.

The script was unusual—a curved, glyphic hand, quickly written, that scratched at Faelamor's memory. No, the thought was lost.

"Not the Charon script," she said. "Why not? Why would she write in a less secure hand?"

"Perhaps she did not want the Charon to be able to read it," Maigraith replied. "But she must have wanted someone to. Why does anyone write the Histories, other than for posterity?" Maigraith took another book down, this from among the earliest. It had been rebound at some time, for the pages were smaller and the writing came up to the binding. "See, this one is in the Charon script too."

There was nothing else in the room save, in the center, a small leopard-wood desk and stool. Carrying her volume over to the desk, Maigraith wiped it clean with the hem of her coat. She sat down on the high stool, turning the pages with one hand while she held the globe up with the other. There were no diagrams, drawings or even doodles. Just page after page of writing and some marks along the top. Dates perhaps. She took it back and got another.

A sixth sense, which came and went in waves in this awful place, told Faelamor that what she sought was nearby. Perhaps related to this sense, the aftersickness was returning. If she didn't find what she was looking for soon, she never would.

While Maigraith browsed, Faelamor went to check the rooms further up the corridor. Her intuition was working strongly now—she found that she could envision what was beyond the other side of each door before she opened it. She did not go far. Outside one door, the fifth, she stopped abruptly.

Something *was* hidden here, in this nest of storerooms and pantries! She set out methodically to find it. In the back of a larder she came upon a number of secret compartments, but did not bother with them. She knew that what she wanted was not there.

She spent frustrating, teasing hours among spice jars and cutlery drawers, and rooms full of cloths and linen carefully folded, but found nothing. Then, as she went through the further door she jumped and cried out. It felt that something soft but spiny had clamped itself to her back. She backed out—there it was again! There was something in the door, or the wall! She traced the surfaces with fingertips as sensitive as a safecracker's. It was in the wall; and it had been concealed in haste, for the plasterwork was ever so slightly less perfect than elsewhere. She could just feel the edge of the new work.

Faelamor found tools, broke the plaster away, cut out the mortar between the stones and levered one out. In the cavity that was revealed she found a small lead box sealed with a charm. To break that hurt her cruelly. But she got the box open. The lid creaked up.

Inside were three pieces of golden jewelry: a heavy chain, a bracelet and a torc, all of red gold. She'd gone into the library at Chanthed looking for information about Yalkara, and the ancient drawings had shown her Yalkara's jewelry, made of Aachan gold. She knew the value of it all too well.

Faelamor picked up the chain and received a shock that flung her through the doorway. She could not get up for quite some time afterwards. The skin of her fingers, where she had touched the metal, was swollen, bright red and crumpled up. A hideous prickling raced up and down her nerve pathways. No matter; she would find a way to handle this gold. She closed the lid of the box, put it in her bag and headed back to the library, very content. She had what she wanted.

As she reached the door, cramps doubled her over, just the

merest forerunner of what was to come. Maigraith was still sitting at the desk going through the journals. Faelamor took up the slim volume again, peering at the strange script. She let out a muffled exclamation and Maigraith stuck her head around the corner. The gold must have heightened Faelamor's sensitivities—the curiosity she'd felt about this script before was now a shout of alarm.

"It rings! It rings in my head like a klaxon." Faelamor was talking to herself, walking back along the shelves of books, checking volumes at random. "These are all in the Charon script, but the last is no script that I've ever seen before, *save on the Mirror!* Yet now I feel that I ought to be able to read it. And I must; what I want will surely be in it."

"Perhaps the chronicler can read it," said Maigraith.

"Llian of Chanthed? Tensor's pander?" she sneered. "I don't think so!"

"What are you looking for?"

"I don't know. Maybe this is the one." Faelamor held up the smaller volume. "I learned a lot from her in our last battle, for she was strangely weak, curiously sluggish then. Not at all like the other times."

She continued browsing, idly picking out a book here and there and putting them back.

That preoccupation nearly proved her downfall, for suddenly the whole of existence shuddered again, only this time much more strongly. Being a master illusionist, Faelamor understood the nature of reality better than any, but she found herself hard put to retain the image of the library in her mind. Everything shivered and shimmered; even solid things seemed not to know their state. The very act of looking at a thing appeared to change it. All the realities connected to that place appeared one after another: the slow drying of the land over eons; the soil rushing off the bare hills in storms, leaving them barren and rocky; the building and delving, from tiny huts of stone chinked with mud to tall towers and the superstructure of the mines; the randomness of human events, of events in that very room.

Even herself she saw there, in a distant age; and Yalkara, tall figure on her stool, writing in her journal. Head down so that her face could not be seen; a fall of dark hair. All the Charon were alike, in that manner. Then she was gone, the room empty again, dusty, still. *So like*, Faelamor thought, shaking with hot and cold chills.

At first Maigraith felt dizzy and had to close her eyes, though that had not stopped her head from spinning. But toward the end her whole body became tense with expectation, like the first part of a sneeze, and she opened her eyes and saw the woman. "Was that your enemy?" Maigraith cried.

"That was Yalkara." Then, in a panicky rush: "Maigraith, someone's inside. They're coming this way!"

"How can that be? Havissard is protected."

"It *was*, but we entered. Events are moving to a climacteric; Havissard is known to be a place of great secrets. Now that Tensor has let loose the secret of gates, others may also be using them. Perhaps someone entered the same way we did."

"Or perhaps what we did let them in."

"There's no time to debate the matter!" Faelamor snapped. "Go back to the gate and prepare the way."

"What about this intruder?"

"I'll deal with it, once I know who it is." She could not resist the impulse to lecture. "Observe! Learn your enemy's capabilities! Then strike swiftly!"

Faelamor opened the small volume, idly glanced inside again and as she did so actuality shivered a third time. The image of Yalkara appeared once more and looked up from her stool, straight into Faelamor's eyes. Instantly Faelamor was speared through the heart by a realization. A tremor passed up her spine. The writing was indeed familiar; she could read a glyph here and there. She closed the book, staring into space and time. To say that she was shocked and disturbed would be a profound understatement. She was terrified, though she could not say why.

Dark rumors from the past rose unbidden. The impossibly

distant past—the time that the Faellem had erased from the annals of their world. Only myths and rumors remained, and cautions.

No time for that now! "Go back to the gate!" Faelamor screamed. "Make it ready *immediately*!"

Maigraith took one look at her face and ran.

Faelamor used what remained of her strength to disguise her appearance. The illusion was not one of her best; not much more than a change of clothes and hair color. She sat staring at the glyphs in the little book, waiting for the intruder while the time stretched out eternally.

He stopped in the doorway when he saw what lay within—a vast library—the storehouse of one person's Histories. He stared, holding the globe high, then moved forward reluctantly, perhaps thinking that it could only be a dream, and a disappointing one. But it was no dream. It did not recede before him. Faelamor studied him from under her hand.

It was Mendark! He could only be here for one thing. That must mean that the Council's own plans were well advanced. Well, she had what he wanted. Be careful, he was very dangerous.

He approached, the unreality that she had felt before spreading out in front of him like a shockwave. Her head spun. She felt that she was losing control. What power had *he* used to get inside? Whatever it was it was still active, and interacting with the protection it was a peril to them all.

Faelamor leapt out, attacking him with phantoms and delusions that even to her own mind seemed twisted and dangerous, nothing like what she had intended. Mendark, taken by surprise, fell and she fled at once, feeling as if she was pursued by the shades she had conjured. Aftersickness was burning, roaring, exploding in her brain. She was incapable of noticing that the little book had slipped out of her bag.

Faelamor came lurching up to the gate, her face gruesomely twisted. Maigraith had never seen her so wracked.

"Is it ready?" Faelamor screamed.

"Yes," said Maigraith with provocative calm.

"Show me the destination!"

Maigraith sent the image, the woven platform suspended above the river, across the link. It was so clear and perfect that they might have been looking through a window.

"Follow me!"

Faelamor leapt recklessly into the gate. Maigraith followed, infected by her malaise, and it grew worse when she realized that Faelamor had vanished. This time the passage was a desperate, unreal one, and as soon as Maigraith was in it she knew something had gone wrong. The link evaporated, then she came out in suffocating cold and wet and dark, an explosion of water that stung her skin like a hundred little whiplashes.

Maigraith felt the water boiling away from her. How could the destination have been so wrong? Cold water burned in the back of her nose. Perhaps she was in the bottom of the deep ocean—a current was pulling her along. Maigraith felt gravel under her feet, propelled herself upwards and her head broke the surface. Rubbing water out of her eyes she saw the platform hanging placidly just upstream—they had come out at the bottom of the river.

Maigraith was not a strong swimmer. She struggled out to lie gasping on the bank. When she recovered her breath she looked around but could not see her liege. Then, downstream, a bundle of rags bobbed to the surface. A feeble claw clutched at smooth rock, then the water pulled her under again.

Maigraith felt that thin hand clutching at her heart. For better or worse she was bound to Faelamor, hating her yet still finding something in her that she needed desperately. Running down she dived back in, found Faelamor underwater by feel and brought her to the surface. Water dribbled from her nose. Maigraith heaved her onto the ground and pressed the water from her lungs.

Lying there on the mossy bank Faelamor looked weak, tired and old. The straps of her leather pouch were gripped so tightly that Maigraith could not prise them loose. What had she found in Havissard? Opening the flaps of the pouch, Maigraith spilled out the contents. It gleamed red against the grass; a heavy rough-cast chain of gold; other, smaller jewelry. The sense of the gold alarmed her—a horrible raspy feeling up the nerves of her arms. What could Faelamor want it for?

Beside her, Faelamor gasped a breath. Maigraith put back the jewelry, fastened the pack and walked away toward the forest. When the river was beyond sight she opened her own small parcel. The stylus was undamaged but water had got into the package containing the loose leaf from the tablet, smearing and twisting the writing into a cry: *Aeolior!* Something wrenched at her heart. She folded the paper over carefully and walked deep into the forest.

33

A Little Rebellion

Faelamor forced herself to hands and knees, choking up mud and water onto the ground. Water and vomit burned in her lungs and up her nose. She heaved until there was nothing left but bile and blood—she brought that up too. Clawing at the grass, she dragged herself away from the mess to the river bank. As she leaned over to scoop water onto her face, the turf was springy beneath her breast. The water was still, a little quiet backwater beside the race that had almost drowned her. Her face was reflected, haggard as death itself, and her pale hair hung down like the unraveled ends of a dirty old rope. Too weak to move, she stared at the wretched old woman she had become. She had no idea what had happened.

Faelamor dangled her fingers into the cold water and sucked the moisture off until she had the strength to get up. Memories began to come back—Havissard. The Aachan gold. The little book, in an unknown script that was hauntingly familiar. The gate going wild. Perhaps the gold had forced it to go wrong. She had no memories after that.

Where was Maigraith? She dragged her head around, which hurt horribly. Maigraith was nowhere to be seen. Where was her pouch? Where was the gold? Faelamor began to panic. Was it lost at the bottom of the river? Or, almost as bad, had Maigraith found it? She recovered a fleeting memory of Maigraith bending over her. Faelamor crawled back up the slope and saw her pouch on the grass, next to the contents of her stomach. She fumbled with the straps, tore them open, felt inside. A wave of relief passed over her when she realized that the gold was still there. Her safety net, if all else failed. But the relief was short-lived—the little book was gone. Where was the dreadful book? She fell back onto the grass.

Cold brought Faelamor out of her dreams. She must have lain there for hours, almost comatose, for the shadows of the trees now stretched right across the clearing. She was freezing, chilled to the core, and she stank of bile, vomit and blood. She was lying in it. It would have been very easy to remain there. She felt so sleepy, so enervated. But a voice kept whispering at her and it got louder and louder until it was a scream: *You are the Faellem. You must go on! You must!*

What was the matter with her? Why was she so weak, so ill from the gate? Faelamor had forgotten how it had wracked her, forgotten that for a day and a half she had forced back the aftersickness resulting from all she had done in Havissard. Finally it had returned, doubled and redoubled, and claimed her. She pulled herself to her feet, swaying and staggering. Not far away was a pebble beach and shallow water. She dragged her clothes off, dropped them on the shore and flopped into the water. It was like being molded in ice.

After washing herself all over—her face, her hair, inside her mouth—she crept out again on all fours. Upriver, the gate structure that had sent them to Havissard and back again still hung between the trees over the water, curving like a smiling mouth. Grinning at her wicked folly. She would never use it again. She left her clothes where they lay and crawled the hundred or so paces to the shelter of woven reeds.

Faelamor was tormented by her blunders. She had nearly drowned, a dishonorable death, a failure of her duty. She kept thinking that, over and over—not that she had nearly died but that she had nearly *failed.*

It was almost dark now. Creeping into Maigraith's sleeping pouch, she pulled it up over her head. It shut out the light but the nightmare of Havissard was stronger than ever. *I am the Faellem,* she told herself. *I may not rest until my duty is done.* Her body gave up and dragged her down to blessed sleep for a few minutes, then the cold flung her into wakefulness again.

She dressed herself with all the clothes she had, heavy woolen socks and boots, gloves, coat, hat. Her belly burned like acid, as if she had burst her insides with all that retching. She forced the pain away but that just brought back the cold lurking in the background. *Fire! I must have fire or I will die.* Faelamor crawled to where dry sticks and kindling were stacked under another woven shelter. Maigraith was so damned efficient! She dragged out wood with her teeth, piece by piece, and set a fire, but though she struck sparks into it for half an hour it would not catch. Her sin had offended even the elements.

Faelamor could feel herself weakening every minute. It was almost as bad as it had been in Thurkad after the Conclave last winter. The nights were not so cold here, at this time of year, but still cold enough to kill her if she collapsed outside. Had she been Yggur or Mendark or Tensor, she might have brought flame out of her fingers, but that form of the Secret Art was barred to her. Then inspiration struck. She crawled to the shelter, finding by feel one of Maigraith's little lightglasses. Even so insignificant a device as this was forbidden to her but what was one more crime? She lay on the floor with it in her hand, the glow stirring and seeping out between her fingers, remembering the first time she had seen one.

Maigraith had been just a young woman—barely out of childhood—when they had gone together to an ancient place in the south, stronghold of some long-dead, long-forgotten tyrant. The people who had taken over his demesne were mere squatters who understood nothing, but they knew how to light the opaline spheres above the doors.

Maigraith, as usual, had watched all this in silence, but on returning to camp she had sat quietly with metal and crystal of various kinds; smoothing, polishing, shaping until she had her own version of a globe. She sat back, examined it on all sides, and touched it in a certain way. It did not light. Nor did the next one, nor the two or three hundred after that. But Maigraith was admirably persistent and, one day, one did light up. The ones after that were smaller, and worked better, until eventually the globes she made were more perfect than any Faelamor had ever seen.

Faelamor had not asked how she knew what to do. Whether it was intuitive, or transmitted in some way across the generations, Faelamor did not know or want to know. The very idea of working with *devices*, of empowering *objects* through the Secret Art, made her shudder. Forbidden knowledge!

Taking the globe between her teeth she dragged herself back to the fireplace. She put it down on a stone beside the wood and smashed it with the back of the hatchet. It burst with a blast of blue-white heat that burnt her fingers and set her coat smoldering up to the elbow. Faelamor beat it out and looked down with satisfaction at the blaze.

After rescuing Faelamor from the river Maigraith walked off into the forest in an uncertain mood, half-joy, half-melancholy. Havissard had been good for her.

Now she had found something that could not be taken from her. She belonged somewhere at last. She was not just a tool in Faelamor's hand. She had a different destiny—she was here for a purpose. Was it tied up with Faelamor? She did not know, only that she was part of a puzzle, perhaps the key part.

Maigraith walked in the forest until dark. As night came down she remembered Faelamor. She felt the outline of the silver stylus in her pocket, smiled and turned back to the campsite.

Faelamor was hunched over the fire, shivering. Maigraith saw that her eyes were turned inwards—she had retreated right into herself. Her lips were pinched blue. Maigraith touched Faelamor's cheek with a finger. She was like a piece of meat in an ice chest.

A pot stood in the fire. Most of the water had boiled away but there was enough for a small cup of chard. Maigraith stirred the big leaves into it, added honey from a comb, squeezing the dark brown stuff out of the waxy cells until the chard was as thick as syrup, licked her fingers, picked out a young wasp that had been squeezed into the mug, stirred the tea with her finger, licked it again and held the mug to Faelamor's lips.

There was no reaction. She prized Faelamor's teeth apart with a stick, held her head back and poured the hot liquid in until it overflowed. Faelamor gasped, choked, spluttered. Her eyes flew open and she looked blankly at Maigraith. Then she recognized her. Maigraith held the cup to her lips again.

"Turn and turn about," Maigraith said wryly, remembering how Faelamor had rescued her from Fiz Gorgo a year ago.

Faelamor did not reply. The cup was soon empty.

"More?"

Faelamor nodded. Maigraith fetched water, boiled the pot and repeated the dose. Two cups later Faelamor was able to hold it by herself.

"My guts are on fire," said Faelamor. She crawled into the shelter and slept until the middle of the following day.

When she arose Faelamor was back to her old self, though still weak. "Knowing how much you hate me," she said, "makes me wonder why you dragged me out of the water. Why you came back."

Maigraith shrugged. "My whole life has been duty. Everything I have ever done has been to meet other people's goals. At the moment I can see no other way for myself. Perhaps I can do nothing else, being, *as you made me*, so incomplete."

Faelamor was not certain what to think about this, but she took it as though her indoctrination, or her compulsion, still held. Then Maigraith stripped that illusion away in a second.

"As soon as you went through the gate," she said conversationally, "I considered breaking the anchor and leaving you *in between*."

Faelamor shivered, and looking into Maigraith's eyes she saw something that she had not seen before. Something steely that she had always thought Maigraith lacked.

"Not even you could have survived that," Maigraith went on. "I considered it seriously, then I recalled to mind the lessons that you taught me. Duty above all. Respect! Honor! My honor, that is, since you have none. And so I let you live, knowing that your goal was a noble one and mine to support it."

Faelamor wondered if she was being sarcastic, or ironic.

"Then prepare to do it," she said, but Maigraith was not finished.

"But be sure of one thing! As you were lessened by what you met in Havissard, so was I increased by what *I* found. I aid you now of my own accord, and if I decide to go that will be of my choosing too."

Faelamor did not feel strong enough to challenge this statement; she merely gave a non-committal sigh which Maigraith could interpret how she pleased. Yet inwardly she was raging. Whatever you have seen of my strength before, she thought, was but a tenth part of what I have at my disposal. Your time will never come! I made you with a flaw so that what you boast about can never happen. When I am ready you will feel that power, and then you will come back, begging to serve me. That is your only duty.

No more was said. There were months of work to be done before the Faellem arrived, if they were coming at all. Things to be found, things to be learned; watch kept on Thurkad and for Rulke. And together they must practice all the skills they needed for her ultimate goal.

Faelamor sat silent, quivering with some emotion that she had been trying to control all this time.

"What's the matter?" Maigraith asked.

"I had a book," said Faelamor, her eyes showing raw fear. "What happened to it?"

"Your bag was fastened when I pulled you out of the water. There was no book in it."

"You saw it!" screamed Faelamor in a panic. "The small book in that strange script!"

"Perhaps you lost it in the river."

Faelamor squeezed her head between her hands. "No! I must have dropped it in the library when Mendark appeared. This is a disaster!"

"We can go back for it if it's so important."

Not far upriver the gate hung between the trees, swaying ever so slightly when there was any breeze, leering at her, a reminder. Faelamor knew she could not use it again. That it had worked at all was surprising, so imbued were her atoms with the prohibition against devices.

"I can't go through the gate again," she said, shuddering at the thought of that sin, and at the memories of Havissard too. "I've too much to pay for already. You'll have to go."

"Me?" cried Maigraith, even more afraid of the gate now. "I can't!"

"Of course you can. You did most of it the other day. Why won't you have confidence in yourself?"

"Because you made me so," Maigraith said softly.

"I must have the book. You'll go in the morning!"

That was that. She had to go—her liege had ordered it.

I suppose I can make the gate work again, Maigraith thought. I did seem to understand it, instinctively. "I'll try," she said.

Faelamor examined her. "I must have the book, but no one must know I have it. And be careful—Mendark could still be there."

Maigraith lay awake that night, mentally preparing herself. After their precipitous return from Havissard things would never be the same between her and Faelamor. She had gained some little thing that she could not articulate; a sense of belonging.

But what did the future hold for her? If she freed herself from Faelamor, what would she do with her life? If she did have a purpose, what was it? Maybe she would find the answers in Havissard. The first visit had been a revelation.

Maigraith fell asleep, to dream about Havissard. Reliving the making of the gate, she found that it came easily to her. So easily that she found herself drifting out of Elludore in her dreams. That frightened her awake, then she put it out of her mind and slept.

PART THREE

34

PRIDE AND PREJUDICE

Shand came wearily up the stairs of the inn and opened the door of the room that was his when he was at home. He put his candle on the dresser, stretched weary muscles, turned toward the bed and stopped.

They looked like two lost children. Llian's head was cradled against Karan's bosom and both were sleeping peacefully. He'd missed them on his lonely journey. He watched them for a while then took up his candle in one weather-beaten hand and went back up the corridor to the open doorway. The light revealed fragments of chamber pot all over the floor. Shand picked up the most dangerous shards and fell into bed. He had done a double march to get here today and was so weary that he did not even wonder what had happened, just went straight to sleep.

Karan stirred. The burden of the night had been lifted slightly—she did not feel quite so alone. It was mid-morning. Downstairs, breakfast must be long over.

Easing herself out of bed, Karan pulled the blankets up to Llian's chin. She dressed quickly in her woolens—green baggy trousers, gray stained shirt, green socks of fine wool, brown boots, jerkin and coat. She was utterly sick of her traveling clothes. Her tattered felt hat she stuffed in a pocket. There was no mirror in the room but that did not bother her, since she seldom saw her own face. Anyway, she'd had enough of mirrors. She brushed her thick hair until it shone, though as soon as she finished it sprang out as untameable as ever.

Passing the next door Karan heard a familiar gurgling snore. Her heart leapt and she peeped in the open doorway. Shand was back! She could have leapt straight onto the bed and kissed him.

Dear Shand, she thought, looking down at her old friend. His hair was grayer and thinner than she remembered, and there were a few more age lines on his face, but his beard was long and luxuriant. It had been summer when he left them in Flude.

"How I missed you," she murmured, and sat down on the chair beside the bed, watching him sleep as he had watched over her in Thurkad. He drifted slowly into wakefulness, turned over and opened one eye. His eyes were green, but a lesser green than hers and deep sunken, which made them look smaller.

"A fine thing to come home to, you two in my bed," he said with a smile.

"Where have you been all this time, and why did you go without saying goodbye?"

"Have you breakfasted yet?"

"No."

"Then run down and rouse out the kitchen, and let me dress in peace. I know you are shameless but an old man has his modesty. We'll break our fast together in the sun, if there is any."

"So little to be modest about," said Karan with sparkling

eye. "Vanity, more likely." She danced out of the way of Shand's casual hand and out the door.

Shand dressed quickly and ducked into the other room. The huge welt on the side of Llian's head was bruised black. Karan's handiwork, but why? Already he had an inkling. He could sense the trouble.

The inn had a veranda on the northern side, closed at either end by a wall, and even in winter it was a pleasant place to sit when the sun was shining. Thick old vines climbed the posts, leafless now. He found Karan sitting on a plank bench. On a trestle before her was a pot of chard, two bowls, a larger bowl with fruit and a platter on which sat a loaf of dark bread. She was cutting slices off the loaf as he arrived. She poured chard the way he liked it, not too strong, squeezed in a few drops of lime and passed it across.

"Llian is not breakfasting today?"

"Llian . . . He's sleeping still. Oh, Shand, I hit him over the head with your chamber pot. It was awful."

"Not *my* chamber pot," he said mildly. "But that's not what I saw when I arrived."

"I'm soft-headed in the early hours."

"And cranky before breakfast," he said, remembering. He pushed the fruit basket toward her. "We'll talk about it later."

"I'm not sure I want to talk about it at all," she muttered. She selected a small gellon, cut the skin away, shaved off a sliver of orange flesh and put it in her mouth. She made a face.

"That's the worst gellon I've tasted in years!" It looked magnificent: large, round and plump, the thin skin bright orange with a red star of seven rays at the base. It should have had a rich, musky odor but this one had no smell at all. "Surely it's not even ripe? Though it's soft enough."

"This was a blighted year," said Shand sadly.

"Still," said Karan, "even blighted gellon is better than none." She took another slice and a sip of sweet chard with it. "So where *did* you go? Did you come back here to find us?"

Shand unfocused his gaze, deliberately it seemed, but said nothing for a long time. From where they sat they could see the roofs of the other houses in the village, and the track winding down in the direction of Hetchet. The path was empty. Chimney smoke rose straight up into still air like signal banners. Karan ate the rest of the gellon and was nibbling on a dark crust before he spoke.

"Not particularly. After Flude I sailed down the Sea of Thurkad, then east up the River Alm, and eventually back to Thurkad."

"Can I ask why?"

"My own business. A pilgrimage of sorts. Nothing to do with ancient relics, if that's what you're thinking. Why did I come back here? Because I live here, of course. But also because I was looking for you two. You seem to have taken rather a long time to come such a little way."

"We took Selial to the Hornrace. She died there and the Aachim buried her at the foot of the Rainbow Bridge."

"That was kindly done."

"She was good to me and I cared for her. And then Llian wanted to go to Chanthed, so we returned that way."

"Hmn," said Shand so coolly that Karan hurried on.

"Did you go anywhere near Gothryme?" Her voice trembled, thinking of her neglected home.

Shand shot her a glance from under bristling brows. "I did!" he said sternly.

"Is there . . . anything left?"

Again that glance. "I wonder that you dare ask, Karan, having abandoned them for so long."

"It was you took me across the sea when all I wanted was to go home."

"Nine months ago! You could have sailed from Flude to Thurkad in a few weeks. You could have been home months ago."

Karan was silent. Every delay had a good reason but she felt that defending herself would be like making excuses.

"Rachis is old, Karan. Faithful, diligent, but very old. All he wants now is to sit in his chair in the sun and dream away his few remaining years. I think he deserves that, don't you? But he's been working from dawn to midnight, trying to recover from the war before the winter strikes, hoping that you will come home and take the job off his shoulders. He does not criticize you yet he wonders why he serves so faithfully."

Karan was in tears. She had neglected Gothryme shamefully. "How is my land? How are my people?" she asked.

"They have not fared so badly, as it happens," he said, brushing the tears away with callused fingers. "Lower Bannador suffered grievously, but the Hills were spared the worst of it. Too far to go for too little, I suppose. That's not to say that Gothryme hasn't suffered. The Ghâshâd came through more than once on their errands from Shazmak. There is ruin enough and many have died. Much you can put right, but some can never be."

"And there my duty lies," she said. "I wonder that it has taken so long for me to see it." She rose abruptly to her feet.

"Sit down! This is no time for impetuousness, no matter how well-meaning. The whole of Iagador is in turmoil. And know that Yggur holds most of it, including Bannador, and he is not inclined to give it up no matter what temporary alliances may have been forged in Katazza."

Karan knew that, too. She was no stranger to the realities of power.

"Besides, there is Llian. He won't be able to travel today; perhaps not even tomorrow."

She screwed up her face. "Let us not talk of that now."

"It must be faced—as Gothryme must be."

"I know, and I do not shirk this responsibility either. But later; I'm too confused. Let's talk about other things, please."

"All right, whatever you want."

"I'd like to know where you've been." She spoke very humbly.

"There was a place I had to visit. A very ancient place."

"So you *were* questing after Aachan gold!"

"No I was *not*! More like an homage to the past. *My* past. Perhaps an indulgence in these times but I had to go."

"Tell me about it."

"I'd rather not. Like you, I am reluctant to face up to my failings."

"Well, what else have you been doing?"

"I visited Thurkad on the way here, secretly of course. Yggur has been back for months. The tales say that he returned like a fury, crushing the rebellious with a fist of iron, casting out the Ghâshâd and quelling Thurkad in an instant. But that's his tellers, rewriting history as usual. The true story is much more interesting, and centers on your friend Maigraith."

"Oh?" It was more than a year since she and Maigraith had been together on the road to Fiz Gorgo. "Tell me about her."

"The story is very strange. She and Yggur were lovers . . ."

"I knew that," said Karan. "I've heard tales about her too, though all different."

He told Maigraith's story, concluding: "She led an army into Bannador against the Ghâshâd and the rebels, claiming that Karan of Bannador was her special friend and she would not abandon her people. You might have been a nobody once, but you are quite famous now in your little country, and even beyond its borders. I heard tales about you everywhere."

"I don't want to be famous," said Karan mournfully. "I just want to go home."

"Well, I suppose it'll all die down over time. Anyway, she liberated Bannador and drove the Ghâshâd yelping back to Shazmak. So, indirectly, you've done your folk good after all."

"Her special friend!" said Karan in amazement. "Well, perhaps I am, since I never knew her to have a friend. What a strange person she is. And she has suffered so. Did you see her?"

Shand shrugged. "I've never met her. Just before Yggur came back she disappeared. And that's all I have to tell."

"Well, I've news for you." She told him what they had learned in the library at Chanthed. "Faelamor was there months ago."

"Grim tidings," said Shand. "And for Mendark too, since it may bear on what he went east to find. Yggur must be told at once. I'd hoped for a nice long rest in Tullin. And that's not all, is it? Out with it."

Karan poured herself another bowl of chard. Her eyes met Shand's. "If we must."

"Let's go for a stroll. Some things are easier to talk about, walking."

She offered Shand her arm. They went around the back of the inn, crossed below the woodheap and struck out across a herbland covered in snow. Soon they came to the Hetchet road, as it was called, though it was no more than a slushy track. The steep slope directly below the inn had once been graveled with fist-sized pieces of rock that jutted up through the mud and made walking difficult. Further down, the track was covered in unmarked snow.

Karan took comfort from the pressure of Shand's broad fingers on her arm. She was afraid to talk about Llian. It hurt.

"I trusted him. *I loved him,*" she said.

"You still do, and all the things that made you feel that way are still there. And all the things that you ignored when you made that choice."

"I hate him! The things that make me hate him I didn't know about before."

"Nonsense. You're acting like a hurt child."

"You never trusted Llian. You often said so."

"I admit it, but I'm prejudiced against the Zain. I make no secret of it. Mendark trusted Hennia, and she betrayed the Council. They're all the same!"

"I don't know what to do!" she cried. "I'm so confused."

They were scrambling down the steep part of the slope. In some places the mud was frozen, old bootprints deep and hard to walk on. Then they would step down without warning into greasy clay that was treacherous. They skidded their way to the bottom, where the forest waited: dark trunks, dark branches, hard dark leaves even in winter, like a threat.

Karan was sorting through her memories, trying to understand what had happened last night.

"He was curious from the moment we met," she said, speaking to herself as much as to Shand. "Impertinently, arrogantly so, it seemed to me. He asked questions that no stranger would ask of another. It shocked me then, though since I've come to learn that it's just his way."

"He is according to his nature—and the character of the Zain. That's what makes him a master chronicler, just as it is what led to their downfall."

"Did you know that one day in Shazmak he actually searched my room for the Mirror? I was furious, though later I realized that Emmant's enchantment had made his curiosity insatiable. I suppose it was the same with Tensor—they both worked on Llian's weakness."

"What was Llian looking for?"

"Something he came across in a book Emmant showed him." They passed under the leaves of the forest, out of the wind, out of the sun. Karan shivered. "He's never mentioned it since and I haven't asked. I'd forgotten about it. He was almost frantic with the lure of it—the key to one of the great mysteries. To the chroniclers, that is—nothing of *real* importance."

"Did he name this thing?" Shand asked, though with no particular interest.

Karan furrowed her brow. She'd been so angry at the time. "He said it was the image of a tablet."

"The Tablet!"

"I suppose so. The key to the script of the Charon, I seem to remember."

Shand gave a great sigh. "I can imagine the passions that such things arouse in a master chronicler. If the libraries of the Charon could be translated it would open whole new worlds."

"I've thought no more about it since. But after Katazza and his dealings with Tensor . . ."

"Remember that Tensor forced Llian to aid him," said Shand.

"At first! I believe Llian did it willingly in the end, in return for what he could learn from Tensor." Karan had thought herself into an agitated state—she couldn't think straight; didn't know what to think. "Whatever the reason," she said furiously, *"he did it!* And that story about how he escaped from the Nightland, how can that be true? How could he get away from Rulke?"

"He was telling the truth *as far as he knew it,"* said Shand. "Look, why would Rulke want to keep him in the Nightland anyway? Maybe he escaped, or maybe Rulke let him escape. What does it matter?"

"Because it's my fault! I left him there. The shame will live with me until I die. And after last night it's tearing me apart!"

She sat down on a log but the rotten wood crumbled, dropping her into a hollow full of icy slush. The trees crowded down, their black branches reaching out for her. She got up again hastily, wiping ice off her bottom, and they continued.

"After what Rulke did to the Zain I cannot believe that Llian would make such a pact," Karan went on, now veering to the opposite opinion. "Coerced or forced, yes! But not willingly. But on the other hand, he is easily dominated. It would be easy for Rulke to impress his will on him. Even Emmant did so."

"I can't follow your train of thought," said Shand. "What happened last night?"

Here the path turned around the end of a ridge, momentarily coming out of thick forest into a clearing. Before them was a steep slope, partially bare of trees, and a wilderness of deep valleys all clad in snow. Shand leaned on a rock and looked away down the slope.

"I'm all confused. He'd been so contented since Chanthed," Karan said, "whereas I've been cranky. I've been having nightmares about Rulke again. We had a misunderstanding—all my fault—and I locked him out of our room. Maybe last night was my fault too! Then we both dreamed the present and the past, when I made that sending to him here last winter. It seemed that the past unlocked the way for the present. Our dreams were linked, and I couldn't break the link, and then Rulke came."

"What?" cried Shand, springing forward to grip her by the shoulders. He stared into her eyes, shaking her in his agitation. "Rulke in the flesh? Through a gate?"

Karan pulled free, suddenly afraid for Llian. "No, it was just an image, but by the end I thought he was going to condense himself in the room." As she told the story Shand's face grew bleak.

"This almost sinks your previous bad news," he said, settling onto a log with his head in his hands. "If only I'd come back sooner."

"It was horrible. I felt split in two, the me of a year ago and me now, and Llian the same. Rulke tried to compel me over the link, through Llian. He went within a breath of doing it, too."

"Why would he want to compel Llian?" said Shand. He looked as if he had just had a very unpleasant thought. Rising from the log, they walked on. "Why use Llian to get at you, for that matter? I suppose it's easier to use connections that are already there than to make fresh ones."

"He would have had me, if I hadn't almost knocked Llian's brains out. Poor Llian! No one could resist that power." Karan wasn't confused anymore. "I've got to get back—I've left him lying up there all alone. He might die." As she spun around Shand grabbed her flying coat-tails.

"Wait, I see it now. You're quite wrong. Rulke has possessed him, as he did to Yggur long ago! Whatever Llian says or does, no matter how convincing his explanations, you must never trust him. He isn't your friend anymore—he's a puppet of a dangerous enemy. Protect yourself against him."

Karan reeled, clinging to a tree for support. "I'm not afraid of Llian. He would never harm me."

"You must protect yourself," said Shand in steely tones.

Her temper flared. "You've always been prejudiced against Llian, because he's Zain."

"I know the treacheries of the Zain better than anyone on this world."

His bitterness shocked her. "I won't believe that of Llian," she said. She kicked a stone, which shot down the track, bounced high and crashed into a branch, sending down a small shower of snow. "When he comes to me, what am I supposed to do? Llian has always trusted me, no matter what."

"But you've just spent the last hour telling me how worried you were."

"I had to tell someone," she wailed. "Leave me alone; I didn't ask you to take over my life." She flung herself off the path into the forest, hurtling up into a thicket where she bogged in deep snow. She hurled it about with her arms.

Shand ran after her. "This is too important to have tantrums about."

"I'm not having a tantrum!" she said abruptly. "I just can't do it, even if you are right."

He led her out of the black forest into bright sunshine. Karan sat down on a boulder of schist, tracing the looping, knotted grain of the rock with a finger. Shand stared down the road, fighting some internal battle.

"I'm going back," said Karan. "Llian's all alone."

"He's all right; I looked in on him before breakfast. We've got to get this sorted out."

"The only way to sort it out is to talk to Llian."

"No!" Shand yelled. Then he lowered his voice. "That will alert Rulke. Say nothing to Llian, I beg you. Pretend that it never happened."

"That's how you solve your problems, is it?" she said angrily.

"It's the best way with this one, believe me."

"I don't believe you; I can't do it."

"You must," Shand repeated in obsidian tones.

"You're tearing me apart," said Karan, banging her knuckles on her forehead. "After all Llian has done for me. If he *has* been corrupted, it's my fault."

"Whatever Llian did was of his own free will."

"You're making a terrible mistake."

"Who knows the Zain better than I do, Karan?" Shand said bitterly. "Watching them has been the work of half my life."

"What if you're wrong?"

"I'm not." He paced down the track then came back, his back bowed.

She stepped into his path. "Well, what are you going to do?"

Shand sat down on bare ice and put his head in his hands. It was hard to get out the words he needed to say. "If this was war . . ."

"It isn't!" she snapped. "Llian is *mine*, Shand, and I will defend him with my last breath, even against you. In spite of all you've done for me and all I feel for you."

"He must be taken to Thurkad and examined properly, with all the tools of the Secret Art."

"And then? What do you do with *my* Llian then, Shand?"

"He'll have to be guarded night and day. *At least!*"

"Be damned!" she cried wildly. "There'll be blood spilled if anyone tries!"

"Karan," said Shand, more gently, "you don't know what's at stake."

"I know what my stake is!" She went down on her knees before him. "Shand, leave him in my custody, please. Let me take him to Gothryme. Even if he is . . . what you say he is, he can't get up to any mischief there. There's nothing and no one to spy on."

"This isn't a game, you know."

"Do you think it's a game to me? Look, can Rulke make Llian do things that are not in his power now?"

"No!" said Shand grudgingly.

"Can Llian use the Secret Art, or wield a weapon as if he was trained to it?"

"Of course not! Possession cannot confer the powers or the skills of the one that does the possessing."

"Then even if you *are* right, all he can do is spy. What harm can he do in Gothryme?"

"And if he escapes?"

"I'll send word instantly, and track him down myself."

"I don't like it." He paced down the track again, arms and legs jerking. "All right, I'll come to Gothryme," he said reluctantly. "But on one condition."

"Anything!" she said unguardedly.

"You must agree to do as I require."

"Of course!" She sighed her relief.

"I saw Malien in Thurkad," Shand said. "She said she might see you in the winter. We'll put him under the guard of the Aachim, if they do turn up, and I'll come home."

"I'll be glad to have them," said Karan. Malien was kin and would understand her view. "Though if things are as bad as you say I don't know what they'll eat. And how was Tensor?"

"No better. No worse."

"Well, what is it that I must agree to?"

They headed back again, arguing all the way, and it was not until they were almost to the inn that Karan succumbed to Shand's demands. She felt as if something inside her had been murdered.

Llian woke with a terrible headache. The bed was empty. Where was Karan? He dressed as best he could. Every time he moved his head it shrieked and whirled nauseatingly. Downstairs he was given curious looks but felt too ill to wonder about them.

It was stiflingly hot in the kitchen. A few spoons of porridge was all he could manage. Lurching outside, he wobbled down in the direction of the woodheap. There he hung over a block of wood, too ill to move.

Later, as he began to feel better, he heard voices from the track below. Karan's voice was unmistakeable. He wanted to run to her for comfort.

"I can't," she said in a frail voice. It sounded as if she was crying.

It took a few words before he recognized the other—Shand! Shand was back! Had he been capable of it, Llian would have leapt out and embraced him. Then he was glad that he hadn't.

"Llian is the enemy now," Shand said in steely tones. "Rulke has surely possessed him. After last night you can never trust him."

Last night? What was Shand talking about? A fragment of the nightmare dribbled back.

"No!" cried Karan. "How can you ask?"

"Llian is no more than a tool moved by Rulke, and a deadly one," said Shand. "Do as I say or our bargain is broken. I'll betray him if you don't. I can't compromise, Karan."

"I thought you were my friend," she wept.

"I am. You must put your feelings aside. The fate of a lot of people may rest on what you do now."

"And Llian is one of them."

"Karan!" Shand's voice was as frigid as a glacier.

She broke. "I will do as you say," she said in agony. Her words froze Llian inside.

"Say nothing to him about it; don't even mention it." They moved on up the path, out of Llian's hearing.

Llian sat there for ages, staring at the tramped-down snow through the cage of his fingers. Karan had abandoned him, cast him aside and he didn't have the faintest idea why. He wanted to flee but was too sick and sore. He wanted to die.

* * *

It was noon and the inn was serving lunch when Karan and Shand came downstairs again. Llian was sitting beside the fire, an untouched bowl in front of him. There was a huge bruise on the side of his head. His hair looked as if a rat had died in it. His skin was a sickly yellow color and his cheeks were burning, fever red. His eyes were red too, glassy, but his hands were blue.

"Shand!" Llian said coolly. "You're back!" Karan would not meet his eye. She had been crying. "It's good to see you, Shand. I need to talk to you." Then he caught Karan's eye on him and scowled. "I've such a headache, and I can't seem to remember why."

He rubbed the bruised side of his head, then winced. His fingers came away with a smear of fresh blood on them. He stared at the stains, looking confused. "I must have fallen down the stairs. I can't remember anything."

"Oh, Llian, what are we going to do with you?" Karan said. He looked sick and sad, and a little foolish, and suddenly her eyes filled with tears. She disappeared through the door, almost running.

Shand stayed behind, plying Llian with wine and talking merrily about past times. Llian could not comprehend what had happened, for he had no memories of the night. One day he had been going along merrily, the next he was treated like a criminal.

He was not fooled by Shand's pretense at friendliness. Karan was hopeless at hiding her feelings. Something had gone terribly wrong, and it had something to do with the wild dreams of last night, but he did not know what.

That night, after Shand went to bed, Llian caught Karan in the corridor.

"Karan, please tell me what the matter is." He took her cold hands. "I've always trusted you."

Karan's hands lay limply in his. She was in agony. If she told Llian, Shand would betray him. She pulled away.

He put out his arms to her. "Please!"

She just stood there. A tear leaked from each eye and ran down her cheek. "Don't, Llian," she whispered. "Don't do this to me. I can't bear it." Then she fled.

Llian was devastated. It was all over. Everything they had made together was broken. What was he to do?

And that night, and for many nights after, in his worst moments he wondered if he might not have betrayed them to Rulke after all, and not even known it.

Karan lay in her cold bed and could not sleep. Why? she kept thinking. Why had Llian done this? Or had he done it at all? She couldn't tell. Once she would have relied on her own judgment but Shand had broken that defense. Why did I say yes to Shand? He's wrong, I know he is.

Please come to me, Llian, she thought a hundred times that night. Come into my bed. Don't say anything, just hold me in your arms and make everything like it used to be. I'll break my word. We'll run away into the mountains where no one can find us.

Then, when dawn was breaking and she still had not slept a wink: Why didn't you come? If only you had come we could have worked this out.

But Llian did not dare. The rejection had broken him. He could not face the thought of it happening again.

35

HOMECOMING

Two days later they left Tullin, heading east toward the pass and Bannador. The sun came out the day they departed, turning the snows to mud and slush. That made the trip harder but they were seasoned travelers now and the week's journey was uneventful, like most of the past months. The last day was the hardest, a slog through mud that was sometimes calf-deep. A slow silent trip, each preoccupied with their own troubles.

Llian had fallen behind. Shand came up beside Karan. It was his first chance to talk to her for days.

"Tell me about the dreams," said Shand. "When did they begin?"

"In Flude!" she said.

"Have there been any more since Tullin?"

She did not feel like talking. She felt betrayed by Shand. The friendship between them had been fatally undermined. She forced herself to be polite.

"*I* haven't!"

"And Llian?"

"He never speaks about them, but he often has them."

They came down into what were called the Hills of Bannador, though they would have been mountains anywhere else. It was a land of steep ridges and deep gullies, barren after yet another dry year—a land dotted with little hamlets and isolated steadings each with its meager flocks of sheep or goats. They met no one that day, for the track followed the stony, waterless ridges.

After a day heading southeast they crossed into granite country: rounded rocky hills covered in straggly pines and broad valleys where there were crops and larger towns. From this point they saw signs of war everywhere—burnt fields and forests, broken bridges, ruined houses and, not far from Gothryme, a village reduced to ashes. The last building had been a stable, for the fire-scarred skeletons of half a dozen horses still lay among the rubble.

On they trudged. The anticipation became a hard lump in Karan's chest, a tingle in her stomach. Even the terrible problem of Llian sank into the background before the prospect of being home again.

They reached the Ryme, the river that flowed through her land, watered the fields around the town of Tolryme and passed out of the valley east toward the sea. Karan pulled her hat down as they entered her town. She did not want to meet anyone, or explain anything, before she got home.

Tolryme was a poor but pretty place, an overgrown village really—a couple of hundred cottages, a handful of merchants, a market square, a library and a temple, all built in pink granite and gray-green slate. It was in sad shape: many of the cottages were reduced to blackened walls. The bridge across the Ryme was broken, the central arch a scatter of stones in the river. That did not matter at this time of year but it would in the spring, when the snow melted in the mountains and turned the Ryme into a torrent.

They forded the river and followed a winding track between high hedges. Through gaps in the hedges they saw trampled crops and the bones of slaughtered stock, long since picked clean.

Gothryme Manor was set in the upper part of a broad valley. The ridges that ran down on either side were grasscovered, their slopes broken with boulders and copses of small trees. They climbed the hill. The chimneys of Gothryme appeared. Home at last! Karan choked back tears. Nearly five hundred days had passed since she'd left with Maigraith for Fiz Gorgo, thinking to be away just two months. How young, foolish and afraid she'd been back then. So what had changed?

Karan felt self-conscious taking Llian and Shand home, seeing every deficiency, shabbiness and rusticity through their eyes. What would Shand, who had traveled the world and seen all of its splendor, who had once been wealthy and powerful, think of her home? What did Llian perceive with his all-seeing chronicler's vision? Would he one day mock Gothryme in some rustic tale, an idle yarn spun in some barroom bawdy session?

Gothryme was small, just a battered keep of pink granite, with younger buildings of the same material extending in two wings from the rear. The keep was more or less oval in shape, and squat, only three storeys. It had a simple conical roof of green slate, a bare flagpole and a brass weathervane in the shape of a flying goose, though it had once been struck by lightning and the long goose neck hung limp.

The wings had originally been two-storeyed, roofed in slate, with small windows on the outside. Sometime later, long verandas had been added on the inside, and the open end enclosed with a low wall to which lean-to trellises had been attached and covered in vines. The kitchen gardens were further up the hill, on the sunny northern side. It all had a rustic, home-made look, but the gardens beside the front door were neat and the gravel path freshly raked.

Behind the garden was an orchard then a steep slope of grass, brown with boulders and huge outcrops of granite.

Half a league further on, a broken cliff wall of pink granite blocked the way to the mountains. A narrow path wound its way up the cliff to the uninhabited uplands, rocky ridges and deep wet valleys, and her magnificent but useless Forest of Gothryme.

As they approached Karan saw that the stonework of the keep was battered at the front and most of one wing had been burnt to a stone shell. The other wing was also damaged, while some of the surrounding walls had been reduced to rubble.

"It might have been worse," she said, though she was shocked at the destruction, and more so at the state of the town below. If this was mild damage, how must the rest of Bannador have suffered? Winter's boot was on the threshold. After years of drought there were no reserves left. There would be famine before spring.

Despite their quiet approach the news had come before them and a small group waited on the front steps. They included Mavid the cook, small and pale with brown flour all over her apron, Nutan and Mara, leathery gnomes who had been gardeners since before she'd been born, Old Mid the handyman and master brewer, as round as the barrels in his cellar, two cook's helpers, one carrying a mop and the other a scrubbing brush, and Galgi the weaver, tall, longlimbed and twiggy-fingered, to say nothing of half a dozen children including mischievous Benie, the cook's boy.

"Karan, Karan!" Benie screamed, dancing around in a circle.

At the head of the group stood Rachis, her steward, looking at least ten years older than when she'd farewelled him last year. Even then he'd been an old man, and looked it. Now he was gaunt, his cheeks sunken and his hair just a few sparse white threads. Rachis shuffled forward, looking beaten down, but his smile was genuine.

"Karan-lar," he said, putting out his long arms. "This is the answer to a prayer. How long have we waited and longed for you to come. Welcome home."

Karan dropped her pack and ran up the steps. "Rachis, I'm sorry! I should have been here."

She flung her arms around him. He towered above her but was so very thin. His embrace reminded her of her childhood. After the death of her father, and then her mother, he had been the only one to treat her kindly.

"So I've said more than once. It has been a sore trial for us, this last year. But having heard your part in this, it would have been the worse had you been here. The Ghâshâd came through quite a few times, asking after you. But for all that they treated us better than Yggur's Second Army did, or his First! Come inside."

"Where is everyone?" she asked. "They are not—"

"We were more fortunate than our neighbors—no one from Gothryme was killed. A miracle! Everyone else has gone hunting or a-gleaning, for we have little left to eat and nothing for the winter. Some also went down to the town to help rebuild."

She went around the rest of the group, Benie last of all. Karan shook his grubby hand. "I missed you, Benie. What say we go for a walk after tea? You can show me the garden and the animals. Tell me, have you been teasing old Kar lately?"

Kar was an old black swan, a fixture on the pond for many a year. Benie burst into tears. "Kar's dead! Those rotten soldiers *ate* her!"

That was what war meant to him and he was inconsolable. She hugged him, shedding a tear of her own.

The weathered doors of Gothryme stood open. They were made of planks thick as Karan's fists, reinforced with iron bands inside and outside, and studded with iron bolts. One door was dented and splintered.

Karan introduced Llian, who was polite but unusually reserved, and Shand, who knew Rachis of course. They went inside, into a round hall some thirty paces across with a curved stair of stone running up the far wall. The flagstones were scattered here and there with threadbare rag rugs. On either end of the hall was a fireplace large enough to roast an ox, but neither fire was lit and the hall was icy.

Karan stood there in silence. "What happened to the carpets and tapestries?"

"Stolen by the soldiers," said Rachis dismally. "Also the candlesticks, the silver, most of your mother's jewelry, and everything else they could carry away. We haven't enough wood to heat the hall. Come into the kitchen."

She followed Rachis out into the northern wing. The kitchen, larders and pantries had not been damaged though there was little in them. One wall was taken up by a huge iron stove of eccentric design, her father's work. A few pots simmered on top. The opposite wall had a pair of fireplaces with roasting spits, and cauldrons hanging from a bar over a meager fire. The stove was warm though, and they all stood round it while Mavid made tea.

They drank it standing up, so anxious was Karan to reckon up the damage. It was considerable. Rachis went through the list while they walked around. "The damage to the northern wing is fairly superficial, but most of the southern will have to be rebuilt."

They passed out into the gardens, which were also in sad shape. Llian gazed around him. "I hadn't realized you were so rich!"

Karan's estate, which had come down to her from her mother's side, comprised the upper part of the valley and the ridges on either side. Most was steep, with scrubby woodland and poor, stony soils good only for sheep and goats. Only a small strip near the river was arable.

In addition she held title to the Forest of Gothryme, an ancient upland wood that extended along the eastern side of the Great Mountains, as well as various waterfalls, streams and a small lake. This forest was almost virgin: magnificent and old, with good hunting and fishing, but inaccessible except by a precarious stair up the granite cliffs, in consequence of which it added almost nothing to her living.

She was also heir to the folly of Carcharon, which was

higher still, beyond the forest and up the dangerous path that led eventually to Shazmak. Carcharon had been built five hundred years ago by her mad ancestor Basunez, at a place which had some kind of cosmic significance to him, if to no other. But Carcharon was utterly worthless and had been abandoned after his death.

"Rich, ha!" snorted Karan. "It feeds us, but there's not much left over to sell, or to buy what we can't grow or make. Gothryme was in debt before I left. Even in the good times, before the drought began, our wealth was counted in silver, not gold." As she walked around, and the toll of the damage mounted, her heart sank further and further. It could never be made good.

"Is that all?" she asked as she and Rachis finished going through the stock books. "What is the state of our accounts?"

Rachis hesitated. To be the bearer of such bad tidings, to confess his failure, was like cutting out his heart. "Grim," he said, hauling out a huge ledger and turning the pages one by one from the very beginning, a good thirty years ago.

Karan watched the years go by with agonizing slowness. Finally he grunted, smoothed down the last page and pointed to the balance with one finger.

"That's all?" she said in a whisper. "One hundred and five silver tars? That won't last a month if we have to buy food." The estate, even if spring was bountiful, would earn no more until mid-summer.

"The war!" Rachis said heavily. "What with fines, taxes, confiscations and the bribes I had to pay to stop the soldiers from looting everything, you are lucky to have anything left at all. Had not your friend Maigraith come at the head of an army we would be living in tents. And since his return, Yggur has taxed us into the ground. See, I have itemized every expense. And I have to say that we are better off than most." He listed a dozen families who had nothing left but the land they camped on.

Karan closed the ledger with a snap. "When do his tax collectors come back?"

"The spring equinox," said Rachis.

"And the assessment?"

"Five hundred and forty tars," he replied mournfully.

Karan went white. "We need more than that to restock, let alone rebuild. Thank you, Rachis."

He nodded and went out, walking very slowly. Karan remained where she was, her head sunk on the ledger.

Shand found her there an hour later. He rested his hand on her shoulder and Karan looked up with a start. She pulled away, still angry with him.

"Worse than you thought?"

"Much worse. We are practically ruined now. We will be, when Yggur's tax collector comes back in the spring. I will have to go to the *graspers*. What will their rate of usury be, after all this ruin? They can ask what they like."

"Hundreds of percent, I should say. Have you nothing that you can sell?"

"Precious little. Most things of any value are already gone. Whatever I can spare will fetch almost nothing, since thousands of other families are selling the same stuff, while whatever I need will cost its weight in silver. And I still owe you and Llian, and Malien, for all the costs of a year's travel."

"For my part, that is forgotten," said Shand. "I can afford it."

"We had this conversation once before," said Karan sharply. Being beholden to him was even worse now. "I pay my debts." How? she thought. How can I ever repay you or anyone?

"Well, who knows what spring will bring?" he said cheerfully. Since leaving Tullin he had behaved as if there was nothing between them. "Come, put your long face away until the morrow. They are preparing a celebration for your homecoming. Don't spoil it. They have had hard times too. The head of the house must smile and set an example, whatever her own feelings."

"I know what spring will bring!" said Karan. "My fortunes have turned. But you're right. Despair in my own home is more palatable than the same thing on the road. No one will work harder to restore Gothryme again."

There was a banquet that night, the best that Gothryme could muster, though that was little. The want and the quality were disguised by plentiful wild herbs and garlic and mustard, and there was wine enough, and dancing and singing, and the kind of high spirits that come with the passing of the storm but before the drudgery of cleaning up begins. After that Llian even did a telling. It was far from being one of his best, but it was the best that the people of Gothryme had ever heard, and they even forgave him his morose looks.

This was where Karan belonged, though it had taken her long enough to realize it. Shand had never seen her so at home with people; so happy to be the center of attention; so authoritative.

It was well after midnight. The party was over, everyone gone to their beds. Karan wearily climbed the stairs to her own room, which was on the top floor of the keep. It had a damp-stained timber ceiling and a wooden floor with cracks between the boards. The walls were undecorated, the hangings all stolen, but long narrow windows in the curving walls looked east, south and west, so it seemed light and spacious. Her bed, a huge square box, had been freshly made, and there was a vase of fragrant winter violets by the head.

She'd imagined her bed for a year. Mostly she'd imagined Llian sharing it, but he'd stayed downstairs in one of the guest rooms. She stripped off her clothes, tossed them into the basket, had a quick wash in freezing water and crept between the sheets, into the hollow at the center of the old mattress.

An hour later, numb with cold and unable to sleep, she got up again. Her mind refused to turn off. Karan emptied out her pack, putting her traveling gear away. When that was done, her hair brushed, the covers smoothed down, her restless fingers came across the blackened silver chain Llian had given her in Katazza. A reminder of happier times. It was the most precious thing she owned.

She took the chain off and let it fall into a pool in her palm, repeating the action over and over. Poor tarnished thing. Silver showed here and there. She rubbed it with a dirty shirt, not successfully, so threw on a robe and padded downstairs to the scullery. Hunting out some silver-cleaning fluid, now redundant since all the silver was gone, she scrubbed away at the chain.

After an hour or so it was almost as good as new, save for tarnish between the braids of silver that she could not get out, even with a brush. Karan held the chain up to the light. It was a beautiful piece of work, a lovely old thing, and as she'd thought, the weave was exactly the same pattern as the Great Tower that she had climbed in Katazza. She supposed Kandor had made it as a reminder of that marvelous structure, though why he'd hidden the chain so carefully was a mystery. There had been thousands of items in Katazza of far greater value.

There were some scratchings on the clasp, still filled with dirt and tarnish. She worked over them with a brush, then cleaned out the grooves with a needle. It was engraved writing, she realized. The letters were revealed one by one. F I A C H R A. Not a name that meant anything to her. She searched for other markings and eventually found a beautifully engraved sigil or glyph, the maker's hallmark. It was rather worn, clearly older than the name. She must ask Llian about them sometime. If Llian ever spoke to her again.

They had reached Gothryme just in time, for in the night the wind came up, howling from the south, a blizzard that dropped a knee-deep cover of snow by morning, and a lot more during the day, though the calendar only said autumn. The season had turned a month earlier than last year.

It snowed for two days, then the sun melted it all away again. No one was fooled—it was warning of a cruel winter on the way, and famine in Bannador. If winter came in earnest in the next few weeks they would very probably starve, for most of their grain and stock had been stolen or sent to the relief of the lowlands a long time ago. That generosity began to seem foolish now. Supply wagons could move down there during the winter, but up here they would be snowed in for months, travel only possible on foot. They could freeze too, with much of the manor uninhabitable and their stocks of firewood destroyed.

They also worried about the Ghâshâd, though none had come through the valley in months. Karan learned that Yggur had a garrison only a day's march away, at Tuldis. She did not find that comforting.

The following days were spent in the hardest of physical toil. Everyone set to, gathering fuel and scavenging for what food they could find, though that was practically nothing after the war. The only other source was the high forest, normally untouched because it was so inaccessible that it was not worth the trouble. Up there were mushrooms and nuts, animals large and small, and fish in the lake. But foraging so far away and carrying it down the cliff was an impossibly time-consuming task. Time they did not have—the next snowfall would cover everything on the ground for a hundred days.

Llian, however, felt much better in Gothryme. Perhaps it was the nature of the place, for Gothryme was not grand, either in size or proportion or ornament, but it had the comfortable feeling that comes with great age and continued use. Its walls were mostly unplastered stone, decorated with a few rustic woolen tapestries and hangings, most threadbare and repaired many times. They were the ones that had not been worth stealing. Its floors were bare stone too, slabs of slate or shiny schist with a scatter of rag rugs.

Perhaps the exhausting toil had something to do with it, for Llian slaved, as did everyone, from the hour before the dawn until late in the evening, long after the early dark. And his were the dirtiest, most menial tasks, for he was good for nothing else. He could not do anything more skilled than mixing lime and sand to make mortar. So he worked, lumping stone, timber and slate, filling buckets with mortar, carrying water or cleaning out barrels.

And perhaps it was the lack of time to think, to brood and bend over his books until the middle of the night, for there was never time for that, and even if there had been, candles were precious and he was far too tired to concentrate. No one in Gothryme cared to talk about the affairs of the world, and perhaps by tacit agreement neither would Karan or Shand. In any case Karan had no interest in outside affairs, unless they affected Gothryme itself. She steadfastly refused to discuss such things.

Or perhaps it was the ambience of Gothryme—some characteristic of land or house that made it a poor place for receiving outside influences. Whatever the reason, neither Karan nor Llian had any bad dreams for some time.

Llian was so much better now that Karan began to doubt what had taken place in Tullin, to feel more and more sure that Shand had been wrong. But she did not raise the issue with Llian, nor he with her. In their desperate struggle to get ready for winter Karan put that fear to the back of her mind. And though their bodies cried out for the comfort of each other he never came to her bed again, nor she to his. The barrier between them was too high to overcome.

"We're not going to manage it," said Karan to Shand, halfway through stacking a wagonload of wood. Her anger had thawed somewhat, since he'd been working so hard for her. "There just aren't enough of us."

Shand grunted as he heaved another length up to the top of the stack. "Talk uses energy," he said. "Don't waste it."

"Well, without a miracle we'll all starve."

The mood was gloomy that night—the whole household infected by the realization that they had enough food for barely two months, even if they ate the precious seed and the few remaining breeding animals that they would need for the spring.

That night Karan called the household together. While they assembled she went down to the cellar and rummaged among barrels that had not been tapped since her father was alive. Surprisingly, the cellar had not been discovered by the looters. She came back with a small cask on her shoulder, which she put in the middle of the table. It was thickly coated with dust, as was her coat and her hair.

"I called you together tonight," she said, "to put our position before you." As she spoke Karan dusted off the cask with a rag. She tapped it expertly and drew off a jug of golden liquid. Pouring a measure into mugs the size of eggcups, she handed them round. They touched their mugs.

Llian sipped his liquor. It was a kind of fortified wine, luscious, sweet and strong.

"Things are very bad," she said. "So bad that we may well starve if we stay here, and even if food is to be had I've no money to buy it. So whoever wishes to go and has a place to go to, leave with my blessing."

Beside the barrel sat a small chest. She lifted the lid. The hundred or so small coins that remained did not even cover the worn red velvet on the bottom. "Here is all the money I have. Whoever would go, take two tars from the chest for your traveling expenses. I am deeply ashamed but I can offer you no more. If we survive the winter the tax collector will ruin us in the spring. Come up, whoever of you would go to a better place, and take what is your due."

She stood back, expressionless, doing nothing to influence them. They must do what was best for themselves. They filed up one by one, young men and women, weatherbeaten laborers and hunters, ancients who should have been in their rocking-chairs for a decade. Even the cook's boy, Benie, came forward.

Llian sat watching Karan. Despite his own feelings, he could not help pitying her. It seemed that she was going to lose everyone and everything. Then to Llian's amazement,

Rachis came up too, slipped his hand in the chest and all the coins chimed. Had Llian a handful of grints to his name he would have flung them in, in spite of their woes. But he had nothing left.

Yes, he did! The silver knob that he had unscrewed from Kandor's bedpost in Katazza, against the time when his wallet must be empty, still lay at the bottom of his bag. It must be the weight of a hundred tars, at least. He ran out.

Karan watched him go, dismayed. Every single person came up, touched their glass to hers and went to the chest. The coins tinkled like bells heard from far away. Llian reappeared with his hands in his pockets and followed the procession.

Just as he put his hand in Llian looked up and caught Karan's eye. She had gone white, absolutely stricken. Despite their troubles, she had not thought that Llian would abandon her too.

The whole room held its collective breath, then Shand lifted the chest and shook it, making the coins cry out in a great voice. He laughed, a rich cheerful roar. Karan looked offended.

"Your people deserve you, and you them," he said, tilting the chest so that they could all see inside. The bottom was heaped with coin, copper and silver. In one corner was a big familiar silver knob, here and there a flash of precious gold, and mischievous Benie's shiny copper grint sat proudly on top of the pile. No fortune, but enough to get them through the winter, if there was food to be had. Karan burst into tears, ran down and embraced them every one. While her back was turned Shand slipped his own contribution into the chest.

36

A LIGHT IN CARCHARON

Karan woke well before dawn to a persistent banging, as if one of the shutters had come loose. Better fix it before it smashed itself to firewood in the wind. Rousing slowly from too little sleep she realized that there was no wind! It was the front door. Someone had been pounding on it for ages. Who could it be at this hour? Every muscle ached from the previous day's toil, but it was time she was up and doing. She ran down the stone stair, wrapping her robe around her. Perhaps the war had started again. Perhaps it was Yggur's tax collectors come early.

At the door she found another small miracle. The threshold was crowded with laughing people. It was Malien and eleven of her Aachim.

"In Thurkad I heard of your troubles," said Malien, "so we came earlier than we'd planned. We're all here, save Tensor, Asper and Basitor, you'll no doubt be pleased to hear."

"How is Tensor?"

"Well enough, considering."

"I can hardly tell you how glad I am to see you," said Karan, kissing each of them. "I don't know how we're going to feed you, but we'll worry about that later. Come in."

"We didn't come empty-handed," Malien laughed. "Look!"

Karan put her head out the door and saw, looming up out of the fog, the biggest wagon that she had ever seen, a vast affair with six wheels and a canvas-covered load that extended a span and a half above the sideboards.

"What's for breakfast?" asked Malien.

"Porridge and pancakes," said Karan.

Malien jumped up on the tongue of the wagon and rummaged inside, coming back with a huge flagon of black syrup. "I've just the thing for porridge and pancakes," she said, and they all followed Karan inside to the kitchen fire.

That night Karan, Malien and Shand discussed the affairs of the last months, including Llian. Later, Shand took Karan aside. "You don't need me now, so if you can spare me I'll go at dawn."

"Go with my most heartfelt thanks," she said, unable to hold her grudge any longer. "Without you I would never have coped. And I know what you put in my chest last night. More than I can ever repay."

"I deny putting anything in your chest," he said with a straight face. "And therefore I beg that you never mention it again."

"Very well. Are you going home?"

He sighed, running thick fingers through sparse hair. "I wish I was. No, I must bear tidings to Thurkad."

"About Llian," she said in alarm. "Must you tell Yggur about him too?"

Shand hesitated.

"Please, Shand. He's much better now. Give me this chance. What can he do here, with Malien watching? Surely even you must admit that you could be wrong."

Shand looked reluctant. "Very well," he said grudgingly. "There is an infinitesimal possibility that I am wrong, and if so it could have very bad consequences. I will say nothing until we next meet, but be careful."

He was already gone when Karan rose with the sun. The weather was good so everyone headed up the cliff path, seldom used, that led to Gothryme Forest. Beyond that the track wound higher and higher, to the long-abandoned fortress of Carcharon, high in the windswept mountains to the west. Karan's father had been slain up here when she was eight. On this path had Karan wandered when she set out to find Shazmak at the age of twelve; and when she left it again, six years later. And this way Tensor had returned to Shazmak the previous year, to try and catch her with the Mirror. Every step of the path was embedded with memories for Karan. But they did not go beyond the forest: Carcharon was a folly and Shazmak was occupied by the Ghâshâd.

Llian felt good today. He walked beside her all the way up, fascinated by the Histories of her family, and noting everything so that he could tell them one day.

For more than a week they were blessed with fine, cold weather, and they collected hundreds of sacks of nuts, still good; several barrels of fish from the lake; dozens of baskets of fruit, most spoiled though still edible—these they would make into jam; and some autumn berries that in the drought had shriveled on the brambles. They also gathered mushrooms, wild onions and edible roots and tubers. And game, more than they expected. Enough, with what the Aachim had brought, to tide them over, unless the winter was very bad, and some to send down to the town.

By this time, prodigious labor by the Aachim had repaired some of the stone walls and put a new roof over them. That would give them five extra rooms when the inside work was done, though they would still be terribly cramped. Then winter really set in and it snowed for a week without stopping. Gothryme was completely cut off.

Winter's fury meant that there was less to do—only emergency work could be done outdoors. The rebuilding went on inside, but now it was artisans' work and proceeded at a more leisurely pace. Some of the Aachim went up to the forest to hunt. The cold meant nothing to them.

Karan spent most of that week sitting with Rachis at the big table in the refectory, surrounded by the records of the past year: ledgers as long as her arm, made of thick homemade paper—her family Histories. In these books every detail of life at Gothryme had been recorded for over a thousand years: births, deaths; crops, yields, failures; stocking rates and breeding records; fires, floods, pestilences, famines, droughts, wars . . .

But every time she sat down to work some distraction arose, or if it did not she found that she could not concentrate anyway. Then, lying awake in the middle of the night Karan looked up and saw that the dark face of the moon was full. Suddenly she *sensed*, what the matter was. In the black abysses of the world another piece had just clicked into place. The enemy was abroad! Karan realized that she had been waiting for it to happen.

Llian went back to his books, reviewing the notes he'd made of the time he'd spent with Tensor, his descriptions of the Nightland, and Kandor's papers too. He worked away at these tasks placidly and methodically, but without fire or any real interest in what he was doing. There was no intensity in him, and generally he put his books away early in the afternoon and sat staring out the window at the snow. He felt terribly sad.

Or he would walk about the house, sometimes browsing in Karan's family archives, sometimes studying the architecture, or just dreaming. He especially liked the old keep, said to be two thousand years of age. Several times Malien came upon him there, lying on the floor looking up at the ceiling, or sitting on a bench staring at a tapestry, absently dreaming.

The night of Karan's premonition he was woken from an exhausted sleep by an unpleasant dream. He sat up in bed, trying to piece the fragments into something that he could make sense of.

He had dreamed that he was carrying wood, stacking it in huge stacks against the stone wall of a woodshed. But it was not Gothryme, for he humped his load along the pinnacle of a dangerous ridge through a gale that wanted to sail him across the sky. Then Llian realized that it was not wood at all, but a piece of strangely curved metal that was cradled in his arms. Every time he tried to put it on the stack, it would not fit and someone shouted at him. He kept carrying his piece of metal back and forth along the ridge, and each time it was a different shape, and none of the shapes would fit where he tried to put them. Then he went back to sleep and the dream disappeared.

In the morning Malien found him sitting on a step in the keep, just staring at the wall. She stood watching him for a while, worrying about him. He looked to be trying to stare through the stone.

"Llian," she said. He did not move. She touched him on the shoulder.

Llian turned slowly, giving her a blank look. "Yes?" he said eventually.

"Come with me. There is news."

She went out and down the corridor. Llian followed, dragging his feet. He was far away, wrestling unsuccessfully with his dream.

Malien turned into the refectory where Karan was working with Rachis. There was a fifth person in the room, a farmer from the barren western part of her lands who supplemented his living by hunting in the Forest of Gothryme.

"Dutris, this is Malien and Llian," said Karan. "Tell them what you saw two days past."

Dutris was a young man, perhaps no older than Karan herself; short and wiry, with a tanned face and hard, slender hands. His hair was almost white, but his beard was dark. He spoke quickly in a soft voice, barely audible from the other side of the room. He was direct to the point of brusqueness.

"I was hunting in the forest. My camp was on the western side. Two nights past I saw a light high up on the old western path. But that path goes nowhere, only to Carcharon. I went to see. There were lights in Carcharon. I dared not go too close. I came down at once."

He looked anxious. Perhaps he had done the wrong thing.

Karan reassured him. "You did well to learn this without risking yourself. Did you see anyone?"

"Once! They were coming across from the track that goes up into the mountains. Ugly people with gray skin, skinny as sticks. Ghâshâd! And the lights were pale blue and burned steady. That's all."

Karan thanked and dismissed him, and turned to Malien.

"The Ghâshâd are coming down the path from Shazmak again. I knew it! I sensed something last night. But why can they possibly want Carcharon? There is scarcely a more inhospitable place in all Meldorin. It defends nothing."

"What is Carcharon?" asked Llian, roused from his indifference at last. "I've heard the name before."

"A folly!" Karan said. "It was a madness of one of the lords of Gothryme, in olden times. Basunez was his name, an ancestor of mine on my mother's side. A necromanter of sorts, a practicer of the Secret Art, and he thought that he had found the perfect place for it—so my father told me. Some places are thought better than others for such business, because of the resonance of the land or the intersection of lines of power, or some such nonsense.

"Basunez divined that this place was the best in Santhenar, at least in the parts of it that he had been to, for the Secret Art. So he named it *Car-charon* (meaning better than the Charon) though whether this referred to the character of the place or what he hoped to do there I never heard.

"Twenty years it took to build Carcharon, a terrible labor, for Basunez was never satisfied. Three times he tore it down to bare stone and built again. It's cut out of a horn of rock in the center of a steep and knife-edged ridge, utterly barren. There is no water there, and nothing grows, and it is exposed to the most violent and bitter winds. Even in summer it's terribly cold, but in winter it's perishing. Every stick of firewood must be carried in by hand, and every bit of food; up a steep and dangerous path. Why would anyone want it? It guards nothing, not even the eastern way to Shazmak. That takes the next ridge south, half a league away."

"Why they want it is of little moment," said Malien. *"They are there!"*

"Basunez's researches came to nought. He never found the secret he was searching for, and slowly went mad in frustration and despair. His servants left him one by one. He lost his fingers from frostbite and eventually froze to death in the worst winter of that century.

"He had made a fortune before he went mad, but every grint of it went on this folly. Our house was bankrupted by the extravagance. After he died Carcharon was abandoned. It still belongs to my family but we do not go there. Nothing remains but the folly of a madman."

"What can the Ghâshâd possibly want with it?" Llian wondered.

"I haven't the faintest idea."

"We'd better send word to Thurkad," said Malien.

Karan could not sleep after that. Had they taken Carcharon to prepare the way for Rulke, or because it was close to Llian and her? That night, as soon as it got dark, she imagined them swarming out of Carcharon, filing down the cliff path, coming for her. Just by being here she put Gothryme and the whole valley in danger.

But that night a runner came with an urgent letter. Mendark was returning by ship from the east; Yggur summoned them to a council in Thurkad.

"That's all I needed," said Karan with a shudder. "I won't go! I loathe Thurkad and I'm having nothing more to do with this business."

"None of us can avoid our responsibilities," said Malien. "That's how this all began."

The news woke Llian's dormant fears as well. His respite was over; the dreams and the torments would soon return. He suddenly knew what the strange dream was all about. The metal things that he had been carrying were pieces of the construct, and in his dream he had been helping the Ghâshâd carry the finished parts into a storeroom. Was that what they were doing now, up there in Carcharon?

37

A Reunion

After a troublesome, mostly silent journey through heavy snow, Karan, Malien and Llian slipped into the city quietly, by ways that Malien knew. They found Thurkad to be bruised and battered but not cowed. Its people were as unruly as ever, and they went about their stealthy and wicked businesses much as before. Not even Yggur had been able to curb their wantonness.

At one of the dozens of cafés on the waterfront they met Shand. He gave Karan the most perfunctory embrace and shook hands with Llian and Malien distantly.

"Is something the matter?" Karan asked as they headed back to his lodgings.

"I'm wasting precious life here, pandering to fools and waiting on villains," he said grumpily. "One more problem and I am off for Tullin, and I won't be coming back."

"Anything *particular* the matter?"

"They're all out for what they can get."

"Who are you talking about?"

"Yggur, Mendark, not to mention Hennia the Zain! She's changed sides half a dozen times this year. Treacherous bitch, like all her kind."

Shrinking visibly, Llian turned away.

Karan tried to cover it up with jocularity. "Well, that's human nature, which is irreducible, as you should know."

"And mine is to go home and hide from my problems. I need Tullin just as much as you do Gothryme."

"Did you speak to Mendark about Chanthed?"

"His ship hasn't come in yet."

Shand's lodging was a disreputable-looking tenement with stained stonework and falling render, a place that looked damp and filthy under Thurkad's perpetually gray winter skies. It was not far from the room where he had nursed Karan back to health last winter.

"What a dump," said Llian, though a year ago it would have seemed a palace compared to his student's lodgings. "Haven't they heard of paint in Thurkad?"

"Are you paying for it?" Shand said coldly.

"I have no money."

"Then keep your thoughts to yourself. I don't want to draw attention to us. Alliances made in the heat of battle, in the trials of Katazza or the desolation of the Dry Sea, need not hold up now that Yggur is back in the seat of his power with his armies behind him."

"Pompous ass," said Llian under his breath.

Karan started to say something, then thought better of it. She hated Thurkad; always had. If the rest of the week was going to be like this it would be unbearable.

However, inside they found Shand's rooms to be well furnished and comfortable, though cold because of the wood shortage. Once they were safely installed Malien left them, going off to see Tensor. Karan stayed inside, since that was cheaper. She often thought about pawning the beautiful chain but could not bring herself to part with it—it was so connected with Llian. Every time she looked at it she remembered climbing the Great Tower, and the night after.

Karan spent most of her time working on her ledger in front of their pathetic fire, a thin candle fluttering in the end of a bottle beside her. She was preoccupied with the rebuilding of Gothryme and the re-establishment of the gardens on the uphill side of the manor, which had been trampled into the ground, though there was not a coin to spare for the work. This work of creation gave her more satisfaction than anything she had done in her life before. This was real. This was what she wanted.

Llian was miserable. He could not bear to be in the same room as Shand, whose contempt was all too evident. Since there was nothing else to do he went out. That was not pleasant either, for it was dismal weather. Being broke, he was forced to tell to earn his drinks, but his audience was only interested in the crudest of talcs. He returned late that night feeling worse than when he'd left.

"Where have you been?" Shand snapped as soon as he opened the door.

"Telling yarns for a few drinks."

"Better not be about the Mirror!"

Llian scowled, began to defend himself, then went into the other room and crawled into bed. He hated Shand.

"He's doing it again!" said Shand. "Blabbing our secrets!"

"You heard him, did you?" she asked acidly.

"I know him, Karan!"

Nothing changed the second day, or the third. As Llian put his coat on, Shand attacked him.

"I'd prefer that you stayed here," said Shand. "This is not a good time to draw attention to ourselves."

"Well, I'm fed up with your dark looks and your conspiratorial exchanges."

"Trust needs be earned!" Shand said angrily.

"Impossible for anyone who is Zain to earn yours! I've already tried that. You've been muttering about my heritage since the first time we met."

"And I've been proven right!" shouted Shand, "as I told Karan in Tullin."

"Shand!" Karan said, but the damage was done.

"So, you admit it at last, you grinning hypocrite! Well, I've known all along. I overheard you agree to betray me in Tullin, Karan. How could you?"

Karan leapt up, knocking over the table in her distress. The candle landed on the rug. Shand sprang to put it out.

Llian gave the pair of them a look that could have burned through rock, and left abruptly.

Karan was distraught. "I can't do this, Shand," she wept. "The two people that I care for most, constantly at each other's throats."

Shand was in no mood to make concessions. "I warned you. I've seen this kind of possession before."

"I prefer to rely on my own judgment. Stop undermining Llian; leave him alone."

"Your judgment is clouded by your feelings toward Llian."

"And yours by your prejudice against the Zain," she shot back. "Damn you, Shand, you're a mean-spirited old bastard. Don't ever mention it again."

Shand was quite shocked, then looked away, went into the next room and closed the door. An hour later he came out again. "I'm sorry, Karan. I've been a fool."

She looked up at him miserably, ran the fingers of one hand through her hair, leaving a tuft sticking up, and bent again to her work. The candlelight turned her hair to red gold.

Shand stood looking down. Oh, for such a daughter, he thought unguardedly. But that thought brought an unhappy one and he reached for the bottle on the mantelpiece. Karan looked up at the scrape of glass on stone. Shand had the bottle to his lips.

He caught her eye, hesitated, then held the bottle out to her with a rueful expression. She shook her head automatically—even half a bowl clouded her thinking, took away her will to work all day and half the night—but saw something in Shand's face and changed her mind.

"Not out of the bottle," she said. She dragged her table out of the way, found two bowls in a cupboard and filled them. They sat together, sipping their wine, not talking. The wine was a good one.

"More?" asked Shand, when the bowls were empty.

"Why not? The first finished any hope of work tonight." After half of the second was gone she put the bowl down. "What is it, Shand?"

He shook his head. His eyes were closed. There was a tear on his cheek.

Her soft green eyes met his deep-set eyes.

"I had a daughter once," he said.

She said nothing.

"She is gone, lost long ago. How I loved her."

His old face was quite broken. A grief that would last for all his life, that had colored every moment of his life since. Karan's heart went out to him. A tear fell on his beard and hung there, a single drop that flamed in the candlelight. Then it ebbed away like the passing of a life.

"My fault it was entirely. I neglected her, then she was gone. One day I had everything; the next: nothing. I can never forget her. Can never forget how I failed to keep my promise."

Karan said nothing, only hugged him.

"She was such a beautiful child." His eyes were blurry with terrible, distant sadness. "When I lost her all the joy went out of the world. It would have been her birthday today."

"That is why you gave up the Secret Art!"

He was startled. "How did you know?"

"You know too much, and you are too old and, dare I say it," she felt self-conscious saying it, and rolled her eyes so he would think it just a joke, "too wise."

"Wise I am not. Look what I've done to you and Llian. I'm sorry, Karan. I will try harder." He smiled at some secret thought. "Sometimes you remind me of her. You're right. In ancient times I did practice the Secret Art, and even had some modest success at it. No one knows that now, save Mendark, and you, and Nadiril of the Great Library. Do not speak of it, I beg you. I had a great love, and I was wealthy and powerful and proud. Too proud and too busy rushing around trying to alter the course of fate. But I minded everyone's business except my own, and with the passing of time I lost everything, even that daughter I loved more than anything. That was lifetimes ago, but still it hurts. I've never spoken about it before."

Perhaps that's why it still hurts so much, Karan thought. "How did it happen?"

"I don't know. The Zain had their revenge on me for something I did to them in ages past, I'm sure of it. Who else could it have been? That's why I've been so hard—well, you know all about that. She was gone, and all my efforts, great efforts you can be sure, discovered nothing. My wealth and power, wisdom—ha!—even the Secret Art, were revealed to be worthless. So I renounced them, and my duties and responsibilities, and took up the simple life in Tullin. No responsibility more onerous than to chop wood and keep the fires going, no duty except to the landlord, in return for meat and drink and a bed. And in truth, I found that the life suited me."

Karan raised a sceptical eyebrow. Perhaps you convinced yourself, she thought, but I doubt that a great past can be cast off so easily. "Then what brought you out of Tullin after all this time?"

Shand stared into the fire. They were burning wood from a house nearby, destroyed in the war. It smoked and steamed, poor stuff with little heat in it, choking the grate with white ash. A sliver of wood was sticking straight up like a spire, and Shand watched the smoke trail up from it, the wood slowly charring. The spire drooped down until it touched the main piece of wood. The smoke failed.

"Brought me out?" he said absently. "I suppose it was your father."

"My father?"

"I knew him well. I told you that once, remember?"

"Of course I remember. It was when we were in Ganport, after you had taken pleasure in my humiliation—the famous bath, *if you remember*!"

Shand laughed and it gave Karan pleasure to hear it. "I could hardly forget it."

"I would not say that we were the best of friends, for we were too different for that. But he was very kind to me when my memories troubled me most. I was shocked to hear of his death—he was the kind of man that you think will live forever. Then your sending from the ruins above Tullin roused me to my responsibilities.

"Once I realized that it was you, the past woke in me. It put me in a great conflict and it gets deeper every day. This hanging about, waiting on the whim of Mendark when I could be minding my own business in Tullin, drives me into a rage!" He banged the table, making the empty bowls jump.

Karan stayed up late, working on her plans until after midnight in spite of the wine, and worrying about how she would ever afford to fulfil them. Shand had been asleep for hours. Llian had not come back. Finally she went to bed, but woke in the night at some noise outside. Her heart was racing, and she felt uneasy. Where was Llian? Doubtless in some low bar, drinking with new-found friends, equally low. She drifted back to sleep.

She was woken in the morning by a muffled conversation outside, then Shand opened the door. She sat up sleepily, looking away from the bright lantern.

"Was that Llian?"

"No, he's still not back."

The night's foreboding stabbed her in the belly. Karan leapt out of bed and threw her clothes on.

"What's the matter?" said Shand.

"Something's happened. I'm going looking for him."

"You'll never find him."

"If I was in trouble he'd come looking for me." She shrugged on her greatcoat, took her hat down off the peg.

"Do you want me to come too?" Clearly he didn't want to, for his eyes strayed to the bottle on the shelf.

"I'd prefer to be alone. Oh, who was that you were talking to?"

"A messenger. Mendark arrived a few hours ago. It's said that he looked very worn."

"Will there be trouble with Yggur?"

"More than likely, though doubtless they'll try to get along for as long as suits them."

She trudged the sodden city all day, asking at every inn she came to, but found no trace of Llian. The backstreets of Thurkad were a labyrinth and her talent told her nothing either.

Karan returned in the early evening, not daring to walk in such places after dark. Saturated, freezing, she was shaking with a chill that was surely going to get worse. At Shand's question she shook her head. "Not a trace. I don't know where to turn. You haven't heard anything?"

"No!" he said.

"Something's happened to him."

"It's beginning to look that way. I hope—"

The tone of his voice annoyed her. "Don't start on that again. It's nothing to do with Rulke!"

"You can't know that."

"I know! He's in trouble. Shand, you've got to help me. You have contacts here. Please, Shand."

He writhed.

"I'm sure my father would have wanted you to."

He twisted, but in the end could see no honorable way out. "I suppose I could ask my old friend, Ulice, if she's still alive. I'll go in the morning."

"Could you go now?" she asked desperately.

Llian went out into the Thurkad night, into the wind and rain and smoke from countless chimneys, which hung in the streets like greasy yellow fog. Contrary to Shand's opinion he did not have any particular destination in mind, as he had only a few coppers earned from a previous begging tale. He was in no mood to repeat that tonight. He wandered the streets for hours, till his wet clothes stank of smoke. It felt as if it was raining misery and it did not stop at the skin—the unhappiness washed right through him, saturating every cell and nerve.

He paced on, head bowed into the wind, an anonymous and shabby figure, pathetic as any of the tramps, derelicts and street people that he passed. None met his eyes nor showed the least interest in him. Why would they? He had nothing to offer them.

Well after midnight, Llian turned into a narrow street that was vaguely familiar. Tallia had brought him here, he remembered, the night he'd sneaked into the citadel just before the disastrous Conclave. Yes, there was the house, still recognizable though burnt to a roofless masonry shell. Llian climbed through a window like an eye-socket and perched on the rubble inside, sheltering from the wind.

There had been a cellar, he recalled, and leading from it, a hidden tunnel. He found the cellar by falling into it, a sudden drop onto rubble that bruised one knee and gashed his palm. Groping around, to his surprise a section of one wall quivered under his weight.

He found a length of candle in his pocket, lit it at the nearest street lamp and went back to the cellar, shielding the flame from the wind and the rain. After clearing away a lot of rubble he was able to lever the section of false wall open far enough to squeeze through. He pulled it closed behind him and stood there ruminating, watching the distorted shadows from his candle on the earthy walls.

The opportunity to get into the citadel had opened up without his thinking about it, but now Llian realized that the archives could hold the answer to a number of his questions, not least what had really happened at the time the Nightland was formed.

He hesitated. Why not? What was there to lose now if he

did get caught? He held his candle high and started up the passage. At the other end he found the depressions in the wall that opened the hidden door, pressed them together and the slab began to rotate at once. Llian kept out of the way, mindful of its irresistible power to crush and maim. On the floor was the evidence; a bloody stain where the guard's foot had been pulverized the last time he was here.

Llian hurried to the archives, then remembered that the door was kept locked. He continued on anyway and was glad that he did, for the door was open and a dim light wavered distantly down one corridor.

After checking that there was no one in sight Llian moved off a different way. The archives were vast and he soon lost himself in them. At the end of the row he came to a vault with steel walls and a complicated lock on the door. The door was ajar. Llian found his curiosity impossible to resist.

He slid in through the gap. The vault was solid steel, floor, walls and roof. He soon found out why. It contained the most secret records of the Council—whole shelves of documents under the heading of the Proscribed Experiments, among other prohibited topics.

Llian felt dizzy with excitement. Forbidden knowledge! He did not consider for an instant that being here was a crime. He failed to wonder why the outside door was open, why the vault door was open, even why such records, which would normally be kept under a charm of obscurity, were unprotected by any spell at all. He took the first book off the shelf and opened it. His hand shook. He began to read.

Time passed but Llian was quite oblivious. Finally, though, something made him look over his shoulder. There, leaning negligently on the edge of the door, stood Yggur. Llian almost jumped out of his skin.

"Hello, Llian," said Yggur with a menacing smile. His cloudy eyes were unreadable. "What are you doing here?"

Llian's terror of Yggur woke. "I'm looking for documents . . . about the Nightland," he said, and knew that it sounded like the lie it was. "I have Mendark's permission."

"For the Council's secret archives? Liar! His ship hasn't even docked! Come along. You'll find my cells more comfortable than you deserve."

He stretched out his arm, clamping Llian's wrist like a manacle, and led him away. Llian expected to be interrogated as brutally as before, but as the door closed Yggur was called away urgently and did not return.

The first meeting of Mendark and Yggur was not reported. They must have reached some agreement, however, for Yggur vacated the top floors of the citadel in favor of his old fortress, though he kept control of the lower floors and the dungeons below.

Mendark, Magister once more, was soon busy in the citadel, renewing all the links of his power. And that was considerable, for rumor had magnified his successes and he was not short of retainers to do his bidding. Yet strangely, no one had seen his face. Orders were issued by underlings, and when Mendark did appear he went about cloaked and veiled.

Karan sat up all night but Shand did not return. Her cold got worse. She was dozing in her chair by the fireplace when he finally appeared, looking exhausted. "Any news?" she croaked. Her throat was burning.

"I found Llian." He took his wet coat off and hung it by the fire.

"Where is he? *Is he all right?*"

"He's in Yggur's cells, in the citadel." He toweled his gray hair.

She leapt up and ran around frantically, trying to find her boots. "We've got to get him out. You know what Yggur will do to him."

"Karan!" he said. "You can't. It's quite impossible."

"Then I've got to see him at least."

"I wouldn't advise it," he said.

"I hope you're not bringing that—"

He took her by the shoulders and brought his whiskery old face close. "I learned something else tonight."

She shivered, hot and cold. "What? What's the matter?"

"Llian's not the only one on Yggur's list. He wants you too, Karan."

Why her? Was it starting all over again? She knew why, though. Yggur had never forgiven her for stealing the Mirror. He nurtured his revenges, did Yggur. He'd told her so.

"I've still got to go," she said stubbornly. "Llian risked his life for me."

"Yggur knows how you think, Karan. He'll be watching for you. It's not a risk, it's certain capture."

"Then, *as my friend*, what do you advise?"

Shand found himself in a difficult position, but it was impossible to refuse her now. "Well, Yggur's distracted with Mendark at the moment. You could try to bribe a guard. It'd take a hell of a bribe though, for the fellow would have to flee and never return."

Karan was silent. She had no money worth counting, but she did have one precious thing left. "Would you do something for me when next you go out?" she rasped, wiping her dripping nose.

"What is it?"

She lifted the silver chain over her head. It was the only beautiful thing she had ever owned, and she loved it more than anything. "Llian gave this to me in Katazza. It was hidden under Kandor's bed. Would you pawn it for me?"

He inspected the necklace. "It would be a tragedy to sell this. It's incredibly old. It's . . ." He looked puzzled.

"I must!" she said.

"What if I were—"

"No! Just sell it."

"Very well, but don't expect too much. It's valuable because of its age, not its weight of silver, but neither counts for much in the middle of a war." He held it up to the light. "The feel of it reminds me of someone I once knew!"

"There's a name engraved on the clasp," she said. "Fiachra! Was that her?"

His hand shook as he examined the writing, then he closed his fingers around the chain. "No," said Shand. "I've not heard that name before."

After he'd gone out she regretted it, but too late to call him back.

Just as Shand returned, Zareth the Hlune appeared at their door, demanding that they report to the citadel immediately. The man was greatly changed from their last meeting, on Tess's boat. His face was sallow and his chin pigtails peppered with gray.

"You!" he cried, shooting Shand a hostile look.

"How was your bamundi?" Shand asked cheerfully, giving the back of his neck a meaningful rub.

"It spoiled before I recovered from the poison," snapped Zareth. "Get moving!"

Karan was shocked that their hideaway had been penetrated so easily. Shand smiled at her indulgently. "But my dear, this is Yggur's city now, and he was always distinguished by the quality of his spies. He would have known where we were within an hour of our coming."

"Then why all the artifice?"

"One does not march into the camp of an enemy and bed down in the adjoining tent. Nothing so offends the pride of the powerful as arrogance in their inferiors."

"But we were allies before," she said plaintively.

"Of necessity; of convenience. Now he has his empire back, while we are weaker than before. Why would he surrender that advantage? This is no game. Get ready; we'd best not keep him waiting." He turned away. "Oh Karan!" he said over his shoulder. "I pawned your chain. It fetched a bit more than I expected. Three tells and a few silver tars." He handed her a small, heavy wallet.

It was an astounding amount of money. Karan took it, feeling desolate. "Thank you."

"Another thing. I spoke to Yggur a while ago."

"You spoke to Yggur?"

"After I learned where Llian was. I've always got on with Yggur, as you know."

That was a black mark against Shand's character as far as she was concerned. "What's Llian accused of?"

"Stealing documents, concealing documents, trespassing in the Council's secret archives, lying about what happened in the Nightland, treachery . . . The list goes for almost a page. It seems that I was right about him after all."

Karan was silent. Why had Llian gone to the archives at a time like this? What was he doing there? How would she ever get him out again?"

He was the first person she saw after they were escorted into the extravagantly decorated Council room of the citadel. Llian was standing between two guards. Shand saw the relief on Karan's face when she realized that Llian was safe. This business was tearing her apart, and there was nothing anyone could do about it. The sooner it was over the better. Llian looked awful. He made to move in their direction but the guard caught him by the collar. Karan ran to Llian but her relief turned to fury when the import of Shand's words sank in. There must be proof of Llian's guilt this time.

"Karan," Llian said. "I'm so sorry. I'm . . ."

She had pawned her beautiful chain for nothing. Karan struck his arm to one side and turned her back on him, rigid as a poker. Llian dropped his hand, his face went blank and the guards led him away.

No meeting was held that day, but the hours went quickly, for many old faces were there. Old friends, and old adversaries.

Tallia appeared, tall and elegant, looking as though she had just risen from her bath. She showed not a sign of the journey to the east, spanning half a year, save that her face and arms were a little darker and she walked with a slight limp. Tensor was carried in on his litter, escorted by Basitor and laughing Asper, whose spiky hair was now cut short.

Tensor looked even more wasted than he had when they'd parted in Thripsi at the end of summer.

Tallia saw Karan through the crowd and hurried across, but she had barely said a cheerful hello when Karan's eye was caught by a couple entering the Council room, a tall old man—an ancient man—and at his side a small slender girl with a long face and shining silvery hair. To Karan's amazement, for Tallia's manners were normally impeccable, she broke off in mid-word and literally ran across the crowded room.

Tallia picked up the girl, whirled her around, then crushed her in her arms. She took the withered hand of the old man in her own hands and brought it to her lips.

"What . . .?" said Karan to Shand, but he was already barging along in Tallia's wake.

"Karan, Shand," said Tallia, beaming. "Meet my most special friend Lilis; and here is Nadiril of the Great Library. Of course you know Nadiril, Shand. Lilis, this is Shand and Karan. They are my friends too."

"I am very pleased to meet you," Lilis said in a high voice. She had quite lost the urchin squeak of a year ago. Now she was self-assured, on the verge of womanhood. "Tallia often spoke about you on the way to Zile. And Mister Shand, I know you're my teacher's friend so I'm sure you will be my friend too."

Shand laughed. Her joy was infectious. "I'm sure I will, Lilis." He shook her hand.

Lilis turned to Karan who was hanging back, feeling shy, especially at meeting the great Nadiril.

"Hello," said Lilis. "I've seen you before, after the Conclave. I was jealous of you, for you were Llian's friend."

Karan was disarmed. You wouldn't be jealous of me now, she thought, then put her bitterness down deep where it could do no harm. She laughed and embraced the child. "Well, we have something in common," she said.

"It's all right! I never had a proper friend before. Now I

have lots. But I am rude. Karan, please meet my teacher, Nadiril. He has been very kind to me."

Nadiril smiled his wispy smile and held out a fleshless claw. His hand felt like Selial's had, just before she died, but Nadiril did not look at all defeated.

"Karan Elienor Melluselde Fyrn, of Gothryme in Bannador." His voice was a whisper, and he creaked when he bent down to her. "There are so many tales about you. And I knew your father. We shall sit down together later on and you will tell me everything."

"Yes," said Karan, inhibited by his height, venerability and reputation.

"Now, I must know, is Llian here?"

Karan and Shand exchanged glances. "He is," said Shand.

"Yes, yes!" cried Lilis. "Where is my friend Llian?"

"Shall I lift you onto my shoulders so you can look for him?" wheezed Nadiril. "No, perhaps you are getting a bit old for that."

Shand lowered his voice. "I must tell you, and you too, Tallia, that Llian is in grave trouble. I am sure that he had dealings with Rulke in the Nightland and is now his creature, body and soul."

"What? *What?*" cried Lilis, who had not caught what was said.

Nadiril put his hand on Lilis's arm and she stopped at once. "A very grave accusation," he whispered. "I don't believe a word of it."

Shand looked taken aback. "Well, we can talk it through later on. You may see Llian yourself and ask him what you will."

"I shall," said Nadiril, "and now I'm afraid I must pay my respects to the great, and take my seat at the Council table. Lilis, I must leave you for the time, but I know you are among friends. Tallia," he said with more than a little pride, "ask her what you will, and you will be astounded. What a student!"

Karan was immensely relieved at Nadiril's words. Believing Shand had always aroused a conflict in her. She resolved to re-establish that strange dream-link she'd made to Llian before her trial in Shazmak, just to keep watch over him without his knowing.

Nadiril creaked his way forward to the main table where the dignitaries were already assembling, though only for a ceremonial meeting. The real business would not begin until tomorrow.

Shand led the others to a lower table, and had just begun to pour drinks when Osseion and Pender came through the door together. Osseion was unchanged, though Pender looked to have lost weight.

Lilis clapped her hands in sheer happiness. "Oh, this is perfect," she said. "I have all my friends together at . . ." Then she broke off, staring through the doorway.

Karan felt goosepimples break out all down her back and arms, though she could not see what Lilis was looking at.

Lilis took a little step forward. Her drinking bowl fell to the floor and smashed.

"Oh!" she said, her long face tight as a drum.

A small man appeared in the doorway. Platinum hair cascaded over his shoulders. His face was long and narrow, the skin stretched tight across cheeks that were pink, freshly scrubbed. The way he stared at Lilis, there might have been no one else in the room.

"Lilis? Is it you?" he said softly.

"Jevi," she whispered. *"Jevi!"* she shrieked, raced across the room and flung herself into his arms like a little silver-haired bullet.

He staggered back under the impact. "Lilis," he whispered. "Just look at you. There has not been a day in the last eight years that I have not thought of you. But I never thought . . ."

"My Jevi, you came back for me. I knew you would! Every night I said a prayer for you, and every morning I tried to think of a way to find you again."

"I did not think to find you so grown up. Why, you are almost a woman."

"I am," she said proudly. "And one day I will be a librarian. How did you find me here?"

"Your friends found me, Osseion and Tallia and Pender, and got me free. You are the luckiest girl in the world. And now that I have my Lilis back I could die of happiness."

For once Lilis had nothing to say at all, but the sun shining out of her face told the whole story.

38

THE BOOK

Maigraith rose, ate a frugal breakfast then walked upstream through a dawn drenched with mist. She was thinking about the art and science of gates. As Tensor's original gate had been made from metal and stone, materials that the Aachim were supremely comfortable with, so Faelamor's was rooted in the natural environment so beloved of the Faellem, the fount of their strength and their soul.

But the Faellem were not makers of machines, and were forbidden to use magical devices at all, so Faelamor was constrained both by inexperience and by the prohibition. She had used a chip of stone from Tensor's original gate in Katazza to spark her own to life. *Like calls to like*, she had said.

A woven ladder hung down from the tree on this side of the river. Maigraith climbed up. The platform swayed beneath her but the chip of stone was not there. Looking down into the rushing river, she knew why the return had gone so wrong. The stone, the focus, must have fallen into the river on their departure, and Faelamor was so inexpert that she had brought them back to the focus rather than to the gate. Maigraith tested the ropes, bouncing on the platform until waves ran across it. This is Faelamor's creature, she thought. I don't like it.

She set to work on the gate, pulling it apart and remaking it, but finally realized that there was still too much of Faelamor in it. She cut it down and it fell into the river, where the current hung it over the rapids further down. Shortly it tore free, tumbling out of sight. Just at that moment Faelamor appeared.

"You couldn't make it work!" she said, critical as always, but her shoulders were slumped.

"It's not mine! I have to make my own," Maigraith shouted.

"There's no time!" Faelamor screamed.

Turning her back, Maigraith set off upriver.

All morning she wandered, not knowing what she sought, only that it must be the right place and she would recognize it when she found it. Upstream the gorge narrowed progressively until there was just a narrow strip of forest between dark cliffs of limestone, stained red and black by seeping iron. As she squeezed between two ironstone boulders shaped like spires, the hairs stood up on the back of her neck. Looking left, Maigraith saw a vertical slit in the cliff, a cave where a fault had wrenched the rock apart. To her right the river raced through a channel cut in rock. Leaf-filtered sunlight made lozenge patterns on the ground. This was a good place for her.

Maigraith put her ear to one of the ironstones, trying to tune herself to the structure as she would to a pebble from which she planned to make a lightglass from. She would not shape this rock, or the other—no time for that—but she sensed out its mineral essence and set to work.

Carefully selecting a pebble from the river, she took a chip from the top of one ironstone and the base of another, and a piece from the rock of the cave mouth. Squatting between the stones, Maigraith chipped away at her four pieces of rock until they were roughly shaped, four quarters of an egg. She smoothed the pieces until the quarters fitted together perfectly, singing the essence of the stones as she did so. The task took all day and part of the next, but she worked patiently, humming to herself, shaping and testing, smoothing and retesting.

Faelamor came and went, chafing at the delay and increasingly wasp-tongued. Maigraith ignored her. Finally she laid the egg aside in its pieces, pulled the basket of silver wire off one of her lightglasses and wove it into a thread which she passed through the four stones, drew tight and fastened them together as one. She warmed the stone egg in her hands and envisaged the four components of her gate—the river bed cut into rock, the pudenda-like cave mouth, the twin spires of ironstone.

Momentarily the egg wobbled in her fingers then lit up like a lightglass. Maigraith moved it between the spires and felt her hair drawn out toward the stones on either side. I can do it! she thought.

She did not tell Faelamor that it was ready. Nor did she feel the need to test her gate in any way. She stood between the stones, staring into the middle distance, at the rushing water not far away, feeling the opening behind her as if it lived and breathed. It felt very peaceful here. She clenched her hands around the egg, then swung them back and forth like a pendulum between the two ironstones. Maigraith had always had a feeling for stone and was sure that she could call what she needed from these. It felt like home here.

The short day faded; mist began to rise up from the river. Her hands glowed red and black. She conjured the most vital image of Havissard into her mind—the bedchamber where she had found the silver stylus and the piece of paper with the mysterious name—Aeolior! She worked through the procedures that Faelamor had shown her so reluctantly: the making of the gate, the way to control the gate. They were as clear as if they had been carved into the stones.

I *can* make this gate work! She focused on Havissard and tried to bring the gate to life. Nothing happened. It was no more than its individual components, half-seen through the mist.

What's wrong? Maigraith began again. Maybe I'm not trying hard enough. She went through the process once more, but again it was lifeless; not even the hint of a gate. Maybe I'm trying too hard.

Maigraith went back to her rhythmic swaying as the mist rose and the light faded.

Faelamor appeared, glaring at her. "You've failed again!" Her face was blanched. She disappeared.

Maigraith let herself drift right into the dream.

I've been doing it the wrong way—Faelamor's way—but of course that won't work with *my* gate. I need something to draw a line between Havissard and here. Her small treasures, the silver stylus and the name, were still in the pocket of her coat, carefully wrapped. Taking out the stylus she held it tip upwards between her fingers, touching the stone. She recalled to mind the room that Faelamor had used as a landing place last time. No, that image was too crowded; she kept seeing Faelamor's tormented face as she leapt back into the gate.

Maigraith focused on another place—Yalkara's sleeping chamber. The stylus had lain there for centuries. That room was not tainted with Faelamor—all the fears and emotions associated with her would not rise up to choke off her abilities, as they had so many times before. Faelamor had saturated her with fear of failing.

Maigraith recalled to mind the way to control the gate. She squeezed the egg, rehearsing the procedures step by step. Ready! She closed her eyes. Yalkara's bedchamber floated before her. Forcing down a momentary lack of confidence, she tried to open a gate. There was no dizziness, no shifting planes of reality, no feeling of movement at all. The image faded slowly from her mind. I've failed, Maigraith thought.

That's all I know about gates. It isn't easy at all. How I sneered at Faelamor.

Then she noticed how warm it was. The air was warm and dusty. She sneezed. Opening her eyes she found that she was in pitch darkness. *Havissard! I've done it!* The transfer had been so clean that she had not even felt a bump as she arrived.

Maigraith put away the egg and the stylus, feeling in her pocket for a lightglass. The one she fished out, she was pleased to discover, was her favorite. It was formed from a single red-brown garnet the size of a small egg, perfect save for one tiny flaw. She had used that flaw to pass a silver thread into the heart of the crystal. The light was a redbrown glow that suited her mood.

The light showed Yalkara's bedchamber, just as she had left it. Havissard was hers to explore for as long as she cared to. At least, Maigraith recalled, as long as she could go without food, for she had brought none with her. She could do what she wanted now; she need never go back at all. Faelamor could not reach her here!

The bedchamber was a dark room—walls, carpet and furniture. The red-brown light from the globe seemed to sink into the walls and disappear. She touched it to more light, but still her eyes strained. Memory told her that it had been brighter in here before. She found a globe above the door and fetched from it a brighter light, white and yellow. She was surprised that it worked. The floor was quite dusty and their footmarks could clearly be seen: Faelamor's little prints passing through, her slightly larger ones going back and forth, the mark of one knee beside the bed.

For the rest of the day (was it day or night here?—she had no idea of the time) she wandered through the halls and rooms of Havissard. She found many things to interest her, for the place was exactly as it had been abandoned. Every cup and spoon remained, every bed and bedcover, every tapestry, every kitchen implement. Even the food survived in the storerooms, though that was long past use, save perhaps for dried-up stuff that she was not hungry enough to try. But somehow she was disappointed. Something was lacking. I expected too much of Havissard. For all the way it calls to me, it's still just an empty place full of old things. Something is lacking, but in me!

Shaking herself, Maigraith headed to the library for the book. She found trackmarks in the dust, a chip from a lightglass, a man's bootprints going right up to Faelamor's bench. There was no other sign of Mendark. Half the day she spent in the library, just looking through the unreadable journals, dreaming. Some were illustrated with sketches, mostly of buildings, ruins and landscapes. They all looked strange. Aachan was a forbidding, inhospitable place, with its black flowers and organic buildings, its mountains like broken glass stuck on top of a wall. But somehow appealing.

Maigraith enjoyed the time in the library most of all, until she recalled to mind the way Faelamor had looked as she examined the smaller book. She could still see her horrified face. Whatever had upset her, she had found it in the book. There was an empty space on the shelves but the small book was nowhere to be found, and she lost Mendark's tracks in a part of Havissard where there was no dust at all.

Maigraith was famished, and she had given her word to Faelamor. If she was to abandon her it would be to her face. She headed back.

To her exhilaration the return was almost as effortless as the coming. Maigraith was now pleased that Faelamor had forced her, as glad as she had been to be pushed by Vanhe. She had learned a completely new skill, all the more precious because Faelamor could never master it. Another step on the road to her new life.

She emerged from the gate between the ironstones, hipheight above the ground. The air popped and she fell the short distance, landing on her knees. It was dark, past midnight. She had been away for more than a day. Suddenly exhausted, she trudged downstream to the camp, threw off all but her shirt then crawled into her shelter. Weariness battled with hunger and won; Maigraith slept.

Faelamor appeared soon after. She squatted in the mouth of the tent, watching Maigraith sleep. Putting out a hand, Faelamor stroked Maigraith's brow, then drew back her hand. Maigraith, Maigraith, I care for you more than you can ever know. I'm a monster, it's true, and I've treated you worst of all. But duty must come first. She bowed her head and withdrew.

Faelamor shook her awake at dawn. "Where is the book?" she hissed right in Maigraith's ear.

Maigraith, jerked awake, rubbed her ear. "It wasn't there."

"Are you sure? Did you look thoroughly?"

Maigraith groped forward in the semi-darkness, put her hand on what turned out to be Faelamor's breast and shoved her away. "I searched the library," she said angrily, moving after her into the daylight. "I followed your path all the way back to the gate. It wasn't there. It looked as if Mendark picked it up."

"Mendark!" said Faelamor, her face slowly drawing into a horror mask. "Was there any sign of him?"

"Footprints, a chip off a globe, but that's all."

Faelamor convulsed, then bit back a scream. Maigraith wondered if she was going mad. "What does it matter?" she said. "How can this old book be so important?"

Waves of red and white pulsed across Faelamor's face. She clenched her fists, then took three, deep, deliberate breaths, trying to bring her panic under control.

"It matters!" she said hoarsely.

"Why?" Maigraith pressed her recklessly. "What are you hiding? *What does the book say about the Faellem?*"

Faelamor exploded. "How dare you question me?"

"I know you're hiding something," said Maigraith, determined to find the answer whatever the consequences. "Is this why you were exiled? Why the Faellem refuse to take you back now?"

That turned out to be one question too many.

"You useless, incompetent fool," Faelamor screamed.

"How I despise you." She shuddered, stumbled away a few steps, then to Maigraith's astonishment her face scrunched up like paper in a fist. The golden eyes disappeared in the folds, her mouth gaped open and a horrible thin, squeaking wail issued out of her. *"No time; no time!"*

"Faelamor, what is it?" Maigraith cried, scrambling to her feet.

Faelamor screamed and screamed, her face like a scarlet sponge.

"Tell me what the matter is!"

Maigraith bent down over her, unable to comprehend what was happening. Faelamor had always been the very definition of control. She tried to catch her liege's hand but a hard little fist struck her right in the throat. Maigraith choked. It felt as if her windpipe had been crushed flat. She fell to her knees, desperately sucking at the air.

The screaming had not stopped for an instant, though now it was growing shrill, cracked, squeak-like. Opening her eyes, Maigraith saw Faelamor staggering around drunkenly through the trees near the river. She's gone mad, Maigraith thought. She ran soft-footed after her.

The sky turned green, then red, then black. Thick red drops the size of melons drifted in the air, illusions exploding from Faelamor's tortured mind. She appeared and disappeared randomly as she passed between the trees, but it was illusion concealing her, raw and uncontrolled, breaking out in spectral waves that saturated Maigraith's eyes with color. She knew that, somewhere within herself, she had the strength to disbelieve them out of existence. She tried to, until her eyes bulged out. Suddenly the colors disappeared.

There was no respite. Now the trees seemed to have come to life, their trunks swelling and contracting as if breathing. Branches thrashed at her—more illusions from Faelamor's deranged mind. Maigraith ran around a massive tree, a branch slammed into her and she landed hard on her back.

She was slow to rise this time. It felt as if she had been whipped across the face. Her breasts felt bruised. Then, as she lay with her eyes closed, Maigraith heard a strange groaning sound accompanied by a rustle-thud! And again, this time closer.

Her eyes sprang open. A branch end was questing about in the air, its jagged tip stuck with dirt and impaled leaves. With another groan it stabbed at the ground not far away, sprang back and sought out in her direction.

If that's illusion, it's the best I've ever seen, Maigraith thought. She lay for a moment longer, getting her breath back; then, as the branch thrashed above her, *What if it's not illusion? What if Faelamor's fit is actually doing this?*

The branch whipped down, stabbing at her belly. Maigraith rolled, felt the jagged end tear through her nightshirt, then scrambled to her feet and ran.

Had it been anyone else in the world, she would have struck them down with the Secret Art. She attempted it but felt no power in her hands at all. Faelamor had made sure that Maigraith could not use power against her.

Other branches lashed at her. She weaved and ducked, then found herself in a clearing not far from the river. Faelamor was reeling about on a stony ledge above the water, her screams reduced to a crackling wail. Her staring eyes passed over Maigraith, who felt the grass stab at her ankles, the stones try to crush her bare toes.

She snatched up a stick lying on the ground. A hailstorm of pebbles and twigs exploded upwards, battering her exposed flesh. Protecting her eyes with her hand, Maigraith kept going, beyond the stony area onto smooth rock.

The storm ceased. Instantly the rock split open beneath her, cracks opening and closing like giant clams. She snatched her foot out just in time. Faelamor was spinning round on the ledge, and every time her eyes caught Maigraith's she felt a stab of horror at what she saw there, a mad world in which every object loathed her and wanted her dead.

The rock moved. Something smashed directly down onto Maigraith's bare foot. She felt the bones break. The pain was impossible to ignore but she kept going, a running hobble. As Faelamor spun round again, Maigraith thumped her on the back of the head with her stick, as hard as she could.

Faelamor's feet lifted off the ground and, still making that ghastly cry, she fell forward off the ledge, tumbled over and over and smacked into the water face first. The scream was cut off and the current pulled her under. The illusions stopped instantly.

That wasn't supposed to happen, Maigraith thought. Her eyes followed the bubbles down to a set of rapids, where Faelamor became wedged between two boulders with her head and chest forced under by the flow. Her legs thrashed uselessly.

Duty suddenly reasserted itself. Faelamor was drowning! Until Maigraith repudiated her oath, face to face, Faelamor remained her liege.

One step revealed that her foot was badly broken. Faelamor would drown long before she hopped down to the rapids. Maigraith did the only thing she could—she stumbled forward and dropped into the river.

Her nightshirt ballooned up around her face, then she struck with an impact that sent a spear of pain up through her foot. Maigraith trod water feebly, just keeping her head up as the current carried her swiftly toward the rocks. The rocks swelled in front of her and she slammed into them, not far from Faelamor.

Maigraith crawled across to heave at Faelamor's legs. She hardly moved; the force of the water was too great. Almost shrieking with pain, Maigraith stood up on her broken foot and dragged Faelamor out of the water.

Faelamor's face was battered and bruised blue all over. Water dribbled out of her mouth and nose. Maigraith draped her face-down over the rock and was about to deliver a hard blow in the back when Faelamor released her breath with an explosive gasp and rolled over.

"You took your time!" she choked. Little and old and

fraillooking Faelamor might be, but she was as tough as the bones of Santhenar.

"This is the very last time!" Maigraith said; then they crawled together to the bank, up through the forest, which had now reverted to inanimate wood, to the camp.

Faelamor gave no thanks or apologies for her fit; but then, Maigraith had not expected any.

"This is a disaster," she kept saying as Maigraith attended to her lacerations and bruises. "A catastrophe! We're doomed!"

Maigraith was sick of it. Her foot was in agony. Why was she working so hard on someone who, mad or not, had just done her best to kill her? "Then crawl away and die," she screamed in Faelamor's face, "and the sooner the better!" Packing up the bowl, the rags and bandages, she began to hop to her shelter.

"What's wrong with your foot?" Faelamor asked sharply, in the hoarse little voice that came out when she was exhausted.

"You smashed it with a rock!" she screamed. "You tried to kill me."

Faelamor knew it too—Maigraith saw in her eyes as the memories of her fit came back, one by one.

"I'm sorry!" Faelamor said. "Sit down. I will attend to it."

Maigraith could hardly bear her touch, but she endured. The bones must be set and she could not do it herself. Faelamor was a healer of rare skill—the foot would recover as quickly as bones could grow together. It would need to, Maigraith sensed.

She sat on the ground, whittling a pair of crutches, while Faelamor put the bones back in place and made a wooden frame to take the place of plaster. Her touch was infinitely gentle. Even her look was caring—until Faelamor caught Maigraith's eye on her—whereupon the habitual scowl reappeared.

"Wear this for three weeks," she said. "Then you may remove it, but treat your foot gently for another two. No jumping! After that it will be as good as ever."

Maigraith tried out her crutches. The frame was gruesomely uncomfortable.

"How are you feeling?" asked Faelamor. "Are you strong?"

"That depends what you require of me."

"To call the Faellem again." For a moment that look of despair was back in her eyes, then she shuddered and became her iron-willed self again.

"I think I can manage that," said Maigraith.

They remade the link.

Hallal? Faelamor called. *Ellami? Gethren, answer me!*

To their amazement, a response came at once.

Faelamor, sighed the wispy voice in Maigraith's mind. *Is there no end to your arrogance?*

Ellami! The voice was like a current through Maigraith's mind. *I need you!*

You need us. How novel! But we don't need you. We refuse you, Faelamor! Your crimes have brought shame on us all.

Ellami! Faelamor begged. *Tallallame needs us. We must find the way home.*

We know that, said the voice, strengthening as Faelamor weakened. *But not your way. Begone!*

Faelamor shuddered, clenching her fists until her nails cut red crescents into her palms. Maigraith, fearing that another fit was coming, withdrew from the link hurriedly.

Bring back the link! Faelamor shouted into her mind, and as Maigraith did so, she continued. *Ellami, Ellami, don't go! A disaster—a catastrophe!*

Oh? said the voice.

It's just another of her tricks, said another, deeper voice. Gethren, Maigraith thought.

I've been inside Havissard, sent Faelamor.

You used a gate! The voice was incredulous.

I had to, since you refused to aid me.

Don't dare blame us for your crimes, Faelamor.

Listen to me. I found a book in Havissard. An awful book, by Yalkara!

There was a long pause, then the first voice said sharply, *What book? What does it say about us?*

Maigraith's curiosity was aroused. Why were they so afraid?

I cannot . . . could not read it, Faelamor sent. *But just the script is a horror. It reminds me—*

Not over the link! snapped the second voice.

An even longer pause followed, as if the Faellem were conferring one among another. *Put the book away in the safest place, Faelamor. Protect it with your strongest illusion. Do nothing to put us at risk.*

The book is lost, Ellami, Faelamor wailed. *I dropped it in Havissard and—*

And? said the voice, now frigid.

Mendark has it, Faelamor wept.

The voice swore. There seemed to be another hasty conference. Then, in tones like a creeping glacier, *These are our orders. Do nothing whatsoever to make this mess worse. Wait upon our coming.*

39

EVENIL

Faelamor sat on the grass, weeping. "This is the worst day of my life," she said after her tears were used up. "To be abused so by my own people. I cannot bear it."

They sat silently for a long time, then Faelamor stood up. "I must go back to Havissard."

"You would disobey their orders?" Maigraith asked. She did not care either way, but she was curious.

"They're too far away," Faelamor rationalized. "They don't know what I know. I've got to recover the book. Quick!" She began to throw things in her pack.

"If Mendark used a gate he could be five hundred leagues away by now," Maigraith said, gathering food, knife, light-glass and all the other little things that Faelamor was sure to forget.

"I don't think so! I don't believe he came through a gate at all. I think he's still there, or nearby, with the book. Send me back!"

"Send you?" Maigraith said. "How?"

"Through the gate, fool!"

"It's my gate," Maigraith said softly. "I don't know that it would work with you."

"I watched you," Faelamor said. "I saw how easy it was for you." She shivered as if afraid of Maigraith's power, or potential. "I know you can do this for me. It's your duty to do so."

Maigraith did not argue. They hurried upstream to the gate stones. She stood to one side while Faelamor squeezed into the cramped space between the stones.

Maigraith was tormented by self-doubt, by mixed emotions. She did not want Faelamor to use her precious gate at all. She hated her; wanted her to die in the gate. And yet she felt the duty of care keenly.

Faelamor stood ready. Maigraith opened the gate and tried to visualize the destination, the library in Havissard, but Faelamor wrenched the image from her and vanished with a tremendous clap of inrushing air.

Maigraith stared at the empty space between the stones. Her head hurt. She was not ready—not nearly—but Faelamor was gone. There was so much that they had never discussed. How was Faelamor going to return? What would happen when the Faellem appeared if she did not come back?

She sat there for two days, staring at the space between the stones. Once she thought Faelamor was on her way. Maigraith tried to take control of the gate but it did not open;

Faelamor did not return.

Ravenous, Maigraith took up her crutches and hobbled down to the camp. There she packed her pack, returned to the gate and tried to open it, to follow Faelamor to Havissard. The gate opened easily but she could not find the destination.

Havissard was completely closed off. Maigraith could not find a trace of it. Faelamor had made sure that she could not follow. After a week of failed attempts she was worn out in body, mind and soul. Initiative deserted her. She could not see what to do. Could not think.

Abandoning the gate, she returned to the camp and began

to make preparations for the coming of the Faellem. That was still months away, the end of autumn at the earliest, but if hundreds appeared they would require food and shelter. Maigraith needed to be busy. She set to work.

Faelamor landed in the library at Havissard, after a journey that she never wanted to do again. The gate might have been lined with spines, for it pricked and stung her all the way. It was Maigraith's creature, one that wished only to torment her.

The minute she arrived at the library, skidding across the dusty floor on her elbows, Faelamor remembered the slim book slipping out of her bag. Mendark's footprints were clear where he had walked across to pick it up. Maigraith's were there too, careful not to obscure the others. Faelamor admired her for her cautious mind, and damned her too.

She followed Mendark's winding path through the rooms and corridors of Havissard. It *was* a tedious day but Faelamor took no shortcuts. Even when it was clear the tracks had doubled back on themselves, she followed them every step in case Mendark had hidden something. He hadn't. Faelamor was able to sense out his path where Maigraith had lost it, though only near the end of the day did she find the greasy chute by which he had made his exit.

Faelamor crawled into it, thinking that he might be trapped at the lower end, or broken on the rocks below. She had the foresight to take out her knife, pressing it against the side to brake her slide down.

At the end she smacked into a hatch reduced to a hinge and two pieces of broken timber. But there she remained, for the protection that Mendark had passed through, by the power of Yalkara's ring, was an impenetrable barrier to her.

Impenetrable but transparent. Looking down, Faelamor could clearly see the bramble thicket and Mendark's body trapped in it. His arm moved feebly; *he was still alive!* Days had gone by but he was still trying to hack his way out. I've got the gold he came for, she thought, and he has the book that I so desperately need.

The thicket might as well have been on the dark side of the moon, for she was trapped in Havissard as securely as he was outside. Faelamor tried every power she had but nothing would allow her passage through the protection.

After the sun rose next morning, she saw several figures slashing their way through the thorn bushes. Faelamor struggled until it drove her wild, until illusions exploded out of her in all directions. She animated the stone in the same way that she had brought the trees to life in Elludore. Contractions began to pass along the chute like the motions of a dragon's bowel.

It could not excrete her though. The protection constipated it. I'm hallucinating, she thought. I'll kill myself if I'm not careful. Staring out, her view sphinctered down to a pinhole straight in front of her, Faelamor saw Tallia and a huge soldier cut down a limp-looking Mendark and carry him away.

Faelamor stabbed at the transparent barrier, over and over, but it was unbreachable. Her guts were burning again. Digging her knife into the wall, she forced herself backwards up the greasy tunnel, crawled to the library and, using the greatest effort of will that she had ever employed, forced open the gate.

This one was not like any gate she'd ever imagined. It was a wet, dripping, organic tube like the maw of a giant snake, one whose gullet dripped acid from the roof. A belch sent acrid, rot-stinking fumes tumbling past her. But it was her only way out. Faelamor closed her eyes, bent forward then forced her way into the shuddering cave. She did not expect to get out of it.

"Take me to Mendark's book!" she shrieked. The gate snarled and hurled her into oblivion, then just before the ultimate blackness she sensed Maigraith trying to bring her home.

She failed. The gate exploded and dropped her into nowhere.

Faelamor had not returned from Havissard. In spite of her sense of liberation and self-discovery Maigraith remained in Dunnet—the chains of duty and responsibility were still strong. She kept on with her work and in her spare time practiced her mental and physical regimen until she was as fit in body and mind as she could possibly make herself.

Autumn passed. Preparing for the coming of the Faellem involved a mountain of work. When that was done Maigraith worked on her gate, shaping the twin ironstones into obelisks, making her controling stone, the four-part egg, more perfect, more attuned to the river, the cave and the obelisks, visualizing as best she could various destinations, and even opening gates to one or other of them. She never went through them though, for the work was exhausting and she knew that every gate was a risk—she might not come out again. For the moment there was no purpose to her life, and nowhere that she wanted to go.

And Maigraith had identified a weakness in herself that she was unable to overcome. Even for places that she knew well, most times she could not conjure up a clear picture of the destination in her mind. It made her afraid of the gate again.

The lonely days passed. Winter came. One day, when the snow was thick on the forest floor, Faelamor returned unexpectedly. Maigraith was pleased to see her, finding her own resources stretched thin by the months of isolation.

"Where are the Faellem?" Faelamor shouted from across the clearing.

"I have seen no one since you left."

Faelamor swore, something that she rarely did. "Then I have hurried all this way for nothing. I called you with my mind, many times. Why did you not answer?"

"I sensed no link," said Maigraith coolly. Why should she be blamed for Faelamor's failing?

Faelamor smashed her fist against a tree, even more uncharacteristic. "Is there food?"

Maigraith turned into the store shelter to fetch what she had. She laid it out on the flat slab that they used for a table: small flat cakes, baked of nutmeal and honey that morning and flavored with the sexual parts of flowers; fish from the river, smoked; pickled mushrooms; wild onions, rather old and withered; the bulbs of a plant rather like a lily that grew by the river, though these had a starchy, gluey flavor. She also had a very mild wine made from fermented nectar.

Faelamor looked at the food with scant enthusiasm.

"I will have tea as well," she said, turning down to the river to wash.

Maigraith was not hungry but she joined Faelamor at the meal, nibbling on a piece of nutcake.

Faelamor finished her meal, wiped her face and stood up. She had not taken her pack off.

"Are you going again so soon?" cried Maigraith, feeling like a child who, though uncomfortable with her visitor, did not want to be abandoned. "Did you recover the book? What news of Mendark, of Yggur?"

"News must wait! It is a race now. Mendark and Yggur are up to something." She turned away.

"I will not be treated like a child!" insisted Maigraith. "Tell me what is happening in the world or I won't be here when you return."

Faelamor scowled, but answered. "I tried to force the gate to take me to the book, but it hurled me out of Havissard into a secret library, one Mendark built, a long way south. How I got out again is a tale in itself. I didn't recover the book. But Mendark is back and I'm sure he still has it. Since then I've been spying on the company's meets," Faelamor said with a little pride. "It wasn't easy, even for me."

She told Maigraith the gist of the tales about Mendark and Yggur, and Karan and Llian too, which were already well known. Itinerant tellers were now spreading them around Meldorin. "And there are most disturbing rumors from the mountains behind Tolryme, where we met a year ago, if you recall?"

"I remember. We met there after you betrayed the Aachim and let the Ghâshâd into Shazmak—"

"I did not betray them—they are not *our* species; not Faellem! I warned Tensor of the consequences of holding me but he chose to ignore me."

"Beautifully rationalized! You went to Tolryme to spy on Karan."

"To search out her ancestry, and learn what you had kept hidden from me: that she was triune!"

"I didn't *know* she was triune," said Maigraith. "And you did betray the Aachim. Hundreds died because of you."

"I warned them!" Faelamor repeated angrily. "Besides, that was a year ago."

"That makes it all right, does it?"

Faelamor ignored her. "Something is stirring near Tolryme, in a place called Carcharon. An ominous name! How am I to deal with that as well?"

"I—" said Maigraith.

"Yes! Go and find out what is going on—it may be Rulke. I've got to go back to Thurkad and recover Yalkara's deadly book. Go as soon as you can."

"I will," Maigraith said.

Then over her shoulder Faelamor said: "When the Faellem come, tell them nothing."

It was the best part of fifty leagues to Tolryme the way the forest paths ran. It took Maigraith ten long days of marching in the cold. On the tenth evening she reached the town just on dusk and took a room in its only inn, a large square granite building that was rustic in the extreme. She longed for a bath but because of the wood shortage that was impossible. The best she could do was an all-over wash with a jug of lukewarm water.

She changed her clothes and went down to the dining room. That was a spartan affair too—coarse bread and a watery stew of vegetables that were long past their prime. As she was mopping up the last of the liquid with a crust a young man limped up to her table.

"I beg your pardon," he said, doffing his cap and twisting it in his hands.

She looked up. He would have been a handsome fellow had he not been so thin, for his brown hair was magnificent and his bones well chiseled. But his cheeks were hollow and one arm was gone above the elbow.

"You are Maigraith," he said.

"I am," she replied, "though I would prefer that you did not broadcast it about. How do you know me?"

"I fought for you at the battle of Casyme last summer, when you overcame the sorcerous Ghâshâd and saved the First Army. My name is Evenil."

"How is it that you are here, Evenil?"

He smiled self-consciously. "This was my home town before I went a-venturing. But one day I found myself in Orist without a copper grint to my name, so I joined Yggur's army and eventually ended up here again."

"What do you do now?"

"I was paid out when I lost my arm—a few silver tars—and now I do whatever I can. There's plenty to do, even for someone with my handicap, but no one has any money to pay for it. And even if they could, there is precious little food to be bought, and hellish expensive. My tars are already gone."

And you are beginning to think that you will starve this winter, she thought. She had seen the same dozens of times, even on this short journey.

"Tell me, Evenil," she said, indicating the chair opposite, "do you know my friend Karan Fyrn?"

He sat down. "No," he said, "though I've heard all about her. I used to play at Gothryme when I was young, but she wasn't there then."

"Is she at home now?" Maigraith asked with sudden hope.

"I don't believe so. I heard she went to Thurkad a while ago." He looked downcast, evidently thinking that he had nothing useful to tell her.

"Have you heard of a place in the mountains called Carcharon?"

"Of course! It was built by mad Basunez. I could guide you there, if you wish," he said more boldly.

Maigraith considered, and the longer she did the further his face fell. He was so thin that he would surely not survive the winter. No, she said to herself, this man lost his arm in my service and now he has asked me for help. I cannot refuse him.

"You can guide me," she said. "But—"

"Oh thank you!" he cried, taking her hand and kissing it, then immediately letting it go. A flush crept up his throat.

"It may be dangerous," she said. "Have you heard rumors about that place?"

"They are everywhere, but here we have more important questions to worry about: what we will eat tomorrow."

"Have you family here?"

"No more, though there is a girl that I would take to wife, if she would have me. Janythe was my sweetheart before I went wandering. We had dreams of a cottage and children, but what use am I to her with this handicap?"

"You are still a man, and in my service now. Go and ask her!"

"After we come back," said Evenil, but she could see in his eyes that he no longer felt good enough.

"Here are three silver tars," she said. "Buy food for a week, if you can get it, and meet me here at dawn."

He did so, carrying a pack and another bag which held the sorriest grain, fruit and vegetables she had ever seen. "It is the best I could buy," he said, "and it cost all of a silver tar." He handed back the other two. "And I could find no meat at all."

"No matter," she said, handing the money back again. "I

don't care what I eat. Keep this, there may come a chance to buy more. If necessary we can hunt."

At Evenil's side a sword was slung off a bit of rope. It was a short ugly thing with notches along its blade, and looked as if it had been used for cutting wood. It looked not much use even for that.

They set out toward the granite cliffs. Evenil must have sensed her mood for he said nothing at all, but he was very attentive to her every need, as he imagined it, pointing out the best route and the best stepping places on the way up the cliff path. Maigraith forbore to point out that she had crossed the known world more than once. He was doing his best to earn his hire.

They were crawling up the last part of the ridge, a knotted club of rock with steep steps cut into it.

"Above this," said Evenil, trying to steady her, though having only one arm it was sometimes at the risk of both their lives, "there is a round place with stone seats where they say mad old Basunez used to stage bloody spectacles for his masons."

"An amphitheater, on this miserable ridge?"

"That is the word. Amphitheater!"

"Then it must be the most dismal one in all of Santhenar." She pulled her cloak about her more tightly but the wind—the incessant wind—blasted right through it. It was a rare sunny day but the sun had no warmth in it and the wind was a wild, wailing, biting, aggressive thing—it hated them for their life and their warm blood and did its best to take them unawares and hurl them down into the gulf. It was almost mid-winter—hythe only a few weeks off.

They gained the amphitheater, made their way across it and peered over the shallow western lip. A narrow path carved atop the ridge crest wound down and then back up to a hideous nine-sided tower. Snow coated its helmeted brass and slate roof.

Carcharon was indeed occupied—two stick-figures, unmistakeably Ghâshâd, stood at the top of a stair by a pair of open gates.

Maigraith and Evenil huddled there all day, watching; a day of the most miserable tedium. The Ghâshâd walked up and down the steps; they paced around the walls; they changed every two hours. Occasionally other guards appeared, patroling in pairs on the walls or sighted through embrasures. What were they guarding?

Maigraith knew that this news would not be enough to satisfy Faelamor. She would have to find out, though the prospect was terrifying. And she had to look to the safety of her faithful guard as well, whose chivalry up here would be a hazard to both of them.

"I'm going up to the gate," Maigraith said as dusk approached. Tiny ice crystals sandblasted their exposed faces. "Stay right here; guard my back! There may be scouts out."

She could see, even in the failing light, that he knew it was an excuse. And he, a soldier once, was humiliated. "Do you obey my orders, Evenil?" she said harshly, thinking that she could not afford him up here. He was perceptive; he realized that too. He bowed his head.

Maigraith crept along the winding path; a precipice lay to either side. For a few minutes at the change of each guard there was a chance to get close, for it was so cold that even the iron-hard Ghâshâd lingered in the shelter of the open door when one pair relieved the other. They still watched, but there was an opportunity. She moved as close as she dared, lying on the edge of the path well below the stair, concealed by the blowing snow as long as no one came down the steps.

No one did; eventually the guard changed and in the thickly falling snow she made it right up the steps and slid in behind a bronze statue of a mythical winged creature. From there she could hear the guards' talk. They were uneasy—perhaps they sensed her. She knew she would never get in through the doors, but spines and rods embedded in the wall offered another opportunity. She began to climb up toward a lighted embrasure near the top.

If the cold had been bad before, up here it was unbearable—the wind hunted like a howling pack and the metal rods stuck to her skin through holes in her gloves. She had to climb around the tower to reach the embrasure she was aiming for, and knew that she hung over the unseen precipice.

Reaching the embrasure, Maigraith slanted her gaze in, keeping out of the light. A big man moved into the line of sight and she knew him at once. It was Rulke, heading across the room. Her heart leapt from side to side; she felt weak, exposed, afraid. And drawn to him too, though that was madness.

Rulke whirled, staring at the northern embrasure as if something had startled him. He had sensed her! She ducked away from her window, the eastern one, and began to climb down hastily. Came a roar from inside—Rulke's voice. She swung from spine to prong, hurrying, taking risks with the icy metal, desperate to get around the corner before he looked out the window.

She heard an answering cry and knew that it was brave, foolish Evenil come to rescue her. In the lights from the open door she saw him running up the track with his blunt sword upraised. His tragic loyalty brought tears to her eyes. They would kill him in an instant. She moved more quickly but was too late. While she still hung four spans above the rock there was a short sharp battle on the path, but the onearmed man with the blunt sword was no match for their spears. One glided into his breast, he sagged down and was toppled over the edge.

Maigraith hung in the freezing cold until the guards had checked the path and gone back inside to report. Then she crept along the track to the point where Evenil had gone over. She found it easily enough, for there was enough light from the windows to show the snow blushing dark in a patch the size of a hat, where the spear had carved him. She looked down, trying to remember how steep it was here, midway between the amphitheater and Carcharon. Further over the slope was gentler, but here it was precipitous. Impossible that he could have survived. She could see in her mind's eye how the spear had plunged into him. He would have been dead before he fell.

She squatted there for a long time, mourning her guard. He had served her to the best of his ability and this was his reward. Nothing she could do about it. Faithful Evenil was gone.

Maigraith could have gone back and slain them on the step, but what would be the point? Her melancholy duty was clear. She must take the news to Janythe, Evenil's sweetheart whose hand he had not dared to ask for. There would be no cottage and no children now. Sick at heart, Maigraith headed back down the mountain.

It snowed all the way home. Maigraith arrived back in Dunnet after an exhausting, slow trek to find Faelamor waiting for her. She had failed to recover the book. Moreover the Faellem had still not come. Faelamor was in a shocking mood, terrified that they might not be coming at all. She had tried to raise them by means of a link but had not been able to get back the merest whisper.

"Well, what did you learn?" Faelamor snarled.

"It is Rulke!"

"You're sure? How can you be sure?"

"I climbed the wall of the tower and looked in at the window. I saw him clearly. I've seen Rulke before, remember. I recognized him at once."

Faelamor was, if anything, even more furious than before. "Fool!" she shrieked. "What if he saw you? He needs your kind just as much as—" She broke off, staring right through Maigraith as if she had just realized an awful possibility. "Why?" she said in a whisper. "Why did he go to Carcharon when he had all Shazmak at his disposal?"

"I have no idea. Carcharon is a powerful place. Maybe—"

"And it's a place that's positively impregnated by a certain family. "Basunez! Galliad!" She grabbed Maigraith by the jacket and shook her. "And who owns Carcharon? Who lives just a step away? Who is a sensitive and a triune, surely just what Rulke requires?"

"Karan," said Maigraith weakly for lack of air.

"Tallallame, Tallallame, your fate rests on the one which is three." The proverb had been old before Faelamor had left her world.

Faelamor released her, stumbled backwards and sat down abruptly on the snowy ground. Maigraith walked away to the river, wondering what the proverb meant.

When she was gone Faelamor said to herself, "The balance has tipped right against me. Rulke was bad enough by himself. With the triune he will be invincible." She sank her head on her arms and rocked back and forth for a few moments, then sprang up again. "I was right about Karan the first time. I must finish her. I should have done so long ago.'

40

DINNER WITH NADIRIL

In the evening Nadiril appeared at Llian's cell with a parole from Yggur. "Come with me," he said. "We have much to talk about."

They went down to the waterfront of Thurkad, to an inn which had private dining rooms. Nadiril was greeted with a bow so low that the doorman's bald pate touched the floor, then they were led to a large room on the second floor. There was a glorious fire. Small-paned windows looked out over the harbor, though presently the view was obscured by sleet whirling against the glass. An aged waiter lurched in with a menu as long as his arm. Llian looked at the prices in alarm, surreptitiously feeling the sad little coins in his pocket.

Nadiril laughed, a rustling sound like the leaves that blew along the streets of Thurkad. "I'm paying. Order the best of everything, if you wish. It all tastes the same to me, but it gives me pleasure to see young folk eat."

Llian had not had a decent feed in days. He ordered soup,

a platter of appetizers and, to follow, the second-most expensive dish on the menu. Nadiril selected the wine to go with each dish. When the first wine appeared, a small jade flask containing a luscious yellow vintage so strong, sweet and thick that it could have been a liqueur, Nadiril fixed Llian with a flinty glare and said, "Now tell me your tale; omit not the least detail. And take my warning to heart. I can read truth from falsehood as I read a book. Give me nothing but truth, as you know it and as you have been taught as a chronicler."

"Truth is what I am searching for," said Llian. "But my tale will take all night."

"You have other appointments?" Nadiril asked with a wry grin.

Llian also managed a smile. "I don't receive many invitations these days."

"Then begin!"

Llian began. A good while later the soup arrived, a honey-colored consommé made from prawn heads flavored with saffron, with wafer-thin slices of marbled egg floating on top. It was gorgeous, but when it was gone he was hungrier than if he had eaten nothing.

By this time he was standing in the dock in Shazmak, telling his tale to the Syndics. *We have heard the evidence of Llian, and it is truth as he knows it,* Selial had said.

"Ha!" said Nadiril. "I see what Karan did, and it has never been done before. An astounding talent. I must speak to her about it."

"The Syndics did not pick it," said Llian.

"Pah! People are books to me. You are not tempted to lie to me are you, Llian? I wouldn't advise it."

Llian caught a glimpse of the hard edge beneath the kindly face. However, the idea of telling even a fib to the great Nadiril was beyond his ken.

"Good! Go on."

They cleansed their palates with eggcups of water of

lime, a misnamed drink if ever there was one, for afterwards his breath made the candles roar.

Llian continued. Shortly the ancient waiter returned, staggering under a tray as wide as a wheelbarrow.

It contained appetizers too numerous to mention. There were nuts glazed with hot ginger or cardamom or bitters; a bowl containing a spray of crisp noodle-sticks in the colors of the spectrum; a side-dish of prawn heads, probably those that had been used for the soup, the empty shells packed with minced walnut, grape and herb stuffing, and beautifully arranged with the long red feelers crossed to make diamond patterns against the white plate. In the center of the tray was an octagonal plate containing raw chacalot cut into perfect cubes, and around the plate were ten dipping bowls. One was filled with olive oil and one with chilli oil; one with rock salt, one with garlic slivers, one with hot bean paste, one with lime pepper, one with crystallized molasses, one with green mint and purple basil in vinegar, one with flaked toasted almonds and the last with mustard seed. And there were many other dishes, spices, sauces and pickles on the tray, some so strange that Llian could not imagine what they were made from.

"How does one approach this?" he wondered, pointing to the chacalot dish.

Nadiril smiled. "Take one of these leaves in your left hand, thus," he said, shaking off drops of water. "With the silver tongs, so, select your piece of reptile and dip it in the sauce of your choice—I prefer the lime pepper—then place it in the middle of the leaf. Then, still only using your left hand, fold the leaf into a neat little parcel and pop it in your mouth."

Llian began loading his leaf with half a dozen pieces of chacalot, each well steeped in a different condiment. The folding operation proved to be more difficult than he had thought, and mixed sauces dribbled down the front of his shirt.

"It is generally thought to be poor etiquette to combine

flavorings in the one leaf," said Nadiril, with a twitch of the lips. He handed Llian a napkin. "I tell you this just for future reference, you understand, since I care nothing for such whimsical conventions. Resume your tale, if you please." He leaned back in his chair, his eyes never leaving Llian's face.

Nadiril had taken only a few mouthfuls, though he sipped his wine with evident relish. The main meal came and went, huge crayfish in a voluptuous sauce. They had such beautiful carapaces, brightly colored in greens and blues and reds, even after cooking, that Llian could scarcely bear to crack his open. He ate every morsel, licking his fingers clean at the end, but a minute later could not have told what he had eaten, he was so involved in the tale. Karan and he were crawling through the caverns of Bannador now.

Around midnight the dessert appeared, an astounding confection: a spiraling tower of iced cream, molded jellied fruit and toffee balls each filled with a different liqueur, all woven around and around with threads of brittle toffee, and topped with creeping glaciers of red and yellow purée, winter strawberries and gellon. It was so delicious that Llian was forced to break off the tale until he was finished. With it appeared another bottle of wine, this one a purplish black with an astringency that contrasted sharply with the sweet fragrance of the dessert.

Llian picked threads of toffee from between his teeth. "You are not . . . tired?" he asked hopefully. Nadiril's questioning was still razor-sharp, but Llian's head was spinning. He had slept badly of late.

"I sleep only a few hours a night, and if I don't get it, it hardly matters."

The tale continued, all the way to the Great Conclave in Thurkad. Coffee came with a sweet fortified wine so rich that Llian again had to stop talking till he had licked the last drops from the rim of his bowl.

"Leave the bottle," said Nadiril to the aged waiter, who

was yawning behind a swollen-knuckled hand. "And another pot of coffee, if you please."

That did them until well into the early hours, by which time Llian's tale had reached Katazza, where Tensor was working on his gate. Llian was beginning to flag badly.

"Ah," said Nadiril. "This I am especially interested in."

He questioned closely as the tale unfolded, and at the end of it, when the gate was made and Llian's final collaboration with Tensor told, he fixed Llian with a penetrating stare. Llian felt more exposed by this kindly old man than he ever had by Yggur's merciless interrogation. "This does not reflect entirely to your credit," said the librarian.

Llian could not meet his gaze any longer. He lowered his eyes, red in the face and thoroughly ashamed. "No!" he whispered. "I was too curious. I would have done anything."

"It is good to truly love your work, but the chronicler must remember that he is also a man and owes a duty to his wife, his family and his people."

"I have no wife," said Llian stonily.

"Of course you don't. I know everything about you. Tell on."

More coffee, and that did them till dawn scattered pink petals across the sky beyond the harbor. Llian was still in the Nightland, for that was a topic of surpassing interest to Nadiril, and he questioned almost every sentence.

"All in all, not entirely to your discredit," he said, when the gate had spat Llian back into Katazza. "I see that you have told me a pretty good swag of truth. But what did Rulke do while he had you in that trance? That's what we must find out. Come closer."

He did something with his hands. Llian slid smoothly into a hypnotic state, and, sometime later, out again. The sun was well up. "I shall have to think more about this," Nadiril said. "I'm sure there is a way to penetrate this veil. Now, what say you to breakfast? This telling is hungry work, I imagine."

Breakfast appeared, porridge with a golden brown well

of syrup and butter melted down through the middle, and a huge pot of tea. The tale moved more quickly now, for the trip back to Meldorin had been relatively uneventful, and before the tea was finished Llian was in Tullin dreaming nightmares about Rulke.

Again Nadiril questioned him keenly, but there was much that Llian simply did not know about that night, and at the end of it Nadiril said, "There is also something here that I don't understand. I can see that it will cost me another dinner or two to get to the bottom if it. Still, the price of truth was always high. Continue!"

Llian finished off the tale and Nadiril's frown grew deeper as he heard of Llian's treatment by Shand and Karan.

"Hmmn. A fine tale. And I believe it too, more to the point. Most of it," he amended.

"You believe me!" sighed Llian. "I had begun to think that I was the monster that everyone makes me out to be. Or might as well be."

"Never think that! Be true to yourself and your calling. Do your work with proud indifference; time will prove you right. Beware to be too curious. And if you ever need help, you have only to ask." He put what seemed to be an extravagant amount of money on the table. "Now, take my arm. Help me back to my rooms. Then, I regret, you must take yourself back to your cell. Your parole has run out."

Llian felt crushed. He had been hoping that his imprisonment was over. "You are staying in Thurkad?" he asked as they went slowly along.

"For the time. The library is in good hands, and this business needs an eye from someone who stands to gain nothing from it. And a word of caution: beware Yggur, and Mendark too."

"Mendark?"

"He suffered a devastating loss in Havissard, as you will hear. He has come back full of fury and bitterness, and knowing him as I do, he will be looking for someone to blame. Be careful."

* * *

It was time for the Council to begin. Mendark was already sitting at the Council table and Karan was shocked at his appearance. He looked like an old, old man who had tried and failed, and could not come to terms with that failure. He did his best to hide it, but not quite well enough. Though months had passed since his defeat in Havissard, the bitterness still showed. She could hardly imagine it was the same man they had traveled so far with. He now looked like an aged, withered raptor. His skin had shrunk tight all over, pulling his nose into a beak, his ears out sideways and his fingers into claws. He moved like a robot, as if his garments were far too tight, and his eyes were as dull as cooked fish.

"What's happened to him?" Karan whispered to Tallia, beside her.

A strange, almost panicky expression passed across Tallia's face, then she turned away. "He had a very hard time of it, in Havissard."

Karan knew Tallia was dissembling but did not press her.

Yggur entered last of all. He seemed not much changed but for wearing spectacles with lenses as thick as bottle ends. He still walked with a limp, though now he carried a cane. Yggur sat at his own small table, overlooking the larger, staring down as if sorting people, but Karan noticed that his eyes did not move.

Watching him, she saw that he weighed everyone at the lower table, his broken eyesight stripping them to their essentials: friend, enemy, troublemaker, fool . . . But when he turned his head to Mendark, a fleeting cold rage passed across his face, a terrible thing to see.

The Council was full of posturing and power games between Mendark and Yggur. Mendark harped incessantly about the past, about his great deeds at the time Rulke was imprisoned and since—his heroism in Katazza particularly. But somehow he was unconvincing, almost plaintive.

Yggur listened in silence, growing ever more irritable;

then, for no reason that Karan could see, abruptly broke up the meet and hurried them all out of the chamber. That night a messenger came to Shand's rooms, to tell them that there would be a small meet in a few days' time.

Shand was furious. "Damned if I will," he roared, shaking his fist in the messenger's face. "If Mendark and Yggur are going to play games, I'm going home."

"I would be grateful if you could stay long enough to dine with me," said Nadiril, who had dropped in for tea. "Are you free this evening?"

"I am," said Shand, suppressing his anger.

"Good! It must be ten years since we last ate together, and there is a lot to catch up on."

Nadiril, noticing that Karan was eavesdropping, drew Shand over into the corner. "Not least this business of Llian. Sometimes I don't understand you, Shand."

"I know what I know!" Shand said stubbornly.

"I don't think you do. Your prejudice against the Zain is quite irrational. Now come, which of us is the more impartial judge of character?"

"You are," Shand said, grinding his teeth.

"So I am, and I say you have done Llian very ill. But we will talk about that over dinner."

That evening they did dine together, a dinner that was almost as long as the previous one, but the old friends fell out at the end and Nadiril went home by himself in the early hours. In the morning a haggard Shand packed up and, telling only Karan that he was going back to Tullin, suddenly disappeared.

That night Nadiril took Karan to dinner. She enjoyed the evening immensely, for he was a charming, sensitive dinner companion. Only one notable thing came out of it, however, when late at night she asked what had happened to Mendark.

"That's his secret," Nadiril said after a long silence. "Though I suppose there's no reason why I shouldn't tell you. Mendark is very old and Havissard nearly killed him. He was forced to renew himself, though he knew it was one time too many. It was not a complete success, and the best spellmasters in Thurkad have not been able to undo the damage."

"Renew himself?"

"We old humans age quickly, Karan. Even mancers cannot live for a thousand years without renewing their bodies many times. But there is a limit and Mendark has pushed beyond it. I can say no more than that."

"Have you done that too?"

Nadiril laughed. "This grizzled cadaver is the original me. One life is enough, for me."

"So that's why Mendark is so preoccupied with his reputation!"

"Obsessed, almost to the point of madness," said Nadiril, then turned the conversation to other topics.

The following day he lunched with Malien and by the end of the week he had dined with everyone who was involved in the affair. But he kept his counsel.

The meeting was held some days later, in a small dark room upstairs in the citadel. When Karan arrived she found Tensor (attended only by Asper), Malien, Tallia, Nadiril and Yggur. Shortly after, Mendark came in, leaning on Llian's shoulder.

"Perhaps some among you have wondered at this subterfuge," said Mendark, standing at the end of the table. Even his voice was different; it was gravelly, like gallstones rattling in a bottle. He cast a scowling glance at Yggur, who was looking down his nose at them from a higher table. "It is well known that I have come back from a long hunt. It could hardly be otherwise, coming as I did by ship, in such haste. And after all the events of the past year, it takes little to set tongues wagging."

"Not to mention the loose mouths of certain chroniclers," snapped Yggur. "Consider yourself on probation, chronicler. Were it not for Nadiril you would be chained to my dungeon wall, not *privileged* to be here as recorder."

"My dungeon wall, as it happens," said Mendark. "You will recall that we separated in Faranda each to undertake our particular purpose. And what have we found?"

"For my part, very little," said Yggur. "I sent trusty lieutenants to Alcifer. What did I find? Regarding the making of flutes, nothing. About the Mirror, nothing. Of Aachan gold, only this!"

Opening his fist, he let fall on the table a ring, too small to fit a man's hand. It rang out, a richer and more mellow tone than that made by ordinary gold. It was a luxurious golden-red, like Karan's hair.

"Are you sure it is Aachan gold?" asked Tallia.

"The color is quite characteristic, though I suppose that could be faked. But I put it to the test anyway. I am satisfied."

"I'm not!" cried Mendark. "Let Tensor verify it in front of us."

Tallia carried the ring down to Tensor. He accepted it with reluctance, but did not even look at it and handed it back at once. "It is," he said hoarsely. She brought it back.

"What do you know about it?" Llian asked Yggur, leaning forward eagerly.

"Not much, though I've had it for a thousand years. I found it in Alcifer just before Rulke was taken!"

That caused a sensation. Mendark leapt to his feet, his mouth hanging open. "You're trying to get at me! Well, it won't work."

Yggur leaned back in his chair, his hands clasping the back of his neck. Light from an overhead lamp fell on the long bones of his face. His eyes were closed but he was smiling.

"You needn't worry, Mendark," he said, in his deep, slow voice. It seemed that he relished the coming contest. "It's just a simple ring as anyone might have worn." He passed it around.

"What a beautiful thing," Karan said when it came to her. It was made of the finest golden wires, woven together into a flat braid of five strands. She slipped it onto her ring finger and held it up. It fitted rather well.

"Look at it carefully, Llian," said Yggur. "This ring was used in the betrayal of Rulke."

Llian pricked up his ears. What had Rulke said about that, in the Nightland? *I was betrayed, and the woman I was to pair with, an innocent, was destroyed.* Clearly there was more to the tale than *The Taking of Rulke* revealed.

"It's much too small for Rulke's finger," said Llian.

"It was a betrothal ring for his bride-to-be," said Yggur. "Seek out that story and you will have another Great Tale. One that has never been told, for it reflects an ugly light on us all."

"Shut up, Yggur," snarled Mendark.

Yggur smiled. "Your reputation will need all the polish you can give it, Mendark, after I've finished with you." He looked directly into Llian's eyes. "In that struggle, Llian, we all did evil in the name of good. To win the war against Rulke, to save our world from him, justified any crime. I would not have the Histories speak false about this matter."

Mendark's mouth had gone as hard as a steel trap, but he said no more. The relationship between Mendark and Yggur was changing. The defeat in Havissard had undermined Mendark, but Yggur was slowly consolidating his power after Katazza and the loss of Maigraith.

Mendark briefly spoke about his encounter with that unidentified woman in Havissard, though he glossed over how easily she had humiliated him. Nor did he tell how Tallia had rescued him from the brambles. He showed the book that the woman had dropped in her flight. "It must be important; why else would she have taken it? But I can't read it."

"What a strange script!" said Llian. "You say that Yalkara wrote this?"

"It would appear so, just before she left Santhenar. Can you read it?"

"I don't know. It . . ." Llian flipped the pages. "It's like a primitive version of the Charon script, which no one can read. And at the same time it has elements in common with the Faellem writing, which I can read haltingly. How can that be? The origins of the two are utterly different. It's also similar to the script engraved on the Mirror, though not the same."

The book was passed around the room but not even Nadiril could shed any light on it.

"What about Shand?" said Mendark, suddenly realizing that he was not there. *"Where is Shand?"*

"He's gone," said Nadiril. "He went back to Tullin this morning."

Mendark swore, but there was nothing to be done about it. "Well, Llian, this can be your next labor. Have a go at deciphering this script."

"You get ahead of yourself," said Yggur coldly. "First we must debate Llian's behavior."

Karan held her breath, thinking that Shand had informed on Llian, but Yggur continued, "After we've finished with Havissard, Mendark."

"Before you get onto Havissard you should know what Karan and I learned in Chanthed," said Llian.

"Yes, Shand told me that, but the meet needs to hear it from your own lips."

Llian told the story, beginning with Faelamor's behavior in Katazza that had first aroused his suspicions, then telling how the original sketches, that showed who had first gone into the burning tower, had been stolen, apparently by Faelamor.

"Oh, well done, chronicler!" said Yggur. "You may yet redeem yourself. You can confirm this, Karan?"

"In every particular," she replied.

"So, we have more enemies than we thought. We'd better come back to Faelamor. On with *your* tale, Mendark. What have you not told us about Havissard, apart from how you got in and back out again? Let's see what you found there. Bring out the gold!" Yggur leaned back with an expectant smile.

Mendark shivered. "How I got in is my own business," he said gracelessly. Then he took command of himself and bowed to Llian. "You have indeed done well, but unfortunately too late. The gold was in Havissard but I was beaten to it by an hour. When I recovered the woman was gone and the place where the gold had been was empty." He told that story, save for parts that showed him in a bad light.

"A convenient tale!" said Yggur. "Don't be insulted, but of course you can prove it?"

"Of course I can't prove it! But if you care to make the journey you can check it yourself."

"Who was the woman? That's the important question."

"We can only guess. My guess is Faelamor."

"Very likely. Well, our plans are scuppered," he said to the meeting, "if Mendark is telling the truth. We can't discount the possibility that he's hidden away the gold for himself."

"We can't," Nadiril agreed. "Though I am inclined to believe him."

Mendark bowed ironically. "But you two are doing Rulke's work for him," Nadiril said. "So let's get on."

"How could Faelamor get to Havissard so quickly?" asked Malien, who had hitherto said nothing. "And how did she get in?"

"To both, the same answer. She made a gate."

"And she was not alone!"

"I think not."

"Hmmn," said Yggur, squinting at a calendar through a magnifying glass. "Faelamor was seen in the camp in Bannador just before,"—his voice cracked—"Maigraith disappeared, and that was only weeks before you encountered her in Havissard. This supports the gate theory. Well, later on we can address ourselves to the question of what she will do with it and where to find her. I think I might take charge of that myself.

"Now we come to the matter of Llian," Yggur continued. "I found him going through the Council archives. What were you really doing there, Llian?"

"I was looking for papers about Kandor."

"Liar! You were found in the secret archives. The vault!"

Llian hesitated.

"Well?" said Yggur. "Your life may depend on how you answer."

"The door was open," Llian said weakly. "All the doors were, even the vault."

"Entrapment!" said Nadiril. "Really, Yggur! This rather poisons your case, not to mention your own credibility."

"I don't know the layout of the archives," Llian continued. "I was looking for the right place when you found me." He reminded them of his suspicions about the death of the crippled girl, and told of Kandor's letter that he had found at the citadel a year ago.

"Why did you not tell me this at the time?" Mendark shouted, banging his fist on the table. A vase of wine toppled, sending a yellow flood everywhere. Papers were rescued hastily. "Show me the letter."

"I destroyed it in Katazza," said Malien. "I thought that box was best left unopened."

"But Faelamor has opened it now. We need to know what the letter said."

"I have a copy," Llian said. "I found it in Kandor's bedroom. As well as a later one to Yalkara."

Karan produced the letters that she had safeguarded all this time and they were passed across the table. Yggur scanned them and tossed them aside.

"A distraction! Let's get back to Mendark. I don't believe—"

Mendark read the letters and nearly tore his hair out. "Why did you not show me this before, Llian? If I had known Kandor's suspicions of Rulke I would have gone straight to Havissard. I could have been there weeks before Faelamor. *I would have the gold!*"

He was consumed by bitterness at the disasters in Havissard and the failure of all his hopes. Yggur's accusations of treachery were unbearable.

Then Yggur stood up and his face was as still as a mask. "I see another possibility," he declared grimly. "Look at the evidence—documents that Llian mysteriously comes across but only tells us about when we force it out of him; conversations that he has with our enemies; things that no one else has ever remarked upon. It's very plausible, as we would expect from such a talesmith. But is it *true*? Would *you* trust someone who had spent days alone with Rulke and Faelamor?"

Mendark tugged his beard anxiously, looking to Nadiril and Malien. "And Faelamor arrived at Havissard looking for the gold at exactly the same time as I did. An unlikely coincidence."

"No coincidence at all," Yggur said coldly. "Llian knew what you were after. We know that he had dealings with Rulke, and Tensor and Faelamor in Katazza. This is the last straw. *I accuse! I say he betrayed us to Faelamor!*"

Llian was speechless with fear. Karan jumped to her feet. "This is outrageous," she shouted. "We didn't see Faelamor in all the months between Katazza and Chanthed."

"She was here only days ago," cried Yggur. "Right here, spying on us at our first meet."

"What?" cried Mendark.

"Indeed," said Yggur, "She and Llian could be speaking together right now, as Rulke did to him in Tullin."

Karan went white. "Who told you that?" she asked softly, thinking that Shand had gone back on his word.

"I did," said Nadiril.

"Deny it if you dare!" Yggur raged.

Karan was silent. "Do you deny it?" Mendark asked her.

"I cannot, but—"

Mendark held up his hand. "Then I must take Yggur's accusation seriously, for all that I know his true purpose—to distract us from his own villainy."

"If you so mistrust Llian, why did you admit him to your councils?" Nadiril pointed out. "And if you do not, where is the profit in this charade? I am not convinced. I see Llian as a pawn between the two of you: each twisting everything to your own designs."

"Llian was in the archives to spy for his master," raged Yggur. "Remember the treachery of Hennia the Zain."

"You call it treachery, when she betrayed us to *you*?" cried Mendark.

"I will not be swayed," swore Yggur.

The interrogation went on for hours, until Llian was a white-faced wreck and the whole room wanted it to end. But Yggur would not allow it. "And there is the business in Tullin. It seems he has betrayed us, and Faelamor, to Rulke as well. The scope of his treachery is truly breathtaking. Once a traitor . . ."

Karan was called upon to tell what had happened that night.

"You cannot force me to give evidence against Llian," she said.

"We can," said Nadiril, "though we would prefer not to."

Llian jumped up. "Tell it, Karan! Bring it all out! Then they'll see that I've done nothing wrong."

He was fatally in error. After Karan told of that night in Tullin, the meet was as shocked as Shand had been. Yggur paled; his cheek began to twitch uncontrollably.

"I was right the first time! We should have finished him back there in the Dry Sea."

"Why is he doing this?" Karan whispered urgently to Malien, who was beside her. "I don't understand."

She whispered back, "Yggur was possessed by Rulke once. He's terrified that Rulke will do it again, through Llian."

"No!" cried Llian, stumbling toward Yggur with his arms outstretched. "Examine me yourself, you'll see that it's all a terrible mistake."

Yggur recoiled in terror. "Back, traitor!" he cried. "Guards, take this man."

A guard stood on either side of the doorway, hard-bitten soldiers each the size of Osseion. The nearest sprang forward and took Llian by the collar. Llian flung himself backwards, the shirt tore and he landed flat on his back.

"What shall we do with him, lord?"

"Put him down," Yggur screamed. "Do it here, where I can see it done!"

The guard put his foot on Llian's neck and drew his sword.

Before anyone else could twitch a finger, Karan hurled a flagon of wine unerringly at the guard. It smashed against his ear. He fell backwards over a bench. She knocked the bottom out of another flagon and darted between the tables, holding out the jagged end.

The second guard drew his weapon. Karan feinted at him with her flagon. He raised the sword to hack off her arm. Nadiril hobbled between them. "Put down your weapons," he roared.

The guard hesitated, looking to his master. "Give the order, Yggur!" Nadiril rasped.

"Go back to your posts," Yggur said, and the guard withdrew, though he did not sheathe his sword.

Nadiril made a quiet hand-movement in Mendark's direction.

The Magister roused. "The threads are tangled, and we are too agitated to sort them out. Take him to my apartments where he can do no harm *nor come to any.*"

"Over my mutilated corpse!" Yggur shouted. "Take him to my cells. The lowest ones."

A squad of Whelm marched in, led by Vartila. They gripped Llian by the arms and led him out.

"No!" cried Karan, running after them, brandishing her bottle. She was remembering how Llian had tried to defend her at the Conclave, when the guards came to take her away. A burly guard took her from behind and disarmed her.

"No need for your guards to assume the whole burden, Yggur," Mendark said smoothly. "Mine will do duty by their side."

He clapped. "Osseion, Torgsted, guard this fellow, turn and turn about. See that no harm comes to him." They followed the others out.

Yggur was furious, but without bloody battle there was little he could do about it. The Council broke up in disarray, its plans seeming no further advanced than when they were conceived months before at the base of Katazza.

41

The Beggar's Curse

The guards hurried Llian through the dark, two Whelm gripping his elbow in a paralyzing hold. They need not have worried. Numb inside, Llian could not even think of escaping.

Osseion came up beside him. "I'm sorry, Llian," he rumbled.

"Where are they taking me?" Llian asked faintly.

"To the citadel dungeons."

Llian fell silent. The guards tramped on either side, their steps echoing off the walls. They clattered down stair after stair, along corridor after corridor, past the cells where Thyllan had incarcerated Karan last winter, then deeper still into a damp basement with a low roof held up by massive columns. The walls were blotched brown by seeping water, and here and there crystalline efflorescences grew out of roof or wall. They passed many a dank and dismal cell, most occupied. Dirty faces peered out of gratings as they passed. Their stench hung in the air like mist.

"What a terrible place," said Llian. "Am I going to be put in one of *these*?"

Osseion opened his mouth then shut it again. Never had duty been more onerous. One of the Whelm spoke from behind him.

"These cells are for ordinary criminals. You go to the dungeons reserved for the blackest traitors, chronicler."

They splashed through slippery puddles, then headed down another stair covered in trickling water to a low-roofed level that was completely unlit. Osseion's big boots thudded against the stone, echoing off the hard walls. The noise woke one of the inhabitants. A scream of despair issued from some subterranean crypt.

"Help me! Let me out! Help me! Let me out!"

The cries came from a grating in the floor, rusty iron bars bolted down over a square hole about the width of his shoulders. Llian shivered. They passed another hole, equally dark and horrible, from which came a frightful stink as if someone had been forgotten and died down there. At the pit after that the leading Whelm stopped. Vartila opened the brass padlock—the only thing down here that was not decayed and rotting—with a long key. Another Whelm appeared with a ladder.

The grating crashed open, the black pit yawned, the ladder was banged in. Llian stared at Osseion, almost vomiting in despair.

"Best go down, Llian," said Osseion, with clenched jaw.

Llian got on the ladder and went hand over hand down into the dark. It stank of mold, damp and old human waste.

"Get off," the Whelm shouted. Llian slipped on the slimy floor and fell to his knees.

His tormentor stuck his head down the hole, holding the lantern in so that, briefly, Llian had the opportunity to inspect his surroundings. The cell was quite large and completely empty. "Better stay on your knees, if you hope to get out again."

The ladder was drawn up. The grating was slammed

closed. The light disappeared. Llian was left alone with only the screams for company.

The dungeon contained nothing; no bed, no chair, not even a toilet bucket. Just stone walls two spans high, oozing damp, and a drain in one corner to stop it filling up with seepage and his own waste. It stank as if it had been used as a privy for a thousand years, and it had.

It was as dark as tar now. Not even the grating above was visible. Llian paced across the cell, and back again. Four paces; four the other way too. He felt the walls, every ell of them, but of course there was no possibility of escape. Walls and floor were stone in massive blocks. The drain was too small for any human to crawl through.

In his time Llian had told many tales of prisoners held in dungeons, but none of them prepared him for the hideous discomfort and misery he experienced there. It was impossible not to dwell on stories of infected rat bites, of prisoners walking on festering stumps because their feet had rotted off, of madness and torment and death. It was evident that Yggur intended to break him as quickly as possible.

After some hours a dim light appeared above.

"Water, water!" Llian shouted.

The light moved slowly down to his grating. "Dinnertime," said a Whelm voice.

Llian was seized by violent impulses. As soon as the fellow came down the ladder he would smash him in the face and swarm up it; he would do anything, he would kill to get out of here. He stared up at the shadow.

A deluge of cold slops struck him in the face. Llian fell down, clawing the muck out of his eyes. A bone cracked him on the back of the head. He cleared his eyes as well as he could, but the stuff had coated him from head to toe, clotted in his hair and ran down his back. He was saturated in the greasy, half-rotten muck.

"What am I supposed to do, eat it off the floor?" he screamed.

His tormentor laughed.

"Please give me some water," Llian pleaded.

"Lick it off the wall," the Whelm shouted back, then the light moved away again.

His further cries were not answered. Absolute darkness replaced the light. Eventually Llian became so thirsty that he did lick the limy water off the wall; so hungry that he scraped slop off the floor and tried to eat it. It was revolting. He choked it back up into the drain. Llian lay down on the wet floor and vainly attempted to sleep.

A long time later he woke to find himself crawling—his matted hair was alive with dining cockroaches. His body crawled with fleas and lice, biting him everywhere, while something rasped at his ear, emitting little squeaks of pleasure. He smacked it away, sending it skittering across the floor. It was a scrawny, flea-ridden rat, and it soon came back.

After an agonizingly long time, Llian realized the futility of trying to shoo the pests away. He lay down, allowing them their way with him. The dining roaches made strange crackling sounds that traveled down into his skull. The lice and fleas made no sound while they ate, but he felt the pinpricks all over.

Sometime later he was woken by a pulpy crunching in one ear. The rat was perched on his shoulder, snatching cockroaches out of his hair. Every darting crunch splattered his ear. His degradation was complete.

If only Karan would come. Surely she must appear. But the miserable minutes stretched out to unbearable hours, and those to days that were nightmares of discomfort punctuated only by the daily deluge of slops from above. The Whelm's aim was unerring; he got Llian every time. But Karan did not appear. Once she would have moved the earth for him but now she no longer cared. She had abandoned him. He made his heart as hard and cold as the walls of his prison. She meant nothing to him anymore.

Karan's dream-link told her only that Llian was in misery. She had been working day and night to get him freed, but her efforts were to no avail. Though she spent the entire three gold tells on bribes, a fortune so staggering that it made her sick to think of it, no one could or would, or dared, do anything for her. Finally, swallowing her pride, she begged to see Mendark. He looked more shrunken and raptor-like than before. He was polite, offering food and wine, but inflexible. She gained the distinct impression that he was afraid of Yggur now.

Malien could do nothing either. The Aachim were without influence here in Thurkad. "There's only one person can help you," she said, "and that's Yggur. But if you do go to him, be very careful."

Karan was afraid—afraid for herself, but there was nothing else to do. The day after that she waited on Yggur. She spent all day and all evening sitting in a freezing room while dozens of others were admitted. Finally, late that night, she was escorted in.

Yggur looked down at her. "I don't believe Llian and I don't trust him. I'm never going to let him go," he said.

"May I at least see him?" she whispered, despairing.

"No," said Yggur. "Now get out or I'll have you too. I haven't forgotten your part in this!"

She hung around the gates of the citadel, but there were dozens of guards, very alert and watching for her. After being warned off for the second time in as many hours she fled. There was only one chance left. She grabbed a few hours' restless sleep then went to Nadiril's villa. A servant admitted her at once. Nadiril was sitting by the fire with Lilis, who was reading verse to him from a scroll. Jevi was down at the waterfront, working on Pender's boat. Lilis finished her recitation. Nadiril corrected minor errors in her pronunciation, her rhythm and her accent, told her to read it again by herself and turned to Karan.

"You've come about Llian."

"These charges are monstrous lies. How could he have had any dealings with Faelamor? It's absurd."

"Indeed it is, but plausible, and Mendark and Yggur are so

afraid of each other that they both believe the absurdity. How is Llian?"

"I don't know; Yggur won't let me see him."

"I'm sure he's being treated well."

"I'm not; I can sense how unhappy he is. Please, can't you use your influence?"

"Poor Llian," said Lilis, laying her scroll aside. "He was so kind to me. You must be able to help."

Nadiril put up his hand and Karan helped him to his feet. "Let's pay him a visit."

There was utter consternation when Nadiril appeared at an obscure basement gate of the citadel with Karan and Lilis, asking to see Llian. He could not be refused, of course, but a Whelm sentry raced off in one direction, and one of Mendark's guard in another.

"Wait here, if you please," said the other guard.

Nadiril pushed him to one side. "Take me to Llian's cell at once," he said in an icy rasp.

"He's not in the cells," said the guard. "He's been put in the lower dungeons."

Nadiril went as rigid as a poker. He marched past the guard, a vast man who could have snapped him like a twig, but the fellow stepped smartly out of the way.

"You can't—" said the other guard, a Whelm.

"Be damned," Nadiril roared. "Out of my way!"

Karan was amazed. She followed beside Nadiril, almost running to keep up with his long strides. Suddenly he did not seem to be frail at all. They went down and down, into a stinking basement. The guard ran beside them.

"Help me! Let me out! Help me! Let me out!" came the hopeless cry from the first cell. Nadiril looked disgusted; Karan was profoundly shocked. Lilis wept.

Just as they reached the third grating Mendark appeared with a troop of half a dozen. Footsteps clattered behind them and from the other direction Yggur's soldiers came running, a squad of twenty led by two Whelm. They stopped just behind Nadiril with their spears at the ready. Yggur limped up behind them.

"What goes here?" he demanded of Mendark.

"I would ask the same of you," Mendark replied.

"I wish to see the condition of the prisoner," Nadiril said in a voice like a breeze stirring wheat husks. "Open it!"

"He stays!"

"Open it!"

Yggur gestured, one of the Whelm unfastened the lock; another brought the ladder. Karan snatched a lantern out of the guard's hand and literally ran down the ladder.

"Oh, Llian," she cried when she saw him, his hair and clothes saturated with rotten sludge. He was shivering. She put out her arms but he would not come.

Llian was hideously mortified that she should see him so foul and degraded. He had thought himself into a state where it was just him against the world.

"Don't touch me," he whispered.

"Llian," she cried, standing like a statue with outstretched arms.

A cockroach crawled out of his hair, waving its feelers in the air. "It's too late," he said to the wall. "You should have come a long time ago. I don't want you now."

"I couldn't. Yggur wouldn't let me in."

From above Yggur's harsh voice came down. "Come out, Karan, *or remain*!"

"Damn you," she screamed, shaking her fist at him. "I will remain."

Llian spun around. Each torment was worse than the one before. To have Karan sharing his degradation would be worst of all. He had to get rid of her. "Go away. I don't want you and I don't need you." Putting his hands on her shoulders, he thrust her toward the ladder.

"You have until the count of three," cried Yggur.

Tears sprang to her eyes. "Llian, what has become of us?" she wailed, then climbed up without looking back. At the top she pushed past Yggur, knocking him backwards with her shoulder. "I'll see that you regret this."

Yggur laughed. "You can't even pay your taxes. You'll be on the street 'ere spring."

Mendark said nothing, but he watched Yggur and Nadiril suspiciously, as if they were in league together.

"I've seen enough," said Nadiril. He took Karan's elbow. "Are you satisfied now?"

"Satisfied?" she whispered.

"Come! We can do nothing here." He bowed to Mendark and to Yggur, took Lilis's hand in his other hand, and went slowly back the way they had come.

Outside, Karan sat down in the gutter with her head in her hands. Wet flakes of snow settled in her hair. "This is a nightmare. I don't know where to turn."

Lilis sat down beside her. "Come and stay with us. Nadiril will help you, won't you, Nadiril?"

He was still as a tree, deep in thought. "What? Yes, of course. Come to my villa. It is quite comfortable, by Thurkad standards. I'll send someone for your things, and Llian's too. We must talk."

A good many hours and one deluge of slops later, Llian was dozing fitfully on the floor when he was woken by the grating above him being opened. A light appeared. Silhouetted in the opening was a bony outline that he recognized as Vartila. A rope ladder was flung down. He climbed it awkwardly, not knowing what to expect. At the top, two Whelm hauled him out, exclaiming disgustedly at his condition and his stink. Osseion and Torgsted lay on the floor, as still as sleep.

"Where are you taking me?" he asked plaintively.

They laughed. "To your fate, chronicler!"

The laughter had an ugly ring to it. Llian knew real terror now. As far back as the Dry Sea Yggur had wanted him killed, to get rid of the threat that he saw in him. The guards led him along corridors that he was unfamiliar with, then out the back of the citadel toward a place with high walls that he knew to be the execution yard.

"No!" he cried, struggling hopelessly with his shackles.

The Whelm laughed mirthlessly and jerked at his chains.

42

THE EAR

The miserable gray light told Llian that it was not long after dawn. It showed the execution yard, a narrow and cramped space forty or fifty paces long but only ten wide. It was surrounded by walls so high that the sun never reached the bottom, and the walls and flagstones were covered in oozing moss. There were sets of manacles all along the long walls, a viewing platform at one end and an execution platform, a dais of gray stained stone, at the other.

A Whelm whose name Llian did not know thrust him sprawling into the yard. He looked around at the dreadful place, the manacles, the stained rock.

"Look up," the Whelm chuckled.

Llian did so and wished he hadn't. The top of the wall bore a single row of gibbets which went all the way around save for the space directly above the viewing platform. Mechanically he counted his way along the row. There were twenty-six gibbets, all but one with an occupant, and some of the bodies had been there so long that he doubled over, retching bile.

"One to go, eh!" the fellow said. "That'll be you in an hour. Better finish your tale quick, chronicler."

Llian groaned. He was utterly helpless. He swung around, aimed a kick at his tormentor and fell over. The Whelm laughed again, a sound like lead pellets falling through an hourglass.

"Dangerous prisoner," he said, pushed Llian backwards against the wall and snapped the manacles over his wrists. "Wait here," he leered over his shoulder. "Won't be long now." Then he went out, crashing the gate of the yard behind him.

Wait here! The humor was so pathetic that it brought tears to his eyes. He wasn't going anywhere ever again. Lucky that old Wistan had talked him into putting his tale down. I wonder if it will be called Llian's Tale when I am gone. Hardly likely! The *Tale of the Mirror*, that's what it should be called, but I suppose someone else will take the credit for it now. I wonder what my friends will make of it? I wonder what Karan will think of it. But the thought of her was unbearable.

Llian struggled against his manacles but only succeeded in chafing the skin off his wrists. It began to rain, then the rain turned to sleet, a normal Thurkad winter's day. More than once he heard shouting in the streets outside, as if a riot was going on. Nothing unusual about that either, in Thurkad. No one came for him. He was freezing. He had only the twenty-five corpses for company, and a crow that perched on the cranium of one of them, prising at an eyesocket. But it found nothing—those morsels were always the first to go. Llian put his hands over his eyes to block out the sight; it would be pecking at his, tomorrow.

The day wore on and before the end of it he was trembling from hunger, for the food in his dungeon had been so disgusting that he had eaten nothing for days.

In the afternoon the wind picked up. The corpses began to

dance, to sway and twirl and flop their limbs back and forth. The puppet dance: it would be him tonight. And if his friends could not, or would not, pay the cost of the rope that had hanged him he would dangle there till the flesh was picked away and the bones fell down.

The corpses were now swinging their limbs about most animatedly, and almost as if his thought had been heard one fell, the body and the head separately, thudding on the flags not far away. The horrid sight made him weep for whatever poor fool had incurred Yggur's ire. He wept for himself too.

Not long after that there came a great commotion from the street. Llian could hear people shouting and running, but the sounds were muffled by the high walls and he could not make out what was happening.

The day dragged on, the sun finally setting without his ever seeing it. Night fell in the execution yard, and such a throng of ghosts came out that they had to jostle and elbow each other out of the way so that they could stare at him. They seemed to find Llian a very singular fellow, but they felt no compassion for him. That is not an emotion ghosts are capable of feeling.

They were a bitter lot, these gaunt specters—not a one had been executed for a proper crime, as far as he could tell. Llian begged and pleaded with them for aid but their ghostly hands could not even catch a snowflake, much less undo these manacles thick as anchor chains.

Well after dark, Llian became aware that the sky was lit in several places, buildings burning. A cluster of ghosts drifted up to the top of the wall, laughing and pointing, but they did not share with him what they saw.

Outside all was quiet now. He had grown tired of their constant bickering and whining. The specters recollected their own miserable lives and deaths over and over, but the agonies of their companions were too tedious to listen to.

"Go away!" he screamed, and that sent a stir through them like a breeze through washing. Eventually they tired of him and did go, and then Llian was sorry. The ghosts were much better company than the corpses.

"What can I do?" wailed Karan. Llian's agony was bouncing back and forth inside her head; she couldn't shut it out. Maintaining the link-monitor over him for so long was exhausting as well as emotionally draining.

Nadiril blew the steam off his cup. "Yggur will be rid of him as soon as he gets the chance."

"How could anyone be afraid of Llian?" said Lilis.

Nadiril strung his chain of logic together. "Remember that Yggur was once possessed by Rulke, who left a hold there that was only removed by Mendark in Katazza. If Rulke has possessed Llian in the same way, which I doubt, he might be able to cross from him to Yggur. The only way for Yggur to protect himself is to kill Llian."

"Isn't there anything you can do?" Karan cried.

"I don't know. I am old, and not strong."

"Do you have . . . *Powers?*" asked Lilis.

Nadiril chuckled. "I do, but none so great that you need whisper about them in so melodramatic a way. I am no necromanter like Mendark and Yggur. We are weak vessels alike, myself and Karan and you."

"But you are cleverer than any of them," said Lilis stoutly, sitting by Jevi's side near the fire. "And Jevi will help us, won't you?" She looked up at him.

"Of course," he said, pulling her close.

"I would not put him in that sort of danger so soon after you got him back," said Nadiril.

"Then you can't get Llian out!" Karan said hopelessly.

"No, *I* can't."

"Can you get me back in there secretly?"

"Possibly, but you can't get him out either. He's guarded by professionals."

Karan sank into black despair.

"But you can do *something*, can't you?" piped Lilis, who

knew Nadiril's ways by now, and his habit of saying no more than was asked of him.

"I left an *ear* on the wall by Llian's cell," he said in tones that were almost apologetic.

"An ear?" said Karan. "What are you talking about?"

"A device that listens for me. It will tell me if anything happens down there. See, here is another." He took a small piece of folded leather out of his pouch. It was like a tiny donkey's ear, complete with hair.

Lilis was fascinated. "And this tells you what the other ear hears?" She put it to her own ear. "I can't hear anything."

Karan sat up. Nadiril laughed. "Do ears speak now? Of course not. For that you need a *mouth*, with lips and tongue." He brought another leathery object out of his pouch, this one like a miniature donkey's muzzle, and set it down on the table.

Lilis bent her own ear to it. "I still can't hear anything," she said.

"That's because no one's making any noise down there."

Karan and Lilis stared at the mouth but it remained obstinately silent. A servant came in with lunch, which they fell upon, for it was well into the afternoon and they had gone out without breakfast. It was simple fare, bowls of soup thick with vegetables, brown bread and cheese to follow. After that they were sitting by the fire, sipping bowls of custard-yellow mil, when a faint donkey voice brayed behind them.

"Help me! Let me out! Help me! Let me out!"

Karan leapt up, spilling mil all down her trousers. The mouth was speaking, though the donkey lips did not move. Underneath that she heard the flapping tread of a pair of Whelm.

Nadiril creaked to his feet. Lilis stared at the mouth in wonder. From it came a tinny bang that must have been the grating crashing open. "Come up!" said a squeaky voice, half-donkey, half-Vartila.

"Look at him," said another Whelm. "What a disgusting wretch! He stinks."

"Where are you taking me?" came Llian's plaintive voice.

Footsteps tramped away down the corridor. "Help me! Let me out! Help me! Let me out!" wailed the mouth, then it spoke no more.

"Where have they gone?" cried Karan.

"I don't know," Nadiril said. "Will you get my cloak, Lilis?" Lilis came running back with it. "Wait here," he said to Karan.

"I've got to come," said Karan.

"Better that you don't. I've many reasons to be in the citadel, but if you're with me Yggur will be suspicious, and may think we know something. Wait here. Be ready to leave Thurkad on the instant. Lilis, come with me; you can be my errand girl. You can come too, Jevi."

They went out. Karan cleaned the mil off her trousers, packed her bag and put it beside Llian's, and sat back down again, waiting and dreading the news.

It was not far from Nadiril's house to the citadel. They went to the front entrance. "Don't say anything while we are in the citadel," he said. "And especially don't mention the ear."

"I won't," said Lilis, clutching Jevi's hand and drawing close, away from the enormous guards. "Can you get poor Llian free?"

"I don't know, child," Nadiril said heavily. "I've got to find him first."

He went up to Mendark's offices, unhindered at any stage. He told Mendark what he had learned, but not how.

"What?" Mendark shouted. He sprang out of his chair, which toppled over backwards. "Llian taken? Osseion and Torgsted slain?"

"Perhaps not slain, but certainly overcome."

"Yggur goes too far!" he raged, stalking back and forth in agitation.

"He lives every day in deadly fear of Rulke," said Nadiril.

"What can I do? I need Llian. Yggur has an army—I've but a handful of guards."

"Make a diversion, one that will occupy all his time, while I find Llian."

"What?" Mendark muttered, pacing up and down. "Ah, I have it! Off you go; leave it to me."

As soon as Nadiril was gone Mendark took out the black opal spheroid and the seven-piece puzzle ring that he had used to magic his way into Havissard. He touched the opal to life, and his fingers writhed with the puzzle ring while he sat deep in thought.

Outside the citadel Nadiril looked up at the window where he knew Mendark's apartments to be. Though the blinds were drawn he saw the room suddenly lit up with rainbow lights. Then it became dark again. He smiled and went to do his own work.

Within minutes flames leapt up from the roof of Yggur's headquarters, from the barracks of the First Army, and even from a corner of the citadel itself. This was followed by mysterious fires in half a dozen strategic places. Rumors swept through Thurkad that the Ghâshâd were invading. People rioted in the streets and not all of Yggur's soldiers could contain them.

Before dawn of the following day the bolts on the door of the execution yard rattled. This time it was Vartila, alone. At least, the figure had the semblance of Vartila, though it seemed taller and moved more slowly. Llian had no fear left; he stared at her numbly as she unsnapped the manacles and picked him up after he fell down.

"Are *you* come to hang me?" he croaked.

Vartila gave Llian her shoulder. "No!" she said, and in the lamplight her face was harder than ever.

"Then who . . ."

She smiled, or attempted to, though the sight was almost as fearsome as her frown. "You are freed. I am taking you to Karan at the gates of the city."

"Reprieved?" cried Llian. "Is this some ghastly joke?"

"No joke! It took me a long time to find you," she said

somberly. "I am sorry. Put on these robes and pull the hood down. No one must see you."

Nothing more was said between them. They picked their way through city streets full of panicked people and soldiers vainly trying to restore order. But every soldier knew Vartila's face and no one checked her. Llian did not even wonder what had happened. By the time they reached the west gate his fear had turned to an all-consuming rage, greater than he had ever felt before.

Karan lay miserably by the fire, where she had eventually dozed off in the early hours. Soon after that she was woken again. Someone was shaking her by the shoulder.

"Karan, wake up," said Lilis. "Are you ready?"

"Yes. Is Llian free?"

"I don't know. I'm to take you to the west gate. There's rioting; half of Thurkad is on fire, and people say it's the Ghâshâd come back. We must be very careful."

Karan, Lilis and Jevi went out into the unpleasant night. Hateful place! Karan thought, longing for Gothryme. Lilis led them to the gate unscathed, where they waited for an hour in sleet and wind. At dawn a tall figure loomed out of the darkness. It was cloaked and hooded, as was the smaller figure behind, but the rust in the voice gave Nadiril away.

"Take him and go quickly," he said in an almost perfect imitation of Vartila's harsh voice. He pushed the smaller figure forward. It was Llian.

"How did you get free?" Karan asked gently.

Llian was in such a state that he could not speak at all.

"What will Yggur do now?" asked Karan of the Vartilafigure, who dissolved into Nadiril.

"After Mendark's diversions last night Yggur has his own troubles. There are horses waiting outside. Go quickly."

Karan was already worrying about that. The escape would have to be paid for. But that did not matter now. Llian was free! She thanked Nadiril and the big-eyed Lilis, and they hurried away.

* * *

Llian had been so traumatized by Thurkad that he had retreated right into himself. On the rare occasions that he came out, the face that he turned to the world was a cold rage against everyone and everything. Karan tried many times to get the true story out of him, but he was incapable of responding.

"No one trusts me, so why should I give a damn about anyone else?"

"If it wasn't for me and Nadiril, you'd be dead!" she snapped.

"I'd be better off dead."

Karan did not know what to do. Constrained from pleading her case any further, she took refuge in silence. No matter how she tried, she could not dismiss one niggle from her mind. Perhaps Rulke *was* his master, or Faelamor, ridiculous though that was. Or maybe both.

Llian could sense this ambivalence in her, and while it was there he could not take the least step toward her. The divide between them yawned as wide as ever.

After days of miserable slush-riding, constantly looking over their shoulders, they arrived back in Gothryme. Nothing had been resolved. Nothing was any further advanced than it had been the previous summer. Nothing changed, but the rumors from Carcharon were stronger than ever. The Ghâshâd had been seen many times, bearing huge loads down from Shazmak. They were preparing something there, but what?

43

POSSESSION

At Gothryme Karan found that the Aachim had made great progress. Three whole rooms were finished and several more were well on the way.

"I would like a quiet place to work, if it can be managed," Llian said, when they arrived. He gave her that blank look that broke her heart, as if she meant no more to him than a plaster statue.

She nodded as if he was of no consequence to her either, and though they were still short of space she set him up in two tiny rooms against the old keep. They were in the wing that had been greatly damaged, the only other occupied room being Karan's sitting room. The place was quiet apart from hammering from the far end, for most of the daily life of the manor took place in the other wing or the keep itself.

Llian's rooms were paneled in wood that time and the smoke of a thousand years had stained the color of coffee. The outer one, his bedroom, had a tiny window, but the study was thick-walled, cold and windowless. It suited his dark mood and he sat there, brooding or writing near a tiny fire.

Karan came in to check on him once or twice a day, or bring him food, for he would not eat in the refectory with anyone else. Whenever she did, she found him sitting in front of the fireplace, though often the fire had gone out. He took no part in the life of Gothryme, and after a few days the manor went about its business as if he was not there. His moody presence cast a small shadow, but the next few weeks were a peaceful time for everyone except Karan.

Every time she closed her eyes she saw Llian, crouched in his freezing room, looking thinner and more tormented. He worked like a man possessed, and perhaps he was. Day and night he wrote, and paced, and wrote still more. He had become an insoluble problem: one so painful that it was no longer bearable. The monitor she'd put over him in Thurkad was wearing her out, physically and emotionally. Eventually she did the only thing she could—she blocked him out and closed down the link completely.

Llian lay in his icy bed, sleeping fitfully only to rouse to cold and misery. Sometime after the middle of the night he woke, or thought he did, to a familiar voice in his head, just a faint little whisper.

Ho, chronicler! It's good to speak to you again. Get ready. Soon I will call you to—

Llian sat up abruptly, panting, but the voice was gone, cut off in mid-sentence. His trembling hands eventually lit the candle beside the bed, but the room was as empty as ever.

He could not sleep now. Llian got out his notes and went on with the tale, though it was many hours before he could concentrate on his work. Memories of Rulke kept coming back.

Llian hid himself away, afraid that Karan would read the nightmares in his eyes and judge him again, but Karan was preoccupied with her own affairs. He did not see her at all that day.

Two nights later Rulke was back.

Chronicler—he was cut off, then reappeared so strongly that Llian could almost see his face in the darkness.

Chronicler, prepare yourself. Get back the link with Karan and bring her to me.

"I won't come," Llian said aloud. "And neither will she."

Yes, you will—

Again the voice vanished. Llian's teeth began to chatter. He could not bear the dark, nor the thought that Rulke would come back. He wanted Karan more than ever but was sure any approach would arouse her mistrust. He huddled beside the dead coals in the fireplace, not daring to approach her now. In a sudden, heart-stopping realization, Llian understood how desperately Rulke needed Karan. Ever since she'd escaped the Nightland, Rulke had been using Llian to get her back.

A fortnight had gone by since their return from Thurkad. Karan knocked on Llian's door but he did not answer. It was dawn. She eased the door open and found him already at his desk. Last night's dinner sat untouched on the table. He was so thin that even his broad hands looked bony, and he had a driven look that she never wanted to see again.

She stood there, watching and remembering, then Llian glanced up at her with a look of absolute desperation. Her innards began to dissolve. The moment was poised. She was about to throw out her arms to him when he swept his papers together with one arm, stood up and shut the door in her face. What had been in her heart seeped down and congealed into a cold hard lump in her belly. She went back to her sitting room. There was nothing she could do.

A few days later Karan was up on the roof, helping to replace some slates that had blown off in the previous night's storm, when she saw two people riding up the path through the snow. She felt a black cloud of foreboding settle over her. She had known all along that Llian's getaway was too good to be true; that Yggur neither forgave nor forgot and sooner or later it must be paid for. Karan wiped dusty fingers on her overalls and clambered across to the ladder, but discovered that the riders were Mendark and Tallia. Physically Mendark looked better than he had in Thurkad, though there was still a predatory glint in his eye.

"We came to find out what's going on in Carcharon," Mendark said.

"Actually, *he* did," said Tallia. "I came as I promised I would, so that you could show me your country."

"Llian is here," Karan said nervously. She was no longer sure what Mendark's attitude to Llian was.

"I know!" Mendark smiled a shark-toothed smile. "Forget it! That was all a misunderstanding of Yggur's making."

A misunderstanding! Karan was not convinced by his heartiness, and it made her smolder that he could dismiss Llian's abuse so casually. But Mendark *was* Magister, and she an almost-bankrupt nobody, so she smiled, led them in to the fire and plied them with food and hot drinks. Mendark showed no further interest in Llian and left at dawn to see Carcharon for himself.

"What's going on?" she asked Tallia as soon as he was gone. "I've been expecting Yggur every day."

"He's got more urgent things to worry about at the moment—wars and rebellions in the south. He's withdrawn most of his troops from Bannador in the last week. Llian's not such a problem this far away."

Karan was delighted to see Tallia, for as her relationship with Llian waned, her friendship with Tallia had grown, built on the foundations that they had set down in Faranda. Tallia was ever kind, ever cheerful, ever dependable. The two had spent much time together in Thurkad.

It remained overcast though the weather was mild. They spent most of the short days outside, riding to Karan's favorite places: a crystal waterfall midway along the cliff, now frozen into a series of icy steps for a giant; a perpetually warm spring issuing from a cavern at the other end; a glade set among the leafless willows on the Ryme. Or they worked on Karan's garden plans, pacing out beds and hammering stakes into the hard soil in readiness for the spring.

Then the weather turned bleak, windy and snowy under an impenetrable overcast that seemed to have been there forever. They had seen neither the sun nor the stars in over a month.

There were eyes in the night. Piercing eyes like the hot glow of the fire. And as the dark hours passed they looked up more frequently, from that inky space where their owner worked invisibly.

Again Llian leapt up in bed, gasping for air. He thought he'd heard someone say *Ahhhh!*, an exhalation of relief right in his ear. Feeling around for his flint-striker, his shaking hand knocked it off the table. After he found it he clicked the striker again and again, but it would not give a single spark. The flint was lost.

Then, groping around with head down and bare backside in the air, he felt rather than heard an amused chuckle that stirred the hairs on his forearm as gently as a baby's breath.

Stop fussing with the candle, boy. I am all the light you'll ever need.

As he spoke, the yellow wax of the candle began to glow from the inside out, and it grew in brightness until Llian had to shield his eyes.

It's time, my friend. Wake Karan, have her link with you. Quickly; this way is terribly wearying.

"I can't," Llian whispered.

Can't, or won't?

Llian realized that Rulke knew nothing of what had happened between him and Karan.

"Your visit in Tullin nearly destroyed me."

It hurt me too, chronicler. I could not move for a week after Karan smashed the link so crudely.

"No one trusts me anymore, not even Karan, and Yggur will kill me as soon as he gets the chance. He's already tried."

Silence in his head as if Rulke was thinking. Then the voice was back, ringing with urgency. *Bring her to Carcharon. Hurry!*

"I won't go!" Llian said. Whatever it cost he would protect Karan from Rulke. "I refuse! I reject you utterly!"

Will you never learn who your real friends are? Then regretfully I must force you.

Llian actually sensed regret, then a terrible pain coursed through his head, like an earache shooting from one side to the other. It was cut off with a cry of pain as great as Llian's own. He blacked out on the floor.

Llian got up in his midnight despair and packed his bags to flee, anywhere. But he was trapped just as he had been in Chanthed a year ago. He had no money nor any way to obtain more. His telling skills would buy nothing in Bannador in this cruel winter—no one had coin for such luxuries. Karan's funds were committed ten times over to Gothryme. Who could he turn to? Nadiril had offered help, but Nadiril was far away in Thurkad, if he had not already gone back to the Great Library.

In the early hours his ear began to ache, a pain that became a throbbing pulse of agony, died away to nothing then began again, and each time it stopped he faced the dreadful anticipation of its coming back. In the madness of the night he once thought about calling Rulke, giving in to him, only he did not know how. Then all at once the pain blew away.

Llian, now wide awake, began to feel the pressure in his mind again. Rulke was calling—another of his waking nightmares.

Good night, chronicler, boomed the voice in his head, the deep, rich and ever so slightly amused tones that were unmistakably Rulke.

Are you ready? Have you done what I asked? Fetch Karan! Make her link with you. I will do the rest.

Llian struggled with his tongue until foam dripped from

his sagging lower lip, but the conflict was too great. He could do no more than grunt.

You refuse me! boomed Rulke. *Karan does not cooperate? Has the famous voice lost its potency? You are less than I thought. Let this encourage you to try harder.*

Llian convulsed, biting his tongue.

Why do you resist? said Rulke. *There's no point. Bring her to Carcharon, by coercion or by force. Don't make me send my Ghâshâd for you. Think what they will do to your friends in Gothryme.*

Mendark had been out for a walk, pacing through the crusted snow as he tried to work out what was going on at Carcharon. Rulke was preparing something there, no doubt about it, but what? Mendark felt afraid, powerless, and the renewed body tired easily.

Shivering, he opened the back door a crack and slipped inside, heading for the kitchen fire and a warming cup of tea before bed. It was very late, past two in the morning. The whole manor was silent. He drank a bowl of stewed, bitter tea, unlaced his boots and warmed his feet on the stove, then set off for bed.

Passing Llian's room he heard a strange sound, like a combination of a chuckle and a cry of fear. Mendark froze with one foot in the air. A light was flashing and flickering underneath the door, far brighter than any lantern in Gothryme.

He lifted the latch ever so gently. The door opened a crack. Llian knelt on the floor, facing away, with his arms out in an attitude that could have been supplication or submission. Across the room an unlit candlestick flickered and flared. Mendark could see no details in the bright, but he did not need to. The room reeked of Rulke's aura.

Kicking the door open, Mendark sprang inside. The light flared so bright that he had to shield his eyes. He racked his mind for a counterspell or a charm of banishment. Finding one, he strained until his brain fumed and his eyes felt like they were boiling out of his head. From the light he sensed amusement. Mendark forced harder, something went snap behind his eyes and the light vanished.

Mendark realized that he was lying on the floor beside an unconscious Llian. He tried to get up but his limbs were paralyzed. The pain in his eyes grew ever worse. Forcing obedience down frozen nerve channels, Mendark gained the door. He stumbled off to bed and, despite his terror, could not get up until the afternoon.

The latch rattled. Llian did not look up. Whoever it was he did not want to see them. The door banged again and the bolt was shot *from the inside*. The back of Llian's neck prickled. He looked up, hoping that it was Karan coming to him at last.

"What did Rulke offer you?" Mendark asked coldly. He looked awful.

Llian almost fell off the bed. He had not even known that Mendark was in Gothryme. "What do you want?" His voice cracked.

Mendark gave a thin-lipped smile. "I want to know what you did in the Nightland. What you really talked about, what Rulke said and did, and what happened last night."

"I . . ."

"Don't even begin to lie to me. Old Wistan was right about you. More than once he cautioned me, when he wrote about your progress. *Genius without ethics is a deadly commodity,* he said. I only let you go so you could lead me to Rulke. What's he really up to? I'll have it out of you if I have to break you to get it."

Llian was devastated by the admission. I thought you were on my side. Can no one be trusted?

Mendark moved his hands in front of Llian's face, a truthreading of some sort, and Llian felt pain as if his heart was squeezed by iron pincers. The pain spread through his chest, shot up his arms, up the back of his neck and flowered at the base of his skull.

"Give me the truth and I will protect you. You know my

word is good—compare me to the Great Betrayer. You Zain know better than anyone how *he* rewards his friends."

Mendark's spell waged war with Rulke's compulsion. Finally it was too much. Llian collapsed, unconscious.

Something was shaking his shoulder, waking Llian out of a sleep all the more glorious for being free of pain and domination. His eyes rolled around his head, focusing on his other nemesis, Mendark.

"No," he moaned, trying to take refuge under the pillow. "R-R-Rulke—" He convulsed, foaming at the mouth.

Mendark saw this as Rulke punishing an intransigent pupil and made his truth charm ever more potent. His face could have been carved out of one of the glaciers in the high mountains.

"What do you want of me? Will I never be free of you?"

"I sponsored you at the college for fifteen years," Mendark choked. "Your meat and drink, your carousing and wenching. You owe me equal service—corrupted though you are."

Llian writhed. Mendark looked into his blank eyes.

"I won't let you destroy the twilight of my reign, Llian."

He set to with his hands and his spells until Llian was reduced to a blank-faced lump, but he could get no further. Eventually Mendark, in almost as much pain as Llian, was forced back to his own bed. He called for Tallia but she had gone out with Karan on a long ride and was not expected back until the following day.

Llian slept all day, if what he endured could be called sleep. That night Mendark came back for the third time. Llian had bolted the door but Mendark came in through the window.

Llian clawed away across the floor in his desperation to escape. Mendark ran him to ground in a moment. The torment began again and this time it would not end.

Karan returned late, but when she brought Llian's dinner tray she found the morning one untouched. Llian was asleep and did not stir. She thought little of it—he often ate nothing all day—and went wearily to her own mattress.

His visitors reappeared in the middle of the night. It went much the same as the previous visits, only worse.

The next afternoon Karan and Tallia were sitting beside the fire in Karan's sitting room. This was a smallish room that opened onto the courtyard by means of long windows, each of many small panes. On a clear day the high mountains could be seen but today it was snowing and a hard wind hurled flurries at the house. All but one of the windows were shuttered against the cold. The end window was unshuttered, lighting the place where they sat. Snow lay knee-deep in the courtyard.

Karan had a ledger on her knee and a pencil in her hand, one minute working furiously, the next gazing dreamily into the fire or through the window. Someone passed along the veranda, unidentifiable under their heavy coat. Tallia was sitting at a small table on the other side of the room, playing a game with counters on a seven-sided board. Something wailed above the wind.

"What was that?" asked Karan, scratching her neck with the pencil.

"Just the wind," Tallia replied. Nonetheless she rose in one swift movement and went out.

Karan could not concentrate on her work today. Since her return home everyone had slaved just to survive, and she had dreamed of having the time to work on her designs. Now she had the time, but no matter how she put the world out of mind it kept coming back. And Llian too. Sometimes she heard him cry out in the night, for his window was below hers, but he did not call for her and until he did she would not go to him; only lie in her cold bed aching for him, yet trying to block him out.

She hadn't seen him awake since Mendark had come back from Carcharon, Karan realized. He'd always been asleep. The last time she'd spoken to him was three days ago. *Since*

Mendark had come back! She dropped the pencil. How could she have been so blind? And she had closed down the monitor over him.

Just then there came the most horrible shriek. She sprang up, scattering pencil and papers. Tallia flung the door open.

"Come quickly," she cried, running out again. "It's Llian!" she shouted over her shoulder. "It sounds like he's having a fit, but the door's bolted."

Their shoulders struck the door together and it burst open. Karan pushed past Tallia. Llian was lying on his side with his knees drawn up and his fists tightly clenched. A gaunt Mendark stood over him like a condor tearing at its victim. Karan could sense a strange aura—Rulke again.

"How dare you," she said softly.

"You don't even know what's going on in your own house," he raged. "I've almost killed myself trying to break him of Rulke."

Karan looked from one to the other. "Why wasn't I told?"

"You weren't here! Rulke has come to him the last two nights, that I know of, but it began long before that." Mendark staggered and had to sit down. "How could you be so negligent, letting him get to this state? How could you not see what is going on under your nose?"

Karan was mortified. "What have you done to him?" she whispered, looking down at Llian with tears in her eyes.

Mendark abruptly sat down on the chair. "I tried to break Rulke's compulsion; force it out of him. But it's not working. Rulke's too strong."

"You're killing him," Karan wept.

"A small price to pay," Mendark said stolidly.

"You—" She choked, then leapt up and seized a heavy poker. Tallia restrained her. "Get out of my house and never come back!" Karan screamed. "Come on my land again and I'll kill you."

Mendark was too worn out to argue, or fight. Contemptuously, he pushed past Karan and went out. "Tallia," his harsh cry came down the hall.

"I'm staying!" she shouted back.

Llian lay absolutely still, his eyes closed. Karan took his wrist in her hand. His skin was clammy and cold; the pulse fluttered as light and as fast as the wings of a butterfly.

"I don't know what to do," she wept. "What's Mendark done to him?"

Tallia knelt down with her hands clasped around Llian's head and her ear to his temple, as if listening to the ticking of his brain.

"Mendark believes that Llian made a bargain with Rulke in the Nightland, and was forced to forget it."

"Do *you* believe that?" asked Karan, tormented by her own inability to decide and desperate for some support.

"I . . . I've an open mind," said Tallia. "There's something not right here." She bent over Llian again. "Mendark's spell hasn't worked." She looked up at Karan's white face.

"Can *you* do anything?"

"It's too strong for me. And there seems to be something else—something that goes against Mendark's work." Tallia strained until her hands shook. "I can't find it. It's hidden in some way." She released Llian's head and stood up. "It's beyond me. It must be—"

"Rulke!" said Karan.

There was no healer in the town, but even if there had been, what healer would know what to do here? Malien had gone up into the mountains with the hunt and might not be back for days. Nothing could be done until she returned.

Llian convulsed so violently that he flung himself into the air. One fist struck Karan in the stomach, knocking her backward into the wall. Her belly felt as if it had been belted with an iron bar. Llian rose to his knees. His mouth was wide open, one hand clawing at his face, the skin tearing beneath his fingernails. The other hand wrenched at his hair till a clump came out, skin and all. His mouth was open, twisted as if about to scream, yet nothing came forth but a horrible gurgling whistle. Foam-flecked slobber ran down his chin. His legs thrashed.

Karan grabbed his arm but in this madness he was far too

strong for her. His hard hand caught her across the side of the head, sending her reeling into the table, which toppled over. Llian clawed at his skull. He seemed to be trying to plunge his fingers right through his head, to pluck out some barbed torment.

Tallia put her fingers against the base of his skull and pressed hard. The noise stopped at once. His eyes slowly closed; his hands fell to his sides. He would have fallen had she not held him under the arms.

"Take his feet," Tallia said to one of the faces at the door. Nutan the gardener grabbed his feet and began to back into the other room, his tiny bedroom.

"He'll never get better in there," said Karan hastily. "Bring him to my room."

They carried him out, through into the keep and up the stair. Llian was not heavy but he was awkward to carry. They laid him on Karan's broad bed. He was in a terrible state. There were three gouges on his right cheek and one on his left, from which the blood wept. Skin was crumpled up under his fingernails. His hands were bloody; in one he still clutched a clump of brown hair. He had bitten his tongue in three places, so that he dribbled blood, and his left leg was locked so rigid by cramp that it could not be straightened.

"What is it?" Karan whispered. "Has he gone mad?" If he had, it was not like any madness that she knew of.

"I don't know," said Tallia, shaking her head. "You'd better tie him up."

Karan sank down on the end of the bed with her head in her hands. How had Llian come to this, to be tied down raging and foaming at the mouth like a rabid dog? Had she helped to make him this way? And what stupidity had made her close down her link? If she hadn't she would have known something was wrong days ago.

She stroked his hand where it lay limp and pallid on the coverlet. She untangled the clump of hair. It was all bloody at the roots, a ragged piece about the size of her thumb-nail. Karan burst into tears.

Tallia found some soft cord, the kind that was used to tie

up a dressing-gown, and tied Llian's hands to the head of the bed. He did not rouse. Karan had stopped crying now but sat listlessly at his side.

"No time for that," said Tallia briskly. "Make yourself useful. Rub his leg until the cramp goes."

Karan was glad that there was someone to give the orders. She lost herself in memories as she massaged the muscles of Llian's calf and thigh—they were as tight as wire—and gently worked his leg until at last the muscles unbound. How she longed for him, just to lie with him, skin to skin, warmth to warmth, touch to touch. When that was done Tallia tied his legs as well.

I've not seen anything like that before, Tallia thought. What can he possibly do that Rulke wants so badly? "Watch him," she said to Karan and went out, closing the door behind her. They took turns sitting beside his bedside that night. Llian lay still for hours, as though in a deep sleep. In the middle of the night he thrashed and shrieked, shouting incoherently, but soon lapsed back into unconsciousness.

Llian woke. It was night. Instantly the imperative was in his mind. *Bring her. Bring her!*

He resisted, made himself mute, stubborn as he could be when he did not want to do something. But his resistance was of no account, broken in seconds by a pain in his head so terrible that it felt like his brains were boiling. He tried to claw at his head, straining at the cords, but Tallia had tied the knots cunningly and they held him secure. Still he writhed, contorting himself to the limit of his bonds. His face twisted, he made the same terrible sounds as before, then slid into unconsciousness again.

This went on through the long night. Karan tried everything—herbs and drugs as they had in Gothryme, or could obtain from the town—but they had no more effect on him than tea. Tallia had many skills and strengths, but none that would permit her to look inside Llian's mind and identify what it was that so tormented him. He kept nothing down but a little broth. Karan knew that the torment would eventually kill him.

He began to thrash again. She would have given anything to end it. Her anger and bitterness had evaporated. Karan knelt over him, weeping, pressing him down with her small body as he bucked like a wild horse. Her tears spotted his twisted face, then he plunged off a cliff into sleep.

It was morning again. Tallia was watching him now; Karan slumped in a chair before the fire. Tallia had never seen her looking more worn. She was exhausted too. Someone came in with tea. When Karan picked up her bowl her hands shook so much that the liquid slopped all over the table. The bowl rattled on the marble as she put it down again.

Later that morning Llian roused enough for Tallia to spoon hot broth into him, but he did not recognize either of them. His eyes turned in on themselves and he went back into the darkness.

"Tallia, please help him."

Tallia held out her hands. "This is beyond me," she whispered. "Mendark's spell forces against Rulke's compulsion and I can't remove either. It's the conflict between them that's doing the damage. You could try giving him a sleeping draught each time the fit begins; perhaps that will give him the rest that he needs. I'll go and get Mendark. I'm sure he's only gone as far as Tolryme."

"You won't!" Karan said fiercely. "I'll never trust him again as long as I live."

"Once he lifts his spell, Llian will be back to what he was before."

"I don't want him back to that! I want him whole again."

"This may kill him," said Tallia.

"And so might Mendark," Karan said angrily. "Every one of my instincts about him has been true."

"Look!" said Tallia. "I know that you have been under a . . ."

"Don't *Look* me," Karan exploded, facing down tall Tallia, who retreated before her fury. "You're not doing Mendark's work either. Go away; leave us alone!"

Llian rolled against his bonds and gave a heart-rending groan.

"Very well," said Tallia with pursed lips, and went out. Then she put her head back around the door.

"There is one way you could try, if you dare, though it would be a terrible risk for *you.*"

"I'll try any remedy but one," said Karan.

"Try to reach him through a link. You may be able to get in under the compulsion and the spell, to wake him. Otherwise I'd say he will not last the week. But don't do it at night-time."

A link! She would try it. But that talent had always been difficult, not to mention unreliable.

The following day Tallia looked in every few hours. By the afternoon the sleeping draughts had done some good; Llian appeared a little better.

"Have you tried to link yet?" she asked.

"Yes, but I can't reach him."

The next time Tallia checked, mid-morning of the day after that, neither Karan nor Llian was there. Llian must have improved considerably, she thought, to be up and about. At lunchtime she asked Rachis where they were.

"Karan and Llian went out early," he said. "They won't be back for a few days."

"*Went out?* Where have they gone?"

"I don't know. She left this note. Is something the matter?"

Tallia scanned the note. *Llian and I are going away for a few days,* it said. *Not far.*

She ran outside. It was snowing gently, but not enough to conceal where they had gone. Out of the trampled snow at the back door emerged a pair of boot tracks that she recognized, Karan's size, and a larger pair. They led up the yard, over the stone wall and directly toward the cliff path that went to Carcharon and Shazmak. She followed the tracks far enough to be absolutely sure, then ran all the way down to Tolryme, through knee-deep snow, to find Mendark.

44

AN INSANE DECISION

All day Karan kept vigil, holding Llian's hand, stroking his forehead or feeding him gruel with a spoon, just being with him and trying to reach him. He seemed better now. Only once did the fit come on him again, though it was a weaker, briefer episode than previously, and a small dose of poppy syrup sent him into a relaxing sleep. No point trying to link to him in that state, but after the potion wore off she attempted to.

She tried many times that day, but failed each time. She kept trying, well into the night, ignoring Tallia's warning. They lay together, Llian in her arms, as night descended. The room became dark as pitch—not a glimmer anywhere. Karan did not move to light a lamp. The dark seemed better for what she was trying to do.

Then suddenly she felt that he was looking at her, imagined that he held both hands out to her in yearning. She put out her hands as well, across the link, and touched him.

Oh, Llian, she sighed across the link.

He spoke as from far away. *Why did you abandon me?*

I'm sorry. I'm sorry. Are you . . .?

I feel very weak. Hold me! I am so . . .

Karan felt as if she stood on the edge of a vast gulf in darkness, one of the enormous canyons that cut down to the Dry Sea. She could sense Llian as a lonely speck on the other side, a sad drab figure searching just as disconsolately as she was. Years could have gone by, so timeless and directionless was her search, but neither could find the way to the other.

A tiny light grew in the darkness, and across that chasm she saw him, an ant-like figure illuminated by a candle-nub of light, a frail beacon in the infinite darkness. He knew it too, for she saw him turn his head her way, and as he did the light that touched him became a blade, then a wand extending out over the gulf. It touched a thread suspended there and like the morning sun on a single strand of spider web the light glided along the thread, illuminating a path across the abyss.

Llian took a step toward it. Looking down, Karan saw the same path before her. She held her breath, then took courage in her hands and stepped upon it. It swayed beneath her and she threw out her arms for balance, and saw Llian do the same, a little stick-figure at the end of immeasurable distance.

She wanted to run and take him in her arms. Llian was clumsy at the best of times; terrified of heights all the time. He could never walk this path. But Karan could only see one step in front of her. Beyond that was half a league of blackness. So she continued, one step at a time, and Llian did the same, and always out in the middle was dark.

Slowly she paced toward the absolute nihility over the chasm. A dozen times Llian swayed and teetered on the edge, and Karan put her fingers in her mouth to stop herself from screaming out. Over the link she sent him warmth and encouragement and love, and each time he recovered and kept on.

An eternally long time later, when the darkness at the center had shrunk to a globe no bigger than a barn, Karan felt a rasp of terror touch the nerves at the base of her spine. It was just a little thing, not like a scream of danger from her talent, but she paused in her step. The thread path quivered under her.

A shiver passed up Karan's spine. Something was not right. There was such a clamor in her head, many voices, but she could not distinguish the words. Suddenly she heard Llian shouting at her.

"Karan!"

He screeched out something else, but she could not make out whether it was a cry for help or a warning, for at that moment a single low note boomed down the canyon and blotted everything out. The bridge jerked then swayed in slow oscillations that tried to tip her off.

Llian fell to hands and knees as the vibrations grew wilder. Then in a feat of daring that she would never forget, he rose to his feet on that single thread, put his hands around his mouth and bellowed at her.

No sound came. Nothing at all passed through the black globe at the core of the bridge. Llian reeled about and she ran forward in a desperate, futile attempt to get to him before he fell.

She ran until there was a stitch in her side. As she was about to plunge into that roiling cloud of nothingness, there came faint to her from one side, the echo of Llian's shout. "Go back, back, ackakkkkkkkk!"

She skidded to a stop, the tiny echoes now tapping at her inner ear from a dozen directions, getting to her where his shout had been prevented.

"Link, link, ink inkkkkk!"

What was he trying to tell her? She could not make it out. Did he want her to try harder with the link? A seed of mistrust began to germinate. She could not rid herself of it.

The black cloud swelled and shrank, pulsing away like a beating heart. She stepped forward gingerly. Another step.

Another echo came to her, the faintest of all, but not even

its reflection from a dozen precipices could disguise the utter urgency in Llian's voice. "Karannnn! Breakkk linkkkk *noowwwww!*"

The echo trailed away to nothing, but not before she saw Llian crushed down as by the blow of a mighty fist. Treachery! She turned and ran. The narrow, slippery path ran steeply up before her, into dark. Often she had to guess where to put her foot, so gloomy had it become. Only a step or two behind her the shadow came, clawing and clutching at her heels. How far down the curve of the hanging bridge she was!

Karan sprinted as fast as she had ever gone. Near the top her feet slipped on the slope. Snatching her heel out of an unseen mouth, she went hand over foot up the path, saw the top, sprang, bounced on the rubbery surface—the link—and rolled back up over the edge of the gorge to safety.

Gasping on the brink, she snapped the link before it was seized. *Rulke! It was a trap!* and found herself back on her bed in the pitch dark, drenched in sweat, her heart hammering so loud that she could hear it.

A comparable shudder wracked Llian. She heard his eyes spring open, though he was not seeing her.

"I will not," he kept whispering, slurring the words. In her arms she could feel his struggle. "I will die before I let you have her." His eyes closed and he slept again.

The veil was torn from her eyes. This was not the action of a traitor, unless Llian was more devious than she could imagine. But she knew Llian better than anyone; his little deceits were quite transparent to her. Maybe they had all been wrong about him.

Karan shook Llian and called his name but he would not wake, and the Rulke-presence did not reappear. Llian seemed more rested now, more like himself. She lit the lamp, bolted the door, cut his hands and feet free and, taking off her boots and socks, slipped into bed and took him in her arms again.

He was freezing! He gave a little whimper, but she pulled his head against her chest, stroking his hair. Her fingers passed over the small bare patch on his scalp and he flinched. She blew out the lamp and pulled him tightly against her, sending him care and protection and love with her body, more secure than any link could be, then he gave a sigh and slept more soundly, more easily.

Someone came to the door, tried it and went away again. She dozed, slept, dreamed, and in the night her dreams changed to peaceful ones. Suddenly she woke, realizing that Llian was awake beside her. It was pitch dark still.

"Llian," she said softly.

He did not answer, but touched her as if trying to speak to her with his fingers. He stroked her nose, her high-arched eyebrows, her cheekbones. Catching his fingers in hers she drew them down to her lips. "Tell me what happened. Tell me everything."

She slipped his hand lower, inside her shirt. His cold fingers lay on her breast, unmoving.

He made a sigh, a little bit of a whimper in it, then pulled his hand away. "You refused to trust me. You preferred Shand's opinion of me to your own. That hurt so much. After he appeared in Tullin you never listened to me again."

"I'm sorry." The words could never express her mortification. "I should have refused him, not that he gave me much choice. But if you could have seen yourself that night—it was terrifying, Llian."

"I know, I remember it now. That night it all seemed so wonderful; so right! But as soon as Rulke called for you, I knew him."

"Called for me?"

"I think it began in the Nightland, after you . . . left me."

Yes, Karan thought. That's where it all started. That was my mistake and this is what it led to.

"I didn't remember anything about that until a few days ago. There was a memory of great pain, and his voice saying: *One day I will call, and you must come and tell me what you know. If Karan has survived you will bring her too, for I need her more than you.* Then more pain. The dreams were just idle threats at first, like the dreams you had last year. I suppose that's the only way he can reach me. That night in Tullin . . . it was a great promise. But underneath it, a long way from the surface, a threat. Then he started calling for you."

"When was this?"

"A long time ago. I can't remember."

"Why didn't you say? Why did you not come to me?"

"I overheard you and Shand in Tullin. You agreed to treat me like a thing possessed by Rulke. I tried that night and you rejected me."

"You cannot know how that tore *me* apart," she whispered.

"I know how it tore *me* apart. I heard Shand calling me traitor and you agreeing, even though you well knew how prejudiced he is. Shand has turned everyone against me. Mendark will end up killing me, if Yggur doesn't. He only let me go to find Rulke and trap me. Did I tell you that? He's just as bad as Yggur."

Karan could hear his feelings of betrayal. Rage exploded from her. "Mendark's gone. I threw him out."

"I desperately wanted what Rulke offered, but not so much that I would give *you* to him. No one tried to help. I was simply accused and condemned."

"I should never have listened to Shand," said Karan, torn between loyalties. "He is a good man, but blinded by prejudice."

"You and Shand were so self-righteous; and everyone else was contemptuous, save for Nadiril. How could you think that I would make a pact with Rulke *for you*, I who am Zain? That lesson was taught me at my mother's breast. I can't deny that I was tempted by his offers, and still am. But I would never give you to him.

"Then Yggur left me in the execution yard with the corpses. No food, no water, just twenty-five bodies swinging in the breeze. Can you imagine the horror of that day? That was when I first realized who my enemies really were."

Karan was wracked, knowing all that he said about her and Mendark and Shand was true. But another part of her could not help but think: "Yes, and yours is a very pretty speech, and that is your art and your trade, even without Rulke putting the words up for you to say." How could she tell?

"What does Rulke want from you? What do you know now that you did not in the Nightland?"

"No more than he might have guessed three months ago. Anyway he doesn't want me."

"What does he want?

"The one thing that I will never give up. You! You have some talent that you don't even know about, and it's crucial to his purpose."

Karan was struck dumb, though her mind was racing in many directions. Rulke had wanted her for a long time. Even back when she carried the Mirror she had wondered why. First she'd thought that he was just after the Mirror. In the Nightland she'd learned otherwise; perhaps that was why she had panicked and fled. Now she understood—he must need her for her rare talents. But why? She could not imagine.

This put Llian's actions in a wholly different light, if he had endured all this *for her*. Either he was as cunning as Rulke himself, or she had him a terrible wrong. All she had was her own judgment. All this might be just another manipulation of the Prince of Deceivers, but no longer could she disbelieve Llian. She would not hide from her mistakes; she would face them. She knew Llian was not capable of something so monstrous.

How cruelly she had treated him. Well, that was over. In support of her, Llian had done many things that were hard and unnatural for him. But never had he judged her or doubted her. He had suffered all this, protecting her, in spite of what she had done to him. She had misjudged Llian terribly. Being Karan she must immediately put it right.

"What if I won't go, and you can't bring me?"

"He'll send the Ghâshâd down for you. He told me so the other night."

It was black in her room but Karan could see in her mind's eye the expression on Llian's face. I don't have to imagine it. I've seen more than I ever wanted to. I will never mistrust you again, not if everyone else on Santhenar does. Not unless I see the evidence with my own eyes.

"Where were you supposed to take me?"

"To Carcharon. That's where he is, or will be."

That explained a lot, though not why Rulke had gone there instead of Shazmak. Maybe mad Basunez had been right after all, thinking it the best place on Santhenar to work the Secret Art. Yet there was no point puzzling about something that could not be answered. The only way to find out would be to go there. There had been much talk at the Council about spying on Carcharon. Karan had even agreed to send up some of her woodsfolk, though they dared not go close enough to learn any more than was already known.

Carcharon was *hers*, and she was outraged that Rulke had taken it, but there was nothing to be done. The place was impregnable, save to a siege of months. If Rulke came for her the whole valley was in peril, whilever she and Llian were here. And just as much peril if they were to flee secretly. What was she to do? There was only one thing she could do.

She jumped out of bed and lit the lamp. "What are you doing?" asked Llian, sitting up. The light hurt his eyes.

"Stay here," she said. "I have to find something."

She ran out in her bare feet. The house was completely dark. Down the far end of the library were big wooden cupboards with wide drawers where maps, charts and old drawings had been kept for generations. There were plans of the holding too, on parchment or canvas or hide, some so old as to predate the construction of the keep. She riffled through maps showing the layout of her land and its boundaries, plans of paddocks and forests, charts showing the heights of great floods, sketches of buildings and gardens long gone. These she put aside, wishing she'd known they were here.

She would look at them another time. But she found no plan of Carcharon.

There was a long chest beside the cupboard. Karan heaved herself up on it with her arms and sat there, rubbing her feet to warm them. The stone floor was frigid. Where could the plans be? Everything of value in Carcharon had been brought home with Basunez's body after his death. Where were his papers? She had never seen them in the library either.

No, wait! When she returned to Gothryme for the first time as an adult, she had found her father's journals. She had often read them, trying to bring him back. Her father had always been interested in Carcharon. She remembered him talking about a secret way into Carcharon.

She ran along the long aisle, lantern in one hand, and crashed into Llian who was feeling his way along in the gloom. He fell, caught a shelf with one hand and held on grimly. The leg that he'd had the cramp in was weak.

"Idiot!" he said with a painful smile. "What are you doing?"

She gave him her hand. "I'm looking for a map of Carcharon, in my father's papers. Here they are."

There were a number of slim journals, as well as a thick heap of papers held together with tape. She undid the tape and the papers spilled all over the floor. It took a long time to search through them all, but no map was found. She sat down on the floor and carefully put them all together again.

"I was sure that it would be here," she said.

"When did you go to Carcharon with your father?"

"I was eight. Seventeen years ago. Not long before he died."

She named the month. Karan tied the bundle up carefully and put it back. Llian took the journals down, one after another, looked inside and replaced them. He riffled through the pages of the third and took out a small folded piece of paper. He handed it to Karan without opening it.

"I imagine that this is it," he said.

She unfolded it. It was a small plan, labeled *Carcharon.* On one corner was a sketch of the fortress and its defenses; a round the outside, writing in a neat hand. "He must have made this himself. The paper is the same as that in the journal. How did you know it was here?"

"It was a logical place to look."

The map had told her what she wanted to know. She slipped it into her pocket. Llian looked faint. She took his hand again and they went back to her bedroom.

"Get into bed," she said. "I'll be along in a minute." She disappeared, returning shortly with a huge mug of hot soup and a slab of bread. "Eat this, then go to sleep. I won't be long." She ran out again.

"Hurry up, it's freezing," he said sleepily, as the empty mug slipped from his fingers.

He had not had a proper sleep since Mendark's arrival. He drifted into dreamland but his sleep was soon fractured. It was so cold in the bed. He reached out for Karan but she was not there. She had never come to bed.

That shocked him awake. Llian limped through the house and caught sight of a small shape at the open back door.

"Where are you going," he hissed into her ear, though it was all too evident.

"Carcharon!"

He clutched at her coat. "That's the stupidest thing I ever heard."

"What choice is there? There isn't one. How can I let him come down here looking for me? How can I flee? The Ghâshâd would tear the whole valley apart."

"What are you going to do when you get there?"

Karan hesitated. No, be honest with him, she thought. Now and forever. "I don't have a plan. I'm going to bargain with Rulke for your freedom."

Nothing Llian could say would make the slightest difference; her mind was fixed. Her strength frightened him.

"You're a fool," he said. "And I'm a bigger one. I'm coming with you."

"Don't be stupid; you wouldn't even get over the back fence, in your condition."

"I'm coming," he repeated, "even if you have to carry me."

She laughed until tears ran from her eyes, then wept just as long. She kissed him on the lips, sprinkling him with her dewy cheeks. "Go and get dressed; I'll wait for you."

"You've already proven that you can't be trusted. You can sit on the bed while I dress. And don't move!"

Grinning, she followed him back and dutifully sat while he got ready, layer after layer of wool, and over all a long down-filled coat and a cloak of waxed cloth. He had to rest when the job was done.

"Can you help me with my boots?" he asked hoarsely.

"What a pathetic pair we are," she replied as she bent down.

She filled his pack with dried stuff from the pantries. They fortified themselves with a bowl of soup each from the cauldron that hung over the fire. The fire was just ash and coals but she dug deep with the ladle and the soup that came up was scalding. It made them sweat in their winter gear. Llian suddenly found an appetite and took another bowl. Karan was busy at the table, scribbling a note for Rachis. Filling a large flask with hot soup, she buried it deep inside her down-filled sleeping pouch. Then they went out, into the snow and the wind, each terrified of what would await them above the cliffs in mad, desolate Carcharon.

45

CARCHARON

"This *is* the stupidest thing I've ever done," said Karan as they headed out into the snow.

From the look in Llian's eyes he was thinking the same thing. Suddenly they were as close as they had ever been. He took her hand; she thrust it into a wool-lined pocket. It was three in the morning. The night was overcast, like every night for the past month and more.

As they climbed over a stone wall Llian was struck by a feeling of having done this before. "This reminds me of the night we met, heading up into the mountains to a destination that only you knew."

She laughed. "If you only knew how I felt when you crashed down my steps. *'My name's Llian—I've come to save you,'* you said, then knocked yourself out at my feet." She giggled at the memory. "And you were sick and sore that time, too."

"Not as bad as this," he said, squeezing her fingers, smiling at his own memories.

They took the path that led up the valley. The dogs barked but Karan shushed them to silence. There was a little soft snow and under that a hard crust from the thaw of a few days ago. Where the path veered up the northern ridge the powder had been blown away and they could walk easily on crusted snow. It was quite dark, but Karan's feet knew the path, well worn from so much coming and going these past weeks.

By the time they reached the top of the ridge Llian was staggering. Karan almost gave it away, but she could not get him home without his cooperation, and his will was like iron. "In life and in death I will never leave you again," he said, and after a short rest he felt able to tackle the relatively gentle gradient along to the bottom of the cliff.

Now each march lasted only a few minutes before he had to stop and rest. After an hour he was utterly worn out.

"I'm sorry," he said. "I can't go any further. Can I sleep for an hour?"

"Of course!" She brushed white flakes off his nose, for it had begun to snow lightly. "I just wanted to get well away from the house. No one knows we've gone, and Rachis won't worry. My note took care of that."

They camped in the lee of a boulder, spread a groundsheet and squeezed together into one sleeping pouch with the other pulled up over it. It was snug but warm. Karan held the soup flask to Llian's lips. A moment after he finished he was fast asleep.

Karan did not sleep, just lay there thinking and fretting until the growing light of dawn showed a field of round boulders thrust up out of the snow, with black shadows behind. Before them was a pile of boulders as big as a temple. A big-eyed owl blinked at them from a hole in a tree.

She woke Llian. "We'd better get on, if you can manage it."

The brief sleep had wrought miracles. Before the wintry sun rose they reached the base of the cliff and began the climb. It was painfully slow, but easy at first, even with the snow, for the cliff sloped back into the mountainside and the Aachim had cut new steps in the stone where necessary.

"Did you tell Rachis where we were going?" he asked, as they rested two-thirds of the way up. Llian's leg was worrying him. He looked up at the remaining third of the cliff path, which was very steep and narrow, with trepidation. Far below, the chimneys of Gothryme were fresh with smoke.

"Of course not, and why would he think this way? I made no urgency of our trip, so probably he won't tell Tallia unless she asks about us. She fell out with Mendark over you but I suppose after this news they'll follow us. Let's get on."

She gave him her shoulder and they made their halting way up to the top of the cliff. Karan had ample time to reflect on the stupidity of this journey. Llian looked like death again. What could possibly be gained from it?

It was mid-morning before they finally reached the top. Before them the forest of Gothryme stretched beyond sight to north and south, while to the west it clad a slope cut with steep gullies. The mountains towered white beyond that. They looked back but there was no sign of pursuit.

The snow was deep and soft here, the walking hard going. They did not hurry. Carcharon was not a destination that one hurried to. Llian's rest stops grew longer and more frequent, but by the evening of that short day they had reached the furthest side of the forest.

There was a small lake on the up-slope side, just inside the margins of the forest. It was called the Black Lake on account of the color of its waters. Surrounded by tall trees on all sides, it must have been fed by a warm spring, for it was not yet frozen over. A small stone pavilion stood beside the waters, so old that even the granite of which it was built was crumbling, though its roof, a series of metal spires, was intact. The side against the water had a balustrade of stone but most of the balusters were broken. Nearby was a pier and a set of stone steps that led down to the water. A tiny dinghy had once been tied to a brass ring there. They camped inside the pavilion, sitting on the steps and toasting bread at a small fire. The remainder of the soup was enough to satisfy them both.

"I often came here when I was a child," said Karan, looking around her. Llian did not answer: he was already nodding where he sat. She helped him into the sleeping pouch and folded his cloak for a pillow. Karan was restless; there were too many memories here. On the other side of the pavilion she leaned on the stone rail. The surface of the water was like a black mirror, so still that the reflected stars were as clear as in the sky above.

The stars were out! The overcast of the past months had cleared. Was that an omen? If so, for whom? She walked out onto the pier and sat with her feet dangling over the edge, looking down into the water. She wondered idly if a surface so clear and dark as this one might not also be used as a seeing mirror. If so, this one surely ought to speak clearly to her, if only she knew what to ask it.

The moon was three-quarters full, and a great deal of the dark side was showing, but it was only fleetingly visible through the tall trees. How well could Rulke really know Llian's mind? They'd only had those few days together in the Nightland. Could he sense how near they were? Did he know they were coming? No way of telling that until the middle of the night. That was when his visitations appeared. Well, she had the poppy syrup for that need.

The map had confirmed what she already knew; what her father had told her. There *was* a secret way into Carcharon. She leaned there idly, musing. The folly of her actions was quite clear to her, but it was her own life, and she would harm no one if she failed—no one save Llian. She put that out of mind for the time, steeping herself in the sounds of the forest and the stillness of the lake. The last time she'd been here was on the way to Shazmak, when she was twelve. The time before that, her eighth birthday. Karan remembered it quite distinctly, and not only for the birthday, the last happy time of her childhood. Just two days later her father was gone, beaten and left to die on a windswept ridge in the snow not far from here. A brutal, senseless crime; he had carried little of value. But he was lost forever. She shivered and turned to the sleeping pouch.

Morning came, and Llian woke first. There was fog in the forest and mist on the lake, a mist that hung low over the water and cut the black to silvery gray. The sun was coming up behind the trees. Karan slept soundly, her arms wrapped around him, just her red hair sticking out of the pouch. Their campfire was still burning, sending a wavering thread of smoke up into the mist. She must have stayed up late. He was inclined to let her sleep, but the smoke might have already warned their enemies. He shook her by the shoulder.

"Karan, wake up!"

She came awake at once. "What's the matter?"

"The fire's still smoking."

She cocked her eye at it. "That was careless," she agreed. "Amazing how quickly you lose your bushcraft. I would never have done that a year ago. But I don't think it can be seen—the smoke's spread out before it gets above the forest. Still, we'd better be on our way, just in case they have a patrol down this far. Put the water on, will you. I'm just going to have another five minutes."

At their halting pace it was the best part of a day's walk from the Black Lake to Carcharon. On the other side of the forest the path diverged from the way to Shazmak and took to a rocky ridge so steep that they had to go up the first part on hands and knees. The track was icy and the wind blew incessantly.

Their trip up the ridge was agonizingly slow, with constant stopping for Llian to rest. He was very tired and weak but would not give in. Karan kept watch for the chase that must surely come, almost hoping that they would be prevented from going further, but there was no sign of pursuit even as they turned up the steeper ridge on which stood the frigid folly of Carcharon.

Now the path became a winding track along the very top of the ridge, like the road up to a fairytale castle. Stepped as if the ridge top had been carved across by successive cuts of a plane, it was narrow and fell steeply on either side into deep gorges choked with boulders.

"I can't think of a stupider place to build a fortress," said Llian. "Why didn't he put it down there?"

"Because this was the best place on Santh for the Secret Art, and *nothing* else mattered."

"But what must it have cost?"

"Not relevant."

They crept on.

"Karan," said Llian unsteadily, a long time afterwards.

"Yes?"

"You remember how I used to be terrified of heights?

She squeezed his hand.

"Well, I'm not anymore. Just terribly, terribly afraid."

She laughed and he did too. "That's a great improvement. Do you want to rest."

"Let's go a bit further."

Here the track was wider, but the broken steps were icy and littered with shattered rock. The fall on either side was precipitous, though layers of rock cropping out of the side of the ridge made ledges here and there. The path grew steeper as they climbed a thickened part of the ridge. It was late afternoon by the time they reached the middle of the bulge, a knotted fist of rock with veins of white and red.

"Above this the path is overlooked by Carcharon," said Karan. "We can't go any further until it gets dark."

Llian's face was pale and pinched. He could not take his eyes off Karan, hungry for her trust and affection. All the while she held his cold hand.

While she was puzzling out the secret way into Carcharon on the little plan, Llian went on all fours up the steps to the top of the knob and saw before him a flared-out ridge top about the size of a playing field, into which had been carved a small amphitheater with stone benches. On the lower side of that a ridge path led down and up again. The tortured rock layers here were blood-red, purple and black, and networked with writhing quartz like veins in an eyeball.

Just an arrow's flight away, Carcharon was more grotesque than he had imagined. The top of the ridge had been cut into a sloping plane, and there Basunez had built an ugly tower of nine uneven sides. It squatted at the lower end, surrounded by an elongated wall that ran up the hill and back down the other side. The structure looked like a sinking row-boat, the stern pushed down by a huge tower.

The tower was built of glassy-smooth gabbro, a striking violet-gray in color. Its walls were covered in clusters of projections: rods and hooks, vitreous spheres and opaline spines like those of a sea urchin. But the clusters were distributed oddly, in no conceivable pattern, and the wind alternately sobbed and shrieked through them. The tower was capped by a spiny helmet of brass, with brass arches sweeping over the walls, and the spaces between the arches were filled with green slate. The lines of wall and tower curved oddly, without grace, harmony or proportion.

Llian climbed back down. "He must have been quite mad," he panted.

"He was, and the family refused to help him. We do not serve madmen. The greatest has a duty to the least, and the least to the greatest, but that does not extend to fools or follies. Duty is not blind in Bannador."

"How did he ever get it built?"

"He brought in masons, carpenters and laborers from down below. The cost was unbelievable. Many of them died on the job, and on his death our house was bankrupt. It took five generations to pay back the graspers and even now we remain poor, for all that we have a lot of land."

"Can't you sell some of it?"

The look that Karan gave him suggested that he was as mad as old Basunez.

"Sell land? Sell *land*?"

Llian changed the subject hurriedly. "Why here of all places? A handful of besiegers could starve him out."

"That wasn't a consideration, as I've already explained. Basunez was a scholar and the ways of the Charon were his special interest. As he grew older this interest became an obsession. He believed that the powers of the Charon came from secret knowledge, and that if he could find out their secrets he could have their power. He also believed that there were nodes of power, places where the nature of reality was different and the Secret Art could be made to work better than anywhere else."

"Like the rift below Katazza," said Llian. "And the gates of the ancients, which could only function in certain rare places."

Karan was not interested in the details. "Anyway, right or wrong he believed that a most potent node lay here. He built Carcharon to take advantage of it. And certainly there is something about the place, for whenever I came here with my father I could feel it. An eerie shrinking and wrinkling of my skin, and a prickling inside my scalp. I can feel it now. I've not felt it anywhere else." Not like this anyway, she amended silently.

The clear morning turned into a wild snowy afternoon, the wind to a gale howling among the rocks. That would provide enough concealment to get near, they hoped. Meanwhile they stayed where they were, for there was no place on the ridge better sheltered than where they huddled. The wind sandpapered their faces with snow grit. It was not unlike a saltstorm in the Dry Sea, with the heat replaced by cold.

Karan looked up at the sky, veiled now by thin hurrying cloud. Llian took off his gloves to warm his nose with his hands. "What's inside Carcharon?"

"The tower, storehouses, woodsheds and other small buildings. There's a water cistern on the western side, cut into the rock. We might poison that, if we had poison, and if we did that kind of thing. And a door leading from the tower into the yard, of course. That's all I can remember."

Llian touched Karan's shoulder, having no idea what she had in mind. "Well!" he said. He was tense, afraid, vulnerable. The more he thought about where they were and what they were doing, the more ridiculous it seemed. Then a sudden biting pain wrenched him and left just as suddenly. He felt for a second the way Shuthdar must have felt in his hideously twisted body before the end. Just a reminder, but it stiffened his resolve. Nothing could be worse than that.

It took away all Karan's uncertainties too. She held him until it passed. Briefly the sun touched her anxious face, then the rushing clouds closed again.

"Take this," she said, bringing out a little flask. "But just a tiny sip or it will make you sleepy."

"What is it?" Llian asked suspiciously.

"Poppy syrup."

"Put it away! I'm going to need all the wits I can muster. So how do we get in?"

"There's always a secret way with us, even out of Gothryme. Rulke may have found it, though Basunez was very cunning. If he hasn't, we'll give him something to think about."

Llian snorted.

"Don't underestimate the importance of surprise," she continued. "We must make him think that we are worth something, and yet he must be sure that we are no threat. He must underestimate us."

"Very well," said Llian. "But when we reach the place, let me go first."

Karan went still. This was so unlike Llian. He was usually so careful of himself. Despite all her vows, a little suspicion rose. Why would he want to go first? No! She thrust the suspicion behind her.

He knew what it meant, her silence and stillness. "Karan, listen! What worse can he do to me than he has already done? When I step into Carcharon it will be a relief, whatever happens next. But why should he have you so easily? If I fail . . . promise that you won't come out unless I fail."

"You have some specific scheme in mind, then?" She had not been able to think of any plan.

"I'll do what I do best, and challenge him for you. Unless you forbid it."

"I forbid it! I'm not some bone to be fought over by dogs."

"I mean to do it anyway. I brought this down on us by my pride and my lust for knowledge."

"You are indeed proud! I might as easily say that I caused it by abandoning you, or by making that link a year ago, or by stealing the Mirror in the first place. I *utterly* forbid it."

"Karan, speak the truth to me." He took her cold hands in his and pulled her close. "Will you be truthful?" Again the slanting sun touched her, making sparks in her eyes.

"Yes," she said, shying away from certain dark corners that were hers alone; reserving a little piece of the truth for herself, just in case.

"When you go in there to meet him, do you have any plan, the least scrap, to get yourself out again?"

"I got away before, remember?"

"That's not an answer. He won't underestimate you again. Well?"

She bowed her head, erasing the sparks in her eyes. This was not a Llian that she was used to, nor one that she could lie to. How she loved him. She burrowed up under his coat, squeezing against him. "I have no plan," she said in a muffled tone. "Not the least scrap. And not much hope either."

"Well, I have."

It hurt. She had come up here to protect *him*. "May I know what it is?"

"It'll be easier if you don't, in case things go wrong."

She slid back out. "Very well! The secret way is somewhere along here."

She frowned at the map, trying to make sense of the directions in a gloomy landscape crusted with snow. Here and there a ledge ran off the ridge crest for a few paces before dwindling away to nothing. "These ledges form a maze, but there's only one way they connect to form a path."

"More like a treacherous game of snakes and ladders," Llian observed unhappily. "Just waiting to skid us over the edge to our deaths."

"Only if we're careless," said Karan. "But I intend to take very good care of you from now on. Back down here a bit."

It turned to be back up, not down. They found the path just as the light began to fade. Holding his hand she crept across the dangerous slope. At the end of the ledge was another, down a step, and beyond that, yet another. Above them Carcharon was hidden by the outward bulge of the slope. Here the steep ground was bare: native rock tortured into folds shaped like waves capped with snow. She picked her way among them, stopped briefly next to a tall rock shaped like a squat lighthouse, then hurried on.

"There is a tunnel," she said. "But the entrance can't be seen from above or below, or the sides."

Unless the rock's shifted after all this time, Llian thought.

Searching among the rocks she found a great folded outcrop of gneiss, the up-slope end of the fold being capped by a flat boulder. After much heaving the boulder swung sideways on pins, revealing a cleft just wide enough for them to wriggle inside. It was hard work getting Llian in. Once inside Karan touched her little lightglass to brightness.

They crawled down a steep slope choked with rubble. After they cleared that they found a low, irregular passage—even Karan had to stoop—that wandered through the ridge, evidently cut through lines of weakness. Every so often it ended in a steeply sloping shaft, and sometimes they had to climb the rough stone. This caused Llian some alarm, though the shafts were not very deep. Eventually they found themselves at the bottom of a much deeper shaft, up which a ladder ran.

"We must be below Carcharon now," said Karan. "Go carefully. Any noise will carry all the way up."

After a climb of many spans, during which time Llian twice had to be tied to the ladder while he rested, the rough rock ended at a counterbalanced stone door. The mechanism was stiff but they raised it enough to crawl beneath.

"Now," said Karan, "if they've found the tunnel—"

That was not something that they could do anything about, and they continued up a stair built in a false wall lying between the outer and inner walls. The treads were just thick plates of rock set within the wall.

They reached the top and saw before them another counterbalanced stone. This one would not move, and several frustrating minutes went by before Karan found the two clamps which locked it. She released them. The merest touch on the rock made it shiver. "It's well made," Llian said in a hoarse voice. They did not raise the door immediately, for he was desperately weary.

"How is your leg?" she asked, making a last supper.

"Very painful," he whispered, stretching it out in front of him. She massaged the locked muscles while he ate his bread and fruit. "I'm so tired," he said, his head nodding.

Karan put her arms around him while he slept all too briefly. Again she did not—she was too afraid. She had a presentiment that it was not going to go well. After less than an hour he woke with a start.

Llian took a deep breath. There was an agonized look in his eye that she could not bear to see. Karan put her arms around his neck, kissing him on his eyelids, each in turn, and then the tip of his nose.

"Whatever I say and do out there," he said, "promise that you will not lose your trust in me. No matter what I say, no matter what I do. I will never betray you."

"I *will* trust you, no matter what." And if you do betray me, she thought, you will wish you had never been born. She hugged him again, just a quick squeeze, then put her hands flat on his chest and pushed him away saying, "Go now." She couldn't bear long farewells, though she knew that she might never see him again.

He cautiously raised the door and pushed it down behind him. When he was gone she lifted it the merest fraction and waited. She could hear, if anyone spoke nearby, but she could not see. Then, ever so carefully, she re-established that thread-like link to Llian.

Llian emerged in a part of the tower concealed by a short wall. He peeped over and saw a large room that took up a good part of the top floor. The room was lit by globes on the walls and hanging from the ceiling, and was decorated with tapestries, some in the finest of metal threads, etchings on black metal and wire sculptures of extraordinary complexity. There were benches and tables on the other side of the room, and machines and devices large and small everywhere. A curving stone stair led to the lower levels. How many Ghâshâd had it taken to carry all this down from Shazmak? A hundred trips, surely.

There was no one in the room. He crept around the corner and saw, in the very center of the room, alien in shade and contour, the hard metal, blue-black shape of the construct. It was the very machine that he had seen in the Nightland, that Rulke had made there in his mind. But that was image, this surely the reality. All the more reason why Rulke should agree to his proposal, if the construct was ready to be used.

He could feel its presence from where he stood. He was drawn to it. It hung in the room, neither suspended nor yet touching the floor. He must touch it, and Llian did, and though it floated there, seemingly it had the mass of a mountain, for it did not even shiver when his timorous hand met its curved flank. But Llian trembled and fireworks burst inside his skull, making him dizzy. For a moment he could not remember what he was doing here. He nearly fell. Then he took his hand away and the construct was just an alien thing of metal again.

A snatch of music drifted up the stair, a haunting wail. Llian felt dizzy, sick and weak, his silly scheme coming apart. What if Rulke found him here, unprepared? Suddenly he heard a clamor below. A flare raced across the sky; he could see it through the window. What was going on? Limping to an embrasure he looked out toward the yard. As the flare died he saw a tall figure running along the wall, then it leapt into the night. It might have been Tallia. Another flare lit up the sky. So they *had* been followed from Gothryme.

Well, the diversion was welcome, whatever the source. He needed a few minutes to recover his composure. Crouching down behind the wall, he took deep breaths, willing himself into the right state of mind. The mind of a teller, the greatest of the age. Beyond even that, the persona of the character he must be to succeed at this. Arrogant, bold, even reckless. And totally convincing.

There came a footfall on the steps. Llian screwed his courage tighter. He was as ready as he would ever be.

Rulke came up slowly, smiling. Even the way he moved had menace. His surprise at seeing Llian there was so momentary as to be almost undetectable. He did not check, nor did anything show on his face, but Llian saw that he was put off-balance and took a little heart from it. At the same time, Rulke's offers in the Nightland came flooding back. The greatest knowledge of the world. How tempting it was!

"So, you *have* come! A clever diversion. Tallia is a worthy assistant to Mendark. Perhaps the student will in time surpass the master if she can bring you in my front door undetected."

Llian's training had given him a certain mastery of his face, so he did not react to this.

"You've brought *her* then? Just in time! In the morning the Ghâshâd were going down to rip Karan out of Gothryme."

It was just a question, no power or force behind it. The tone of one conspirator to another. Yet Llian could barely restrain himself from screaming out: *Yes, yes, I've brought her, she's hiding there behind that wall.* Perhaps Rulke already knew.

Llian stepped forward, assuming a facade that he did not

at all feel, drawing it on like a second skin. Arrogant. Insolent. Cocksure. Rulke had stopped two steps below the top and their faces were on a level.

"I have not," Llian said, and in a gesture of calculated indifference he leaned on the top rail of the stair, looked down past Rulke and yawned. Rulke was not moved, but his carmine eyes narrowed and in a gesture equally lazy he put out his fist and began to squeeze it tight. The pain began in Llian's head, but after what he had felt before it was only token pain; he was better placed to resist it now. His arrogant persona shrugged off the pain, though inside he worried that Karan would sense it and come out. He put out his own hand, the fingers up. *Stop!*

Rulke was intrigued. He withdrew his hand. The pain was gone. "This is a change from a few days back."

"Perhaps what you sensed a few days back was only what I wanted you to," said Llian. He screwed his courage up another notch, made himself more arrogant; more insolent yet. "I have an offer," he said.

Rulke laughed with genuine amusement.

"Or rather," Llian continued, "I should say, a wager. A challenge!"

"I make no bargains," Rulke said. "You will give her to me anyway."

"I *give* you: *nothing!* I did not bring her. I am not such a fool. But I can. She is utterly captivated by me. She will do anything for me *now*."

Llian was very convincing. In her hiding place, Karan winced.

"But you cannot find her. At least, not in time." Llian was gambling that Rulke's need for Karan was urgent, that he required her for some purpose related to the construct, and the opportunity must be taken now. But if he was wrong, if Rulke had time enough . . .

"I can destroy you with such agony as none have ever experienced," said Rulke, pounding one fist into the other with a smack that echoed off the walls. "I *will* have her."

"I know what you can do. Who does not? But destroying me does not get you Karan. She has a thousand hiding places in Bannador—your people failed to find her before, remember. I am a gambler, though. We can be of benefit to one another, and get some amusement from this situation as well. You have been locked up for a thousand years. Let me entertain you with my proposition. You have something that I want. You made an offer back in the Nightland. The best bargain is where both parties get what they want."

"The best bargain is where I get what I want and you are reduced to slavery," said Rulke gruffly, yet Llian could see that he was intrigued. "Make your proposition."

"I challenge you to a telling! We each have skills in this arena. Should you win, I give her to you. Should I win, you give me what I want, which you know is the Renderer's Tablet that will allow me to decipher the Charon script, and rid me of this curse you put on me."

"Two prizes! For one who bargains from a position of such weakness you are truly arrogant."

"I am a professional. I must have my fee."

Rulke roared with laughter. "You amuse me, teller. I'm glad you came. But the Tablet—that secret may be given to none!"

"Then it will be all the more valuable for me. You offered it before, remember. Besides, it belongs to the past, while you are the future of Santhenar."

"Once given it cannot be taken back. Who knows what the future holds. The damage that could be done to our species is too great. Anyhow," Rulke rubbed his jaw, considering, "I find the scales to be out of balance. What more can you offer?"

"If I lose, I will give myself as well."

"The scales do not even quiver! If you lose, I will have you anyway."

"A willing servant is worth a hundred slaves. I think I could provide you with some small amusement."

"Even so, I would not give away the secret of our script for so puny a servant, so little an amusement."

Llian was about to make a better offer, his final, when caution prevailed. This was going too fast and Rulke was controlling it. He must not seem too eager. Llian shrugged. "I can wait," he said. "I would dearly love to have the Tablet but I can spend my life without it. There is no fun in the wager if I have to risk a tell to win a grint."

"Yes, and I can wait for another thousand years if I have to. My need is nowise urgent."

They stared at each other. But *could* Rulke wait? And if he could, was he minded to? A thousand years is an eternity, and the wait might have given Rulke eternal patience. Or it might have broken it. What he did next would give him away. Llian was very skilled at sensing the mood of his audience, and he sensed that Rulke was lying. That it was urgent, that Rulke's opportunity would not come again for a very long time. But he must make himself impassive, emotionless. Llian began a tale in his mind, one so familiar that he could continue to tell it to himself even while his thoughts were elsewhere. It was a trick that he used sometimes to calm himself and blank out all outward expression.

Rulke was still staring. Llian lay down on the floor and closed his eyes. The tale reeled off in his mind. Surely Rulke did not know what to make of him. No enemy had ever behaved like this before, and he must be wondering if Llian had some power that he knew nothing about. The Zain had always been hard to read. Minutes went by.

"If you feel outclassed, I would be prepared to give you a handicap," Llian said quietly from the floor.

"I need no handicap!" Rulke roared. "I accept your challenge. My conditions are these:

"One: The Ghâshâd will adjudicate. They are mine, you will say, yet their code of honor is rigid. They will judge fairly. There will be three judges. I believe that you have met them all before: Jark-un, Yetchah and Idlis. And Idlis, the least of them, shall preside. His vote will be counted only if the others disagree;

"Two: If I win, I have her and you as well;

"Three: If I lose, you go free and I permit you to have what you want, even her, though that would inconvenience me sorely. But should you choose the Tablet, that secret you must buy, and the price is Karan of Bannador.

"That is the offer. You have one minute to consider it. If you do not accept, I shall personally go to Bannador and bring her back. I have the time."

Had he won or lost this round? On the whole Llian felt that he was ahead. A greedy look came into his eyes but was quickly hidden. He considered aloud. "She has given me much sport and no little amusement. So much that I have become quite fond of her. I am minded to say that you ask too much."

"You're unconvincing, chronicler! I know how you lust for my knowledge. You compromised yourself back in the Nightland. Had you not done so, neither you nor Karan would be here now."

Llian was so shocked that he almost gave Karan away. How could Rulke know? Did he know? "She isn't *here*," he said.

"You have ten seconds," Rulke scowled.

"Then I accept your terms," Llian rushed out at the last moment, trying to look panicked. Rulke wasn't reacting the way he'd expected him to. "The amusement that she offers can be bought easily enough. No one can say that I didn't try to save her. Ah! But how we have tumbled, she and I. I will miss her for *days*!"

Behind her rock, Karan started. This stretched her promise to the limit.

"But Santhenar is bursting with young women eager for a chronicler such as I will be. For the Tablet I would give you my mother," and the naked greed burned in his eyes now. "No master chronicler has ever had such a prize. I will build my own college; Chanthed will be just an outhouse—"

"What do you take me for, chronicler?" Rulke said coldly.

The flow of words dried up, and the self-confidence. Llian looked like an uncertain boy.

"That kind of talk doesn't impress me," said Rulke. "If I believed it for a second I'd put you out the door. However, having seen you and Karan together, I know you're putting on an act. And it's a good act. Perhaps you *are* the one to tell the Histories of the Charon after all. The telling will show your quality. Let it begin!'

46

The Telling

Rulke bounded down the stairs, calling for his Ghâshâd. Llian had an attack of nerves. Had he made things better, or worse? Previous experience suggested that Rulke was not without honor, but was he? He recalled Karan once saying that the Whelm did their master's will in all things. Did they still, now that they were Ghâshâd? And even if they judged fairly, what tale could he possibly tell that would move them more than their master's?

And what must Karan be thinking, crouched behind her slab? He had better win.

The judges had taken their stools. A dozen other Ghâshâd were assembled in two rows behind them—gaunt, cadaverous faces all much alike, save stocky, round-faced Jark-un. All were still; all silent. Rulke had changed his clothes—the black replaced by trousers and shirt of indigo silk, with a crimson sash and a flaring cape of the same color. The silk shimmered with every movement. He looked magnificent.

"My tale," said Rulke by way of preamble, "is not a tale of Santhenar. It is a tale of the distant past, when I was young and we were newly come to Aachan. Once we had a world but we lost it, treacherously cast into the void. Do you know about the void, chronicler?"

"Not as much as I'd like to," Llian murmured.

"It is a *nightmare* of savagery! A million kinds of creatures dwell there, each preying on the others, each changing constantly in a desperate attempt to survive. Intelligent creatures as well as mindless beasts. You know how great and powerful we Charon are, chronicler, but we were not good enough to survive the void. We died there, a million of us, dwindled to nothing. We were almost extinct! So we determined to conquer, to possess, to strike down the enemy first. Never to yield! Never to trust!"

He bowed his head for a moment, then looked up into Llian's eyes. "The tale—my tale—is how we found another world, and how we took it for ourselves. The tale is *How the Hundred Conquered a World.*

"How we hated our barren bright rock in the void," he cried in an over-loud voice, "where the sun-splash was like splinters through our eyeballs and the seas had boiled themselves into the air long ago, leaving only a gluey muck with the taste of clay. How we crouched there, clawing at the sky in our resentment and despair!

"Then a chance came—an opening to another planet. Someone looked out into the universe, and his inquisitiveness and his longing left a track that identified his world."

That had been Xesper the Aachim—Llian recalled Tensor cursing his name on the Dry Sea.

"We followed his artery back and found—Aachan. We knew that no other chance would ever come. *Aachan!*" he sighed, with the air of rapacious sensuality that so characterized him. "Such a darkly fecund, luminous, erotic planet. How we coveted it!

"In the void we had lost our previous name. Now we gave ourselves the name *Charon*, for a frigid moonlet at the furthest extremity of the void, to always remind us how far we had come, and what we had come from.

"I flung myself into the indifferent void—we did so, every one. We thrashed across non-existing dimensions that extend twice five ways at once. A black whirlpool beckoned to me. I leapt toward it. It hurled me into a tarry ether that burned and choked and blinded—hurled me out again. *Rejected me!* Raking intangible black clots from my nose and mouth, I spat in my hand and washed my eyes. Still I could not see or feel or hear or breathe. My feet moved past my head; my head went past my feet. The very brain seemed to spiral in its socket, then with a sordid *plop!* I bobbed to the surface of an ebony pond and floated spread-eagled on an elastic interface.

"I rubbed my eyes. They rewarded me with Aachan. Ours. *Mine!* Only the Aachim between. I lay sprawled in an oily bog. The stars flamed, opals on sable. A delicious cold aroused my skin with fire; the bog moved and a thousand reeds caressed my naked loins, cool and darting as an adder's tongue. The blood pulsed sluggish in my veins, moved in viscous spurts, sighed in my head. I abandoned myself.

"Time moved, but I did not. I was lost within a lethargic, sensual dream. Before I could bring myself to rise from my bed the small sun began to stroke the sky, and the underside of the leaves above gleamed with blood. The landscape was revealed, soft and round, luscious as the bottom of a maiden at prayer. I could have mounted a tree, even a rock."

Rulke was all aglow, his handsome face alive with the memory of that far-off time. The urgent lust of his youth was like a flame, waking an echo in those that watched. The walls of the tower seemed to expand and contract. Llian stirred, uneasy. The Whelm watched, mostly impassive.

Karan, crouched behind the wall, felt the skin on her arms rise in goosebumps. How long had it been since she and Llian had made love? Months! She wanted him now with a passion that was quite reckless.

"But already our chance was fading. We were so few—we must take the surprise to them; must strike with violence!

Then the chilling thought—where were the other Charon? Surely they must be near. If we had not come through together . . ."

Suddenly he leapt halfway across the room, crimson cape flaring out from his shoulders. "I sprang out of the bog, flung off the slime. My toes curled around the ground beneath the ooze and I was off, running through the humid cool dawn. Naked we came to Aachan, and weaponless. Clothes we could do without, but weapons we must have, for the owners of this world were many. We were but two hundred, all that remained of our species.

"Before me was one of the upright stalked things they called a tree. There had been none on our scalding rock. A part of it hung over. I smashed it off with my fist, making a snowfall of leaves in my hair." Rulke struck the construct a mighty blow; it rocked in the air. "I shaped it roughly into a club, a cruel sharp knot on the large end. But was I a beast, a thing without dignity, nobility, culture? I flung it away. Until there was a weapon to suit I would use my hands.

"The breeze sighed, plucking the leaves from my hair. How full-to-bursting life seemed! Before me was a long soft slope of grass, and at the top a structure, perhaps a dwelling, for it was small. A thing of domes, curving into one another. To you, Llian, whom I know to be a student of the whole, it might have looked like the kidney of an ox. To me it was less than the sum of its parts, and the parts had the shape of a ripe woman's behind. I was up there with no more sound than smoke in a still sky.

"The place was open. Good; they must have nothing to fear! And yet, weapons hung in a hall. I did not take them and run, as I should have; I was curious to learn about these people. It was still dark inside, but my eyes adjusted. There were many chambers in one part of it, like a hive. I went from one to the next, bringing death like a wasp; to men, to women, even to children." His eyes flared fire. Llian had to turn away from the conflagration. "Why did I do that? I often wondered, after. I would not do it now; not on the innocent. I remember the feeling though—a killing urge, a lust for death, a violent sensual thing linked to that other lust that had been strong in me since I woke, too long in the void. They were proud, those Aachim, but unused to death. Not till my hands were at their throats did they know me and why I came.

"In minutes the chambered part was a charnel house. I stood there panting, looking down at my work, trying to know my enemy. They were strong beautiful people, soft of skin and rich of voice even when my thumbs were on their windpipes. The kind of beauty that does not fade with age, and slowly even in death. Here was one, naked in her bed. I might have yet . . . But no. No time for that!

"The other part was open, as if I was within a shell of many chambers. I went past a place where flame swirled in a box made of glass. There were rugs on the floor, beautiful in pattern and color; tapestries woven with metal threads; sculptures of metal and stone; carvings, paintings, calligraphy. I saw more beauty in this house than on the whole of that cinder that had been our world. Well, thus far it had been easy. Aachan would be ours this day.

"Perhaps the passage had drained me, or the thicker air intoxicated me. I felt exhausted, starving. And I had blundered badly, for one was left alive. Maybe she had come in from outside—I'll never know. She just appeared on the far side of that open space. She was one of the smaller ones, and quite beautiful, though her face was twisted horribly in her silent grief. Karan looks very like her," he said, turning to Llian. "Even to the color of her hair. I was moved at her grief, though I was the cause of it. I have seen her likeness more than once since. My harbinger then, but no more. Elienor, Elienor!"

Out of the corner of his eye Llian saw Idlis rise to his feet, his thin-lipped mouth hanging open.

Rulke continued. "She had her hand on a metal plate—a mirror, I later realized—and was speaking urgently at it. Was she calling to other communities? If so I had made a grave mistake and risked all. She must die. I leapt across the room and knocked her down, but she was very fast, and in the hand I could not see was a long broad knife, wickedly sharp. As I struck her she stabbed me between the ribs and wrenched the knife, cutting open my chest from front to back. The knife jammed in my ribs; she scrabbled across the tiles and was gone.

"She had killed me, surely. The air rushed out of my lung in a humid cloud. I staggered across the room and fell down on a bench, gasping for air. My side burned like acid. Pink foam oozed from the wound, and a terrible amount of blood. I lay there gasping; dying; watching the blood ebb from me to make beautiful ruby patterns on the white floor.

"I was so weak that a child could have slain me with a butter knife. I swooned, but jerked awake almost at once. Swooned again.

"Who knows how long I lay there, but the blood underneath me would have filled a drinking bowl. My feelings were indescribable. The enemy was warned. Hours I had dreamed away in the bog; more hours in this killing frenzy. The Charon were doomed and my follies were the cause, *my lusts!* How could two hundred overcome a million?"

"A fear rose up in me that was the worst fear of all. This day would see the Charon extinct—our species gone from the universe forever.

"But we Charon never give up. While I lived, duty must be done. If I could drag myself, I must add my weight to theirs. This was an imperative so strong that only death could stop it. That cinder in the void to which we clung had seen our ruin. Now of the once numberless Charon only a handful remained, barely enough to renew ourselves on another world. There had been other times, other chances, and we had gone out in our twos and threes and fours, trying to find a way. But none survived; none returned to lead us to a new home. This was our last chance, but only if most of us survived. Now surprise was gone; I had thrown it away. A mere thousand of them and we would be extinct. Extinguished!

Expunged!" Rulke's face was wracked, the face of a man in the last throes of crucifixion. *"No Charon ever more!*

"I heaved the knife out in a gust of blood. Almost fainting, I pulled apart the lips of the wound to see how badly I was damaged. Very badly. There was a hole in me that you could have put your foot in. That last wrench had cut through my ribs, so sharp and heavy was her knife. Some cut-off pieces of rib floated in the wound. I put in my hand and pulled them out, feeling around in the cavity to be sure I had them all. Underneath I could see the flaccid pink thing that had been my lung."

He tore open his shirt. A thick, ugly scar extended from below the nipple, under his arm and halfway to his backbone.

"What did we know about the Aachim and their world? Only that their most important city and seat of governance was in this part of the country. We had directed ourselves to it, as near as the unstable void and our own imperfect knowledge would allow. But something had separated me from my fellows. Perhaps that streak in me, that has always directed me to strike out alone, sent me to this place instead. Distantly I could sense the other Charon and their peril. A vast threat was building against us, a force of overwhelming strength. We were unarmed. I felt the pain again, the surety that our kind would be annihilated. I could not allow it. That pain was worse than the agony in my side.

"I forced the pain down, considered what to do. Probably the others had come out together to move on the capital in darkness. That had been our plan—to seize their most sacred place, and their leaders. But I had violated the plan, given away the surprise. I sensed that things had gone wrong from that moment. I must act as if I was our only hope. I must allow nothing to stop me. *Nothing!*

"First, the wound. About the lung I could do nothing, only hope that time would heal it. It must weaken me greatly. But the gash needed to be held together, and the bleeding stopped. I had no needle or thread, nor wits to search for either, but necessity made a way. In the large room of shells was a sculpture of gold wire, a most beautiful thing, as fine as gossamer. I smashed it apart, wove wire together to make a golden thread, seared this in a flame, punched holes in myself with a sliver of metal and sewed the wound together again with the wire. I felt some pain before that was done," he said in a profound understatement, "and the wound bound up with strips of cloth until no blood came through.

"Among the dead there were ones that were almost of a size to me, and I took the robes from one, the boots from another and strapped the knife that had so damaged me to my leg. I took no other weapons; I had no strength to carry them. The woman I had lusted after lay there, one hand flung out toward her child, and she was as beautiful as before, and as dead. But now my passion was spent, as if the knife had cut much lower.

"There was no room for pity but I did regret. I picked up the dead child and gave it back to the mother, covering her nakedness with a sheet before I went out. I can still see her face, and the child's." He shook his head as though to clear the memory, then bowed it in a minute's silence for his victims.

"The killing lust was gone and has never returned. I have killed since then, in self-defense or in the heat of battle. Necessity makes us what we are, not nature. But no more for the joy of it. Never after.

"I went out of that place to the top of the hill and looked down. Would that I had done so before. Below was a city which I knew to be their greatest, though it was not a big place. The Aachim never made cities like the fecund cesspools of Santhenar. But a metropolis nonetheless, many thousands. On the uphill side was an open space with five sides, and behind that a great public building. A strange beautiful subtle place, unlike any I have ever seen. But you know of their genius in that way.

"The eyes of the Charon are keen. As I came down the hill I saw fighting in several places. We had been split into groups, each surrounded by a multitude of the enemy. The warning had come in time for them to rally. Need was for a daring stroke, and it could not wait. We were being slaughtered in battle. What if they put the prisoners to the sword? I could not bear to think about it.

"I went down the hill as quickly as I could without attracting attention. I am not dissimilar in looks to an Aachim, though bigger than most. You wonder, Llian? Ah, but the Aachim were bigger then. In robes and boots I was not challenged, even after I came into the streets of the city. But I could feel the agony of my people. The tide had turned against us; the Aachim, despite that they had no enemies, were well prepared. As soon as the warning was given they flocked to their posts, while most of us were still naked and weaponless.

"Often that day I felt the death cry or the sudden absence of a friend, as if a part of myself had been erased. At last I reached the center. With each breath I could feel the blood turning to foam in my chest, bubbling horribly. The pain was unbearable; I felt that I was slowly drowning. No matter how deep I breathed, the air was not enough. Blood poured down under my robes into my boot, squelching as I ran."

Rulke relived that moment as if he was actually back there. "I must rest. It feels as if I am dying. The air is turning the color of blood, the people before me breaking into strands and streaks. I sit down. But my people are dying every minute—I may not rest! I get up, force myself a step, then another. Each yard is my world; my past and my future. Nothing exists but the next."

He stared blankly at Llian, then recovered and reverted to the teller. "That was hard, but to do it without looking like a madman, a white-faced, staring, jerk-limbed puppet, that was much harder yet. But I did it, making my gait smooth, knuckling my cheeks to bring the color into them.

"Now I heard angry voices in front of me. A great militia surged forward, herding my people into a tight knot. I could do nothing here. Were they to be slaughtered I would die with them, for there can be no greater pain than to be the last of your kind. I prepared to hurl myself forward. But no, these Aachim were folk bound by codes, or at least rituals, and there was to be a trial. So I gathered from what was happening, though I could not understand their speech. Two guards took hold of each prisoner and they were led into the vast hall. I followed.

"Inside, my small hope became no hope. There were more than a thousand Aachim in the room and many times that number outside. How few we were—a hundred gone already; only a hundred left in the universe. No hope! My exhaustion and pain suddenly came down on me. I clung to the wall in a shadowed alcove, sucking in air, every breath agony. Were it not that many of the Aachim were in a similar state it would have given me away.

"Nothing happened for a long time, then the angry buzz of talk died away. Over the heads of the crowd I saw two people, a woman and a man, come onto the dais behind the prisoners. They entered without a retinue, but with great formality. I saw what we had understood from our spying, that they were greatly reverenced. Both were quite old, but moved regally. The room was absolutely still. They sat down and the proceedings began.

"The woman spoke, and the man. Then the woman again. Though I could not understand their words, I found a sudden hope. This pair were too greatly reverenced by the Aachim. Their weakness, my opportunity! I knew not how, but that I would leave to the instant.

"Now my people were being called to account, one by one. In turn each of them was led forward, a charge read out, witnesses spoke briefly, each had a turn to speak in their defense, and many did, defiantly, though surely their words meant nothing to the Aachim. After that the two on the dais conferred, the woman signaled and the prisoner was taken to the other side of the room and held under guard. This was done with deliberation. The whole proceedings might take another three hours, I calculated, though perhaps it would be quicker at the end. I allowed myself but two.

"I slipped back out the door, too hastily, for one man looked at me curiously as I passed. Perhaps I had committed an error of discourtesy, or protocol. I went around the further side of the hall, which was a huge building of metal and stone, and found that at the rear there were smaller buildings attached. Even walking up that gentle slope wearied me, but only when I tried to climb onto the roof did I appreciate the toll that the wound had taken of my strength.

"Only will drove me now, an urge so primitive that it could not be stopped save by my death. I reached the roof of the smaller building, my heart threatening to burst out through the hole in my side. Each gasp for the air that would not come whistled in my chest. I sat down on the roof. Once more the world took on a rarefied view, as if I observed it from a distance. I saw myself take off my boot and shake out quivering clots of blood the size of placentas; they went splat! on the roof. I stared at the horrid splashes, unable to imagine that they had been a part of me.

"A man, the one who had noticed me in the doorway, was creeping up onto the roof. I stared at myself staring at him, willing my arm to move. The man must have thought I was mad, standing there with my blood and my boot. A woman appeared beside him. From their looks they were brother and sister, and she the younger. She was in no doubt as to what I was. Her hand dropped to the knife on her belt.

"I willed my arm; it heaved one of those bloody jellyfish at her face. It shocked her, the red mess wobbling in the air toward her; she slipped and I kicked her in the belly with my bloody foot. Not a hard kick, but she fell backwards off the roof and didn't return. The brother cried out and flung himself forward, onto my knife. I let him come until he sagged down, then I turned away to the higher roof.

"By the time I reached it I'd lost all sense of time—all how, all why, all when, as if my conscious mind had passed the quest on to a deeper, less articulate, more dogged self.

"I had become a machine, blindly carrying out each task

until it was finished, then supplied with a new one until it in turn was done.

"Eventually I reached the roofs above the dais, as near as I could judge. These were made of thick metal, which in my state I could not shift, but the valleys between the roofs were lead that I could cut with my knife.

"From there I was able to gain access to the space inside. I clambered in, creeping along beams of metal and timber until I judged that I was above the dais. It was dark inside the roof, but not pitch dark.

"The ceiling of the hall was made of metal panels, pressed into intricate patterns. I prised up the edge of one with the knife and put my eye to the sliver of light.

"The judging seemed to be nearly complete; there were only a handful of Charon on the near side. But I was some distance from where I needed to be.

"Suddenly the pain was back, a terrible desperate pain that would not allow me to think. It went, then it came back again. I could not even remember who I was.

"By the time it receded I was too weak to crawl the few paces that I needed. My boot had filled with fresh blood. Inspiration took me! I tore off the boot.

"I poured the blood onto the panel. It made a small pool there, about as much as a full tea bowl. I forced a corner of the metal down and the blood began to drip through the ceiling, right onto the table, the papers and the presiding Aachim.

"I did not look down, but the sudden silence, and the tumult that followed, told me what I needed to know. Later I learned the sensation that the blood had caused—a symbol of doom and disaster. The diversion gave me the minute's rest that I needed.

"I dragged myself along until I was directly above the spot that I wanted. The panels were soldered with lead. I sawed it away from three sides.

"I judged the fall once more. It was a long way, five or six spans at least. Wounded as I was, the fall might well kill me. Certainly I would break bones.

"I swung myself up above the panel and clung there. My side wailed in agony; my head swam; my stomach heaved. I spewed there on the beam. No time to rest; they were hurrying through the judging, upset by the omen.

"I dropped, crashed through the panel and fell like a stone, down and down, onto the center of the long table. It split beneath me and the legs at one end collapsed. I felt the most shocking pain that I have ever felt, and looked down to see the shattered ends of my thigh bone protruding through the flesh. The golden stitches along my side burst open; red foam sprayed across the table. I wept bloody tears. The two venerable Aachim stared at the gruesome wreck before them. They were too shocked to move. With the last vestige of will my body could summon, I swept them into one arm and put my knife to their throats.

"The Aachim were staring all, their agony seemingly as great as my own. My eyes picked out a single face in the crowd, the red-haired woman who had wounded me that morning. Her eyes were sunken as craters; her face as blanched as the white of an egg. I had obliterated her house. Elienor! I pity her now. I spat blood on the floor and spoke to her, to all the Aachim. My voice was a whisper, but that was enough.

" 'Throw down your arms!' I cried. 'The Charon have come to Aachan, and it is ours.'

"To my surprise they made no resistance. The rest took only a minute, and then—blessed oblivion."

Rulke came back to himself slowly. He looked to Llian. "So it was that a hundred captured a world. *The Hundred!* So the Charon survived. That is my tale. Every word of it is truth.'

47

THE REPLY

Llian bowed to Rulke. His face was austere, but inside he was exultant. Rulke's had been a masterly tale, a barbaric splendor, and none who heard it were unmoved. But for all that, it was a simple tale, a performance. A tale told too well, too truthfully, and to his challenger rather than his audience. Or rather, he had told his tale as if the audience was Llian, perhaps unconsciously seeking to impress the great teller. And he had, but watching the faces of the Whelm, Llian had noticed that they were shocked and disturbed by something Rulke had described.

I know what moves them, Llian thought. It was Rulke's selfindulgence that had put the Charon in such a dire extreme, necessitating his heroic acts, and this jarred against the rigid codes that were everything to the Ghâshâd. To them duty was all, but Rulke had failed that duty. He had put his lust, his glory, his honor before the survival of the Charon, and his reckless courage had not redeemed him in their eyes.

Llian threw out the tale he had been mentally rehearsing

and began to construct another. At the same time he worked to suppress his personality as much as possible. The Ghâshâd were an ascetic, sober folk who frowned on pleasure and frivolity. *The message, not the telling!* No rhetoric, just a plain tale with a meaning that they could not fail to understand.

"My tale begins long afterwards," he said in a soft, neutral voice, "almost at the time of the Forbidding. And the subject of my story is an entirely different people: not great, not proud. Their vision had a smaller compass. Theirs was to serve. Duty, loyalty, honor: that was what their lives were made for. And they were called Myrmide, a word which in their tongue meant to serve and to obey without question.

"Where they came from, no one knows. They settled in the southeast of Lauralin, beyond the land of Ogur and the Black Sea. A small, slender, black-haired people they were, and at first the cold troubled them terribly, for the place they had been driven to was under snow for six months of the year, and the sea covered in ice for four. The Ghâsh Peninsula, that place was called, and still is."

Rulke sat bolt upright on his stool, frowning. He knows what I'm up to, Llian thought. I'm not going to get away with this.

"The full name was Ghâsh-ad-Nâsh, that is to say, fume-and-fire, for the long extension of that land into the Kara Nâshâl (the Smoking Sea) was dotted with vents from which liquid rock flowed, and steam, smoke and ash blasted into the sky. But later they found this place much to their liking, for there were secret valleys where the springs stayed hot even when the sun had set for the long winter and the ground froze as hard as iron.

"One peculiarity these Myrmide had, and that was this: they must have a master and a purpose, else they were nothing. Their whole lives, pride and worth were invested in such service. Their master at the time of my tale was Bandiar, a minor necromanter but an important person on the peninsula, though the world would never have heard of him if it had not been for Shuthdar.

"After Shuthdar fled to Santhenar with the stolen flute," Llian glanced at Rulke, who was watching him keenly, "he was ever hunted. Eventually he fled to backward places where the people were uncouth and spoke strange languages, but the result was always the same. Toward the end he ended up in the Ghâsh Peninsula, and even there he was harried. Shuthdar was old, tired and crippled now. His life had been one bitterness piled on another until he came to hate all things, including life. The only thing in his life was his beautiful flute."

"*My* flute," said Rulke, almost inaudibly.

"He took refuge in a cave on that frozen shore, where one day Bandiar found him and brought him back to his fastness. Why did Bandiar do so? He too lusted after thc flute, though he was clever enough not to show it. If he treated Shuthdar kindly, asking nothing of him, Shuthdar would in the end come to rely on him utterly.

"But Shuthdar, though decrepit beyond imagining, had a mind as mad and sharp as a pin. In his life he had known many kinds of people, but they had all wanted the one thing. He knew that Bandiar was no different.

"From the moment Shuthdar arrived he caused trouble. He was paranoid and cunning, wicked and malicious; a creature of perverse and deadly lusts. In the dark corners of the castle none was safe from him: neither girl nor crone, old man nor boy, nor beast neither. Though he was crippled and moved with a crabwise scuttle, when hot in his lusts he could scuttle with frightening speed, and those withered arms were strong as spring steel.

"But Bandiar would not stay Shuthdar in any way. He excused all these crimes as the small failings of a genius, so that Shuthdar took delight in each new and sordid escapade that went unchecked. His excesses became marvels of theater and exhibitionism, and soon all learned to keep clear of the dreadful thing."

Llian saw on the faces of the judges only contempt for such a master, for as the servants had a duty to the master, so the master's duty was equally sacred. Now to draw the next link.

"The Myrmide were a people inclined to melancholy. Outside duty their only pleasure was music. Their music was beautiful but doleful, like dry wind among ruins; like tapping on icicles. Apart from music they wanted but one thing: to meet their master's purpose as best they could, and never question it, not even when it became clear that the one Bandiar fawned upon was a malicious creature who considered nothing but his own desires; who took all and gave nothing.

"Time wore on and still Shuthdar stayed, for Bandiar had power to protect him from the wolves that had tormented him in every other place, and wealth to gratify even his most sordid whims. But the absence of any check and the gratification of every whim gave Shuthdar license to think of excesses so abominable that eventually not even the most degraded would come to him.

"What can Bandiar have thought each time Shuthdar came whining and accusing him? Let us be charitable and imagine that he thought: 'Just this once will I indulge him, and surely he will give me what I want.' Whatever, events took a nasty new turn. Young people began to disappear, taken by force. At first they turned up again afterwards, after a day; a week; or a month. Some told tales of unspeakable degradation, but others could not speak at all.

"Bandiar's subjects beat on the great doors of the stronghold, demanding Shuthdar's head. Bandiar refused them, coldly. The Myrmide, who were servants, soldiers, spies all, remained loyal to their master. They drove the peasants away with fire and terror, out into the snow. Even little children they struck down, for this showed best how committed they were to their master's purpose.

"Then the people did the only thing they could. All power and wealth resided with Bandiar, while they had none. They would not risk their children any more. Weeping and wailing they abandoned their lands and homes and withdrew into the mountains, and many died there in the winter. But theirs is another tale.

"Now the Myrmide began to feel an agonizing doubt—that the master they served so loyally was a fool who was made a fool of. But this doubt, this disloyalty, they suppressed."

Llian paused to grasp a mug of water. The trials of the past week were catching up. He barely had the strength to stay on his feet. What was worse, he could feel his control of the tale going. He crashed the mug down, then continued.

"All Bandiar's ends were now directed to getting the flute, or the secret of it, from Shuthdar, and in this Shuthdar played with him most cunningly, and took much amusement from his game. Every now and again he would give Bandiar a clue—a word, a scroll, once a lengthy book full of strange diagrams and descriptions of alarming or abstract processes. But the clues only led into a maze of intersecting puzzles and paradoxes, for Shuthdar had made them all up. When Bandiar complained, Shuthdar would insult him or mock him for being a fool, and then, apparently relenting after days or weeks, would give another teasing clue that seemed to offer a resolution of the puzzle, but in fact led ever deeper into the morass.

"The Myrmide were caught up in their master's great project. They saw the researches, the collaboration (as they thought) with Shuthdar, the steady accumulation of work, the ever more intricate models and devices that Bandiar made, all having the appearance of working, with parts that moved and even the production of strange though transitory effects. But in the end—*nothing!*

"Then in their innermost minds a little germ of doubt flowered—that they were made fools of. And this led to a heretical thought, that it was not right to use such means to gain his end; that Bandiar was corrupt. But after all he was their master, and without him they were nothing. And he had a good and noble purpose, this secret of the flute, worth any sacrifice. They put aside their doubts and continued to serve."

Llian looked to his three judges. Jark-un's face was hard as stone. Clearly he thought the whole business was a nonsense. Llian knew that he would never sway him. Yetchah had a mobile face for a Ghâshâd, reacting each time he highlighted the Myrmide's dilemma. What could he say to play upon her sensitivity? And Idlis—he looked as though he had been put on the rack, but Llian judged that it would take a most exceptional tale for him to go against his master. So be it.

"Now among the Myrmide was one called Nassi, a young woman, and she was accounted the least of them, for she was neglectful of her duty, and this brought shame on her and on all the Myrmide. She was not wicked, though they said that of her; nor lazy—they accused her of that too. She tried to be a good Myrmide, a good servant, but her work was never done for dreaming, or fretting about right and wrong, or just sitting in a warm hidey-hole reading the stories of other lands and other peoples.

"She had a ready smile and a warm heart; she was generous and laughed a lot. In short, a thoroughly wicked, wilful and unpleasant Myrmide. The others set a better example: they were very stern. Occasionally one or other of them would smile a thin smile but they never laughed. Yet they had a duty to her too, and they never tired of beating her, to teach her her duty. This went on even after she became a woman taller than many of them. But she was big and plump, with a cheerful round open face, and though the beatings hurt her they did not curb her spirit.

"One task she did well, and that was maintaining Bandiar's workrooms, though there she found an interest in his work that went beyond the duty of a servant. The Myrmide rebuked her for this; then, realizing that Bandiar was pleased to have her help and liked her for her good humor, they saw that it was, on the whole, a good thing. Bandiar often talked about his project to her with barely a hint of condescension, for she had a quick mind.

"As time went by the two became closer than may be wise between servant and master. Nassi came to revere her master, yet she would never share his bed. The Myrmide took her aside again. Was there nothing she could do right? She treated Bandiar as a friend, and that was wrong, but when he wished her to do her duty in his bed she refused. There were more beatings, which Nassi endured with good grace, and life went back to what it had been before."

Llian knew that in his weariness he was losing his train of thought. The tale was rambling. He forced it back on track.

"Shuthdar disliked Nassi, for she was the one person he could not fool, and his suggestions to Bandiar that he be given her had been curtly rejected. Even Bandiar would not agree to that. Shuthdar began to lurk in dark passages through which she might pass, hoping to waylay her, but after her first escape she kept to the lighted ways and took great care of herself.

"There came a time when Bandiar had to go away for a month, and as Nassi by now had few other duties, she spent most of that time in his workrooms, for he had asked her to put in order all the papers related to his great project. Nassi first read enough of each to understand where it belonged, but she began to see a different pattern to the one Bandiar had derived. Doubtless she had made a mistake. She was just a Myrmide, and a lazy one at that.

"Nassi went over the collection again, carefully, sitting by the fire in Bandiar's study, a big jar of his sweetmeats beside her, or a box of pastries lifted from the kitchen during the night. Days of reading and eating went by and still it would not fit together the way Bandiar wanted. But it began to fit all too well another way.

"She lay in the darkness of her room, unable to sleep, turning the pieces of the puzzle over in her mind. More days passed, in which she scarcely slept, pulling the models and machines apart and remaking them in new arrangements. Finally there was no doubt. The purpose that had sustained Bandiar for years, into which he had put his labor and intellect, and most of his wealth, that he had pursued at the expense of his subjects, the Myrmide and all honor and decency, was revealed to be a cruel hoax whose only purpose was to expose his folly.

"Nassi was struck to the core. Her life and the lives of all the Myrmide were undermined. They had corrupted themselves for nothing. Like Bandiar, they were nothing; *a hollow people!*"

Llian looked into the eyes of the judges, one by one. Had Idlis taken the point? He couldn't tell, but Rulke had. He was scowling fiercely at Llian, his fingers tearing paper into tiny strips, then across. The floor around his stool was littered with confetti.

Llian scanned the judges once more. Yetchah was turning, he was sure of it. But the other two, still against him. Well, at least Idlis would be forced to cast his vote. Was there anything that would move him?

"Nassi called the Myrmide to a meet and told them what she had discovered. The Myrmide were shocked, for what she said found an echo in their own fears. But they were outraged too, and humiliated. They stopped their ears against her words, beating her for the betrayal of their master's honor, the dereliction of her own duty, and her meddling, and threw her into a dank cell at the bottom of the stronghold until Bandiar's return.

"These dungeons were a place much to Shuthdar's liking. He often came down to cling to the bars and cackle at her, for though she discomforted him with her clear sight, he was secretly delighted that someone had seen his joke. She seemed more worthy of his heritage than any other he had met. She understood the complex dimensions and secrets that his mind encompassed, yet she wanted none of them. Perhaps he could corrupt her too.

"He came night after night, whispering the dark secrets of

his trade to her, hoping to make more mischief between her and her master. This place wearied him now.

"At last Bandiar returned and called the Myrmide to account. Nassi's crime was so unspeakable that the Myrmide would not tell of it, only pleaded for her death. Bandiar, however, called another meet and bade her say what she had done.

"She told her story again. The papers were brought down; the models too. Nassi showed the way Bandiar had put them together, how she had changed them, what they did now. She drew it all together, revealed the plan and the malicious joke that it showed. Their master, their whole lives and purpose: *nothing!*

"There was an agonized silence. The terrible humiliation was plain on Bandiar's face. The Myrmide prayed that he would deny it.

" 'Master,' they cried. 'We do not hear this. Tell us that it is not true. Allow us to punish her for this vile deceit.'

"They knew it was true. They could read it in his eyes.

"What could he say? A word, even a gesture, would have been enough. Bandiar hesitated. He could scarcely bring himself to utter the lies they wanted to hear. His face looked about to crack apart along the seams of mouth and nose and eyes. Finally he spoke.

" 'My dear Myrmide,' he said, smiling a false smile. 'How could . . .?'

"Then Shuthdar lurched in, whooping, gobs of rusty slime dripping from his iron teeth.

" 'It's true!' he cackled in unholy glee. 'What a joke! The best I've had in a thousand years! And when it comes to the register of fools, the tale of Bandiar and the Myrmide will stand for another thousand.' He gasped and wheezed, a peal of mad laughter echoing off the walls.

"Bandiar could hardly deny it. He shuddered and stood up. " 'Yes, it is true,' he said, and his face showed the contempt he felt for himself and for the Myrmide too. 'I am a fool, and you are fools for serving me.' Putting his weapons on the table, he walked down among them.

"They could ignore the truth no longer. They fell on him and hacked him to death, every one of the Myrmide having a hand in it, save Nassi. She stood to one side, staring at the bloody corpse, shocked into immobility. She had cared for Bandiar. Surely he did not deserve this.

"The Myrmide turned to the other two and would have done the same to them, but Shuthdar had seen what must come next. With his nails he slashed Nassi's bonds and cried, 'Come with me, child. There's no place for you here anymore.'

"She looked at the Myrmide and then at Shuthdar, and put out a plump arm. Shuthdar gripped it in his iron-hard claw, and with the other hand brought out the golden flute and put it to his lips. The Myrmide drew back in fear. Then Shuthdar blew one-handed a haunting melody, a tune that lived forever in those that heard it, and then he and Nassi vanished."

Still there was no sign of what Idlis might be thinking. The tale is already too long, Llian thought. Draw the moral, and finish it!

"The Myrmide looked down at the red rags that had been their master, sickened at what they had become through serving and obeying without question. They had committed the ultimate betrayal.

" 'We take no master ever more,' they cried. 'We are Myrmide no longer. We are *Nunst* now and forever. From nothing we came; to nothing do we return.'

"Then they went back to the Ghâsh-ad-Nâsh, crouching among the rocks and snow, the fire, fumes and ice, and that is what they became, Nunst. *Nothing!* Creatures of shame and guilt and fear, no longer having the will even to be, and now they are gone to nothing. The Myrmide are no more. The only trace of them—a curious custom that still lives in that part of the far south—is that before each meal the people make their Atonement, though for what, none remembers any more."

So they do, Karan thought, crouching in her hiding place, remembering Hassien, that thin, dark-haired, strong-willed woman with the sibilant accent, who had done just that on the ride in Pender's boat to Sith last year.

Llian looked around at his audience. Had he done enough? Too late now, if he hadn't. Rulke's face was almost purple, but the Ghâshâd were very still.

"And Nassi? She survived, though she did not stay with Shuthdar after they reappeared a long way away. She went alone out into the world, becoming a necromanter and a wise woman, and lived to a great age. She died at the time of the Forbidding, it is said, but the house that she founded at Saludith is still there. That is my tale."

Llian bowed to the three judges, to the assembled Ghâshâd, and to Rulke. Rulke did not bow in return. The allegory was not lost on him.

"I notice you dared not say 'every word of it is truth,' " he cried in a black voice. "That is no tale. It is a fable, constructed out of oddments to play on the fancy of the Ghâshâd. Ghâsh-ad-Nâsh indeed! Look at him, Ghâshâd—*the chronicler is a cheat!*"

"It is a tale," said Llian, "and based on truth. That is the sacred code of the teller. The teller is free to tell his tale in whatever fashion he choses, the only burden being that the story may not be improved at the expense of truth. There is a Ghâsh Peninsula; there *were* a people called Myrmide, that served Bandiar and killed him, and are now gone. The Atonement is *still* made, in that land."

He looked toward the judges. They consulted one another.

Karan held her breath. If he succeeded in this she would never doubt him again.

"We lived in the south. We know the facts to be true. We judge it to be a tale," said Idlis after a long pause.

Rulke's face went very hard. "Then cast your vote," he said harshly. "And remember this, Ghâshâd! Twice you failed me with Maigraith. Do not fail me again."

There was a moment of absolute stillness. The globes on

the walls bathed the room in a brittle ice-blue light. Llian heard a small noise below, the sound of a door closing quietly.

Jark-un spoke. "My vote is for the tale of Rulke," he rasped. Llian had expected that.

Rulke looked to the second. "Llian of Chanthed," Yetchah said with a sigh, her almost pretty face distorted under the strain.

Every face turned to Idlis. He had a nose like a hatchet blade—big, sharp and curving. The rest of him was as hard. *I am the least of the Whelm—so I must strive the harder.* That was how he had described himself to Karan long ago. How would he strive this time?

Karan vainly tried to restrain her thrashing heart. Idlis was an honorable man, though his code was impossible for her to fathom. She tried to reach out to him but only met blackness.

Llian could see that Idlis was twisted on the horns of his conflict, duty versus honor. The scars on his face grew purple, the flesh around them white beneath the gray skin. The planes of his face flexed. How to reconcile duty to his master and his requirement to judge fairly?

"There is little to choose between the two," Idlis said. He spoke very slowly and distinctly. The one is the *tale* of a fool, and the other the tale *of a fool.* I choose the tale and not the fool."

"What is your vote?" shouted Rulke, quite unsettled.

"I judge Llian's to be the better."

The silence stretched out like the moment before the hangman's trapdoor opens. Jark-un slid off his stool, turned and smashed Idlis down with a tremendous blow to the face. "The president is indisposed," he said. "His vote is invalid. I cast his vote. The challenge is lost."

Idlis crawled off, blood dripping from his lip. Jark-un drew back his boot. The Ghâshâd let out a collective hiss and he turned away. "Healer, heal yourself," he said.

"The Great Betrayer!" Llian sneered at Rulke. "Your tale reveals you, just as much as your servant's actions. A self-indulgent fool whose folly puts all at risk and then must make himself the hero to save it. That is not the kind of master that the Ghâshâd waited for, all those centuries."

Jark-un's fist swung again and Llian found himself on the floor, spitting blood.

"Enough!" snapped Rulke. He strode to one side of the room and pressed a tiny plate. The slab behind which Karan listened swung up. She tried to dart away, but was stiff from hours of crouching there, and Rulke had already touched another plate. A second slab fell behind her.

"Take her!" he roared at the Ghâshâd. "Take them both."

The subdued Ghâshâd hesitated, shamed. Rulke had offended against their honor. He was their perfect master no longer. But still their master, and they obeyed.

48

The Temptation of Karan

They were thrown into a dark room that was very cold. Llian was dazed from the blow; it was some minutes before he even knew where he was. Cold seeped through his side where he lay on something icy, but his head was cradled in warmth and softness.

He opened his eyes. They were in a gloomy room, the only light coming in through oddly shaped slots in the wall. His head was in Karan's lap, her hands running backwards and forwards through his hair. Realizing that he was himself again, she smiled and put a cool hand over the bruise on his cheek.

"The wheel turns, and turns again," he said. "Isn't this how we met?"

She kissed him on the forehead and on the eyelids and then on the mouth. Desire for him burned like a furnace. She kissed him on the throat, toying with his shirt buttons with her free hand.

"Ah, but I didn't know you then and admired you too

much. Talk about the tale of a fool! Was there ever a bigger pair than us? You overlooked the obvious defect in your plan—that you bargained with the Great Betrayer."

"Yes, but how did you like the tale?" he asked weakly.

She laughed. "What an ego you have! I thought it well enough, though I probably would have voted for the other." Then she pursed her lips, frowned like a schoolteacher and spoke, deliberately pedantic. "Yet since you ask, there were several points I would bring to your attention, thus: the beginning was unsatisfactory, both because of length and for its dubious relevance to the theme; there was much repetition of phrasing and of ideas; the parallel between the Myrmide and the Ghâshâd, and between Nassi and Idlis, was far too unsubtle; your reference to the ritual of Atonement was incorrect in a technical sense; the ending . . ."

"Enough!" cried Llian, pretending rage, though one hand was busy at her waistband. "Have you nothing good to say about it?"

"Well," she replied, helping him with her fastenings, "as a cautionary tale it was well tailored to its audience. The other points I pass over, all save one. The challenge is finished; we are still here. What do you have to say to that?"

"Hmm," said Llian. "I knew there was something that I'd forgotten."

Karan burst out laughing, and Llian was smiling too. One of the Ghâshâd looked in through the peephole to see them laughing and fondling one another, and thought them a very strange enemy.

"I can't help wondering if you might not have distorted the truth a little in your tale," she said shortly.

Llian reluctantly raised his head from her breast, pretending to consider the question. "Perhaps I did . . . cheat a little. I told no falsehood, but the fragments I wove together did not all belong, and I embellished them somewhat. I think that, on balance, I have severely broken the first Rule of Telling."

"Rule of Telling!" snorted Karan, pushing his head back

down again. "Only the totally amoral, such as chroniclers are, would seek to so mystify and entangle what is, after all, an act that every one of us engages in. In any case, to cheat your enemy is not a crime. I would do it without a thought. But to cheat the Great Betrayer—I think the chroniclers might even make a tale of that. But only a minor one," she amended hastily.

"Telling is an ancient and noble art," said Llian pompously. "What the vulgar masses do is not telling."

"Am I one of the vulgar that you sneer at?" she asked with a wicked grin. "And yet, there is another act that everyone engages in. Do you call that vulgar too?"

"Not when I engage in it," he retorted.

Karan rolled him onto his back. "Enough," he cried, "I submit."

Sometime later, tracing his fingers down her naked throat, Llian realized that something was missing. "Where's your silver chain, Karan?"

"I pawned it in Thurkad. It nearly broke my heart."

He just looked at her. "For me? Back then when you so mistrusted me?"

"I still *loved* you. I was afraid. I spent the lot on bribes, trying to get you out of Yggur's dungeon."

"How much?"

"Three gold tells."

"Oh!" he said, quite stunned. "What a waste."

"I'd do it again." They lay in each other's arms for a pleasurable while, then Karan said, "Actually there was something about that chain that I was going to mention ages ago. I'd forgotten all about it."

"What was that?" he asked drowsily.

"The maker's mark—I know how interested you are in old writing."

Llian wasn't particularly interested in hallmarks of obscure silversmiths, but he opened his eyes. "How did it go?"

She traced a complicated sigil in the dust of the floor. "No, that's not quite right. She rubbed it out and did another. On the third attempt she got it right.

Llian sat upright, staring at the mark.

"I'm sure I know that sigil," he said, scratching his head. "Was that all?"

"There was also a name, although it seemed to have been put there later, for the engraving was rather quavery. The hallmark was perfectly engraved. Fia—Fiam—Fiachra! That's it!"

"Fiachra!" Llian literally leapt in the air. "Are you sure?"

"Yes. The name was as clear as new, so it can't have been worn for long after it was put there. The hallmark *was* worn, though. Who was Fiachra? Another of your girlfriends?" she murmured slyly from under her lashes.

"The crippled girl who was murdered in the tale!" he exclaimed. "And the hallmark—I remember it now. It's the 's' glyph—Shuthdar's trademark."

He limped back and forth in a state of high excitement. "The chain must be ancient, if Shuthdar made it. He must have given it to the girl just before he destroyed the flute. And that must be why Kandor designed the Great Tower of Katazza following its pattern. I wonder why? I've got to find it, Karan."

"It's gone," she said, slightly bothered by this obsession.

"When we get out we'll ask Shand where he pawned it. Maybe the broker still has it."

"Maybe," she said doubtfully. There was only one way that they were ever going to get out of here, but Karan did not want to think about that.

They had a few more hours together, then two guards burst through the door and tore Llian from her arms.

Karan was alone with her fears for half an hour, whereupon the guards came for her too. They led her back to the room where the construct squatted in the air. She was just in time to see Llian dragged onto a metal plate set in the floor. Karan lunged against her guards but was powerless.

Rulke stood on top of the construct, brandishing his fist. She did not hear what he said, for the machine shivered the air and Llian disappeared. Almost immediately Rulke and the Ghâshâd held a hurried conference, the realization dawning that the construct had not worked as planned, that no one knew where Llian had been sent to.

Just thinking his name was like a cry of abandonment. Cold fear made her stomach ache. Rulke shouted at squat Jark-un, who scratched his hefty backside then climbed under the construct, pulling at something dangling there. The result was not successful. Finally Rulke got down to see for himself. There was much loud talk and taking apart pieces of the construct and putting them back together again. Karan had time to compose herself. She would not let him know that she was worried about Llian, even that she cared.

Ghâshâd ran back and forth. She recognized several of them from her adventures in the caves of Ashmode. Idlis, of course, now with scabbed lip and swollen cheek, scrawny Thassel, Rebban the pink-eyed albino and a wild-eyed, shavenheaded, fanatical young woman whose name Karan did not know.

The difficulty seemed to be resolved. Rulke gave orders, inspected the work, leapt back up again and caressed his levers. He smiled—evidently the repairs had been successful. The Ghâshâd filed out; she and Rulke were alone. She watched him with narrowed eyes, knowing that he would expect another attack, but she was planning nothing. What was the point of escape? None, until she achieved what she came here for. She was not afraid for herself any longer. She had gone beyond *that* fear.

In his dealings with Llian, Rulke had often worn an expression of amused contempt, but he was watching her so warily, stood so cat-like on his toes, that she was suddenly struck by the incongruity of the situation. Karan smiled: he was afraid of what she might do next. Well, perhaps not afraid, but uncertain. She did not fit the pattern of his other enemies. And having heard his tale she understood why her appearance worried him. If he only knew how fortunate she'd been before, how little an enemy she really was.

He looked disconcerted by the smile. Evidently he wanted something from her and wasn't sure how to get it.

"Why do you smile?" he wondered aloud. "My power over you is absolute."

"And yet you're uncertain," she replied. "You worry about what I'm going to do and it amuses me to see it. I'm like an archer who has shot her only arrow and can but wait with empty hands."

He said nothing to that and after a long interval she asked softly, "What do you want of me?"

Now it was Rulke's turn to smile, for her voice had cracked on the last word. He took her by the shoulder and led her to a couch on the far side of the room, where a small table was set with dishes of food. She sat down as far away from him as she could get, rigidly upright. That amused him too.

"I might put you to a number of uses," he said, giving her an ambiguous glance.

Karan stared right into his eyes. "Be sure that if you try, my knife *will* cut lower than Elienor's did," she said coldly.

Instantly he trapped her two hands in his and, smiling at her helplessness, relieved her of the knife.

"Don't mess me around!" she said furiously. "You brought me here for a reason. You think that I may have a talent that you need. If you cannot even send Llian where you want, how can you hope to direct the construct to those far-off places that are your real destination? That's why you want me."

Rulke's smile thinned. "They briefed you well."

"No one briefed me. What else could you possibly want *me* for? Sensitives are rare. I also know that my abilities cannot be compelled. I'm no use to you unless I'm willing."

"Perhaps you underestimate my powers, or my need. I forced you before!"

That showed a misunderstanding of what had happened that night above Narne, but she felt no need to correct him.

Silence. For a long time she thought of nothing, all of her feelings and fears turned inward. Rulke watched her without speaking. Briefly they heard shouting and a bright light drifted in the sky—another flare. Rulke was standing with his back to an embrasure and the light made a halo around his curling hair, so black that the glare caught the sides with the blue of oiled steel. His face lost all definition but his eyes glowed brighter than ever. Then the light faded.

For a moment she saw him clearly, every pore and lash, every scar and wrinkle, and was amazed to realize that, after all the slurs on him, he was noble. Such strength there was in his face; such power in his eyes; such clarity of vision. His eyes caught hers and she felt the power of his animal magnetism. Then he smiled, just a bare twitch of his lips, so that she caught a glimpse of white sharpness and was afraid that there was a predator within.

Rulke was watching Karan just as carefully. She looked little and young. On the human side she was of no great lineage, he was thinking, for he'd had the Ghâshâd find out about her. Just an old family, barely civilized by his standards, and prone to madness, as the one who'd built this pile had been. But her father went all the way back to Elienor herself. Yet there was a conundrum too. Where had her sensitive talents come from, especially her astounding ability to link? That was not an Aachim talent. It was scarcely credible that she should have such a talent at all, with *that* lineage.

Still, whatever the source, he knew of no other with the talent he had sensed in her in the Nightland. There might be others but it would be a long task seeking them out. He did not have that time. He had to find out more about her.

Karan was still staring at him. Her eyes had a liquid vacancy and she swayed, looked puzzled and bit her upper lip with her bottom teeth, rueful and uncertain. She shivered. The cold was piercing here, for the room was open to the elements. She wrapped her arms across her breast and sat down, confused and on the edge of panic. She might have been a baby confronted by a jackal, so totally was she at his mercy.

"I see what you want," he said. "You want to go back to Tumbledown Manor, with chickens roosting all over the house, and breed up brats with your chronicler mate."

Karan colored. "Why do you sneer and rubbish my life? You've talked enough about perpetuating your own kind. But now that I'm here I will do what needs to be done. Tyrants must be opposed else we will all be slaves."

"Slogans! Here is another! Freedom is anarchy and does none any good. Only I can offer the peace and security you crave."

"You offer slavery and death," she snapped.

"You've been taken in by stories told to frighten children. Why would I destroy what I wish to rule? Under me there will be no war, no little nations fighting among each other and wasting their strength in conflict."

"You will destroy all our works."

"The beauty of Santhenar is in its culture and diversity. I would foster that, not destroy it. If you knew us, you would know how much we care for art and history. I offer peace. Once I have mastered the construct I plan to order Santhenar. You may have a part of it, if you aid me."

"Your reputation does not incline me to believe your promises. I want no part of your world."

"Not even Gothryme?"

"Save what is already mine."

"Then you may keep Gothryme, little as you want, if you aid me. If you do not . . ."

"Then we are back to threats. I prefer you in your true colors."

"When Santhenar is mine there will be the peace that you crave, that it has not had in five thousand years. Who else can do it? Not Faelamor—she cares nothing for this world. What she will do, if she achieves her goal before I do mine, will destroy your planet.

"And your other friends? Yggur is empty; a bitter, twisted

fool. He has no vision for Santhenar. His wars and schemes are but a tool to get at me, and if he ever achieved his goal he would collapse like a pricked bladder. Tensor? Utterly wretched and hopeless. What little the Aachim had, following him has stripped it from them. Name someone better."

"Mendark?" she said, though the name was bile in her mouth.

"The man is corrupt to the core! Look at Thurkad under his rule and you know what Santhenar would be brought to."

Karan had no answers.

"There is only me," he said gently.

"What do you want?"

"Didn't you listen to my tale? I want a future for my species, nothing more."

"History tells different!"

"Because the chroniclers blacked our name to satisfy their corrupt masters."

"How can you say such things? Only hours ago you boasted of the plunder of Aachan."

"We were violent once, in the youth of our civilization, but we had to be to survive the void. No more. We came to Santhenar to make good a mistake—my own, I admit it—but what followed was not of our making."

"The Ghâshâd terrorized my country in your name," she said. "Bannador is ruined. Thousands are homeless."

"The Ghâshâd exceeded their authority and have been punished."

"And you will make good the damage?"

He was silent. "Insofar as it *can* be made good, I will do it," he said at last. "If I should win!"

Peace, thought Karan. If only it could be so. But she said, "Once you are master you will become a despot. The Histories tell us that is the way of power."

"Damn your Histories!" he cried. "What you most desire is almost within my grasp. Will you help me to attain it?"

He saw that she was tempted and was hard put to conceal the desire in his eyes. "To think that all my plans rest on you, little pallid creature that you are. Life burns so feebly in you old humans. Fifty or sixty years, a hundred at most, and you are done. Even those mancers among you who have taken the gift of greater life grow tired and cannot hold to their purpose. Look at Shand, look at Mendark, and compare what they might have been to what they are. Little wonder that your scope is so limited, your achievements so puny. I have been burned in intense fires, quenched and forged anew. Not even a thousand years can separate me from my vision."

Karan turned away and rested her arms on the cold sill of the embrasure. A few stars still shone in the east, against the dawn, but even as she watched a wedge of cloud moving down from the mountains blotted them out. The light from inside picked out the spiraling motion of small hard flakes of snow.

She turned and looked up at him. "But you are the Great Betrayer. I am not persuaded." She walked unsteadily back to her seat.

"Then I will force you." His eyes gleamed.

"You are so arrogant! You understand nothing of my nature."

Karan was astounded by her boldness. To think that she had been troubled by Emmant once; now she defied Rulke himself. But her resistance was hopeless, as she knew. Given enough time he could overcome anyone.

"I've wondered about that. Who *are* you, Karan? There's something in your heritage that I haven't found out."

She started. *Triune!* She could never escape from it.

Rulke shouted down the stairs. "Jark-un! Find where the chronicler has got to and bring him back!" He looked back at Karan. "You won't be so defiant with my boot on your lover's throat," he said softly.

49

Out of the Frying Pan

The guards hauled Llian back to the construct chamber. Once more he felt the unbearable temptation to do whatever Rulke wanted, and have his reward. With what the Charon could tell him, there was no doubt that he would be the greatest chronicler of all time. Of all things that might have happened, he was least prepared for what did occur.

"So you're ready to do my will now?" Rulke said, leaning negligently on the side of the construct. "It's too late! I have no further use for you, liar and cheat that you are. How could I ever have thought to let you tell our Histories? You're rubbish, and like rubbish I throw you away. Get on the plate." He pointed to a hexagon of dark metal set in the floor. It had not been there earlier.

All Llian could think was: *but I don't want to go.* He opened his mouth; shut it again. "No," he said, with just a trace of the insolence that had so helped him before. "I have not been paid."

"What did you expect from the 'Great Betrayer'," sneered Rulke. "Cheats don't get paid."

Jark-un dealt Llian another blow to the side of the head, then Yetchah dragged him onto the plate and flung him down. Rulke leapt into the high seat of the construct, a mighty bound twice the height of his head, and took hold of the levers.

Llian rolled over and pushed himself to his knees. He felt dizzy and sick. Rulke was shouting down at him, his face alive with fury. He rolled the palm of his hand across a rod tipped with a silver knob and the construct sprang to life. There came a rumble so low that it was more a feeling than a sound. Every object in the room, even the walls, was distorted, the very light twisted in its path from one place to another. The plate beneath Llian began to grow warm.

"Here is your payment," Rulke shouted. "You're the very first! Make a lie of this to dismay your friends in Thurkad."

He swept his hand down on the silver bulb. Llian's guts twisted horribly and he was flung through a vortex of nothingness out of Carcharon.

This time he did not lose consciousness, only emerged from a state like amnesia to find himself embedded in a bank of snow. His nose was bleeding. This doesn't smell like Thurkad, he thought. It was still dark but there was enough light to make out benched rock and, in the distance, the unmistakeable outline of Carcharon against the snowfields. He lay on the crest of the amphitheater, right above the ridge path where Karan and he had waited yesterday.

I don't think *that* journey will dismay my friends, Llian thought. Red lights glared through the windows of Carcharon. So near! He had to get back to Karan.

Llian crawled forward, found nothing underneath him and toppled onto the highest bench of the amphitheater. He felt dreadfully tired and weak. He could have slept in the snow. He did.

He jerked awake. You can't sleep here, you fool! Standing up, he saw a tiny light zig-zagging up the ridge. He watched it listlessly, wondering if it was the Ghâshâd come to take him back, unable to care if it was. No, they wouldn't come that way.

"Further up, I think." It was Tallia's voice.

Tallia! She was taking a risk, carrying a light up here. He hardly had the energy to call out; his whimper was torn away on the wind.

An answering shout. Llian lurched to his feet and fell down again. Then Tallia was lifting his head, shining a light into his eyes, wiping half-frozen blood from his face.

"It's Llian," she called over her shoulder.

Another shape labored up through soft snow. "He seems to be all right," she said. "Are you all right, Llian?"

"I just want to sleep," Llian groaned. Every part of him ached.

"Where's Karan?" said a rough voice—Mendark's.

Llian did not dare open his eyes. Just the sound sent shivers up his spine.

"Where?" cried Mendark, shaking him.

"Carcharon," Llian croaked. "Rulke wanted her all along."

"What happened?" Tallia asked urgently. "Why did you come up here?"

"Karan knew a secret way inside," Llian replied, utterly exhausted. He tried to explain, but even to him the story sounded as if he was making it up. He sagged against Tallia and gave up.

Tallia examined his face, using a narrow beam of light from her lantern. The abject Llian of the past months was gone. Though weary and battered, he looked more assured now. She wondered why.

"I don't like this," said Mendark. "Hold him while I bind him."

"On the top of a mountain?" Tallia said sharply. A rectangle of light appeared at the gate of Carcharon, illuminating the winding path, then disappeared. "What's that? There's someone coming."

Mendark flung himself at Llian and shook him so violently that his teeth rattled together. "Once a Zain always a Zain," he cried. "You've betrayed us again."

Tallia hauled him off. "Leave this to me, Mendark!" Her tone did not admit of argument. "Keep watch, they must have seen my light." She pulled Llian up by the front of his coat. "Get up. Can you walk?"

He mumbled incoherently, able to think of nothing but sleep.

She took his arm. They staggered along the back of the amphitheater. "Your explanation will need to be a good one," she said in his ear. Her voice was chilly but he sensed that she was willing to listen.

"I would never do anything to harm her," said Llian. "You know that."

"I'm not sure what I know any longer."

He started on the story, but he was only up to the point where the two of them left Gothryme when Mendark caught them up.

"Quick! They're coming," he said.

Llian spun around and fell face-down in the snow.

"Trying to get back to Rulke, eh!" said Mendark, lifting him up. "I'm tempted to push you over the side."

"Rulke treated me more honestly than you ever did," Llian said bitterly.

Tallia ran around the rim to see how close the pursuit was. Mendark held Llian by the arm, but he had no intention of going anywhere. She came racing back.

"They're after us! Five, maybe six of them."

Llian wondered why Rulke would throw him out and then come after him straight away. But perhaps Rulke did not know where he had ended up. Perhaps he was just chasing the others away. There were too many perhapses.

Tallia sang out. "Mendark, hold them off. I'll take Llian down. Meet me by the Black Lake."

"This place is undefendable!"

They hurried across the high back of the amphitheater,

onto a buttress cut by icy steps that led onto the ridge below. At a point where the buttress pinched in on the slope on either side to allow no way past, Mendark stood firm.

"Go down," he said. "No, wait!"

"What is it?" cried Tallia, trying to make out his expression in the dim light.

"I've just had a horrible thought. Shand once said that Rulke didn't have the talent to use the flute."

"I remember."

"Then maybe he needs a sensitive for the construct too. And this wretch has just delivered Karan into his hands." He cursed. "Why did you interfere the other night? I'd almost broken him."

Tallia was silent, shaken.

"How could you do this to me?" he raged.

"To you?" she cried in equal fury. "Don't you ever think about anyone else?"

They had not gone much further before Llian was stricken by the terrible pangs that had so wracked him in Gothryme. He fell down among the rocks and snow, clawing at his face.

"Light!" Mendark snapped.

It had begun to get light but now the overcast swept back in, dark and dense, like night falling again. Mendark spread the wings of his cloak around Llian. Tallia let a little chink of light from her globe fall on his face, then put it away again quickly. The wind had come up and dark clouds were racing down from the north-west, obscuring the stars and the moon. A flurry of hard snow, pellets on the wind, stung their faces.

"How far back are they now?"

"Top of the amphitheater. Too close!"

"If only it would snow properly," said Tallia.

Mendark looked up at the sky. "It won't," he replied. "Not enough to aid us, anyway. There's too much wind."

"Help us to the bottom of this steep bit," said Tallia, "then hold them off."

Llian sat up. "I'm better now," he said shakily.

"What was that about?" Mendark asked, taking his arm roughly. "Are you having trouble with your new master?"

This was too much. Llian raised his hands and clubbed Mendark on the side of the head, a feeble blow but one that caught the old man off-balance and nearly sent him tumbling down the steps.

"You deserved that," Tallia said coldly. "We don't need any more trouble. Do something to keep them back."

"This close to Rulke? The risk—"

"Well, take the risk, dammit. The way you go on about your place in the Histories . . ."

"All right!" he snarled, and disappeared back up the ridge. Shortly there came a blinding flash of light and rocks crashed down into the gorge. Almost immediately someone appeared above them.

"That was quick," said Tallia. "What did—?" She flung herself flat on the ground. Something whirred over her head.

Llian could tell from the lanky shape against the dark sky that it was a Ghâshâd. The man sprang over a boulder straight for Llian and heaved him effortlessly over his shoulder. Llian let out a squeak. Tallia dived but the man swung his leg like a scythe, sweeping her feet from under her. She fell heavily and began to slide across the steps, frantically trying to gain a purchase on the ice.

She gave a pained cry then skidded head first into a rock.

Llian's captor began to run back up the path. Llian heard Tallia gasp, "Mendark!" but no more.

The Ghâshâd's boots slapped the snow like paddles; his breath was a piston-beat in Llian's ear. Soon the path became so steep that he could not carry Llian up it. He flung him down on a patch of ice, breath hissing from nostrils crusted with icicles. Llian stirred and a boot slammed across his wrist. The man picked him up and continued on.

50

The Seduction of Karan

"You won't help me then?" said Rulke.

"I can't!" Karan replied.

"Not even for Llian?"

All along she had known it would come to this. "Some friend, after the way he spoke about me." She began to sweat.

Rulke showed his teeth again. Perhaps it was meant to be a smile; perhaps a threat. "An *intimate* friend, and the telling only the minor part of his performance. Why do you think I put you together in that cell?"

Her heart leapt out of her chest and lay on the icy floor with Rulke's boot on it.

"He's gone, but I *have* him still." He touched his forehead. "You will do what I say. Embrace the task willingly, else I tear the mind from his body before you. I will, if I have to!"

"Then you will *never* get what you want!"

"Don't dally with me!" he cried. "I can torment him for a week, a month, a year!"

"He's gone!" she said furiously. "You've already sent him away."

He pulled a device out of a pouch in his cloak, two short tubes of metal joined side by side, with glass in either end. "Put these to your eyes, and look over there!"

Karan looked through the glasses and at once Llian sprang into view, stumbling through the snow. Illuminated by some abnormal light, he was quite clear to her, yet his companions were mere shadows against the darker dark.

"Where is he? That's . . . *that's the amphitheater!*"

"So it is. My construct didn't work as well as I expected. It needs tuning. When I get him back I'll test it properly." He gripped Karan's shoulders and pulled her face up to his. "You can't bear to be parted from him, can you?"

She had to force herself to look him in the eye, not to shrink away. "It's tolerable, to keep him out of your reach."

"Remember Gothryme, remember Tullin!"

"How do I know that what you show me is real?"

Rulke grew impatient. "It's real—see *this*!"

He wrung his hands right in her face. Through the glasses, Llian convulsed, his mouth wide open in a silent scream, and fell down in the snow tearing at his head. She had seen that before. It was far too horrible. She put the glasses down but the image stayed in her mind. Llian's silent cries wracked her.

"Is *that* the reality that it takes to convince you?" he shouted in her face, so close that she could feel the heat of his breath.

"You boast about honor but you're just a sadist."

That struck him in his core. "I'm not!" he cried. "The very future of my species is at stake."

"I've heard that before!"

"Have you?" He thrust his face against hers, staring into her eyes. She did not look away. "Would you not do the same if the life of your child was at stake?"

"I don't have a child," she gasped, trying to get away.

"But you want one, more than anything you have ever wanted?"

"Yes!" she whispered.

"What would you *not* do to save its life?"

"Very little," she admitted.

"As with me! Do you need any further demonstration?"

She shook her head. "I know your work," she said. "I've seen enough of it."

"Then what is your decision?"

"I cannot make it."

"I have no time for this," he snapped, wringing his hands again.

Llian's agony surged back across the link. Karan almost fainted with the pressure of it.

"Leave me!" she screamed.

Rulke made to wring his hands a third time, and in a fury she swung her fist up at his chin. He was caught by surprise, but ducked out of the way. He laughed, genuinely amused, ruffled her hair as if she was a child, then went down the stairs, leaving her cold and alone in the big room. She was caught and they both knew it.

Karan sat on the cold bench. Llian would be better off dead. What point her resisting any longer? Perhaps Rulke was right anyway; perhaps Santhenar would be the better for his rule. How could she tell? Even the wisest, the most learned, could not foretell the way the future would go. Why should the choice come down to her? She didn't want any of this—only Llian.

How much Llian had brought to her life. How much he had done for her. What she most thought of was his tenderness, his gentleness, and the clumsy, laughable, idiosyncratic way that he did most things, save his art. She did not have the will to hold out any longer. Once she would have thought of the greater good, but no longer. Why should she not consider her own little world and her own happiness?

But something still nagged at her. Why was Rulke in such

haste? He insisted that he had plenty of time yet he pressed her very hard. And it had been the same in his dealings with Llian.

Ghâshâd came and went, cleaning the table, packing unidentifiable items inside the construct, removing others.

She went back to the embrasure. The snow had stopped but the wind still howled in the roof. The clouds that had previously covered all the sky were now torn into rags through which the moon could be seen, high above. On the other side the sun was rising. She mentally reckoned up the days until hythe, mid-winter's day. A week. What a winter it had been; what a year. Would the next be a better one? It could hardly be worse. Yes, it could be very much worse, and that depended on what she did in the next few days.

The clouds thinned and she saw that the moon was past the three quarters. It was a long time since she'd seen it, with the continual overcast; not since she'd returned to Gothryme. A full moon in hythe—that would be a good omen for the new year. But that set her to thinking. What omen was that connected to? She leaned far out, the cold wind biting her cheeks.

The moon in hythe reminded her of a rhyme she'd heard somewhere. The dark face of the moon was waxing. Bad luck! Whatever the phase of the moon, whenever it showed the dark side was an ill-omen. But when the full moon showed only the dark face—which only occurred a few times in a lifetime—it was an evil omen. Though Karan did not set much store by omens, she shivered at the thought.

Then it all fell into place. There had been something about the full dark moon after she and Llian fell through the gate into the Nightland. Yggur and Mendark had talked about it once. Suddenly she understood why Rulke was in such a hurry. The moon would be full in about a week. Hythe was a week away too. She squinted against the wind. By the look of the moon, it would be fully dark in a week too. A full dark moon on hythe, mid-winter's day, might only occur once in a thousand years for all she knew. And that was the prophecy—the day that Rulke would come out.

Rulke *must* be ready in a week. No wonder he pressed her. Until now he had played with her, but time had run out. When he came back up the stairs it would be to force her, savagely if he must. Little time for her, either.

The hairs on the back of her neck prickled. She turned slowly, knowing already what she would find there. Rulke! He stood close behind. Huge. Magnificent. Terrible. How could she even think to oppose him? Surely he knew everything, even what she was thinking. What did it matter anyway?

He said nothing but clasped his hands, and the tormented image of Llian was back in her mind though she had put the glasses down a long time ago.

"Look at him, tearing his hair out. Why do you let him suffer?"

No one should ever be made to suffer so, she thought. You have taken away my last restraint. He is mine and I will have him.

"There is a price," she said fiercely.

Rulke frowned. "Another game? What is the price, shade of Elienor?"

"No game. Give me what I want or you get nothing."

He looked tormented. "I haven't got time for this, Karan!"

There, it was out in the open.

"My Ghâshâd have taken him back; he will soon be here." He raised his hands.

Karan was on the edge of panic. At all costs she didn't want Llian to see her dealings with Rulke. He would never forgive her. She spoke quickly. "Do that again and you get nothing. I can hold out against you for long enough. The dark moon will be in hythe in a week. All your preparations must be made in seven days. You cannot teach me to work with the construct in a few hours. Pay my price."

He looked surprised. "You're smart too! Perhaps I'll make do with what I can compel from you."

"You can *compel* nothing useful from me. I, too, have been forged in intense fires. I can turn off my gift in an instant. I did it before, after Narne, and couldn't find it again for months."

"What is your price?"

"All compulsion must be taken from Llian."

"Never, else how will I get you to do my will?"

"You can torment me, threaten my lands, my people. But until he is free you get nothing."

She could see his impatience now. "Very well," he said. "What does it matter? I have no further need for him, and much else to occupy the part of my mind dedicated to his control." He waved his hand. "It is done."

"We are linked. I say it is not done."

"You bluff. I sense no link."

"You cannot," she guessed, "now that you are out of the Nightland. Do it."

Rulke wrestled with himself. How he hated anyone to get the better of him. Yet he must not let pride stand in the way of the ultimate goal. What did anything matter but that? He nodded. His eyes went blank, his lips moved, he looked deep into her eyes. For a moment everything swam before her but she wrenched her mind back to the task.

"It is done."

"I am not satisfied. Do it again."

He smiled. "I've a price too, since we've come down to the final negotiations. Tell me who you really are."

He'd hit on the only thing that she did not want to give up, even for Llian. If he knew who she was, he'd use that too. Was Llian worth that sacrifice? She looked away, clenching and unclenching her fists.

"Well?" he asked softly. "I won't harm you."

Karan bit her lip. Was anyone worth that much? Was Llian? "I am triune," she whispered. "I have a Faellem ancestor. My third name is Melluselde."

His reaction was not at all what she'd expected. Taking

her in his arms he hugged her to his vast chest. She struggled helplessly. "I'm so sorry," he said. "I truly am." He let her go.

She fell down, gasping, not game to ask what he meant. Rulke performed the operation of release a third time, and this time it seemed better to Karan, more complete. She could not see into Llian's mind, but over the link she felt the great relief, the lifting of pressure that he had been under for half a year.

"Well?"

"I am satisfied," she said from the floor.

He smiled and there was relief in the smile.

"Are you still going to bring Llian back?" she said.

"Do you want me to? Will it help you do my work?"

"It will make it ten times harder."

"So I thought. He'll lose his good opinion of you if he sees what you do here! In that case, I have no use for him anymore."

"Good." She closed down the link between her and Llian, just in case. And in case one of her stray thoughts got through. Rulke was right. She was mortally ashamed of what she was going to do. Then, thinking about the prophecy Rulke had spoken in Katazza, she was reminded of Shand's reply.

"There was a foretelling about the triune and you, was there not? Shand said it:

"Break down the golden horn,
Wish the glass unmade,
Fear the thrice born,
But beware the thrice betrayed."

Rulke laughed. "An old Charon fable, but he's got it mixed up. He should have spoken it to Faelamor, not me. I'm not afraid of you, Karan. Now, do your part." He gestured to the construct.

She had almost forgotten it. But now she was struck by the incongruity. "Why do you dwell in this frigid ruin when the whole of Shazmak is available to you?"

"Before the Forbidding we traveled by gates," he explained, "in those few places where such devices would function. Gates can only be made in certain places, and only lead to certain places, and since the Forbidding it is many times harder to make them. The Aachim set up defenses against the use of gates, in Shazmak and all their cities. We have not yet broken the defenses of Shazmak and until we do I cannot take the construct there. Besides, Carcharon is a superb place to use my construct, perhaps the best in Santhenar. In that, at least, your mad ancestor was right.

"So here, piece by slow piece, I attached the reality to the pattern that I brought from the Nightland. There the reality could not exist, so the construct had to be made here. And you are the sensitive who will seek out the Way between the Worlds and tune it to the destination."

"You would go between the worlds?"

"I would, and you will find the Way for me. I will make you great. No one has ever accused me of betraying those who served me faithfully, no matter what my reputation with my enemies. Cast aside your petty dreams, your petty alliances, and follow me."

No point in further delay. "What would you have me do? Why me?"

"Because you are triune. But rare and precious as triunes are, you are not just any triune. You can link! And most of all, because you are a sensitive. Only you can sense out the Way. And, I have to say it, the irony drives me powerfully."

"The irony?"

"That you, who are the very image of my nemesis, the beautiful Elienor, shall be the one who opens our way into the universe."

His eyes glowed; for a moment Karan was caught up in his majestic dream. And it had to be said, she wanted to find out about her triune talent, whatever it was. She had yearned for it ever since Tensor revealed the truth to her. She looked up at him. The magnificent, terrible eyes caught her. She shivered again.

"I will do it," she said. "Show me to the machine, and the working of it."

51

THE DARK OF THE MOON

Halfway up the knotted ridge below the amphitheater, Llian's captor slipped on black ice and fell heavily. Llian was hurled off his shoulder, slid off the path and jammed between two boulders. The man came to his knees, gasping for breath. Not even the iron-hard Ghâshâd could run up this slope under such a load. Blood poured from a wound on his scalp. In the ghostly light of the darkening moon it looked black.

Groaning, Llian tried to get up, to find nothing underneath his legs. He was wedged by the shoulders between two rocks, without the strength to pull himself up that half a span to safety. The Ghâshâd started toward him then staggered back as from a blow in the chest. The clouds parted. The dark moon brought all his bones to the surface, dancing like an animated skeleton. The dance was a struggle with someone who could not be seen.

The Ghâshâd roared his pain to the skies. From not far away he was answered, and answered again. The falling snow was lit by a series of flashes. Llian hoped it was Mendark. The Ghâshâd fell to one knee, went over on his back, rolled over and his arms rose and fell. He seemed to be banging something against the ground. There came a dreadful groan and Tallia appeared beneath him, unable to hold her illusion under the weight of his blows. He was cracking her head up and down against the ice.

She was failing. The Ghâshâd was going to kill her. Dragging himself onto the track, Llian heaved a rock at her assailant's head. The reaction sent him slipping backwards, he wedged between the boulders again, then ever so slowly his weight began to pull him through.

The rock struck the Ghâshâd hard on the ear. He yelped and let go of Tallia's head momentarily. Straightening her legs, she shot him backwards off her.

He landed on his back and went skidding head first down the slope. He glanced off a boulder, clawed at the ice and slid gently over the side. Llian heard a thud, then the rattle of stones. The wind soon blotted out his ever more feeble cries.

Tallia lay groaning on the icy step.

"Help!" said Llian faintly.

"Give me a hand," said Tallia at the same time.

"I can't; I'm slipping." He moved an arm and slipped a bit more. "Help! I'm going to fall!"

With an almighty groan she crawled across and extended her hand. Llian moved his other arm, slipped again and his weight pulled her with him.

She cursed, twisted on the ice and thudded into the boulders that Llian had been jammed between. The gentle shock was almost enough to tear his hand out of her grip, she was so weak. "I can't hold you, Llian."

Llian's legs thrashed, dislodged a clump of snow and found purchase against rock.

"I've got my foot on something," he said.

"Then push with all your heart, because I'm done."

He strained, found another hold with his knee and thrust

himself up between the rocks to safety. Tallia released his hand and lay down in the snow.

Llian lifted her head. Her face was covered in blood.

"Thank you," she said.

"Thank you!" He wiped the worst of the blood away with his fingertips. "Are you all right?"

"No, I'm not. Give me a minute."

"It'd better be a quick minute; there are more of them. Take my hand."

Leaning on each other they lurched down the ridge. They were off the steep part when another spasm gripped Llian's heart like a squeezing fist. He sank down on the ground, holding his chest. The pain was short-lived; soon they were able to continue as before. Shortly after that there was a wrenching, disorienting feeling in his head, and again he had to sit down with an attack of vertigo. Then it was gone.

"It's gone! He's gone. *He's gone!*" It was beyond comprehension, but it had happened. Tallia slammed her hand across his mouth.

"Quiet, you fool," she hissed in his ear.

Llian calmed down. "Rulke's completely gone!" Karan must have succeeded after all.

"*Then he's got what he wants!* What's he going to do next? If you can walk, let's get down into the forest as quickly as possible."

"Walk!" cried Llian, barely able to restrain himself. "I can run. I can skip all the way, turning cartwheels."

In spite of her misgivings Tallia smiled. She had recovered enough to walk unaided. However, when Llian began to dwell on Karan's probable fate, he began to cry silently beside her. She took his arm.

They went more quickly now, after some hours reaching the forest and creeping gratefully into its protection. There they worked their way to the rendezvous, a place not far from the Black Lake, made camp without a fire and Llian sat quietly in Tallia's sleeping pouch, for it was intensely cold. He told the rest of his story, and at the end of it, as Tallia asked no more questions, made himself as comfortable as he could and closed his eyes. The euphoria had worn off leaving him weaker than ever.

The forest was dense here, except for a small clearing west of them, where a grand old tree had fallen, opening the canopy to the sky. Llian was too tired to sleep, too afraid for Karan. The bright nebula was setting, passing across the clear part of the sky, crimson and white and with its scorpion tail high. He shivered, and just then the three-quarter moon came out from behind a rag of cloud. His eyes closed.

Tallia was almost as weary, but she had to keep the watch. After a struggle with her eyelids she went the little way to the lake. The water was freezing around the shoreline. Scooping a handful onto her face she washed the blood off. Her nose, cheek and forehead were bruised raw. She wiped the water away before it froze, then hurried back. Llian appeared to be sleeping. She resumed her watch. Her face hurt.

Llian's sleep was disturbed by terrible dreams. He snapped awake. The moon and the nebula were moving into conjunction, the moon cupped within the up-arching sting of the scorpion so that it was briefly completed, a full moon, red and black. He felt a chill of foreboding. Then it was just the three-quarter moon eclipsing the nebula, merely a glowing patch of gas, and the two moved apart again, the nebula sinking behind the trees, the moon falling toward the west.

Laying his head on his arms, Llian tried to sleep, but sleep would not come. He knew why Rulke had freed him. There was no more need. Karan had agreed to do what he wanted in exchange for Llian's freedom. Time was running out.

But Llian's mind was not on the coming cataclysm. That was for others to consider. What had Rulke done to Karan? And what would he have *her* do?

Mendark came through the trees, his boots going whuff-whuff in the snow.

"What happened to you?" he said sharply, inspecting Tallia's battered face with the lantern. "Did he—?"

"One of them caught me. If it hadn't been for Llian I'd be at the bottom of the gorge now. What's doing?"

"I lost them eventually, though it was hard work. I had to use a powerful magic. Then they found me again but all of a sudden they seemed to lose interest. When I doubled back here they kept right on, returning to Carcharon. Phew! I'm too old for this business."

Llian spoke up. "Just before Rulke used the construct, he said, 'Make a lie of this to dismay your friends in Thurkad.' If that was really his intention the construct failed badly."

"That much I believe," said Mendark. "I felt the disturbance that it made."

"And I'm free of him," Llian replied. "He's completely gone now."

Tallia looked questioningly at Mendark. He shook his head. "I can't tell, save by pressing him with my own Art, and I'm too weary. But even if what you say is true, Llian, you've done other things these past months that cannot be dismissed so easily, not least taking Karan up there. There must be an accounting."

"I agree," said Llian coldly, "and we should examine your part too! Listen—Rulke is vulnerable, with only a few to defend him, and the construct faulty. The time to strike is now, if you are ever going to. Call Yggur up from Thurkad. A forced march could bring him here in less than a week. Call Shand as well. The three of you could stop him."

"Shand would not come," said Mendark, "even if we could get a message to Tullin in this weather. Even if Yggur came, leaving his empire unprotected, this is not a battle to be won with arms. To defeat Rulke we must match strength against strength, device against device, talent against talent. But we have no device, while he has his construct."

"It wasn't working properly," said Llian. "I can speak with some authority on gates, having gone through quite a few this year. He's afraid of us, and vulnerable."

"He's probably fixed it already! Such arrogance, a mere chronicler telling *me* what to do! Speak no more lies."

Llian was desperate. If they left it until after Rulke used the construct he would never see Karan again. But that argument would never convince this desiccated and frightened old man. He had one last try.

"Remember his prophecy," he cried, "after you flung him from Katazza. The dark moon will be full in six more days, on hythe."

Mendark made a dismissive gesture, which Llian misunderstood.

"Did you not see the moon a few hours ago, three-quarters full, in conjunction with the scorpion. That is a pointer . . ."

"Enough of your omens and pointers!" cried Mendark in fury. "How dare you lecture me, who have been Magister for a thousand years, on the phases of the moon. I've known it was this day all along."

"You must—" Llian cried desperately.

"No more; your chatter enrages me."

Mendark whipped the rope around Llian's hands again and gagged him so thoroughly that he could barely breathe. Tallia looked doubtful but Mendark spoke curtly in her ear, with much gesturing to the east, and to Carcharon, and at Llian as well. She answered him in a voice equally stiff, threw her pack over her back in one effortless movement, and was gone.

"She goes to take the alarm to Gothryme and Thurkad," said Mendark. "I stay to keep watch. You stay because there is nothing else to do with you."

The next days were unbearably nerve-racking. Several times each day, after securing Llian to a tree, Mendark slipped away. Once he was gone all night. On the fourth and fifth days after Tallia's departure he did not return until well after dawn. Llian was beginning to fear that he would starve to death while the world fell into ruin around him. Mendark said nothing further, in the brief moments that they were together, nor answered his incessant questions.

On the seventh morning, Mendark returned with a retinue.

Tallia had come back. With her were Osseion, Yggur accompanied by Dolodha, Vartila the Whelm and a troop of guard, their backs bent under enormous loads. Shand was there too, as well as the Aachim from Gothryme and even Tensor in his litter. They too had noted the phase of the moon and what it foretold. Tensor was escorted by Asper and Llian's nemesis, Basitor. Nadiril was also in the party, along with Lilis and Jevi.

They met on a hill which gave a view of forest and river and lake, and in the other direction the ridge and Carcharon and the white slopes beyond which seemed to go up forever.

Shand and Nadiril, friends once more it seemed, slowly climbed up to them. Lilis was holding Nadiril's hand, looking anxious for his health. Jevi held her other hand.

"Aren't you going to rescue Karan?" cried Lilis, jumping up and down.

"We don't have the strength, child," said Nadiril, warming blue fingers over the fire. "Hush now, until we find out what Rulke's defenses are, and the number of his forces. Nothing is going to happen while it is light. What's going on here, Llian?"

Llian told how Karan had brought him back to life, and her plan to go to Carcharon to save him and Gothryme from Rulke.

"That's Karan all over," said Shand. "I've no trouble believing the story."

"You challenged Rulke to a telling?" whispered Nadiril afterward. "Oh, tell me! What a tale—omit not a single word. I feel almost young again at the thought." And indeed his face was quite animated.

Llian told Rulke's tale and his own, and the aftermath, to the astonishment of all and the delight of Lilis, who sat at his feet in the snow in an attitude of hero worship.

"Set him free," said Nadiril. "Every word he spoke is truth. When this is over, Llian, there is an honored place for you at the Great Library."

Llian could scarcely believe that the months of ostracism

were over, that he was accepted again at last. Even Basitor shook Llian's hand.

In the afternoon they headed up the dangerous track to the amphitheater, the Aachim bearing firewood on their backs. There was no sign of life or movement at Carcharon. As moonrise grew nearer the tension drew tight as a bowstring.

"So that is Carcharon," said Yggur, who looked as if the scorpion was about to strike him again. "What a mad, evil place."

"I've not been here since Karan's father was killed," said Tensor.

"I'd heard he was killed on the path to Shazmak," said Llian.

"Only in the general sense of the term. He died at the very doors of Carcharon. It never made any sense. There's nothing to attract thieves and vagabonds up here. Lift me up," said Tensor.

Asper took one end of the litter and another Aachim, yellow-haired Xarah, the other. They raised him high. Tensor stared at Carcharon for a long time. He looked up at the moon. "Doom!" he said. "And now Karan is up there. She won't come back either! Put me down again."

As they lowered him, Xarah slipped on an ice-glazed rock. The litter tilted and tipped. Tensor instinctively snatched at Llian's coat to save himself. His grasp tore the buttons off and the chain Llian wore about his neck broke. The jade amulet fell onto the snow. In the dim light it gleamed a luminous green.

"What's that?" cried Yggur and Shand together.

"It's a good-luck amulet that my mother gave me," said Llian, stooping to pick it up.

Yggur's boot went over it, then he bent and reached for it himself. He snatched back his hand as though stung. "No, it's not!" he said. "It's enchanted."

"Faelamor did something to it in Shazmak," said Llian, "though Malien took that charm off on the way to Katazza."

"So I did," said Malien. She picked up the amulet without taking any harm from it, and held it to her eye. "It's like the one you had before, but this one has the mark of Rulke. In some strange way it is Rulke. This is a deadly thing, Llian; where did you get it?"

"I've had it since I was twelve."

"Not this you haven't. It's come out of the Nightland and Rulke made it, that's certain."

"What is it for?" said Shand. "An *ear* that can hear from afar? He might have heard all our councils. He might be listening to us now. Oh, this is rankest treachery!"

"It's not an ear," said Nadiril. "It's just—"

"Shackle him," cried Yggur, all his terrors coming back. "Why did you not heed me before?"

"Hold on," said Nadiril. "Let's not allow fear to overrule our common sense."

Everyone examined the amulet, save Yggur who could not touch it, and Tensor who would not.

"What do you think, Mendark?" asked Shand, passing it over.

"I agree that it has the mark of Rulke, though I can't *sense* any harm in it."

"Give it here," said Nadiril. He inspected it for a long time. "Shand is right. This could be deadly and until we know exactly what it is, precautions must be taken. I'm sorry, Llian." He tossed it down and ground it under his boot, but it merely sank into the snow.

In a few brief minutes Llian had passed from euphoria back to despair. He stood spread-legged while a stormy Basitor put iron shackles on him. The freezing metal burned Llian's skin. Mendark thrust the key into his pocket.

Llian sank down into the snow, oblivious to everything. He was finished this time.

The amulet had shattered the company. They milled about on the back rim of the amphitheater. No one had any plans or any ideas. The sun began to go down behind the mountains, bleaching the rugged range into black cut-outs against the purple sky. Carcharon became a gothic nightmare dark against the snow.

A little shadow appeared beside him. "Llian," came Lilis's high voice.

"Yes?" he said.

"I believe you, Llian." She thrust her cold hand into his. There was something hard in it.

Llian hugged her to him. "What's that?"

"It's my knife. Hold still while I get these chains off. Then I'll make a diversion while—"

"Thank you, Lilis, but I can't. Karan is up there. I can't leave her."

Lilis stood with him until it was fully dark, a glow beyond the eastern horizon heralding moonrise. As if they had been set ablaze by the motion of a single lever, lights sprang up in every room of Carcharon, dark red flares that shed an uneven and wavering illumination. The dark moon itself could have been rising inside the fortress.

The lights faded; the tower went black, then as though stimulated by the flares, the weird projections on the outside of the tower glowed faintly luminous. They faded. Momentarily Carcharon was surrounded by a shimmering green aura. There was a drawn-out instant's silence.

Without warning a sun lit up the very top of the tower, sending out splinter-bursts of magenta light that had them shielding their eyes. The tower began to deform, waves pulsing through the stone walls. The waves rolled up and down, faster and faster until the whole tower vibrated like a tuning fork. The foundations began to give out a reverberating rumble, so low that the rock beneath their feet shivered in sympathy.

The rumble became a hum, then it shot up the register, now a squeal like fingernails on a blackboard, then a shriek like a knife skating across a windowpane. A gold filling in one of Llian's teeth vibrated, a horrible itchy ache. The noise became the high-pitched wailing of a million bodiless souls abandoned in the void, and rose beyond their hearing.

Silence fell suddenly. Everyone could feel the pressure building. Then the spiny helmet-roof of the tower of Carcharon burst open, spraying green slate through the air like confetti. Broken slate rained down on the snow. The brass helmet became unseamed, and each segment curved outward on its arches, folding down like the petals of an opening flower.

Something dark thrust its way up through the wreckage of beams and brass and metal that had supported the roof. Something that bent the light all around it to a focus: a lens of light that stared at the company like an unforgiving eye.

It was the construct, and Rulke stood on the top of it, holding the levers in one casual hand. Standing beside him, small and pale but with her red hair flaming in the unearthly light, stood Karan.

"Karan!" Llian screamed. She stared straight through him and did not reply.

Mendark stood like a mummified raptor, bony hands hanging in hooked curves, sunken eyes staring. In his despair the renewal was failing rapidly. "No!" he whispered, and fell down on the ice.

The construct swung around in mid-air so that the light lens pointed directly toward the company. Between Llian's feet the amulet burst into flame and melted its way down through the snow.

"Go back!" cried Malien to Rulke in a frail voice. "You cannot stand against us."

"Can't anybody do something?" wept Llian.

"Not *here*; not against that," said Yggur, surprising everyone with his calmness. The moment he had dreaded for so long had finally arrived. He had resolved to face his fears and die.

Rulke said nothing. His silence mocked their helplessness more than any words could have. Then he flung his arm out, pointing straight as a lance over their shoulders.

Llian turned to the east. The shackles seared his ankles and he stumbled, clutching at Lilis's shoulder. The clouds were gone; it was a cold clear night. Dark patches of forest were visible in the starlight, and a glittering cable marked the path of the Black Lake stream through the forest. His upraised hand was trembling. The others followed the direction of his gaze beyond the silver stream, beyond the forests all the way to the curve of the horizon.

The moon was rising, its huge blotched face lurching into the sky, seeming to hang there a moment as if the climb was beyond it. A dark red spot had moved up to its uppermost rim. Llian caught his breath. Now there was only a finger's breadth to rise, now only a sliver. Now the whole great circle hung in the sky, the horizon a tangent. And there they saw it: the matching black spot, the smaller twin, touching the horizon. The twins were visible at once. And it was midwinter's night. The dark face of the full moon was in hythe.

"The first since the fall of Skane," said Shand. "One thousand eight hundred and thirty years ago. And that too was foretold."

They all fell to their knees. The weight of the prophecy pushed them down into the snow.

"All hope is lost," said Shand. "The one who was to be the Restorer is dead."

Ulsh turned to the east. The shackles seared his ankles and he stumbled, clutching at Clu's shoulder. The clouds were gone; it was a cold, clear night. Dark patches of forest were visible in the starlight, and a glittering cable marked the path of the Black Lake stream through the forest. His upraised hand was trembling. The others followed the direction of his gaze beyond the silver stream, beyond the forests all the way to the curve of the horizon.

The moon was rising, its huge blood-red face lurching into the sky, seeming to hang there a moment as if the climb was beyond it. A dark red spot had moved up to its uppermost rim. Ulat caught his breath. Now there was only a finger's breadth to rise, now only a sliver. Now the whole great circle hung in the sky, the horizon a crescent. And then they saw it: the marching black spot, the smaller twin, touching the horizon. The twins were visible at once, and it was [illegible] light. The dark face of the [illegible].

"The first since the Fall of Sethra," said Shurat. "Eight thousand eight hundred and fifty years ago. And that too was foretold."

They all fell to their knees. The weight of the prophecy pushed them down into the snow.

"All hope is lost," said Shurat. "The One who would be the Restorer is dead."

THE END

OF VOLUME THREE

VOLUME FOUR

THE WAY BETWEEN THE WORLDS

concludes The View From The Mirror Quartet

Glossary

of Characters, Names and Places

Aachan: One of the Three Worlds, the world of the Aachim and, after its conquest, the Charon.

Aachim: The human species native to Aachan, who were conquered by the Charon. The Aachim are a clever people, great artisans and engineers, but melancholy and prone to hubris. After they were brought to Santhenar the Aachim flourished, but were betrayed and ruined in the Clysm, and withdrew from the world to their vast mountain fortress cities.

Aftersickness: Sickness that people suffer after using the Secret Art, or being close when someone else uses such power, or even after using a native talent. Sensitives are very prone to it.

Alcifer: The last and greatest of Rulke's cities, designed by Pitlis the Aachim.

Almadin: A dry land across the sea from Thurkad.

Ashmode: An ancient town looking over the Dry Sea.

Asper: An Aachim healer, one of Tensor's company.

Assembly: The puppet government of Thurkad, dominated by the Magister on the one hand and the Governor of the city on the other.

Bannador: A long, narrow and hilly land on the western side of Iagador. Karan's homeland.

Basitor: A bitter Aachim who survived the sacking of Shazmak.

Bel Gorst: A pirate captain living in Crandor.

Benie: Cook's boy at Gothryme Manor.

Berenet: Formerly the second of Mendark's chief lieutenants, now allied to Thyllan.

Blase: One of Tensor's Aachim band.

Blending: A child of the union between two of the four different human species. Blendings are rare, and often deranged, but can have remarkable talents.

***Booreah Ngurle*:** The burning mountain, or fiery mountain, a volcanic peak in the forests east of Almadin. The Charon once had a stronghold there.

Calendar: Santhenar's year is roughly 395.7 days and contains twelve months, each of thirty-three days.

Calliat: A philosopher and mystic of ancient times. See **Forty-Nine Chrighms.**

Carcharon: A walled tower built on a rugged ridge high above Gothryme Forest. It was constructed by Karan's mad ancestor Basunez at a node where the Secret Art was especially powerful.

Chacalot: A large water-dwelling reptile, somewhat resembling a crocodile.

Chanthed: A town in northern Meldorin, in the foothills of the mountains. The College of the Histories is situated there.

Chard: A kind of tea.

Charon: One of the four human species, the master people of the world of Aachan. They fled out of the void to take Aachan from the Aachim, and took their name from a frigid moonlet at the furthest extremity of the void. They have strange eyes, indigo or carmine, or sometimes both together, depending on the light.

Chronicler: A historian. A graduate in the art and science of recording and maintaining the Histories.

Citadel: The Magister's palace in Thurkad, an enormous fortified building of baroque extravagance.
Clatcher: A kind of crayfish.
Cloak, cloaked: To disguise oneself by means of illusion.
Clysm: A series of wars between the Charon and the Aachim beginning around 1500 years ago, resulting in the almost total devastation of Santhenar.
College of the Histories: The oldest of the colleges for the instruction of those who would be chroniclers or tellers of the Histories, or even lowly bards or king's singers. It was set up at Chanthed soon after the time of the Forbidding.
Compulsion: A form of the Secret Art; a way of forcing someone to do something against their will.
Conclave: A forum held in Thurkad to resolve some crisis. It is arbitrated by the Just, a selected group of judges or high officials. The last Conclave was held to resolve the ownership of the Mirror, but Tensor used his potency, laid everyone low and stole it.
Construct: A machine at least partly powered by the Secret Art.
Council; also **Council of Iagador, Council of Santhenar, Great Council, High Council:** An alliance of the powerful. With the Aachim it made the Nightland and cast Rulke into it. After that it had two purposes—to continue the great project and to maintain the watch upon Rulke.
Crandor: A rich, tropical land on the north-eastern side of Lauralin. Tallia's homeland.

Dolodha: A messenger girl; one of Yggur's servants.
Dunnet: A secluded land within Elludore Forest.

Elienor: A great heroine of the Aachim from the time when the Charon invaded Aachan.
Elludore: A large forested land, north and west of Thurkad.
Emmant: A half-Aachim, librarian at Shazmak, who conceived a violent lust for Karan and attacked her. She killed him in Thurkad.

Faelamor: Leader of the Faellem species who came to Santhenar soon after Rulke, to keep watch on the Charon and maintain the balance between the worlds. Maigraith's liege.

Faellem: The human species who inhabit the world of Tallallame. They are a small, dour people who are forbidden to use machines and particularly magical devices, but are masters of disguise and illusion. Faelamor's band were trapped on Santh by the Forbidding, and constantly search for a way home.

***Farsh*:** A mild obscenity.

Festival of Chanthed: An annual festival held in Chanthed in the autumn, at which the Histories are told by the masters and students of the College.

Fiz Gorgo: A fortress city in Orist, flooded in ancient times, now restored; the stronghold of Yggur.

Flute; also **golden flute:** A device made in Aachan at the behest of Rulke, by the genius smith Shuthdar. It was subsequently stolen by him and taken back to Santhenar. When used by one who is sensitive, it could be used to open the Way between the Worlds. It was destroyed by Shuthdar at the time of the Forbidding.

Forbidding: See ***Tale of the Forbidding.***

Forty-Nine Chrighms of Calliat: A series of linked enigmas and paradoxes so complex that, thirteen hundred years after Calliat's death, only one had been solved. Maigraith has recently solved many of them.

Fyrn: The family name of Karan of Bannador, from her mother's side.

***Gah*:** An insulting term for one of the old human species, who are generally considered to be inferiors.

Galardil: A forested land, east of Orist.

Galliad: Karan's father, who was half-Aachim. He was killed when Karan was a child.

Gannel: A river beginning near Chanthed and flowing through the mountains to the sea at Ganport.

Garr, Garrflood: The largest river in Meldorin. It arises to the west of Shazmak and runs to the Sea of Thurkad east of Sith.

Gate: A structure controlled by the Secret Art, which permits people to move instantly from one place to another. Also called a portal.

Gellon: A fruit tasting something between a mango and a peach.

Ghâshâd: The ancient, mortal enemies of the Aachim. They were corrupted and swore allegiance to Rulke after the Zain rebelled two thousand years ago, but when Rulke was put in the Nightland a thousand years later they forgot their destiny and took a new name, Whelm. Roused by Rulke through Karan's link to Maigraith, they became Ghâshâd again and sacked Shazmak just before the Conclave.

Gift of Rulke; also **Curse of Rulke:** Knowledge given by Rulke to the Zain, enhancing their resistance to the mind-breaking potencies of the Aachim. It left stigmata that identified them as Zain.

Glass: Colloquial term for the Mirror of Aachan.

Gothryme: Karan's impoverished manor near Tolryme in Bannador.

Graspers: Moneylenders.

Great Betrayer: Rulke.

Great Library: Founded at Zile by the Zain in the time of the Empire of Zur. The library was sacked when the Zain were exiled, but was subsequently re-established. Its current librarian is Nadiril the Sage.

Great Mountains: The largest and highest belt of mountains on Santhenar, enclosing the southeastern part of the continent of Lauralin.

Great Project: A way sought by the Council to banish the Charon from Santh forever.

Great Tales: The greatest stories from the Histories of Santhenar; traditionally told at the Festival of Chanthed and on important ceremonial occasions throughout Santhenar.

A tale can become a Great Tale only by the unanimous decision of the master chroniclers. In four thousand years only twenty-two Great Tales have ever been made.

Grint: A copper coin of small value.

Gyllias: The Recorder.

***Hakasha-ka-najisska*:** A forbidden potency (mind-blasting spell) developed by the Aachim against the Charon. Zain carrying the Gift of Rulke are immune to it.

Hassien: Pender's wife, who left him in Sith.

Havissard: Yalkara's abandoned stronghold near Tar Gaarn. Havissard is protected by a mighty spell and has not been entered since Yalkara's departure three hundred years ago.

Hennia: A Zain. She was a member of the Council of Iagador.

Hintis: An Aachim who was killed in Katazza. He was a friend of Basitor's.

Histories, The: The vast collection of records which tell more than four thousand years of recorded history on Santhenar. The Histories consist of historical documents written or held by the chroniclers, as well as the tales, songs, legends and lore of the peoples of Santhenar and the invading peoples from the other worlds, told by the tellers. The culture of Santhenar is interwoven with and inseparable from the Histories and the most vital longing anyone can have is to be mentioned in them.

Hlune: The lanky people who rule the wharf city of Thurkad and control all ship-borne commerce there.

Hornrace: An impassable chasm linking the Seas of Thurkad and Qwale with the Dry Sea. An unimaginable torrent flows down it and over the Trihorn Falls into the Dry Sea, to disappear without trace in that arid waste. The Hornrace was once spanned by the Aachim's glorious Rainbow Bridge.

Huling's Tower: The place where Shuthdar destroyed the golden flute.

Human species: There are four distinct human species: the

Aachim of Aachan, the Faellem of Tallallame, the old humans of Santhenar and the Charon who came out of the void. All but old humans can be very long-lived. Matings between the different species rarely produce children (see **blending**).

Hythe: Mid-winter's day, the fourth day of endre, mid-winter week. Hythe is a day of particular ill-omen.

Iagador: The land that lies between the mountains and the Sea of Thurkad.

Idlis: Formerly the least of the Whelm, also a healer and longtime hunter of Karan and the Mirror. He became Ghâshâd and went to Shazmak.

Jark-un: The leader of a band of the Whelm, once rival to Vartila, but now a Ghâshâd. Unlike others of his kind, he is short and stout.

Jepperand: A province on the western side of the mountains of Crandor. Home to the Zain; Llian's birthplace.

Jevi (Jevander): Lilis's father, taken by a press-gang seven years ago.

Kandor: One of the three Charon who came to Santhenar. He was killed sometime after the end of the Clysm, the only Charon to die on Santh.

Karama Malama: The Sea of Mists, south of the Sea of Thurkad.

Karan: A woman of the house of Fyrn, but with blood of the Aachim from her father, Galliad, and old human and Faellem blood from her mother. This makes her triune. She is also a sensitive and lives at Gothryme. Karan helped Maigraith to steal the Mirror of Aachan from Fiz Gorgo, and escaped to try to take it to Faelamor. She has been pursued ever since.

Katazza: A fortified city built by Kandor in ancient times. It was constructed on top of a volcanic mountain on Katazza Island, and was the capital of Kandor's empire of Perion, before the Sea of Perion became the Dry Sea. Katazza was abandoned after Kandor's death.

Lake Neid: A lake in the swamp forest near Fiz Gorgo, where the half-submerged ruins of the town of Neid are found.

Lar: A honorific used in Thurkad.

Lasee: A pale-yellow brewed drink, mildly intoxicating, and ubiquitous in Orist; fermented from the sweet sap of the sard tree.

Lauralin: The continent east of the Sea of Thurkad.

League: About 5000 paces, three miles or five kilometers.

Librarian: Nadiril the Sage. He is also a member of the Council of Iagador.

Library of the Histories: The famous library at the College of the Histories in Chanthed.

Lightglass: A device made of crystal and metal that emits light after being touched.

Lilis: A street urchin and guide in Thurkad, whose father Jevi was press-ganged.

Link, linking; also **talent of linking:** A joining of minds, by which thoughts and feelings can be shared, and support given. Sometimes used for domination.

Llian: A Zain from Jepperand. He is a master chronicler and a teller of the Great Tales. A great student of the Histories.

Magister: A mancer and chief of the Council. Mendark has been Magister for a thousand years, save for a brief period when illegally overthrown by Thyllan. After the Conclave he escaped from Thurkad to Zile, and then led his party to Katazza.

Maigraith: An orphan brought up and trained by Faelamor for some unknown purpose. She is a master of the Secret Art. After the Conclave she became Yggur's lover, though the liaison was not entirely successful.

Malien: An Aachim; Rael's mother; once consort of Tensor.

After Tensor's rebellion in Katazza she took over leadership of the Aachim.

Mancer: A wizard or sorcerer; someone who is a master of the Secret Art. Also necromanter.

Mantille: An Aachim; Karan's paternal grandmother.

Master chronicler: One who has mastered the study of the Histories and graduated with highest honor from the College.

Master of Chanthed: Currently Wistan; the Master of the College of the Histories is also nominal leader of Chanthed.

Meldorin: The large island that lies to the immediate west of the Sea of Thurkad and the continent of Lauralin.

Mendark: Magister of the Council of Iagador, until thrown down by Thyllan. A mancer of strength and subtlety, though lately insecure due to the rise of his longtime enemy, Yggur.

Mirror of Aachan: A device made by the Aachim in Aachan for seeing things at a distance. In Santhenar it changed and twisted reality and so the Aachim hid it away. It also developed a memory, retaining the imprints of things it had seen. Stolen by Yalkara, the Mirror was used by her to find a warp in the Forbidding and escape back to Aachan. After the Conclave, Tensor stole it, took it to Katazza and in it found the secret of making gates.

Moon: The moon revolves around Santhenar about every thirty days. However one side (the dark face) is blotched red and black by volcanic activity, and because the moon rotates on its axis much more slowly, the dark face is fully turned toward Santh only every couple of months. This rarely coincides with a full moon but when it does, it is a time of ill-omen.

Nadiril: The head of the Great Library and a member of the Council. Nadiril took on Lilis as his apprentice after she came to Zile with Mendark and Tallia.

Narne: A town and port at the navigable extremity of the Garr.

***Nazhak tel Mardux*:** A book of Aachim tales that Llian committed to memory in Shazmak. Also called *Tales of the Aachim.*

Nightland: A place, distant from the world of reality, wherein Rulke was kept prisoner. Rulke used the power of his city-construct Alcifer in an attempt to break the Forbidding, but it failed. The Council used the Proscribed Experiments to force Rulke into a bubble formed out of the wall of the Forbidding, then collapsed it to form the unbreakable prison of the Nightland. In Katazza, Tensor made a gate into the Nightland to drag Rulke forth and revenge himself upon him, but only succeeded in letting Rulke out.

Nilkerrand: A fortified city across the sea from Thurkad. Thyllan's refuge, from which he raised an army to invade Thurkad.

Old human: The original human species on Santhenar and by far the most numerous.

Orist: A land of swamps and forests on the south-west side of Meldorin; Yggur's fortress city of Fiz Gorgo is there.

Osseion: The captain of Mendark's guard, a huge dark man who helped Mendark escape from Thurkad and accompanied him to Katazza.

Pender: A masterly sailor who carried Karan and Llian from Narne to Sith, and later to Thurkad. After the Conclave he helped Karan and Shand to escape from Thurkad, and was subsequently hired by Mendark.

Perion, Empire of: Kandor's empire, which collapsed after the Sea of Perion dried up.

Pitlis: A great Aachim of the distant past, whose folly betrayed the great city of Tar Gaarn to Rulke and broke the power of the Aachim. The architect who designed Tar Gaarn and Alcifer, he was slain by Rulke.

Portal: See **gate.**

Potency: An all-powerful, mind-breaking spell developed by the Aachim as a weapon against the Charon, but effective against all but those Zain who bear the Gift of Rulke.

Principle of Contagion: One of the principles of the Secret Art, that objects once associated continue to affect each other after separation.

Proscribed Experiments: Sorcerous procedures designed to find a flaw in the Forbidding which could be used to banish Rulke forever. Hazardous because of the risk of Rulke taking control of the experimenter.

Rachis: Karan's steward at Gothryme Manor.

Rael: An Aachim, half-cousin to Karan, son of Malien and Tensor. He was drowned helping Karan to escape from Shazmak.

Read: Truth-reading. A way of forcing someone to tell the whole truth.

Recorder: The person who set down the tales of the four great battles of Faelamor and Yalkara, among many other tales. He is thought to have taken the Mirror (after Yalkara finally defeated Faelamor and fled Santh) and hidden it against some future need. His name was Gyllias.

Renderer's Tablet: A semi-mythical key to the secret script of the Charon.

Rula: The Magister before Mendark. She was regarded as the greatest of all.

Rulke: A Charon of Aachan. He enticed Shuthdar to Aachan to make the golden flute, and so began all the troubles. After the Clysm he was imprisoned in the Nightland until a way could be found to banish him back to Aachan. When Tensor opened a gate into the Nightland Rulke was able to escape.

Rustible: One of Pender's crew on *The Waif,* a lugubrious pessimist.

Santhenar, Santh: The least of the Three Worlds, home of the old human peoples.

Sea of Thurkad: The long sea that divides Meldorin from the continent of Lauralin.

Secret Art: The use of magical or sorcerous powers (mancing). An art that very few can use and then only after extensive training. Notable mancers include Mendark, Yggur, Maigraith, Rulke, Tensor and Faelamor, though each has quite different strengths and weaknesses. Tallia has considerable skill but as yet insufficient training.

Selial: An Aachim woman, leader of the Syndics in Shazmak, who escaped after the city's fall and accompanied Tensor to Katazza, but could not come to terms with her failure to control him.

Sending: A message, thoughts or feelings sent from one mind to another.

Sentinels: Devices that keep watch and sound an alarm.

Shalah: A young Aachim woman, twin to Xarah.

Shand: An old man who works at the inn at Tullin and is more than he seems. A friend of Karan's late father, Shand rescued Karan from the Conclave, smuggled her out of Thurkad and accompanied her on a trek all the way to Katazza in the middle of the Dry Sea.

Shazmak: The forgotten city of the Aachim, in the mountains west of Bannador. It was captured by the Ghâshâd, after they were woken from their long years as Whelm.

Shuthdar: An old human of Santhenar, the maker of the golden flute. After he destroyed the flute and himself, the Forbidding came down, closing the Way between the Worlds.

Siftah: A fishing town on the northeastern coast of Meldorin.

Sith: A free city and trading nation built on an island in the River Garr, in southern Iagador.

Skane: A city that fell the last time the full dark moon was in hythe, 1830 years ago.

Span: The distance spanned by the stretched arms of a tall man. About six feet, or slightly less than two meters.

Stassor: A city of the Aachim, in eastern Lauralin.

Syndics: A ruling Council of the Aachim, sometimes a panel of judges. None can lie to them in formal trial.

***Tale of the Forbidding*:** Greatest of the Great Tales, it tells of the final destruction of the flute by Shuthdar more than three thousand years ago, and how the Forbidding sealed Santhenar off from the other two worlds.

Talent: A native skill or gift, usually honed by extensive training.

***Tales of the Aachim*:** An ancient summary history of the Aachim, the Nazhak tel Mardux, prepared soon after the founding of Shazmak. Llian read and memorized it in Shazmak so he could translate it later.

Tallallame: One of the Three Worlds, the world of the Faellem. A beautiful, mountainous world covered in forest.

Tallia bel Soon: Mendark's chief lieutenant. She is a mancer and a master of combat with and without weapons. Tallia comes from Crandor.

Tar: A silver coin widely used in Meldorin. Enough to keep a family for several weeks.

Tar Gaarn: Principal city of the Aachim in the time of the Clysm; it was sacked by Rulke.

Tell: A gold coin to the value of twenty silver tars.

Teller: One who has mastered the ritual telling of the tales that form part of the Histories of Santhenar.

Tensor: The leader of the Aachim. He saw it as his destiny to restore the Aachim and finally take their revenge on Rulke, who betrayed and ruined them. He is proud to the point of folly.

Tess, Tessariel: A fishing captain working the bamundi schools out of Ganport. She helped Shand and Karan to escape from Ganport, across the Sea of Thurkad.

Thandiwe: A student at the College in Chanthed and friend of Llian.

Thel: One of Tensor's Aachim.

Three Worlds: Santhenar, Aachan and Tallallame.

Thripsi: A mountainous coastal region at the northeastern tip of Meldorin, chiefly noted for its fishing.

Thurkad: An ancient, populous city on the River Saboth and the Sea of Thurkad, known for its wealth and corruption. Seat of the Council and the Magister.

Thyllan: Warlord of Iagador and member of the Council. He intrigued against Mendark and briefly overthrew him as Magister, but after Yggur captured the city he retreated across the sea to raise an army.

Tirthrax: The principal city of the Aachim, in the Great Mountains.

Tolryme: A town in northern Bannador, close to Karan's family seat, Gothryme.

Torgsted: One of Mendark's guard. A cheerful, reliable fellow who agreed to pretend to betray Mendark and take service with Thyllan, so as to spy on him.

Trazpar: A solar still.

Triune: A double blending—one with the blood of all Three Worlds, three different human species. They are extremely rare and almost always infertile. They may have remarkable abilities. Karan is one.

Tullin: A tiny village in the mountains south of Chanthed. Shand lives there.

Twisted Mirror: The Mirror of Aachan, made in Aachan and given to Tensor, who smuggled it with him to Santhenar. Like all objects taken between the worlds, it changed and became treacherous. So called because it does not always show true.

Ulice: Proprietor of a cellar bar in Thurkad, and an old friend of Shand's. She can get anything, for a price.

Vanhe: Marshal Vanhe, one of Yggur's mid-ranking officers, forced to take command after all of Yggur's generals were killed.

Vartila: The leader of a band of the Whelm. She remained Whelm and served Yggur after most of her people reverted to Ghâshâd.

***Voice*:** The ability of great tellers to move their audience to any emotion they choose by the sheer power of their words.

Void, the: The spaces between the Three Worlds. A Darwinian place where life is more brutal and fleeting than anywhere. The void teems with the most exotic life imaginable, for nothing survives there without remaking itself constantly.

Vuula Fyrn: Karan's mother, a lyrist. She committed suicide soon after Karan's father, Galliad, was killed.

***Wahn Barre*:** The Crow Mountains. Yalkara, the Mistress of Deceits, had a stronghold there, Havissard. A place of ill-omen.

***Waif, The*:** Pender's third boat, formerly a blacklisted smuggler's vessel, *Black Opal.*

Way between the Worlds: The secret, forever-changing and ethereal paths that permit the difficult passage between the Three Worlds. They were closed off by the Forbidding.

Whelm: Servants of Yggur, his terror-guard. See also **Ghâshâd**.

Wistan: The seventy-fourth Master of the College of the Histories and of Chanthed.

Xarah: A young Aachim woman, twin to Shalah.

Yalkara: The Demon Queen, the Mistress of Deceits. The last of the three Charon who came to Santhenar to find the flute and return it to Aachan. She took the Mirror and used it to find a warp in the Forbidding, then fled Santh, leaving the Mirror behind.

Yetchah: A young Whelm woman who hunted Llian from Chanthed to Tullin.

Yggur: A great and powerful mancer and sworn enemy of Mendark. Formerly a member of the Council, he dwells in Fiz Gorgo. After Karan stole the Mirror his armies overran most of southern Meldorin, capturing Thurkad. He and Maigraith became lovers. Yggur hates and fears Rulke from the time Rulke possessed him before he was imprisoned in the Nightland.

Zain: A scholarly race who once dwelt in Zile and founded the Great Library. They made a pact with Rulke and after his fall most were slaughtered and the remnant exiled. They dwell in Jepperand and no longer make alliances.

Zareth the Hlune: One of Yggur's lieutenants, whom Shand poisoned with octopus venom to prevent Karan from being discovered on Tess's fishing boat.

Zile: A city in the north-west of the island of Meldorin. Once capital of the Empire of Zur, now chiefly famous for the Great Library.

Zurean Empire: An ancient empire in the north of Meldorin. Its capital was Zile.

Guide to Pronunciation

There are many languages and dialects used on Santhenar by the four human species. While it is impossible to be definitive in such a brief note, the following generalizations normally apply.

There are no silent letters, and double consonants are generally pronounced as two separate letters; for example, *Yggur* is pronounced *Ig-ger,* and *Faellem* as *Fael-lem.* The letter *c* is usually pronounced as *k*, except in *mancer* and *Alcifer*, where it is pronounced as *s*. The combination *ch* is generally pronounced as in *church*, except in *Aachim* and *Charon*, where it is pronounced as *k*.

Aachim Ar'-kim

Charon Kar'-on

Fyrn Firn

Iagador Eye-aga'-dor

Lasee Lar'-say

Maigraith May'-gray-ith

Rael Ray'-il

Whelm H'-welm

Xarah Zha'-rah

Chanthed Chan-thed'

Faelamor Fay-el'-amor

Ghâshâd G-harsh'-ard

Karan Ka-ran'

Llian Lee'-an

Neid Nee'-id

Shuthdar Shoo'-th-dar'

Yggur Ig'-ger

A Preview of the Way Between the Worlds

The Final Book in the View From the Mirror Quartet

The construct slowly revolved in the air above the decapitated tower of Carcharon, a menace that warped the very light around it. Rulke stood tall on top, holding his levers in one negligent hand, the other thrust out at the rising moon. The dark face, mottled red and purple-black, heaved its pregnant mass over the horizon. A hideous omen—the moon had not been full on *hythe*, mid-winter's day, for 1830 years. Rulke's foretelling was already coming to pass. *When the dark moon is full on mid-winter's day, I will be back. I will crack the Forbidding and open the Way between the Worlds. The Three Worlds will be Charon evermore.*

Karan, chest high beside Rulke, was a stark white, staring shadow surrounded by a corona of flaming hair. Llian ached for her, but even if he could step through the air between them there was no way to wrest her free. No one would help him now. He was a pariah, accused of betraying Karan to Rulke, accused of being Rulke's spy. Nothing would convince the company otherwise. Wherever he looked he received dark looks in return, especially from Basitor the Aachim, who had hated Llian since they met, and blamed him for the death of Hintis in Katazza last summer. Basitor would kill him given the least opportunity.

Llian had only one friend left, little Lilis, but what could she do? What could any of them do? The most powerful of their world were here but not one of them—not Mendark, not Yggur or the crippled Tensor, not Tallia or Shand or Malien—had the courage to use their powers against Rulke and his construct.

The construct rumbled; the stone walls of the tower wobbled; wavering discharges rose up from the spiny protrusions embedded in the walls. The Ghâshâd guards, stick-men and stick-women, resumed their posts, pacing the walls with stiff-limbed gait. The red glare from inside faded and flared, faded and flared.

Llian eyed the construct. It was an impossible thing, made of metal so black that it stood out against the night sky. There was nothing on Santhanar to compare it with. It required no beast to pull it; it had no wheels; and yet it slipped through the sky like silk. It hung in the air like a balloon, though Llian knew it was heavier than a boulder. Longer and broader than a wagon, its sides bulged in complex shapes that were alien then curved away into corrugations underneath. The long front soared up to a flaring binnacle crammed with knobs and wheels, behind which was a thicket of levers, a place to stand and a high seat of carven serpentine.

And Llian knew that the inside was just as strange, equally packed with controls and glowing plates, for he had seen it in the Nightland. But evidently Rulke preferred to ride on top where he could display, and dominate.

"Karan!" Llian sang out in anguish. His voice echoed back across the amphitheater to mock him.

Karan must have seen him, standing there on the rim, for she went quite rigid. At the same instant the construct lurched beneath her. Her arms flailed. Llian thought she was going to go over, then Rulke jerked her back. She looked up at him, looming head and shoulders above her, and spoke, though her words were not even a sigh on the wind.

Yggur adjusted glasses as thick as bottle ends. When Rulke first appeared he had resolved, at last, to face his fears and die rather than be overcome by them. But already that resolve was weakening. "Look at them together," he said, grinding his teeth. "He has possessed her mind. I can feel it, the way he possessed me for so long."

"I hope so," replied Mendark in an even more chilly voice. "Otherwise Karan has betrayed us, and must be punished."

"Don't be so free with your judgments, Mendark," said Malien, but her voice showed her own doubts.

The way they talked was horrible. Llian was stabbed all over by painpricks, as if his blood had crystallized to needles of ice. He sucked at the air but could not fill his lungs. Everything wavered; he felt faint. Then Yggur blew all that away in an instant.

Yggur took Malien by the arm. "Who is your best archer?"

"Basitor has the strongest pull by far. But I should say Xarah is the most accurate at this distance. Xarah!"

Xarah came forward. She was small for an Aachim, not much bigger than Karan, with limp hair the color of mustard and a scatter of freckles on her cheeks. She looked much younger than the others.

"You are the best among you?" Yggur asked, his fists clenched, knuckles white.

Xarah looked down at the snow, fingering a bracelet on her wrist. She knew what was going to be asked of her. Then she gazed up at the construct, gauging the distance. Only Karan's head could be seen now.

"The best that is able," she said. "I can hit any target in Carcharon from here."

"And on the construct?"

"An uphill shot, but yes, I can do it."

"Then put an arrow in Karan's eye, for pity's sake. For her and for us."

She did not move. "Do it this minute!" he cried again.

Xarah shivered. She looked up at Malien, her midnight-dark eyes expressionless in the red light.

"Do it!" Yggur cried, and there were flecks of foam at the corners of his mouth. He looked as if he had just fought a monumental battle with himself, and lost. Terrified of being possessed again, he would do anything to avoid it.

Malien put out her hand. "Stay, Xarah!" she said.

Mendark had summed the situation up too. "Rulke has made an error of judgment. Quick, kill her and we strike a monumental blow against him. He will still be deadly, but not invincible."

Llian staggered between them, the ice-crusted manacles tearing his legs until the blood flowed. He took no heed of that pain; it was nothing beside what he was feeling inside.

"No!" he screamed, crashing into Mendark, who cuffed him to the ground.

Nadiril the Librarian was bent right over on his walking staff, looking frailer than ever. Shand, a head shorter beside him, held his arm. Lilis stood by Nadiril, hopping from one foot to another, fretting for her teacher.

"This deed will come back to haunt you," said Nadiril. "She—"

"Just do it," Yggur screamed.

"No more will I do evil," said Malien softly, "even if the greatest good of all comes out of it. Xarah, put down your bow."

Tensor slid his legs over the side of the litter and with a convulsive wrench forced himself to his feet. He was as gaunt as a skeleton now, the once huge frame nothing but bone and sinew, all twisted from Rulke's blow in Katazza last summer. Leaning his weight on Asper the healer, Tensor wobbled across. Llian tried to claw his way over the snow but Basitor's huge foot slammed into the middle of his back, pinning him down.

"A chance," Tensor rasped. "A chance sent for my torment! What evil did my forefathers do that I should suffer so? Do you give the order, Malien?"

"No!" she whispered, and a tear froze to crystal from each eye.

"You have always been true," he said, clinging to her for a moment.

Letting her go, he took a lurching step toward Xarah. He wavered toward her like the grim reaper, an animated skeleton covered in skin. She stood still, watching him come, the long bow hanging down in one hand, the red-feathered arrow in the other. At the last moment she tried to put them behind her but the look in his eyes paralyzed her.

Tensor plucked the bow from one hand, the arrow from the other. The arrow went to the bowstring; the string was drawn back. Llian's arms and legs thrashed as if swimming in the snow, but Basitor's boot held him in place.

"I'm sorry, Karan," said Tensor ever so gently.

"Shoot, damn you! cried Yggur, shaking so hard that his head nodded like a child's toy.

Karan's red hair looked to be on fire in the boiling glare from the tower. Her face was a white blotch, but Llian had no doubt that Tensor could hit her eye from here. Before he even released the arrow Llian could see it flying straight and true toward her lovely face, to spear straight through her skull with a shock that would carry her backwards off the construct, to her death onto the rocks at the bottom of the gorge.

A Fantastic New Tale from Rebecca Neason

The Truest Power

In the grand tradition of Andre Norton and Katherine Kurtz, Rebecca Neason returns to the wondrous world of *The Thirteenth Scroll* in an amazing new adventure of fantasy and magic. Rulerless Aghamore totters on the brink of catastrophic civil war, even though the blind seer Lysandra, her wolf companion Cloud Dancer, and the priest Renan have found Selia, the young girl who possesses the innate wisdom to save the land. If Selia cannot overcome the many obstacles and demonic magic that bar her path, Lysandra's recurring visions portend that the moment the girl accepts the royal scepter, Selia—and all hope for Aghamore—will die . . .

ALSO AVAILABLE FROM REBECCA NEASON:

THE THIRTEENTH SCROLL (0-446-60953-6)

"This enchanting tale of magic and prophecy . . . will delight readers of high adventure and fantasy."

—*Realms of Fantasy* on *The Thirteenth Scroll*

"The kingdom of Aghamore is territory worth exploring at length . . . with fascinating creatures and terrains. . . . This is a narrative that deserves to be played out in full."

—*SF Site* on *The Thirteenth Scroll*

AVAILABLE AT BOOKSTORES EVERYWHERE FROM WARNER ASPECT

1200